CIVIL
WARS

CIVIL WARS

a novel by

Rosellen Brown

ALFRED A. KNOPF   NEW YORK

1   9   8   4

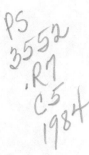

THIS IS A BORZOI BOOK
PUBLISHED BY ALFRED A. KNOPF, INC.

Copyright © 1984 by Rosellen Brown

Library of Congress Cataloging in Publication Data
Brown, Rosellen.
Civil wars.
I. Title.
PS3552.R7C5   1984   813'.54   83-48866
ISBN 0-394-53478-6

Manufactured in the United States of America
First Edition

for Virginia Barber
with love and gratitude

I will call the *world* a School instituted for the purpose of teaching little children to read—I will call the *human heart* the *horn book* used in the School—and I will call the *Child able to read, the Soul* made from that *school and its hornbook*. Do you not see how necessary a World of Pains and troubles is to school an Intelligence and make it a soul?

> Keats, in a letter
> to his brother George
> in Kentucky

"Sometimes in his arrogance he has more anxiety for the world than for himself."

> Kafka
> "He" (*Aphorisms*)

Some of the people and places in *Civil Wars* began in memory, but every one of them has been transformed into fiction. Resemblance to "reality" is therefore a shadow that has persisted: my characters are intended only to represent themselves.

RB

CIVIL WARS

The first time Teddy made love to her—hunkered at the edge of a cotton field near Winona, Mississippi, in an ancient borrowed car twice as big as his own, on a seat that smelled of goats and hay although she trusted it had been occupied by neither—he gave Jessie his working definition of politics.

Politics, he said when they had grown quiet and contemplative, is a man and woman doing what we just did without as much as a sigh or a whisper because their kids are lying all around them listening whether they want to or not. And if they rear up, and if they cry out . . . It is also a man and woman, he said, doing that slowly, slowly in a big white room with a Boston fern in the window and a quilt—say, a red comforter, goose down—at the foot of the bed. Alone except for a cat curled at their feet. Their children are down the hall. No, their children are in another *wing*. That is politics too: the cat likes what they're doing, in spite of the fact that they've nearly thrown it off the bed it comes and walks on their chests, sniffing. That cat is the beneficiary of caste and color and economic good fortune.

Jessie assumed that was the kind of analysis, shocking down here, that Teddy must have used on a dozen willing girls and women. He was famous, at least locally, and had had as many as he'd wanted, or so she was told; so she could conjecture. At least he carried himself that way. And most of them would have been astounded by the change of focus from their bodies to the body politic. All his charm lay in that surprise, in the breadth of his passions.

Surely he must have expected her to widen her eyes and murmur how she'd never *thought* of such a thing. Giggle of outrage and approval. But she had grown up on such ideas—just the luck—and had had Marx for a familiar. That, lust and politics, was her father's kind of analysis and it was right and relevant and murderous and oblivious to reality all at the same time. Teddy, don't, she said to him without explanation. By which, taking his hand and putting it back where it belonged, somewhere between herself and the smell of that barnyard, she meant, Teddy, do. She could tell by the infinitesimal hesitation of his body that he was disappointed in her. Another man had gotten to her first and ruined her for ideology.

ONE

There was nothing she could do—she caught the boy red-handed. He was kneeling in front of a cabinet in the den (behind its sliding door their raggedy liquor collection and a pile of ancient magazines with their pages violated, torn out for urgent political purposes, covers dishevelled), and he was apparently concentrating so hard he didn't hear Jessie bang her groceries into the kitchen, cans rapping hard on the table, and come walking all the way down the long living room. Why she came she would never know; say she was drawn the way a reader looks up suddenly into watching eyes or a sleeper, stared at, awakens. Something told her, some faint buzz of disturbance in the air. Long drink of water in dungarees and sneakers, unruly head of curls like the sun coming up behind her head. Her sneakers made her silent.

The children weren't home from school yet, so she got to stand alone and watch the boy in a brand-new red satin track jacket bright as a flare, opulent-looking, reach his hands into their cabinet, shuffling the bottles around. Shoulders down, intent and not in any hurry, he uncapped a small bottle of the most wretched apple wine Teddy's mother had given them, eighty proof sugar. What a thing to go for, a true corrosive with no compensating soft edges. He flung back his head and drank, letting his eyes roll back to their whites as if in relief of something. Oh, he drank it down like milk, she was already preparing to say to Teddy when the time came. Poor dumb baby, she thought, seeing his dark brown Adam's apple bounce and shine, thought how it must be scouring his throat like furniture stripper! He licked all around his lips for more, then put the top back on the empty bottle and spun it—good habits, toilet trained at a year, no doubt, his mama would be proud—and she waited for him to notice her.

Strange for her, for she was often the noisiest one in a room, but she couldn't, confronting this boy, make a sound. It had nothing to do with fear, only with fascination and a terrible sense of command. (Down here, she remembered dimly, white folks aren't afraid of black folks and that's the truth.) There was something intimate, though, about seeing him in the act of failing at what he was doing; she was regretful. She was embarrassed. Unless he had a gun. But that's always the case, anyone can have a gun, you can be brushing your teeth in the morning turned away from the world and somebody can have a gun. She had lost friends that way; had, a dozen times, almost lost a husband. (But not to black folks. *What is this?*)

Still she wanted to watch him notice her, it was only fair to make him share her shock. He concentrated well. She wondered if he could read. If he did he would be a lip-reader, though: he gave off related small sounds of frustration under his breath, *mmrh* and *hss* and *thhh*, because all he encountered in those cabinets was the collected evidence of Mr. and Mrs. Theodore Carll's sobriety and their relative impoverishment: all they owned were books. On the tall shelves, *The Art of Mexico* (a gift), *Emerald Island* (remaindered), *Calligraphy for the Young* (inkstained). The *Missa Luba* (a Vox Box, cheap). Below them, paperback, thumbed, *Pedagogy of the Oppressed*, *The Burden of Southern History*. Misplaced ironies. Thinking that, she clicked her tongue to the back of her teeth impatiently, and woke him from his dream of plunder. He looked at her and his eyes and mouth opened as if on one hinge.

They had their confrontation. She ganged up. "Sammy Hines," she said sternly. Not that she knew him but his shiny red back said HINES 27 PUMAS in navy blue, and *she* could read. He was in Andy's class, she knew that name. He lived on the corner behind two or three cars in various stages of decay and cannibalistic dismemberment. She knew his mother and his grandmother to say hello to—both were tiny and one was bald—and had worried on occasion about how many generations were camped in that little bungalow till it must have begun to feel like a shack again, familiarly oppressive.

If things had been different, if things with a capital T had been even a little bit ideal, Sammy Hines could have smiled, showing those luscious teeth—he had a wide and perfect mouth and should have been rich from his contract with the American Dental Association for a ten-ad package, with residuals. But if he'd had to burgle, he ought to have been able to say, with aplomb, "Oh, Mrs. Carll, there you are. I'm waiting for Andy. He told me to hang around till he got here." And flick his cigarette like a movie star's. But that supposed a world he'd never dreamed of; and he had no cigarette. Andy and Sammy Hines had never exchanged a word, unless it was a hostile one. That much she knew. Sammy, summoned to attention by the white lady in the dungarees and sneakers, taller than he was, smiling but surely not meaning it, responded as he had been trained. He opened his pie-plate eyes and said, "Yes 'm."

"What in the hell do you think you're doing."

He ogled her, his eyes going up in his head like a mockery. Was he supposed to be a slave or merely a child? "Don't show me the whites of your eyes, please. Just answer my question."

He shrugged then, looking down. The catechism mortified her. She asked a dozen rhetorical questions. He answered none. "Do you know what Pumas means?" She was running out of sensible demands.

Catechized, Sammy had time to regret his respectful attitude. He stared carefully ahead as if he had developed an interest in *The Plays of Jean Genet*. He had a perfect head, she was compelled by her attention to notice, fine boned yet secure, the eyes slightly slanted above the wide flanges of the cheek bones. Are there no rewards for natural perfection? The answer to that was easy. Not at the wrong time in the wrong place.

Then Jessie was forced to ask, "What have you got in your hand?" He had a fist at his side.

"Ain't got nothin." He flung his words at her as if the whole mess were her fault. How could she deny him a fist under the circumstances?

"The other hand." Schoolmarm. Mother. Honky.

"Nothin." He looked like a figure in a dance, hands open stiff at waist level.

"What about your pockets, then?"

"Sheee-it," the boy mumbled and turned out the pockets of his metallic jacket. They were full of the flotsam of his daily life: cigarette wrappers that unfolded with a sound of licking flames. A treadless Tootsie Roll. Two cents that rolled wantonly across the carpet. He was not a winner, not a young man on whose person one would expect to find the evidence of successful strayings from the strait and narrow. No condoms. No valuable merchandise with its price tags on it, no impressive sums of money.

"You ought to find a better way to spend your afternoons. You're not very good at this."

He stood tight through her attempts at sympathy. What could she do with him? Bring him to the police for a whupping? Make him write "I will not break into houses" a hundred times? Carry him home by the ear? His mother would cry or sigh or curse him or curse God, and under her breath curse Jessie, did it really matter? When it came to governing he was long gone. The women would mourn; were there any men at home? Among the people who picked at those beached cars she could not remember seeing anyone out of his teens.

"What do you think I should do with you, Sammy?" she asked him. "You say."

The shrug. She couldn't tell if he was stunned by terror like a bird caught in the house, or bored by her irrelevance. His face was wiped clean, like any adolescent's accused of anything. In any event, participatory discipline was lost on him. Goddamn. Jessie was accustomed to passion, one way or the other. In spite of herself she reached toward his shiny red sleeve. Index finger, middle finger, thumb, she pinched him and pinched him till she heard the bubble of pain break from her own throat.

Sammy Hines of the Pumas, smiling slightly, held on.

She pinched him again, going for his eyes with hers. His mouth moved once but he had nothing to say to her. She was afraid she would beat him up. Somehow she had made a contest of this, as if it weren't clear which of them was guilty. She pinched, turning her fingers like a wrench, until his eyes widened, but he never did say a single word. And she floated in a pool of unthinkable punishments—was there murder so near the center of her? She terrified herself. She could do anything she wanted to and no one in the world would hold her guilty—was that what it felt like, multiplied by the hate factor, the suppressed terror factor, to feel immunity? Was that what the sheriffs carried inside their sweaty shirts, and their deputies right out there on their sneering faces, the knowledge that when you've got a black man (not to mention a black boy) at bay, you make the rules?

She let him go.

Eyes on her face, aggrieved, he rolled up his shiny sleeve and looked at his arm as if it might show him a purple butterfly. "Huh. Dint even make a mark." Not even a two-minute crease. The dark skin glowed as if he polished it every day with a cloth.

"And now you can get out." That felt like a line from a movie. She opened the back door, which he had forced so that its metal plate was bent, but had closed neatly behind him.

"How the hell you want me to get *out* of here?" He looked at the shoulder-high fence that enclosed the yard. "I got to go over that?" For the first time Sammy Hines looked alarmed. "Can't I go back around out to the street?"

"You came over it, now you can take yourself back where you came

from." Let someone else catch you, she was thinking, one of your own—
she averted her eyes from this but it was true—who'll know what to do
with you that you might take notice of.

The boy put his hands on his hips and commenced to argue. He wasn't
as grateful for escape as she'd have expected. She did not want to spell that
out for him, already her face was turning the colors of humiliation, pale
splotches like thumbprints on her cheeks.

"You want me to get caught in somebody's fuckin yard?" He was shouting at her.

"You've already been caught, in case you hadn't noticed."

He smiled sourly. "No, I ain't noticed." Then he took off in a slow
slouch across the scuffled dirt in no kind of hurry. His slick jacket glowed
red hot going over the fence. It left an afterimage behind her eyes.

.   .   .

She couldn't call Teddy, who moved around the state all day, so Jessie
called Andréa, her neighbor and friend.

"Shit," Andréa said, which had once, a long time ago, been a hard thing
for her to utter: she was born "seditty," as some say down here—white
gloved, cool, clean, quiet. Her daddy taught Beowulf at Jackson State. She
had doubtless been the one little girl in school (it was a school run by nuns)
whose braids didn't muss and who would have turned grave tremendous
rebuking eyes on the likes of Jessie. Her skin was the most luxurious brown,
it made Jessie feel her white self mulched under a board, a rock, a layer of
hay. They had all laid hold of her in the old days—Tommy who married
her, Teddy who married Jessie, and a dozen others—and sort of stretched
her fine limbs open to the sun. So she put on overalls and neglected her
nails, stopped doing violence straightening her hair. She got knocked around
plenty and slept on the floors of a dozen jails like the rest of them. And
learned to say shit, a fringe benefit.

"What did you do with him exactly?" she asked when Jessie called her
on lunch hour at her law office. "Lock him in the laundry room to cool
off?"

"No," Jessie said. "I let him go. I sent him away to rip off somebody
else's house, I guess. If he was lucky everybody was out. He's probably
passed out in somebody's carport by now from all that apple wine."

"On an empty stomach. Oh, honey . . ."

"What 'oh honey'?"

Andréa had a liquid sigh. "You got your husband's dumb liberal soft-
head do-good condescension in you. It has finally set in. Dry rot. Worse

than termites. You should have sent that boy to the *po*-lice." She didn't like to sound like a woman who had argued before the Supreme Court; she said it made her itch.

Jessie's sigh.

"You know he's a complicated case, your man, and now you want to wake up sounding just like him. Be easy to take *him* for the New York boy the way he likes to forgive niggers their sins."

"But?"

"But underneath it all—" She made her voice scratchy and reluctant. "Under it all I think he does those backbends 'cause he really hates us deep down like the Miss'ssippi boy he is. And he's afraid of that."

"Could be," Jessie said, weary. She had heard this analysis before. She'd even used it herself. At the moment it was beside the point. "Andréa," she told her. "Either we move out of that house or I'm leaving him."

"You've said it before, hon. You want to know when the last time was? I got it written down here someplace."

"I know."

"You're going to leave Tommy here alone, only white man for a mile around?"

"He can hide behind you, pal, you've got the right kind of face for that neighborhood. We can't hide behind each other."

.   .   .

She would never know if he was in their hire, Sammy in the shiny coat. Had he been sent to trash the house and gotten waylaid by the apple wine? She would never know who "they" were, or even if. But paranoia is like hypochondria: it produces genuine pain, genuine fear, and relieving it is more urgent than accounting for its origins.

They had been getting phone calls. At the beginning these had been pleasant enough, had come in the daytime or right after dinner, like civilized business conducted from an office desk: Would Mr. and Mrs. Carll like to sell their house? Well, if they hadn't thought about it, wouldn't they perhaps like to take some time to do so? Eventually one of these callers worked himself around to the suggestion that the carefully integrated neighborhood was by now down to two white families. Had they happened to have noticed that? (One and a half actually; there were Andréa and Tommy and their baby, Cleo, two to one black. They were here because it seemed safer to integrate privately, in your own family, where the neighborhood was already mixed.)

Sell now while you can still get value for your house, said their caller.

An unidentified voice that was, your everyday blockbuster busting in reverse, all whites out by sundown, to whom Jessie quite firmly said no thank you. We like it here, she told him. We like our neighbors. Are you implying, she asked, that property values are dropping as blacks move in? The caller was black but whatever he thought he did not find it to his immediate advantage to defend the honor or the economic viability of his race.

Then there began (although they didn't think of it as *tactics*) an escalation over one weekend: first the pre-dawn phone calls. Dark night of someone's soul—next-door neighbors, to whom they loaned barbecue lighter, three-way bulbs, even (occasionally) money? The phone would be full of breath, hot stifled breath moist as a child's, and that was all. Teddy would answer. He tried reason, mockery, anger, his own answering silence. The caller would give them a few nights of perfect sleep, the way a junkie lets his body clear out so he can start again with a little jolt. Working on their tolerance. Fine-tuning their vulnerability. There was no one it might not have been. But, irritating though it was, the attention still seemed random.

The few (integrated) acres Jessie and Teddy, Andy and Lydia lived in showed up on the maps as a self-enclosed, self-satisfied round, a little labyrinth of "lanes" and "terraces" in whose quiet streets that led nowhere Jessie could imagine teaching Andy to drive any day now. It was called Briarwood Acres or Meadowview Shores or Pinewood Village—some combination drawn in two random parts from a hatful of perjuries—but she insisted on calling it Plywood Barracks.

The whole development was one slipshod house on one repeated lot, actually, a simple tune played again and again to a slightly different accompaniment: yellow brown blue shuttered gabled trimmed. The Carlls had a modish bare wooden lattice beside the living room window; nothing would grow on it, as if the grass were poisoned. Tommy-and-Andréa's wore an aborted dormer with no room behind it, stained an ersatz redwood. They were flat-out little houses easy to pull in on a WIDE LOAD trailer behind a car waving hot orange flags.

The curtains in Plywood, Jessie had begun to notice, were getting frowsy— loving thy neighbor, she thought, had better not include loving her curtains. A fact, not a judgment. (Nonetheless she felt that lurch of guilt, to which she was becoming more and more immune.) Fiberglas; shiny; mostly white on white like certain men's dress shirts. And like certain men, she could not help but continue, unevenly hung. Further fact: cars were proliferating on lawns. Up on blocks they stood, announcing their disintegration as if it were a community project.

("Jessie." Teddy's voice, the soft Southern diphthong making her name endless, convoluted. The patronizing Southern grandmotherly instruction. "This is a class problem, not a color problem. Really. Your father would writhe to think you've forgotten everything he taught you."

Really.)

All she meant was that there were things she could dare to think and say that, having said them as a bigoted child, Teddy could never say again. And the time had come, she kept saying, for them to leave Mississippi. It was unnatural for them to persist. If they did not leave the South—if they did not leave the state—the "if" a compromise, of course, bargaining chip of the nonnegotiable, as if she had already given something valuable away— then they would have to leave this neighborhood.

But Teddy had a list, a little bit like the Pope's index and just as futile to appeal, of forbidden topics and general thematic areas which he made clear caused him distress. Jessie believed he thought they should dishearten her as well. This, she thought, was a poignant, childlike attitude and it seemed to her to embody a common quality of impossible longing among Southerners that she had not grown up having to confront in New York. (Her parents had tended to the opposite assumption, which had its own dangers, that everything ought to be faced, confronted stark naked as it were; and very little slipped by in modesty even when she was too young to see such sights.) But it seemed easier to build bypasses around reality here than up north—like those houses without foundations, one could throw up an instant structure to contain any wish. "If them troublemakers would only go away we'd be just *fine*." (Teddy right there in their midst, one of them and yet not one of them!) "If our niggers was left to themselves, why, they wouldn't be none of this mess." Or even "any"—grammatical politesse didn't enter in, this longing crossed every boundary.

Even at its best, the Barracks had wounded a certain aesthetic pride of Jessie's—this after the willing suppression of any interest in mere beauty over the last fifteen ascetic years. But for a long time it was the only integrated neighborhood in Jackson and so, in a sense, they had no choice but to live there. And most of that time it had served their needs. Andy was a baby there, and then Lydia, and the place was just big enough—easy to keep decent, which was important because Jessie intended to ignore it utterly, and Teddy, most days, gave little indication that he noticed where he lay his head; lace pillowcases or none, it was all the same to him.

The first time they met the house with its dark trolley-shaped living room, its boxy lines and charmless unprovocative corners—the kind of design manufactured not by an architect but by a mortgage and loan company—Jessie hated it extravagantly. But it was clear even then that this block that curved and bent around its modest lawns and incipient hedges, whose plumbing had advanced beyond drainage ditches, whose houses abounded in aluminum-frame screen doors and matched windows, electric ranges with timers and little built-in bathroom heaters that glowed bright as an open hearth—these were dream houses on a dream block, and she had a nerve.

Black and white, to a one her neighbors had not been born with a guarantee of any kind of housing; some had grown up moving every season, staying ahead of their debts at the boss's whim. Plantation and trailer park people, shotgun shack people. Mrs. Lutie Coleman, just behind and two houses to the right, had lost child and two-room shack to a tornado up around Tolewood, she would tell you that within the first two minutes of any conversation. Others had always had a place, one way or another—the use of a place—but it would have been grim enough to make Plywood Barracks feel like Camelot. She knew that without needing Teddy to remind her. Privacy, the shiny brand-new, choice of colors, of wrapping and trim! And only the bank at the other end of their right to stay, no boss who would throw you off if he didn't like your tone of voice. (You didn't talk to the bank. If you happened to, surely no tone was required.) In her first season in Mississippi, Jessie would have been awed at the privilege of living with folks who were at home in their first real house.

Now, jogging them out of calm and sleep, someone seemed to want the house back. Their neighbors were the bosses all of a sudden, and they were telling Jessie and Teddy, children and cat, insistently but ambiguously to get off the land, and fast, never mind how their blood had watered the soil.

No they're not, Teddy insisted. Somebody only wants to make a buck. We move and they double the price and sell it to some other poor sucker. That game. It may be nasty and venal but that doesn't make it racist. (He was always careful not to make that correlation. Jessie was, apparently, no longer careful enough.)

"It is not heroism," she said, "to live in a cardboard house, in a place where white folks are an endangered species. Tell me, are they calling everybody else on the block at three in the morning?"

He looked pained when he answered that he didn't know because—and he gave Jessie a point by default—he hadn't talked to anybody on the block for at least a month.

.   .   .

The morning after Sammy Hines got nothing but their wine, Andy went out back to fetch his bike for the ride to the high school. Jessie heard a shout and before she could get to the door he was in the kitchen, eyes wide, fair cheeks flushed. He dragged her out onto the steps without a word.

It could have been an arrow protruding from someone's flesh, the shish kebob skewer, shiny silver, that poked all the way through his bicycle tire. It hung out at an angle like a loose spoke.

"Looks like the work of Injuns," Jessie said, her breath going out of her. She felt herself deflate as if she were the punctured tire.

Andy was leaning against the house in a posture of exhaustion; he looked like someone who had ridden his bike a hundred miles uphill. "Funny."

"No, I don't know who," his mother told him then, "so don't even ask me. Or why either. Your father and I seem to differ on why these days." That actually had a more ominous sound than she'd intended: it seemed to imply there were threats on all sides, out there under cover of darkness and inside too. She let it stand.

Andy was fourteen, tall, still blond though his hair was darkening realistically toward Jessie's, the glamor of his childhood over. But he was also soft featured, fine skinned, somebody's lengthening little boy. His emotions washed easily across his face like water in a tipped dish. Now his astonishment had passed over into outrage.

"Let's go around and see if we can find the ones that match." He tugged at the alien thing, which did not give.

"Like Cinderella, you mean."

"Yeah, let's just knock on everybody's kitchen door." He was trying to brace the wheel against his thigh, for leverage.

"I don't think they'd like what we've got to offer as a prize." She bent to help.

When finally he drew the skewer free, long and pointed, a faceted weapon that seemed to have held their names invisibly pinioned behind it against the tire, she felt the first wave of real terror wash up, turning her heart with it and casting it back down.

Andy studied the skewer as if it were a dipstick that would show him exactly how much hate was there to be measured, and how thick. Would someone come next to shoot them while they slept?

The weapon, as if bewitched, was turning slowly back into a kitchen tool. It gave off menace, a sort of luridly inappropriate anger, but, Jessie thought, getting a hold on herself, it was too trivial to threaten murder. I want to go home, she did not cry out to her son who was standing beside her in need of impossible reassurance. I want to go home, she thought, and this is home and I recognize none of it as mine!

. . .

The problem—half the problem—was that her husband was home already and Jessie was not looking for reasons to leave him. He was born, in fact, near the center of Jackson in a house that had finally disappeared for a branch bank parking lot—the New South marches on the Old South like Sherman to the sea, and everyone's "history," even Southern Obsessive, goes up in bulldozer dust. Then, while his father was in the army, overseas, they—Teddy, his mother and his sister Alexis—moved to Yazoo City to live in his grandmother's house.

The old house could have been anywhere, it was dark and roomy and had a porch. But this grandmother's house could only have been here, a meager hot-zone house with no foundation, one of those oversized wooden bungalows with little half-story pillars from porch rail to roof. It was a perfectly middle-class house, only old, which corresponded to a very particular sort of New York apartment in Jessie's mind, with a certain clean closed-off smell on the stairs and little octagonal tiles on the hall floor. But she was shocked by its alien Southern look every time she came to visit, perhaps because she was expected to find a way to feel at home in it; it was, after all, in her family now. It was the house of people who eat Hopping John flavored with pork sides for good luck on New Year's Day. Whose relatives, either close or distant, have double names, Jimmie Lee and Katie Sue. Who are still and always will be privately appalled and bewildered that, Jew that Jessie is, outlander (and not even beautiful to explain it all), their Teddy had married her. Well, shock for shock. They were all stunned at each other's intransigence.

Jessie tried, a thousand times, to picture Teddy as a boy in that house. When he was about nine, he had found two Civil War bullets on the lawn under an oleander bush, shining at its roots, he told her, like the rain-polished bulbs of some unfamiliar flower. Of course he did. She would bet there wasn't a child in this state who missed that experience—it was like a confirmation. The Military Graveyard in Vicksburg is a place to play soldier: you climb the rises, picture the faded slate blue uniforms of the intruders, fall over dead. You can see the live war as a gash in familiar landscape, blood spilled on someone's farmland. Even Jessie was moved when she saw it because the brows of those hills were so tender and domestic, and the gravestones had dates on them so cruel.

At first she had found that exotic, thrilling, *defining*, and that was where the trouble came in, now that she couldn't remember how they were planning to make a long life together out of those differences: she, Jessie Singer from Bronx Science, mascot of her father's Party cell, and Teddy Carll the Confederate child growing up to be a moral Yankee with those hard little bullets lodged in his flesh somewhere, surrounded by the scar tissue of his reform. His family weeping for him as if he were dead. The first time he went to jail his sister wrote him to say she no longer had a brother.

But Jessie was not a New Yorker any more. It was not an even balance. Hers was the accent that had yielded and lost its corners in all these years, not his; it was softening to the local pudding. She was, she thought, without having crossed a national boundary, an expatriate. Yet Teddy was still, and always would be, however much at odds, a local boy. And so would their son and daughter be, a good ole boy and girl.

.   .   .

All Jessie's architectural preoccupation, needless to say, was metaphor. The incidental conditions of a desperate person's life can be coaxed into metaphor to see if they might, that way, yield up a little clarity. She understood that. Still, as conditions, they do persist.

They were, she understood all too well, she and Teddy and all their kind, obsolete.

Recently she had seen an interview with a writer in which the woman had said, By now, "writer" is what I am, not what I do—something like that. It was a toneless statement, which Jessie rather resented. She couldn't get a hint of whether the writer thought that was good or bad.

She knew what she thought of it: Teddy and she were what they once were, not even what they were today; surely not what they were doing. What they were was famous (*he* was); brave (both of them, she intermittently); endlessly endangered. They had spent an enormous amount of time holding the hands of strangers and singing, or urging them to song. Most of the hands were black—Negro at the time—and horny hard, like crocodile skin, with work the likes of which Teddy and Jessie would never know, unless as an affectation.

They had spent their honeymoon in jail, which made them an object of what was then the best kind of community notoriety: amused sympathy, throaty knowing laughter because they were somewhere in the vicinity of sex, balked sex, yearning, the one recognized universal; and anger that once again the peckerwoods were messing around with somebody's freely made plans. That time in jail Jessie remembered waking up at the far point, deep point, of their hunger strike—this was LeFlore County and they went hungry for thirteen days—and in the blue of early morning touching her knees and feeling a shocking narrow knob of bone, like the wooden handle of her

old umbrella. Teddy was on the far side of brick and steel, asleep on the
floor in the company of men. (White only. Even for the likes of those
niggerlovers and longhair jewcommie bastards, the primordial separations
prevailed—they were in something like a four-square box: two for white
and two for black.) Sometimes they could hear the others singing; they knew
they could be heard. They used the local names in their songs, sheriff and
whatever deputies they could call on: *Ain't gonna let Jim Pigott turn me
'round, turn me 'round, turn me 'round.* It was a form of noble cursing,
secular prayer.

Jessie remembered that confrontation with body—her own, light-headed,
pared down dangerously—better than she remembered her confrontations
with Teddy's, though that may be because that long pleasure had gone on
all these years. And she remembered the press of general affection, the sharp
quick hugs of the men and the sweaty bosom-to-bosom embraces of the
women, better too. All the free-floating sensuality of her first few years in
Mississippi blended: approval, relief, concern, loneliness, terror, fury, and
pleasure in hearty company. To have lost it was like, at the other end of
the scale, having lost the very particular touch of Lydia and Andy in their
infancy, mouth on her breast, light fingers on her cheek. She could still
miss it so sharply a weight inside her would shift, it was keen as a stitch
of pain, when she let herself.

But she did not let herself. Not very often. Her children were half-
grown, and the days of Earnest White Girls for Integration were over. Even
if it weren't that *Time* magazine and its accomplices tended to think in terms
of The Year Of and The Decade Of, history, public and private, did move
in its own natural waves, peristaltic, Jessie supposed, as real time digested
them and reduced them to ash and offal. They were all new cells now, twice
new, since all that.

. . .

Teddy was a campus traveller for Marathon Books. He did colleges,
and some high schools, good, bad and indifferent. The only thing to be
said about the job, after taking careful note of the regularity of its salary
and the safety of its execution, was that it was entirely innocuous. Benign.
It seemed not to call any principles into question. Neither, of course, did
it defend any.

When he was hired on as a salesman, Teddy struck his interviewer as
a gamble: he was too smart for the job (although not smart enough to know
how to hide it) and he seemed to alternate between a ferocious energy and
an equally ferocious indolence, or apathy. He had a long and complicated

radiating scar on his cheek which creased the side of his chin and neck, and was apparently doomed to stay the approximate blood-gorged color of private parts. All this clearly pointed to what is called, in women and in employees, a "mysterious past" by those who are about to become entangled with them.

When he was asked why he wanted to be a drummer—because a salesman is a salesman, even if he is taking one order a week on a Rolls-Royce—he simply and rather curtly repeated what he had already said: yes, it was true he had a master's degree in sociology, but that is a rather unuseful possession unless one wants to teach; he did not want to teach; he wanted to stay in Jackson; he knew the state well. He was not a fugitive. He could speak about books with conviction. And this was no summer job: he was looking for something reliable.

The interviewer was too polite to say there was something fishy in Denmark but, in his office in Memphis, he noted that down, in code. He thought, the impression he makes on me will be the one he makes on buyers—well, he seemed, if suspicions were suspended, earnest enough. Had a wry crooked smile, a slightly outslung lower lip that gave him a stubborn, amused look, as if a cigar store Indian were close to laughter, and that healthy head of dark hair. Was tall and tall people command attention (although perhaps not men quite as skinny as this one). Still there was an Abe Lincoln charm. . . . Didn't dress very well but that wasn't very important down here. A good voice. Confidence, though not a salesman's razzle dazzle, more a comfort with speech as if he had been a debater or the teacher he did not want to be, a patience when he demonstrated how he would explain a table of contents that was like an enthusiastic and graceful invitation. His eyes were good: they lit at his own mention of four-color illustrations and technicolor bar graphs. He would do good presentation workshops. There was something both childlike and grave about him. The interviewer hired that and hoped no terrible secret had slipped past.

Only one thing, Teddy had said.

Here it comes. The interviewer poised his pencil above his codes. He had explained the commission carefully.

The thing was that when it came time to sell books to the Council schools and segrated academies, someone else would do it. He would be vigorous in pursuit of new sales, in picking up lagging old sales, but no private schools. His eyes did more than light up at that, they throbbed with a feverish urgency. They were what you might call inflamed.

The interviewer was a recent emigre from White Plains, New York; he was not as surprised as others would have been. The structure of Marathon

Books, as it happened, could accommodate another man to do the "non-affiliateds" over a large area—both of them smiled at the word.

"Thank you," the newly hired salesman said with such a boyish grin that the interviewer wondered if he had saved an endangered life.

Now Teddy had a satchel full of textbooks, their edges neatly cut, pages combed, a class operation. The publisher was a decent one, as publishers go. Once Teddy was well established and his old notoriety acknowledged, he was in New York at a party that came in a package with a sales convention and the president of the company hung at his sleeve all evening so that he could flagellate himself for "never having done anything—nothing but give money, which is easier for me than breathing!—for what I believe in." This could only have meant the South; pickaninny children, cotton choppers, something like that. Everybody needs a Lincoln Brigade to regret not having joined. These are the people who sent down money all those years, through thick and thick. (In thin, the checks tended to slack off a lot.) Teddy refused to reassure him, which he seemed to like, only it made him all the more abject. "Don't be ridiculous," Teddy had said. "What would you have *done* down there?" But usefulness was beside the point. The man had passed up what is known now as a "peak experience," emotionally speaking, and passed it up for what, for *what?*

Teddy, long past his peak experience, didn't sell much science, mostly history and "language arts." A little philosophy and ersatz economics to the colleges. Mississippi, western Alabama, southern Tennessee: he spilled out the goodies on all kinds of desks, big battered wooden ones; sculptured, shaped like kidneys in the offices of the vain; fiberglass like the muzzles of boats. He gave away hundreds of samples. He had to smile, thinking of how warmly the department heads greeted him in the ordering season. Ole Miss, where he had logged so many hours in demonstrations once upon a time he deserved to have a building named after him. USM, where he'd been chased down every narrow street in his car, past Fraternity Row and the chicken fry, and finally pulled into somebody's garage, cut his lights, and lay down on the front seat out of sight. Alcorn A & M, a black school where he was warned, more gently but no less firmly, never to set foot again because his presence was compromising, provocative—effective—dangerous to their state financing. How much easier it was to be welcome. His business went up twenty percent this year, twelve percent last year.

Jessie's work, on the other hand, was almost invisible. She taught second graders in an "alternative school" that was not as subversive as some people wished and others feared, in a building given to them, cast off, by the board of education. Its pipes leaked, its rear half seemed to be cracking off, in winter its heat was unsteady (to put it generously). But she was not even certain that was sabotage, they flattered themselves to think they mattered enough for that. She feared it was only inefficiency. All schoolchildren are hostages to red tape and fiscal insufficiency.

While she was content to tell people that she now found herself harvesting this modest garden, sweetsmelling and colorful, this crop of small children who danced to her tambourine and made marshmallow krispies and learned vowel sounds with her because it gave her pleasure day by day, it had taken Teddy many years to be able to tell people—simply to say, I sell textbooks—without going into a defensive history of his job record since the Movement. The dominant expectation, of course, was that one would be doing something in the People line, which is not much shorter than it ever was. Something distinctly nonprofit. The nonprofit part rarely sprang from the assumption that you have to be one to know one, but rather from the simpler more cynical recognition that some crazy fools will do anything to lend a hand, dirty work and all, for next to no salary, paid in the scrip of purity and purpose. They are the kind of people who are embarrassed by money, a dead middle-class giveaway. Poor people are not embarrassed by money and are contemptuous of those who are.

The best Teddy could do, by way of alibi, was to remind people of his accident. Oh yes, everyone remembered cheerfully. You died! They brought you back. Right, it was all in the papers. It was, and everybody knew it was no accident, it was somebody called the Higgs boys down from Carthage to do the job. The locals gloated, New York and Washington were outraged. There were still a few people he met who thought he had stayed dead; maybe some who thought he should have.

Well, he learned to tell his listeners. The part that was never in the papers was the part that came after the headlines (LAZARUS RIGHTS WORKER LOSES SUIT)—the plastic surgery, the lingering infections under the skin and his face forever tortured with scarring, the time with no job, no money, the long parade of hospital bills. And the insurance company wouldn't even pay for the car that looked twice totalled. They found a loophole somewhere between Intentional Foul Play and Acts of God that would show a confirmed troublemaker like Teddy Carll right out of the office into the cold.

No way he could hang around one of those long-suffering low-paying professional-altruist jobs when all that hit, he would explain. Anyway, he never did fancy a job with an in-out box and a water cooler. You already gave, someone would say consolingly. I gave, Teddy would agree. No— they *took*. Laughter all around. During these conversations Teddy's stitched-up face would begin to itch. Under the places where the surgeon had stretched tissue, added skin, stuck on flesh like a baker mending broken pie dough with moist fingers, his body would speak up: pain, real pain, it would say. You didn't imagine this. But you take it in vain if you think it's an excuse for going soft, joining up. Who did you say you work for?

He had always felt guilty for having been brought back to life. Some weren't. It's a feeling of soldiers everywhere who come back without their friends. Guilty, and then regretful: what for? What for? Jessie had watched him try to find a way to assuage the itch that was trapped inside his healed-over cheek like a moving parasite. He couldn't touch it, couldn't get to the solid behind the shadow to scratch it insensible. What was I raised up from martyrdom for, he would think. To sell history books that slap the sixties away like a hovering deer fly in half a page? To keep a special line of biology texts in the trunk of the car that neglects to mention evolution?

Teddy, these days, every day, came home from work enclosed in the bubble of his routine. Brown car swings into the driveway. Pause while he collects his papers and samples and order books. *America Then and Now. Science for Tomorrow (With Graded Workbook)*. Car door slams like a muffled explosion, the sound a firebomb used to make coming through a window. Thirty seconds, stuck screen door opens with a wheeze. Teddy buttonholed, each day, by the newspaper lying on the coffee table, just in off the porch where it is still thrown, in this age of automation, by a real newsboy on a (ten-speed) bike. Teddy in his baggy suit, subdued by it, reduced in scale. His tie off, either in his pocket or loose around his collar like the stole that hangs around a priest's neck.

When Jessie puts her head out of the kitchen and sees him poised for his minute and a half over the raucous headlines of the *Jackson Daily News*, the back of his jacket creased in large and little folds like some natural landscape viewed from above, papers falling every whichway from under his arm—maybe this is why she always greets him foolishly, clowning, doing a schottische, or clicking her heels together, coming forward with a carrot in her mouth like a rose—she feels such a lurch of disappointment that it winds her, a blow to the stomach. She can feel it fresh every day as if for the first time. Travelling salesman! (A cat-call.) Even the car has the antiseptic quality of something rented at the end of a plane ride into alien territory: it is scrupulously, unnaturally clean, another uniform. But her husband! Her husband was a very young man in dungarees—overalls sometimes, though he tended to leave that to his black friends. (Negro then. How long since they had known any Negroes?) He had such unlikely grace in his long knobby legs, his angular hairless chest, Jessie felt for the look of him now and the look of his practical neatly groomed car the way someone must feel for the lost beauty of a sick and agèd body, such welling hopeless pain.

But she forbids it. Most of the time, she forbids it.

. . .

Because Teddy had been a cowboy once. He and Skelly Washington, surrounded by their minions, were the Tolewood organizing project—they burned up the ground they walked on. They pushed their matching straw hats back on their heads (Skelly's brim with two precise holes edged brown-to-black the size of shotgun pellets) and they led the way, their bodies the vanguard; people fell in behind. There was something for everyone: Skelly dark brown and compact, efficiently made, an easy smiler with a dazzling smallboy grin, who made every black mama want him for her son, except the young ones who simply wanted him.

And Teddy's long unfrightened chin was at the level of Skelly's eyes. He was a different model of vividness, who made things look easy. Teddy's idea of masculinity, if it was an idea at all, was what Jessie—in time, not at the beginning when she was beguiled by it—called Old Gallant. It was an assurance-giving kind of confidence that swept people along as if in its wake, promising that the waters had been tested for invisible cross-currents, not to mention predators; the food already sampled for taint; the rotten floorboards danced upon and found sufficiently firm. He had, in fact, been his own scout into virgin territory, morally speaking; had been, after all, the first embattled rebel in the recent history of his family. (Earlier, there were stories, only after a full century become a source of amusement, of a great-great-grandfather who thought it a mortal sin to raise a gun to anyone, Civil War or no Civil War, who let himself be taken prisoner without resistance; and there were the usual wastrels and suicides who seemed at a distance more eccentric than tragic.) But Teddy had had to make his own way toward a definition of what mattered to him. Perhaps he had that cordial host's bearing for no reason but that he needed to escort others in the footsteps he had (not easily but so laboriously) made. Perhaps his weakness was the undermining side of his strength. Having made these footsteps, and made them wide and deep, wasn't enough. He needed followers.

He and Skelly had thrown away enough energy between them to light up a town the size of Rolling Fork. Jessie, who looked energetic because she had so many opinions, in fact indulged a thousand second thoughts and tired easily; she saw the cowboys as human batteries, charged by the very act of motion. Teddy could be in Clarksdale and hear about a problem in

McComb—that was more than a wish away—and there he would be, mysteriously seated in someone's living room at his peculiar angle, down on his coccyx, legs out straight, on an ancient sprung couch or on bare floor, with pointy knees up under his chin, arms around them, and he would be talking too much, twitching with a kind of afterburn of adrenaline like a dieseling motor that would not shut off when the key was turned. Finally he would settle into silence, would listen to others, would ask an occasional question or suggest a strategic gambit—would subside. Teddy's energy had to be banked or it flashed too hot.

Past tense, all that.

Now all that was left was a terrible weakness, Teddy's perpetual willful hopefulness. He was the kind of good man whose instincts, if not whose behavior, she would trust to the very death; given the necessity that he shortweight someone, it would always be himself. No matter what, she would never stop respecting that absolute integrity, that one unnegotiable. Life was a constant redressing of the balance, from rich man to poor, an endless bucket brigade, all that water sloshing over the side of the pail as he handed it on, soaking his raggedy shoes. He looked to Jessie like an astonished angel—there was something wide eyed, struggling for balance about him, a little high waisted up there on his stilty legs, as if the actualities of his life and the lives of others were breaking upon him too rapidly, full of absurdity, and he could only stand open mouthed, or laugh with a sort of stunned wonder.

When he delivered his famous speeches, all those eyes, and Jessie's, on him in churches, in people's parlors, in his great moment at the Democratic Convention in Atlantic City, what gave him his charisma had never been force and lofty entreaty—it was always a gentle bewilderment at the wretchedness of human behavior. It was a quality that made people identify his emotions as their own. Probably because his racial decency was born again, not automatic, his talk was full of questions, full of logic and reluctant pain. *I am one of those who can't go home again,* he would say: *my mama is deathly ashamed of me when she ought to be proud I've redeemed the family name.* He never seemed better than the people he addressed. This became quite calculated, at a certain point: canned spontaneity. But it was more genuine than most of the shuckin and jivin going on around him, and it seemed to bring the most humble, frightened audiences to their feet.

And oh, he had been beautiful in action, fierce and undeterred by doubt. Jessie knew that she had a weakness for fame that buckled her like an unreliable ankle, set her listing toward its source, no consultation with her will. (Later she would realize that such abjectness ran in her family; she had her mother's hunger for masculine heroes.) But he was good at what he did, and what he did mattered. She had, early, watched him lead a charge of small children out across the green in Peachtree where they hunkered down and spent the day on strike against their segregated classrooms. His speech, shouted out over the heads of adults and children alike, had been quoted "widely," as *Newsweek* put it, the one that ended, "These are the children born into bondage who shall deliver their parents into freedom"; subsequently it had been referred to as his "born into bondage" address, became an artifact with a life of its own. He hadn't written it down, it had been improvised on the spot, but someone had it on tape; it turned up in anthologies as an example of Southern white eloquence, second only to black eloquence in the recent history of persuasion.

Nonetheless what Jessie remembered of that day was the sight of him holding the children's hands, fitting them two at a time under one arm, carrying another who clutched him ungently by the ears, dragging along three or four who held on to his belt and his shirt: Teddy Carll as camp counsellor. One of the littlest children had started to cry in the face of the crowd, the stomping applause, perhaps at a glimpse of the tan sheriff's and highway patrolmen's hats, broad and flat as toadstools, visible behind the clot of spectators. She had watched Teddy put down the child he was holding and matter-of-factly take up the boy who was in tears, talking to him all the while; he had walked with him, stroking the child's bare brown leg and ankle, to the ravelled edge of the crowd and out, vanished while they were still calling him back to the center, his neck bent with attention. The little boy was howling in his ear and he was nodding, slowly, gravely nodding. His concentration was the thing she had first loved in Teddy: the inclination of his head in that necessary direction without fear of looking sentimental, whether it was challenge or rescue, instruction or correction, or, blessedly hers, the infinitesimal patient breath-held palm and finger touch of his love.

But one side of his face, not the ruined one but the one shadowed above his eye by his immovable cowlick, had seemed to be collapsing after all these years of surprise, caving insidiously into a permanent squint, an ironic twist. It was the kind of change that tends to be noticeable only in photographs: then and now. A matter of centimeters. His face had somehow sought its own emotional level. Jessie, pained, called this the Northern side of his face, the neurotic perplexed side that was not at home with what it saw, though she knew that was somehow self-serving; it was, of course, the native-born heart of him that had suffered most. Approaching middle age

(protecting himself against her? she wondered, hurt) Teddy looked perpetually piqued. Jessie heard herself turning into a nag.

Still, she could catch him at his old self sometimes; Teddy undepressed,
unpreoccupied. Inside, when he'd been home from the road an hour or two,
Teddy slowly began to take on his familiar outline. He would shuck his
work-clothes for khakis, put on his sneakers and challenge Lydia, say, to
jog around the block with him. "You're a lump, kid." She loved it when
he taunted her. "You're one of those eleven-year-old washouts who pants
after twenty yards." She threw a towel at him and bent down to tie her
running shoes blushing with pleasure. The rhythm of Teddy's absences and
returns was just odd enough that it made his presence a special treat after
he'd been away a few days. Leaning down, extending one leg that looked
endless beside Lydia's, he would bounce over his knee. Lydia, her eyes on
his face, would do the same, her small rump rising and falling as she stretched
out her tendons. However irritating he might be about other things, Jessie
thought, he had never treated Lydia like a son manqué. I gripe too much,
she would lecture herself while they loped past the front window, Lydia
trying to match her father's stride, leaping from foot to foot like one of the
airborne lighter animals. I do not want to be one of those irritable kvetchy
dissatisfied princess-wives whose husband is never *making* enough—money
for some, prestige for others. What for me, she wondered. Purity? Moral
brownie points? No, usefulness. He was rusting with disuse. Longfellow
said that, or Tennyson—those poets with three-syllable names were all the
same to her. Whoever he was, he was talking about Ulysses.

. . .

Later, when they had made up, Teddy told Jessie why he was so angry
at her.

He had been coming home elated from the delta, driving fast and ef-
fortlessly from flat to hill to flat again because it was a day on which
everything had come together and made something like lost sense to him.
It took very little—less and less in hard times—to touch his gratitude as if
it were a place on his body.

The mediocre department chairman at a mediocre junior college—it was
possible that he was being generous with the adjective—had been in the
process of buying one mediocre freshman comp. book for every student in
the entering class. Then, flipping through the text for the last time to see
what selections it contained he had stopped and said contemplatively, half
to himself, "Black Boy." He was a hard-sweating blond young man who

had a wedge-shaped body, very wide in the shoulders, all his sensitivity gone to his narrow feet where he could keep it secret. He had a pastel face: pink skin, powder blue eyes, pale yellow teeth. "That'll be an interesting piece to do with them, won't it."

Teddy had made inquiry, then, about his background, had been told how he was another of the ones—there were so many, Lord, and they had surfaced so slowly—who had lost his innocence, at seventeen, at a biracial conference of Methodist students in Washington; had discovered the sweet harmony that descended on him when he was convinced what it would mean to love all men as he had been instructed throughout his life in church. ("It's the literal-minded among us who've caused all the trouble, don't you think? Who hear the word and believe it?") How he had seized the black and human hand of the boy who stood beside him and had not been destroyed. This bore out Teddy's conviction that certain experiences acted like cancers, only benignly: who knew when, fifteen, twenty years later, their effects could work up to the surface and subvert the orderly function of anyone's cells?

And Teddy had cried out, forgetting that he was a salesman who worked on percentage. "Well, buy the whole damn book for those kids then. Don't read these paltry excerpts."

So they had made a list together of six books the freshmen ought to read to jimmy open their minds, none of them published by Teddy's company. "*Patterns of Culture*," Teddy said with a surge of memory, "to show them how many worlds there are. And Skinner, maybe"—and so on.

"You're a hell of a businessman," the department chairman said, shifting his weight a little on his oppressed thighs.

"A nonprofit service," Teddy had said, smiling from a different source than he did when he made a sale, and put away his order blanks.

So he had come home thinking, Better, better. Slowly but surely. This was not the kingdom of grace yet, but wasn't it fair to think he had helped slip a resistance fighter behind enemy lines?

But this is what he found on Willowbrae Drive.

Jessie sat on the single step of the slab porch and waited for him now, the day of the skewer incident. She knew it was mean-spirited but she was eager to enjoy catching him off-guard with her news of the morning's depredation. Lydia, who was eleven and tall like her parents, put her dark head out of the house, holding the door open. "Can I sit with you, Mama?"

"Sure," Jessie told her and pulled her out with a little wave. Now the moment would be ruined by her daughter's softening presence; she would be rendered a shade more humane, watched and protective, both.

"I didn't even use to know when your daddy was coming home in the old days," she said, the "daddy" sitting differently in her mouth than it had when she was a child: it had become one of those sops to Southern speech, no longer a simple reference; had become a word she would surely go on using for Lydia's father if she was still around when Lydia was fifty. "He would ride off someplace and I'd stay home and just pray he was coming back again." A history of the Movement through the eyes of The Wife, who had sat all day in the little Freedom Library checking out whatever they owned, gifts from Northern friends who had cleaned out their attics: Book II of Henry George's *Single Tax* and *The Compleat Angler* of Isaak Walton, to small boys who could hardly read "cat."

"And then that time he didn't."

Lydia nodded. The repetition of family myth, Jessie thought, is all they have to prove we weren't always as we are now; that and photographs and the unwarranted faith children have, in thrall to whatever illusions they are handed. It would have been easier to believe she had forever been a nag and Teddy her bored and resistant husband, just as if the issue between them were her lust for a "better" neighborhood or an all-electric kitchen.

Lydia gossiped without stopping to breathe: there were a lot of things that were not fair today, specifically that Sheri had come to her birthday party but had not invited Lydia three weeks later to hers. There was also the new arrangement of seats in school that put her in the middle of a mess of boys, bad enough, but they never turned down their noise and she couldn't even get her work done let alone enjoy a human conversation. Did it sound like a punishment, she wondered, for some obscure sin? She was afraid to ask her teacher for fear those sins might be insidiously multiplying. Injustice steeped in her eyes like tea in two cups, darkening them.

Jessie sat guiltily organizing her own grievances. She made herself listen, off and on, but this was one of Lydia's self-propelled monologues: an occasional grunt of reassurance seemed to be sufficient.

Andy, still at school right now for tennis practice, was Lydia's representative to the world-at-large. There wasn't much he could not do—he was a promising soccer wing; he acted (*Twelfth Night* these days, softening Sebastian's syllables no way Shakespeare had ever intended, but with a gentle conviction); he fixed as many minor motors as his father ignored; was at ease with the silent underwater conversation of computers; played the clarinet serviceably; swam; was neither contentious nor lazy nor, in spite of (because of?) his trayful of talents, particularly ambitious either. He even fought with his sister, as if to forestall accusations of primness or unhealthy perfection.

He was modest and splendid and essentially a stranger to his parents because of it. Andy had always been the kind of child Jessie worried about, superstitiously: she sometimes thought, bending to kiss him goodnight in his neat quilt-covered bed, that she could see him reflected in the unchanging past tense after some unthinkable accident or illness: what a fine boy he had been, the kind this country needs, a model son, friend, brother. She believed, helplessly, that danger most often shadows the undeserving. It seemed, all too often, to be so, though statistically she knew she was not on firm ground.

But then came passionate Lydia to remind them how much chance there is in children; that was the relief of having more than one of them: Lydia they recognized. She was tense, skittish, lonely, focussed. Her depressions were more extreme than her brother's; so were her ecstasies. From very early on, she drew uncanny pictures, adorned the margins of her books with tiny hieroglyphics so composed and controlled they hardly seemed the work of a small child. Unlike her brother, who was enchantingly gregarious and had spent his childhood in the laps of everyone who dared sit in their living room, Lydia tended to stay at one remove and study the company. Sometimes she would color in laboriously, with her ubiquitous set of brightly colored markers, an intricately beautiful dress or suit (she seemed to intuit the shapes and designs of most of the world's native fabrics and costumes) and try to draw the visitor inside the clothes: brown faces and white, thin friends and affectionately rendered fat ones; all was duly noted. Then Lydia would gravely hand the unwitting model a piece of typing paper with some gorgeous bit of finery perfectly centered on it. Like a servant, she would seem to evaporate then, soundlessly, before she could properly be thanked; there was something impersonal about such giving, such unself-conscious genius, as if it were a natural duty, like saying hello, goodbye, can I get you anything? Complimented, people went home and put up Lydia's posters of themselves made glorious. There are many ways to find oneself well liked; the children had mastered diametrically opposed means. The ingenuity of the race, Teddy and Jessie agreed, was humbling. Teddy was simply proud of Lydia. Jessie tended to be terrified and relieved on alternate days, considering her future: she had been born to her own style. Assured though it might be, it was too early to take bets on her profession; but that unpremeditated style was as immutable as her face.

Lydia had continued on about the putrid boys at her table who seemed inclined these days to talk about nothing but jock straps. "Have I ever seen one of those?" she asked her mother, then, "Here he comes!" Lydia cried as the car appeared around the corner with Teddy's shadow sitting straight, alone.

How relieved Jessie used to be—this was long before Lydia—to see his old black Buick pull up to the deplorable ditch that went past their house in Tolewood, that unpainted town shack that stood shoulder to shoulder with its neighbors. They had been so close they could hear the pork chops popping in their fat on the stove next door; could watch old Ti Anderson pee a lovely glittering arc off his back porch every morning at the same time precisely, a ritual watering; could hear it sizzle as it hit the thirsty ground.

Now the brown car stopped with a grunt of exhausted springs. Teddy got out fast, smiling, and whirled Lydia around. Her skirt flew out in a white blur like a color wheel. "Brought you something," he said and with a flourish produced from behind his back a single peacock feather so long it bent its eye side down toward the pavement as if it wanted to graze there.

"Mom, look!"

Lydia took it from him and waved it before her mother's eyes so that Jessie felt a mild breeze that tickled her nose. "Did you buy it or find it?"

"Saw a peacock right in the road." He drew Lydia to his side and whispered the story especially to her.

Jessie, purposely not rising but sitting huddled over her feet to warn him she was not to be courted when he finished courting his daughter, was thinking that men stopped making love to their wives—or, rather, started making love to others—when their wives began to be to them too much like their mothers. It hardly seemed fair to be forced to scold a man she had no desire to mother. But she picked the cold silver skewer off the concrete and held it up in the air without a word, so that she could watch Teddy and register an instant's recoil and then a long bewilderment. As always she feared the day he would stop wanting her. What if she came to that point herself? If this endless past tense in which he believed hardened—petrified—into history and lost its capacity to move her? It was so dangerous a thought there was something titillating about it.

"What in the hell is that?" Teddy asked in a tone that implied that, having been mad yesterday, she was only a shade madder today. He squinted at it.

"An object of destruction, my dear," she answered in a witch's cackle, and meant it every way she could. She approached the car, which was still clicking and crepitating, cooling down, and aimed it like a cake tester at the front left tire. "Let me show you how it works."

Teddy looked, watching his wife's display of anger—she put the fine tip of the skewer gently against the gray alligator skin of the tire and then threatened to pound it in with the flat of her palm—as if he felt that leap of terror from groin to throat of a man, after so many years, about to be set upon by a mob. Not that she might puncture the tire (because she was not insane), nor that he understood that the skewer had been deployed against them as a statement, hysterical and unwarranted. It was, perhaps, that he saw how Jessie stood at a very far remove from him and looked uncharacteristically triumphant. Whatever sorrow she might have felt at such a distance was nowhere visible in her challenging stance. Well, she could not have ordered up a better set of arguments for her cause than these petty terrorist attacks.

Nothing that had hurt them in their marriage, they had always thought, had left a permanent chip missing, a measurable rift. If anything, their losses had driven them together: Teddy's accident, his succession of unsatisfactory jobs, their disappointment over the wearing down of the Movement's passion, their bitterness at the betrayal of old friends—they walked this charred landscape hand in hand, and hadn't it always bulwarked them to share each falling from the grace and the intensity of their beginnings? Tenderness, after all, is the child of vulnerability, not of perfect strength. If each had been asked about a favorite place on the other, a tangible spot which brought forth their protectiveness just at the point where it touched provocation, Jessie would have chosen the back of Teddy's neck, that pale slender narrow part that connected the weighty dark head and body so problematically and could be stolen up on without his suspecting: it was a boy's neck always. As for Teddy—well, the most secret inner flesh of Jessie's thigh, of course, all the way around under the buttocks: what is more private, more delicate, less capable of defense? The dearest part of anyone is always the one most intimate, in greatest contrast to the visible, assertive anatomy of the public person.

Therefore it would have made sense had Teddy felt an ominous premonitory chill watching Jessie fool with the skewer. She twisted it to shine and shine again. They were in the middle of something that had not begun today—nothing ever begins fresh today—but she was almost jolly with it. She felt herself empowered.

Teddy held his daughter in the crook of his arm and scratched his head like a country boy doing sums. Lydia put her arm around her father's waist and looked up at him as if he might have an answer. "Honey," he said, "can't you just hear Verona saying—" and he pitched his voice a little bit high and hung his head on the side, disarmingly— " 'Dear hearts, your presence testifies! Staying put *exactly* where you are not wanted. Making yourself a splinter in the public's hide.' "

Jessie stood beside the car flat footed. "Sure, I can hear her. I can also hear her saying, 'Now you all got to remember that nine tenths of what you do is in your *timing*. Do the right thing at the wrong time, you might as well have stood in bed.' You've heard her say that, dear heart. Don't you think your neighbors here have got enough on their minds without needing a lesson in integration?"

Lydia looked from one to the other of them—the terms of their argument were very familiar and they didn't worry her disproportionately. Often the sound of her parents' voices in this mode (a shade irritable, carefully, not viciously, mocking, ultimately like a single voice trying both parts impartially) was almost soothing. Children will adapt to anything as long as it holds no shocks or hard surprises. And in this case it assured her that both of them were home here with her, working something out. It was only their way.

"You're not the one who's here when these things happen, Teddy. I am and your children are. And we, conservative as we are, have not enjoyed these confrontations as much as you seem to."

Teddy was abstracted. Jessie knew that look: he was picturing a meeting. Whatever the cause of these incidents, racial or economic, they were victims of a plan to oust them. These menacing occurrences were not coincidental. Therefore he would speak. Andréa and Tommy would speak. Jessie would not ask to, or want to. Maybe Jug Dixon of the Interracial Committee. They would ask their neighbors if they knew they were marching time backwards, undoing as they went. That foolishness. They would try to chasten without scolding, take the audience gently over to their side, strengthen their exposed flank. But of course the troublemakers would never be at such a meeting, they never were. He looked, suddenly, tired; it was the low blood sugar time of day. Later they would argue: a man comes home in a celebrating mood and meets that face. But not yet, not before he replenished his energy.

"What are we having for dinner, shish kebob?"

Jessie handed him the skewer with a grand gesture and he knighted Lydia Lady Carll. She curtsied low before him, her knee almost touching the concrete of the driveway. Then they went inside laughing, filling in the distance fast as if it were a hole they had dug on a sandy beach and they didn't want anyone else to come along and trip in it. Jessie's hand was on Teddy's back gently, apologetically, as they went into the house.

. . .

At dinner Jessie watched his attentiveness to Lydia, as though she could hear him say, I am not in bad with every woman in the world. No one was more present to his children than Teddy when he wanted to be, or as absent. He was like a cat who would not necessarily come when called. But she had always been jealous of his days "on," the bicycle rides into the country on the other side of the reservoir, all of them carrying parts of a picnic in their knapsacks. She would watch his face as they extracted bread and cheese from one pack, tomatoes and cookies from another and lay them grandly down. She would watch their faces, too, when he would lean over on one elbow and ask them if he had ever mentioned the time he and his cousin Billy Walsh had dynamited a rattler's nest: that was too good to be true, he and Billy Walsh appeared to have spent their entire childhoods together enticing innocent creatures to their destruction. Jessie was sure he had read about the way to entrance credulous children, Southern style. Or he would take them to the zoo to spend hour after hour in front of a single animal's cage until they had its attention, until they were part of the view for the hippopotamus or the monkey, who would slow down, stop twitching, come to have what looked like a talk. They found places to pick raspberries, to see ice cream in giant vats and get a free paper cup's worth, to ride on a monorail some eccentric had built out of scraps in his own backyard in Carroll County. He had taught the whole block the game of running bases and took them over to a good grassy place where they could flop without burning up their pants knees.

Teddy knew all sorts of things, too: that it was just possible there had been human sacrifices at the Indian mounds in Emerald, and Civil War history which could almost make them cry: the Union and Confederate soldiers coming down to the same stream to wash their clothes on opposite shores and stare at one another in the slowly lifting mist of morning. He had lurid tales of early Jackson that made it sound like New Orleans at its seamiest: a block-long building lost in a game of poker, a woman sold by her lover to the highest bidder, "a white woman with the most beautiful pale cheeks anyone ever saw, they were like gardenias—she had been made to grow up with a net over her face to keep the sun off. And the man who won her wanted her to marry him in a huge ceremony to which she would have to come naked so everyone could see how lucky he was!" The children would stare, embarrassed but afraid to take their eyes off him, for fear they might miss something. "Only the minister wouldn't do it, in fact when he heard about it he kept the woman from having to marry the gambler at all, even in a wedding dress." And there were duels, the story about the second who said to some boys in the crowd, "Don't watch from the trees, gentlemen, my man has terrible aim." And the congressman who came out against dueling—there was a great deal of it, a cross between Continental and Wild West honor—and had to fight a duel to defend himself! Teddy could describe the pistols, silver and mother of pearl like sacred objects; once, he said, he had held one and pretended to aim it. It was so heavy he had to steady it with his other hand.

Maybe, Jessie thought, he secretly enjoyed the life of a salesman, the professionally likable man. Maybe all those years of exhorting like a preacher had turned into this simple story-telling, the charm he dumped out of his salesman's case along with his order books. Like a bad marriage, the job might gratify needs he didn't even know he had.

And once a year on a spring Sunday he led them all on what Andy and Lydia called their annual Confederate Pig-out. They would dress in their most formal clothes—Lydia even wore lace-topped ankle socks—and go down to Captain Billy Bob's in Pecanville to sit at a round table and watch the food of the collective South circle in the center, slow as a fan, on a lazy Susan. There was ham and golden fried chicken, a dozen vegetables cooked into sweet collapse, every variety of aspic with marshmallows, Jell-O jewels with canned fruit glowing through their sides, and every kind of biscuit and lard-rich pie known to the kitchens of the state. Helpings were unlimited; Teddy said such generosity was the cook's way of getting even with centuries of employers' stomachs; the apotheosis would be the first intestine to burst right there in the dining room between the wooden rung-back chair and the thousand-times-laundered white table cloth.

Teddy wore a bow tie to Billy Bob's, no matter how warm the day; if he'd owned one of those slouched forties fedoras he'd have pushed it back on his sweating head and lit a cigar. At the round table where they sat among strangers, they were allowed only a few topics of conversation: the prospects for next year's football season, the high points of the last; the social lives of selected relatives; the sales at the best of the Jackson stores; and the speculations of the weather bureau about the kind of day Easter would be. After the first few outings, Jessie threatened not to come any more. "You can spoof this place, it's yours," she told Teddy. "It's all a little like who can call who 'nigger.' "

"But the kids love it!" Teddy would complain innocently. "We're giving them everything they miss growing up in the house of cynics. Lyddie gets chucked under the chin by old ladies with their glasses on a string, and men with big bellies talk to Andy like he's going to be a hell of a linebacker someday."

Finally it became clear to her that Teddy loved the hotel dining room himself; that its wooden floorboards and the walls extravagantly papered with framed newspapers and photos of local celebrities, athletes and politicians of repulsively reactionary stripe, county beauty queens and civic leaders in suit jackets that could have been Teddy's father's—he loved all of it and loved it straight. These Sundays were a long dream of his enemies at home, who had once been his friends. She found herself thinking, one time, as they stood at the huge brass cash register paying the extraordinarily modest bill, that he was like Tom Sawyer at his own funeral: something in him was full of shame and unrequited love, honor and embarrassment confounded, and he could only watch it from afar, pretend not to be there. He had sat with one arm behind each of his children's chairs, proudly, protectively, and if someone asked him a question from across the table he answered smiling, a good genteel boy, a finer son, without an ounce of irony in him. His mother, Dorothea, would have been proud. On those days the children would feel his gaiety and they'd laugh a lot together, and Jessie could see that in an odd way Teddy was right: mockery was only one part of all the day was about, he and the children actually needed to visit this palace of ritual decorum. Finally she took refuge in the role of quiet wife, dutifully sitting, stiff as a glass plate photograph, beside her exemplary children.

.   .   .

Contemplating the nastiness of their situation, Jessie was bemused. What a peculiar bind she was in. Would there ever be a time when she was in the right place at the right time with the right assumptions? Teddy's optimism could be as debilitating as her pessimism.

She had met him, for example, when he knocked her down—that was simple. But what she was doing on the floor in that classroom in Ohio, and what he was doing there standing over her—that took more than a little explaining. (The children liked to hear all this, even the painful parts.)

Jessie had arrived—this was June of the summer of 1964—at the scene of her real life in her red Volkswagen with its one green fender that hung like a single leaf on a flower blowing South. Half the campuses in the country had committed their able-bodied students, like villages their soldiers, to the second Civil War; they were being waylaid for a week in Ohio en route to their destiny. The planners had found the most typical college—so Jessie reported to her parents on the phone, appalled, derisive—the kind of campus she had studiously avoided when she chose to commute to City College in New York. Probably the idea was to break them in slowly, to bridge the gap between the protected life that had held most of them until a few weeks before and the wilds of Mississippi.

She had just been sprung, as she liked to put it, from CCNY, where she had managed as disruptive a career as she could, short of expulsion: arrests for civil defense drill violation, for anti-U.S. speeches during the Cuban "troubles," for any little thing that could keep her vitriol level high and active in fairly quiet times. She was not a Communist, her father had made that mistake for her, but she thought of herself as tough and unsentimental, as callused as her feet in their incessant sandals were callused. Hardened by good wear.

But this was definitely the outermost chamber of the mystery: the colonial brick dormitories, the mazy crossing of a dozen cement paths in front of the regulation chapel. A crayoned sign said ORIENTATION. It could have been an orientation to anything, she had thought: graduate school, a chess tournament, a summer school where the grinds pushed ahead and the goof-offs fell a step further behind. There were arrows in chipper purple and green. She could see suitcases lying open, trustingly, on the beds that were visible through open doors, and cameras with their straps dangling over the side. There must have been a hundred guitars. They had meal tickets and name tags waiting for them, as if for a celebration dinner, and they had pictures taken holding their names under their chins the way convicts held their numbers, mugging, some of them (probably the most frightened) smiling grimly, not smiling at all. (Defensively: I never smile.) They bristled with opinions, challenges, self-satisfaction. Some looked as solemn as refugees. Jessie decided not to smile but to laugh outright, to dare her destiny, although she had to go through a little buck and wing in her mind—it's hard to laugh at nothing, hard like tickling yourself, she thought. (Where is the picture? the children had asked. Be glad you've never seen it, she said. They only used the ones of the people who didn't come back; Andy Goodman's she thought. He had stood on that line two weeks before her.)

Her roommate had been a transparent-skinned blond girl from Des Moines named Lynn who arrived behind so many valises she had enlisted the help of not one but two eager boys who followed her around the whole week. She looked right through both of them. Eventually they became friends with each other, for consolation. Within half an hour Lynn had thrown up her lunch. ("Barfing in the john" she called it, which made it sound like something you did at a fraternity party after too much sangria. Her short blond hair stuck to her ears with sweat, Jean Seberg playing Joan of Arc.)

She tried to mask the problem with half a bottle of Muguet des Bois but she was, Jessie had thought, recoiling, like someone pregnant with fear. Every meal faithfully traced its way back up to remind her that her body had some rights in this matter too: she might volunteer herself for death but who said *it* had to follow?

The more she shrank, of course, lost somewhere between her good intentions and what she dramatically called her "body's betrayal," the bolder Jessie felt. It was a set-up. Lynn sounded to the emboldened Jessie like an old lady who could no longer get around. Wasn't that the outline of a Peter Pan collar across her shoulder bones the way some girls had bikini straps against their tan? Given such frailty, she thought, she would never stop tinkering with her hide, toughening it, roughing it up.

Jessie made up rules for her as if she'd heard them certified by an instructor in some previous course in life-saving: IF IT FRIGHTENS YOU TO CALL HOME, DON'T! The poor girl's mother ritually offered up her father's heart, every time Lynn called, laid it right on the line for her: "If you really *go there* after the week in Ohio, he is going to *die* and I am going to blame you." That, at least, was what Lynn heard. Others had terminally anxious grandmothers and terrified siblings and all of them seemed to circle around the home phones wringing their hands in a clamorous chorus. "So don't call," Jessie cautioned. "Send them a postcard: GREETINGS FROM OXFORD, OHIO." "What do your parents say?" Lynn would ask Jessie just to pick at her sores a little bit. "Oh mine—well, they've been there." That was as tactless as Lynn could have hoped from her. Her mother *had* literally been there—in Alabama in 1935 doing literacy work, nobly failing. "What does that mean, you were a 'red-diaper baby'?" Lynn asked earnestly, whereupon Jessie simplified vastly: her parents emerged as battered heroes who ought to have inspired ballads. It had been years since they had been involved, in fact; had been anything but disgusted with politics. Her mother had credit cards; once a week, she had a *maid*. Still she wished she could have explained to Lynn that being in Mississippi was for her a kind of obedience too.

She listened to some stirring speeches and was awed by the speakers because they had lived in unspeakable danger. Teddy was one of them. But the content of the speeches was redundant: Jessie did not believe they could learn anything useful about where they were going; what they needed was on-the-job training. Nor was she the only arrogant one on campus. "No, I don't find Negroes repulsive," said one girl in the circle, smiling. "I actually would say I find them quite attractive." Then there was a boy, one of those pink-blonds whose face is always red, who had an Adam's apple that protruded like a perpetual hard-on. "What I want to do is to teach the Negro that Christianity is his most dangerous myth. Historically it has been disastrous for him to identify with his keeper's religion." And so on. Each of them had a leitmotif and dutifully sang it; they simplified themselves and they simplified each other. Surely, Teddy had known, they simplify *us*. Some girls talked lovingly about their maids, others boasted that at their college a Negro was student body vice president. There were so few blacks in their backgrounds, none could be spared for obscurity. Jessie had never thought much about it but she found herself having trouble calling up more than one or two distant Negro faces from her parents' years in the Party—one man who showed up in their kitchen for the endless friendly ideological harangue that was a sport of her family and their friends, and was not made to feel notably welcome. A very light-skinned girl in her high school debating club who probably had one black grandparent. Jessie's record was every bit as blank as anyone else's—it was an amazing discovery since, had anyone asked her, her enormously inflated sense of social virtue, which was like an inherited, unexamined family fortune, would have brought forth piety, even outrage.

Now, too late, she gathered around her some of the odd lots and broken sizes, the Lynns, who were imprinted to her, a long-necked creature of decided opinions and no wiles. Others who'd had some political experience did the same. They spent their time like manic-depressives, sky-high on the singing, which felt like an aphrodisiac that stimulated some long-submerged feeling, a longing other than sex. They were spurred on by the staff's talks about history and purpose and just as suddenly laid low by the discovery that there had been rancor and worse—nothing less than strife—over the decision to have them there at all. It was shocking: they were the contested spoils won by one side in a skirmish, and both sides were stuck with them. That was something they tried not to think about, how their trainers saw them as summer school kids.

They watched, with the attention they had given their studies, stark black-and-white films of beatings and demonstrations, acres of heads which rose and fell from the mass like chocolate pudding at a rolling boil. They heard the names of eighty-two counties that fell loosely into two categories, "regular English" like Calhoun and Hinds, and all the rest Indian: Pontotoc, Issaquena, Yalobusha. "We'll never learn those!" Lynn wailed, her eyes big with alarm. "Why do we have to? This isn't school!" Because everything depended on the distinctions; these were jurisdictions, fiefdoms. Cross a county line and the air changes, they were told. You will know them the way you know your brothers' and sisters' names or you'll be in trouble.

Whenever Jessie closed her eyes she saw Negro women washing their clothes on the rocks of a river. She saw Ross Barnet standing quite literally in the narrow door of a white clapboard schoolhouse, a hand on either jamb. Those were the things she thought she knew. She tried to memorize the *Summer Volunteer Handbook*: *Do not carry any object that could be called a weapon. (This includes cuticle scissors, penknives, etc.) Watch out for suspicious actions of cars and for vehicles with 2-way radio antennae.* She was an obedient girl, she wanted to swallow it all down. Do not throw apple cores in the street, she told herself. Do not sing in public. Go directly to jail, do not pass GO. Do not collect two hundred dollars. Do not go gentle into that good night. I should have a last fling, she thought, like a soldier on his way to boot camp. I might not survive these rules. But she knew she'd be good at them, she was good at tests you couldn't study for.

One night she had it out with a young woman named Edith Eddy, who had a huge voice, church grown, who loved to use it to humiliate the volunteers. Jessie marched over to her at dinner one night—her whole table watched the encounter—and accused Edith of wanting it both ways: we came to help, invited, and we are repulsed, derided, laughed at. What the hell, she demanded, is going on here? Are we going to risk our lives or are we not?

"I never wanted you-all," Edith Eddy told Jessie coolly, a large woman in overalls, whose bust was at the level of Jessie's chin. She used her whole body like an unconcealed weapon. "Some did, some didn't. You-all more trouble than you'll ever work out to be worth, if you don't mind my saying so. Or even if you do. I never made it no secret how *I* felt."

"Just because you were born poor," Jessie said.

"Who said born poor. You think we're all alike. Just black," she said. "I got everything to gain, everything to lose. You got nothin much to give, and that's the truth." Edith's table mates were not so blunt, they soothed Jessie a little, they soothed Edith a little. Edith, here we *are*, somebody said. One of them was Teddy but she didn't notice him then, not yet. He told her later, Your chin never quivered. Damn right, Jessie said. If she had brandished that breast at me another minute, I'd have bitten the goddamn thing off.

One morning, early on, Jessie went looking for a roomful of freedom school teachers: they were going to "do" Mississippi history, learn what they might need to run a rudimentary classroom with no money and no books. "Do what the spirit say do." She opened the door to what she thought was the class and was set upon with a samurai cry, full force, the wind knocked out of her, her clipboard flung, her arms surprised up like a flight of birds. Teddy against her chest for the very first time. He wrestled her down and as she crumpled he was shouting, Cover up! Don't leave yourself open. Don't flail, protect yourself!

But she had flailed. Then she had cried. Picking herself up from where he had her pinioned, knee on her groin (but forbearing—he was, she noted, very well controlled), he could have raped her, maimed her, cut his initials in her cheek. She was easy game, and the whole class laughed. He let her catch her breath, then pulled her up and turned to them. Easy to laugh, he said, but if I come out around a corner and jump on you sometime, from behind a tree, a wall, you better know what to cover. Laughing is good for two kinds of people, fools and wise men. Take your pick but don't be too easy on yourselves. . . .

Jessie brushed herself off, muttered to him what class she was looking for and left disgraced. He did not apologize: he had only been doing his job and he tended to concentrate hard.

But here was where the complicated part began to come in. He had been doing what he saw as his job, frightening his students, then smoothing their feathers back, giving them what little he could of his mastery of certain kinds of situations, saying, This will help you to survive, this is a jeopardy worth surviving.

When they were making the assignments finally—who'd go where, do what, who could take the stress of a bad place like McComb, who needed experienced command when lives hung on it, their own and others', whole communities who weren't looking for trouble—Teddy alternated between the necessary bravado and the heart-stopping humility. He wanted to keep his fingers crossed, he told her, not for luck but the way children did it, telling a lie with hands in a knot behind their backs, not to *mean* it. To make these fates provisional.

There were an even dozen drop-outs who were going home, and he couldn't mock them: enough of the brazen ones ought to be going home, instead of coming along to be nurtured and protected, dropping the load off their shoulders every time they took a step. Coming along didn't guarantee that you were wise, or even smart. That little bitty Lynn, he said to Jessie, who was your friend? "She tried," he told Skelly, who was making fun of her pathetic white-girl pallor. "She didn't have to be here at all."

"Damn right she didn't. Eatin our food, warmin a seat, should of stayed the hell home, she could mince around on them lil pink toenails. Phuh." Skelly made a spitting sound. A girl like Lynn was an ant beneath his shoe.

Teddy wouldn't apologize for her, or for any of the other white folks. He was absolute about what mattered, but the way you found your way onto the path, and then worked up the strength to follow it. . . . You did better being flexible about the details. Sometimes he felt like a preacher, saying Arrogance never won a true heart. Some of his friends, after all, called Martin Luther King a sucker. If that was irreverent or unpopular, so much the better: reverence was undemocratic. If anything made them revolutionaries, it was that they would slay—well, nearly slay—for democracy. They were nonviolent, they would sit on their fists, but they would not talk about loving the people they were merely too prudent to hit. Martin and the Mahatma were in some other place, serene, sublime. *They* were still seething, in the first glory of their power. They were not about to subvert that power with love, except for their own.

Not too many people were patient about the pain, but look, Teddy said, look, to his black friends, who got to tell stories out of their childhoods over and over again and everybody listened. You are *born* to this. And even you have all those people out there in the fields, in their cabins, in Missy's kitchen, who are afraid to come with you, right?

Right. They got their reasons.

Of course they do. And you coax them and cajole them. You put a cotton sack over your shoulder and you go in there with them, looking like one of them, and you go up and down the rows with your clipboard in your hand taking names, trying to get them to stop for a minute and just meet your eyes. And when they do, you see fear and you see confusion, you see all the things they don't understand that you're asking them to be part of. So you don't say, Join up, be a kamikaze for freedom, all you say is, Brother. Sister. Come to the church tonight. Register, put your name down. Nothing more. One thing at a time.

Right.

Right. Well, look. White folks are my people. (It cost him something to say this, not only to his friends but to himself, because he hated so many of them to the bottom of his bowels. So many would kill him if they could. But they were. They were his people.) They don't *have* to come over on our side.

They do! You crazy, man, they *do*. They can't abuse us like they do and stay human!

So that was where they bought in with Martin, even the tough ones who never said love. That's what you think, Teddy would say, but say it wincing. Maybe not human in our terms. But human enough in theirs. That's a sentimental cliché: they can go right on eating and working and screwing and even going to church Sunday morning, and making a hell of a lot better wage than your family, I'm not talking Klan, I'm talking just folks, and when they die they still get buried with honor and people still grieve for them just as if they were human. It's a pretty good facsimile. They don't have to stop and give it a human thought until they *want* to. So don't shit on the ones who stop and think. They choose that. They elect to do it. They can afford to, and you and your folks can't.

Oh, they would say. Listen to him. Noblesse o-bleeeej.

He had lost a lot of his power in those talks, pilloried as an apologist and worse: not altogether trusted. But Teddy was not Carl Stickney, who had grown up in Cambridge the son of a liberal political science professor, or Manny Wasserstein from Queens with his little goat's beard, both of whom, good strategists, were in favor at the moment, while he was not. He was not to the manner born in matters of social justice and he saw what he saw from a flatter angle, closer to the earth, like a ray from a declined sun. He thought of himself as an exemplar of a white man who had chosen with no gun to his temple. If they knew his mother, saw her in her hat on the doorstep of the church, having prayed him away . . . We need one of those signs they put in diners, he told Jessie bitterly: NO CREDIT GIVEN HERE. If they knew the racist things he had thought as a child, which he would never repeat, even to make his point . . . Could he never repudiate them sufficiently, not even if he gave his life?

The only people who seemed inclined to sympathy these days were the Northern white kids, whose presence he had fought for. He'd rather have had an equal number of Southern white kids instead, who would go back to their own hometowns, who knew how shaky it felt, sometimes, to be a new convert, cut away from how many years. But not yet, not yet. That would come, it was slowly beginning. Meanwhile, he was here, wasn't he? Meanwhile, having capitulated and accepted these white students for the sake of the publicity and the protection they would bring with them—the power they possessed without deserving it, for which they would never be forgiven—Teddy's SNCC friends brought him word of every reject, every scared bird who turned tail and scuttled on home. When the girl from Smith said that "au contraire," she loved Negro men, they looked at him and smiled as if she were his sister, who had just serviced the regiment.

One night he found himself spilling it all, like the leeching of a wound, to a New York girl, a long tall Sally with a headful of tan curls. Little

Orphan Annie. That was how he saw her. She was a shade more canny than the rest, with a long background of disillusioning Party history which she liked to advertise even though she claimed it came to nothing—nada! rien! And when they finished walking, end of the line, on this campus path that jutted into empty space like a narrow dock over water, she wanted to be kissed. He had, in his own mind at least, long since jilted his fiancée Lenor, who was back at Millsaps in summer school taking the math she'd flunked because she was with him all the time. But even if he hadn't, all this Jessie wanted was a kiss from a suffering Southerner. He had poured his aggrieved heart into her hands, which could hold none of it, but he had done it in earnest and she was trying. He thought he must look like a damn fool or a hero, and knew he was neither. But in spite of the fact that she'd rather find herself some black stud—when in Rome they all did—nonetheless he had kissed her, he said, because he could not afford to be one degree more lonely than he was just then. And she had said one good thing to him on their way out there. She had said that pretentious nonsense about the Party, rien, nada, but then she had smiled at herself and changed it. "But look, you know, it's like family, your past. You're made of it. It's there whether you ever acknowledge it or not, or love it or hate it or find it boring or embarrassing, right? It doesn't need your approval, but denying it won't make it go away." How the hell did she know that? She had arrived thinking she knew almost everything; his corresponding arrogance was to believe that she and all the other innocents had come knowing absolutely nothing, that *this*, his, was the only genuine experience. He kissed her for that sad and surprising and perfect paradox, and when she laughed he thought about telling her she could ruin her reputation standing so close to the resident reconstructed redneck. Instead, with a nudging sense of relief that someone trusted him even if she had no rank, he had closed his eyes on everything and kissed her again.

. . .

Many years later this recital of what Teddy thought had happened drove Jessie to laughter every time, laughter because the anger that massed in her chest, her throat, had nowhere to go. She let it break in the heat of her mouth like an ice floe dissolving. True, she had been naive. And arrogant. And hungry. Correct, correct. And he had had everything: experience, courage, pain, openness, and that infinitely touching grown boy's body she could never have enough of. But were those two who spoke and held each other without breath and finally pronounced themselves in love only their own ideals for which they had found a willing embodiment? Were they stand-ins for real people who were somewhere else, like those paste diamonds some women wear while their priceless diamonds doze on velvet in a safe? If Teddy was only the hero and Jessie the groupie, *who* had married that afternoon in Tolewood in white Mexican wedding shirts and dungarees under a sign that substituted for a wedding canopy: ONE MAN + ONE WOMAN = TWO VOTES? And what if one ideal accidentally marries one real person? One round and one flat—she remembered something from a college class on the novel—didn't Dickens make flat characters? It had begun to occur to her early on, and she suppressed it, that when she looked at Teddy in a group or even alone, at rest, what she was seeing was really a painting, or a photograph of a generic Early Movement Hero, the shadows his nose and his eyelashes cast altogether hypothetical. Was he shallow, or only grandly deluded to think that where he lived now, in 1979, could make a difference to anyone? Sometimes she thought of the animals who'd survived in the thickets of genetics, the first mutant long-necked giraffes who didn't starve because they could eat from the tops of the trees, who miraculously had the qualities they needed for one time, one place. Teddy, perhaps, had such qualities, deep but narrow. Courage was not what was needed now, nor even obstinate integrity. Perseverance was; there was ample work for the detail men, and the ones with a good grasp of economics.

.   .   .

A week after the skewer found its way into Andy's tire and out again, Teddy went out in the morning with his case of sales ledgers and ball-point pens and started up the car. From the kitchen Jessie could hear it grind and stop and grind again. It was October, the morning damp and a little chilly, but even from there she could tell it was a very peculiar noise, no cold-weather cough. After two gnashes Teddy had apparently had enough, he had stopped trying. She went to the front door expecting to see the hood up and the top off the carburetor while he poked around to adjust the air flow.

But he was around back, peering down the gas tank. She watched him run his fingers hesitantly around the edge, very slowly, not wanting to know. Slowly he tried his fingers, two against the thumb, making the sign that is used, colloquially, to say *money*. The graininess. *Ah yes*. From the front door she had to watch him put one hand to his forehead and steady himself. What can you kick, Teddy, the tires? The garage door that would answer like thunder, like shaken tin in a school play?

Sugar in the gas tank, a great favorite in the fat years of demonstrations and immune reactions to demonstrations, had been the petty irritation that wore them down most viciously. There was no danger in it, not to the person, which left all their energy intact to mourn the violence to their depleted wallets. And it could happen again and yet again: Manny Wasserstein had lost two engines in his Kharmann-Ghia before he got a gas-tank lock. It was yet another coward's gambit—they would come out of an evening meeting or a church on a green and peaceful Sunday morning, breathe deeply after the tension of having failed or having succeeded merely in getting inside, finding the door unbarred, and if nobody had stayed with the car to threaten a confrontation, someone would surely have dosed the tank with half a bag of sugar, its dregs in a little ant-trail down to the gutter where it glittered like black glass finely ground; or they'd have left a bed of nails point-up around the tires. Sometimes the bag would be crumpled right there behind the wheel but the best jobs were the careful ones, invisible until the motor was clotted, fouled, killed thoroughly dead. Perfectionists cut across professional lines. Teddy had lost one good motor. Together they had run off some teenagers once who were bending over Jessie's VW like attentive surgeons. That time they had found no sugar; they searched for a bomb. Two young boys around Andy's age, she reflected now—Andy hadn't been born at the time—had gone loping down the Sabbath-quiet sidewalk toward the church to mix with their well-dressed elders who had perfected their own more polite intangible sabotage: *I am here to tell you that you and your friends will not be welcome to worship here with us this morning.* She and Andréa holding hands on the steps like children sent away from a house without candy on Halloween; Teddy red-faced, fists in his suit-jacket pockets. No one appreciated what it cost Teddy to put on his one presentable suit that had attracted the breath of rage and derision and murderous intention and held it like smoke in a crowded room, absorbed into the very texture of the fabric. She had given it to Goodwill years ago when it was clear he would never wear it again.

Now this, Jessie thought, is the kind of moment that tests a marriage. She was not a subtle wife, she cried when she needed crying and had been known to stamp her foot. But this time she flattened her back to the door-frame and just held on.

He was standing bent over the roof of the car like a man being frisked by the sheriff. Teddy was more subtle than Jessie—not more high strung, only more easily reached, if not persuaded, by nuance and civil suggestion. He had grown up with more manners than she had; her father had thought them superfluous, like religion. In addition to the burden of the message, this was such a sickening way to deliver it. (Although which was worse, she asked herself, that the vandals knew the specific history of sugar in the gas tank or, more likely, that they did not?)

On the phone to Andréa and Tommy a little later—they were the first to hear all the Carlls's good news—Teddy said this was a sort of Dixie kneecapping, done in the dark and not even acknowledged. They hate us, he said, because we are still true to the faith: we are reminders. And Jessie thought, how smug he is. How he turns blind obstinacy into a virtue. He will make it his heroic duty, now, to overstay his welcome.

"True to the faith?" she echoed, when he'd hung up. "What's that supposed to mean?"

Teddy looked at her disconsolately. "We moved in here for a reason, a long time ago. Is that right? We believed in integration—"

"So? There are a lot of integrated neighborhoods these days, Teddy. Not only in name like this one. A lot of Jackson is getting—"

"But listen. Listen." He took Jessie's hand as if he were going to lead her physically to an understanding. "Just the way we moved in here once to make a point when that was difficult, we have to stay now when it's difficult again."

"You're using that pedagogical tone on me. I can't stand it when you do that."

"Am I right or wrong?" Teddy looked hard into Jessie's eyes; he was trying to shame her.

"No easy gestures," she said.

"No easy gestures."

"But you let yourself off too easily. You don't *do* anything, you just *live* at this embattled address, is that it? That's enough to satisfy you?"

"Well, we're good at doing that, so why not? You give testimony with your body."

"That's such ancient rhetoric, Teddy. Is this a sit-in, right here on Willowbrae Drive? Shall we invite our white friends over to lie down on the doormat?"

Teddy had let go of her hand. He clasped his own two hands together and suddenly looked like an anxious Indian or a man at prayer. "Please don't push that way, Jess, okay? I don't need pressure from you just now, I've got enough of my own. All right?"

"I'm sorry," she said, humbled by his humility. "But do you? I'd love to see some of it sometime. I'm not trying to score points, Teddy. Really I'm not. I'm only worried about the next half of your life."

"That's a little grandiloquent, isn't it?"

She shook her head and stood against him and felt his heart, muffled by bone and skin and shirt, invisible where she had to believe an answering pressure beat.

TWO

When the phone rang in the kitchen, late in the afternoon, its hoarse voice was nearly overlooked in the squabble of radio noise. Lydia, just this year, had discovered rock music and with the help of her small transistor she took it with her wherever she went, except to flute practice; like a belled cat you could always hear her coming.

This particular afternoon just before dinner she had been making chocolate pudding with the music blaring while Jessie picked up in the living room, muttering to herself about its hateful shape and mean size. The phone rang and Lydia went for it with the music still turned high. Then she called to her mother to take it, more in confusion than urgency. "Some man from Birmingham, something—I don't know." Shrugging, she handed over the receiver. Jessie pointed to the radio with her free hand and shook her head to quench the noise a little.

And it was that, some man from Birmingham with a high pinched voice, pinstriped, and he was telling her, without the grace of preliminaries, that Alexis and Roger Tyson were dead on a highway somewhere (she did not catch where) and that Theodore Carll was listed somewhere (she did not catch where) as Alexis's brother and, as such, was he correct in assuming that Mr. Carll was head of the family?

Well, Jessie sputtered at him, well, she didn't know. Now let me see, she said stupidly, as if he had asked which magazines she subscribed to, and tried to remember something about Roger's family. But there were too many fences to leap over without even a chance for a running jump. Panicked—out of practice with emergencies, at which she had once excelled for sheer familiarity with blood and bail—she went blank. The question did prevent her from thinking of handsome vigorous irritating Roger alive as poor Roger instantly and unexpectedly dead, at least for the duration of the phone call. Well, she began again, a meager bit of memory filtering through like a dim light, his parents, his father, it was a military family. She remembered a photograph Alexis had brought over to show her mother, the kind they would have kept in the den if they had a den: a set of matching crewcuts, father and son, with an invulnerably coiffed woman between them like a shared spoil of victory.

Yes, the man answered. He was impatient with her insufficiently enlightening detail. His father the colonel lives in Wiesbaden, Germany, retired, and his mother is dead, as is his brother, a soldier in what he called, quaintly, the "European War."

"And on Teddy's—my husband's—side, well, his mother lives in Yazoo City."

"And I understand is not well—"

"Right. She's had a stroke."

"I understand," the small voice said again with something like distaste. Would Jessie ever catch up with him? "In which case it is necessary for your husband to contact me as soon as possible."

"He's not—" she began. Teddy was not easy to reach when he was out on the road.

"Sooner, if possible. There are funeral arrangements that are best made by a member of the immediate family, and the disposition—"

Lydia, who was stirring the chocolate pudding over the fire—it was her blow struck for authenticity that she refused to use instant—had come to a standstill, frowning exaggerated puzzlement at her mother. The conversation, from a distance of ten feet, would have made no sense, must have sounded casual, or peculiarly defensive. At that point, watching Lydia trying in vain to read her face, Jessie remembered the children.

"They are all right, they are with friends for the moment," the man told her with alarming simplicity. "You will have to see to them as well. So you see, I would say speed is of the essence here."

She told him she saw. She gathered what details she could and promised to try to find Teddy, who could have been anywhere between Memphis and Clarksdale, after dinner to go obediently to his motel room or maybe to the movies or to see any friend within a radius of fifty miles. She recognized what was of the essence but could not promise to be able to honor it.

Then she went and held her long-legged daughter in her arms, backwards. Frustrated, Lydia had resumed her stirring and she faced away. Jessie held her tightly, crossing her arms on the narrow chest and told her that her Aunt Alexis and Uncle Roger were—all of a sudden—no more. The child could not pretend to be overwhelmingly grieved by the news because she had never known them at all well, and because—there was, of course, reason for that—most of what she could remember hearing from her parents was far from good. Nor had the aunt and uncle approved, even the meagerest bit, of them. Jessie was caught in a cold flush of hypocrisy, wishing they had been more tolerant of the differences that loomed between them, although they were far from trivial. Nothing but an ultimate like this, though, and a vestige of fearful sentimentality in its presence, could make her repent a word of disapproval.

"But what about Helen and, what's his name—that O'Neill!" Lydia suddenly said, squinting, remembering her only cousins.

"What about them, what about them, oh what about them!" Jessie crooned to herself, rocking her daughter to her. Teddy was out on the road somewhere, suddenly like a fisherman on the high seas, his wife and children pacing the widow's walk, anxious for a glimpse of mast. They clung, over the pot of burning pudding, in terror for their lives.

.   .   .

Now they were in the air. Their children were back on solid ground without them. The separation, at this particular moment, made her uncharacteristically nervous. She had always been relaxed about what some call "parental obligations"—Andy went to demonstrations on her back, in his little blue baby carrier; Lydia had gone to work with her even as a baby to her jobs in daycare centers where babies were welcome, no matter whose they were.

But those were not, in the end, separations. Those were enactments of a special closeness, which was a different matter, wherever it might lead them, even into danger. She could not pretend to like abandoning them right now, of all times, in somebody else's kitchen while their father and she went to Birmingham to settle the permanent absence of their niece and nephew's parents. Oh, the irony if something terrible were to befall *them*, or their children. Sometimes you heard of the rescue party perishing. . . .

Lydia and Andy were with Andréa and Tommy and little Cleo who was just learning to walk and would keep them amused, and they would be better than fine. Teddy had considered driving to Birmingham straight from Grenada where Jessie had found him watching television blankly in the Twin Pines Motel, what else, half asleep. But it seemed as efficient to come home and fly over together in the morning. It was not efficient but, Jessie understood, he didn't want to go alone.

They sat in the back of the plane (she insisted, desperate; it was one percent safer than the front), held hands for warmth, and poked at the cool clinkers of their feelings.

"I'll never know," Teddy said, looking out at the low hills of eastern Mississippi, "if Alexis by herself would have been so unyielding, if she hadn't already been married. She never *was* by herself, is the thing, I think starting from around thirteen or whenever she began cultivating her little patch of boyfriends, she never had to be alone or think a thought of her own."

"You don't think that's too much of a cliché about docile Southern womanhood."

"I'm not talking about docility, not one bit," he said, and lifted their joined hands and brought them down on the armrest in between. "I never said there was anything docile about Alexis. I only mean she could fight like a hellcat for somebody else's convictions. She never grew up the heavy racist on the block, believe me—a lot of that was neither here nor there to her, she was busy thinking about proms and getting her hair to curl right, it was always curling under when it should have been over, or up when it should have been under, I don't remember. She used to cry a lot about it, though. But along would come somebody with some consuming passion— golf, I remember once, with some red-headed guy from Greenville, all she would do for a year was buy golf clothes and practice her putting in the bedroom—and then there was a dog-breeding phase, of all things. Alexis and her thousand things you never wanted to know about an Airedale. You know what I mean."

She did. The ambitious girl, shaking her glossy curls, making herself soft, Silly Putty, in whatever masculine hands. And Alexis, apolitical, had met Roger at Ole Miss and had been formed. Deformed. She had gone to Sophie Newcomb first, a long way away in New Orleans, and had come back quietly after two years. No one except her mother knew why; not, at least, her brother. But of course a broken love affair was the one direction in which anyone's imagination could flow. Its predictability took all the sting of shock out of it. Everyone had seen that sort of thing before: perhaps a Catholic, perhaps a very poor boy from an impossible family . . . To leave a college because it didn't have a good political science department would have been something of a scandal; to leave because your heart was broken in two by a recalcitrant fullback, well, that would never raise an eyebrow, that would be worth packing your trunk for.

So she came back to Ole Miss, chastened, and there, quick before she had to discover solitude, she met Roger Tyson, who had pale eyes in a sunburned face, and a chin that looked cleft by a well-aimed axe. He was the most presentable, promising, straight-and-narrow bigot anyone could design, with one of those little gold pins between his tie and his collar button, there, Teddy had supposed, to suppress an active Adam's apple. She was tall and thin, pretty and nervous, with black Irish coloring, no Irish ancestor in sight, and transparent-skinned hands and a long flat behind; she carried the hard stiff-clasped purse of a middle-aged woman. Jessie remembered best her first impression of Alexis: that she had a certain noisy charm, hilarious, hysterical busyness in company, as if her gaiety had to keep a roomful of visitors (especially the masculine ones) afloat on her buoyancy alone. She had seen it often in Southern woman and had been astounded at how little that energy carried over when they were alone; it made her nervous. She was quiet in Alexis's presence; felt bound to offer an alternative example of femininity.

Likewise, Roger was quiet with them. But his was the quite simple silence of loathing. Forced by his wife to speak, he was at pains to tell them that, having strained hard and overcome the inhibitions of his upbringing, he had been one of the rock-throwers at Ole Miss when Meredith was there "hiding behind the federal marshals." It was bottles, actually, he had told them, precise as always. "I have never been one to throw a brick." They missed the import of the distinction but his general turn of mind had always been sufficiently clear. In any event, he had grown out of his youthful excitability, back into the family's military discipline: the Citizens' Council was for adult rebels who could encourage action but could restrain themselves, who could leave the violence to others. In college, the obligation to throw rocks (no, bottles) did not devolve on any particular class, it was a democratic sport. But as a businessman, with his name on a letterhead and his gentlemanly reserve restored, it was a responsibility he delegated to those who didn't have to grow up and make a living. Perhaps he even gave aid and comfort to the Klan, that was not something one casually knew.

This meeting and the unlikely discussion, after all those years of angry silence, had taken place at the bedside of Teddy and Alexis's mother, to which they had been called impartially. (By then, Vietnam had been added to the stew of animosities.) Was it for the benefit of the children, Tysons

and Carlls, a way of marking the boundaries clearly now that Dorothea Carll's stroke had restored them, reluctantly, to diplomatic relations
and common decency? Roger, Teddy said, was merely peeing a circle around
his history as a defender of the faith.

.   .   .

On the plane Jessie dozed and dreamed. Roger and Alexis and her mother
and father were all in the Fifty-ninth Street subway station in New York,
the IRT with its ancient mosaics. They were sitting on a bench facing
straight ahead in that dark tunnel, ill-lit like somebody's hall stairs. And all
at once down into it came a TV crew carrying klieg lights, and suddenly
they were illuminated, their faces chiseled with sharp shadows. They sat
there as in a tableau vivant, shoulders touching, strangers, her father in a
broad-brimmed forties hat, her mother dressed like a teenager, like someone
just a little bit older than Lydia, in a tee-shirt. Alexis she couldn't make
out but Roger was looking straight up, his face tormented—there could have
been two hands tight around his neck, to judge from his expression, but he
sat quite decorously still. Then the crew passed on, leaving them in the
dimness again. Her head fallen against the plane window, Jessie opened
first her eyes and then her mouth, full of the spittle of a stolen nap, and
wondered if the town to the left of the wing was Meridian, notorious in
memory like some city desecrated by bombs in World War II—the "European War," Mr. Reidy had called it—one of those historic markers in the
minds of schoolchildren, who have long since lost the context. When it was
announced that they were making their approach to the Birmingham airport
for a moment Jessie couldn't remember why they were going there.

.   .   .

They didn't know Birmingham. They had driven through it en route
to other places; had been in Selma, of course, and a town called Eutaw,
pronounced Utah, where a group of them was meeting, many years ago,
to discuss strategies of voter registration. It seemed, very early on this
morning, as might most cities that haven't fully awakened, secret and in-
turned, the neon of its motels still on in the brightening gray, a melancholy
sight like lamps in the rain. As for the rest, they couldn't make out its face:
provincial cities are so much like provincial people, eager to announce their
similarities when it is in fact their idiosyncrasies that make them interesting.
They were, remarkably, too early to meet the lawyer, Dick Reidy, in
his office; so they asked the cab driver to drop them at a Dunkin' Donuts

far down at the end of the street where the buildings dwindled low and random, thinning out at the margins of the business district.

"What's the difference between one of these places in Birmingham," Teddy asked Jessie, looking over the selection with his eyes narrowed critically, "and one in Pocatello, Idaho?"

Surely they didn't have hush puppies in this place? Or—she didn't know.

"About fifteen hundred miles," Teddy said, unsmiling, and pointed out to the waitress a whipped cream puff that Jessie considered truly disgusting for this time of morning.

.   .   .

This Reidy, whose voice on the phone had been so thin and picayune (whom Jessie had classed with Roger: tightass, narrow and crewcut, a third Smothers Brother), in fact was a big swarthy generous-looking man, like a Turk or an Armenian, with an overhanging cliff of graying hair. Surely he had played football somewhere along the way. He was their age, at most a few years older, but he seemed, to both of them, in his shirtsleeves and dark striped suit pants, the kind of adult they would never be.

"How did they die?" Jessie wanted to know first thing. She hadn't had her curiosity assuaged yet; all they had was an unsupported sense of crisis.

"How did they die," he repeated speculatively, as if he had to think about it a while and decide. "I played golf with Roger last weekend, no, weekend before last," he said, looking away. "He beat me to last a lifetime, I remember saying to him." He breathed out hard and closed his eyes for a minute on his frightening prescience, then opened them as if they had cleared of the scene. "Then this past weekend they went out to a conference, an insurance conference, in Seattle and Alexis went along because she told my wife she was tired of never getting to see other places. They were supposed to stay till Wednesday, I think—and they rented a car, you know, the way you do." He sounded apologetic, justifying. "And that was that." He looked at both of them: did they understand how simple it was? "Head-on, on the highway, at a good speed, they said. They were coming back from dinner. It was raining. That's about all we know. I suppose there will be an accident report if you wanted to—"

They shook their heads. No, no, nothing like that. Only if they had to, for the insurance.

Now Jessie could tell, from the way his voice had shrivelled during this short speech, how it was emotion that had constricted him on the phone, making him sound like a Dickens clerk. She was touched, but then felt foolish: why shouldn't Roger and Alexis have had friends, and the friends be moved by their catastrophe?

Teddy was very quiet beside her. They were assailed with details: the arrival of the bodies by plane, the location of the cemetery, a reputable funeral home. Reidy asked, with genuine concern, whether Teddy's mother ought to come to the funeral. The nerve in Teddy's damaged cheek fluttered with anxiety or distaste, perhaps with sorrow. If Jessie had had a kindred scar that worked for her as a visibly beating wing of her emotions, it would have done the same. Who *are* these people? she was asking herself. Before the reconciliation in her mother-in-law's hospital room, had they not gone something like twelve years, fourteen years, without an acknowledgment of life from those two, disowned for the shame of their sympathies? Why were they here to oversee this most intimate moment, having been so estranged when they could all speak for themselves? Reidy had left the office to retrieve the will from the giant gleaming safe they'd glimpsed when they arrived. Jessie, still queasy, looked at Teddy. "Do you think it's really *appropriate* for us to take care of these details?"

Teddy looked grim. "Around here, blood is thicker than any known substance you can name, Jess, you know that—alcohol, holy water—" Perhaps the list would have gone on: hallucinogens, cyanide—but Reidy returned, puckering his mouth in a nervous gesture that signalled a kind of reluctance, tapping the folded document against his hand in a tidy little beat. He had something to tell them; he was hanging back.

"Now," he began, and stopped. Looked for his chair, backed into it, turned his eyes on an old dark map, Alabama 1900, that hung beside his desk, a translucent parchment full of hairline cracks, color of a fat-soaked brown paper bag. Alabama 1900 was overhung with storm clouds; had this been the color of the air? "I can't help thinking you're going to be surprised by this," he finally said, wearily, as if he'd been climbing stairs. "I can't pretend I wasn't. We discussed it when they made out their will, I asked them to think about it very hard. *Very* hard." He was ticking the words off dismissively, as if they were a bothersome routine, da-*da*-da-*da*-da-*da*, but it was somehow clear they were not. "You need to know this now rather than later, I think." Again he stopped.

Were they leaving a million dollars to the NAACP as per instructions in a dream?

"Um," he tried again. "The Tysons, Alexis and Roger, I should say"— and he looked around guiltily—"have made you the legal guardians of their two children."

Is blood thicker than air too? Then all the prudent planning in the world can be undone just so. Is that why Jessie gasped for breath, lost it, gasped again? It would not help to say, "That is a very bad joke," or to turn and run away like a cornered child who spies an opening. Apparently they understood that; they sat still, obediently, as if the rest of their lives had not just altered abruptly.

"This is not going to be an impossible situation," the lawyer said, "but it is going to be extremely—"

"Is that in the will?" Teddy looked as if he were going to stand up and knock down a few chairs. His face was an alarming red.

"Well, yes. It is, and we discussed the alternatives at some length, as you might imagine."

"Legally binding? You can do that unilaterally?"

"Perhaps this is not the time."

"Well, when then? Can you just give your kids to someone—" He looked at Jessie, trapped at the eyes. "This is bizarre."

"Teddy," she said. "Mr. Reidy." Belligerence seemed altogether pointless. This man did not seem like an antagonist. "Can you tell us what they were thinking when they made this—whatever it is, this clause?"

He appeared to be making an inventory of all the things on his desk, but it was too neat to occupy him for long. First they were to understand that no one ever expected such a thing as this to come to pass. Not ever, really. (Teddy and Jessie dimly understood that.) So it was really, in their minds, moot.

Moot. It was a wonderful word, altogether funny, something a cow does, or a small horn. Moot-moot. Mute, mute. Jessie tried to concentrate but she could not look at what was there before her.

Then after that, if he could hazard a guess—

Go right ahead, what the hell. Hazard. She reigned herself in.

They were, to put it simply, which was perhaps how it ought to be put at best anyway, family. There were a lot of impediments between the members of a family but Alexis firmly believed—Jessie saw a young, flighty, worried, unserious girl, worried about things she could hardly imagine, and wondered what belief might have felt like to her—that they were finally beside the point. Matters of lifestyle, matters of taste might be ephemeral. . . .

"Beside the point?" asked Teddy, sitting back weakly. He looked like a young boy in the principal's office, falsely accused or falsely denied. "How could she have thought it was fair to her children to inflict them on us, or us on them? She disowned me—and then us, both of us—when my mother did. She wrote to me that she didn't have a brother any more, and she'd try to forget she ever did, she was going to tell people she was an only child."

"But you had your reconciliation after a while," Reidy insisted calmly.

Teddy's cheek throbbed once, Jessie imagined, for every word he did not say in reply. Reidy, she supposed, thought he was seeing the Democrats and Republicans in debate—but no, that wasn't fair. He would have to understand how shattering this estrangement had been; it was simply not to his advantage to acknowledge it.

"What about their good friends?" Teddy persisted. "I mean, does guardianship mean they actually have to come live with us? You're a good friend," he said, and the lawyer tensed defensively. "Can we choose someone for them to live with? Would that be within our rights?"

"Well, perhaps she thought she could see where the line is, even between good friends. Most of their friends—"

" 'Finally beside the point,' " Teddy was repeating softly to himself; he had decided, apparently, that the key lay there. "If the things we had between us, the impediments you call them, were 'beside the point,' I'd like someone to tell me please just what the point *is*."

Reidy looked out his window, another impossible escape, and slowly back again. "I wish she were here for you to ask, Mr. Carll. You may imagine how I wish that." He was a decent man, courtly, perplexed, and difficult to hate. Probably he had argued with Alexis on this issue and had lost. But neither had he offered to adopt her children if the question ever ceased to be "moot." He did not try to protect himself from Teddy's anger and derision; it could only be that he sympathized with it.

"And Roger?" Jessie asked.

"You might say, if you wanted to put it rather too bluntly, that Roger didn't have any feasible alternatives."

Peculiar. It was not one of those families where the husband, called The Husband, is the one who lacks alternatives. They had never seen him at a disadvantage.

"Let me suggest that you look at the situation this way, if I might. It is my feeling, it was my feeling when we talked, I should say, that your sister thought—or perhaps she only hoped—that certain of those wounds had begun to heal between you. Over time. That there might have resumed a kind of—tacit peace? Does that seem plausible to you? And so the children would in fact be in friendly territory, in a manner of speaking, with family that they knew."

"Jesus," Teddy answered, a cry, and covered his face with his hands. Reidy was a clever man to put them on the defensive, to lay the perpetuation of hostilities in their camp. "What if we refuse? For their sake or for ours?"

"You could petition the court. Of course." He graduated from one voice to another like an actor doing a whole scene by himself, playing all the characters. That line was delivered thin lipped, disapprovingly. Since he did not elaborate, it was clear he was trying to discourage them from seeking a reversal.

"How old are they now?"

"Seven. Or no, just turned eight, and thirteen? Helen and O'Neill?" The question marks were immensely tactful, as if to say gently, of course you remember. "The girl is the older."

"But Teddy," Jessie said, surprised. "That has nothing to do with it. That's like haggling about the price—"

"You have a right to an opinion too, you know." He meant to be sympathetic. "Can you do this? Can you see us doing this? And Andy and Lydia?"

She nodded dumbly. Which would be running out on him, saying yes or saying no? Love, she might say, is thicker to me than blood. "Oh Teddy" was all she could utter for fear she would cry. She waited a full minute trying to force the burning fist down, out of her throat. "Don't make me decide. You know what I'll say—"

"This is not a decision, is it?" Teddy asked the lawyer then, sitting back in his seat, defeated. Even the lick of dark hair that bobbed on his forehead looked subdued. "It's a judgment. No, a sentence. It's a life sentence. And we just have a little time to get our affairs in order. Right?" He was talking to Reidy as if he were a political antagonist, Jessie thought, embarrassed. Again, how his skills had outlived their usefulness! How badly they fitted him for the world after his moment!

"A life sentence, Mr. Carll. Ohhh, I don't think I'd put it that way," Reidy said sadly, benignly, and opened his hands in resignation.

"I'm sure they are very nice children," Jessie began and then stopped for the sheer stupidity of the remark. "When we get used to the idea a little . . . This is a shock." Teddy stared hard at his wife, challenging her to persist in her banality. "I'm sorry," she said, "none of this is—"

"Don't say a thing," Reidy told her, and they all stood. He put one hand on Jessie's shoulder and one on Teddy's, as if to join them to each other. "Don't even trouble yourself to find the words because we all realize there aren't any."

.   .   .

Their children had no guardians. That was no oversight—they had lived, when the children were small, in a close community where everyone was prepared to run a few steps to cover for someone else. They knew dozens of children, mostly black, who were not being raised by their parents, though many were loved *in absentia*, and some were even reclaimed when the tide of practical difficulties turned. (Likewise they knew couples who'd lived separated by thousands of miles, like Sicilian or Algerian workers saving their Swiss francs, and for the same reason—he has a job here and she has a job here, and both are supposed to feel grateful. Meanwhile, there are visits: all those unwilling divorces.) Teddy and Jessie had kept two children for a while, Sandra and Jodene, whose mother was seventeen and needed a mother herself. They were very little and all Jessie remembered of that year was wiping twice as many tails and noses and putting her arms around a long succession of warm burrowing animals, her own among them.

Perhaps they should have seen to their children's security, especially in the days when they courted danger so routinely. But—well. Everything was so unpredictable, there had to be that faith. God, or a good friend, or a distant cousin, will provide. Insurance companies generally will not. Otherwise they could not have done the things they did.

.   .   .

"Andréa?" A yellow telephone, one piece for dialing, listening, talking into, lay in her hand like a split fruit.

"Hey, honey. Your kids got off to school okay and we're going for pizza tonight, so I think they're glad you're gone, if you really want to know. How you doing?"

Jessie was quiet; her friend said her name once, tentative.

"André, wait a second, I think I'm going to cry."

"You mean you're feeling sad all of a sudden for those folks? Is it *sad* over there?"

"It hasn't occurred to me to be sad, I think the two of them are probably only over St. Louis by now. We had to get the funeral home to go meet them at the airport."

"Well, I'm glad you didn't have to do it."

"And the funeral's tomorrow?"

She sighed. "I guess so. But, listen." She told her about the children, tried to say Helen and O'Neill. It took an extraordinary imaginative effort. How could she make sense that could be shared? She could hardly call her own babies by their names when they were born, before she had seen them and touched them all over with her own hands again and again. And even then . . . There was so much to be gone through with these new children before they were to be called by their names; somehow they were still generic.

Bless her friend, she did not try to read them their legal rights. Perhaps, Jessie thought later, it's because she is used to such shifting arrangements of guardianship, such reciprocity. Jessie and Teddy had succored dozens, hundreds probably, when the Movement was most fluid—all those meals, those beds, those desperate midnight consultations when someone's life was falling to bits or the strain of incessant danger was pressing one of them into collapse. But they all went home after a while. Somebody else was their real mother, their real father. On the other hand, Andréa's mother had kept all sorts of relatives on and off through the years; her family had always sounded astonishingly, admirably elastic. It wasn't easy, Andréa used to say, but it wasn't unusual enough to deserve special comment, either. Jessie had discovered, confronting the looseness of such arrangements, that the demand for privacy is the first thing that separates the true middle class from the marginal. Andréa's father was a professor, but his brothers and sisters were forever in debt, in trouble, in need, and he was the stable protector.

"Don't say anything to the kids, please, André. This is so unfair to them too. I feel like we've *all* been in an accident."

"Now don't go get yourself worked up again. Don't think about it like it was some conspiracy to sabotage your family."

"Well—André, these are little rich kids who go to a seg *academy*, they—"

"Well, nothing. Why don't you think of it this way." That was the phrase the lawyer had used too; people were going to come forth now, one by one, Jessie thought, they were in for it, with alternative improvements for their attitude. "It isn't any great fun to get wiped away out on some highway far from home."

"I wouldn't want to try it close to home either. Remember, I know this guy who was legally dead once at a very early age—"

"Okay. And that isn't even the same because *your* guy knew what he was up against. His was what you call a calculated risk. He was in a dangerous business. You think these folks were expecting their kids to be spending next weekend in Jackson on Willowbrae Drive?"

"Do I hear you urging compassion on me? It's too *crazy*, André."

"Compassion isn't one of my big words but, I don't know, hon, this seems like one of those times that sometimes comes along when it doesn't seem too useful to play the purist. Or the smartass. If you know what I mean. No offense. But there's kids in this up to their necks."

Good Christ. Jessie thought of them, then, on Willowbrae Drive, blond and contemptuous and affronted, looking out the window at the laundry on the neighbors' lines. If *they* were too white for their neighbors these days, the Birmingham cousins would be something like transparent. Was she exaggerating the threat from the midnight phone-callers, the backwards blockbusters? Or would they wake in their beds, white faced, bleak faced, stuck all over with those silver skewers like voodoo dolls?

.   .   .

When Jessie was a teenager and asked herself what death might be, one of the possibilities she liked was that she might have died already, who knows when, and not realized it. *You go right on with things*, or so it would seem, only there is a difference because it is all an illusion, you are not really there. Life and death as subjective realities—it was a beguiling idea, her least depressing.

The next few days she knew she had been right: she had died at some undisclosed moment and now it was only her body that was going through these motions, disconnected. Teddy had died with her. They were the ones, not Alexis and Roger, who arrived in the hold of the plane in crates, duly labelled, and their spirits absently watched and tried to care, like live souls.

The funeral home people began it by making an odious request. This was going to be strictly closed coffins, they said, they were not even going to try to make repairs. But still, they thought, still it is always nice to be buried in some favorite garment. "It is always nice," Teddy repeated, looking as if he'd been hit by a heavy object.

"Always," Jessie agreed. "Whatever happened to shrouds?"

"Shrouds?"

"Do you have to be Jewish nowadays to be buried in a plain white winding sheet, or whatever it is? My grandmother was buried in a shroud. It was very nice, considering. I mean, there was something—elemental about it."

"Beyond fashion."

"Right. Two thousand years of unchanging fashion."

They grinned wildly at each other, sticky, morbid, nervous, trapped, infantile, every conceivable thing but suitably sober. Nor will a motel room tend to lend ballast to one's sense of reality. The prints on the wall were Southern Capitol Buildings I Have Known. What Jessie really needed was to have Teddy make love to her with the drapes drawn closed, those heavy drapes most favored by motels, lined with something colorless for the light sleepers, for the adulterers, all that anonymous beige. They could be themselves a while longer, unchanged.

"And they want us to go *get* something to dress them in?"

Teddy nodded.

"Can we take someone along? I wouldn't know Alexis's favorite outfit from the thing she hated most in her closet. I'm sure I'd choose an atrocity."

"Not that anybody would know. Well, we'll call somebody. We can call those people the kids are staying with, they must be close friends. And maybe we can talk a little about this other thing."

"This other thing. You mean Helen and O'Neill." She made herself.

He rubbed his eyes. It had been at least three days since morning.

. . .

They stood before a very wide closet whose louvered doors had been pushed all the way back.

Alexis's friend, Judy Carmichael, was just plump enough to give herself a lot of grief—she had mentioned it twice in twenty minutes—but as if for compensation she had the sort of fabulous pink and white skin that reminded sallow Jessie that "complexion" was a big word down here, not something serviceable to keep your bones in and your organs out of view but a thing of beauty in itself. Her wide placid face seemed to be upholstered in silk. One could imagine someone loving her for it.

She gave to the closet situation the precise quality of attention one usually reserves for museums. She had indicated somehow, without words, that she was not to be hurried in her deliberations; there was that figurative rolling-up of the sleeves that meant business.

Jessie and Teddy left her there, working at the chiffons. Besides the little double-knit pants suits that seemed a travesty to imagine spending eternity in, like a bank teller or a stewardess on the job, Alexis seemed to have—to have had? (the verb was still indeterminate as if her existence in the past tense had not quite been confirmed, the book only slowly closing on her live presence)—an unaccountable quantity of blowy chiffon gowns in all the colors of those pastel button candies Jessie used to pluck off paper when she was a child—Easter parade colors.

They wandered slowly through Teddy's sister's house like insomniacs. The times since Alexis's marriage they had been forced to meet, few as they were, had always been on the neutral turf of their mother's house with some soporific like a Thanksgiving turkey between them. That was a far better strategy for friendly relations than sitting the Tysons in the living room between the two ancient SNCC posters in their silver frames. (Those absurd frames that signalled to Jessie, though not to Teddy, that, having made them into expensive artifacts, it was time to jettison them. That angry, heavy-lipped and heavy-lidded woman in her ambiguous African turban/American headrag, holding a naked child on her arm and staring over all heads into an unimaginable future; the old man in the slouch hat sitting with his cotton hoe, smiling to himself like someone with a fine secret. A framed revolutionary poster, Jessie believed, is a contradiction in terms.) In any event, entertaining Alexis and Roger in their house was no way to find common ground.

In Yazoo City, the one thing they shared was at hand, a childhood among familiar objects, the amused memory of ordinary animosities, brother-sister frictions. The only charged moments came when someone's name was thrown up casually by the tide of conversation—who knew just where that person's political color might actually enter into the living of his life? "Did you hear, DeeDee Olsen finally got tired of who they were making her teach and who she was having to teach *with*, and so she's kind of retired. She's taking real estate. She says she can choose her own company and her clients can even be better than *she* is." Teddy would weigh innocence in one hand and cunning in the other, and the scale would slow and balance, with perhaps a slight tilt toward naiveté. Either Alexis had an unreliable memory, or a guileless loving one: Teddy was her little *brother*, wasn't he?

Nor would having them here in this long low expensive house have advanced deep friendship, but there wasn't much incitement in it: the politics of refusers is less visible than that of advocates. From this side, it was only taste that seemed to have strewn the path from Birmingham to Jackson with impassable barriers.

"It's all swaddled," Teddy said, a kind of awe in his voice. "All this wall-to-wall, ceiling-to-floor busyness. What do you think might be the harm in a ledge that doesn't have something on it that you have to dust?"

"Well, it helps when you don't have to dust it yourself, doesn't it."

Each room was a showcase for a few authentic-looking antiques, surrounded by chunkier, shinier, false examples of the period (whichever one it was; Jessie didn't know Queen Anne from Queen Victoria). Cups in a row on the buffet, ladder-back chairs dutifully arranged, nosegays of dried flowers and pewter bowls. She felt she had been here before, the ideal was to recreate other people's houses, not to make one's own; it was to say the words tradition had said a thousand times. Yet it was pleasant, she thought;

not interesting but comfortable. Just because it paid obeisance to a different ideal, she ought not to condemn it.

"It's the 'doing,' I think," Jessie said. "You've got to make it look like it's been thought about, worked on, and it's come out like some magazine you've seen. You've got to justify something or other. I forget just what."

"Not working, maybe. Do you know she never worked, except I think way back before the kids when she did a little something for Roger at his office."

"Well, plenty of people don't work. I'm sure none of her friends worked. But it looks like she spent a lot of time with swatches of material, matching everything up, this chintz and that gingham. That would take me two lifetimes."

"No, I'm just thinking. Those kids must be used to a full-time mama, you know—full cookie jar and Cub Scouts and all. Not the kind of kitchen table that's always full of school announcements and report cards."

"You're probably right."

"Maybe they'd like to go away to school, have you thought of that?"

She hadn't. "That" looked fiercely, suddenly, like a coin of vivid light at the end of a mile-long mine shaft. To think that they might, themselves, be an uncle and aunt again, the day-to-day, hour-to-hour needs of these children seen to by many sets of professional parents to whom it came natural, who existed and were chartered and state approved and even paid for that purpose. They could go live their lives in a suitable atmosphere, in a world as white as goose down.

"Then again," Jessie said. "To send them away just now seems a little barbaric."

"It seems a little British, anyway. They send their kids off in the best and the worst circumstances. There's no such thing as not being ready."

"Nonsense. Where would English fiction be if unhappy little boys weren't forever being sent off to these wretched mean-tempered prisons with tyrannical headmasters and never enough to eat between floggings?" She thought of Jane Eyre. "Girls too."

"Is that what you have in mind for these kids? You want to be their evil stepmother?"

"It was *your* idea."

Teddy walked into the kitchen. She stood behind him studying the scrubbed counters and the methodically ranged spices in clear plastic, the cookbooks, the three little framed recipes on one wall: CHOCOLATE MOUSSE with a pen-and-ink picture of a moose. DIVINITY flown over by a small white angel with a golden halo and a fairy's wand, and PIGS IN A BLANKET, fat and jolly, tucked under plaid. The potholders in this kitchen hung matched, one a mushroom, one a tomato, on good firm cloth, so clean they seemed to be for exhibit, not for use. Potholders might have been a minor distinction between Alexis's kitchen and Jessie's—her mitts were catch-as-catch-can, with burnt brown spots on their sides; lived-in, one might generously say— but she could be rendered defensive very easily by such differences. Ideology failed her in spotless kitchens. That she was alive and Alexis was not was an unfortunate fact, but it seemed an unfair advantage and incidental to her judgment on herself.

Alexis, she thought, standing between her matching refrigerator and wall oven, how do I invoke you? How do I make you real to myself, and make what is happening real? This was the one room she'd thought she could rub, like a lamp, in her imagination—these shiny, loved and tended surfaces that had absorbed so many of Alexis's hours—to call her forth. And still she wouldn't come. This whole thing was no joke but it persisted in *feeling* like one. This, Jessie supposed, was what she had done with her shock.

She and Teddy stood in what must have been an uncharacteristic silence in that family kitchen and privately lectured themselves about meanness and their shared habit of supercritical appraisal. Jessie imagined someone standing in her kitchen, emptied of household noise and extenuating chaos, and it made her cringe. Teddy bent over a brass magazine rack in which every spine stood straight and dustless, and flipped slowly through something with a blue cover. Then anger began to radiate off his body like heat off the hood of a car in summer, wave on wave. He had found some justification for his contempt. He began to whistle quietly, randomly, as if that were a cooling mist of water he threw on his heat. "Hey look, it's *Bigot's Digest*. 'Race Mixing—How to Beat Them at Their Own Game!' 'Sex and the Civil Rights Saints!' What do you know. 'Martin's Other Life.' "

"Yesterday you'd have been laughing."

Just as well they weren't laughing: Judy Carmichael came in then, a dozen-shades-of-robin's-egg-blue gown on one arm and silky pink shirtwaist dress on the other with what seemed to be birds of paradise roosting on the skirt. "Do you think somebody who was really gay and loved to laugh whenever she possibly could would care more about dignity right now"— she jiggled the sky-blue-pink birds, who leaped under her hand—"or just out-and-out beauty?" and she waved the chiffon which flowed obediently, like a magician's scarves.

They sighed, both of them, the closed ranks of sobriety.

"I'm not sure she's caring much either way," Teddy said crisply. Jessie thought that was cruel, to Judy if not to Alexis, but he was only being matter of fact.

Judy straightened her plump shoulders and gazed boldly back into Teddy's face, as if steadfastness might intimidate him. "Thank you," she said with dignity. "I think I understand that as well as you do. I don't appreciate you condescending to me just because—" But she stopped there, tantalizingly. Someone was rattling the back door.

Having seized control of the house by sheer moral superiority, Judy thrust the dresses at Jessie and went into the pantry to the door. A dark figure entered, taller than Judy and bent a little in her direction, and they could hear Judy say, "Oh here you *are*, Lurene!" in a stricken voice. "Of course, nobody would have *told* you. Oh my dear—" and she seized the arm of the black woman in both her hands as though when she heard she might try to get away. Details poured forth. Judy seemed to be in possession of many more than the lawyer had thought seemly to repeat, and then Jessie thought, No wonder I couldn't find Alexis in her kitchen. I should have remembered *she'd* never be the one who polished it to this spit-shine. If I'd rubbed a little harder I would have gotten Lurene.

Lurene's tweed coat parted to show a dazzle of uniform, like a dark cat's white chest. She was a fine-looking woman of about Jessie's age, medium brown and serious, with worried, close-together eyes and her hair in a white net, so that it looked snowed-on.

"Lord!" she said whenever Judy gave her the space to speak in, and "Lord! Lord!" again, her palm flat against her cheek. The two of them mimed sorrow and astonishment. What must Alexis have been like among them before she vaporized into a cause for ritual grief? There were real tears on their cheeks. What did her "girl" think of her? Would Alexis have been one of those "enlightened" employers who paid in social security scrupulously and gave good references and bonuses as well as outgrown clothes and middle-aged furniture? Or had Roger kept her pure of liberal decencies?

Jessie knew Teddy well enough to see he was desperate to distance himself from this household; he had the avid look of a little boy who was about to announce he'd gotten one hundred on his spelling test. Judy introduced them very formally. Teddy's name, if he'd dared hope it had penetrated, meant nothing to Lurene. Oh the short shelf-life of notoriety! Teddy was like a man who'd committed a crime, he so loved peering into people's eyes to see if they had somehow sniffed him out. No matter that he is proud of his past and deserves to be, Jessie thought irritably, it comes to the same anxious lurking.

She hoped Judy was going to consult Lurene about what Teddy was ghoulishly referring to as "the going-away outfit." She didn't. She decided she'd better go in to choose a suit for Roger—that was going to be simpler, since they were all matching copies of the same statement: PRUDENCE. IN-OFFENSIVENESS. CAPITAL. She had told Lurene to go to Mr. Reidy for whatever monies were owed her—monies in the plural, a sudden rain-shower of tangibles. Perhaps there would be something else for her, she suggested, when the will was read. One never knew, she said, implying that, in this case, one did. "Mrs. Tyson was so devoted to you." This was a good job to lose, then, to such an abrupt turn of the wheel.

"Wait a minute, Lurene," Teddy called out to her as she started off toward the rear bedroom to begin on the inventory Judy had suggested to her: Linens. Silver. Clothes. It would be a month's work just counting it. He sounded every bit as peremptory as any employer. She turned to him coolly, then, to this Southern man, this white man, probably expecting another detail of the termination of her employment.

"Hey, Lurene," Teddy said with his most luscious smile. He looked to make sure Judy was long gone. This was going to be unsayable, his wife thought; also unnecessary. "My sister and I were not very close," Teddy told her in an odd voice, conspiratorial and a little wheedling, as if he wanted something from her, though whatever might it be? "We had a lot of political differences, I guess you could call them. We—differed on questions like, oh, voting and integration and—"

Lurene, as tall as Teddy, put her head back, or rather her chin up, as if to say "So?"

"And I'm—" He was uncharacteristically hesitant. "I'm wondering if you felt like—oh—you've been dealt with decently while you've been with her. I'd understand if—"

"Well, what could you do for me if I told you no," she asked matter-of-factly. "Say she beat on me or spent all day yelling, not much you can do now to set it right, is there?" He couldn't tell her he was only indecently curious.

"Possibly the question of that will, what Mrs. Carmichael was saying?"

"Oh, the will." She shrugged. *Teddy*, Jessie thought, embarrassed. "I seen plenty of wills before. She probably just leaving me a couple her old party dresses and some coats or something from Mr. Tyson for my husband, they about the same general size. I would have wound up with those anyway when the styles come around and change. You wait long enough you *inherit* everything without nobody dying, it all look silly a year-two later. Then, you here you get to take it on home." She shrugged again, her other shoulder.

"What, I suppose I mean, to put it in plain English, Lurene, is that my wife and I and Mr. and Mrs. Tyson had different feelings about having a woman like you come in and clean their house for them, and about every conceivable other thing concerning the life of black people."

Lurene shifted on her feet. She looked at both of them without relish. "It's a job. What you apologizing for. Concerning the life of black people, we need jobs just like everybody else—more, maybe. Only if they treat you decent. Which they did." Jessie could see her draw herself up with suspicion, cautious but unwilling to let his condescension implicate her. She was not going to say more than she had to for civility's sake. "Now, see, I got to go talk to my friends work for other ladies, see if they can find me another halfway decent place."

"This was a decent place, then," Teddy asked again. His face was bright with an illicit curiosity.

"It was all right. I liked Mrs. Tyson, she was a real nice lady. She laugh a lot. Ain't this thing just terrible though—she sure 'nough didn't deserve no ending like that. Not even he did." She rolled her eyes like the servant Teddy did not want to see. There was no way to judge whether her feelings were counterfeit; she had no reason to lie, no reason to tell the truth.

"Is there something you'd rather do, Lurene? Do you have any other ambitions for yourself?" Jessie wondered if he was thinking about the will. Did he expect her to trade in her mop and broken-in shoes and go to college?

Well, she had always wanted to work for a mortician, she said. That was something to lean on and you got plenty of respect, like being a preacher. No, not a teacher, never! Couldn't stand children all day, bad enough when you got seven at home and a three-room house. That's why cleaning a decent lady's house wasn't as bad as he might think, except sometimes when the kids were biting. Somebody else's kitchen's plenty peaceful. Teddy, who had not been able to knock down a wasp's nest of grievances, looked bereft. He smiled wanly, as if this were what he had hoped to hear.

Teddy, Jessie thought, you are such a fool I can't believe it. As if he had something *negotiable* here with this woman! He was not about to ask her to register to vote or to come to a meeting of the Freedom Democratic Party! . . . What was the habit of his cowering soul that made him have to announce his good intentions like that? To keep the woman from feeling alone in the world? To ingratiate himself and his own little ego? Or it was simply that he had his lifetime of whiteness to live down, and would never do so. He was maimed, she thought, positively maimed by the need to repudiate the distance between himself and a woman like Lurene.

Sometimes Jessie saw a little drama in her mind, the kind everyone has read about or seen in the movies: her husband is an earnest young priest, that was easy to imagine, doing God's work in every dark corner. And his superior, a craggy old man with noble laughlines and a secret drinking problem (Spencer Tracy? Barry Fitzgerald?), orders some humiliation, or a change of parishes, because the young priest suffers from the sin of pride. His vanity is the sliver under the thumbnail of every good work he does. She wondered if Roger, his nemesis, could have been an ounce more self-righteous in his defense of the race.

Judy had returned from the bedroom with the laying-out clothes, ghostly and grown over like pod-people, in dry cleaner's plastic. "I'm just going to have to let the mood overtake me," she announced, sighing. "About Lex's dress. I'll decide for her at the very last possible second."

"That seems like a good idea," Jessie said out of the vast blank place from which most of her conversation was coming. "Judy, we need to talk about the children a little bit, I think." They are not, she wanted to say, part of this fashion show.

Judy sank down at the round white Formica table, settled with the heavy lightness of a hot-air balloon under its soundless parachute. She put her chin in her hand and her round shoulders rose against her padded neck. "What do you want to know about them? They're very good children. I mean, I know you must think I've got to say that but they are. They're good in school and they're real good at home." She spoke in a small, defeated voice.

Never mind how their definitions of goodness must differ, "good" like "nice" and "interesting," enraged Jessie with its passivity. Why use it if it weren't intended to mask a complex truth, perhaps an ugly one?

Judy lifted up her plump velvet face, in which the small features seemed implanted like tufts in a Queen Anne chair. Tears massed in her round blue eyes. "I just feel—you know—like Alexis is out and she asked me to drop on over and do this little favor for her? Pick up this dress to go out somewhere *nice* in?" She began to cry softly into the fist of one hand, at first a ladylike and restrained weeping that brought islands of petal-pink up out of her cheeks. But as Jessie sat with no words to offer, Judy's grief began to rise from its submersion and break above the surface of her propriety, shaking her in her seat. She was not so much noisy as full of movement, she swayed like a cellist who cannot escape the weight she is holding but strains to the left and the right as if to see beyond it. Every joint in her generous body seemed to flex simultaneously, an agitation Jessie feared would send her flying into separate parts. She found her own eyes growing damp and her chest filling as if she had swallowed a fist. Apparently the spectacle of sorrow could undo you, you were susceptible to the sight and the sound of it, even an anonymous one. As for this—one friend mourning another, a loss intimate and unassuageable—she felt herself gazing on Judy almost fondly, on her neck and elbows and her uncontrollably twitching foot that kicked against the rung of her chair as if it were trying to restrain her.

. . .

After all of which Teddy suffered. Jessie saw him wrestle with what he had done and her anger dissolved into concern that hung just at the edge of pity: what would feed this man for the rest of his life? Surely he was not doomed to a career of stealing memories like hidden sweets and hoarding them for the sour or the famished days?

It would have been too easy to admit what he had seen in his wife's shocked face, and to agree with her: that his behavior was reprehensible. He could not have enjoyed the twist of disgust on her mouth while he drilled Lurene that way. Either he was malicious or out of control, but he never inquired which and she never bothered to specify. She supposed he couldn't help himself. Meanwhile, poor Lurene, poor Judy Carmichael! Teddy continually assumed women were easily manipulated when in fact they were only easily affronted. Each time he was surprised. If they didn't find him charming and persuasive he tended to pedal too hard, come home panting, sweating like a marathon cyclist, stinking with effort. She sympathized, off and on: baffled passion is what makes exhibitionists and midnight callers, snipers and mercenaries; in Teddy's case it had made him tedious sometimes, and he knew it as well as she; tedious at best, and occasionally offensive.

But everyone gave up too easily. This was why he never apologized to Jessie, tried to think of his diminishing stature as his sacrifice. He too saw it like a religious humility. Nobody cared sufficiently. He told her that she didn't; it was an attribute of character, not of choice. *She had never lost enough*; she was an innocent. If she'd had a damaged child, would she not have loved it inordinately, when others found it hopeless? Well, then: his life was the damaged child and its twisting course his passion. (She called him sentimental. After a certain point she said, nobody would care if Robert E. Lee was your grandfather, but her heart rose in her chest with grief for him.) These were things he tried not to say out loud, but that she made him say, so that she might remember why, in spite of all, she loved him.

. . .

That night in the motel, conciliatory, he reached across the bed for Jessie. It was a question—if he'd done something unforgivable, she'd have turned her back and given him insensible curls. She answered him by moving into the space of his arms. So. She needed what he needed, a sign of life and a promise that, whatever this was, this Birmingham business, they were in it together.

Teddy, after all these years, still made love voraciously, with perfect concentration, the way he had first kissed Jessie on the campus path in Ohio; she thought, often, that it was the only enterprise of her own life whose intensity had never dimmed or faltered. Still, when they entangled their long limbs in the comfort they could rely on but never predict in its shape or duration—when they moved their hands tenderly and firmly along all those rewarding surfaces—both of them were beset by distraction. It was as if they were out in the open somewhere stung by implacable insects.

After the accident, when his body had healed but his shocked spirit was sodden with depression at what might have been—what *had* been for an instant before the reluctant doctors had reached down and grasped his disappearing self by its last half-inch—he had lain still in Jessie's arms and felt nothing, nothing but his own breathing. Making love was too much an abandonment of the body and his control over it, his presence in it, that he had lost and then by luck been given again. He was going nowhere out of himself if he could help it. Even sleep frightened him. He woke himself every hour or two just to see if he could climb back into consciousness unaided. So Jessie had let him be for a long time, let him fall asleep against her shoulder, so relieved to have him there alive and sewn whole. Then he went through a month of trying and failing, half-restored, wanting but not being able to give or take pleasure. It was not surprising. Jessie soothed him and waited for the easing of the death sentence to come clear to him, for his nerves and muscles to believe it.

When he returned to her finally, tired of remembering, it was with gusto, which she met with her own: the two of them, matched and angular, took up their sweet deliberation of each other's secrets. They liked to laugh at the unlikeliness of their skin-and-bone unsexiness, how they excited each other but would look terrible in anonymous black and white, Teddy's knees, Jessie's hipbones. White folks don't know how to move, huh? Teddy would say, moving with Jessie toward some unimaginable fulfillment. You move any better than that you'll kill me dead, Jessie would answer. Flat out. Nothing left for the buzzards.

But tonight, both of them were pinched and prodded by a hundred irrelevant details. Teddy touching her breast, kneading it, feathering it with his fingers, bending to kiss it, make it stand firm for him, Jessie only saw

Lurene staring at them, saw Judy Carmichael in her flowing robe and peeked inside at a bosom white and soft as a seagull's, imagined the perfume that leaked from her, a time-release capsule of suffocating Avon. Squeezed, she would feel like Wonder Bread. She saw all the drawers under Alexis's kitchen counters pulled open, their contents perfectly arranged; saw Lydia looking at her as she handed her last week's allowance, oddly—looking levelly but oddly at her. Jessie began to move more urgently beneath him and she gave herself for a few seconds, with an effort, to the dampness, the pull, the furious rising itch to be over the top and down in a thousand rainbow shards. But there was such static in her concentration, she knew she was going nowhere: there like tardy guests were Alexis and Roger, only their faces, busts on a wall plaque with their edges smudged. She saw the awning of the funeral parlor on West Ninety-second Street where she had said goodbye to her grandfather when she was seven: a blue awning that covered the front walk as if it were the roof of a tunnel. She had thought the awning beautiful, elegant, the kind of embellishment the best stores in the city had, all along Fifth Avenue where they never shopped, and those steep Park Avenue apartment houses around the corner from her mother's girlhood building. When I met you, Teddy had told her, I always pictured you standing out under a great awning talking to your doorman. Her doorman! Down two blocks from where she lived the hulks of the shipping companies lined up against the Hudson like a row of death-dark Quonset huts; they had exotic foreign names that made her dream of being a stowaway. Jessie touched Teddy then out of sight, pulled him from her just enough to lay her fingers around him gently, then tightly, while she scrambled up a steep incline like a guilty child. "Teddy, come back to me," she whispered to his cheek, against her own distraction, and, gratefully, retrieved himself from wherever he had been, he came.

. . .

They are young children, Jessie thought, but they are suddenly more experienced than the lot of us. It is the next thing to dying themselves, isn't it, it is the single nightmare. We cannot imagine our own extinction—moot, moot!—but our parents' . . . She was going to be afraid of these children, they are like radioactive objects, she thought, won't they sizzle with danger, with danger survived? They will be blessed. She expected ancient grizzled faces. This is a boy who must have loved his father's shoulders, they were his saddle, he spent such time fitted onto them, feet in his father's hands like stirrups, they were his crow's nest and the ocean of the world lay all around. (Roger's shoulders—he was so tense and proper. Well, God knows.)

Or she—*Helen*, Jessie made herself say, *Helen*—wouldn't she have spent so many hours lost on the shank of a single one of her mother's deep brown hairs, the small soft parcels of hair that lay this way, that way, intricate, each hair like the dot on a newspaper photo, the line on the television screen, in itself negligible but combined with others like it an array, a totality, a *hairdo*. The pretty woman coming in the door of the school auditorium, at last, while Helen sank down with her bells and triangle for the Christmas Festival of Carols, hers. The cap of curls hers, closely analyzed, fingered, each curl poked around a thumb, a pinky. Her mother's the hazy face she saw, waking her on the day of a picnic, waking her to the smell of waffles or the turkey already started in the oven on Thanksgiving morning.

Extrapolation. What does Lydia think of, animal baby, when I am far from her? Jessie lay on her motel bed and indulged the question. By now Andy was somewhere else, of course: surprised to be touched, embarrassed, threatened, and then unpredictably needy, sorry to be too large for a lap. The gangplank was so narrow between parents' and lovers' touching, and he was just beginning the slow jerky walk out there, suspended above cold waters, strangers' indifference. Maybe Helen's begun that walk herself, Jessie thought; maybe not. O'Neill at seven, eight? She went blank trying to imagine holding him, blank like someone who's forgotten her times tables. The knowledge was there, she had only misplaced it, wait. A little time all around.

If they are strong enough to survive what is happening to their lives, Jessie thought, and there put an end to her own thoughts, they will be too strong for me.

.   .   .

Jessie, in bed, in the dark room in the morning: one by one again the awful imaginings piled up on her with the immovable weight of too many blankets. Irony could not penetrate the airless room; she lay flat and took in stark fact: Roger and Alexis on a rainy highway—didn't it always rain in Seattle, or at least seep?—and a wall of car (truck?) ahead of them or drifting alongside, a tidal wave cresting over their window, that gruesome crushing clang of impact and that trapped refusal to believe turning in half an instant to certainty, and no way out. Of course, of course, she would think if it happened to her. At last. So this is how. Yes, Teddy had said, that's the way it was when I felt the whole car buckle: well, yes, here we are, it was only a matter of time. Is that the death wish or is it only the voice of probability, pragmatic, resigned, the timbre of it achingly familiar, like a voice you'd heard all your life, neighborly, unexotic? This was too frightening to think about, she couldn't decide whether she was inside looking out (and her stomach lurched) or outside looking in. (Which was bloody and eerily silent and left her feeling guilty for having eyes to view the carnage. She hadn't known them well enough to see them when they could no longer see themselves.) She pictured the children instead then, whole: Judy sitting them down to tell them what had happened. O'Neill looking frightened at Helen because there was something peculiar about her, about indolent laughing Judy gone so tense and pale. She stared at Judy's eyes (whose powder blue Judy dressed for so that they seemed to be the same shiny material as her blouse, nylon eyes) but couldn't get her mouth to say the words. She could not watch the children's faces try to take it in. Jessie was awake and in control but the children turned their heads away and Judy's mouth opened and closed, opened and closed like a puppet's whose ventriloquist has been struck dumb. Everything would be different now, the sky they saw would be changed. Jessie remembered when she was little—O'Neill's age or so—she had prayed her mother wouldn't die because she'd have to ask her what to wear to the funeral, and if her mother was dead, how could she ask her? Oh the fledglings, she thought, only half their feathers in and no one coming back to them! If it happened to Lydia and Andy she would never want to know. Inside the car, then, the high wall of her annihilation upon her, that was the view she would pick, to be spared knowing what her children—it all flashed round again fast, a merry-go-round—would have to know.

· · ·

Helen was a cameo. Although Lydia was their idea of beauty in a child— vivid, with Teddy's coloring, her curls glossy black and thick, and their long legs, Jessie and Teddy prepared to appreciate this face, the containment, the withdrawal of it. Helen was pale, small featured, graceful with her hair drawn back, a little bloodless—neat like French schoolgirls one had seen—but she would be a lovely woman. Had she always been so indrawn and silent? Well, she was not O'Neill's age, why should she make social conversation? State of shock, they told each other. State of siege. She has been maimed.

Judy said, "Here are your Aunt Jessie and Uncle Ted," smiling, urging recognition, embrace, comfort. O'Neill was lying on his stomach in her den, in front of the TV. He raised one arm but did not look at them for more than a stolen second. The arm lowered itself, like something subsiding by the force of gravity alone.

Helen was watching the Carmichael dog sleep. He was a Labrador and he was running in a dream, his shiny black haunches moving. Once in a while he sighed like something in captivity that would not be reconciled. Helen turned her eyes toward them but said nothing. They stared at the dog as if they had come all this way to see him.

. . .

The children sat beside them looking untouched, waiting for something visible to happen. A hard light glanced off the tops of their parents' coffins like light off a newly waxed dance floor. The lids were shaped like some kind of roof—hip? Gambrel? Jessie sat very straight and worried the question the way a tongue might worry a ragged filling in a tooth: kept at it and kept at it. Roger and Alexis were made into figures of Biblical proportion; their habits as loving parents were reviewed, as loving spouses, as loving children and siblings. The young blond minister, who frowned like a worried child delivering a school report and met every eye as he had been trained to do, worked carefully, earnestly through the eulogy according to a plan. He seemed to have laid his template across the two lost lives and now was darkening in the spaces one by one: a general assertion, a specific instance, a general assertion, a specific instance: attention to the civilized growth of their children, ballet lessons all the way across town; Sunday school attendance charted, gold stars, dire warnings; these beautifully *dressed* children, who were presented to the world to be loved like the golden prizes they were seen to be. Seen to be, Jessie thought. Seen to be. By whom? A strange distant locution. Time (daughterly) logged at mother Dorothea's bedside; Alexis's willingness—*whither thou goest*—to accompany Roger from Mississippi to Birmingham (conjugal), so that his work might, like a transplanted green flower, prosper. Roger repotted.

Siblings, Jessie said to herself—what about that one live so-called sibling? He did not reappear with his details pinned on like a donkey tail, he had been mentioned as a general but not substantiated as a specific: Teddy exhorting an audience, upturned faces, all of them black, to rise and rattle the bars of their lives. He was an unmentionable.

And Roger as devoted citizen, a fund-raiser par excellence. Two weeks ago to this day Roger Tyson had donned a football helmet and run with the ball, burst through the goalposts, in the Birmingham Southern gym to kick off the United Way fund drive, and what a smashing start it was. The mourners sighed. The Lions, the Rotary, the Elks would miss him, not to mention the Citizens' Council. (Jessie understood that the Lions really roared when they got together, they might raise a communal bellow at the loss of their fellow fund-raiser. What did the Elks do, run?) It had been said in the halls of power that Roger Tyson could get a pledge of good money from a stone, signature and all, because, quiet though he may have been, when he *believed*, he *believed*. (She waited for the echo of the congregation but, though the rhythm demanded it, there was none. The mourners' decorum was astounding; they were sober as Puritans.) Roger had his strong feelings about the world's predicament and he was a serious searcher after solutions. No specifics there either: no bricks or beer bottles, no white sheets, no anonymous phone calls. Strong feelings = murderous certainties? The furrow between the young minister's eyes deepened, doubled, perhaps at the willful suppression of the enlivening details. And now he consigned them to Jesus.

Jessie looked around at the children. Their profiles, from where she sat, were flat, two-dimensional, uncomprehending. She wondered what they would remember of the day. Everyone in recorded literature recalled the smell of flowers, how overpowering it was. White carnations in the parlor. Senses overcome by heaps of roses, the sweetish smell of putrefaction became a garden. She smelled no flowers although bouquets were propped on both sides of the coffins like mounted fireworks about to spin on their stands. The children would wonder, which way were their heads? Why were the coffins closed, why exactly, not why *generally?* What if you died when you had to go to the bathroom—at least that had preoccupied Jessie when she was their age—would you be uncomfortable for all eternity? Do they have their shoes on? Everything, Jessie thought, the difference between useful truth and useless mystery, everything turned out to be specifics.

. . .

Jessie imagined Alexis as a young girl just at the age when she was coming into her adult self—Alexis standing in her room one Sunday morning in a half slip with small green flowers on it, or ivy. Her pale skin began at the elastic, she had nothing on above it and she was beginning to "develop"; she remembered her own nipples like woody brown burls, remembered exactly how they had changed shape from when she had been a little girl going topless into the water in panties with lacy seats. It was the difference between lips drawn back in a smile and pouting lips, rounded and full. Alexis would not have known her door was open, she would have stood staring into the mirror almost blankly, learning, maybe memorizing, herself. Her brother would have watched from the hall, not breathing. He had never seen her so intent. Teddy, in turn, would have felt that stirring in himself that brothers were not intended to have for sisters, but it would be tempered with something tender, protective, wouldn't it? If she could cause such feelings, she would need protection. They were both riding out on a make-shift raft, Jessie thought—thought it now, how it would have begun then when all he could concentrate on was his blood rushing shamefully up; but they were, they were children still hand in hand going into a tossing stream without much to support them but animal courage and the toothpick raft of their healthy bodies. Those little—incipiencies—those gentle inflammations, had disappeared like all the rest, had resolved themselves into her visible life. Inside whichever coffin was hers, Alexis was taking her full hard finished breasts down with her into nowhere. Poor Helen and O'Neill. She wondered if they would come home with her holding hands, and if they did, could they hang on long enough to be a help to one another?

She closed her eyes for a full minute at the edge of a chasm of grief. But the organ had begun to play and it so offended her, its swollen pulpy chords and sumptuous cadences presumed so on her tolerance for melodrama, that when she opened her eyes she had banished that sentimentality, the breasts, the hands. Alexis and she were not really alike in any way that mattered. Teddy's sister had had a choice and had chosen to hurt him, hurt her, and, by her allegiances, wish evil to a million others, to live hurtfully. *Watch this*, she thought. *You don't have to forgive her just because she's dead.*

.   .   .

Teddy and Jessie stood near the door accepting condolences. People were sincerely moved. The words sudden, awful, shock and children recurred and recurred, and a few of the sincerely moved even ventured to embrace them in spite of all, out of feeling for family: they would have chosen guardians exactly as had Alexis. Bewilderment ran high, and personal terror: every illogical turn of the wheel, like a criminal on the loose, is a threat to the general peace.

It was like a party without a host or hostess. "Thank you for coming," Jessie found herself saying by default. "You're very kind. Thank you, thank you." She felt herself studded with false pretenses, like a clovy apple.

The children, fair, contained, stood off to the side. They seemed to belong to no one. Teddy, far more uncomfortable than they, smiled once at O'Neill, brilliantly though without any noticeable context. O'Neill, who was stolid, with protectively rounded little shoulders, stared back, his eyes round, no recognition in them and no pity, either for himself or for Teddy. He was wearing what must have been his Sunday suit.

When they were ready to go to the limousines, Judy Carmichael came and put one child under each arm. "I'm going to send them home now with the Swensons, they'll take them back to our house with our kids."

"What do you mean," Jessie said, suddenly awake, realizing she had been in a mild brain-sleep. "Aren't they coming to the cemetery?"

"Children, you go on outside there in the lobby with your friends, now. We'll be right along." She waved at them as if they were pigeons. "Go on now." She had all the sweet dictatorial habits of the kind of second-grade teacher Jessie most reviled. "My Chilton and Bud will go on with them."

"Why didn't we discuss this? Listen." At times like this she could feel how her enunciation, compared to Judy's plummy speech, was as hard as a truncheon. "Their parents are being *buried*—they can't miss this."

"Well, precisely," Judy said. "They are surely too young to have to cope with such a gruesome thing. You-all make it sound like some wonderful treat." She sighed with sudden comprehension. "This is some of that new kind of thinking the psychologists would all like."

"Look, even children—especially children—have to cope with it. How will they ever understand, their parents get on a plane and they never see them again, and they don't even know where they end up? That's the kind of thing that can have a terrible impact on a child."

Judy Carmichael swallowed once, something medicinal to judge by her face, and cast around for reinforcements. Her pale skin returned the light; she was like a broad-faced bulb, a floodlight, glowing. "Let's just see if we can find us an objective bystander—oh, Dick!"

Dick Reidy, large and sorrowful St. Bernard, loomed before them. Judy put the question to him—should these children be brought to see their poor parents put down into the *ground?* Jessie, like a defense attorney, opened her mouth to object. "I suppose this is why you do make guardians, so somebody has the right to decide. They are coming along, because if they don't come, if you send them home to read comic books or watch 'Little House on the Prairie,' there will always be a mystery about their parents and it will haunt them someday. I've seen it." She had never, in fact, had occasion to see it, but that did not mean she wasn't sure it was true.

Dick Reidy raised an arbiter's hand, the size of a shovel. "Why don't you compromise—take Helen along and send the little one home. Judy's right, you know, he's so young, you don't want to be responsible for causing him nightmares."

"Jessie, you just don't remember Alexis and Roger that well, you—"

"Shit," said Jessie and saw their eyes enlarge like small flames she had blown upon. A newfangled word. They thought she was being frivolous because she was so tenuously related here. They wanted to remind her that she had no rights but the legal ones, and none at all that she wanted. "Oh, forget it," she said. "Take them home, put on their little Hollie Hobbie nightlights. And don't let them know anything's changed, so they can think they've just gone crazy overnight." She backed into the minister trying to escape, and he put his arm around her solicitously, took her into the web of his robe for comfort, where it attached his arm to his body, like a bat's.

.   .   .

They had to talk with the children.

"No," Teddy amended, irritable with tension. "To have a talk with them. That's not at all the same." He suggested neutral territory, whatever that might be—the Carmichaels' yard, perhaps, or a little park they had seen a few blocks over, that had white stone tables and funereal hedges.

"Oh God," Jessie sighed. "Neutrality again. No strong stuff. You're as bad as that Carmichael woman. Why don't we at least give them a chance to see their house again before it all gets dismantled? If they want to."

"I suppose. But that's nothing like living another day in it. I hope that's not what you think you'll be giving them."

Teddy so feared a certain kind of confrontation he was eager to meet in public, Jessie saw, where propriety would force its own constraints. He was like a man who had stopped getting any exercise, whose flexibility was gone.

"Teddy, what are you afraid of? Are you worried that you might feel something for these kids when all those years of good Movement training tells you you ought to despise them?"

"Why do you assume I'm thinking about how I feel?"

"There was something in your eyes. I don't know. I'm sorry. I wish," Jessie said, looking into space, "we could let them stay here a little while, maybe live with someone, to cut down on the abruptness of it all."

But Teddy shook his head. "Just think about your children, Jess. Just picture them. Could you really cut down on the abruptness if we suddenly went—" He snapped his fingers in the air, made a bright popping noise that did not convincingly obliterate them.

"Well . . . but this way everything goes at once, their friends, their familiar places. It's the worst nightmare I can imagine. Can't we just slow it down a little?

"Have you heard anyone offering to keep them?"

She shrugged. "We could probably find someone who'd rise to a month or two. Judy, maybe. I'm sure we could."

Teddy considered. "Well, do you think we should consult the kids?"

"The kids?"

"They ought to have a say—"

"Oh, Teddy. Jesus." She covered her face. "We are so *inept*. Emotionally, I mean. We are so inexperienced. You can think you've been through a lot, but then none of it applies! *I* don't know. I don't have any idea whether they could be trusted to know what they want." She held her sides and moaned as if her stomach hurt. "I feel like a child myself."

Teddy was silent.

Jessie was remembering how it had come to her with astounding clarity, in one of their sloughs of depression, that the ebb of political movements is not so much ideological as it is physical. That exhaustion, body and soul weariness, ought to be the name of the villain that undoes progress, preempts choice. Armies do not turn back so often as they stumble and fall back. Standing, men sway and dream of sleep. Now, she thought, the reason we are surely about to botch this moment in the lives of these children is not what it is going to seem, years from now. There is always that secret ingredient that leaves not a chemical trace in the leaves of the family history. Which is why we are so unsympathetic to old mistakes—the elements of innocence simplify and disappear; they can never be reconstructed.

May we, she thought, not cynically, be forgiven if we guess this all wrong.

One of the things I always like to visit at the Carmichaels is the cat because we can't have one (O'Neill and his pesty allergies). Now there are the kittens. They gave most of them away but they still have two. I'm not sure the little black one ever caught a mouse but about an hour ago she brought me a lovely snake that I think lives under the rock near the fence. I grabbed her by the neck and the snake dropped out of her mouth. I locked her in the house and then I sat on the stone step of the porch studying the snake to see if it was alive. Pushed at it with a stick, it didn't even twitch a little. Was it losing its shine? I thought so— Daddy once said a dying fish's light was going out. I used to watch them (fish) in the boat when Daddy caught them, usually they stopped panting first and it took a while for this sort of wetness to change and then you could see how fat the fish was or if you would have to throw it back. But the snake. It was in a strange position too. Would a snake keep its head draped over its body like that? Like half of a square knot. There may have been a dent in its skin or there may not have been but I could see at least there was no blood. But I was staring at it, trying not to get too emotional, like a scientist. Who knows? I thought. Stunned snakes might not flicker when you stare at them. It didn't know I'm not a cat, or worse. A house fly landed on it where it is sort of braided and I noticed even its eye did not change direction. A bad sign. Why did I let the kitten out to do damage? Silly. I was trying to concentrate on all of it to keep steady but then I started crying again. Remembering listening to Judy Carmichael on the phone telling somebody that we lost our parents out in Washington on a highway, no, the state, she kept saying, not D.C. as if it mattered. "Lost them" is such a dumb thing to say for it. And now everyone treats us like little toy lambies huddling together all soft and woolly. At the funeral it wasn't the staring, it was all the smiling that made me feel funny. Like if they look happy you will be too.

So Judy went right on, she always just rolls past every subject like a tank, how her next-door neighbor died three weeks ago, suddenly, at her meeting of the Rebekahs. Reaching for a canape. (The cat is crying to come out again, hitting the screen door with her tail, she is mad.) Someone that surprised me by coming to the funeral was Tina because her father I thought was taking her to Kentucky after he got divorced from her mom. But she was there, that was very nice of her to come. Well, everyone who isn't dying over here is getting divorced. It is no coincidence Mom went with Daddy. And my friend Manda's grandparents are dying all over the place, there's that too. She is in the hospital and being rich won't help her, he is at home, Manda says, his legs are gone all of a sudden and not showing any signs of wanting to come back. This is not as funny as it sounds. If I cannot stop crying I don't know what will become of my pride. Daddy said no matter what happens crying shows no faith in Jesus who knows what is best at any given time. I wonder if he had anything like this in mind.

When I stopped the snake was halfway into the hedge. There was like this dark skinny shoelace showing out behind. We will go on living, I sort of know that, and maybe that is better and maybe worse. I hope O'Neill won't have an attack. He can't cry, I mean shouldn't, because of his lungs, it starts him off at wheezing sometimes. There is a lot of noise behind me but the cat is not getting out again today—let her be punished. She does not know what irrevocable means. (I do, it was Word of the Week just last week and I got it right on the test but I didn't know how soon I would need it.) I mean the cat doesn't care. She only wanted to play with the snake irrevocably, what she knows about killing is all an accident. Let the snake stay under the rock healing up, dear God I pray, and teach it to be careful. Let these tears stop. If Jesus really cares. If they can't stop, please, please let them be invisible like everyone else's.

I have to go. Judy is taking us over to our house to see it one more time. Then I think they (Aunt Jessie and Uncle Ted) are coming for us. Later.

The children chose to come; they wanted to see the house again. Jessie asked Judy to take them over; she had a feeling, hard to justify but firm, that she and Teddy ought not to be associated too closely with that farewell.

.   .   .

When Helen and O'Neill came back, Judy, without consulting them, brought out milk and chocolate-covered graham crackers. This she accomplished briskly, as if it were a daily task, producing matching cornflower blue mugs, arranging the cookies in a fan pattern on their dish. Then as she turned to go, as if an invisible rain were falling, causing them to soften and run, the angles of intentness disappeared from her features and her face became all circles, pious and regretful. "I'd best leave you-all now, I think," she said in a sweet girl's voice. She had prepared the statement so that it came out round and finished, like the arrangement on the plate. She was a methodical woman.

They faced each other, but if there was about to be an interview it was unclear who was to ask, and who answer, the questions.

Helen kept her eyes on the milk in her cup. She shook the mug or, rather, rocked it gently, one palm resting protectively beneath, as if it were a glass with ice cubes in it. But it was quiet. There was nothing in her even-featured face that looked especially sad; she was like someone who had been roused from sleep or summoned in the midst of deep concentration, whose pupils were only slowly adjusting to the light. She was not about to yield herself up just yet.

O'Neill's almond eyes, though, were red and his long lashes wet and separated. He had sat down angrily, abruptly.

There was no way to touch the enormity of it. Humbled, Teddy and Jessie sat quiet. Every second of their incompetence seemed to them barbaric, but saying the wrong thing, they were sure, would be far worse, they could rip off skin and draw blood where silence only left a dark and aching bruise, the flesh intact.

Finally, when she could bear the tension not an instant longer, knowing that Teddy could survive longer than she without the diversionary solace of words, Jessie took a wracking breath and said, "I hope you could feel—" she looked at Teddy, panicked, not at the children—"could find the memory of your being together in your house." She didn't mean to sound so much like Judy Carmichael for whom the right thing to say was the most orotund and meaningless. Had she whispered those words haltingly to her own children, surely they'd have understood; have grasped her distress on their behalf, if not the exact meaning of the statement, and they'd have given comfort back, shared it around, meager though it was, by answering. That was a good part of what loving was—trusting someone's intentions, knowing good faith when it came, however feebly and raggedly, toward you. Well, why should these children trust her? They were not her children. Like birds or animals who are right to be wary of the friendliest human gesture, they had themselves to protect, not the feelings of strangers.

Helen flattened her delicately drawn lips into a straight line, half smile, half grimace. (They didn't know yet that this was her favorite gesture, emphatic but ambiguous.) O'Neill looked around the kitchen avidly, probably hoping to be saved.

If the elders were silent long enough, would the children speak? It was cruel to put forbearance to a test.

"We are, we will be happy to have you with us in Jackson, you know," Teddy said with his eyebrows up disarmingly, so that he looked like a young boy selling raffle tickets on a corner, hoping to make a killing. "But we want to make sure that's the best thing for you right now. So soon." His Southern had come forward, except for the you-all, Jessie thought, which would have been a form of outright bribery. "Because there are other possibilities."

The children continued to say nothing. Owed something, owed so much, perhaps they felt they did not have to give back the small change of casual response.

Jessie put her elbows on the table, her temples in her hands, in hopeless determination. Helen looked surprised. She moved her chair backwards an inch or two. "Do you think—we really thought we ought to give you a chance to think about this and talk it over—if we could arrange it, would you like to stay in Birmingham a little bit longer, until you feel ready to come over to us?" She wished she had spoken more slowly; it all seemed to tumble out too fast, too casually. It struck her as unfair that such a crisis as this had never happened to her before, no wonder she was unprepared. Stage plays, in the hands of amateurs, came out this way; the talk and the action bunched up like traffic.

O'Neill's eyes blurred over. He bounced the front legs of his chair on the linoleum, his body a stutter.

"You can choose, you really can," Jessie assured them. "If you don't want to leave everything all at one time . . ." She dwindled off. There was no way to name the alternatives without reiterating the unspeakable.

"Who would we stay with?" Helen's thin voice, a sharp edge at best, came to them as a surprise, they had resigned themselves to conducting a sort of double dialogue with vicious circumstance, into which the children would not enter undefended.

"We could work that out. . . . Anyone you'd like to, I imagine. Everyone would be happy to have you."

Jessie saw instantly that she had made a bad—a careless, an overeager—offer. Because, didn't anyone mean no one, emotionally speaking? Such indifferent generosity must seem an affront to Helen's particularity. "Oh, we're the ones who don't have any parents," Helen said wearily in confirmation, as if she had been dragging herself through that condition for years. "Come here, O'Neill." She got up slowly and took her brother's bare arm in her hand where its vivid tan against her paleness made them look like distant, tenuous relations, cousins, perhaps, as Lydia and Andy would be.

"Come out here and talk to me," she coaxed, not gently. O'Neill looked at them reproachfully and followed his sister into the pantry, where Judy Carmichael kept full shelves of canned goods lined up so perfectly their labels were like one endless ribbon, merely indented with shadow between the cans. There was a year's supply of toilet paper glinting in its wet-shiny cellophane skins, and dog food, cat food, enough for a kennel. Efficient woman, Jessie thought, under that silk and silliness. She dealt briskly with her two rowdy boys—what would two more children be to her?

The Tyson children stood behind the door, which moved like a rudder to left, to right as they leaned against it. When one of them grasped at the knob it made a metallic squeak that displaced air. A verdict was being passed on them, Teddy and Jessie felt, although that was hardly the point, and they knew it. O'Neill gasped out, through tears, that he wanted to ask his mother. He was shushed into hiccups, and then was quiet. It was in this interval, when she imagined Helen discovering herself the closest thing to her little brother's mother and feeling for the implications, that Jessie's own hot tears welled up and coursed down her face from a dozen outlets, the way, so long ago, her breasts had surprised her by giving milk from every inch of nipple, a general and generous seepage and drenching. She kept her hands on her face and let the tears gather behind them until they were slippery and sticky. She was wiping them dry with her thumbs as the children emerged from behind the door—ridiculous, as if they had taken a vote for class president!—and she turned to hear their consensus.

Helen lowered her eyes like someone making an admission for which she would be blamed. "We decided we might just as well come."

"Do you think—" Teddy began.

"There's no sense going on here like nothing's different." She looked up at them, a quick glance at each, and then down again as though their faces reflected an uncomfortable light. "We wouldn't kid anybody."

"Kid anybody!" Teddy said without thinking. Jessie winced at the rawness of it. But he went on gently. "No, you wouldn't, I don't suppose. Or yourself either." In their presence Teddy looked mournful; it was when they were out of sight and he was preoccupied by *whose* they were that his feelings went dry.

"So we might as well come," O'Neill said brightly; he made it sound like a promising project. He took a very deep heartening breath in which he looked ready to list the virtues of his choice, but let it out slowly instead and sat down to eat a cookie and study the table. His chin twitched evenly as if he were chewing with his front teeth, behind closed lips.

"You're going to get fat, O'Neill," Helen said with harsh sisterly smugness. "Mom warned you you better start thinking early." She looked at them briefly, then back to O'Neill. "His daddy went through a period of the most disgusting *fat* when he was a boy. I'm glad I never knew him then."

"Oh, let him have a little sugar," Teddy said smiling, pained. "This is no day to worry about that."

O'Neill smiled back at him and at his sister, who had simply been trying to assert authority as if to put a seal on her maternity. He took two cookies which melted instantly in the burning palm of his hand. He raised his fingers as if to hide his face. His eyes closed in ecstasy, then, he licked the hand clean.

Well, we decided to go to Jackson. They gave us a choice of now or later. Everything that looks like it would be the same (our friends, and everything) wouldn't really be the same any more at all. I wish somebody here like Julie Ann's family would say We will keep them and adopt them and all, then I would at least have a sister I like, and her mother and dad are ok. But no one is saying that. I suppose family is family and an uncle feels an obligation. Anyway this is what their will said and they never asked us. Why would anyone else want us forever just because Julie Ann and I went to Sandbox nursery school together and kept on being best friends. Even with blood vows I guess that isn't family, I didn't make the vows with Mr. and Mrs. Sandifer!

I can't think about Mom and Daddy and those two in the same thought, though. Truly they (my aunt and uncle) are such dinks. They are different but sort of the same too: both are tall and skinny, they are like these dumb pine trees or something, Jessie has this sort of small head on a long body and sort of medium hair with a lot of curls like Annie. (Only not red. No particular color—blah.) And he has very dark hair, straight, he looks more like an Indian. And he has this awful scar, it looks like his whole cheek was in a meat grinder and then was pushed together like hamburg. It is disgusting. I don't know how anyone can come near it. She has this jerky New York accent that is so strange, she says things like "chawclit" and "I'm tawking to you," you can see her whole mouth come tight together like for another language altogether.

It is all so totally absolutely not real when I realize we are going to live in their house like we belong to them that I am not even upset about it! I know I won't but I keep sort of expecting to wake up and say What a terrible dream, I almost believed it for a while, and then I would apologize to Mom and Daddy for blotting them out 1-2-3. O'Neill is the same, I think, because he isn't really very upset either. He cried a little today and wanted Mommy but I'm sure he believes she'll be back when this bad joke is over. He's a lot worse when Daddy gets mad and smacks him or he gets grounded for doing something outrageous. (Just last week the way he cut that old chair with his Swiss army knife. He is still not allowed to watch t.v. Daddy's curse from the grave!!!) He's been getting lots of attention in fact and people are giving him candy (which is like smiling all the time, what does it have to do with anything to keep your mouth happy?). So he'll probably end up more spoiled than ever.

Anyway if these two only knew some of the nasty words that were said about them in our house they might not be trying to be so nice. (I see them trying, I can almost guess they aren't using their natural voices on us, being so c.a.r.e.f.u.l.) I won't even repeat the words Daddy used. Mom in the last year or so was on him a lot for calling them those things, and was even sort of protecting my uncle, saying what he did was right in the end, even if she didn't agree with how those people tried to do it. It was one of the many things that was eating up their love like burning acid.

P.S. When Judy took O'Neill and I back to our house it didn't do *any good. I could not look at it like it was any way special, it was just our house that I have lived in since we moved to Vestavia from on the other side of Birmingham when I was too little to know. Maybe you have to believe things in your sleep first or something. Did she expect me to go around saying Dead Dead Dead! over everything, or kiss it goodbye, the mattresses and the toaster? The furniture did not speak a single word to me and I also felt Judy kind of wanted to hurry so I couldn't wait for feelings to begin to like come up slowly out of the fog. The only time I got a little weak-kneed was when we went into the sewing room and there was so much of Mom's unfinished business lying all around, and all those windows she loves looking out on the sunlight. (I mean, loved.) There was half a dress pinned on Aunt Maud (what we call the dress form) and the leotard she was decorating for my ballet recital was just all kind of bunched up on the table with the silver edging hanging down, it looked like an icicle, where she must have put it down just for a minute and now I can't believe will never pick it up again. (I am reading that sentence over and over but it doesn't make any sense at all. It is just these words.) She was in that room, though, I could feel that when I was there, a little. I could hear a thousand things she said, like the way she cursed because the thread on the machine always broke and she couldn't fix the tension without a screwdriver. But O'Neill was always taking the screwdriver away to fiddle with an intergalactic something-or-other. Then she would laugh and say Don't tell your Daddy you heard me saying this—and then she'd say it and wink. That was the closest I came to feeling anything the least little bit strange in there, though (and only for a minute). I am already making her into memories and that is so awful. Like I am admitting she is only in my mind now. I can't admit that but I don't know what I can. I am old enough to know what it means—she is dead, that means I will not see her again. And if I think anything I do will matter to her that is only because I know I will see her in heaven. But it does not feel real at all. When I get this far I have to change the subject.*

I think Judy was disappointed.

"I will take my mother's clothes," Helen said the next morning. "Some of them. She had very good taste."

"What is going to happen to the dishes." "What is going to happen to the sheets. The television sets." The questions appeared rhetorical. There were three television sets; one was recessed into a wall, like a statue in a niche.

O'Neill said, "Take a match and burn the house up. You could put it under the stove. Or the curtains."

"He wants his chance. He once started a fire in the curtains," Helen said calmly. "That was when he was little. And he was in a lot of trouble. Weren't you, O'Neill?" She was packing piano music into a large plastic bag with a picture of a modern church on it and script letters that said *We Try Harder.*

Teddy tried to help but he was not much better than useless. He got to sit in the kitchen reading about the economics of the New South in a pamphlet called "What We Must Do" that grudgingly admitted the mid-nineteenth century was a thing of the past. He tipped his chair back to read it. Niggers (cf. Nigras) had been transformed into welfare chisellers and could thus be identified and eliminated. Women who reproduced like rabbits were to be dealt with scientifically: the final solution. Deficient children drank up resources like chocolate milk and nothing remotely like gratitude emerged. Teddy saw great bubbles of gratitude, a general foaming-at-the-mouth, from the tattered little devils.

Teddy was a fast reader. When he skimmed a document like this one, his eyes flicked across the page with nervous speed so that he looked like a man with twenty seconds to devise an escape from a cul-de-sac.

O'Neill, who had an elf's face and elf's ears, lay down in the middle of his parents' bed. He sank into the mauve and lavender quilted bedspread, which puffed up all around him like angry skin around a splinter. He slept. "Let him," Jessie said to no one.

.   .   .

Assignments had been given out, with Judy as the straw boss. A neighbor was "doing" the garage and Dick Reidy was investigating the safe deposit box. He was the executor, the one who understood its language. Lurene, who had her language too, would pack boxes of household belongings and haul them—where? An auction, someone had suggested. In the will, everything significant went to the children, but who would get the electric knife, the steak knives, the bun warmer and the lawnmower, the blankets, the andirons, the toilet brushes? What becomes of it all? Jessie asked out loud, horrified. Can't we pack it up and bury it with them like the Pharaohs' pottery dishes? Her father's old asceticism shadowed her like a Depression child's anxiety at running up a debt: how can one go to the nether reaches

unaccompanied by the electric sandwich-maker and the wok? Body was like
a tail of tin cans tied to the soul, all right. But earthly possessions—was it
Thoreau who said you should own no more than you could pull behind
you through a narrow hole in the wall, a mousehole big enough for your
shoulders (and the shoulders turned, Jessie thought, as they are, gently, at
birth)? Can't you walk clean, out of your life? Half the possessions in this
house were registered by number in their manufacturers' files: they lived a
shadow life elsewhere, their permanence guaranteed, or at least warranted
for ninety days, though their owners' was not. When Roger and Alexis
came back as ghosts and poltergeists and flung around the appliances, they'd
better remember that warranties only cover normal wear.

Meanwhile (Dick Reidy, executor, suggested), they would melt it down
to money.

. . .

One of us should stay, Jessie announced. One of us should clear up the
practical details and get to know the children a little and the other one get
our kids prepared. After an early conversation to assure them they were
there and safe, they had put off talking on the phone to Andy and Lydia,
seized by panic at the thought of telling them how they, all of them, had
been overcome—by what? The sentence had no ending. Teddy said it was
ignoble to be afraid to talk to your own children about anything, but he
was, he admitted, ignoble and afraid.

"You stay," he said, hiding behind his incompetence again. "What do
I know about the value of guest towels and Teflon pans?"

"What do I know?" asked Jessie. "We don't have any guest towels. Or
Teflon pans."

"Look, I'm going to take O'Neill's advice if I stay here. I'll get a match. . . ."
Teddy hated things: would not shop, wore the same clothes with a look of
sublime indifference like a priest in a shoe-length habit, for years at a time,
into fashion, out and in again. He could have lived in a tent, a tent with
bookshelves, would have been happier in one, where the minimum sufficed
and that the pure utilitarian. He would have invented, had he been able,
the can opener that unplugged drains and washed clothes, the all-purpose
hammer that took out splinters and made duplicate copies. Lacking these,
he tended to have as little to do with tangible necessities as he could arrange
by making such a fiasco of repairs, improvements and household solutions
that he was exempted as a kind of mercy to the handicapped, and a mercy
to the house. He was not the one to inventory a dream house.

Furthermore, Dick Reidy had shown him the Tysons' will.

"Just boilerplate," said Reidy. There was a paragraph concerning char-
ities—Teddy felt the hair on the back of his neck rise. This was like giving
money to the Third Reich. He laid his forehead on his hands, which were
on the desk joined in what might, for another man, have been prayer. For
Teddy it was control they were grasping for, grappled together; it was a
holding tight. The National Association for the Preservation of the White
Race. Americans for a Renewal of States Rights. "I've got to get away from
here before I do violence," he said. "Jess, I think you're a patsy, that's what
I think. Running your fingers through the enemy's underwear. Let's both
just leave. Walk out. Take off."

"Spoils," Jessie said shrewdly. "Two down, how many to go."

"Please."

"You might as well go home before I take a match to *you*."

"Taking home the enemy's kids. I feel like it's been a long time since
I've seen anybody I *love*."

"It's been two days, if you don't count me. Look, Teddy, why are you
jeering at me? For a serious man you can be an astonishing asshole, did you
know that? What do you suggest we do with these children of your enemies?
You're the one who talks about blood being thicker than school paste."

"I don't know. Give them to the people who're preserving the race, let
them be Exhibit A and B of racial purity. Deal with them scientifically,
like welfare chiselers who reproduce." He did not look happy with himself,
saying this.

"I'll drive you to the airport," Jessie said. "Now that we own two more
cars than we did the day before yesterday."

"Now that we own two more children."

.   .   .

Driving back from the airport, she imagined how Teddy would very
soon be circling over Jackson, looking out his tiny window at evergreens
that grew in tufts bright as broccoli. Her mother used to put baking soda
in the water, cheating, to keep the broccoli just that optimistic green. (Jessie,
come in here and let me show you how to wash these dishes! her mother
would say innocently, dozens of days. I already know how, thanks. But it
wouldn't protect her.)

The Pearl River below would be brown. It always looked as if it had
been dragged inside out, all the blue on the underside. There would be a
good deal of starting-our-final-approach shuffling around him, a couple of
young businesswomen probably, booted and tweeded, getting into their
coats, snapping their attaché cases closed. A different species from Alexis,

surely. Pitney-Bowes, Digital, This-Tech and That-atron. There would typically be only a few blacks on the plane, looking so dignified they appeared to have swallowed their teeth. When they spoke to one another, they seemed to expect to be heard, discussing with apparent pride college budget deficits or promotional strategies. By the time they were on the ground they'd have gone on to growth projections.

In the airport he would be greeted by those cases of metal shovels in primary colors, each standing, in red or yellow or blue, propped beside a card that celebrated another hole in the ground: new wing of the medical center. Arts complex. Dig we must. See how we burgeon, Jackson waxing.

Nonetheless she knew that Teddy couldn't walk through here without seeing the old rest-room signs in his mind: WHITE MEN   COLORED. He had seen them all his life, before he'd noticed. After he'd noticed, he had gotten hit in the stomach in that corner, hit, hard, on interstate property, hit under federal jurisdiction. Sometimes his chest constricted at his memories, he told her he could feel a band of numbness circling front to back as if his heart were all scar tissue. Yet he feels happy to be home each time, he always is. She goes white with anxiety before the glass windows. There are peculiar cozy areas set aside for waiting, little platforms; she tensely eyes the families gathered on the patches of rug watching TV as if they were at home, or the kids beating on the pinball machines. All of them are on home territory; only she feels, perennially, like someone arriving in Mexico or Greece, prepared to be under a strain, to have to concentrate hard to be sure she understands, though what it is she doesn't understand she will never be able to say. But Teddy will be home.

The last time they flew in there were two black women, dressed up, bright colors winking out under their somber coats and a dozen gold chains over their chests, waiting with them for the van into town. Then they were joined by a young white girl in jeans and a black man of about thirty with a conservative Afro. (Processed hair rides the bus, by observable rule. And only smokers sit in the back. Before her stroke there had been times when Teddy's mother had wanted to travel somewhere and, not eager to spend the money on plane fare, had stayed home. "The backs of the bus seats are greasy with their *hair* pomade, Teddy," she had said. "Really, you might try to understand.") Teddy had smiled at the two women. One nodded curtly, as if to dismiss his attention. Too bad there were no babies, Jessie thought. He did really well with babies, nobody minded if you tickled them with your eyes. He waited for the women to get into the van, sit back on the slick seats, cross their ankles demurely, or settle with their legs parted comfortably, and then he hauled himself in beside them, trying to look neither too comfortable nor too uncomfortable. But he was always conscious of how he might seem, he was never done with that, knowing where his legs were, his hands, his eyes. She watched him watch himself when they were in public, making casual overtures carefully, like a flirt. A professional integrationist, Jessie called him with her chilliest Northern superiority. She made it sound like *whore*. What would happen if he were himself? Who, what was himself, what was he holding in suppression?

Oh Teddy, go on, she thought wearily now. You do the best you can. She'd been weakened by the last few days: her irritation was surely excessive. Alexis's face flickered past, early Alexis. If you do a little better than you were born to, that ought to be enough.

. . .

Teddy took the children out for pizza and told them, very methodically, he said, that they were going to have a sort of brother and sister.

He called Jessie when they were in bed. "Not necessarily asleep, I'm not sure I'd be asleep if I'd just been told all that." He brought out a very long sigh of relief to be done with that part of it.

"Well?"

"Well. I'd say Andy's eyes sort of lit up at the challenge. You know how practical he is. What will it mean on a day-to-day basis, right? Where will they sleep? He sort of blinked once for every question, like he was crossing it off. What grades are they in? Will we still do things like this—go out for pizza? Go to the movies?"

"You mean will we suddenly be all cramped and poor like some of those families he knows where there's more kids than money?"

"I suppose that's what he meant. I said, don't you even want to know what flavor of pizza they like? I mean, if both of them like anchovy, you know, he's going to be outvoted."

"Did he laugh?"

"He sort of—I guess you'd say he groaned."

Jessie imagined how Andy, from within his own skin, peering out through his own gray eyes, innocent and curious, would see no humor in the question. It was, she supposed, his instant flexibility at play. He took the events of his life at face value—one long swallow of information, a little emotional rearrangement like finding a new place to store your bike, and he was beginning to get acquainted. "How could we have produced such a well-adjusted child?" Jessie asked.

"If that's good adjustment."

"Well, true. Where does he put his doubts, his refusals? It's daunting, isn't it?"

"It'll be god awful if he ends up taking everything anybody dishes up to him and just files it away neatly as a necessity. But I don't think that's what he's doing, I think he's just—he's trying, that's all. I think he understands very wisely and decently what this is going to take out of him and all of us and he's not going to waste any time kicking against it. Not until he has to."

"And Lyddie?"

"Oh, baby, Lyddie had a gratifyingly hard time with it, if that's what we want to see. Forbiddingly hard." He stopped to remember, breathed out hard as if he were cooling his upper lip, said, "She just stared at me like I'd done something—dangerous. I mean—I remember she was holding this piece of pizza in both her hands and she froze just that way." The slice—Jessie was trying to be there—with its swirls of red and yellow like a Jackson Pollock—would have been an arrow with its point aimed at her mouth. She would have had her perplexed look: why is he telling me this? Does he expect me to believe him? Jessie had seen that look that was interchangeable with the one she produced for every new math lesson: you turn it upside down and *multiply?* Unlike her brother, Lydia took nothing for granted, neither good nor bad. They had seen endlessly how she seemed to need to construct her security from scratch every other day, count her parents, touch her belongings all over like a lover, have a reassuring conversation with her cat, drag him in to sleep on her stomach as if to weight her down with the certainty that he existed and, existing, loved her best.

It was unclear, Teddy said, which Lydia was having the greatest trouble assimilating: the instantaneity of catastrophe from the point of view of Helen and O'Neill or of Lydia, Lydia herself, her life, her place, blooming and singular, in her parents' eye, her possessions, her place in the world's eye. Jessie wished she had been there; she'd have taken her daughter's cool dry hand; the slice of pizza would have rocked in the other and collapsed onto her napkin. Her eyes would have swamped with tears and so would Jessie's and together, biting their lips, they'd have worked to keep them from falling. Lydia would have been afraid they'd be angry with her.

"So there's Andy standing there, you know, in this posture that says 'I will be a guide,' he's trying to ignore the terror he sees in Lyddie's face, you know. Keep real far from it."

"The family Boy Scout."

"Don't knock it, we might need a little of that for a while. So then Lydia tries to hold us to the original deal. She says, 'Mommy didn't say any of this when she called.' "

An accusation full of hope. "Did you tell her I didn't know? We didn't?"

"Of course I did. Then she said, 'Well, wouldn't they rather stay where they know everybody? Maybe they won't like it here.' "

And so on, Jessie saw, desperate to undo it. She thought of the scene in the Superman movie where destruction gets played backwards: where California heals, the crumpled fender straightens, mutilated bodies unbend, where spilled blood finds its way back into its veins like toothpaste miraculously restored to its tube. Ah Superman. Real coffins stay closed.

"And then when she was out of ideas she just said in this little voice, 'Daddy, I want to go home now.' So we go to the cash register and I put my arms around her and I say something like 'Honey, think how sad it is for them.' And she's talking into my chest, you know, all damp and teary, and she puts her head back and looks up at me and she says, 'Do they get to be orphans now?' " They laughed.

She envied Teddy his connection with the children; alone and responsible in this strange place, in this room that passed as casually as money from hand to hand, she felt like a combination of mother and orphan, adult and child, half sorrowful, half grateful for all she still had waiting.

.   .   .

To be able to wake at the other end of this! To forgo both the melodrama and the trivia and say, Oh children, this is going to be so hard, and thereby, for proving you understood, to be exempt from living it through. What was the other end, though? When would they be finished with each other? Alexis and her brother Teddy had seemed irrevocably sundered, hadn't they, and look now. Family you were never finished with; absence of family goes on forever—either one a doom.

Jessie, in the shower, soaping the familiar surface of her skin with the tiny motel soap like a perfect stone in her hand, was seduced into a peculiar appreciation of all she could feel, minutiae, that was recognizable. There was a special delight in being alone with herself. (Judy Carmichael had offered her a guest room. The Tyson children were in their friends' rooms on the floor in rainbow-striped sleeping bags, as if they were enrolled in a long-drawn-out slumber party. She saw Judy shadowing her, voluminous as an old-fashioned nun, a voluptuary nun, in her flowing caftan dressing gown. She would offer, would demand, that they share truisms about motherhood and wash them down with bourbon camouflaged in something sweet.)

At least, she thought, the contours of her stomach hadn't changed with the advent of these two new children. The straight strong bones of her thighs, the rocky knees with their amusing facets, the lifelong lines at wrist and elbow, hers like fingerprints. She thought of Alexis—could never manage Roger, could never find a point of contact, of vulnerability in him as she could with Alexis simply by virtue of their shared sex. She thought, that is, of Alexis whose fingerprints were already beginning to fade like the writing—CASHMERE BOUQUET—on the wet soap closed in her fist.

.   .   .

She let them take a lot of gear. They loaded it into and onto the station wagon, which was coming home with them. (For the moment and perhaps forever the white Corvette was not.) But she looked at it with trepidation: their house was so small! Andy and Lydia had learned to divest themselves of outgrown books and games for want of storage space; they had learned not to be sentimental. But it was hard to order these children, who were going to be lonely at best, to leave behind the piles of boxes they claimed to need. What Jessie wanted was the kind of precise information that had been extinguished with their parents. (Not that they were, just days later, the same children their parents had known.)

O'Neill, for instance, had a house, made of aggressively firm cardboard, that he would not give up. "Look," he said, taking her arm and dragging her through it, "look, it's got a mail slot and these electric wires and a real closet! Look, you can walk into it." She understood. But it was such a strong house, standing so unassailably, she told him, they would never be able to break it down. "With pliers?" he asked, very suspicious. "With a monkey wrench? My dad's got all that." She wanted to stall him so that, when they returned after a while to claim what they had to leave today, he might have forgotten or outgrown it: it would take up an entire room at home! A real room for a pretend house. What household economy.

Helen stood silently on the path beside an oleander bush half-reduced by October to bare twigs. She was wearing dungarees and a Snoopy sweatshirt: Snoopy upside down on his doghouse saying SOME DAYS AREN'T WORTH GETTING UP FOR.

"Do you want to sort of—say goodbye to anything, Helen?" She was thinking of how hard it had been for her to leave any of her apartments as a child. When her father had gone into hiding and they had left West Eleventh Street to live for a while in Brooklyn on Eastern Parkway, where they tried to "start from scratch," her mother had called it, pretending to be a recent widow, out of reach of neighbors' gossip, she had walked very slowly down the dark front steps, at a dirgelike pace, touching each bar of the banister as if she were patting the heads of her faithful retainers. Her attachments had been so deep, she sometimes thought, because an only child needs receptacles for the energy that brothers and sisters expend so casually on each other.

Helen, however, stood in her caul of silence and simply shook her head. She did not seem to feel she owed explanations. Her silence had an intensity of its own; it had nothing in common with passivity.

O'Neill was in a flurry, running in circles. "I can't find my calculator." He said it three times, with a rising intonation, and then butted his head into what would have been his sister's lap, had she been sitting. She shouted for him to stop. "Maybe Lurene knows where it is." She twisted away.

"But where's Lurene!"

Helen shrugged.

"She's not here today, O'Neill," Jessie told him. There was such disruption inside the house they would never be able to find a small quiet object. "We've got a calculator at home, we can find yours next time, or have her send it to us. She can mail it."

He stamped his foot on the concrete path. "She wouldn't be able to mail it, dummy, a nigger wouldn't know how to do that. That's complicated, it would have to be all padded in a special box to make sure it didn't get busted, and it needs the adapter, and she wouldn't do that."

Jessie opened her mouth to begin on him but she stopped herself. Futile lessons, moral indignation and realignment, those were Teddy's department. And this was not a time to scold. "Let's get in the car now," she said, just that, and wondered if she was letting them both off easy.

.   .   .

O'Neill waved at his neighborhood as they wound out through it. Once he pounded on the window, although Jessie saw no children his size that he might have been saluting. There were some dramatic houses and some absurdities, like an Italian villa painted a rash Mediterranean pink, color of rambler roses, which sat beside a Swiss chalet A-frame built of creosoted wood, color of telephone poles. It was not a modest neighborhood, however silly its excesses. Lawn predominated, professionally kempt, unlived-on, an elaborate frame for the house at its center. She was going to need all her control to ride them down Willowbrae and not apologize for it as she apologized to herself. If she could lay bets, she would expect O'Neill to make retching noises in the back seat, and Helen would blink to herself, sealing her vision back, and say not a word. She would suffer it like a banished princess sent to live with paupers in the woods. (No one ever wrote about the suffering of those patient selfless princesses. Cordelia, or the one whose father disowned her until he learned the true dearness of salt and summoned her back again, did they have crying fits, hypochondriacal pimples, bloody vengeful dreams? Who gives up a kingdom without backtalk?) If Helen stayed silent, would she be dropping acid or slicing open her wrists at sixteen?

Jessie tried six subjects, and then she turned on the radio. The mention of Lydia's cat, Mickey Mouse, had brought forth a graphic confession of O'Neill's severe allergies, with dramatic examples. No, the Carll children did not go to Sunday school, but the Tyson children might continue if they wished. No, they did not eat steak or chops every other night, who could afford such a thing? We could, the little boy said unabashed. (They were going to feel martyred, starved to boot, on macaroni and cheese and brown rice. They would never believe they were still in America.) O'Neill's in-nocence was appealing—he seemed too young to be malicious and in addition he was Alexis's son, she who could be so guilelessly, so whimsically insulting. But there was not going to be any escaping its scattershot, no matter his intentions. She and Teddy could take it, she supposed, but Andy and Lydia were going to have to tough it out.

The radio introduced into the closed car the voice of an evangelist that rose and rose, higher and higher, like a tightening guitar string. They were sinners on C, eligible for moral repair on E, lucky to be in God's good graces, humble, on A. By the time he had seen to their salvation they were an octave closer to heaven. God bless his listeners; likewise the feed he advertised. It was God-given good and your chickens and hogs, he cried, will *know* it. She turned the dial to international godless rock. *"If you think I'm sex-y and you like my mon-ey, come on, baby, let me know!"* The children said nothing and then the Interstate opened before them and took them in, disclosing nothing.

Modest farmland, modest wooden houses, white and grayed white, like something laundry soap could never soak clean again. Tin roofs rusted orange and burnished brown, like uneven copper. Indifferent green sweeping off vague as a painted set in both directions—just as the secret life of a country is in its small towns, so the life of the towns is on its back roads facing nothing. When she and Teddy and their friends were in danger, years ago, the federal highways were the most exposed, fifty percent safer. Teddy got his on State 49. Tommy and Andréa had been clubbed good, once, in the dark of an underpass leading off Interstate 55, but that was *off* in a place where light couldn't reach and the traffic was nil for ten minutes at a time. They'd have done better in the fast lane, but that would mean they could never get off to go home. . . .

What was Alabama, what faced the other way? The original Black Panthers, from Lowndes County, had painted, for anyone who would listen, a mirror image of Mississippi, different in detail, identical in spirit, not quite real when it reappeared, defined under a layer of journalists' adjectives—corrupt! violent! passive! loving! brave! vindictive!—that were really composed of thousands of facial expressions, attitude of dozens of shoulders in public places, numbers of listeners, sympathizers or hecklers who showed up for a church meeting or a roadside white-sheeted torch-carrying rally. . . . Helen was tapping her on the shoulder. She said something urgently while Jessie explained to herself that the girl didn't have anything to call her— neither "Aunt" nor "Jessie" nor any other noncommitted thing. It seeped through to her only slowly that the quiet voice was giving an alarm: O'Neill was about to be sick in the car. She cast one quick believing look at him (both his hands were on his mouth and his eyes bulged above like cartoon circles) and they swerved to an instant grinding stop on the macadam shoulder. "Open up the door! Get out in the air, quick, you'll feel better."

The boy swung out, corduroy legs first, and stood breathing deeply with his face turned up, like a true believer come to be blessed. Color seeped back into his cheeks; his ears stayed a pinched porky gray. He jiggled from foot to foot and bobbed his head. Jessie had had a toy once that looked like that, a paddle on which half a dozen wooden chickens rhythmically pecked corn. *Go to him*, her maternal voice urged, while the chorus of her teacher's instincts echoed behind. She had seen so many dozens of children pass before her over the last few years, as if she were a general reviewing troops. They had lived for a year at a time in the carefully focussed light of her concern, the bedwetters, the high achievers, the touchy siblings and glorious finger-painters, one boy with perfect pitch and two girls who would have been gymnastics champions if they'd been born elsewhere and another color. There had been borderline brain-damaged, borderline geniuses. And the stunned ones, silenced or made manic by divorce or abandonment. All of them, whatever their qualifications for affection, had had easy access to Jessie's concave bosom and her long encircling arms. Sometimes she felt like a mother monkey. Can't I, she begged herself now, watching her pale-faced nephew bounce from leg to short leg as if he had in his nausea somehow also caught a mortal chill, can't I go put my arms around him now when he feels so awful? This poor sweet cracker child.

She could not. She watched him over the littered roof of the car from her own side and saw, as she had feared, that he had taken on for her the telltale characteristics of assigned work. Coercion. She had not done as well in college as she might have because of her built-in resistance to requirements. She had ceased to love making love when the two of them were earnest about also making a baby. She knew it was immature but she liked and needed the idea of emotion freely given. (Would she have been one of the resisters, then—a Roger—when it came to accepting new times, integration, voting rights, all the rest, where the law comes first and the order comes down that you will learn to live with it later? If she'd been born where they were born? Is that what it is, she had often wondered, secretly ashamed, consent freely given? License to remain unmoved, unmoving?) She can love her students, those petitioners for endless warmth, because she has chosen them en masse, a sort of class action charge on her instincts, appeal granted. But this . . .

Helen had stepped silently out of the car and gone to her brother. She did not look at Jessie—they had their own undisturbed habits after all— and she picked up his small pointy chin in her hand so that she could study his face. Jessie could not guess what she saw there.

"Would you like a soda, O'Neill? That ought to make you feel a little better." Jessie had learned, in her years of dealing with people she was obliged to like, that a gesture of friendliness could cover a gaping absence of feeling, at least for a while.

"You-all think you could keep one down?" his sister asked him gently.

"A Sprite," the boy said, leaping toward the car. "Let's us find a Sprite, okay? And y'all can get a Mountain Doo-Doo. That's what we call it, Mountain Doo-dee-doo-doo-doo." He was revived. Jessie sighed and checked off, on the list she had prepared like an empty ledger in her mind, one minor trial survived.

. . .

Almost survived.

She took the next exit and they were, in a quarter of a mile, in the Alabama she had accused of facing the other way. They had gone from the frontage road in the direction of what felt like town. The sign had said LUCAS, ALA., POP. 211, and there, she supposed, the town was: A gas pump and a little cinderblock house with a Drake's Cakes sign crooked in one window and, in the other, a thoroughly inaccurate clock above a directive to Join the Pepsi Generation. (Would Lucas, Ala., have a branch?)

She pulled up out of range of the pump. Tires and random discarded car parts, rusty as a red tide, and a bumpy wave of mattress springs, pots and yellowed papers, stood fixed in the field—she expected that if she looked hard she would see roiling movement, something boiling up from below.

"This place int going to have any!" O'Neill shouted in alarm. "Anyway I'm not going in there."

A shambling old man began his slow approach, dragging a sludgy windshield rag in his hand. He was dark as bittersweet chocolate and wore a hat that looked like a soft-sided gray bird.

"Have any cold soda?" Jessie asked out the window.

"Yes'm, sure do. S'inside there." He indicated the blockhouse store. "I go getch somethin, tell me what y'all want."

"What did he say?" O'Neill hissed. "I can't ever understand a country nigger."

"No, that's okay," Jessie told the old man. "I'll go on in. I'm not sure what else I want."

The man touched his hat and stepped aside deferentially as she got out. The children cowered, or so she thought she could feel as she walked away. Did they think he was a Mau-mau with a spear behind his back? Or was it disgust at the junked, heaped, soiled, conscienceless yard, which was like the entrails of some large thing violently ripped out and flung into the wind and then blown back, and which their parents would have driven on past, clicking their tongues at the barbarism some people prefer.

Inside it did not astonish Jessie, though it would have the children, to find a store with a thousand items piled in the dusty half-light. She loved this kind of place, how there would be uncountable surprises in here like abandoned loot found scumbled together in a robbed tomb. Used carburetors and Campbell's pepper pot. All-Bran. Denture cream and Wild Turkey. Galoshes, slumped against each other with their tongues hanging out. Playing cards. A full display of Wonder Bread in its primary clown-suit colors, work-gloves and kitchen pails, and, hanging on a far wall, a cellophane packet containing a fire-engine red harmonica. A silt of road dust and sheer distilled time had settled over it all, like the soft filter of a movie camera being kind, rendering everything vague, and vaguely beautiful, abstract. The motes in the air were visible and busy, they seemed to swarm with amoebic life. A sprigged curtain separated the store from a hidden rear. The old man, still holding his rag, made change for Jessie's Yankee Doodles and sweating bottles, mumbling and mouthing while he wrote out the bill, pressing down hard, on the empty margin of the *Birmingham Times*. He double-checked.

Like Teddy that day with Lurene, she wished she could give him some sign. *I am not who you think I am. I know who you are.* (Do I?) *Those rude children do not belong to me. Trust me. I am not now nor have I ever been a White Lady.* Didn't he think it peculiar she would stop at his store, his station, afloat here like a ship broken up on the shoals? Well, it was nothing like that to *him*, it was his home and his livelihood. And for all she knew, desperate white folks came by fairly often in search of phone or bathroom or a Baby Ruth to help them stay awake on the endless stretch of road. They could, after all, go anywhere they pleased; he was the one who would think twice about going to their gas stations, and likely decide against it. She was flamboyantly polite saying Thank you.

She handed over the sodas and the crackling cellophane of the cakes to the children.

But they would have none of it. "You'll get poisoned on that!" O'Neill said, accusing her with a twisted face, then sitting wrapped in his arms, the chill returned.

Helen simply shook her head when Jessie held out her Mountain Dew. She let O'Neill do a lot of her talking, a lot of her belligerence.

"You've got to be kidding!" Jessie sat down on the passenger side of the front seat, and swung around to face them. "Now tell me, really, what do you expect to happen."

They would not speak. She felt defeated.

"You think because you don't like the looks of this place—because it's not Howard Johnson's or Stuckey's or something—that you can't trust the soda? This came out of a bloody machine, and I opened it for you on the machine! You want me to do it with my teeth?"

They sat closer together, their elbows touching.

"I see," said Jessie, moving into the driver's seat, tilting her own head back to receive the scrape and rasp of the cold bubbles, "that we're going to have quite a few little things to talk about when we get home." As if that tone, in a home not theirs, would do anything but harden their hearts and stiffen their necks. It was too soon for this. She started the car and they headed back toward the highway. Jessie's own heart, not hardened, not yet, was pounding so wantonly she thought she might lose control of the car and finish the job Alexis and Roger had started on their little family—deliver their children to them, scathed, scratched, scourged. Little racist fools. Monkey see, monkey say, monkey do. Provocateurs.

. . .

The finish on the road changed slightly when she crossed into Mississippi.

WELCOME TO MISSISSIPPI
THE HOSPITALITY STATE

The sign was framed by painted pillars, a magnolia in the center. No more magnolias, what they needed these days was hard-cash tourists. The children slept, far from any home.

How many years would it take, Jessie wondered, to feel Alabama in its intricacy? Know the counties, the fractions of the counties, which were hospitable, which were best to circle around the long way? That was the way she had known Mississippi for years, it had lain in her mind under an invisibly veined survival map, each line a rumor, a fact supported by a documented event or a body. Her mother had been in Alabama as a girl, a young woman, doing literacy work, that was the odd thing. Unlikely, she of all people (devoted now to the life of apolitics, credit cards, forgetting), and also unlikely the endless repetition, the foolish succession of the seasons of conscience: spring, summer, fall, winter, lovingkindness, isolationism, desperation, independence, help-thy-neighbor, throttle him until he breaks. She liked to think of herself as independent of her parents but she is here, isn't she, their daughter, doomed to be here or somewhere like it sure as the daughter of alcoholics drinks, or the suicide's child takes refuge in self-destruction. She had arrived in 'sixty-four among hundreds of people her age whose assumptions about the world she shared. More or less, as it happened, but certain of them had been unquestionable. But her mother at nineteen . . . she had arrived as a free lance, so to speak, part of nothing but the general post-Depression desperation to make a mark, cast a shadow in blank space.

Mother and her starlet's face. She had tried to evade it, had been a serious young woman who bit her lip and ruined her looks. She liked to wear soft fluffy sweaters that made her breasts perfectly round like something drawn with a compass. Well, Jessie did not know that for a fact but she had seen pictures: her father had shown her the pictures, often, proud of her beauty, a man who loved to love women. And he had described her, fulsomely, provocatively, as if she'd been a lovely possession that cast glory back, like a light, on its owner. (Her father, who despised ownership of property!) What, in fact, do I know about my own life, Jessie thought, and I was *there?* Her mother used to counter her husband's praise by telling her daughter what a blight her face and body had been. Envious, siding with her father, Jessie would never believe her.

In one picture, which Jessie kept on a shelf in the bedroom, her mother is standing entirely alone on a frozen dirt road near Eula, Alabama, wearing a short sailor's pea jacket and a man's gray scarf. Jessie has tried to imagine who would have taken such a picture—possibly the driver who dropped her off there to do her poor day's work? Probably she wanted to send it North to scare her parents. Her good winter coat, Jessie imagined, was at that moment hanging on a hook in the room her parents would keep for her, with hope and without bitterness, on Seventy-fourth Street off Madison Avenue, where she would not admit she lived, where she did not live for almost six months. That coat would have had a fur collar, that room a bed piled with carefully husbanded European comforters, stacked and indulgent, ready to soften her sleep so that she doesn't know which direction in the world she is facing when she wakes—a cloud. She woke on it, under it, nauseated when she was at home. It was her curse, she said, another piece of unappreciated good fortune like her pretty face, it was like being drugged and she thought it was intentional. She could not bear to be disoriented. (But Jessie, as a child, has slept under the comforters; her mother's mother saved them, and she as a girl slept under them guiltily, apologetically pretending to be rich.)

So she carried her well-kept face, *shana punim!* from that dark and ponderous apartment, joy of her German father, prayer of her German mother, and it took all her effort to make it ordinary. In the pictures it is scrubbed and her dark wavy hair is scraped back into a rubber band: an anachronistic look. This is 1935 when every girl wears some kind of lovelock loose around her face, flirty, frivolous; but she, Elizabeth Forbath, has achieved the look bobby-soxers will have ten years later, clean and innocent, or of her own daughter in yet another ten—except for the lilylike pallor no healthy woman knows how to, or cares to, achieve today. She is clutching a leather briefcase under the arm of the pea jacket and she is shivering because it is winter in Alabama and not what she was led to expect. Where are the trees that have made the South famous in her mind? Where are the flowers? The sky is the color of pork. That is a detail Jessie remembers— how the sky was the color of pork and her mother had never eaten pork but had seen it in the windows of butcher shops on Madison Avenue where her own mother never shopped. Now she was seeing it on dinner plates in Alabama; it was a measure of how far she had come from home. Why weren't you in college, Jessie used to ask. But college was remote, not automatic, then. Girls didn't necessarily go, nothing was certain but marriage for that generation. So many other middle-class German-Jewish girls had gone to Barnard, stood for mass portraits on the steps of the administration building in white blouses and dark skirts, hiding their dusty hands behind them. The time wasn't right, is all she ever said. I had to do what I did. (*That* was a familiar argument.) And then she had met Jack.

The car drifted down the highway toward town, past the new restaurants that burgeoned and duplicated themselves and sat smug in their trendy names, services to accompany all the new growth of Jackson in every direction. The way every new subdivision used to need a church and supermarket and a school, now it had The New Deli and The Steak Pit. Plays on words in The New Mind. They were all theoretically integrated, no one would come out with a flit-gun the way they did fifteen years ago and spray down the air around your table to make the room fit for decent habitation, nobody would set on you in the parking lot, but there were precious few black faces behind those clever heavy menus. Well, it was a question of comfort in the end, not the self-conscious defense of rights but the chance to freely choose pinto beans and greens and fried chicken over a Szechuan buffet or a bagel breakfast, among friends. No one could legislate style.

So, Jessie thought, they would begin something tonight, all of them together, though God knows what it would be: a family shaped like a camel, all unmatching parts, by unlikely collaboration. She worried about herself; she also worried about Teddy. Just at the point where his feelings ought to be fluid and tender, that was where, more finally than she, he came to a brick wall. His was not merely congenital obstinacy. He had marked himself as a man who would escape middle-age panic only because he'd already had his case, early, and therefore his immunity. He'd managed his young man's hysteria—the crisis, the climacteric of the useful self—at thirty. Any man, she had to suppose, who is returned to life and lives to wonder why will not be surprised again by weariness or stasis. An extreme sense of safety, the numbing of certain nerve ends, follows an extreme danger.

But now. Helen and O'Neill, those frail grafts, will have to take, and she and Teddy will have to water the soil and keep it fertile, and they will have to refuse to hate them for their need. They had been approaching, slowly and with contradictory feelings, but nonetheless inexorably and therefore with an acceptance of the rhythm of it, the end of family. Andy would cut himself loose in a few years—he was getting remote in a spotty way already, drawing in, thinking for himself, keeping busy with his friends, reveling in his awesome set of competencies. And then Lydia would be a teenager: she had the beginnings of breasts, nubs under her sweaters the breadth of raisins. She was rewarding to be with, and not as a child is rewarding, but as an interesting and unpredictable companion.

But Teddy . . . Sometimes he talked about rejoining his old life somehow, although he did not know how or where; not a single one of the current

not-for-profit commitments was dazzling enough. They were, he said, for
the long-haul folks, as if he were talking about truckers; it didn't bother
him not to be one of them. Maybe the Peace Corps—Tanzania, Namibia,
Brazil. (With all those twenty-two-year-olds? Jessie would ask, incredulous.)
Lost once more among dark faces, slick bodies, to live as a well-fed ghost
among the starving millions. Something wholly unfamiliar, anyway, whose
exotic particulars would overwhelm his cynicism. He would use it differently from the twenty-two-year-olds, he insisted. Something that, however
much he knew it underneath, would at least be so novel and demanding,
day to day, that he could immerse himself in the cold-water shock of its
challenge: dictionary, rite, geography, everything fresh but the stink of
politics, the subterranean unchanging part. Jessie, he assured her, would
come along. Even though she thought she was happy teaching, immersed
in the day-to-day that added up to a sufficient sum of meaning, he didn't
take her satisfaction very seriously. Their rhythms were similar, he told
her, although she seemed to have come to the end of Mississippi before he
did. Nonetheless, he assured her with unnerving confidence, you will come
with me; you will still be here and when I'm ready to go to some unpro-
nounceable village in some jungle, that will be the year you will have had
enough of buttoning children into their galoshes and wiping their fingers
smeared with ice cream and graham cracker.

Jessie slowed for her exit. Once in a while she had seen highway signs
that threatened drivers that their speed was being clocked by air. (She had
never actually noticed a low-flying radar plane but that was a different
story.) Taking the banked exit carefully, bearing these sleeping children,
who were in every way but the technical, strangers, she felt herself spied
upon from above, though not for anything as inconsequential as her driving
speed. God looked down on some strangers, no doubt—you get what you
think you deserve; Alexis and Roger must have felt themselves so observed—
though she had a feeling that radar planes with the power to issue summonses
probably frightened more people, on balance, than heavenly surveillance.
(That was her New York cynicism; down here God was still the ultimate
summons-server.)

Careful measure was being taken of something she couldn't see. Now
what? she challenged whatever looked down on the roof of her car. All bets
were off. Their profession, for a while, would be Parents. Parenting, that
offensive, illegitimate verb that made a state of being into a continuous and
improbable act, the kind you could study in school, get an advanced degree
in. Beginners, Intermediate, Advanced, Graduate Parenting. She had to

tighten her grip on the wheel to keep from turning the car back onto the highway again, straight on down toward the Gulf of Mexico.

.   .   .

O'Neill had been asleep as they approached the house, thus depriving Jessie of his first spontaneous response. Helen, as one might expect, offered nothing. Jessie had begun to prattle when they turned off the highway, commenting on what were distinctly not landmarks of the neighborhood. In the silence the turning signal, a green tic on the dashboard, made a sound like a discreet "tsk, tsk" of disapproval. She was still talking when they drove down Willowbrae, around two small black boys doing wheelies on their bashed-in bikes. One raised his arm in an ambiguous salute, somewhere between a wave and an assertion. Helen stared straight ahead, as if not seeing it might make it all go away.

She shook her brother. "We're here," she whispered, pummeling his small shoulder.

"Where?"

"*There.*"

O'Neill sat upright dramatically and glared out the window. "You're kidding me. Oh. No!" He held his hand on his chest and slumped over stricken. This was supposed to be funny. What is this moment like, Jessie wondered—not like arriving at summer camp, two months in a piece of the country (patrolled waterfront, canteen privileges) picked out of a brochure! Not like a new neighborhood to which your parents move you carefully swaddled like a valuable possession, having brought along the family's dental records and given every magazine subscription department six weeks' notice!

O'Neill peeled his fingers from his eyes, one by one, and looked at the house head-on, straight into the lattice whose sparse summer vines, all branch and empty stem, in this season appeared the victims of root-poisoning. Helen's hand, tightened on his forearm, exacted a petulant silence. Possibly they expected nothing any more, having been so unaccountably punished, body and soul, for nothing they had done. They did expect something though, and, seeing where she had brought them, there was no doubt they were disappointed. Jessie, who hated the house more than they ever could, tried not to feel hurt.

Lydia, official greeter, had made a welcome sign for the front door. Somewhere between her original impulse and its execution, inhibition had overtaken her. What was usually its own reward was her extravagant use of color (so that her birthday cards seemed to trumpet their promises of pleasure, her DON'T FORGET TO WAKE ME FOR MIDNIGHT! last New Year's Eve was a winter garden, her GET WELL QUICK to Andy for his three-day flu was nearly exhausting in its variations on the spectrum from ROY through BIV). But these gambits must have seemed too celebratory for this occasion. Then again, she seemed to have reasoned, black would be unseemly and would only depress them further. Jessie smiled to see her compromise: she and Teddy were not the only ones whose complexities and second thoughts made out-and-out feeling a struggle. Oh Lydia, she thought, dear Lyddie, trying so hard to get it *right*. There was a large gray bird, a sort of gull-cum-pigeon, with a neck full of subdued color like an oil slick, flying in, full steam ahead, from the right-hand margin. In his mouth he held a banner wafting out before him, on which the plainest most dignified letters announced WELCOME TO HELEN AND O'NEAL. (Perhaps he was used to misspellings.) She had written in shyly, for the sake of thoroughness, WE HOPE YOU WILL LIKE IT HERE across the bottom in a deep purple that probably stood in her mind for gravity, earnestness, the altogether antifrivolous.

·   ·   ·

Precisely as she would not have had it, that was how it happened that when Jessie's children returned, later in the afternoon, from soccer and puppets, the presence of the Alabama cousins already seemed to be everywhere in the house. Every bit of airspace had been absorbed. If they had not been supplanted—but they had better not dare indulge such an absurdity, Jessie thought—then they were, at least, mightily surprised and inconvenienced from the very front door against which leaned, inside, a guitar in a light blue case and a carton full of striped knee socks and pastel nightgowns.

Lydia came in looking eager nonetheless, but self-consciously, like someone who has had a talk with herself before she put her hand on the doorknob. Where was Helen? O'Neill, Jessie knew, had gone out into the backyard with Mickey Mouse, even though she had reminded him of his allergies. "Come!" she called out to Lydia, who stood just inside the front door like a guest uncertain of her welcome. "Come, honey, we're making a grand gala welcome dinner and I need your help."

Lydia looked at her silently. Then she said meekly, as if it were an unpopular opinion, "You're home."

"Oh my God. Of course we're home. Honey, hello!" Jessie gathered Lydia into her arms, so embarrassed that tears sprang to her eyes. She held her daughter locked extralong until the tears subsided. Lydia was impatient;

she shifted feet inside her mother's grasp like someone swallowing in the middle of a kiss.

"Let's see if we can find Helen," Jessie offered, chastened.

Stiffly Lydia said, "First I've got to put my puppets away."

The usual challenge was to drop them in the least convenient and most conspicuous spot, her two papier-mâché Indian dolls in their diaphanous saris. She was working up a play about two girls, one upper caste, one starving caste, both as beautiful as unicorns (no visible scabs on the poor one). Today she hugged the two of them against her chest, protective, and headed for her room to check it, Jessie assumed, for invaders. One tan face loomed back wide-eyed over her shoulder as she disappeared, its nail-polish caste-mark bright as a receding tail-light.

They found Helen, stalled approximately nowhere, in the tiny hallway between rooms. If she wasn't hiding, neither was she stepping forward. Probably, Jessie thought, she wanted to be discovered. Jessie had her hand on her daughter's shoulder; she felt Lydia stiffen as if they had encountered a total stranger standing alone in the dark. "Look, Helen, here's Lydia!" she said cheerfully, though the last thing Helen needed was an introduction to the girl who lived here.

A small dry-mouthed "Hi" came out of the shadows, less than a syllable.

Lydia's obligatory "Hi" was even more timid. Had her hand not been resting on her daughter's shoulder Jessie would never have heard the word; instead she felt Lydia's body rise a fraction to let it emerge, then close around silence again. She restrained the impulse—it took unnatural discipline to squeeze Lydia's bony shoulder blade and keep on squeezing until an enthusiastic greeting was extruded. What amazed her later, when she told Teddy how they had stared with unrestrained curiosity into each other's faces, was how, being children and closer to their true instincts than to propriety, neither of them felt the least obliged to smile. She was the one to smile, with false delight and with a desperate hope they were too innocent to need, until she felt ashamed and suggested that Lydia could help her cousin move her shirts onto the extra hangers she had found in Lydia's closet.

Back in the kitchen Jessie basted two chickens and stared at the pale goose-pimpled skin. For the first time she recognized, to her faint surprise, and to her surprise at that surprise, that six people was more than a welter of emotional complexities, it was a damn large family. These two small fatty chickens would not be enough; their plump clammy breasts and shiny drumsticks, purplish bone at the tips, would make a terrific appetizer. Then everyone would wait, casting their eyes about nervously, for dinner to begin in earnest.

Judging by the thickness of the atmosphere in the living room, where Andy stood with his shoulders back as if for inspection and his voice lowered as far as he could convincingly push it, where Helen and O'Neill simply stood like exhausted shoppers between their bags and boxes, the house would not be big enough either. She strained to hear their conversation but it was too sporadic to register at a distance. O'Neill seemed to be saying something about cars, real ones or Matchbox or dreamed-of. Andy was naming their cars, with years, to no audible applause.

She called out to Helen to come help set the table. The girl came to her in her bubble of containment and took the dishes out of her hands without a word. The hands that did so were delicate as a dowager's. Jessie showed her where to put them. Curious, she thought, that both the haughty mistress of the house and the proud servant might go about their business equally enveloped in such quiet, uncompelled to make conversation, certain of the impenetrability of the wall between them. Without caste-marks.

. . .

Dinner was formal; they might have been six people eating, each alone, at separate tables. These children must have had a long history of correction, a starching and ironing of mind and backbone; it was chastening. Jessie found herself wishing this small boy would, accidentally or otherwise, knock over his glass of apple juice. He was no longer a scion of the military.

The single moment of visible life occurred when O'Neill gestured toward the collage of photographs that hung just within eyeshot in the den. It was a mélange in glossy black and white and the pointillist gray of newsprint— friends, heroes and heroines, mementoes. There were babies now grown and the faces of certain of the illustrious dead. It was a wall that, in spite of the addition of the children's school pictures each year (inanely smiling or stubbornly scowling in alternate years), tended to change less and less with the passage of real time.

"Oh," Andy began, "those are a lot of our friends. My parents' old friends, people they knew—" He inclined his fair head toward his small rosy cousin with a look of Boy Scout helpfulness.

"You got a lot of nigger friends," that cousin told him amiably. "You got somebody up there that looks just like Lurene. You know Lurene?"

Teddy put down his fork, an old-fashioned movie tyrant about to explode into comic indignation. Jessie put her hand on his arm. She watched herself, and felt like the matching old mistress who could be relied on to be more permissive and pitying and to feed such small mischievous boys cookies out of the jar in the pantry when no one was looking. But, let Andy do it, is what she meant when she shook her head.

"Hey, you watch that," Andy did say.

O'Neill looked blankly at him, but with some curiosity. Truly, he did not know what to watch.

"We don't call people 'niggers' in this house," Andy told him with startling simplicity. For that moment both of them, Teddy and Jessie, thought the whole insane situation worth living through (as if worth entered in, as if their evaluation could conceivably matter), just to have had the incomparable opportunity to hear the ease and sweetness of their son's warning. He had not lorded it over O'Neill, hefting his greater power to assure the boy, or himself, of it; nor did he slap his hands from a height: he had stated fact—*we do not*—as if it had been *Watch out for the hot water, it comes out strong,* or *Be sure the cat doesn't get out.* Their faces burned with a painful pride.

Helen made her way through her chicken and rice slowly and method-ically, one of those eaters who turns over everything on her plate for in-spection the way she would a body, face down, that needed identifying. It made her look suspicious, even paranoid: ground glass was it, or hair or garden dirt? It seemed understood that O'Neill would be the one to venture forth, blunder and be driven back, while she was the steadfast protector who risked nothing on speech but would wait for him faithfully to return from his reconnaissance flights to the far end of their tolerance. Delicately, she forked her chicken skin inside out and slowly, frowning, raised it to her mouth.

After a decent interval, in which O'Neill did not defend himself, Lydia asked some questions. She was assembling an impression, or trying to, gamely, but she lacked nearly everything she needed. Without apology, sitting very straight, she got down grades and favorite subjects, for her invisible questionnaire; hobbies, the exact level of Helen's accomplishments *en pointe*, the number of extant comic books in O'Neill's collection, the names of his best friends and his worst. "You're thirteen?" she asked Helen baldly. "And you're—?"

O'Neill looked at her silently.

"Seven? Eight?"

"Eight. I was eight on August the seventeenth," he told her solemnly. "My half-birthday's February seventeenth." He had granted her the official power to question him thus.

Helen watched, faintly amused, distinctly a member of the adult camp, even if she would not approach it. The few firm unadorned words about her dancing were all she volunteered. When Lydia pressed her for the names of her friends—this was important, she seemed to say by her insistence, it would confer some form of sharable reality on her cousin to know that she had walked to school, whichever school it was, with Bobbie Lee and Patty and sat at lunch with Claudia, hating Jeannine—Helen only shook her head.

"Just tell me their names, you don't have to say anything else about them!" Lydia was so good herself at providing random details that she could contentedly fill in their contours as if they were a set of paper dolls to be colored in.

"What are their names to you!" Helen finally cried out, shaking her head as if to throw off it something that had gotten caught in her hair. "What're they to me, I'm never even seeing them again anyway!" She looked at all of them, then, accusingly; leaned her forehead on the palm of her hand so that it looked like one of the weighty pink-white peonies that Jessie futilely tried each spring to prop on a forked stick. Thank God, Jessie thought, and watched the girl's defenses fall around her like the petals of the peonies, pale but tinged with the vividness of blood at the edges. Silence and perfect composure were too dear, too potent, too enticing to be used by a child who hadn't even begun to grieve yet.

We are there. I tried to write in the car but it only made me dizzy. Then O'Neill almost upchucked and I thought I better not chance it and get sick myself. (He is still little enough so she might forgive him if he did, but I would be in Disgrace.)

I don't think we can do this. It is too horrible here for me to even say. They live on a nigger block and in a little, it feels like about the size of a trailer. Seedy would be Mom's word. Not a thing I would call really nice in it anywhere. How do people live like this? I cannot believe my mother would do this to us, maybe she was never over here and saw how they live. A lot of books and the rest old and dreary and piles of things on cabinets. Papers and open books turned over to keep the place. Some wooden statues, I think from Africa (Andy says). No matching furniture. In the bedroom they just pull the covers up (if that). No bedspreads anywhere in the house.

For another thing no one goes to church, not even Sunday school. Instead of God they seem to worship: Colored People, any and all. There is something sick about this, not that I can't stand being around them, I am about ready to have some in my class, that's all right, as my mother *said they can be there and don't have to be my good friends. But with these people it is something crazy, with pictures up the way I have Jesus Christ. I wonder if they would be Negro if they could. Even their children are nuts on the idea. They made a scene when O'Neill said Nigger and I wanted to scream "Who says you're so great and know what's right" but I didn't. This is not my house to object, I have some manners that say keep your mouth shut far from home.*

Lydia I haven't seen since she was really little. She is okay, I guess, only she has this kind of nosy stare, like: what are you doing? Her eyes pop a little but with very pretty long lashes like petals on a flower. I hope we don't get thrown together a lot just because she is a girl.

My cousin Andy seems conceited. He is tall like his father only quite blond from somewhere (?) and really cute. But he looks like he thinks he's something, the way he flew at O'Neill. (It's too early to tell.) My poor baby brother. I talked to him later to tell him it's okay, what do we care what they think, but he already forgot it. He is different from me, Mom used to say he is the rooster and I am the brooder, and it's probably true. He has no grudge pocket and I'm all bulging with things I carry around with me from one day to the next whether I want to or not.

They keep asking a lot of questions, but just in the middle of getting ready to answer every time this huge tiredness that feels like a rock just rolls over me and makes it hard to answer. My chest and shoulders get very heavy. I feel I am going to fall asleep. It isn't anything to do with boredom, maybe it's more because I will never ever get these people to know who I am. Helen Marie Tyson. ME. I don't know what it is. It just overwhelms me. I wish I could just check off on a long list what I like and don't like and they would gladly leave me alone. But that wouldn't be ME either. (Does it matter that I didn't know who ME was before? Probably!) I don't know what I mean exactly. Only I wish they would send me off somewhere alone, it will take such an effort to realize what a thing has happened. I keep promising to think about it. I just don't have the spare energy to get to know everybody and have them know me. Who wants to know them anyway. We have got nothing for each other. I only want to go to bed and sleep.

When I say my prayers (I will in a minute when the light goes out— O'Neill and I are in their t.v. room and I feel like we're (1) in the middle of everything and (2) keeping them from watching t.v. even though they say they don't watch any programs after their kids are in bed) I will truly pray the Lord my soul to take. I don't want to live in this horrid place!

I don't want to think about why I am here. And if they had to die, I should too because of what I had to do with it. I will close my eyes and hope it is still true the way it was in old stories that people can just will themselves never to wake up. I am certainly tired enough to sleep 1½ eternities.

"I believe I have figured out what 'jaded' means," Jessie told Andréa, sitting down at her friend's kitchen table. "It means that it's getting harder and harder to surprise me, even with a one-two punch."

Andréa snorted through her nose. "You mean to sit there and say you're not surprised by the size of your immediate family these days?" She poured coffee, her firm round arm familiar as Jessie's own beneath its rolled-up sleeve. Andréa wore men's white shirts, shirts that looked masculine, as uniforms to ward off attacks on her efficiency.

"Sure, I'm surprised by it. But I'm bored by it too."

"Bored! Now don't that beat all. What do you mean you're bored by it?" Andréa as mother. It was a role she relished; she could be down-home and lawyerly at the same time.

"I mean I'm—not engaged, somehow, emotionally."

Andréa shook her cropped head. At its blurred edges, light came through her hair. "Ain't that some luxury now. How many people you think are engaged by their little passage through this world. Do I have to say it? What if you were starving? *Jessie*. What if you were my Aunt Shy, lived in that cabin out of Belzoni with one leg and a busted water pump, two goats and commodity beans all those years. And a thousand other ones worse off than that, think Aunt Shy's got it pretty good. What you talkin about, girl? You do disappoint me sometimes." Her voice rasped. "You'd better get out in the field again."

Jessie looked into her long lap. Andréa's Aunt Shy was famous among them; for all anybody knew she didn't exist. No one would be able to understand it, then, if Andréa couldn't, how the disengagement made itself known in proportion to what she felt called upon to feel. To all the exclamations—"Oh dear, the poor darlings!" "I am so terribly sorry, Jessie, really—the loss must be unspeakable, oh, *both* of them. My dear." Like a motor or a mule, her feelings seized up. The little boy in his blazing white jockey shorts, the slanted wings of his shoulder blades working as he washed his hands with admirable, unlikely thoroughness. Helen's profile that made her think of a fine crystal bell, something transparent in its curve, hard and soft at one time.

"Oh the round of school beginnings. Changing dentists. Finding Helen ballet lessons. O'Neill's allergies. Making room for all their junk. You haven't been through all this a couple of times and *done*." She dwindled off. "What do you want from me, Andréa, moral perfection? I feel like a camp counsellor."

Andréa regarded her coolly. "You're making yourself do this."

"No. But I'm letting myself." She clapped her hands together as if it were cold in the room, left fist into right palm again and again. "God, I feel like we're on a stage, what is this?" She looked around her as if there might be a cast of characters hidden in its cupboards. Or as if there were an audience somewhere silently listening to this exposition.

"You're letting yourself—is it because they're little bigots like you say? And you want to punish them?"

"Oh, Andréa, I don't know. You'd love it, though, I know, hearing them talk about nigger this and nigger that." It continued to seem strange, though she would not think of it except at a distance, that she was less forgiving of their intolerable habits than Andréa.

"Well, just how many niggers you think they know? The kitchen maid? The gardener? The local bag-lady? You're going to have to bend their pale little ears back with some of the sweet truth, lamby. They'll have to learn the lay of the land if they're going to live on it."

"Yeah? Come to dinner tomorrow night, okay? You and Tommy. Come give them Mama Andréa's introductory geography lesson. Let's see if they turn over their soup bowls in your lap. Maybe Helen will refuse to serve you." She laughed.

Andréa put her coffee mug down slowly and laid her hand lightly on her friend's wrist. "Jess, you look to me like you're in the middle, right about in the eye, of one hell of a deep depression, not what you're calling this deep ennui. Am I seeing right? Otherwise you'd know you're a hell of a lot bigger than they are."

Jessie lowered her lids on cold tears. "Oh, a pep talk is just what I need. I don't *care* how it works out, that's the thing. Is that depression? I don't want to convert them, or rescue them, or even make them happy. I just want it to be over."

"What's *it*, baby. Tell me when you'll know it's over."

Jessie shook her head, stricken wordless to be taken at her word. She was losing maturity and steadiness the more she needed them. She sighed hugely, hopelessly, and told the truth. "It'll be over when it hasn't happened yet."

"Oh." Andréa was disappointed. She took her concerned hand back.

"You expecting another phone call. Think that lawyer's gonna call you up from Birmingham, tell you it's okay, you can come out now."

Maybe, thought Jessie, pulling herself in tightly as if she could shrink her rib cage and all the competent organs within it so that she could pass for a rather large child, maybe I can run away.

.   .   .

But that ended it. She was not going to let anyone else get the better of her, morally. If morality was what was at stake. Whatever was. Teddy could be as squeamish as he wanted to be, as absolute and untouchable, but she would chasten her impatience. She walked down the block from Andréa's house, headed around the corner. A nest of little boys called to her out of a tree and she strained to hear what they were shouting but missed it, and just as well. The houses seemed to be shrivelling for the season as cold took the softness of leaves and flowers and left the meagerness of the architecture to show like poor slight loosely strung bones, chicken or child.

Maybe, she lectured herself, maybe we are all tested in our lives (she did believe that—even without God, she believed it) and, like one of those nasty fairytale tricks, we don't know which event is the true test. Why assume that lying on jail-cell cement was the hardest thing you would ever be asked to do? Terror was accessible. It was short lived and specific and shared, shared all around. A communion. There was no shame in being afraid to die or be maimed. It was possible, after all this time, to see clearly, for example, and not in caricature, the peculiar blue eyes of Sheriff Dickie Wing of Indianola: they were periwinkle, violet, the color of a late afternoon summer sky darkening toward its daily storm. The color of Elizabeth Taylor's eyes, framed all around by intricate folds as if by rumpled bedsheets. And she had stared into them fascinated, acknowledging their disembodied beauty even as he reached for the hand that held her tin dinner dish and plunged her arm, to the quivering elbow, into boiling water. "Now you wash it real good, just like at home," he'd whispered. "Better." His eyes had widened to mock her as her own widened. But then it was over and her arm tingled and flashed, pain and numbness, as if the water had been ice. And everyone in the cell had to do the same. There was a low moan, humiliation, anger, disgust, not pain. Still, still . . . Surviving together, they were shriven. They were exhilarated. That pain only became part of the history of their endurance; and it became one more thing to laugh about later, in self-congratulation. Who but someone who was never there would call that difficult?

But this now: would they eat a vegetable dinner? *That* was difficult. Beets, baked potatoes, okra and tomatoes? O'Neill and his steak. She did not *want* to accommodate him. Let him accommodate her.

Here it is, here comes our humbling, she thought, and turned in at the driveway toward their house, that brown freight-car stalled in its barren yard. She would endure it for her pride's sake only, would practice buoyancy as a discipline. (And would she wind up sounding like Alexis, giggling on through no matter what? Like a halfback, strong-arm circumstance as she swerved around it in an end-run and kept moving?) If pride made these orphans tolerable, so much the better. If it didn't, they would all have a smaller portion of sweetness and so be it.

Had a dream so horrible I can't write it. Woke myself up so I wouldn't have to finish it and layed awake until morning all damp, thinking I was getting my period and soaking their couch straight through but I wasn't. Covers too heavy, Jessie heaped them on so I couldn't move. I don't think they had a lot of blood, Judy said my mother died without a single trace on her (then why couldn't I look in the coffin?) But my dream was about fountains and fountains of it, Daddy's throat especially, like a stuck animal, and they floated away on it. I thought they would go out to sea on a red wave. And the other cars on the highway honking and turning like in a whirlpool. It was raining. "Borne away on the tide of the Lord / And never looked back, looked gladly forward!" If they knew the end had come, did they embrace Him gladly? I wish I knew that. I don't think they would have had time to be anything but scared. Every Sunday morning we would sit in church singing how we are prepared. But were they? That way? So sudden? No one can ever know.

Everyone here had to go back to school today and work and O'Neill and I get one more day at home to do Nothing. I looked around while Brother Bear watched soap operas. I asked him what he thinks about this place and he just said it's ok but my teacher said little kids don't have any sense of time, like what is forever or even past tomorrow, so I am asking the wrong person. Wait till he figures it out!

On Teddy's desk, which is the sloppiest one I ever saw (really foul) there is a folder marked T.C. PUBLIC INFORMATION ACT *and inside has a list of (I think) government spying that shows the kind of illegal things my uncle has done. Secret meetings and phone calls where they were probably planning riots and everything. He has put explanation marks* next to a lot and red question marks are bleeding all over. And he has a lot of doodles, mustaches and faces (men and women) and a hand grenade (if I know what one looks like. Or else it is an armadillo). This folder is just lying there in the middle of everything marked up so it looks like a joke but it's on official stationery.

So basically Daddy was right about such people as trouble makers. I'll bet he (Ted) is secretly glad Daddy is dead because there is one less Enemy around now. I feel I am stolen into the real enemy camp now and I wish I could sabotage or some other way ruin Teddy's best layed plans. He has pictures of Martin Luther Coon and the Kennedy Bros. Corp. (like Daddy used to say) on his wall in frames like saints. The whole corner where his desk is (in our room where we are sleeping) makes me nauseous.

Then I went into Jessie's closet. I was hoping there were no spiders in there, lots of corners around here could use a Lurene to keep them squared off. They are all webbed with dust and filth. This poor woman doesn't wear anything except blue jeans and sloppy shirts that would fit a scarecrow better. And crazy colored tights like lollypops. I can't help it, that makes me think about my mother. I don't think in a way that gives me a picture but I keep thinking of whole kinds of Beauty, for instance, that are all gone now. Whole places she made in my Life, that are sort of hollow now, and everything spotless to boot. An example of what I mean:

Her clothes. Everything she had practically was soft, she believed in making every possible thing feel good, different kinds of material, silk and quiana (I want to name a baby Quiana). Melting and creamy. And everything with that sweet spice of popoorie in a silver dish or a small cheesecloth bag that she once said was like a kiss she layed on each pile of things, that would be closed in a drawer. She made all this her work of Art. Jessie spites all that with her drawers all ashambles, and her shoes (sneakers, etc.) tumbled in the bottom of the closet like it was the charity bin in the church vestry.

My mother knew all about makeup too and would do Makeovers of her friends who were always so grateful. It was a talent God gave her. She made Judy's nose look narrower and sort of turn up at the tip and a few women got rid of some of their double chins and eyes too close together, all with the tricks of the trade. These are the things women owe it to themselves to know and everyone who has to look at them. Nothing obvious in her makeup, you could hardly tell she was wearing blusher or eye shadow (for occasions only). Jessie I see just throws water on her *face in the morning and rushes her fingers through her hair and all you notice coming towards you is these two turquoise legs (or whatever stupid color) and maybe big sloppy silver earrings. The Natural Look. I'll bet deep down even Teddy would like a woman who payed some attention to herself.*

Teddy seems to travel a lot, even more than Daddy ever did. (He is some kind of a salesman.) I wonder if he has a lot of different wives, "one in every port." Maybe those are women who smell of Topaze and Arpège in the cracks of their arms. And have something besides jeans and jeans skirts in their closet. A laugh on her Natural (ugh) Look.

I wanted to write to Julie Ann and Bonnie etc. but when I think about Birmingham it hurts. I can't say what I mean by "hurts" except I want to squint my eyes and look away in another direction. Later I will think about it but now I just feel sick and excited, nervous like something is going to happen, even though the worst has already befallen. But it keeps feeling like nothing happened yet. It is coming at me. My stomach feels all shaken up. So I am putting it all out of my mind.

No home there
No home here
No home anywhere
But Jesus

THREE

Shock is exhausting. The children needed a rest. Was there, could there try to be, such a thing as a slow transition from life to life? From the intimate logic of one place, one intricate set of comforts—faces, voices, hands, the grasp of a customary bed and chair, the way the faucets turned, the precise angle of sky always visible from the bedroom window, the worn route to school, so on, so forth—to a new logic?

A slow transition? But didn't they need to be rejoined, instantly, to their ongoing present, without having to feel themselves out of time? Still, somehow, vitally attached to daily movement and accomplishment?

Meanwhile, someone ought to show them Jackson. But they weren't tourists. Someone ought to help them settle in. But there was no space to settle; their belongings stayed ignobly in cardboard boxes—Seagram's, Dewar's—piled against the baseboards. The hall looked like the annex to a liquor store. Someone, then, ought to take them away to Disneyland, to Acapulco! For punctuation, to open a more natural space between past and future than the brutal crack that ran the length of their lives right now. Passivity, if not exactly celebration. A time for letting their defenses down.

How? How? How?

They were not doing this right, and they would all regret it. But whose life is so elastic it can be stretched, doubled over, pulled open, held there, closed again, and *now?* "This is one of those times," Teddy objected. "Latr we're going to wonder why we couldn't have managed it." But he had to work and so did Jessie: they were quite ordinary when it came to that. The ideal—say they could agree on one—was a luxury reserved for coupon clippers. And such a luxury, convenient as it might be, they did not really want.

.   .   .

Jessie stalled at breakfast. She wanted them to be good and late for school. The task of registering Helen at her new junior high had fallen to her, as if she had no job to go to. Teddy had taken off at dawn for a workshop presentation of his new "old math" books in southern Tennessee; he could not wait around to take Helen in. "Another English muffin?" She reached the open box toward Helen who ate her muffin and jam as warily as she'd approached her dinner. Lydia and O'Neill would simply have to stay home and wait for her.

Even late, after the crowds of kids who, passing each other, had bucked and hallooed and clinked shoulders like wine glasses in an endless toast to friendship, they were self-conscious. Helen's eyes were wide with apprehension. She had the look of Dorothy, after that severe blow to her head, just arrived untrusting in Oz.

An extremely tall black boy was walking very slowly across the main lobby placing one foot before the next as though he'd been sent to measure it off by paces. He towered over Jessie, who towered over Helen. Jessie asked him where the office was although she knew—a little casual speech could sometimes soften the wary. The boy looked Helen over brazenly before he answered. Then he tilted his head to the side in an odd position, condescending because it was so coquettish.

Jessie had thought she should go alone to register Helen so that she could talk openly about her to the administrators and to her potential teacher. But Teddy, as always, had been adamant: there was nothing she was going to tell anyone about her that Helen could not hear. She even had a right to speak for herself. How else would she learn to trust them?

Now she came forward into the office at Jessie's side, with the expression—a tense poise, a transcendent tolerance for whatever would overtake her—that Anne Boleyn and Lady Jane Grey might have worn to the executioner's block. She looked as though, given a chance to say a few words, she might make a dignified speech of farewell to her beloved earth. Jessie wanted to squeeze her arm, in its blue-striped oxford blouse, and commend her for her bravery. But that admission would, she knew, be undermining for both of them.

A young black woman in a plaid jumper smiled at them, offering up for their admiration a set of fine gold inlays. She took down the information about Helen's previous schooling without a lost beat for curiosity. Her school had not, like some, been called a Council school, proudly acknowledging its patrimony; it was only the Sunnifield Academy, which sounded good, small, expensive, and only incidentally—only if you wanted to think about the probable implications of those qualities (which the young woman clearly did not)—in business for the sole purpose of keeping white children separate from black. As it happened, Barber, the junior high school to which she and Teddy were consigning Helen, would also cease to be integrated fairly soon if it lost any more white faces to private school and to other neighborhoods. So Helen would be welcome as another white survivor. It was preposterous that she was helping to hold the line, but there it was, an immutable demographic fact.

Teddy knew the principal here, though Jessie had only met him once or twice, at anti-war demonstrations; she wondered if she might just have a word with him. The young man, Curtis Hover ("rhymes with Rover, folks, sorry, not with Lover"), had been moderately active in his student days at Jackson State—nothing to rumple his clean shirts excessively, but still he had worked hard and been on the right side (or at least on Teddy's side) of a number of issues. That made him radical by public school standards. It was surprising that he had gotten this job, and that he had kept it.

Jessie and Helen studied a bulletin board, office notices on salmon, canary and robin's egg paper, while they waited for him. Jessie considered sending her off to the lobby to look at the student art exhibit while she confided in Curtis just what kind of swan they had here, and why. But that was too easy. Would this, though, be too difficult for Helen? She read a mimeographed challenge to the office staff from the board of education to reduce waste, conserve postage, cut down on their use of ditto masters, and pondered: would it give her a little kick in her complacency to meet this presentable young black man, shake his hand, see how he takes charge? Had she ever had occasion to touch hands with such a man? Jessie had repeated to Teddy what Andréa had said: who has she been encouraged to see but servants, derelicts, posters of sullen young men wanted for armed robbery?

Curtis Hover came striding out of his little office smiling and gravely shook Jessie's hand. She had to introduce herself by way of Teddy, whose name brought forth from him a friendly exclamation. This was an old boys' network of a brand-new kind. They went into the office, took seats on old wooden slat-backed chairs, exchanged a little gossip. Curtis asked Jessie to tell Teddy that there was going to be a commemoration of an old shooting, Wednesday night, in South Jackson. "Remember Atecia Burrow?" Jessie remembered; she said they would try to be there. Their conversation floated on a succession of names like something borne up comfortably by water. She could see that he viewed her as an emissary of her husband but there was nothing she could say to that.

Finally Curtis sat back and asked what had brought them in today. He was an admirably relaxed young man, clean featured and alert, mustached, the color of strong coffee laced with heavy cream.

Jessie carefully, soberly, told him the circumstances of her niece's arrival while Helen sat without expression as though the conversation had not gotten around to her yet. Curtis promised to select a teacher who could help her make the best adjustment to Barber; named some of the extra-curricular activities the school could offer—the trophies were beginning to pile up in the case out front; invited her to come in to see him if she was having any problems whatsoever, although he looked faintly amused as he suggested it: did one report to an enemy general about the behavior—the existence—of his minions? Then he asked her, in the padded voice of an earnest therapist, if she could foresee what her problems might be. It was an inappropriate question but Jessie had the feeling that Curtis was trying to prompt the girl to speech, any speech, even the catharsis of anger or .refusal. He seemed to be telling her that she would not shock him with unruly feelings, that she could trust him to take it, understand it, even forgive it, whatever it might be.

She was, however, a child and perhaps such unsolicited kindness put too intolerable a burden on her. Her eyes brimmed uncontrollably. She shook her head and her mouth stretched tight in what looked like it could be, but was not, a smile. At last, not to affront him but to save her last remnant of control, she turned her head sharply over her right shoulder, showing him only the flawless pale skin of her soft cheek.

"Well, probably I shouldn't even have asked you to think about that. My mistake. We aren't going to dwell on the negative here, okay? We're just going to try to make you feel right at home. I can take you on up myself to the class I think you'd like best. . . ." He was rising, smiling. She wiped her eyes with her fingertips.

Which meant, since things are relative, even pain that feels absolute and irreducible, that Helen flung out to her Aunt Jessie a long look that was like the disappearing hand of her drowning self. Could she not, would she not, somehow, in spite of all, save her? Curtis Hover had put his bleached pink palm, the color of the bottom of a conch shell, on Helen's thin sleeve. Helen stared at it.

"You'll be *fine*, Helen," Jessie said to her and held her cold hand in both of her own. She took advantage of the moment and lifted it to her lips, kissed it as if she were sealing a bond between them, precisely because she knew Helen felt herself betrayed. The girl went like a prisoner of war, stumbling a little, pretending she'd been roughly pushed. A prisoner taken in trade for nothing, her bitter eyes insisted. Curtis Hover led her away, and since the bell had just ripped through the office with an almost human shriek, it was into a bobbing tide of bright colors and many more dark faces than light, which closed behind her as if she had truly drowned.

.   .   .

That was the easy part.

The hard part was to admit, walking slowly back to the house, that Andy had despised this school. With all his background of ease among all kinds of people, and his forbearance, decency and goodwill, Andy had graduated gladly to the high school last June, where there promised to be some breathing room. It was pot and cocaine in the locker room, it was his own abused frailty on the ball court, and the fact that he was not precocious with girls, with beer, with anything except, perhaps, certain undiscussables close to his heart—it was all those things that strained and worried him and made him wary. He had friends, of course, both colors of friends, but there were periods when he woke for school with dark patches under his eyes and pleaded to be left in bed.

It was a nasty position to be in, the defender who needed defense himself. When he got tired of fighting, he quit the clubs that stayed all white on technicalities, or did not try out for the ones that were only black. Last year he had quit Scouts too because meetings had begun to feel like an endless day in court: defenses, hair-splitting interpretations of the order to open the door to Scouts of all colors. He did not enjoy being the prosecutor. But staying out of trouble didn't make him comfortable in the locker room, his thin white lengthening chest so fragile amidst those of the bigger boys, who had trust in their strength. He was forced to give over his money only a few times, occasionally his lunch, and the lock from his locker once, nothing worse.

It was only, he told his parents, that the black boys made him feel like a little pansy; when he did well in his classes they tried to make that a confirmation of his weakness. He wasn't sure they were as bad as they liked to sound, but they still could humiliate him with a single glance, and exclude him, harshly, from their majority. His best black friend, Raney (Dungeons and Dragons champion, math whiz, newspaper editor), was mocked too, and more so, for spending so much time with white boys. Worst of all, though, Jessie reflected, there was a hesitancy in Andy's manner when he confided these incidents and how he quailed before them. Did he feel he was failing them when he showed his wounds? Were they disappointed? Or worse, in the way of children, whose attribution of power to adults is so confused, so helpless and absolute, wasn't there a hint in his guilt and distress that somehow—not literally, but in spirit, in that ideal place where there is not an inch of distance between *hoping* and *making happen*—that this whole damn integration business that afflicted his days was *their* idea?

Dear God, how have I sinned to deserve this punishment? I don't understand, and who is supposed to explain it to me?

Every single face there (school) is black except maybe 1% or so. I never knew there were so many different shades of colored until I was having to walk side by side in the halls. (And the whole school is so big I will never learn where everything is. It is a big yellow brick building, very official looking like a state capitol or something, and stands on a hill all by itself. But what a waste inside.) One set of bathrooms on each floor, a cafeteria that almost made me sick, this sour Chinese food and orange soda pop sticky on the tables. The girls' room smelled of sweat and "bathroom" with cigarette smoke everywhere and maybe worse. You could hardly even see. Wet toilet paper and towels mashed into balls on the floor, one of the faucets stuck and the sink overflowing. Noisy girls splashing in it. They made me think of little kids at the wading pond. Just pigs at a trough. Someone flicked water at me and I raised my hand and almost hit her. Then she stared in my face and I don't know who looked most scared so I just ran out. I wouldn't want to get jumped on by a pack of them, there is a certain meanness in them, and when they laugh or joke it is like a treefull of hyenas.

My main teacher is white, it is a man named Mr. Prouty, young, in khaki pants a teacher at Sunnifield would never dream of wearing. He is sort of nice looking but has a wall eye and it is hard to tell who he is calling on. (He is Math and Social Studies and a colored woman, Miss Conrad, is English.) Mr. Prouty made me want to die in a corner, he made me stand up in front and say my name and answer all these dumb questions so my "classmates" could get to know me, like do I have any nicknames and what do I like to do after school and do I have pets. I could tell, they could care less that this white girl has a paperweight collection and guitar and takes ballet. Then he kept saying he couldn't hear my answers and I finally just stood there. Those times I just go blind and deaf and my whole body is like a piece of solid waiting. I didn't know where I was or if the building was burning I don't think I could have moved. When he gave up on me he came and tapped me on the shoulder and I sat down. Probably he did it to be nice but I can see since my Mother and Daddy are gone, the more people try to be nice the worse they make everything.

There were so many brown faces all around the room seemed actually truly dark. I am not imagining it. They are still on reviewing decimals and fractions! At home I was half way through Algebra I.

Miss Conrad just ignored me. That was perfectly fine as far as I was concerned. There is one other white girl in that class, a fat tub of lard named it sounded like Abneice or something. With that kind of name maybe she is one of them only very light. (?) And I thought, Oh no, if I have to be her friend. She was wearing a quilted dress with a bib like an overalls dress, and looked twice as fat as she probably is. I am sure her and the other Whites who go here just can't afford the private Academy. I don't know the social studies they're doing, is another problem. This is the War of Versailles or something, these treaties and all. Help!

When we had to pass classes, I didn't know where to go and this big Negro boy (must be a basketball player) came and asked what my program card said, he would help me. His name was Don. His friends were all giggling away and pointing at him but he showed me Room 202 which is like an auditorium where they were having a speech about Career Opportunities for the future, and high schools for special talents and all. I wanted to say My career opportunity right now is I want to be dead. How do I go about "achieving" my goal, can you help me? I found a seat on one side almost by myself and just sat and didn't listen. The audience made more noise than you would believe throughout and no one even told them to stop or else. There doesn't seem to be a lot of discipline and the teachers look right through the mess to the other side. Mr. Prouty's eye went round like a lighthouse beam but he didn't say a word.

I sat and made some decisions: I am going to go here for about a week. Then if it isn't any better (it won't be) I am just not coming any more. Once in a while I'll come in to be safe so they don't get suspicious. What do I have to lose? Jessie I call my Betrayer because she knew what I thought when she brought me here to school and wouldn't listen. So if she finds out, good. Then maybe she'll pay attention to my wishes. I get

the feeling she and Teddy are busy guessing our "needs." Well, mine is
to go somewhere like my school at home. (She probably sees that as my
"wants," not my "needs," so too bad.)

Jessie, pulling on violet tights the next morning, thought hard about
O'Neill and decided he was like a wheel—if she could get him rolling, his
momentum would carry him forward. This year she was teaching third
grade and he was going to be in her class, her care. She was filled with hope.

Therefore she took his hand, going into the school while the morning
was still damp. Lydia ran on ahead, out of their sight. Outside, the building
looked like the *ur* school: it was blocky and red brick and its long windows
were the kind one would expect to see decorated with matching construction
paper turkeys a little nearer to Thanksgiving. Inside, as it happened, no
two children dared execute precisely the same turkey: at the alternative
school that was called cheating, not art.

They were early. Jessie pushed open the heavy door, which Lydia had
let swing shut behind her to show her independence. She brought O'Neill
right up the stairs where, at the broad landing the purple and yellow and
magenta mural the children had made hung colossal, seething against its
black background. She had always thought of it, hoping it was no sacrilege,
as an inside-out *Guernica*—not a cry but a happy shout—of utopian life, a
lively dream of the joyous peaceful village, the angular figures celebrants
all, kneelers and leapers and bareback riders of every shape and race, pea
green, orange, throbbing violet a little bit like her tights. The mural put
skin color in perspective.

"What's *that*?" O'Neill asked, stopping short as they got to the landing.

"Well, what do you think?"

He rolled his eyes once, like someone being drunk, and stared, smiling.
"Some bad draw-ers?"

"Look. Where's the sun?"

He searched, bending and thrusting his head toward it, exaggerating his
movements as if study were an activity that used every muscle. "It's all
over—there's four-five-*six* suns! They've got six whole suns. Is that supposed
to be six days on there? Or they would be pushing each other right out of
the sky." He did a bump to one side, a bump to the other. This was one
clever child.

"Might be. See, and there's color all over everybody. Does that look
like a happy place to be?"

O'Neill licked his lips as if they were an ice-cream cone.

They continued up to her room. She would register him later, on her own time. She planned to get him set up before the others came, and to give him permission to work by himself all day if he wanted to. He looked like a child who could concentrate; he had his own ideas. She wanted him to stockpile some of that good feeling about the place before its peculiarities struck him. Six suns' worth.

By the time the twelve other third graders arrived, O'Neill had begun to build himself into the corner, turret on turret, blond hardwood post, beam and porch. By recess, he had pulled from her basket of miscellany an endless blue scarf that he laid out carefully around the base of his castle for a moat, and had not built a drawbridge over it. When everybody took out their snacks and gathered around him to get a good look, his castle drew all their attention, like a fine suit of clothes on a grownup, or a gorgeous tie. He took one end of his rumpled blue rayon water and flicked it like a leash to make it flow. He was sitting with the castle in front of him by then, between his legs, his giant belly; he was safely on the other side of it. He gathered up and kept all their compliments, did not reject even the awe of Tyler who whistled through his missing teeth, or Rhonda, or any of the black children. He only smiled, a victim of his vanity, and lowered his head to a dozen petty refinements that remained to be made by three o'clock.

I am becoming a whole new person. I can feel a hard shell growing and it will protect me, and O'Neill too if he needs it. (He says school is ok, he doesn't like the Negroes in his class but there's more white kids and then he makes a muscle as big as a grape and shows me.) I asked him if it felt like a nightmare, and he said they get chocolate grahams with their milk for snack and they have less workbooks. It turns out Jessie is his teacher, you can't get away from her. But he doesn't know what to mind and what not to mind. Little kids, even smart ones, are surprisingly stupid.

I am going to sleep now. Mostly I sleep. There is nothing else I feel like doing. Lydia offered me her bike—mine will be coming soon, whenever our furniture arrives—but I don't want to see this city. She says there is a lake nearby although it isn't beautiful, she even admitted that. It is behind a chain link fence and is industrial on the other side, which you can unfortunately see. It gets dark early, though, and that's fine with

*me, so I have an excuse not to do anything. I do not feel real. That's
all I feel. Floating. There is a book on the shelf above Teddy's desk on
the ruins of the Mayans and I am this girl I found in old Palenque, it's
called, bathing in this mist that never stops except for a while at High
Noon. I meet my love behind the ball court and we go in the high grass
and lie down. I am strong and keep him at arms' length but he loves
me and I have to make promises. (What did the Mayas wear? I have
no idea!) Every time he touches me the rain begins. It sifts down fine in
our eyes. (It rains every day in the Yucatan like here in summer.) With
this dream I fall asleep in his arms every afternoon before dinner. Then
when Jessie comes home I set the table (that seems to be my regular job)
and she just yaks away. I don't feel like I have to answer her. Not to be
difficult, only because there is nothing I want to say.*

A box arrived at the door one afternoon. "The 'Ups' truck!" O'Neill
shouted and ran to sign the clipboard next to the proper X. "It's from it
says, um, Singer," he called out to Jessie, the box blocking his face. "What
Singer? Is it a real singer?"

"Oh it's your—" Jessie removed it from his hands. "It's Andy and Lydia's
grandparents, their other grandparents."

"Shake it!" He contemplated the brown carton the way a starving child
might eye a side of braising beef. Jessie didn't want to disillusion him but
if her mother's package was typical it would contain a set of towels (bought
at an irresistible sale), a fine shirt or a beautiful slipover for Teddy (a futile
inducement to reform his appearance), and for the children an item of
clothing or perhaps a book or two not necessarily calibrated to their current
ages and interests (although Jessie was more sympathetic than they were on
that issue; they were in no position to appreciate how quickly the phases
of their taste flew by, to be replaced by their polar opposites).

Sure enough she watched O'Neill's expectant smile dim as she lifted out
Elizabeth Singer's touchingly irrelevant offerings: for herself an off-white
lace-encrusted half slip she would have no occasion to use unless she took
up another life; for Teddy a pair of brown velvet moccasins—house slippers,
apparently, since every part of them was soft as a tongue—that he would
sooner wear on his ears than his feet. And the real purpose of the offerings,
four matching oxford shirts of the most conservative standard light blue
with rather unsubtle red monograms where the heart would be: A, L, H,
O. A gesture in the direction of togetherness, a way of saying Welcome.
"Well, O'Neill, look!" Jessie forced herself to exclaim. She tried to shake

out his shirt with a flourish but it was pinned in half a dozen places. By the time she'd found all the invisible silver pins her fingertips touched tiny blood-spots onto the sleeves. But he surprised her by actually liking his shirt. He compressed his chin into his neck and crossed his eyes trying to catch sight of the gothic O on the pocket, his little fish of ego hooked in the first throw of the line.

When Jessie pulled up the tissue paper that had fallen from the pile of shirts she found a manila envelope with her name scrawled across it in red. In small letters her mother had written in her genteel script: *Cleaning out some closets, have too much junk. Do you want these pictures? Don't know if they have any value for you. If not, feel free to chuck them out.*

How unsentimental of her, Jessie thought, holding each snapshot toward the light at an angle to cut the glare. There was Jack Singer and cohorts on what must have been the Staten Island ferry, most of them sitting back on the bench against the railing laughing, Jack to the right, the angle of his body easy, his lumber jacket open, white pants baggy. And here was her father holding up a fat baby Jessie, making an astonished bug-eyed face at her; she, in a bonnet, the center of a daisy, grinned out of her jowls. And oh, she thought, smiling at the brownish snapshot, its edges serrated like the teeth of a knife, her father's vivid face so young her breath went out of her. His mouth was open, slightly, on some imperative. Even in this photograph, engaged rather than angry, he had that air of authority that comes of belligerence controlled, of anger that makes useful energy as a kind of by-product of ferment, like bubbles. (His anger had usually been for people in groups too far away to have names or faces, and for his parents who had worked too hard and died too young and whom he seemed to blame, somehow, for their own doom. For their acquiescence.) How can we, Jessie thought, staring at his lively face, escape the conclusion about our parents as about ourselves—that the attraction is first sexual, that everything more rational and dignified and publicly justifiable comes after the first fact? Her mother talked about how she had listened to him beat back Troskyites and anarchists, and mere pathetic "Bad Deal" reformers like herself. But her eyes, no escaping it, it was still clear in the twentieth telling which Jessie had ritually demanded, her eyes were surely on his head, which was already nine-tenths bald, but all the more handsome for that—bone pure, insistent, attentive—and on his strong hairy arms.

In the last of the pictures she saw her mother, Elizabeth—was she Singer yet, or still Forbath? This must have been soon after her Alabama winter because she is still wearing that cocky little pea coat that her beauty makes stylish. Just around the time this photograph was taken, Jessie speculated, her mother would have been informed with perfect certainty by a forceful young man named Jack Singer that programs like hers were doomed to failure, failure was too good for them, by the New Deal death wish. Reform was another word for appeasement; it was an anaesthetic for the masses. The National Youth Administration was an insult, and at bargain prices. The CCC camps were—what did he call them, not co-optation, that was a newer word, another generation's word. But that was the point, wasn't it—it was a very old story. There is perfidy everywhere, Jack Singer had said, and the president (her mother's hero!) is the Hero of Perfidy, who promises to build the vehicles that will carry the country to its salvation but who conspires to leave out half the bolts and screws. Whenever she had heard this as a child, and that was often, Jessie saw cars like the Fords and Hudsons and Pierce Arrows that lurk in the background of this handful of loose browning photographs, but all of them racing along a cliff with their wheels rattling off, their bodies quivering and shedding doors, glass, lights. A macabre comedy, and the president laughing over his cigarette holder while it happens. Keystone Cops.

Her mother was by now, of course, back up in Manhattan after that one endless Alabama winter, feeling like a pebble thrown up from under the wheels of something large whose whole shape she could not see from where she was. It was that sabotaged vehicle Jack Singer talked about, she supposed, rattling toward its ruin. She was angry that anyone would send the likes of her, new graduate of Girls' High with a smattering of typing and Pittman shorthand (whose shadings and subtleties were said to be like Japanese watercolor painting) to such a wasteland. Winter hardfrost aside, it was like a desert there, so parched it couldn't even absorb her earnest efforts to be helpful. Jack laughed at the word helpful, it was a sissy word for a sissy program, it was a word for children. But Jessie, she had said each time she told the story, my eyes were stung with what I saw! Rats under wooden porches. A picture of a lynched man's corpse though, thank God, not the corpse itself. Faces in the windows of such battered buses, blue city-to-city buses, that looked like ghosts . . .

Jessie stared into the black and gray and white face of her mother, also a ghost, trying to see if anything she had witnessed had surfaced in the large pale eyes with their extravagant Pre-Raphaelite lids. What she ought to understand about her mother, perhaps, after years of thinking of her as a model rebel, married but not safely married, to a printer and a Communist, not to the upwardly mobile middle-class professional her parents had raised her for, is how much energy had to go into the preservation of her seriousness, her gravity, even, from assault. That effort might have saved her from unquestioning thralldom as a beautiful object, as an amiable hausfrau who could use her money for maids and mink stoles, but it was not necessarily sufficient to bring her safely to another place. She was like a refugee who had escaped across a dangerous border but who had never quite arrived at the country she'd dreamed of. Her resources had been, in the end, finite. And Jack had mocked her best, her hardest moment. Now, so many years later, she had become what her parents had intended for her in the first place.

O'Neill, who had gone off to show his shirt to anyone he could find, buttoned wrong over his red sweater, had come back to shake Jessie's arm. "Do you think it should be 'O N' on here? I think my letters are O N, it's not just the same kind of name everybody's got, like Andy or Willie or something."

Jessie resurfaced in his vicinity. She took a deep breath. "No, that might look sort of like a word, don't you think? 'On'? You wouldn't want to confuse people, would you?"

"What's all that stuff?" he asked, tugging on the hand that held the photographs.

"Nothing," she said, "they're nothing at all that you'd find interesting." Why did she have them at all, so unceremoniously bundled off to her? The tyranny of nostalgia around this place was one thing, hard to breathe in, but "feel free to chuck them"? Next time she spoke to her she would have to chastise her mother for unwarranted casualness in the face of her own history. Painful or not it wasn't an old coat, you didn't just give it away.

.   .   .

Jessie came home late from an after-school meeting to find the house in a state of suspension: the children's jackets and other proofs of their presence were scattered everywhere but the children were not in sight. She called out and heard a vague response from the room that held, these days, Helen, O'Neill and the television set. There they were, all of them gathered on floor and couch, attentive the way Andy and Lydia used to be early on Saturday mornings before the pagan altar of the cartoons.

"Oh, Mom, this is so gross!" Andy called to her. "Hurry, you've got to see this." There was a sound of retching and awed wounded cries of the sort Lydia liked to make before the atrocities of a football game. She put her bookbag down and rushed obediently in to see the first of the pictures of the Jonestown suicides. She had heard reports, aghast, on the radio but without graphic proof. They were face down, most of them, a city of sleepers so casual, arms around each other, black and white together, legs at ease, no one arranged for the formality of death but caught—it all looked reversible, as if one and all they might still stir and wake, stretch, rise to reconsider their hasty decision—napping.

Jessie felt the wind pummelled out of her. It was infinitely harder to believe such a thing when you could see it and everything seemed recognizable except the instinct that laid those people down. The children (who never watched the news! How had they known this would be on?) made one endless outcry of disgust and fascination, each contributing democratically. Lydia, finally, leapt up with her hand pressed against her mouth, and ran from the room to be sick somewhere else. Jessie went to comfort her, quite content to give up the commentary that followed the silent viewing of the carnage—self-inflicted but no less carnage—in funereal tones that sounded less sincere than they no doubt were. As she started down the living room she heard O'Neill asking earnestly, "Is that what dead people look like? Don't they look any different?" His voice was quiet but it was not casual. No one answered him. Jessie hurried on to find Lydia leaning against the bathroom wall, breathing hard, in tears of outrage and bewilderment. "I don't understand how anyone can want to die like that," she said very quietly, reasonably. What had Helen been doing, Jessie asked herself, smoothing back her daughter's curls, feeling her own stomach heave. Just sitting, her legs discreetly under her, silent as a hole in air? A black hole, collapsed in on herself, daily tighter and smaller and more and more impenetrable. She was the only one of them who had not cried out her refusal at the sight of the hideous stillness in the pens—they looked like a fairground where the 4-H Club showed its spring lambs in hot competition—a whole city fallen dumb forever on the patchy grass.

. . .

Of course they liked to eat. Teddy and Jessie shared with their generation that pleasure in the sensual that came down, in concrete terms, to the ownership of fresh ginger, a good Vindaloo in a bottle, even a bread pail for six loaves at a time. Sometimes, when they contemplated this pleasure in a world that fed so many of their neighbors on food stamps, they were inhibited by guilt, but it was comforting to know that a satisfactory stir-fry dinner actually took less beef or chicken than a single hamburger, American style.

In any event, they rarely had time to eat together elaborately: someone was always headed for the door just as the others pulled up their chairs. Teddy, for instance, on the evening of the demonstration Curtis had told Jessie about, assembled a cold cheese sandwich while Jessie stood mixing hamburger patties in her big stainless steel bowl. He dropped some lettuce leaves on it like jungle camouflage.

"Oh, you mean I didn't need this extra pound of meat," she said to him as he stood against the kitchen door chewing. "You won't even be here."

He shook his head and took down the jar of instant coffee. "You're sure you don't want to come. There're going to be people you'd like to see."

"I do want to, but I don't like leaving all these children here. It's too soon for that."

Teddy stood filling the kettle, muttering angrily that he thought they had long since passed the crib and bottle stage. He turned off the water with a hard tug. "Jesus, they're not brand-new babies. Andy can keep everybody in line. And Helen's probably an ace baby sitter too, you know."

But that wasn't what she meant. She did not want to leave Helen and O'Neill in a house without parents, whether they took notice or not. The idea depressed her. "Someone will wake up with a nightmare."

"Jessie." Teddy stood still holding the kettle at waist level as if it were a lantern. "Hey, let's take them along. O'Neill and Lydia at least."

"O'Neill!"

"Yes, ma'am?" O'Neill called from the living room where he had been lying on the comics trying to make himself into Silly Putty. Before Teddy could give her a detailed, principled reason for the random idea that had formed itself on his tongue, she turned to put the hamburger meat away. Why argue? They could eat downtown for a treat. The boy might as well see how wide and deep it was, this life he'd been kidnapped into. Was it sadistic to think that?

Lydia was exhausted and seemed to be getting a cold. (Jessie suspected she was fighting off depression with secret sleeplessness. Often when she was anxious she seemed to hold herself back from sleep the way some children held their breath, a withholding of trust.)

"You go," Jessie said to Teddy and took the hamburger meat out again. Water droplets had condensed under the plastic wrap she'd stretched across the top of the bowl. It seemed to be raining under there. "Take O'Neill. I want to see"—she knew how callous she must sound—"I want to see what happens."

But as Teddy and O'Neill were putting on their jackets she turned and saw Helen watching her. She couldn't even begin to decipher the expression she saw—was it more than curiosity? What did she look like in Helen's noncommittal eyes? What did she *want* to look like? She didn't know, but it was not Wife in Apron Saying Goodbye to Her Man at the Door. "Wait for me!" she shouted and went for her coat. "But dinner—" she began.

"It's all right," Helen said to her laconically. "I know how to make hamburgers."

"Will you be all right? Because—"

Helen shrugged. "Why not?"

O'Neill reminded Jessie of a dog they'd had when they were just married. The dog might be eating, sleeping, running down the street with his pack of friends, but if you said "Car, Willie!" in a voice that meant business, he would leap gratefully to your side and come anywhere with you. He would stand stiffly on the back seat, knees locked to keep from pitching forward, and stare at the scenery with the raptness of a ship's captain sighting for land.

O'Neill sat beside them now with glowing eyes. All of them were in the front seat, shoulder to shoulder; Teddy had his boxes of textbooks in the back. O'Neill didn't come up much beyond the top of the door. Jessie wanted to touch him the way she would her own children, for his warmth if not for her own, but she was shy. He sat tight.

"Hey, you want to sit up a little higher?" Teddy asked him. "You're going to miss a lot down there. We'll get you a pillow or something for next time."

"Or you could sit on my lap," Jessie offered.

"In the Corvette, I can see everything. When are we going to go get it?"

They hadn't given it much thought.

"My dad always took me places in it. He let me steer it. I always used to drive home all the way from Frontier Avenue and I used the signal. One time I even backed it up."

"Well. We'll have to go over and get it then, we don't want you to forget how to drive." Jessie was thinking how she had never been in a Corvette but Teddy had owned a Triumph once for a while, before her time, till somebody took it to New Orleans and totalled it against one of the pilings on the Pontchartrain causeway. The power of the car, he would say, was like cold water streaming off you when you drove, it poured down your sides and washed you clean. Sometimes, on a straight delta road, he could get the speed up now but the damn Valiant started to kick back at about fifty-five: it said I'm a family car, man, don't *push* me like that. It said, Hey, friend, that's *dangerous*. It had a small safe neuter voice. Jessie thought she might have liked the Triumph: very little sped past her these days.

The best thing of everything he could remember, like the moment runners speak of ecstatically when they break through time and space into another element, were the times when he was outrunning a car full of s.o.b.'s, even a sheriff, doing eighty-five, doing ninety, and he'd pull the handbrake and spin around on a dime, a perfect 180 degrees, and then pass them going back through a wall of dust. Their astounded faces—sometimes you could get a millimeter-of-a-second's look at that confusion, somebody in the car flipping his head around in disbelief. That was what he was getting ready to do when the Higgs brothers got him, and nudged him off the road—well, it wasn't a nudge at ninety—and into the kudzu.

"We'll go get the car one of these days," he said to his nephew. "Then we can ride around together and you can show me some of your tricks." But possibly, Jessie thought, that would upset him when they really got down to doing it, make him grieve for his father. They would have to discuss it.

But the boy was looking out the window avidly at the dark houses with their meek lights glowing. His neck and shoulders said nothing about his state of mind except what Jessie had seen at school, and had made good use of: that he was a child who was led forward into each moment by irresistible eagerness; that certain griefs and injustices—perhaps memories but perhaps not—did not clutter his mind yet. He was already outrunning himself.

They were coming into town on North State Street where the funky old houses were, the tall chipped narrow ones with pillars that had once been grand; that had gone through rooming house sag, divided into a dozen rooms with eccentric landladies and inadequate plumbing; that were good for nothing now, before their next reclamation, but antique shops and cheap hairdressers.

"Let me tell you where we're going," Teddy said gently to O'Neill. He told him that once a terrible thing had happened near this place, this very night five years ago. Two young girls named Atecia and Joyce—girls only a little bit older than Helen, high-school girls—were walking along the sidewalk coming home from a friend's house just around suppertime. And just when they got near the railroad track—"We'll go over it," he said. "You'll see, we have to pass there on our way"—some men went by in a car, men who didn't even know them, and shot at them with hunting rifles.

O'Neill had turned to watch him, looking across Jessie, who was going to let Teddy do this. His eyes were rough spots of gold in the dark. "Did they get 'em?"

"Jesus," Jessie said. "This kid would side with the robbers against the cops."

" 'Get 'em?' Why should they have got 'em? We're not talking about ducks, O'Neill. They weren't doing anything. They were just walking and talking. Maybe they were laughing."

"Oh," said O'Neill, dampened. "But they must have been doing *some-thing*."

Teddy glared straight ahead. Jessie looked from one of them to the other. There was so little traffic after rush hour that Jackson, evenings and weekends, became a small town. "They were just walking," Teddy said evenly. "But they were black girls and some men thought—think—it's all right if you kill black people even if they're not bothering anybody."

Now we will see, M. Rousseau, Jessie thought, if a child's natural goodness will bubble up like a fountain when it is set free of evil influence.

O'Neill turned back toward his window, out of which there was nothing to see across the flats but the distant lights of downtown like a midway. The road was bumpy out here and the grayness of the open lots made them endless and ominous. They clattered across the bridge that spanned a creek nearly invisible in this season; every spring it flooded the nearest downhill houses so that they could reappear chastened and reborn just in time for Easter.

"Look. There's the railroad crossing coming up. See, there isn't anybody around, so a coward could do anything he wanted out here, and then he could run away." Teddy's voice tensed on this kind of recitation: Jessie could see how he felt a primitive outrage begin to move inside his stomach, ready to come to a rolling boil. "Yes, one of them did get killed. Atecia. She just fell down right on the other side of these tracks and she probably never even knew what happened to her. And Joyce got very badly hurt but she was all right after a long time."

O'Neill had turned to look at him, silent, his eyes round under his bangs. They drove for a few blocks till the dreary houses began to thicken around them. Then he said, kicking his legs up and trying to touch his toes, "You better find a gas station pretty soon."

"Why? They'll have a bathroom where we're going," Jessie said. "Do you need one?"

"My daddy says you should never let it get below half empty, and look where *that* is. That red needle."

"It's fine," Teddy told him. "Don't worry about it." Was the boy afraid of stalling in the vicinity of murder or was it the sudden flash of memory of his father as king of the road—dethroned, uncrowned, the Corvette out of combat under a green plastic tarpaulin—that made O'Neill sigh once and seem to deflate? They were all still shy with each other. He leaned his head against the door until they pulled up among the other cars beside the drainage ditch and stopped.

.   .   .

It wasn't a demonstration, as it turned out; it was a mournful private ceremony made public, a volunteering of grief to be handed around a small circle. The loaves and fishes of loss and outrage, forever multiplying. They had hoped, for O'Neill's sake, that they would find themselves at a rally, invigorated, ignited by numbers. But that was foolish. Of course. What would they be protesting? *Everything* was nothing to protest.

Joyce, the girl who had survived the shooting, lived in Detroit now but she had come home to visit her parents, and all of them were here, right down the block in Atecia's house to honor her memory. It was one of those gatherings that makes confident people awkward because they will always talk too loud in a room so tiny, and awkward people resigned because no one, not even the lords of social gatherings, seems able to master discomfort.

The room was a small gray square, lit by a dull ceiling fixture, that felt like a slightly enlarged elevator. The speckled linoleum had dashes of color on it, distributed like cupcake sprinkles. A picture of the slain Atecia stood forward on a little table with a black moire bow tied across one corner on the diagonal, in the spirit of a well-wrapped present. She was—had been— a lively looking long-necked girl with slightly Oriental eyes and parted lips, photographed in her blue high school basketball uniform with an indistinct expression in her eyes, as if they had already been moving away from the photographer's—a picture taken halfway between here and there, accidental, like her death.

Teddy met a few people he knew, old N-double-A folks, who still took themselves, like him, to dispirited meetings like this out of loyalty to the people who had lost something, someone, and who pretended to have grown and gained and somehow prospered because, they had been repeatedly told, sorrow conveniently waters the roots of wisdom. While he talked with them in an unnaturally subdued voice, Jessie watched Atecia's mother, a tiny woman wearing what had to be a wig because its lush shine did not seem to reflect sufficient inner vigor to account for it; it was like a wildflower, a sport, waving over dry and weedy ground. She came and took Teddy's hand, and then Jessie's, nodding as she had nodded all around at anyone willing to come out tonight. Although the woman probably didn't know their names, Teddy gravely introduced his nephew O'Neill Tyson as he would have had O'Neill been an adult and a dignitary. The formality seemed to do the old woman honor.

O'Neill stared at her as if she were a brand-new species. When she reached out and put a hand on his fair straight hair, he tensed. But the politeness that had run deep in the channels between generations in his family was a form of discipline so potent it appeared to precede even passionate resistance. The boy stood still and bore her hand like a patient horse, with his eyes cast down.

Frank Dixon, known as Jug, of the Committee for Interracial Reconciliation, came in just as they began to arrange themselves to hear the
memorial. He made it a habit to sneak in, bearing his huge body as lightly
as a dancer's, on tiptoe, wherever he went: his schedule did not allow for
early arrivals. (Still he never left before he'd made contact with everyone
in the room.) He put his arm around Jessie's waist and pressed with the
whole fleshy strength of it, to the elbow. He cuffed Teddy on the shoulder
from behind. He was a huge Arkansas farmboy who looked as if he must
be wearing overalls under his corduroy jacket. Like Teddy, he had grown
up in a place where his adult devotions were heresy, but neither trusted
the other entirely, as if they were converts to competing sects of the same
religion. There had always been so much of that (and the opposition, as it
always does, waited to see if they would snuff each other out). It was tribal,
and from a distance, worse than absurd: costly. As for Jessie, she saw Jug
as a man who was no friend to women, least of all the ones he plowed and
fertilized more casually than a farmer any field. She pitied his wife, Jo, who
seemed too smart to have put herself in the way of such constant inconstancy.

This evening she felt herself (and Teddy and Curtis Hover, who stood
with his hand on his wife's shoulder halfway into the kitchen) much bigger
than everyone else who had come out for the ceremony. Or was it that they
were the only young people there? (Young?!) Joyce—she didn't know her
last name—was a large woman, and pregnant, so that her red and blue
checkered maternity blouse rode straight out below a broad white collar.
But everyone else, the minister who invoked God's protection, the neighbors
who nodded after him, trying not to wonder where God was the day the
girls fell in their tracks, all of them had a frailty—perhaps it was only bone
weariness—that seemed to Jessie a sign that, having changed so little under
the pressure of fresh grief and anger, nothing was ever going to change in
ordinary times like this. Not for households like this that still, within the
city limits, had drainage ditches out in front. This generation would be
extinguished by time like a candle in a bell jar. Atecia's mother would go
to her grave, wigless and mostly bewildered by her daughter's violent blame-
less end, not even angry any more. She had tried anger but it hadn't helped
much.

Joyce, on the other hand, seemed to believe in the cathartic power of
justified rage. You would not want to end up on the wrong side of *her*,
Teddy whispered half-admiringly; she looked capable of saying anything
that might wound, in a voice that could penetrate steel—she seemed almost
cheerful in her wrath, as if it gave her physical relief. Would she always
have been like this, given, by coincidence, a cause sufficient to her outrage?

Or had events enlivened her? Jessie thought she recognized a born hellcat, one of those feisty girls with a voice on her at the age of five. She admired that even as she might try to stay out of her way. A stiff white-girl's pageboy hung out around her head like an umbrella, and her round eyes were circled with what looked from a few feet back like Vaseline but was probably more like lavender eye-shadow. Making her thick presence glamorous was a thankless task Joyce had taken a swipe at; but she had at least made herself look decisive. She had *mass*. A black star.

And therefore she launched right in without looking at the picture that stood meekly beside her in its ribbon, or at the minister or at Atecia's mother, who sat on the couch like a small obedient girl with her hands loose in her lap and her ankles crossed.

"Been a long time since I sat in this room here with my friend Atecia," she said, looking straight ahead at no one's eyes. "Sometimes I think back, I can't even remember her real good, to be honest. Maybe Mrs. Burrow can, I hope she can, cause, after all, Tecia was her *baby*. But I can't and I tell you that right out. A lot of things been happening to me since that evening out on the track back there." She cast one arm loosely to the side. "For one thing I quit that dumb school and for another I moved up to Detroit to live with my brother, some of you remember my brother Bubba. He work at the River Rouge plant, the Chevy plant, and he got me a job. I got a kid and another one on the way. Feel like it's halfway here tonight." She laughed and put one hand on it in case anyone had missed it. "But all's I got to say is, see, I got to do all that and everybody else in our class at Central got to—they ought to have about a hundred and fifty kids between them by now if they got a one, and it's only a few years gone past. And them white girls who went to that same school with us too, they got them a whole generation too. Now one other girl I know of, she died, she got blood poisoning or something, and some of the boys in accidents and one in an army plane that blew up, at least I think I heard that. Tomkins Paul, that was. And probably more in the army too, I don't know cause I haven't been around here much to keep up.

"But here's what I'm saying. Out of all the rest, there's only one who never got to have kids or a man of her own or make some money and save it up for something she be needing—nothin. Nothin. High scorer on the ball team, real good with her fingers making stuff, whenever we had to do that, she could work your hair like nobody you know in any beauty shop—so she walk home from her friend Beverly's house, she hurrying cause she got to get supper for her mama after work?—and that's it. That's it, no more chance to do *nothin* and I'm here to tell you they never found the motherfuckers who done that to her. All right? I got a real good description of that car, it was a red Ford with a beat-in fender and special chrome on it and a two-way aerial, and I even seen a little of who was in there before I went out, but they never even went and looked." Her voice was so firm it flew out among them like a solid sphere. You could hear her shouting at her lover or her children in that raw righteous way. She could probably sing out and hold up all the altos. "Bastards never searched *nowhere* for *noth*in. So when they tell you everything's good with us down here—*which* they are saying—even up in Detroit where I be livin now—just because you can buy a greasy hamburger at Woolworth's and they went and hired a couple of niggers over at the hospital or something—you just think about my friend Tecia that some cat finished her off before he went home and had *his* supper just for the hell of it, like some men, they take a shotgun to a deer or a duck flying over a swamp. And you can just hear them laughin, right? Score one. Like droppin a basket. I could hear 'em in that car hootin and hollerin, I ain't about to forget that dirty sound." She paused for what seemed like her first breath.

"Well, I go to church, I been goin all my life and I got to ask Jesus *why*. If you bad you suffer, fair enough. But what if you never did no bad thing to nobody. I got to tell you—" She turned toward the minister who stood, small and brittle in his dark worn suit, with each hand tucked into the opposite armpit, his chest shielded. "I stopped going to church after Atecia. I was in Saint Dominick's hospital felt like forever, and when I got out and I was still in bandages, looked like some kind of ghost, I just couldn't find no answers to fit that question. I won't attack nobody that believes, but I— *me*—I couldn't listen to no more folks telling me everything's got its reason or its season or what-all it got in the Bible. Folks that wrote the Bible never had no dealings with the Jackson Police Department. I never saw Ecclesi*a*stes get hit in the back with no firehose, get shot out of ambush just when he's walking on down thinkin do we have hot dogs tonight or maybe just grits and a little leftover ham hock?"

Joyce cast her eyes around the room. Then, as if for the first time, she seemed to notice that her audience was made of particular faces. Her gaze hooked on O'Neill who was standing in front of Teddy, shifting from rapt attention to a fascination with the fingerprints on his thumbs, which he held side by side, like levers, to study, and pushed together hard to see if their shapes matched. When he looked up, Joyce caught his eyes.

"See now, what if I took and aimed at that nice little white boy there—" She pointed to him accusingly. "See, he just standing there up against his daddy, he ain't causing no kind of trouble, all right? What if I just took and emptied my barrel into him all the while he standing looking at me all wide eyed. What you think his daddy do if he could get his hands on me? And you think anybody *stop* him?"

It took Jessie a few seconds to understand what she had said; when she had, the hair on her arms, on the back of her neck, bristled with revulsion. What the hell kind of thing was that to say to them—would they be here if they deserved that? Teddy, who had stiffened with anger, opened his mouth to object.

But "He's not my daddy!" O'Neill called out to her in his high clear voice, angry on his own behalf. He stood up very straight and prepared to defend the distinction with a pugnacious chin.

But Joyce was not interested in details. "Ever who he is. Don't matter. You know what I mean."

There was some uncomfortable shuffling of the feet of the polite and the fearful, who did not like to give offense to friendly white folks. "I only mean, I touch a hair on the head of some pretty little white boy, I ain't never gonna see another sunrise. You know how many black bodies they fished up out of the rivers when they went out lookin for them three civil rights workers back there? The ones they kept sayin got 'slain'? You know they pulled em up in halfs, in quarters, they got hands and they sure 'nough must have dragged up some privates, and then some boy's head up in the Big Black, just the head, never could make out who it was. And nobody ever went around, called that poor child 'slain,' all dignified and public, and the president say 'Ooh' and the FBI say 'Aah,' and all the newspapers come running with their pad and pencil. Just another little bit of fooling around scaring someone for the hell of it before supper, like I said, practicing foul shots. Well, I ain't offering to shoot no little boys here—I'm sorry, sugar, I didn't mean to scare you." She smiled at O'Neill but it was not a warming smile. She rested her hands comfortably on the mound of her stomach as if her own child might need reassurance.

"But you-all know what I'm saying. I'm saying Atecia Burrow, you died for nothing and no one. I don't think *voting* gonna help that. I don't think *integration* gonna help. Cut down on strangers but it don't cut down none on enemies that I can see. In Atlanta they killing innocent children. In Buffalo they cutting out their hearts with a penknife, fathers and sons. So what do I say? We victims that day out on the tracks, we victims right now. And you got to lie to yourself if you think the changes amount to more than a pocketful of damn pennies."

And she turned her back on the room and walked past Curtis Hover and his wife and into the kitchen. The audience rippled and breathed out, hard. Atecia's mother stared at the minister uncertainly, a plea—this was her house—but he looked as if Joyce had had him by his collar and shaken the words right out of him.

Teddy might have stood up and led them the way they wanted to go, back into comfort and hope, but he looked winded. Jug Dixon, a white minister's son, did it: somebody had to. He swung his huge bulk out of his little bridge chair and put both hands up in a gesture that said Not so fast. Where do you think you're going, racing off into despair like that? Every mass meeting had to be turned into an instrument to be used; every grief had to have the passion threshed out of it, to feed the hungry flock. Jug rolled out his testimonials to improved relations, the annotated symptoms of change, true and not true. His office existed to document progress, not defeat.

Teddy was taking in short gulps of breath as Jug spoke, as if he were suppressing a response to each sentence. Jessie recognized the habit: he was like a runner setting his feet in place. When Jug sat, to polite applause, Teddy pulled himself out of his chair slowly, looking reluctant, putting all his weight on the back of the chair in front of him. "Can I just say another word or two?" His hesitancy was feigned. There used to be times when he'd travel two hundred miles so he could sound as if he didn't dare stand to make a few tentative additions to the business at hand.

"You know, I have the feeling you're going home discouraged," he said quietly, finding some eyes to look into. "Am I right about that? And I hear the sound of disappointment here tonight." Jessie could hear the old rhythm beginning to beat, the preacher's emphasis, the half black, half white jazz-in-the-mouth syncopation he used to do so well. "Well, let me hear it!" he called to them, nodding. "If you're holding grief to your hearts, let's get it out here and look at it. Don't take it home unspoken, it can eat at you that way, it can bore a deep hole in your chest and you'll never get free of it."

Nodding overtook the audience, sorely relieved, and the singsong repetitions of church. They began to call out to him.

"Listen! For every lie they tell down in the capitol building these days, I'll tell you one truth. Did you know—" and he was off at a clip, into statistics for school enrollment, for graduation, for job availability. It was his salesman's job: who could tell if he was lying or telling God's honest truth, Jessie thought. She wouldn't trust him with his own name when he got started on his forward roll; somewhere between education and demagoguery he was trying to salve their pain. It hurt him, he said, that their problems depressed and did not enliven them to action.

"Ten years ago in this state . . ." And out came the numbers, maybe fanciful, maybe scrupulous, of welfare cases. The numbers were different now, lower, but since employment figures were up, wasn't it clear—well, didn't it seem likely?—that those numbers had moved off the ranks of need and discouragement into those that brought home paychecks and paid their own way now? Likely or not, the audience was rapt. This had nothing to do with Atecia but it was soothing and made them feel better about coming out tonight. They sank back almost imperceptibly and folded their hands in their laps, passive before the proffered facts. The old minister in the first row had placed his hands on both sides of his dark jacket as if he were supporting the paunch that came with his sudden sense of well-being. "This time, now, in 1979, if someone did what they did to your daughter, Mrs. Burrow—may Heaven forbid it, but if they dared to—don't you agree they'd have a harder time?" Teddy looked at the tiny woman but it was with his public gaze that saw no one, as if blinded by footlights. "Now we have some protection of our jury system, so that there couldn't *be* an all-white jury. Now we have—you have—enough political power so that the police chief *answers* for his investigations. Even though there are a hundred, a thousand things we still have to do, time has *not* stood still. It may be fashionable to say that nothing's changed but . . ." People loved to think they were moving against fashion, it was bracing to the ego to feel brave and independent. "Atecia Burrow's death is only one of the atrocities that have finally weighed down one side of the scales of justice so that . . ."

They could hear Joyce whistling in the kitchen, banging drawers closed. Atecia's face, still and forever distracted as she turned away, bounced in its frame when Teddy pounded his fist, vehement on behalf of three hundred and eighty-seven black elected officials and one mayor, on the little table that was its altar. It almost fell over. He caught it and held it straight, his knuckles showing over the Woolworth gold.

The small crowd's applause fell around Teddy with the steadiness of a hard rain shower. A few people stood, clapping strenuously right under their chins, beckoning to the rest of the congregation to do the same. Teddy's eyes shone back at them and he nodded, suddenly diffident, as if the whole performance had somehow slipped out of him unbidden. Well, all of it—most of it—was true: progress was like the glass that was half full or half empty. She couldn't accuse him of cynicism, really, and he was beautiful at full gallop. It was only that there weren't many assemblies of the passive who would let him stroke them without recoil these days. The moment was too easily his.

"He finished?" Joyce asked, leaning out of the kitchen. She smiled innocently and, reassured, slipped back into the crowd.

Jessie stood with O'Neill and considered the woman's wanton self-delighting cruelty: nasty though it was, she was right, she could not do to O'Neill what O'Neill's father, say, might have done to her. And for all Teddy's decency and its statistical ballast, these people, in this little house, were not living in the grace of hopefulness. Jessie stood with one arm across O'Neill's shoulder, her wrist on the boy's small chest. The thin skin of her pulse point could pick up the distant lunge and flutter of his excited heart. Jessie had long since given up thinking some blacks would ever stop hating whites, all whites, no matter who; she differed with Teddy right there. She remembered all too well the zeal with which their friends, most of their black friends with the exception of Andréa and a very few others, had refused to speak to them in 'sixty-seven, 'sixty-eight. She had held out her hand to a man whom she had admired since those weeks of entry into the Movement in Ohio, and—she was not about to forget the icy shame with which she retracted it—he had raised his own out of his lap, reluctantly, and gave her his flaccid pinky to shake.

O'Neill, standing at the ready, was intrigued now with the proceedings. He leaned against Jessie trustingly, Jessie's fingers laced in his, as though having publicly declared Teddy not *his* father, he could stand closer to the two of them without yielding up anything that mattered. He was waiting—or so it seemed—for that lady, or some other one, to stand up and single him out again.

.   .   .

"Teddy," Jug Dixon said, one foot on the seat of a folding chair, his hound's-tooth pants leg drumhead taut over his bulky thigh. "Good words there, buddy. You should have been a down-home preacher. Look, we got to get together." That was Jug's perennial way of saying hello: it was as if his whole life only stretched out in front of him as it was promised in his little flop-eared black appointment book. Nothing ever happened in the present. He liked to construct events in the proper sequence.

"I'm here right now," Teddy said disingenuously, smiling as if he were O'Neill. Jessie was usually too irritated with Jug to say more than hello to him.

"No, man, listen." And Jug bent his head to Teddy's. His large lids came down halfway over tremendous dark spaniel's eyes. Everything was confidential for Jug; the day of the week was a secret he might leak to some but not to others. It was a question of keeping up contact, this perpetual urgency.

"Listen, I got an idea in the middle of this thing here—" He cast one arm out to take in the room and just missed cuffing the minister in his wire glasses. "Frankly"—he lowered his voice—"I don't think this kind of chicken-shit get-together does anybody any good at all. If anything I think it's got a depressive effect, am I right? Except for your little uplift there, I feel like I've been underwater for an hour and my skin's beginning to pucker right about now."

Teddy shrugged and nodded. He was watching O'Neill, who was accepting a paper cup of something from an old lady with her glasses on a pearl chain. People who passed stopped to pump Teddy's hand and thank him; he smiled back, flushed like a man who had done some righteous exercise.

"Well, lookit," Jug continued, and slid his cheek up next to Teddy's so that they were facing the same way. It was the way conspirators would pass a message in a crowd, lips closed, when they weren't supposed to know each other.

"I got this idea for a grand gala demonstration. We haven't had a real good one for so long damned if I can remember back. Right? You can't name me one that really pulled out the troops and spread as much joy and fight as a sixth grade football game." He rubbed at an imaginary spot on his rock-solid thigh, humbly; picked, rubbed and smoothed, to give him some point of apparent concentration. "War stuff, maybe, a few years back, but that was different folks. Anyway—what we need—I was listening to what's her name, Joyce there—is a holiday like an Unknown Soldier's Day." He sketched something in the air, the vague shape of the day. "Only this is the Unknown Victim's Day. Not Schwerner-Chaney-Goodman, not— you know—Mrs. Liuzzo or Reverend Reeb or ole Herbert Lee. I mean, like she said—who ever paid any tribute whatsoever to all those missing ones who just never turn up again? Or the bodies that by the time they surface you can't even tell whose son they were any more only what color their grieving mother must have been."

O'Neill was drinking the last of whatever was in the cup. He was chatting quite amiably, amiably enough, apparently, to deserve a refill. Either he was very early into the con game of disembodied charm or there was hope for his unformed soul.

"Business must be slow, Jug." Teddy took his cheek away.

"Damn straight. Feels like we're making horseshoes or piano rolls or something these days. Just as much grief and trouble as ever but nobody wants to hustle for it. And they won't send money either."

"I'm not sure times are ripe for your anonymous skeleton game. Is that what you want to stir up these days?" This was usually Jessie's line of questioning. Teddy winked at her.

"Well—if we could get exactly the right kind of publicity on it." He grunted at the futility of that. "Like the little lady says, people like to believe all that progress bullshit you gave them. Whole damn country thinks folks are all living like Laverne and Shirley in their Beverly Hills condo. They want to believe these kind of folks you got tonight, all humble in their little shirt-cardboard lean-tos out here in this neighborhood that ought to been condemned years ago—they like it this way or they'd go get them one of those high visibility new jobs uptown. Can't you see that Mama Burrow in her snappy little uniform with the gold buttons, down at the Delta ticket counter smiling into her computer?"

"Yeah, but you're not really suggesting we start celebrating all that old violence. You trying to give the Klan ideas?"

Jug shrugged. "Mobilization." He raised his eyebrows hopefully, wiggled them, then lowered them the way Groucho did when he wanted to undermine his own words.

"For?"

"Four? What, four?"

Man wasn't even concentrating. "No. Mobilization for—? You got together a program since I saw you last?"

Jug clapped him along the side of his upper arm muscle, getting ready to dismiss him. "Matching up the action with the need's the least of our problems, Ted-o. Just get the troops *moving*. Forward thrust. Passion. Desperation."

"Bullshit." It was time to steal O'Neill from his circle of old lady admirers and take him home to bed.

Jessie couldn't stay quiet. "You don't mean any of that."

Teddy gave his nephew the high sign. "Yeah, Jug. You just love a parade."

Jug sighed. "No, I don't mean it. I know confrontation time's over and probably just as well and I know my goddamn letterhead's got two colors of hands shaking on a deal. Peace first and then negotiation. But you know and I know which hand's getting the short end and supposed to be glad to get it. I wish I knew how to give a hotfoot to this town just once before I quit and go back to the farm." He put his forehead against Teddy's to make a secret out of inarguable fact. "We got a case of low-level narcolepsy here. Lots of sleeping at the switch."

O'Neill came to stand with them. "You giving somebody a hotfoot, can I help?"

"Leave it to Beaver," Teddy said.

"I'll call on you to light the match, little mister," Jug told him and poked a fist into his ribs. "You can light it and we'll all hide someplace together and watch what happens." He ruffled Jessie's curls and walked away. She watched Jug make his rounds of intense, apparently random conversation. That whole absurd proposition could more easily have been put to Teddy as the question it was: what's your pulse rate these days, Teddy Carll? How do you read the signs? Any pressure building up around the fault-lines that I ought to know about? He was supposed to be flattered that Jug would ask him, since, even if he still had a good voice he had no more constituency any more. Now that the life and death urgency of their old alliance had dwindled, Jessie could allow herself the full weight of her distrust: Machiavelli among the Tinkertoys, Jug was. Should she pity or fear or merely revile him, that guide to the labyrinth, whom no one would follow?

Mrs. Burrow kissed him when he left. Teddy was silent as they crossed the scrappy patch of grass to the car. When they had sat down he said, and Jessie breathed out hard with relief, "What an asshole. Has he gotten crasser than he used to be or was he always a clown?"

He didn't wait for an answer. "He's right about the hotfoot, God knows he is *right*. But there he is in the do-good business and I swear Lyddie's doing more for human relations just by lending some kid her pencil in school."

Jessie pulled herself closer to him. She was so relieved that he hadn't taken Jug's bait that she was reconciled for the moment. He had more than principles left, he had some pride as well.

．　．　．

Helen was sitting up in the kitchen when they came in. She looked to Jessie like one of those censorious cheated-on wives in a cartoon; she only needed cold cream and a hydra-head full of curlers.

Teddy squeezed O'Neill's shoulder, a salute to some bonding chemical the evening had released in them. The boy went off to his sleeping bag in the den without a word of encouragement.

Jessie watched Helen for a full minute from the doorway.

"What is it?"

The girl sat stonily with her hands around a mug of warm something.

Jessie hurried to her side and shook her shoulder. "Helen, *what* is the matter?"

Helen didn't look at them. "Someone was peeping in the window at me," she said quietly, as if she were confessing to a crime.

"Oh shit," Teddy said.

Why did it so often seem that good spirits were followed—tail-gated—by bad? Jessie's heart somersaulted.

"I was getting ready to take a shower. I was in the bathroom with no clothes on. And there was someone at the window."

Teddy breathed out again. "How did you know that? Didn't you have the window curtain pulled?"

"That's not something you dream *up*, Teddy," Jessie said impulsively. "She knew, that's all."

"Well, *I* don't know." I don't know her is what he meant to say. "Are you going to make this into a woman's thing? 'All of us can tell when one of you beastly males is watching us from the trees you live in'?"

Jessie put a protective arm around Helen and stood her up. "Let's go to bed now. We're here and nothing can happen. Okay?"

With a look of unconvinced resignation, Helen and Jessie walked back toward the den; Jessie could see her filing away the event and Teddy's refusal to believe her. She carried herself and her silence like someone with good cross-indexes of injustice and short weight. Jessie soothed her into bed, wishing she could feel, at least, that fear had made Helen vulnerable; but it seemed in fact to have stiffened her neck.

But, Jessie reflected, she was surrounded by such stretched-forth necks—the Bible talked about pride that way. She had worked with friends, Andréa and half a dozen others, for example, to set up a Rape Crisis Center a few years ago and now they were planning an adjunct house for battered wives, and hadn't Teddy seethed at every hour it took her away from home? It was as if he were, in some remote way, on the side of the assaulters and batterers. Some obscure pride in him was affronted, though if she'd been doing something solely for blacks he wouldn't have said a word. Alienation of affections, he would say, treating it like a joke. But he was angry, no joke, and she couldn't counter his nastiness because she had no key to it.

"How can you be sure she's not some hysteric about her body?" Teddy objected, when Jessie came back from comforting Helen. "I mean, a teenager who's finally got a little something to protect?"

Jessie laughed drily. "That's ridiculous. I don't have any trouble believing her at all. It isn't as if this is the first thing that's happened here, you know."

"But did she actually see anybody? I'm getting tired of all this anonymous menace."

"You mean someone's face? No. But she told me she saw a sort of glint across the glass. She turned the light out because she said she felt someone out there. And she pulled back the curtain and then she said there was definite movement, like a ripple in the window. Something taking off across the grass."

"Something with broad black shoulders, undoubtedly, and his big black pecker in his hand—"

"*Teddy.*" She made a sour face at him. "Sometimes your impeccable aristocratic manners get away from you."

"How come every Southerner's got to have aristocrats in his family that you can hold up to him the way all you poor Jews have a great and famous rabbi salted away somewhere. A million and a half wisemen." He raked his fingers through his hair. "Well, look now. She's figured out where she *is* by now, wouldn't you say? Don't you think that would make her feel like she's—I don't know—surrounded? Unprotected, at least? On the night Mommy and Daddy are away? Even if he is a poor apology for a daddy. So here she is home alone, all that fair flesh and somebody's coming to get it. She probably thinks we're about ready to offer her up to the neighborhood anyway. She has to go to *school* with them."

He turned away from her and put his long fingers through the handles of the hanging cupboards. He looked like a man doing exercises, head fallen forward between his shoulders. Exhaustion. Defeat. "Look," he said to the cupboard. "Whether we're all about to be raped by bogeymen or whether she saw Mickey Mouse chasing a chipmunk out there, you and I know we've got to move. All right?"

"Well, thank you. You've finally grasped it."

"We've got us six people and a cat living in this doghouse here, and we're not shackpoor, however it might cost us the pride of empathy to admit it. We have two extra dependents and a wagonload of money comes riding on their heads. To be perfectly honest. A station-wagonload full of their flotsam and jetsam and a bankbook full of money to make some readjustments in their name. For their sake."

Jessie looked at him steadily. It was like watching a large slow ship heave around into a bay that had been empty, awaiting its arrival. "Well, if you've thought that all along, why are you only admitting it now? Do you enjoy making me into a shrew?"

"Oh Jessie," he said quietly as if he had given it so much solitary thought he could barely speak of it out loud. "This isn't between us, it's between me and me. You're the one who seems to want to make it into an endless confrontation."

She stood her ground. "But you've—"

"I've had to reconcile myself to a lot of things, okay? Don't be so damned egotistical, I haven't been trying to undermine *you*."

"All right. Fine."

"Not everything in a marriage is communal property, you know, every feeling, every opinion."

"But that leaves me very lonely."

He looked down at his feet. "I'm sorry if it does. I haven't been trying to do that. It just might occur to you that I'm pretty lonely too."

She made a movement to reach out to him.

"So let's get on to the next step." He snapped to attention and she drew her hand back. "We'll get us one of these places with a thousand yards of frontage and a kidney-shaped pool. We'll go get the Corvette out of mothballs. We'll get another phone and list it in the book under 'Teenagers.' We'll—"

"Jesus! You make me dizzy, you know that? There I thought you were coming around graciously to my point of view and then you have to undo it. That's an interesting kind of domino theory you have. I don't know if you ought to go to work for the State Department or for *Better Homes and Gardens*." Easy, she was thinking. Much easier to let him have his sarcasm, blame the space problem and get on with it. Even if the dialectic her father believed in had swung like the sharp-edged pendulum it was, its razor side to their necks, let Teddy think they needed two extra bedrooms, whatever it took to get out of here intact. Let him mock the need if that helps him get through this. So the neighborhood would be black again, closed, thoroughly regressed to a segregated haven. She ached for him, for the stubbornness of his vision; let him ache a little for her, for the ease with which she yielded. How had she ever dared to think their differences would be complementary rather than divisive?

Teddy lifted his head and smiled at her dimly, self-deprecatingly. "End of an era," he said, lifting one closed hand halfway between a fist and the gesture of a man drinking a toast.

Let's hope, she longed to say. Oh pride, she thought, bloody pride, and put her arms around him. She respected him despite all. Every virtue is a vice if you pinch it too hard. She had never said she was a martyr. He had never said he was a pragmatist. Maybe they could find some space to meet in the middle.

Andy came in around ten and we talked a little bit. He isn't so bad, really. He is very busy at school—an all-around student, I guess—and he is in, of all things, a Shakespeare play. I don't know any boys who would do that. He has a part called Sebastian (sp?) in 12th Night and he did some for me. He has specially nice warm eyes, blue-gray like a baby, they must have never changed, and kind hands. (I am not saying that because anything else is wrong with the rest of him.) He told me his mother and father want us to be happy here and they know it isn't so easy. I only laughed, thinking "Happy!" "I'm a long way from happy," I told him "but that is probably to be expected." I didn't really want it to seem like anybody's fault when it probably isn't. Then he went to bed, giving me a very long look but without saying anything else.

Then It Happened. I was going to take a shower. And there was a figure out in the backyard in the dark, and it was looking in! Its shadows sort of rippled across the glass. I put my clothes back on and went running out. By that time Jessie and Teddy were coming in and I could see Teddy didn't believe me at all. To be 100% honest I can't say I am so sure. But there was something moving before I closed the curtains and what else could it have been? Some man, probably a neighbor or their son on the lawn, and I was a white girl and there was every bit of my white skin showing. And I didn't want to tell Andy, I think I would die of embarrassment first.

Well, it is so clear Teddy doesn't have any patience for me. It isn't like Daddy who could get angry at more things than you could ever imagine, because Daddy had this thousand Rules and he would usually be upset because you broke one. Teddy you can't predict. Why was it my fault? There was somebody out there and I was holding my clothes in my hands!

So Jessie got on my side. This is very familiar, I have been through it already and I am an expert at seeing it happen. Actually I thought I heard that fathers and daughters have sort of a special thing about each other (Eodipus?) but you would never know it in all the houses I go into not only me but my friends too, their fathers are the ones who get on them and ride them about Infractions (Daddy's word). Some don't like their moms too, but my mom, I almost wrote "is"—was always fine except when he had all of us afraid. Which was all (most) of the time. I remember once when my african violet died I was sure he killed it yelling. If you can make a plant grow by talking to it and saying nice things, who says it can't be scared to death too.

But anyway, Teddy. I can see him get this disgusted look that says All women. Leave me alone. I will be glad to. But I don't want her all

*friendly just because she has her problems with her husband. Leave me
out of it too. I am not here to help them in their arguments together.
(Like, I'm not sure Jessie believed me either about the peeping Tom but
she wasn't telling Teddy.) I will never trust any man because from what
I see they make all women sneaky.*

Jessie woke at about two-thirty and lay listening to a radio playing at
full volume—maliciously? indifferently?—in a house across the yard.
Whichever it was it made her angry. Someone who worked late or didn't
work at all. Maybe they should all move to Maine or North Dakota, now
that they were leaving here: some place where they would all free-float,
exiles like Helen and O'Neill, where questions of color would never arise.
If they moved to Quebec they could all be hated together for not being
French. . . . WOKJ came across the fence in a scatter of sounds, mostly
saxophone. She saw Teddy and Skelly Washington sitting head to head
over the two-way radio in the Freedom House—the same scatter of sounds
sometimes, if there was interference, that weird mix of bands that made
you feel crazy, smooth blend of unrelated conversations, popping syllables
like spliced tape. Like throwing pebbles of sound and watching them hit
the ground and scatter. Shatter and scatter. Used to feel like they were
locked up on a submarine together, Teddy would say. None of the women
touched the machines unless they happened to be the only ones around.

Where the hell was Skelly now? Los Angeles, when last heard from.
Gone so Christian he must tack himself to a cross to sleep nights. The last
time they'd spoken to him, he had called to plead with Jessie to convert.
Had threatened. Had offered to come by—you'd think he was around the
corner—and bring pamphlets. "Sounds like you're selling insurance, Skell,"
Teddy had said, trying to laugh.

"I *am*, man. I *am*. Don't you laugh at me. This is the *only* insurance
policy. You got this, you don't need nothin else. Jesus's the best policy
anywhere in town."

"Is it my imagination or does it sound like you're wearing a jacket and
tie? Skelly?"

He laughed his old laugh, close to the ground, warm in his throat. Skelly
was small, built dense as a fist; even his hair hugged his head tightly,
efficiently, a cap to be worn in all seasons. "Sound like you can see me—
my uniform, man. I got to meet strangers out on the corner, I got to look

convincing. Decent." Skelly had gone years with one pair of jeans and a
dungaree jacket that had taken his shape; they could stand without him in the
room, cracked and softened and capable like the skin of his weathered hand.

"But meanwhile, man, that Jewess you living with. You got a Jewess
the mother of your children."

Dorothea Carll would say that too. Teddy told him to stop. Told him
another word and he would hang up.

"But I'm talking to you for your good and hers, before it's too late and
there's no turning back. This is the revolution, that other stuff was just
toolin up."

Where would he be now? At Eldridge Cleaver's right hand? Feisty,
angry, would he have walked open eyed into a knife in a barroom? Dropped
the pentecostal flourishes and taken up selling real insurance with cash-in
privileges?

Whoever had turned on the radio doused it now, one long dying squawk
of static. The old Skelly, the other cowboy, in his disintegrating straw
farmer's hat, smiled at his partner the way he had always smiled, like a
little boy, all the way past his pointy dog teeth. He is so long gone, Jessie
thought—they are—so never-was, in memory, they might as well be a dream
or dead.

. . .

O'Neill sat on the edge of Andy's bed, glowing, his arms pulled tight
to his body as if a single movement might upset a delicate balance. Andy
was rummaging through a desk drawer whose clutter reminded Jessie that
he was, thank God, far from perfect. "I'm giving him my stamp collection,
is that okay?"

"Of course. Why not?"

"Is it a—like a *real* collection?" O'Neill asked. "Or is it all Canada and—
did you send away for everything?"

Andy pulled a whole overflowing drawer out and carried it to the bed.
"No, it's got lots of cancelled stamps that really came through the mail.
African and all kinds of European. Look, Mexico. We've got friends all
over."

"I have some of my grandpa's from Germany, but that's all." O'Neill
sent Jessie a look of transport and then turned back to his cousin. There in
the circle of Andy's light and effort he sat, all his edges turned in. Andy's
approach, the logical one, was to try to keep a number of balls aloft at once,
each recreational, big brotherly: stamps today, a promise of softball tomorrow and before they went to bed—Jessie groaned and removed herself

from hearing distance—a belching contest for big stakes: Andy had a Reese's for the winner, to be adjudicated by the two disgusted sisters, who squealed and covered their ears. When O'Neill won (forty-three) he stood perfectly straight like a choirboy, his eyes squeezed shut for better concentration. The girls tore out of the room making retching noises. When Helen came upon Teddy in the hall she turned an extravagant pink, then a more worrisome white like a slapped cheek and ducked away, murmuring apologies.

. . .

Jessie looked for the hallmarks of misery and strain in the children. She did not know where to look: they were other people's children after all, and though every thirteen-year-old or eight-year-old had certain habits in common, there was no such thing, she knew well enough, as the generic child. Some of their idiosyncrasies were of no significance and she let them pass without comment. O'Neill insisted on rising from his bath to clean off the dirt of his own bathwater with a quick shower. Helen wanted baking soda for her toothbrush instead of toothpaste. O'Neill was faithful to his habit of forgetting at least one necessary thing when he left for school with Jessie and Lydia in the morning. Helen could not eat breakfast comfortably, she said it stuck in her gorge.

It was the larger questions that dogged Jessie: O'Neill could concentrate on play but not on work. His capacity to read came and went like the sun in winter. He picked fights and then blamed anyone in sight for landing the first blow; yet there never seemed anything dangerous in his anger, he seemed to be playing with mock violence as if it were another diversion, a toy.

One morning Andy found him standing at the end of the kitchen rapping with his knuckles on the cabinet door as if he expected to be admitted. He told Andy that he liked the sound his fingers made, thick and hard and final. But Andy watched him strike every wooden surface as he crossed the living room and duly reported to his mother his suspicion that his cousin had a fetish. Jessie, scrutinizing him, could never catch him at it. Either a single day of heavy superstition had assuaged his hunger for protection or he was watching Jessie watching him and would not be captured.

In general the children were scrupulously polite to each other. O'Neill tended to be sillier and noisier outside his sister's line of vision, and Helen more remote, sealed into her envelope of self; together both seemed to breathe more evenly, O'Neill to keep his voice down, Helen hers up. She bossed him, as Lydia liked to put it, sensitive to the weight of an elder on her own helpless shoulders. But O'Neill, who didn't accept much direction from anyone else who was not unequivocally adult, rarely balked when she ordered him to do (or more often, not to do) something. Probably, Jessie told Lydia, he likes to have someone in his own family caring about him enough to make demands. Lydia took that up: "Maybe when Helen bosses him it feels good, like a heavy quilt on you when you're cold." Oh, the chill wind blew through Jessie when she heard that, the wind of fear and danger that might ever separate her from her wonderful child.

But Jessie could see Lydia brace herself before she approached the Birmingham cousins. She didn't look jealous of her possessions, or of her parents' attention, she looked, more simply, vigilant and ill at ease. And she had been sleeping badly, her face soiled looking, smeared under the eyes.

Jessie took her downtown to the dentist one afternoon. Lydia held her hand like a younger girl and wanted to stand against her whenever the two of them were idle. "What is it, Lyddie—is something bothering you?" They were walking from the car to the dentist's building, which was called— Jessie was always amused when she said it—Magnolia Towers. What was she *doing* here?) Lydia looked chilled and miserable.

"No, I want to hold your hand is all. Can't I do that any more? Just because I'm not youngest now?" She took her hand back and put her fist in her parka pocket.

"Sure you can, honey. I love it. But I have a feeling—"

"Well, I don't like to go to Dr. Schmitz. I can't stand that rubber thing he puts in my mouth."

"But you've been looking queasy and not just now."

"What's queasy?" Lydia's eyes were everywhere; she wasn't listening. "The last time I told him I couldn't breathe with that thing all over my mouth he asked me if I was afraid of small rooms."

"Are you having trouble with Helen and O'Neill being around? Are you missing things the way they were?"

Lydia had pushed the heavy door open with all her strength and was holding it, breathless, for her mother. She said, "Oh—I guess it's strange to think they're not visiting. I mean we'll never be just *us* again. But . . ." She kept her head down and her eyes averted.

"But?"

"But it's what I—oh, you'll get mad and I don't blame you, I'm horrible, the things I think, I'm selfish and—"

"What, Lydia? Don't tell me what I'll think, let me decide that."

They had stopped in front of the elevator. No one, Jessie was relieved to see, stood with them.

"It's just that—" Lydia looked desperate. "They *scare* me. I'm sorry. . . ." She began to poke at her eyes, anticipating tears or stirring them up. "That's not very nice to them but it's like—I just lie awake at night and I think maybe, like, I'm going to catch bad luck from them somehow. And then what would we do? I can't look at O'Neill being crazy and—like, *happy*— or at Helen, when she's using my mirror or getting washed or something, or when she was trying to string her guitar—I'm sorry, I'm trying not to, but I keep thinking they're orphans, real ones, she's not a fairytale princess or something, they've got nobody, only us and we don't even know them, really. And maybe it could—" She looked away from her mother, in whose eyes she could behold, if she wanted to, the most uncensored fear for herself and for her children, a general moist forgiving pity. But it was true, Jessie thought, flinching: having the Birmingham cousins in the house was like feeling a continuous finger-touch of dire possibility on her own cheek, her wrist. They were reminders, scarred as Teddy was scarred by what had seared the flesh of their lives closed, rough, over a wound. If children were easy to love in their innocence, their—well, she thought, it was a form of emotional virginity, wasn't it?—then these children, victims of such brutal thievery, were all the more difficult to love when they needed love most. They could not be sufficiently provided for. Lydia, looking at them, put her fingers to her frail throat, afraid. She knew with other children that they shared her world; all of them guessed together, and some ignored, their futures. They spent hours engaging the outsize questions: what will you do? Where will you live? Who will you—this was occasionally supplanted these days, in sophisticated circles, by *will* you?—marry? And along came O'Neill and Helen and they were like the victims of rape or flood, strayed into the wake of adult catastrophe, still looking like children as if they were devious, hiding under their ordinary skin the flaying they had borne.

"Does Andy?"

Lydia stamped in her Chinese flats. "Oh, he doesn't care. I don't think he ever stopped to think one single time about how come they're living with us. He's just so busy being—" Lydia waved her hands in the air, and left her judgment hanging.

"Busy *being*," Jessie said, smiling. That would make sense: he was neither introspective nor vulnerable, but he was sensitive and sound. And he was always somewhere else. Like a father who gives gifts in place of himself, Andy had lately presented to O'Neill not only his stamp collection but his old baseball hat, a Chicago Cubs pennant he had mysteriously acquired, a splinted hockey stick and a clock he had once taken apart but never reas-

sembled, its parts carefully but uselessly husbanded in a box with a combination lock O'Neill was learning to open. He had promised O'Neill his
magic set on his birthday. But all that served beautifully, these were symbols
O'Neill loved and fit himself between. They bore Andy's warmth and the
impression of his admirable body and that seemed to be all the closeness
O'Neill wanted for the moment. Teddy he more or less ignored.

"Lyddie, I understand what you're feeling. You shouldn't hate yourself
for that." She put her arms around her daughter just as the elevator, sighing
and lunging, dropped down toward them and two panting teenaged girls
in flapping pea coats came through the lobby at a run to catch it. "We have
to really try, though, both of us, not to be frightened of something that
isn't their fault." She didn't know what to suggest: contamination by Fear
and Pity, what would the antidote be? Time? Dailiness? Maybe the slow
slackening of their own disgust at what had befallen them. (Helen's, she
amended. O'Neill was something else again, but Helen, she suspected,
harbored an instinct toward vaguely justified self-blame.) She would observe
it and try to hold Lydia's distaste back until Helen's dwindled; until, she
thought, Helen became herself again and not a freak bent out of shape by
premature sorrow.

.   .   .

Well, what, Jessie asked herself, prepared to argue for as many answers
as she could find, what *should* the life of a child be like? There was a generic
quality to the inquiry that made her shy back like a horse with a snake at
its feet. She was an intensely pragmatic person who had grown up in a
house which was as thick with dogma as a church; as a lapsed ideologue
she tended to steer clear of as many abstractions as she could.

She, for example, for all the peculiarity of her household, had not been
unhappy as a child. Only that she had pictures of Gus Hall and other pin-
up favorites of the Old Left taped to her wall the way most girls kept
baseball players or movie stars. Her friends in school had never heard of
her heroes or derided them if they had, but she loved to get a glimpse of
them at meetings or, best of all, walking to or from the door of, say, the
Manhattan Center: ordinary men in overcoats and crushed fedoras, who
crossed a threshold and were transformed into honored speakers rapturously
applauded at the podium. Sometimes their pictures appeared in the *Worker*
or the next day's *P.M.* And that was miraculous to her: that she had seen
the man in the humble flesh and here he was, shown around the world-at-
large in this shadowy form. People wanted to see him even in a poor gray
copy made of dots and spaces.

She had spent so many hours of her childhood with the backs of her calves pressed hard, for coolness, against the gray metal folding chairs of Union Square meeting halls. The wooden floors in all those upstairs lofts reminded her, in a logical confusion of senses, of Klein's, which was downstairs on the Square—that hideous, nauseating weight of three dozen winter coats tried on in search of a good heavy bargain. (Her children would never understand, she loved to tell them, how the nylon parka was a breakthrough that brought them greater personal comfort than anything Galileo had ever done for them!) But she had made the best of those evenings of rallying, analyzing, proselytizing: there was excitement and her family's peculiar kind of honor—it was probably what church felt like to Ann-Marie and Kathy, her Catholic friends, the conferring of a state of smug blessedness—to be found under all those woolen piles of words, if you could only dig deep enough. She loved to applaud the speakers, she would wake from a doze to hear someone's treachery being rehearsed or someone else's courage, just in time to stamp her feet and bounce exuberantly on her hard chair. From her early vantage point the only disadvantage of her parents' dedication to the Party was that her father came home late from meetings too many days of the week; not only did she miss his company but he ate reheated casseroles with crusts on them and she was the one who was left, fairly early on, to dig away at their caked sides with a Brillo pad.

What else, what else could she remember? Riding to the end of every subway line with him to see what was out there. His whiskers that grew so magically that she would run to him every evening to whisk her hand across his cheek just to feel the burn. Her father's irritability: it was only politics and Party matters that made him curse and rage to himself dramatically as if he were on a stage. He held arraignments and trials directed half to her mother, half to himself. He rarely began at the beginning, so that Jessie could never determine whether these were narratives of actual events or of events as Jack Singer would have had them. Jessie's mother treated these outbursts as if they were a periodic form of indigestion; she mumbled unintelligible comfort back but knew its limits and let him rave.

Those were times when he was unapproachable but it had to be remembered—this was part, now, of her lecture to herself—that children justify much more outrageous sins of their parents: fathers who take their little girls to bed, mothers who compete like playground rivals, behavior that is negligent or devious or intended to wound. How could she not have forgiven the occasional inattention of this passionate man who, standing at the door in the morning, would tell her he was sallying forth? Who was surely a genius and a savior of invisible people in uncountable numbers?

(He explained to her there was a difference between "people" and "peoples." His particular influence seemed to be on behalf of the peoples in the plural, who languished the whole globe over in the chains, also invisible, of tyranny.)

It was only the final inattention, the insult to their love for him, love in the singular—were they not as legitimate, the three of them, as any abstract Albanian family with half a dozen children?—that she would never forgive. It was the choice he had made, or allowed to be made for him, from on high, where the idea of family was a negligible inconvenience from which a man could be separated quite casually, that set the distance between them which the passage of years would never close. Perhaps it would have befallen them anyway as she grew and became critical. The pity of living only once is that there is no way, ever, to be sure which sorrows are inevitable.

The night before he disappeared he had tried to say something important. It was the first time he'd ever failed to utter a single word that made sense to her: what he was doing was—apparently—unutterable. He was so clumsy and earnest all he did was confuse and frighten her. It was a long time before she heard the word "underground," and just as well because, without the letters and little presents she began in time to stockpile, sent from postmarks that her mother told her were not correct, she'd have been certain underground meant dead and buried. But when he vanished she did not feel ambushed, taken by surprise. What she felt was betrayed: he had for the first time known something he hadn't wanted to tell her. Whatever was taking him away from them had begun by changing him.

That night, when she was nine, Jessie was lying on her parents' bed listening to the Cisco Kid. Her parents had the bedroom, she had the living room couch, but she was allowed to play in their room. Cisco was calling everybody hombres and his voice, which she heard on Monday, Wednesday and Friday, throbbed at the radio's lower registers, familiarly, comfortably, like her own father's. These days, in fact, she was hearing Cisco's somewhat more often: her father was on his way out to work at the print shop when she awoke in the morning; he was spending more and more time at Party meetings at night. When she kissed him on his bald head he looked tired but he pretended her kiss woke him and put him back on his horse, and straightened his saddlebags. If Jessie were to draw a caricature of her father as she remembered him from her childhood, it would be nothing but a smooth round skull, fringed with coarse hair, and a thin mustache of the kind that has gone out of style now except among certain suspect populations (the Spanish, the Arab) but which was a movie star special in the thirties and forties. (Inside the covers of Dixie cups, she could remember the vanilla and chocolate ice cream waveringly divided, how most of the sepia-colored faces of the actors had her father's mustache: Robert Taylor! Helmut Dantine! Brian Donlevy!) And then those muscular veiny arms under their patient tracing of cross-hatched, curly hairs. Her well-brought-up mother and those particular ropy arms. Her father and her mother Lizzie's pale skin, the clear nearly forbidding purity of her hair pulled back from her forehead, like an impossibly even shoreline seen from a great distance. . . .

Her father had come into the bedroom just as Cisco told Pancho the poisoner of cattle was loco but he wouldn't get to hurt any cows again. Half the evil connivers on the show were loco; a few were desperate because their wives or children were sick; that left a small remnant for pure unmotivated greed. Jessie wondered if these were the proper proportions in New York City or only on the range and in the badlands, whatever they were, where no one had been scolded in the name of Marx and Engels. She wondered if her father, had he lived in olden days, would have been like Cisco.

"Jess," her father had said in a voice peculiarly weightless. She wanted to put her hand on his forehead, he sounded warm and sticky, but she felt constrained to let him say what he had come to say. It had been another late evening at work; his dinner had waited, crusting over; her mother had muttered about his bosses, who were milking him dry. Who would be "the first to go," Jessie wondered, the bosses or the landlords?

Her father asked her a few questions about her day, her friends, her schoolwork. He kept his hand on her arm, though, as if to prevent her, physically, from leaping into detail; she could tell when he was only pretending to listen. When she told him about her trading card collection, toward which she showed an unbecoming covetousness, making deals and trading up like an experienced capitalist, he frowned. He hated Monopoly and this was only another variation. Later, she would respect his fervor; but now Jessie alternated between guilt and irritation. She had a friend in school who came from a very orthodox Jewish household, and she felt the same alternation when she heard the details of Hannah's life: belief, impatience—the prohibitions! the anxiety! the familiar pleasures! When your parents were *believers*, there were so many ways for you to end up in the wrong. . . . Nonetheless, Jack Singer politely listened. She didn't know much about why grownups feign attention, but she could feel the absence, the place held open by his own concentration, like an empty room somewhere between his asking and her telling. Her words came back to her unheard.

Then he said something uncharacteristically sentimental. She was alarmed by the tenderness of his words because he was always direct, cured to a leathery hardness. "Jess, you know, you're the only reason I ever knew that could make me want to stay home from work a long time and just play with you. Be here with you."

She had found this an odd and, much as she loved him, a not altogether pleasant idea. Her father playing jacks? Making deals for her trading cards? These werethe days when the only fathers who played with their children much were disabled, or "charming good-for-nothings," which usually meant drunks who couldn't hold a job. She laughed because she didn't want to hurt his feelings. She wanted to ask him, please, what was going on, why he, who was always so careful to be understood, had stopped making sense, but he was talking faster and faster. Or she only remembered it that way, like dominoes tumbling forward, pushed from behind, unresisting. He was spinning a veil to put between them. She clung to his hand—*what if*, he was asking, *what if*, and then *what if*—and she let herself be embraced roughly and held, while Jack Singer looked over her shoulder into the middle distance, which was a wallpapered with baby blue Irish harps.

He was a father vigorously possessed of opinions, but rarely did he burden her with homilies. He spent a great proportion of his waking hours in the company of argumentative friends and family, comrades who conducted themselves like affectionate enemies, sat at the round wooden kitchen table and bickered and guzzled tea. Stalin, Truman, Ike, Korea and Palestine-turned-Israel. Many unnamed insults and injuries called "compromises" and "sellouts." They were not people anyone would give advice to, they could take care of themselves: they took care of unions, didn't they? Of locals, of strikes and rallies, occasional subpoenas. Uncle Moe was a blacklisted phys. ed. teacher from City College who had a job as a waiter. Lenny Moskowitz had been in jail at Dannemora and was not considered a convict but a hero. Aunt Faye used shocking langage to describe the behavior and the deserved fate of most of the world and then turned to Jessie, who was helping serve, to accept a Danish—"Only a half, mommele, cut a little piece off that for me, will you?" with sweet composure, smoothing Jessie's unruly hair.

There was a tiny Italian man name Gia-something—Giacarlone?—who once brought over a kettle of spaghetti that smelled foul to Jessie, who had never encountered Parmesan cheese; recently there were matching twins from Kentucky who looked like dry twigs and spoke about coal miners all the time. These were the people who filled the evenings of Jessie's days. When she was grown she asked herself whether she had known them, really, or had only seen them in the movies and imagined them back into her life.

Either more people seemed, on the surface, stereotypes or, after so many years, she had drawn in the real faces with clichéed features. Had there really been a melting pot right there in her kitchen on West Eleventh Street? Only when she saw her Mississippi friends in the news, and recognized that peculiar *rightness* they had about them—as if they had been well cast in the parts of themselves!—Skelly, Varona, Fannie Lou Hamer, Amzie Moore—she understood how it was the power of their visible roles, the real occasions for their heroism, like giant outlines against which they, smaller, stood that enlarged them into myth. So she kept her small band of mythic comrades in her mind, half as they were, half as their position in her life demanded them to be. And how, she wondered, did they keep their own day-to-day reduced selves? Gracelessly, like Teddy?

Jack Singer had seemed to conduct these voices as if they were an orchestra, changing subjects and calling on people to say what they thought or ignoring them and talking about them after they went home. She got the feeling that new visitors were being given a test but that no one had warned them first: they passed or failed innocently. The ones she never saw again probably got zeroes.

That happened once with a newcomer, a handsome young Negro man with a high peaceful forehead that Jessie kept her eyes on—it was like something in a painting, serene and saintly. But the man himself was high strung and tried to talk endlessly about the special problems of the colored people. She had never heard some of those things before. The very air in the room seemed to vibrate with her father's irritation. Everyone shouted the man down. "No distinctions, no special citizens, not even any nationality!" her Uncle Moe had cried out, waving his arms as if he were leading them in the Internationale.

"The first thing, look, religion separates," her father had said very patiently, in a patronizing tone he never took with her. "What does Jessie learn when she goes up there to P.S. 2? She comes home the first day of school with a complete list of differences like a guide to a flower garden: 'In this row we've got Jews, in that row Catholics. We have a Protestant teacher and the man who cleans up after school is a Negro named Mr. Naglie and he always shouts at us to pick our papers up off the floor, so everybody calls him Mr. Nigger.' " They fought over this for a while, Jessie's father and his friends crying out for the abolition of all distinctions and the Negro (whose forehead turned out to have as prodigious a capacity for worry wrinkles as her grandmother's, whereupon he lost all his specialness for her) arguing for tolerance of differences, encouragement of differences. "We are equal but that don't mean we're the same, that's two altogether different things." They had him outnumbered. A sour belligerence floated on the atmosphere between them—what was the difference between the times when they were amiable about their beliefs like people playing stage roles, when they seemed to agree to disagree, open handed, and this, a fight with real fists? Was it that they thought the Negro man was different from them even though they didn't believe in difference? How could that be? The whole argument, she had thought, would be something just next to lying.

Jessie sat on her customary stool, leaning on the wooden counter, pretending to do her spelling homework or her arithmetic, and when there was a half-second lull in the argument for the drawing of breath and the redeployment of ideas, she ventured, "But Daddy, even if Mr. Naglie came and told us he wasn't a Negro any more nobody would believe that. Not even the dumb little first graders."

Everyone had laughed, her mother and Aunt Faye had exchanged looks of pride, although Jessie thought her remark true, not funny. Worst, her father had applauded. He liked her to disagree with him, he talked about it as if it were good exercise, but the kind without a destination. Running barefoot in sand. She wanted to be right; apparently that was something hard she wasn't quite ready for yet. Or it was something they didn't like children to be. But she was in training.

One thing she was right about, though: something was peculiar. The day after their uncomfortable talk in the bedroom, her father was gone. At the door, after school, she heard a dramatic sweep of organ music, disaster time on "Helen Trent." Her mother was supposed to be at work in the principal's office at the junior high on Ninth Avenue. Right about now she would be hanging up her Mother Hubbard and punching out on the time clock. "Wait, wait," the music seemed to be saying as she turned the key in the lock. "Worse and worse," it cried. She came through the vestibule and saw her beautiful mother at the kitchen table, the blood drained from her face. When Jessie stopped to figure, many years later, she discovered that her mother was in her mid-thirties when her husband fled into that middle distance he had been studying in the wallpaper of the bedroom. That pale skin of hers, that almost forbidding purity that Jessie envied, turned out merely to have been that of a young woman—how could a man leave a woman as good and beautiful as her mother? It did not seem possible.

Jessie stood in the middle of the linoleum in her short white socks and her navy blue windbreaker with her hands in her pockets trying, since she could not be delicate and lovely, to look like a longshoreman. (She had her father's face and nobody's body.) She was told, implausibly, that her father had gone on a trip. That left her mother's tears to be explained. He had abandoned them, clearly, and her mother was going mad with grief. They were going to move, she said. This is a long trip, the one he's on. She held Jessie's hand and seemed to take support from it herself. Brooklyn might be a nice place to go; Aunt Faye was finding them an apartment as close to Prospect Park as she could. Everything was going to be all right. He loved her, he had said to tell her so. Her mother even smelled different: it was either fibbing or crying that smelled strange to Jessie—a sharp electric odor surrounded the two of them as if there were some wires, wires of connection, perhaps, or wires that conducted heat from body to body, burning where no one could see them.

.   .   .

It was a paradox, a fortunate one, perhaps a defensive one, that out of sight, her father began to lose his absoluteness for her; he was drawn back into the haze of relative judgment. And relatively speaking, she decided at twelve, when he came home from his pointless hiding, he was a fool. Or he was easily prevailed upon to take himself too seriously—a different kind of fool. These were, without a doubt, her mother's categories, which she had heard in an undertone like a language registered in sleep, osmotically, on one of those under-the-pillow tapes. She was not about to accept without irony the Central Committee's conviction that social justice—Revolution!—demanded her father's absence from her for two years. Whatever reality the world possessed, when her father went underground she began to see the entire plot as a fiction, a conspiracy whose sole end was to ruin her happiness and her mother's. One man, an ordinary one whose whiskers grew ferociously every day when he was at work, who picked his teeth with the corner of a folded-over matchbook, who always forgot to put down the toilet seat when he was finished with it, much more ordinary than the Famous Speakers, that one man who was not Gus Hall or Bertrand Wolfe (Jack Singer's picture had never appeared in any newspaper!) could not serve the world better out of sight than in it.

What, precisely, did his flight preserve? The skins of others, who did not have to flee? He would have gone to jail, her mother said. We'd have lost him anyway, for longer. We'd all have been ruined. Sacrificed. He'd have been another hero-convict, like Uncle Lenny Moskowitz, Robin Hoods in baggy work-clothes. Thus had she been the grieving Madonna the day of his leaving. But she was angry at him too. Her anger was greater by far than Jessie's, because it was not diluted by bewilderment—and it became the medium in which they both lived, breathing but not thriving, like fish moving dully through stagnant water. Just at the moment when ideological zeal might have sustained her, Elizabeth Singer's blinked out, a vital source of power gone. They huddled, in their new basement apartment on Eastern Parkway—Aunt Faye had been as good as her word, they were near the Park—but for a long time Jessie was too depressed to go outside. It must have been a month before her mother dragged her, sullen and slow, like a toddler having a tantrum, up to the obscene statue—naked soldiers—at Grand Army Plaza. What was she doing locked in the house? She strained to remember. Was she trying to be "underground" too?

Her mother had had to drag herself back to Manhattan each day until she could find a job closer to home. Jessie had no idea how she managed the absurd cloak-and-dagger secrecy of her husband's absence—probably she never mentioned it, or she made up a story of divorce or a serious illness to account for her red eyes, her fatigue, the look of devastation that Jessie remembered best, that yellow-tinged pallor the exact color and frailty of paper white narcissus. Jessie would be home from school—her new school— long before her mother emerged from the IRT. She would return from marketing, arms full of groceries the two of them could only plod through slowly, with the appetites of self-punishing depressives. Jessie had no curiosity about the neighborhood; she did not want to make friends to whom she would have to tell elaborate lies, and then (she had gotten caught up in enough white lies to know) have to concentrate to keep them consistent. It took less energy to be alone, and energy was what she could no longer spare.

She pictured her father locked in a room somewhere—Pennsylvania was her choice although she could never say why; it sounded distant and deep in woods to her, pine groves of very tall thick trees that admitted no ordinary sunlight, only a Hansel and Gretel sort of forest gloom, mushroomy and dense—and she thought she might be able to imagine with all her power what he did with his time and do it too. She built houses out of her trading cards, which had lost, overnight, all their value as social currency. She slept. She studied her fingernails, saw they were becoming delicately ridged, like the embossed paper napkins they used at dinner, and remembered that someone in school had told her, once, that ridges were a sure sign of vitamin deficiency. The same messenger of doom had demonstrated for her what the jagged sound of pneumonia breath was like; she spent a long time each day testing her breathing, hoping for the worst. How could it be, she wondered, that her father had not been the hub of her life, and yet his absence deranged the whole wheel as it yearned to roll evenly forward? Not having recognized their existence before, suddenly she had no motive power and no steady direction. She had needed him there so that he could be invisible, was that it? All the forces balanced evenly? That was just possibly a definition of security. A negative definition. Not plausible—this she was thinking now, having thought nothing then but how uninteresting everything was under the gray wash of her listlessness.

She and her mother pretended Jack Singer was dead, when they spoke to their new neighbors, freshly dead, to account for their general air of dishevelment and depression. They did not "mix," as Aunt Faye put it. Elizabeth Singer disappeared from rallies and Party meetings as surely as if she too had buried herself alive, nor did her old friends follow her to Brooklyn to see her. This she alternatively interpreted as prudence for her sake and prudence for their own. It made her even angrier.

Why hadn't he taken them along? All Jessie ever got for answer was a punishing look as if she were hurting her mother intentionally and could stop if she only chose to. But she needed to know, was he *doing something*, some important job, in which they might participate inconspicuously, or *doing nothing*, merely hiding, from which they would distract him? Would he simply arrive in their living room one day like Rip Van Winkle, rubbing a hundred years of sleep from his eyes with his fists?

Because she had been promised by her mother that he would return. He wrote her casual cryptic letters behind those misleading postmarks that continued, oddly, in the vein of their final meeting in the company of Cisco Kid, as if she were a tiny girl to whom he had never spoken about Lenin and Trotsky, revisionism and the Hitler-Stalin pact. He seemed to have forgotten that she was ten years old, and then eleven and even twelve. Distance and his own desperation appeared to have diminished her, in her father's eyes. Probably he needed the sentimental perfection of her babyhood. Probably he felt, even if he did not think, that when he came back to them he would not find her aged; changed; independent.

But he did come back, and she had always known he would, otherwise she could never have been so guiltlessly angry. Jessie and her mother strengthened themselves on their anger, battened on it as if it could restore their strength. He had excluded himself from their life for the sake of an idea whose time had not come and perhaps should never come; obedient to the order of people they had never known; so much the worse for him. Wars separate families, Elizabeth Singer told her daughter, but no one calls them good. Necessary, maybe, but necessary evils. Your father is a cipher, a nothing, a clerk in the order of things. He is being sacrificed. All the cowards have scattered and they have taken their slaves with them, for fear the slaves will tell stories on them. *He could have said no. He could have said, If I go, my wife and child go too. We could have gone away somewhere, all of us, until they forgot about him.* They made this decision whimsically—

Jessie thought from the sound of that word that it had something to do with music. And he did not refuse.

So they struck out into their nonpolitical life like nuns who have quit their convent. The board of education was not cooperative and would not arrange a transfer to the office of any Brooklyn school, so Elizabeth Singer found a job selling robes and underwear at Abraham and Straus, where she was given a discount on everything she bought. She approached this perquisite as if it were a personal gift whose giver would be offended if she did not take advantage.

The two conspirators began to amass goods—if anything, Jessie feared the giver of the gift might take her mother's employee discount card away from her for abusing her privileges. At first she had to be wooed: even for the girl who had lusted after "Blue Boy" and "Pinky," the best trading cards in anyone's collection, this sudden proliferation of clothes and furniture (a new set of rattan chairs, upholstered in orange and yellow flowers with a matching table and a marvelous giant silver candlestick lamp) felt exactly like what it was: intentional disloyalty to her father. This was a binge, she could tell that even at ten—the kind children indulge in when their parents are away—and it made her feel shaky and lonely for the old days, when no one gave much thought to what her father had always called ephemera. (She didn't know what the word meant but it implied contempt.) They had gone too quickly from not wanting what other people wanted to burying themselves under it so that now they felt all the weight of these objects but not their textures, none of their distinguishing charms. Jessie thought nervously about the winter coats she had despised at Klein's—how they had pressed her shoulders down and winded her with their practical weight. Yet she'd rather be there searching for a bargain that would last at least two years (big in the shoulders, and hope for a hem) than here in the oversized dressing room at A & S trying on yet another blouse that she didn't need. It was embarrassing; she could feel her mother's anxiety. "Here, try the one with the ladybugs," her mother would say, sitting on a stool. Only her heavy comfortable shoes gave her away as an employee, not an independent shopper.

"What am I going to do with another blouse? Who wants to wear *bugs*?"

"They're ladybugs, they're supposed to be lucky. You'll change more often, the way you're supposed to."

"There aren't enough days in the week."

They were walking on Jack Singer's grave. That was the meaning of Elizabeth Singer's preoccupied stride across the beige carpeted floor to the station of the cashier that was lit with a little bulb, a pair of children's blouses and a pleated skirt over her arm, with the defensive speed of a woman who fears she will be stopped, arrested perhaps, where she is not supposed to be. Who is prepared to brazen it out.

They also began to make forays into "the city" to do things together that Jessie's father would have called frivolous: Radio City and the Roxy. (Jessie bought a picture of the Rockettes for her wall.) They went to see "My Friend Irma" being broadcast at the CBS studios, where Marie Wilson stood very straight at her microphone wearing a blouse with a Peter Pan collar just like Jessie's, turning the pages of her script carefully, silently; where joining the audience to applaud on cue made her feel privileged and disappointed at the same time—it had never occurred to her that the audience was a calculated part of the act. But she hugged her mother's arm as they sat in a perfect vacuum of attention and tried not to cough or wriggle. This was nothing like a speech in a dim hall about Stalin, Hitler and Ribbentrop, although that audience too seemed to applaud on cue.

One time, just before Christmas, they even went skating at Rockefeller Center in new woolen slacks with rented skates, and her mother giggled like a young girl, caught somewhere between her authority and her ineptness. Afterwards, having decided that the hot chocolate in the café tucked back just outside the ice-rink was for "a different class of people," they walked on aching ankles down Fifth Avenue in a misty darkness that spun aureoles like tears around the lights but would not let down its snow. All of New York seemed to have gathered on this street to see the extravagant window decorations in the stores—it made Jessie mourn for all those lost years when she hadn't so much as dreamed such pleasures existed. She felt like an immigrant waking up, awed, in a land of milk and honey. For Jessie the afternoon, which had lengthened magically into evening, was an episode of high glamor, especially when it ended in the comfort of this populated darkness, but like every other thing her mother gave her these days, there was a suspect quality to it, waiting always like a depressing room she had to return to no matter where she'd been: that illicitness, that fevered devotion to having fun, when fun of this sort was, as religious prohibitions had it, "expressly forbidden."

Not that Jack Singer would ever have criticized what they did, even if he thought they were wasting money frivolously. (*His* family outings had always been intellectually nourishing and, not the least of their attractions, free.) But her mother urged her to write to him all the details of their good times, of their betrayal. Dutifully he wrote back that he was glad she was having fun, was getting out, was enjoying herself and not brooding that he wasn't with them. "That's guilt talking," Elizabeth Singer said bitterly. He did not say a critical word, nor did he tell her he felt left out or forgotten. ("He wouldn't dare," her mother said.)

Jessie would send her letter off to an address she knew bore no relation to her father's "whereabouts," as they said on "Sam Spade" and "Mr. Keene, Tracer of Lost Persons." It took an overwhelming effort, as if she were pushing a Prospect Park boulder uphill, to write a street address and try to picture the envelope falling through a real mail slot onto the floor, or slipping into the slit in a narrow brass box with a buzzer at the bottom, when she knew he was in another city altogether. Maybe someone would destroy it or worse, tear open the envelope and read it. She felt as if the real letter were a lie too—the real news went to him at his real address, in an imaginary envelope. She could get it to him by will alone, only he couldn't dare acknowledge it out loud. This was her matching disloyalty to her mother— that secretly, wordlessly, in her bed at night, she told him she was unhappy, that she disowned the matching skirts and blouses, the new radio, the extra playing cards, the hamburgers at luncheonettes. She had even bought her first banana split, an extravagance so huge and foreign she couldn't enjoy eating it. She wondered sometimes in a fit of guilty honesty whether she delivered these confessions—or at least unburdened herself of them—to keep on his good side because he would come home someday, or if she really was only trying to say she would rather have her father than a closetful of outfits and a whole box of soft-centered candies of her own: acknowledging the competition but awarding him the prize.

Eventually they relaxed into a steady rather uneventful life, the widowed wife, the half-orphaned daughter. It was only a life conspicuously without politics, with little outer dimension, as if news of the world might seduce them back or contaminate them with its complexities and its power to evoke bad memories and make demands. They read no newspapers, listened only to Gabriel Heatter on the radio.

Altogether they did not make coming home an easy thing for Jack Singer: he was going to suffer ill-at-ease among their dustable objects, as if he had penetrated the dormitory room of two college girls who rarely studied. Jessie had forgotten how serious her mother had been, how artificially she had plunged the two of them into this banality, all for the sake of dramatizing hurt. Except for Jessie's presence she had expunged him and his influence, had said to her own parents *You were right*, had laid herself down on the other side of the question What Has Value? Things she could buy had value. What a superficial renunciation it was, Jessie thought now, what a convenient erasure for a woman who had grown up in material comfort and denied it, with whatever misgivings, for conscience's sweet sake. Jack Singer's apostate wife.

But when he came home he too had had enough. He came back a civilian, as it were, his ties severed, his loyalties worn thin, depleted by distance. After all the justifying he had done to keep his ideals alive in spite of the revelations of the forties that had sickened and depressed him, he had been punished. His presence in the "dead file" of the Party after a while had become a self-fulfilling prophecy. He was, to them, like a drowned man. That they had been the ones to hold his head under did not change the fact: he was of no more use. There was no more Party for him, and only a corner of Union. He was on the way to being rotund, and a little bit shinier about the head than Jessie had remembered. He had a wary look, the outer edge of something vanquished in him: not that he had not led a life for two years—there were short-term jobs, there was apparently a woman, probably more than one, he made no secret of that. No one had inflicted celibacy on him. He had not lived in a cabin in a pine grove. He had been in Cleveland, Amarillo, Salt Lake City. But he had forfeited his high-spirited, idealistic, dedicated little family for something that had not happened, his wife was right. His dedication and sacrifice had gone unnoticed and unclaimed. He had allowed an unnatural break in the rhythm and when he sat down at the new Formica kitchen table and contemplated the self-satisfied small smile of his wife and on his daughter an angular face, her hair skinned back in a ponytail so that her features seemed to puddle up close to the middle, handfuls of breasts and even a voice with an unfamiliar inflection—that was Brooklyn—he knew he had made the one mistake of his life. They did not trust each other: he had abandoned them and in return, they had abandoned him. Anything could happen—they would let it. They had not waited. His devotion had repudiated them; they had repudiated his devotion.

Starting then (or for all she could know it, starting the day two years earlier when he left them) Jack Singer had the subtly diminished, invalided restraint of a man who had suffered a grave heart attack. He was active, he did not make public statements of regret, he railed and muttered and refused to cast a reformist vote, but there was something like a scrim between him and everything he looked at. He came home faithfully every evening from the print shop where he worked, like a man who has given up his mistress, but they would not have missed him had he lingered for a meeting. Jessie wondered if they were cruel but there was no way to trace her way back to see her father's face: he had passed from the center of her line of vision.

Jessie had always heard that a parent's dying, for a child, seems like a form of abandonment, intentional, unresisted. Leaving aside the positive attraction of heaven, it must seem impossible to kidnap a grownup who didn't want to go.

Two parents dying?

Did Helen and O'Neill think they were hideous children, then, who had frightened their parents away? That they didn't deserve to keep them?

She had always known that her father would come back: she could hate him purely. Meanwhile he sent her sandalwood soap, the first ball-point pen she had ever seen, Mexican jumping beans. Crackerjack love. What in the world did Helen and O'Neill know, or think they knew, or need? When they lay in their rainbow sleeping bags at night in this endless emergency shelter, did they listen hard and hear nothing in the air saying their names longingly, delivering an urgent message?

Because, for better or worse, Jessie thought, nothing was being said.

.　.　.

Jessie came upon O'Neill near the coat hooks at the close of school. It was a rainy day and he had, like all the rest, come in with his sneakers crusted with mud—whose mother insists on galoshes these days? Who even owns rubbers? He was patiently banging his shoe on the floor when she walked past him. When she crossed back he was scraping at it indolently, looking elsewhere. She opened her mouth to ask him if he was planning to stay the night when she saw what he was stalling openly, shamelessly, to study: Derrick's mother, a very tiny, very young blond woman in a pink slicker, whose hair mounded up like a pile of fresh plane shavings, tucking in Derrick's shirttails from behind. Her hands worked over his shoulders rapidly, he wasn't a boy but a bolt of something inanimate, and not very delicate, about to come undone; as if she were a cat mother whose kitten's fur needed an unsentimental sprucing. She turned him around abruptly.

Jessie watched O'Neill banging his sneakers together, his pace slowing to an irregular stutter. He stared at Derrick and his mother with his body very straight and stern, as if in resistance, arms remembering to move only once in a while. When they were gone (unceremoniously, without good-byes—typical) he held the soles of the shades-of-blue shoes together, perfectly still, a pair of cymbals that had made their gigantic noise, and he attentive, feeling the reverberation flow up his wrists into his arms.

At noon today I walked out of school. Nobody saw me. (Anyway, who would care?)

There isn't much around the school except houses but I didn't think

I could breathe any more in there so I walked up and down these dull streets for about an hour and then just went back and waited till the hall was full and slipped in. It is sweaty in school and the floor wax just comes up in my nostrils and feels greasy like lamb fat. I am beginning to recognize a feeling I always have. It is like when you have the flu and you can't find a comfortable position to lie down in or sit up, and yet it doesn't hurt either. It is: no place to rest and feel good. I don't know if that makes any sense but that is the best I can say it. So if someone says she is feeling grief that her mother is dead (I never said I would be sorry if my father walked off the edge of the world and disappeared, in fact I am quite happy and relieved), if they look for grief that is not at all what they will find. Not very dramatic. "Sorry."

There is (1) No place to put my clothes. I am tired of having boxes. When is my furniture coming by van? "When we move. There is no room here." Let them try to live like this in a box.

(2) No privacy. I don't hate O'Neill but I am going to. He gets up at night to pee. He breathes hard. He plays early in the morning, what's his hurry? He invites the jerky cat to sleep on him and then wheezes because he is allergic to him (her?). I know sometimes I'm not altogether fair to him because I admit it, I want him to grow up fast now so he can help me. But sometimes I know he takes advantage of being "the little one" and just fiddles around or does dumb things and I don't feel like I can do that because to them it is convenient that I grow up fast. They didn't know they were getting two little children, after all.

I'm going to have a nervous breakdown before we move. It is like a motel room here. At night sometimes Teddy sits and works at his desk and I have to pretend I don't want to go to sleep. "It's okay, I'm not tired." O'Neill sleeps right through. I feel like I always get to bed too late or get up too early. Altogether I wish I could think of some way to get out of here but I do not want to be one of those runaways who go to Chicago or New York and get into drugs and maybe worse, and have to "crash" any where they can. I am thinking of writing Judy Carmichael to take us back but if Jessie and Teddy found out I would be in some peck of trouble.

Andy talked to me again, he invited me in his room. He sat real close and first he told me, like about his other grandparents, how they used to be Communists and proud of it, but are not any more for some reason. I guess they finally saw the truth. Then I told him about mine, living in Germany, and Gran dying when I was pretty little. And how we were planning to visit next summer. Then he said, Remember, we

*have some grandparents that we share. It's sort of hard to remember that
actually—now that we have moved in with them (him and Lydia) they
seem more like strangers than like cousins who you like to know are out
there but you don't ever think about them much. I didn't even know
how my Mom's Daddy died till Andy told me—he just went away to a
conference in Biloxi—some kind of engineers—and they were staying at
his favorite hotel right on the Gulf and he ate a big company lunch (he
was round as a barrel) and they had a little free time so he went swimming. And that was when he had a Major heart attack right in the pool!
Which is too gross to think about, do you die first or drown first? Do
you sink or float there like a fish on top? But anyway, that was that.*

*Andy has this sort of half-crookedy smile he must have learned from
his father (or else it comes with his mouth), only it is more sad with
Andy, sheer nasty with Teddy who looks like it is wrung out of him
against his will by how stupid the whole world is (except of course him).
I said "Everybody in this family seems to go away and die out of sight."
I guess I sounded "bitter" but who could blame me. "It's like cats having
their kittens," Andy said and then looked like he wished he had never
tried to say anything funny on the subject.*

*So to make it up (I think) he asked me did it feel funny to talk
"casually" about dying like that and I said I didn't think about it any
more than he did when it was a grandparent or someone unless I knew
them well. "But your parents?" That is always first on his and everyone's
mind, they can't see me any more without thinking it. I said I couldn't
think of my parents as dead either but that was different. That I just
couldn't even if I tried. I said it isn't real to me, not as real as their life,
it is a blank idea if there is such a thing, and anyway if I make that
my one subject, like an obsession, I won't have any other life. And I
might as well have died too. So I just will not.*

*I also told him about Christ and how Christ is a bulwark against
pain. I have to say he didn't look very convinced. For one thing he is
$\frac{1}{2}$ Jewish! It is easy to forget, him being blond and not looking it. He
said Jessie's family never really had any religion they believed in, since
Communists are Godless I know, but it's there somehow. Like at Christmas I would see that some things made her uncomfortable. (But maybe
all religions would, Jewish too?) Still it's just like being colored is there
like a curse in your veins, even if you don't think of yourself that way.*

*I also asked him did he have any nigger friends. (I did not call them
that!) He said sometimes. "There is one boy you should meet, he is really
neat!" His name is Raney, I don't know why he is so neat but maybe I*

will some time and see for myself. I had to go. He touched my hand with his, sort of side to side, I don't know what it meant, it was more friendly than sexy, but he is the only person I have met here who makes me believe I might feel good again some time.

Being with Andy made me think about when Tim Knight kissed me after the time we went swimming. I don't know if you could call it a skill exactly but I think I am going to be good at that. He was surprised I knew all about kissing (French etc.) because he is a lot older and I never kissed anyone before. It was like that song in that show they did at the high school, it was just doing what comes naturally. I don't really think of Andy that way, more like a brother, but wouldn't it be funny if we ever got to like each other that way living so close to each other. Things like that do happen. It would be so convenient it would almost be like if we were married! (secretly)

They have this friend Andrea who is Negro, who is married to a white man, Tommy. No one here thinks that is the least little bit disgusting and anyway if I asked Andy, say, what could he tell me. You can't tell someone why you don't think something is horrible. O'Neill and I are reduced to giving each other these looks. I feel like a spy in the house. Even O'Neill sometimes surprises me, he is not particularly loyal. Jessie asked him would he go to somebody's house from school if they asked him—this was a kid named Willie Washington, very original, so three guesses! And he said "Oh sure Jessie. I would." Even Mommy never said we had to go far enough to be friends. I do not believe in self pity but I am very very alone here.

It was, inescapably, time to visit Dorothea, the single grandmother shared by all the children. Watching them dress in the morning Jessie felt distinctly unrelated to herself, let alone the rest of them. She sat on the high stool in the kitchen and sipped tea, receiving their requests for help and for judgment with a rare detachment. There were, she said to herself, a great many mothers who set out to have this many children, who did not feel it peculiar to be responsible for a third of a dozen haircuts, parkas, Dramamine pills, adjustments and satisfactions, not to mention the nether reaches of personality.

Teddy was out getting the oil changed in the newly annexed station wagon. His sister, who had been in charge of it, had run a tight ship of a household but her car, it was becoming clear, had suffered absent-minded neglect. Teddy said, "No comment," and narrowed his lips censoriously as he always did in the presence of routine feminine abuse of the automobile, which he considered a secondary sexual characteristic.

Jessie studied the traffic patterns, how the two girls did not consult each other over clothes, over anything; how, in fact, they gave each other a rather wider berth than their two narrow bodies demanded. Watching them, at different stages in their vanity, trying on and discarding shirts and sweaters, Jessie found herself thinking that the cousins actually bore a strong resemblance to each other in style if not in appearance: both, she suspected, were so afflicted with a conviction of their worth and of their worthlessness, simultaneously, or in relation to these judges but not those, to that standard but not this, that they bore themselves—their slight bodies—like precious liquids in a shallow bowl. She knew her own daughter well enough to recognize that Lydia's constraint was unnatural, an ostrichlike performance intended either to discourage her cousin's approach or to deny her existence altogether: if I do not move she will not see me. If I do not speak she will go away. Lydia alone on a morning such as this would have hurried around the house locating lost socks and trying on hair ribbons, singing with, at, the radio noisily, bothering her brother. This morning she dressed with the preoccupied gravity of a bride. Helen did the same, her back to all of them, her face to any and all mirrors.

O'Neill got himself dressed in his corduroys and a yellow alligator shirt and sat down on the couch with a comic book. His legs stood straight out as if splinted. He did not look up until they were ready to go. When Teddy came back the boy made it clear he was affronted that the car had gone anywhere without him. "I even know what kind of oil it takes, the station wagon and the Corvette aren't anywhere near the same!" He gritted his teeth, half-serious. He would like to have dared to be serious. "I bet you went and put in the wrong kind."

Teddy apologized. The truth was, he had forgotten he had this new son. Andy hadn't followed him around for years, and he had put behind him the blessed irritation of moving always with that shadow that hung just in back, beside or in front of him, that buzzing swarm of activity and questioning. "The car needs a tune-up, you can come in with me next week," Teddy said to make amends.

"Maybe." O'Neill shook out his comic book as if he were opening up a paper bag, mimicking and mocking the adult gesture at the same time. Sometimes he wore his precociousness disconcertingly like someone in drag, who was and was not what he seemed; who had contempt for what he longed to be. "I'll come if I can." Teddy looked at Jessie and then at heaven above.

But it was Andy who fascinated Jessie. He came out of the bathroom looking furtive, his clothes a shade neater than usual—he had just begun to make very specific demands of whoever folded the wash fresh from the dryer: the creases in his khakis were becoming a preoccupation. When Jessie stood near him she discovered the cause of this morning's odd self-consciousness.

It was aftershave (though he didn't shave yet, and, fair as he was, would not for a long time), a bottle Dorothea had given Teddy last Christmas, blue as peacock's blood, in glass the shape of a full-rigged galleon or a pirate ship. Its smell clotted in the nostrils like ether.

Jessie felt, watching him walk the full length of the house with a peculiar tense gait, as if his tremendous feet had been bound like a Chinese lady's overnight, that he was changing before her eyes, growing plumage—or, rather, just out of her sight behind the bathroom door. It was as momentous as the loss of virginity, she thought, shocked: the day he could feel himself looked at (pray God, appreciatively) by a girl. Or the day he *wanted* to be. That would make Helen something like a spy, willful or otherwise, in their midst: a presence forever felt, even when it didn't try to be.

She turned her mug over in the sink and watched the cold dregs pour out, color of bourbon. *I am an innocent*, she thought, *mother of innocents. I am not ready to let him join in that dance yet*. No wonder the boys at the junior high thought him a child—he was only now becoming half a child.

And maybe, she thought, Teddy was right, almost right, about Helen and that prowler: what she really felt was not a stranger skulking around the back lawn but her cousin in his room, lying stretched on his bed like a victim, staring at the thin wall no more than a membrane between them.

FOUR

Teddy had always had to court his mother, to solicit her good feeling. This was sheer habit on Dorothea Carll's part, a style to which she had become accustomed early, that overrode every expectation of fortune or status in her life. She was the youngest sister of four, called Sissie in fact, and she had been spoiled almost by formula: if eldest sons expected the kingdom, youngest daughters kept the imprint of the crown on their tender flesh.

Teddy's childhood had been a ritual of carrying her bags and baskets, dragging out chairs for her, spreading blankets, dusting off benches. The first time he saw a full-dress opera he recognized that space the others kept clear around the soprano's long wide skirts: it was the self-same empty ring that had moved with his mother, and kept her loved but slightly remote. She was blond and tall and had been lovely, sharp featured, pointy nosed and pointy chinned, with bright full flushed cheeks that seemed to belong on a lusher woman, and a full wide mouth—her looks were emphatic and inconsistent, and to further confuse things she spoke and acted like a vague pastel girl whom confusion did not embarrass; in fact she seemed to think it becoming. Now, reduced by her stroke, she still seemed tall, even in her wheelchair; her height had never been in her legs. Her features still bore the strength and regularity belied by her behavior. (Her mother, Teddy's Grandy, had ridden herself forward through an unpleasant life with the sharply cut unrelenting profile of a ship's prow carved to look human. She had been a strong woman whose favorite activity was "taking steps"—she took steps about every situation that displeased her. Perhaps belles, like ambitious businessmen, alternated generations.)

The stroke had only accentuated in Dorothea the torpidity and dependency she had always indulged. Secretly Jessie had thought she must be the most wickedly happy of women, the kind who will admit to no joy but who cannot help but experience it, great draughts and gobbles of it, because everyone, helpless, is doing for them exactly what they ask. If people earned their ends (and Teddy rejected her contention that they did: his father had died in an instant, apparently, an indifferent sort of death about which nothing could be said except that, characteristically, he had bothered no one and had not been forced beyond his sunny disposition into profound contemplation)—then Dorothea Carll had tailored her illness to her needs. She was waited on hand and foot because it was hand and foot—right and partial left—of which she had lost the use.

Teddy and Jessie had been at her house a few months ago in the sticky days at the close of summer, minus the children. Aunt Tush, as always, had been in harness: nurse, hostess, companion. She was like the one sister in a family who has been given to the church because she was judged—somehow, for reasons long since made obscure by virtue of her indispensability—dispensable. The one small, frail bird among them, she made her sister Dorothea look like an eagle. She had never married, had never gone away, had worked for many years in a law office through successions of partners, devoted to each in turn, silently, impartially, with a half-smile of approval or expectation. Teddy, growing up, advanced from an early apprehension that Aunt Tush was a saint to a later one that she was a "sap"—that was a big word then—and had finally watched his opinion stop, wavering like the spun dial on a game of chance, somewhere on the line between admiration and disgust at her acquiescence. And if he didn't comprehend her motives for living a life of endless ill-rewarded availability, he was certain that she made it possible for Dorothea Carll to go on being vague, demanding, invincible.

Tush was at the door nearly before Lydia had raised her finger to the bell. She beamed at them without words and bent to look full in the children's faces—for Andy and Helen she didn't have to bend at all—and murmured melodiously the way a wood duck does, deep in her pendulous throat.

They all trooped in to see Dorothea, who sat in front of the broad living room window frosted with light. She was faced to look out, so surely she had seen them arrive, but she did not turn to them as they came in to her. By now—her stroke long since having settled such deficits upon her so that if it hadn't begun so it was as much a state of mind as a condition of body—she didn't seem to mind drifting, being caught looking at the wrong thing, asking the wrong question, forgetting what she had just said. These lapses were probably, her doctor explained, the result of genuine misfirings and blockages in the brain, numerous tiny strokes that flicked away at her connections, loosening them rather than ripping them full out. But they were so familiar, so—consistent—that Teddy was sure there was a fraction of the willful in her refusal to connect and stay connected. Whenever he alluded to what she called "the troubles," as if they were in Belfast, a shooting, a jailing, an action of his own that she despised, her eyes began a slow float to the farthest wall.

She turned her large head toward them now, over her shoulder, her body in its chair still facing out as if at a second-string family of children and grandchildren. Teddy bolted in front of the crowd of them and put his arms around her shoulders, bending at the waist. "My baby," she said into his plaid shoulder, "my baby." Alexis, he knew, was the baby she meant, and had not had a fair chance to say goodbye to. What he had told her on the phone from Birmingham she had barely seemed to comprehend; when he had called her from home to see how she was assimilating the news she had seemed disconcertingly cheerful, as if the worst had passed, perhaps in her sleep. She was blank but steady. Her voice no longer had the flexibility to contain emotion; it was a monotone and moved in constraint, like her body.

Now, crying against his chest, her immobile body hard as a tree, she caused her son to look overcome for her: though he had lost something very different, his mother had in her way lost both her children, two out of two. Teddy and his alien wife, his alien friends, his doomed habits that would yield him up to the devil, holding the hands of his filthy black allies. And now Alexis, the good one, punished. "Why?" she demanded. "Tell me why."

"No reason," he whispered to her. "No reason, Mother."

"I'll tell you," she said bitterly. "It's to punish me. Haven't I been punished enough, Jesus? My husband gone, my legs gone, now my baby gone!" She looked at him as if he might have an answer that he was with-holding. Tush had got her gray blond hair nicely waved and her cheeks powdered so that the creases were smoothed; they looked the way clay looks when someone has raked it gently with a fork for texture.

"We've brought all the children, Mother," Teddy said, stepping back. It was a statement of fact and a warning to her to summon up some dignity. "They're doing real well, considering."

"Well, let me look at you, then," she said irritably, and turned to gaze on the huddle of them standing there looking accused and possibly guilty.

It was one of those moments that demand grace, when love is an un-protected emotion, a frail wire with no sheathing of convention to keep its heat in, or the air's chill off it. It was insufficient that they knew, in a general sort of way, that she loved them (grandmothers love their grand-children, especially when young). It was hard to look at her face, which had a twist to it not quite severe enough to appear the result of her illness. Instead she seemed implacable, dissatisfied, and what could they assume but that they were to blame?

Teddy, feeling foolish, stepped into the breach, scattering cheer broad-side. His mother didn't hesitate to place the burden of her self-centeredness on the children. Sorrow would be appropriate, even anger. But she, a woman of seventy-three, ought not to be their competitor for a sense of abandonment.

"Oh my dears," she said, ignoring him, looking from O'Neill's trapped eyes to Helen's, "your beautiful mother!" This could have been meant as consolation, Jessie thought. But no, it was again a cry of unsurmounted personal outrage: their mother had done something foolish and selfish—it was enough to make one stamp one's foot!—and she was not about to be forgiven for it. They looked more frightened than pained, and said nothing.

Excused, they bolted and were visible through the front window walking slowly down the street, Andy and Helen in front, Lydia and O'Neill behind, subject to distraction by odd bits of glitter on the sidewalk, in the gutter.

Jessie excused herself to see if Tush needed help in the kitchen. She prided herself on having contrived to spend the fewest possible moments in her mother-in-law's presence, but so skillfully, subtly, that she could never be accused of having fashioned an escape. In addition to her problems with Dorothea's self-centeredness, she found Teddy's answering mask of vivacity unnerving. He sounded like a man high on something that made him irresponsibly, inappropriately happy. Poor Teddy, there was no way to get through such a day intact.

The kitchen was as brightly lit as an operating theater. Jessie stood between the wall that held Tush's obsession with wrought-iron trivets, heavy and dark enough to be weapons, and the opposite wall that was dressed up in her prize-winning collection of crocheted potholders. There were little Aunt Jemimas in red dresses and white aprons with black pug faces that looked as if time were causing the disintegration of their solid bulk into lace. There was a painstaking version of a lattice-work state capitol building, and a full-color Ross Barnet hung by a long loop of yarn. Among the bulldogs and poodles dangled one pied brown spaniel head whose faithfulness was sewn into a permanent silver sparkle in his eyes.

Tush gave Jessie a short hug and looked at her with satisfaction.

"Oh dear," Jessie said, looking down on the old woman's head, which might have been covered with crocheting itself, so sparse was its web of hair. "Tush, how has she been?"

"How has she been." Tush proceeded always by repetition and incorporation, like a slow and careful learner. "Jessie, I have to tell you I can't honestly say. She's been fretful as a baby since Teddy called that day, but she won't talk directly about it. I wouldn't even swear to you, if you put me on oath"—this was her favorite expression, perhaps learned from or for her lawyers—"that she even understands what's happened." Tush's eyes filled with tears; if Dorothea didn't understand, she understood for two. "You know that some of her faculties have been a little bit . . ." She cast a dismayed, betraying look at the door to the living room. "A bit slippery, I'd call it. Not gone completely, you know, but not what you'd want to put your faith in either. I would have to call her—unreliable."

Jessie commiserated and helped Tush spoon the dressing out of the turkey into a silver serving bowl. Some people's lives, she thought, are too quiet to deserve a bold and splashy word like tragedy, but what would be a proper description of this tethered service Tush would neither escape nor ever be properly thanked for? For every thought Dorothea would not devote to someone else, Tush gave a minimum of two. Jessie saw that her hands had begun a discreet shaking since their last visit: each finger jiggled at its own pace, gently, like the leaves of an aspen. What would become of Dorothea if Tush had to retire from caring for her?

"She thought," Tush said, grasping the locked shin bones of her turkey in one hand, "she thought Alexis was coming over today."

Jessie gasped. "How do you know?"

"Oh, she said so, just as if it wasn't anything very special. She said, let's remember to show Alexis the new damask cloth from the Ladies' Rummage—just like that. But then she found me looking at her."

"And—?"

"And she gave a little whimper, sort of to say, 'Well, all right, if you think we oughtn't.' Because I think she was remembering how Alexis never thought she should buy used items like that, she thought it wasn't becoming."

"Well, did you say anything?"

Tush looked down at her fingers, observed them doing their dance and closed them into fists. When she reopened them the tension had brought them to a tentative stop. She regarded them distantly. "Oh, Jessie . . ." She gave a tired sigh. "I thought, Tush, dear, just let it be. Why pain her? My feeling about these things is what I suppose you might feel with a little child, I thought, if she doesn't see it then she must not be ready to see it.

And then someday she may. But why does she have to have a perfectly clear picture of how she stands right in harm's way?"

Tush's hushed voice, that innocent insistence, stilled Jessie's desire to argue the point. Why, in fact? Teddy would be furious, for the thousandth time, that his mother could justify a convenient blindness in herself to be spared the grief that made monkeys of the rest of them. But really, what could be the absolute virtue in truth? She couldn't remember. For a functioning mother or a nine-to-five worker or whatever, it was inescapable; reality was. But for Dorothea Carll, retired from any kind of active duty, sitting in that chair with her sight and hearing blinking on and off again like Christmas tree ornaments, what difference did it make what she comprehended? All words were shadowy, fleeting. Could she, by not knowing, hurt anyone more terribly than she would be hurt by knowing? Let Alexis live.

. . .

The children returned hungry from their walk. The dinner was eaten, as it is always eaten in the course of such visits; the turkey, which looked as polished as the side of a violin, and the low-salt dressing, the dumplings, the blueberry pie, seemed to be what they had come all that distance for. Tush's cooking had made so many adjustments and compromises, of which she was no longer aware, for the sake of Dorothea's dietary restrictions, that it had taken on the anonymity of hospital cooking. She did not think to apologize for it.

O'Neill seized the salt-shaker and flapped his whole arm back and forth over his plate, casting salt on the table cloth and into his water glass like a magician laying down a spell beneath his hand.

"O'Neill," Jessie said, and was surprised to see that he took correction from her without so much as a challenging look. He offered the silver shaker all around and put it silently down.

"We're going to move, Mother," Teddy said in Dorothea's direction, his voice loud although she was not deaf. For once there was honest news that she might welcome.

"To Birmingham?" She was feeding herself carefully, opening her mouth wide to receive the fork in her left hand wherever it might happen to arrive.

"*Bir*mingham." Teddy and Jessie locked looks.

"Well . . ." Dorothea was watching her hand as it lowered its fork, the way she might watch someone of uncertain intentions about to do something to her, ready to suffer it but not to approve it. She tore her gaze away. "Well, to be near Alexis. And Roger, not least."

Helen, who had been excavating her food in her familiar way, began to tear at a knot of turkey skin. She pursed her lips to work at it and dug away with her fork until it scraped against the plate with a subdued shriek.

"Their—where they're buried, you mean?" Teddy asked, his voice light, eyes closed as if that might extend his patience.

"Where they have their lovely house. Maybe they could help you find something like it." She smiled brightly; her teeth were still perfect. "It was an architectural original, you know."

"Oh Jesus," Teddy said. Tush had told him, years ago, how she had actually seen Dorothea having her stroke, how they had been talking on the porch and suddenly, without a break in the conversation—could redheads successfully wear pink? He would always remember that—she had stopped making sense. In full drive, the gears had stopped meshing. Eventually she had gotten sense back, though never again the sound of conviction in her voice; it was her ability to stand and move that had disintegrated. Now, he thought, they were all party to another accident, the continuing one that in time, not long now, would bear her away. Her age and her condition were like an army of ants carrying her off piecemeal.

Jessie had not yet told Teddy about her conversation with Tush. "They can't do that, Mother," she said gently, as vaguely as she could.

"If you can ever be induced to be friendly with your sister again, she and Roger will be as fine as friends to you, I know it. Identical, I should think. You are just about over all that now anyway, aren't you? Dear? Your foolishness? Those people seem to be doing better than you are these days, without your help." She laughed a dry laugh at her joke.

Teddy put the fingers of his left hand across his mouth and pushed them tight. There was no way but this, manually, to insure his silence. (His mother had taught him to do that very early—they called it The Muzzle. When he was saying something that offended her she would hold up a finger and say, "Teddy, put on the muzzle!" and that would end it.) The family, Jessie was thinking angrily, the abstract words running as far from her as horses seen in a field somewhere, grazing under distant trees, the family exists to perpetuate reduction, intimidation. Teddy came to see his mother, whom he had loved and obeyed but never liked, only, it seemed, to be reminded that he was going nowhere, was running on a track without beginning or end: that for all his world-saving he was a small recalcitrant boy no better than O'Neill and nothing he could ever do would make him more. She could not resist making him so. Hopeless, hopeless. And Alexis had learned obliviousness from her mother, and triviality, the way she had learned tatting and buttermilk biscuits. Her acceptance of the teachings had been cheerful, not petulant, but it came to the same thing: a turning of the back, an about-face, on real life.

"Well, we're moving right in Jackson, Mother. A bigger house. A neighborhood I think you'll like."

"For the children. They have to watch their fingers in the grater, you know."

He was tempted to think she was taunting them in that deadpan voice, but she had an eager comprehending look. Even her one drooping eye seemed to be making an effort to open wide.

Teddy sighed. "For the children. Right."

"And what about the grater, Teddy?"

Pure poetry. He looked at them one by one as if he were polling them. They all looked attentively back, Andy and Lydia smiling a little, but only a little, embarrassed. She is yours, all of you, Jessie wanted to say, to O'Neill and Helen especially: she is not our crazy burden visited upon you like all the others, the social aches and pains. Teddy, her son, smiled at Dorothea without words and nodded, and she seemed satisfied. It was in her power to be easily placated.

"The pie, dear," she said to Tush, who rose obediently to bring it in.

. . .

O'Neill and Helen stood one behind the other in the hall to the bedrooms, studying the photographs hung just above eye-level. "Mom looks plain silly," Helen said to her brother. "You think she really ever wore her hair like *that?*" Alexis in a pink formal with spaghetti straps, her matching pink arms thin and exposed, a small girl's, hands joined meekly in her lap, as if to deny the sophistication of the dress. Her hair in a beehive, spun high over air, made her face tiny.

"Mn-*m*-mn," O'Neill answered in the approximate inflection of "I don't know," high on the middle syllable. "She looks like you in that."

Helen laughed, obviously pleased at the thought. "Oh, I don't think so."

They seemed to sway together, raptly. Teddy watched them, and Jessie too, from beside him. She felt, all the time, that she was on the other side of a glass through which she could see but not touch them. They lived sufficient unto themselves, inside a different medium.

"How come there aren't any pictures of you?" O'Neill asked him when he saw Teddy watching.

Teddy came toward them out of the underwater green shadows. Jessie hung back, feeling that she had found her proper relation to this family: it was invisibility. Teddy sighed and didn't answer. After a while he said, "Because my mother and I—your grandmother—had a little while there when she didn't really want to think about me much. I was doing some things she didn't approve of. So—I guess, she just took the pictures down and she never bothered to put them back up again."

"Maybe she ripped them up into shreds." O'Neill offered this with his usual impartial enthusiasm.

"Maybe."

"Well, then, you ought to get her some new ones now that she likes you again. Were there any pictures in a uniform? Like football?"

"I was too light for football. I played some basketball though, I wasn't too bad." Teddy laughed. He had never spent much effort on sports, he had been a full-time moralist all the way back, like someone who was going to grow up a preacher: some things were frivolous. Most things. He had been student government president in high school and very proud of himself too. (In retrospect, he told his children, he'd been obnoxious, puffed up with his own importance.) His uniform had been a suit and a white shirt; all you saw when you looked at him was ears. Ears and a spiny cowlick. He had been roving reporter for the school newspaper, *The Clarion*, had walked around, smug, provoking the townspeople with questions like "Who is Trygve Lie?" and "Do you think the U.S. should be involved in Dien Bien Phu?" and when they shrugged, uninterested, he wrote angry editorials about Apathy, Indifference, Individualism. He read Emerson, Thoreau, all those Yankees. His hero was Tom Watson, before Watson's populism turned racist. Oh, he was earnest, he and Jessie were a pair, separated by so much space, so many details of geography and circumstance, but both of them hard-breathing, grim in their rectitude and charming in their energy, charming because people would follow charm. Ambitious. Morally ambitious.

"Oh look," Helen said, "one picture." Then she stopped abruptly and sighed as if in defeat—she had forgotten that she meant to show no enthusiasm in Teddy's presence. It was true, there was a family picture, Dorothea in the center with the enigmatic mouth of a Madonna and his father beside but slightly behind her, barely touching her shoulder. His father's face, benign, all on the horizontal, is the kind *New Yorker* cartoonists draw to represent the Average Republican—except that down here the Average Republican is a Democrat. Teddy sits at his father's knee, Alexis at her mother's side, the immutable sexual separation already in force, looking elective, looking somehow natural and jolly, a Carll family tradition. Teddy is about ten: clean-faced boy, dangerously skinny with faceted cheeks, and his hair razor-cut, so that he looks like a dwarf marine recruit. His mouth seems to stretch from one ear lobe to the other, like his father's his face all side to side while his morose mother's is up and down. Alexis is all braids and complex braces of skirt straps, dressed in an alpine costume. And knees. She shows knobby little-girl knees with the shine of cheeks on them.

"We were younger than you-all in this one."

The children worked hard at the picture, mining it for something they could believe in of their mother's, their uncle's, their grandmother's vanished life. Jessie, still behind the door jamb, feeling like an eavesdropper, was assaulted with such sadness that she felt, for one long moment, that it was cruel, more corrupting than pornography, to show this thing to young children—what could it do but lacerate them with all the forms of obliteration that awaited them: and you, my lovelies, and you, you too . . . But it was not themselves they were seeing, they were too young to make such a leap, still too literal minded for that.

"O'Neill favors Grandy a lot more than I ever thought," Helen said. It was the most unguarded sentence she had ever spoken to either of them. "Something about his—I think the space between his nose and his upper lip. And the forehead, somehow—"

"Naw!" O'Neill slapped at her arm.

"Naw? Why naw? You don't know what you look like, *you* can't see it."

"I'd rather look like my daddy."

Helen gave him a condescending look. "Rather hasn't a single thing to do with anything. Where do *you* live?"

O'Neill puffed a few times like an engine preparing to depart from the station. He had come to the end of his concentration and he slapped her one more time to seal the end of the discussion.

Alone with Helen, Teddy seemed to cast around for another comment that might prolong this intimacy. "Your Grandy was a very good-looking woman. It's sad what's happening to her."

Helen looked at him with her eyebrows at a critical angle. "You talk about her like she's somebody very far away from you. You don't sound at all like she's your mother." She blushed as she finished, at the enormity of catching an adult in his emotional inadequacy. When her face colored, the delicate center ridge of her nose went pale, like a tensed knuckle.

"Oh, Helen." He paused. Then, Jessie thought sinkingly, he lied. "I think it's a—kind of self-protection, do you know? She's too hard for me to look at right straight on. And because I know what's bound to come soon." The piety was absurd: his mother had cast him out, it was simple, almost Biblical. She was a woman who could not love him more than she loved her gnarled view of the world. And so, equally simple, he would not love her, would not allow it. Could he not understand it as well as she did? Jessie wondered. For she knew that children are not the only ones who can be cast out and never reeled in again. And now, far down, leagues under, was this lassitude. She wondered how much he loved anyone or anything when he labored under his veil, this incessant cloudy weather. As if he touched all of it with thickly padded fingers: flesh, adult's or child's, Jessie's own, all of it receded from his grasp, this one great callus, this thick horny residue between.

"You certainly know what it feels like to protect yourself against things you don't want to think about."

Helen looked at him warily. "Why do you say that?"

"Well, I don't see you mourning your parents very openly."

She looked away toward the opposite wall, which was an endless display of green cannons, piles of perfect balls heaped at their sides like limes in a market. "I don't want to talk about my parents. If you don't mind."

"Or if I do. That's what I mean by self-protection. Don't you know it would be better for you—"

"No, I don't know," she flared at him angrily. She had a way of holding her head so steady that her mouth seemed disembodied, like a puppet's. "If you want to know, I think they're in a better place. I'll see them there if I ever get lucky."

Teddy opened his eyes and mouth simultaneously. He looked foolish— a comedian doing a double-take—and closed his mouth into a grin. "You're serious."

"You're not serious. You're never serious." She looked bitter; she had held in so much she ought to feel murderous.

"Nobody's ever accused me of that, Helen. I think we must be serious about different sorts of things."

"You're not serious about Christ."

"No. No, I'm certainly not, nor ever said I was." He took a deep despairing breath. "I figure there are a lot of sufferers who are still alive and could use all the attention they can get, without any distractions."

"Christ is not a distraction."

Helen and Skelly—what an interesting combination that made, Jessie thought: zealots of opposite colors. Harlequin and Columbine, kneeling in their black and white costumes. Had she been suppressing this, then? Was this getting her *through*? Was she lying in her sleeping bag every night praying her way out of the black tunnel of her outward life?

"Where have you been with this before, Helen?" Jessie asked, announcing her presence.

She smiled to herself. "It isn't anybody's but mine. I don't owe it to anybody to talk about how I feel."

"No, but to yourself."

"Myself . . ." She shrugged and let the word darken, like a small light dimming. Then she walked away from the two of them, down the hall, backwards, ostentatiously dramatic, till she was drawn back fully into shadow, leaving them alone with the cannons.

.   .   .

Now they were moving on down the highway, through falling light, toward home. Andy and Lydia had begun a song about fish-heads, had tried to teach it to O'Neill (there were only two lines) and had given up because he was clowning and refused to get it right. There was a lot of noise, jagged shards of it glittering without end. Jessie sat beside Teddy, casually telling him stories about school, which was at the moment in its first pocket of uneventful quiet: parents happy, children happy, the board of ed. momentarily invisible.

Teddy listened for a while and then, without prelude, said, "Do you know, when my daddy died, my mother told me just pretend he was a dream?" He didn't look at her, kept his eyes dutifully on the road. " 'That'll be easier,' she said, 'pretend he never really was, you made up that nice man who came home from over there'—she used to sort of say that like it was the *song?*"

Jessie stared at him.

" 'With all those li'l gifts he had for you, and he seemed to stay a little while and then last week, why, you just finally opened up your *eyes* and now, you see, he's gone!' " He shook his head and breathed out hard. "A man's whole reality like a bubble or something that blows off into space and pops without even snagging on a solid goddamn branch."

"God," Jessie commiserated. "Only your mother. You know, I'm surprised she never became an addict of some kind, an alcoholic, maybe. One of those professional escape artists—she certainly has the right temperament for it."

She drowsed a little in the chilly dishwater gray of evening, thinking of the way the darkness gathered between New York buildings, so much deeper, more absolute than twilight in open country. Evening from her window on West Eleventh Street was like a massive pencilling-in with a number 2 laid on its broad side. . . . Lazily she wondered if Teddy's father, had he lived, could have swayed Dorothea from her self-righteous cruelty to her son. Had his father lived and his mother not, would he have been wholly orphaned (when a lot of pushing came to a lot of shoving) by a single death? Not a man whose widow teaches his son he was only a pleasant daydream. . . . But Elliott Carll would have been more moderate; he was from Gulfport, and Gulfport had always lacked the purity, the fierce concentrated isolation of the inland places—there was that east-west highway that had always blown "foreigners" across the state, right along the coast; houses and hotels and beer joints on one side, the broad sweet-looking polluted Gulf on the other; there were military installations stocked by Yankees, and shipyards. They had had to put a good face on down there— if not good, then better—and they had suffered, too, the real influence of broadened experience.

The car sped along between the great ravines of kudzu in its wild and lonely winter incarnation as moon landscape. Ghostly, gray brown, disappearing into the dark, it lay thick as an entrapping net over the rolling molded hills. Then Jessie, gasping, smashed Teddy in the arm between his shoulder and his elbow and he woke up. Which is to say, Jessie realized with a forward heave in her chest like the kick that sometimes woke her from a dream of falling, that he had been asleep. The front wheels had just crossed the white outer line; they were heading toward the dead gray mat of kudzu at a fierce speed.

She had cried out "Hey!" like an order. When he saw what he had almost done he shuddered, apologized vaguely and was silent. Jessie was not. "How could that have happened? You're not here by yourself, they're making all this racket!"

The children hung over the back of the seat to hear the details.

There were none. They begged Teddy to tell them—was he tired? Did he want to stop for coffee? An adult in trouble, having done something unforgivable—that was in its own category of vengeful excitement, a paying back of a little of the world's power to their empty pockets.

"You've already landed in a ditch once in your life," Jessie muttered, her arms around herself protectively. "That ought to be enough for any one man."

From the well of the car came O'Neill's voice, asking about the circumstances of that "landing in a ditch." Had he really? And lived? Had *not* lived? He demanded details.

Andy gave him a guided tour: the Piggs boys, he and Lydia called them, but they were really the Higgs brothers, from Carthage. The chase on that deserted stretch. The gnashing sound of locked fenders and the extraordinary dust rising like a plume of smoke when one of the struts gave out and the car rolled off—no, leaped off like Evel Knievel—into the kudzu, which was green and springy in that season, a million million leaves under the high noon sun. The next car along had been sure it was an explosion! (God, how they loved the story.) And then Teddy, extracted from the clenched wreckage, dying, dead.

"You were *dead?*" O'Neill shouted and beat his fist on the top of the front seat. He had thrust his way by knee and elbow between Lydia and Helen who were wincing at him and elbowing back. No, it was Lydia who was elbowing; Helen had her eyes closed so tightly her cheeks looked as if they'd been gathered with thread pulled too tight. They bunched under her eyes like an old woman's, or an apple-head's. Jessie was on the verge of an angry speech, Teddy could read that from the way she sat forward tensely holding on to the hem of her skirt, but she said nothing.

Dead about the length of time he just slept, Jessie thought. Went deeper down is all, and came up slower. "Old history," Teddy said. Jessie could see that he didn't want to talk. He had frightened himself into a beating of the heart so violent it took all his concentration to prevent it from making his shoulders and his knees twitch, jiggled on insistent strings. He could .have killed them all. Or some of them, selectively. Oh she knew he loved them. Or some of them, selectively. (All he had ever wanted to do was love more people than he knew, and take care of them somehow.) Since he was a man who spent most of his time in his car—locked like an astronaut in this absurd position, feet forward and flexed, hands gripping an indented wheel, one elbow at a time rising, falling, as he corrected its movement, eyes forward and only forward—she thought he would do well to understand exactly what had overcome him. Tomorrow he was going down to Port Gibson, then on to Laurel, down the straight strip of 61, across on 84 and back, the numbers endless, endless all the green pines and bare brown twigs and houses and crossroads slipping past, pulled past him like yarn past a hypnotized cat. Could he be trusted alone with himself?

Worse. Although he probably could not have named the impulse to close his eyes and float in a carful of his most beloved, there was something lodged sharper than a bone in the bottom of his throat that made the act anything but random. Jessie knew the feeling: something about losing yourself, something about abandoning direction, control, concern, even that love you worked at so assiduously. Especially that love. There was a word for it. She knew that if she said that word to him aloud he would lift his hands from the wheel and bring them to his eyes, no matter how the car might lurch to a thousand pieces, and—right there between the dry sweeping ridges of kudzu to the left, kudzu to the right—begin to cry. But she didn't know what the word might be, or if, knowing it, she would trust him with their lives and whisper it to him.

Teddy is so dreary and preachy, he should be my father's brother not my mother's. I told him he was not serious about Christ and I could see him trying not to laugh. Just wait, the day will come when he is least expecting it.

The worst thing my mother ever said to me once (when I was very mad at my father because he did some stupid thing, I think it was the time he gave our puppy away without telling us about it) was "You are contemptuous." (I had to look it up in my dictionary.) Sometimes it may be good to be c. but mostly she meant it is not a nice characteristic. Teddy is c. all the time and of everything. His face is set in this little snide almost-grin so he looks like he is enjoying it when you are uncomfortable. He is like one of those people who loves to set up practical jokes against their friends and watch the water dribble out of the cup and down their new dress, or put something horrible-looking on the floor and let you step in it. We had an argument (well, not quite but it was not a friendly talk) and he I am sure thought he was speaking like an adult to an adult. Why are you not in mourning for your parents? Like, who do you think you are, you are as lowdown as Cinderella? And his eyes get mean and fixed and that disgusting scar fills up with little, like, pockets of blood something half cooked and half raw. How can he tell me how I "have to" feel about anything? He doesn't know anything about me or about them.

On the way home he nearly crashed the car and Jessie said he died in an accident once. Could that be? And is alive? Then maybe he thinks he is his own Jesus Christ the Savior, since he died too and is still here. But the thing is, could someone have saved my mother and father??? I don't want to know! So then I look down at my brother and I keep thinking he wants to say to me, "Maybe they are really alive! Out in Seattle! Maybe they woke up!" But he wouldn't dare sound so stupid. So then I had to put my arm around him and just pat his head and say "Oh dear little boy, my little brother, O'Neill." That was all I said, not why. He tries not to but I could see every little light of hope flashing inside his eyes and face and I had to be the one to put it out. It wasn't my fault one bit but it made me feel old and cruel, like a stepmother.

She ought to have been looking for a house, but finding a ballet school was easier. Of her whole list—

FIND HELEN A BALLET SCHOOL
FIND HELEN A CHURCH
FIND <u>HELEN</u>

—it was surely the finite one. When she asked the sort of friends who knew about things like dancing schools, they gave her an unedited list. ("Jessie, it depends on the *child*.")

But Jessie did not know the child. She saw her narrow shoulders and long slender hips, knew how the mother had been shaped, assumed Helen would go on being moulded in her approximate image—that pear-shaped bottom that not gravity but genes had elongated. But all she saw was the child's spirit beyond a haze and that confident secretive walk, as if she were the virgin in whose lap the unicorn would someday lay his head. As if she knew it.

There was even, Jessie thought, the distinct possibility that this ballet business had, in the absence of the girl's visible "real life," taken on a spurious life of its own. Whether or not it had ever been more than a casual interest, one of those *de rigueur* exercises in grace and social poise imposed by her class and her mother, she had no idea. When asked about her interest in resuming her dancing, Helen assumed the verbal equivalent of the non-violent position. That left Jessie the policewoman who drags the supine body away and does with it what she pleases.

But the air between them had to be filled with something. She would rather drive Helen to ballet, or have her go downtown by bus, than see her come home from school and sit, without complaint, without energy, on the end of Lydia's bed, as she had been doing. (When Lydia was home, she simply vaporized.)

The dancing schools had remarkably unappealing names: the Merl-Ann School of Tap, Toe and Baton. The Fedrova Academy (promising?). The Ar-kay-gee Russian Ballet Institute. The Y. The single school that appeared on every list, with stars as if it were a plush restaurant, was the School of the Dance Center downtown, part of the new arts complex that was Jackson at its most cosmopolitan. Apparently it was a ballet school in earnest; the others were neighborhood fancies. Jessie had seen news stories about the Dance Center's recitals in the paper, not tiny announcements but real press releases.

They went to see. Helen stood straight and kept silent, venturing no questions during interviews, no comments afterwards. A prima ballerina dignity. The one thing these establishments had in common was a beguiling quantity of loose and billowing fabric, as though their claim for art could be secured solely by their freedom to flow, to refuse to crop and stifle. The studios had the look of the bedrooms of arty small-town girls who had sworn an oath never to cut their hair or wear tailored clothes. Well, of course— these were the girls, grown older and heavier in the haunch. These were the girls who ran them. There were colorless chiffon scarves in the untended reddish hair of the aged Mme. Fedrova, whose round Russian accent was by now hopelessly tainted, stretched horizontally like a slack muscle, by her years in the South. A swathe of dusty tie-die hung from push-pins on the shiny wood panelling of Ar-kay-gee, surrounded by dozens of small clipped magazine photos, their edges curling up, of dancers slicing through air, and, less ecstatic, Polaroid prints of the Ar-kay-gee children in recital, done up in their extravagant tutus like poodles in jackets.

The directors of these schools conceded, one after another, that the advanced student—she was always referred to as if she were theoretical, or at best in another room—might find herself more and more alone as her prowess increased. The good students were peeling off; it was tempting but impolite to ask Where to? She hoped they might tell, spontaneously, but not one teacher did. All of them hoped to acquire a good dancer to cheer them up for a while, even if she inevitably joined the exodus. It had to be the Dance Center, of course; of all the schools, that was the only one that required an audition.

Jessie brought Helen to her try-out on a sharp blowy day. It was an early afternoon at school for her: her children were doing projects with another class and she was dispensable, though she'd have liked to have been there to watch O'Neill put the final triumphant touches on the "painless mousetrap" he was building. (It was a cage with a door that fell like the blade of the guillotine but was meant to be benign; the worst it could do to a mouse, he had decided, was knock it unconscious for a while. On the side he was planning to paint a mouse in boxing trunks falling backwards, seeing fluorescent silver stars.)

Jessie waited outside Helen's school, slumped behind the wheel of the car. Her own children, who tended to be enthusiastic and demonstrative, had never made her feel quite so "maternal" in the negative, stereotyped sense as Helen. O'Neill, complex though he might be, was transparent and bracing as cool water. Though you might have to ask him things because it would not have occurred to him that you didn't know, and though, understandably, he gave the feeling from time to time of a child who was "not himself these days," he did not seem particularly to value withholding, or to make of silence an act in itself.

Were those things, as Helen practiced them, the way she had been before, or was it all anger and depression? She had a distinct right to be whoever she had been previously. Even to be who she had to be now. Of course. Though, conceived that way, they sounded to Jessie like masks or stage roles or worse, personalities granted and reclaimed like the objects of ghostly possession. But Jessie wanted to *know*. It was not yet time to contact the Birmingham friends to discuss her, because Jessie did not want to make the problem sound worse than it was. Things were nowhere near the alarming stage yet; furthermore, she knew that impatience was now and ever had been her own—well, one of her—besetting flaws. But no orphanage, she thought, would send a child forth so little heralded by description or encouragement.

She watched the closed dark green doors of the junior high school buckle, quiver open, then fall shut again as if someone had lost heart. There was a long gathering pause and finally, with a hoot of triumph, the whole side wall of the school seemed to give way. The students, more colorful than a circus, erupted with the urgency of escapees from a burning building. They milled and seethed. A black boy, whose purple pants glowed so violently they willfully seized attention, seemed to walk without an upper half; a girl and boy who had come as cowboys matched from perfectly creased hat to silver belt buckle no smaller than a warrior's shield to pointed-toed boots. The vanity! The money! She would not like to have confronted such vivid Hollywood self-assurance in an eighth-grade classroom. The words "savage glitter" occurred to her, sitting with her knees bent a little against the bottom of the steering wheel, making folds in her skin. She had heard them once used to describe a book, but here it was in life at Barber Junior High. No one would leave the cowboy and his girl alone, they walked out toward the sidewalk escorted, it seemed, by ardent fans.

Helen had detached herself from the tangle of vividness and was coming toward her, light as a leaf and dressed like one in subtle shades of tan and green. Robin Hood colors. She walked with her head down. She muttered "Hi"—"Ha" to Jessie's ears, which could still be surprised by the sounds she was not born to.

"Ready?"

She shrugged.

"Are you nervous?"

"I never went to an audition before so I don't know what to get nervous *at*."

"Well, that's a positive approach. A lot of people get nervous when they don't know."

Helen looked at her neutrally, her books balanced in her lap, her toe shoes in a black and yellow box on top of them. Jessie chatted about the buildings they were passing—a tolerable conversation one would have on a bus with a stranger. Well, what did she expect, intimacies at three o'clock, between social studies class and warm-up exercises?

The Dance Center looked as serious and impersonal as its name. It was new, carefully colorless, full of textures in careful unspontaneous juxtaposition, carpeted up to the door. They watched a young black man in leotard and tights walk past with a woman in a soft and clinging plum-colored practice outfit. Jessie could have watched the young man move back and forth forever while she analyzed his beguiling stride, half ghetto bounce, half well-schooled European slide. They must be, she thought, instructors. Their camaraderie—the very presence of white students in his classes—there was no going back on it: Roger Tyson's nightmare had turned into casual reality.

Two other girls were trying out: one was only about nine, round as a tub, with Dutch-boy-cut light hair and fat rings around her thighs like a proliferation of garters. The other was a tall black girl, a few years older than Helen, whose hair stuck out in two little Olive Oyl screws behind her ears. She was in her leotard and had her pink ballet shoes tied on by their pink ribbons when they came in; she was stretching out at the barre, raising her left leg gravely, with infinite ease, and then her right. She had her head inclined so that she seemed to be listening to each leg as it passed her ear.

Unlike the studios where the dancers had to come already dressed and leave perspiring, there was a dressing room. Helen went into it without a word. Jessie stood looking at the dance posters, at the clean pale legs and the cloudy skirts, that tea-rose kingdom removed from the grime of the world. This studio had the same clean feeling, though its newness and formality made it more clinical than magical. Jessie had always liked the discrepancy between the gunmetal gray of backstage, that Navy Yard bleakness or the unadorned workmanlike echoing wooden spaces of practice rooms, and the rarefied beauty of the diaphanous lifting bodies seen from the balcony. Practice and performance were so wonderfully unalike. Ar-kay-gee and the Tap-Toe-Baton Academy had neither.

Helen came out of the dressing room walking splay-footed in her hard-toed shoes, making a slapping noise. She went to the barre on the opposite side of the room from the other girl, who had laid her leg along the barre and was bending to her knee. The round child was leaping without grace and without apparent training down the wide center of the room. She was having a good time. Jessie watched Helen rolling down from her toes and up, down and up, her face wiped blank. Ballet was the perfect place for that cryptic look of intaken breath that would never be released. Her face that did not acknowledge effort.

The teacher, who suddenly emerged from another door, was, to her surprise, male. He was curly haired and rumpled around the eyes, neither young nor quite middle-aged: in him too there was a quality of suspension, perhaps of the perfect body aging less quickly than the face, the skin. He called the three girls together, more or less with his wrist, and after a minute had released the youngest one, who glared at him and beat her arms like an indecisive pigeon against her sides. Then, as her mother began to approach the viewing window to claim her, she surrendered and went in to change her clothes.

Jessie saw that the black girl's mother had seated herself, in her coat, on the long vinyl sofa against the wall. She sat beside her and they talked with their faces straight ahead so that they could watch the girls as they began their elaborate graceful charade, following directions.

The other dancer was named Valerie. She was from Los Angeles, she had gone to a professional children's school, and she was very very good.

"Whyever did you move to Jackson?" Jessie asked, trying to indicate that she did not really belong either.

The woman was wearing a greenish tannish tweed coat Jessie could never have aspired to and had lovely high cheekbones across which lay a sprinkling of freckles like cinnamon, accented by perfect makeup. She smiled crookedly. "My husband's job is not one anyone would leave, no matter where they sent him. I think he'd have gone to Australia if they had wanted him to. Wagging us all behind him." She named his company. It was one of the hot properties that had set cranes against the Mississippi sky, and undoubtedly Valerie's father was a very visible figure against that same sky, now that the company needed black faces.

"And Valerie goes to—what? Murrah?"

The woman looked at Jessie critically and said without much pleasure, "And Valerie goes to Murrah."

"Have you thought of sending her away to school?"

She sighed. "Next semester, you may be sure. We thought we would give it a try. But—" She raised her commanding eyebrows and shrugged.

"There is not a single element in that school that I am pleased to see her associate with. To be perfectly honest. And that unfortunately includes the faculty, so-called."

Jessie smiled and said nothing. She didn't much like to hear anyone talking about elements instead of people, or so-calling anyone either: she and hers had been so-called in the Jackson newspapers a few times too often. Still, she thought, what a shame the whitest of the white folks couldn't hear how their children didn't measure up. What would they say? And when they saw that child do a tour jeté or a double entrechat?

Jessie didn't know much about ballet but it was clear that Helen had a gift. Her fluorescent cool became incandescent, it gave both heat and light every time she turned her pale face to Jessie. Her features seemed more and more general, somehow, their outlines blurred, as if she were every young girl moving, leaping, and her long neck was revealed to be a graceful stem of rather remarkable length and suppleness, from which inclined that face made gentle in its absorption but not tentative, never tentative.

When the two girls had been dismissed to get into their street clothes, the instructor walked out to speak to the mothers in the gallery. He was rapturous, could not have been more pleased, could not wait to meld them with the class at large, which, of course, had started together in September, many continuing from last year. But "no problema, no problema." He was Spanish; his name was Juan Echeverria. Up close he was somewhat older than he had seemed. His face had many smile wrinkles, like cracks in sturdy pottery. He clapped his hands together like a child promised a new toy. "Beautifully matched, these two, although the—ah what, Valerie?—she has the more of experience. But not to worry," and he touched Jessie on the shoulder reassuringly. "Your daughter, she would to come along soon. She may be a bit early for the *pointe*, but not so bad as I sometimes see. Quick. A strong body, not so light as it look when she is in her spins out there." He touched himself in various places—the strong places?—with the speed and practice of a genuflecting priest.

"And strong head I think too, no? Both of them—smart, strong, not bad training as you expect. A good day, two long-leg girls from careful teachers who had guard their turn-out. You know how some people talk about overlooking—no, overseeing?—that turn-out, it is like guarding a young girl's virginity!" He laughed. "Very careful. Very devote. Ah— devoted." And he kissed his fingertips. What must he make of Jackson, Jessie wondered. And vice versa. Meanwhile she pondered the idea of the sacred turn-out. She had always associated it with voting day.

Valerie's mother had a great many questions for him. Jessie, not the mother of her candidate and therefore not schooled in the jargon of the trade, had none. She watched the slow trickle of the next arriving class— these were younger girls, bright eyed, well dressed, many of them black —surely an "element" that could not affront Valerie's mother. Jessie studied the group as it spread to take over the room. How extraordinary to dare imagine, fifteen years ago, that tiny brown girl with the blue plastic bubbles holding her hair out in stiff plaits, shaking the arm of that redhead, and the redhead turning to greet her with a shout of welcome. They were raucous and relaxed. This is what it was for, she thought, all of it, what Teddy call- ed progress in that speech at the memorial, oh Teddy, this moment when they don't know anyone is watching, these skimpy little bodies in their tights and leotards. Forgive me, forgive me my cowardice, and my impatience.

.   .   .

When Jessie, pushing the heavy lobby door open, said "Well!" she meant, And so that's settled.

"Well," began Helen slowly. "I think Fedrova."

"You think Fedrova what?" The cold air shocked her through her open jacket so that she felt her breath gone.

"The one I like best. I think that's the one I should go to."

Jessie stopped dead. The car was—somewhere—but she couldn't begin to remember where. She was stupefied. "*Helen—*"

The girl looked at her, then widened her eyes as Jessie must have done, and wiggled her head at her, shaking it rapidly the way a dog shakes in its fleas, mocking. "What are you staring at?"

"I am staring at you. You are telling me that you choose that weary, dusty Fedrova and her Isadora scarves and her little gang of amateurs over *this?*" She pointed back over her shoulder where the Arts Center had begun to hulk low and blue gray in late afternoon shadow.

"You said I could choose the one I like best. You said that to me dis- tinctly." The pique in Helen's eyes was something Jessie hadn't seen roused before: an excited shine that narrowed her nose and promised temper and spite in small flying pieces like shrapnel.

"Well, yes, of course I did, but I assumed—perhaps incorrectly—that you had some taste and could exercise adult judgment. Could you perhaps try hard and tell me *why* you prefer Madame Fedrova over this clearly superior place?"

Helen reverted to her single solution: she shrugged and tried to seem stupid. Jessie thought she might like to knock her up against the wall and ask her to shrug again while she stood pinioned there. "The atmosphere," Helen muttered finally, a sop.

Jessie plunged her cold hands into her pockets, where they smashed up small nests of shopping lists and candy wrappers. "Might it just be possible that the part of the atmosphere you don't like here is that all those children are not white and rosy cheeked like you?"

Helen gave her one brief and possibly frightened look and cast her eyes down, stubbornly, to her sneakers. They were running shoes, actually, Jessie noted, and they had some color of stripe that crisscrossed them intricately, like a highway interchange, faintly glowing in the banked light. "Is that plausible?" Badgering wouldn't help, but what could help *her*, and blot up some of this anger? "You are going to give up a professional opportunity like this and go waste your beautiful talent in a two-bit enterprise up over a typewriter repair shop, with an old out-of-shape woman whose only claim to fame, I suspect, is that she was born—a hell of a long time ago so that she doesn't even try to bend over any more—in a country that has a tradition of great dancers? All because there are some children here that you don't want to be friends with?"

Helen chewed on her bottom lip and waited her out.

She went on, and then went on some more. She tried to stop herself— this was a habit that Teddy called her Rhetorical Front, and warned her was counterproductive; it was exactly like his Rhetorical Front, only less frequently resorted to. She could feel the anger sizzle through her fingers; she raked everything in her pockets to shreds. Then she remembered that the car was down the block and around one corner and they walked there, she speechless with rage, Helen drawn back into herself, lagging a step behind as if to announce a terminal lack of connection with this stranger who dared to harangue her like a mother.

They rode home in a heavy silence. Jessie put on the news and Helen either slept or pretended to sleep. Jessie saw the two girls, Helen and Valerie, undressing side by side, legs emerging from their corduroys, long washboard rib cages covered with tender adolescent skin, but secretly strong, the man had said. He would be disappointed: he was seeing ribs and backbone, what flexed, what retracted, with what ease. How could he have guessed that Helen would not so much as touch the long bones of Valerie's clean pale hands for love or art or money?

This dancing. Here is a poem. (If I give it to Jessie, maybe she will understand. But I would cut off my feet before I give it to her.)

I love it
And I do not love it
To see my body whirl around
Weighing nothing
Without a sound
And all the perfect dreams of beauty
Pink petals, mine all mine,
Hidden in my heart will shine.
But it is like bending
Under a whip
And tying your self in bondage's grip.
The most difficult thing in this world.
Beauty should never be easy.
Beauty should be fun, not work.
Beauty should not have exercises
And a judge and rules
You cannot dare to shirk.
I want to be special.
I do not want to be special.
I want to be special.
I do not want to be special.
My choice is like a neon light
Blinking on and off
Yes or no
By day and night.

Jessie is c. like her husband. She automatically assumes I am such a racist and complete bigot that I would not want to work with this Negro teacher I saw and these students when that is not the First and Only Thing I am capable of seeing. But oh no, try to tell her anything. I would never give that poem to her or mention "fear" or she would use it against me some other way. She insulted me. I do not owe her an explanation, just let her think whatever she likes to. Uninvolved will be my way, the Cross I bear. I deny myself church and pray alone. Or they would get too much satisfaction thinking they found out one of our NEEDS *and they are taking care of it. No way. I deny myself comfort of any kind. In a little while if my dear mother came back to me—say she really was saved like O'Neill dreams!—she would no longer recognize me.*

O'Neill had never finished his mousetrap with its portrait of the reeling victim seeing stars. That Friday afternoon, instead, while Jessie and Helen went downtown to the dance audition, he had ripped open Tyler Holloway's lip and loosened the last of Tyler's stubborn baby teeth. This Jessie learned from a huge clamor of self-righteous children when she set foot across the threshold of her classroom on Monday morning. No outraged parent had called over the weekend to demand reparations or even apology; nor had any of her fellow teachers let her in on the atrocity, although they had many times, in meetings, agreed that the only punishment worth meting out, to disobedient child as to disobedient animal, is the one that directly follows the crime, lest the power of cause and effect be hopelessly vitiated. O'Neill, needless to say, had not "told" on himself.

Jessie felt as though she had stepped off a curb into heavy traffic. Every child clamored, some tugged at her arm, a few at her thighs, and Ophelia threatened to untie her dungaree wraparound; all of her, hands included, was twitching with outrage. Out of range stood Tyler of the newly told tale, smiling shyly and proudly, his lip still swollen, still blue and crusted with scab, and behind it—he grimaced, or smiled to show her—his now-famous tooth hung crooked on a string of skin. Any boy who had not lost it nobly in a fight would have removed it forty-eight hours ago.

O'Neill, not canny enough to lie low, had sailed in with her, casual. Possibly he thought the statute of limitations in the permissive unthreatening alternative school would not bring last week's debts forward to blight a fresh week. Possibly he felt, as they say of psychopaths on the way to execution, no remorse.

But he seemed suddenly to have discovered ordinary danger: he took one step toward Jessie, his head near her crook of elbow, then one back, having remembered he would get no solace there. Then he bolted and ran out of the room. "No!" Jessie cried, even before she heard the thud of the children's sneakers as they turned to pursue him. "You stay right here, all of you. We don't need a mob running around out there."

They were crestfallen but they obeyed her. (The school was not as permissive as it seemed for lack of authoritarian nagging.) They would have loved to play hound on the trail of a self-confessed sinner.

Jessie let him go. She only hoped he wouldn't leave the building. (Interesting, she reflected absently, that she was thinking the usual: how she would have to answer to his parents if he left school and got into any trouble.) She settled the class, which would not really settle, at its first work of the morning, forgoing Circle Time when they exchanged the shinier remnants of their weekend excitements, and called Tyler to her so that she could hear the story.

It was classically simple. They had somehow got in each other's way, first over the paint pots, then over the hammer which O'Neill had held on to although Tyler was using it, and with which he had pulled Tyler forward halfway across the room as if he were an intractable nail in a board. "Why didn't you let go?" Jessie asked, smiling.

"Wasn't his hammer, that's why. I was using it. He try and take it right out of my *hand*." Tyler had been pulled against a table, someone's finger-paint had splashed out and all around. "And then he start up cussin me and cussin Ophelia, it was her paints, and then everybody just come and jump in!" Tyler still looked secretly pleased with himself. He had triangular eyes whose wide centers ignited with pleasure as he spoke. This white boy was in trouble for messing with him.

Jessie cuffed him on the head and called him a good sport, and in the interests of justice, promised that O'Neill would be punished on two counts, grabbing someone else's property and calling names. "Okay?" she asked Tyler. He expressed doubt by looking away, fixing his eyes on the cylindrical cubbyholes that held piles of construction paper and scissors. It was because, give or take a few details that didn't concern Tyler, O'Neill was hers. Was a swift kick in her credibility.

On her way down the hall to find O'Neill, she stopped in to ask Mary Frances, who had been the teacher in charge, her version of what had happened on Friday. Tyler's version was seconded. There were some details of the "deplo-rable" racial epithets O'Neill had brandished. Although there were always children for whom this experiment in benign education did not work, there had never, since the alternative school took over this old building, been the sound of such nasty words echoed wantonly between its walls. Or so she was given to believe.

Mary Frances was very young and had a head full of fizzy little ringlets that reminded Jessie of bubbles in champagne; they made her own curls feel old and relaxed, stretched out and easy. In fact, Mary Frances acted like those bubbles—a squealer-in-glee, a clapper-of-the-hands, an enthusiast of a peculiarly childlike sort, she had had trouble, quite often, establishing her authority over the children. ("With!" she would say. "Not 'over,' 'with!' " which was part of the problem.) "I suppose he waited till you were gone, Jessie," she offered, her eyes round like her perfect carbonated curls. "All the things that came spilling out—I have a feeling he's been sort of storing it up, you know, just waiting for an opening."

Jessie nodded grimly. "Did he say anything to anybody besides Tyler and Ophelia?"

"Willie, I think, because Willie came to Tyler's defense. And because— you know—" As if Willie's blackness were suddenly too embarrassing to mention.

"Better and better."

"He's got a lot of anger in him, Jess. I mean, I felt like I was just handling a firecracker there for a while. That child has a really tense *back*."

"What did you do to him?" His back was the least of his problems.

"Quarantine. But it was almost the end of the day. I told him you'd be mighty disappointed in him."

"Did he laugh?"

Mary Frances sighed and adjusted the sash on her complexly printed skirt. She wore lovely antique dresses to school to please herself, since no one else would much notice in the drafty old building, and sometimes she had trouble not stepping into her drooping hems. Right now she had blue poster paint on her lace cuff, delicate as the edging on carnation petals. "He said, 'Good.' And strutted around a lot, like a little cock, when I took him out of there. I believe he really thought he had accomplished something."

"All right," Jessie said, turning to mount her chase. "Here comes."

He was in the boys' room but she knocked once, announced she was coming in, and came. He didn't resist; she wished he had so that she could stay immersed in the easy part a little longer. He was sitting on the wooden slat-back chair under the window exactly like a felon who has decided the chase is over, that he would rather suffer than be shot. The high white urinals on the far wall looked like Roman artifacts, fountains made quaint by time. A trickle of water ran down on one of them teasingly; it had left a permanent streak of chlorine blue.

"O'Neill," she said sadly, knowing her sadness would only irritate him further.

"Jessie," he answered. "Aunt Jessie? Mrs. Jessie? *Who* Jessie?" He looked perfectly earnest, waiting to be told who, ready to go beyond the moment into the inescapable issue.

Standing, shocked, in the wooden doorway, neither inside nor out, and wondering how one could tell a red herring from any other kind, she couldn't even begin to answer him.

O'Neill is getting to go back home with Jessie. She very carefully explained to me she wants some time with him alone. (He is having "trouble" in school whatever that means. I'll bet they give him a lot of reasons.) And she also thinks he might feel better if he sees his old friends for the weekend. She didn't ask me. But I decided I would not want to go anyway. That is not my life any more. Period. My life is nowhere. What is the sense of thinking of anything from before, those friends won't do me any good now. My mother can't come to me to talk or go choose a dress with me or go to the pool or anything so why be distracted by those things that are only memories? I am concentrating on today and tomorrow. I can't touch a memory with my fingers or close my hand around it. If I tell Bonnie and Julie Ann how awful this place is what can they do? Feel sorry for me, just what I need. I am going to grow up without pity.

Out on the road, Jessie and O'Neill were developing a game together. Every time they approached a town each of them would name one very specific thing—you could hardly call them sights—they planned to see: because it was raining, it was a woman with a blue umbrella; in Yazoo City, a stone church; in some of the smaller towns it was a FOR SALE sign, a barn with a painted advertisement on its wall, a dead tree. There was no point whatsoever to the game, which was why they liked it. Jessie, in this month and a half, had always been too busy to play with O'Neill, he had missed that time in her life; and it kept her, too, from directing his reluctant attention to this or that atrocity of a house or a rusted tin trailer or a bedraggled child walking in the distance, it damped down the Walker Evans vision, that dreary clarity that Teddy tended toward. As for O'Neill, he hadn't had much occasion for laughing lately, his good cheer was a muscle growing slack. So their searching, finding, mischievous cheating, ungrudging surrender—there seemed to be no blue umbrellas in use these days; perhaps, Jessie suggested, there was an ordinance forbidding them?—was tonic for both of them. Towns that had once been impaled on the map of her mind with pins (Skelly got his windshield busted in Dandelion; Butts is a speed trap and then you're in trouble); she rode through this time looking for lightning rods, sows in a pen, backhoes. She felt hypnotized by such frivolous concentration, felt a cooling hand placed over the back of her neck and held there.

She didn't get to go places much any more: Teddy did all the driving and then, on weekends, wanted to bury the keys to the car. Wasn't that why Alexis had taken that trip with Roger—to "get away"? If you believed in fate, you would have to see what happened as punishment. But for what? Today she believed in blind chance.

"Coca-Cola sign!" O'Neill called out. "I got it!"

"You got it!" Blind chance, or chance that sees moving shadows and lunges for them as if they were prey?

. . .

They were going to spend the night at Varona's. She never saw Varona any more, and missed her. She was one of the touchstones, the incorruptibles, of all the women she had known the dearest teacher. She made them all look callow. But Jessie had to prepare O'Neill for this visit, or he would find it strong medicine. She told him this was Andy's godmother they were going to see, told him she was black and large and grand and looked, maybe, like an African princess. "Only she likes to laugh," Jessie said, "and she's very nice to little boys. She has two of her own." She hoped she could engage him, distract him, with details.

"What are their names?" O'Neill asked obediently, grabbing at the passing straws. Perhaps he was trying to imagine small black princes like the blackamoors on the lawns in Birmingham.

"Matthew and Simon. Only they're grown up now, they're probably not there these days. I don't know. And Varona's an important lady, now. You know what, O'Neill," she said solemnly, "she's the mayor of her town."

He did not look particularly interested. "Backhoe!" he shouted when they passed a prehistoric-looking long-necked machine standing silhouetted against the dimming light.

"Too late," Jessie teased. "Game's over." If she'd been a praying woman, she'd have prayed along about here, she thought, when she saw her old favorite cypresses knee deep in the river where it began to look like Louisiana bayou country. They were about fifteen miles south of Wolfville when it started: the delta road curved right along the bank, not so marooned, so parched and inland for a while. The trees were sunk in still water up to their leafless middle branches. When she passed them in sunlight it looked as though the whole town, or at least the side that was all dark faces, had gone and walked into the Yalobusha to be baptized. God, she had forgotten! Pass them by quarterlight as they were doing now, a long day in the delta, a glow was oozing up from the river and there was the whole town, one by one, all in the near dark out there, drowning.

O'Neill didn't ask any more questions about anything as unlikely as an African princess ruling a delta town but when they arrived in Wolfville and ribboned through the soggy rutted streets where people still stood and watched each car go by for want of better entertainment, he said to Jessie, and wrinkled his nose at what could have been an obnoxious smell, "She can keep this town, boy. Anybody could be mayor of this junk pile if they wanted. You could be mayor, even."

They got there just at dinnertime, which was not what she had intended; but it would have been much too pointed an insult if Varona found that they had stopped to eat. Jessie walked with O'Neill up the two steps to the concrete porch and knocked with her knuckles on the white door, whose paint was feathered and cracked like an old enamel pot. Then Varona had her in a hug and Jessie was introducing O'Neill who stood unyieldingly stiff beside her, his eyes wide and unblinking. She felt a ripple of spiteful pleasure at the boy's discomfort—let it be cauterized, contained. Let him not repent but simply learn to walk out of it like a shed skin, his father's meanness and contempt. There was no one Varona could not charm.

Last time Jessie had seen her she was in a leopard-skin robe, bobby sox peeking out at the hem. Today she stood deep in flowers, colossal poppies with bright leonine heads, yellow and pink. "Well, come on in, y'all, outta that evening chill! You letting it in my living room if *you* don't care." Her hair was back behind a white band, well greased for company. That rich brown bobbing head seemed to Jessie never to age or change.

"You coming, O'Neill?" Jessie's voice was matter of fact. But O'Neill looked angry: everything she had told him in the car was beside the point now that he stood in the aura of the actual woman. His face was strained as if he had been plunged into cold water without a warning. Jessie bobbed from foot to foot, ill at ease with her conscience: she believed in assent, consultation, discussion but—oh, this was Teddy, what she abhorred in him—after the consultation she expected full consent. That was not exactly democracy. Now she seemed to be perfecting the aim of her cold-water arm. "O'Neill, you are letting in the *cold*."

The boy, looking down at the ground, came sullenly in and closed the door.

"Well, let's looka here," Varona said, smiling full at him. "I guess you'd be called the new boy in class. Hey, you like pop?"

O'Neill shrugged and kept his eyes down, a form of disrespect that could pass for shyness in a pinch.

"That mean a no or a yes? 'Cause I got two kinds of stuff in here—let's see—what is it?" She went to the refrigerator. "A root beer and a Pepsi, I guess it is. My boys get home before you make up your mind you won't get no second chance—"

"Root beer." He caught Jessie's eye as if to plead forgiveness for not being absolute in his refusals. "Please."

Varona had pork chops and a pot of beans for them. She put some A-1 on the table and sat down but she didn't eat. The boys were both crosstown, Simon at work at the Piggly Wiggly ("Make a grownup feel like a little kid every time you got to say that!" she complained and laughed) "and Matthew with his girlfriend. He always with his girlfriend, you know that little Gerry Starkweather? If they ain't made me a grandmother out there—he got him a truck, would you believe?—then one of them's gotta be sterile for sure. 'Cause Matthew—you remember Matthew?—he don't *talk* enough to take up all this much time. Man of action, so we can guess what the action gonna be!"

"Remember I told you Varona's the mayor of this town," Jessie said to O'Neill, scooping up some beans on her fork. "You're eating with the honest-to-goodness mayor."

O'Neill looked all around the little square table covered with woodgrain contact paper before he stared gravely up to study Varona's face. He must have been adding together into a woeful sum his contempt for navy beans served from a black pot, and the little pile of white bread, the grayish bones of the chops that lay like the picked corpse of sparrows in his plate, and putting it against whatever beginner's sense he had of the dignity of a genuine mayor. Varona watched him piecing it out and smiled so hard, so encouragingly, her gums showed.

"Honey, after this here child goes on to bed I'm gonna tell y'all what mayor comes to around this place so you don't carry no fancy ideas on home with you." She rose, this time letting her weariness show, and the price of her good cheer, and put some coffee water into a pot. "Y'all don't mind boiled coffee," she assured Jessie. "I don't seem to have patience to fiddle with one of them real pots. Down there at what they calling City Hall—" she snorted out a plugged laugh—"we got us one a them Mr. Coffees. I want you to know we got a *integrated* coffee machine, water comes down the same sprout for them and me and we got our little mugs all lined up in a row just like chickens in a roost. Just think on that. Lordy, Where Will It Lead?"

How many layers down did that depression go, Jessie wondered. She helped O'Neill into Matthew's bed right after dinner, Varona assuring them that he'd had his lying down for the day, with a gear-shift in his ribs. O'Neill, it was clear, wanted to crawl away anywhere he could; he did not want to see Varona or her house or her son's silvered track trophies. He pulled the quilt up to his chin and closed his eyes like a child in a game imitating a corpse.

They sat down at the cleared table. "Well, Jessie, I tell you, they got us just as bad as before. *You* know that. I suspected when I won this damn fool thing they had to be letting me win it, that was the only way, they ain't no less clever than they was before so that only mean they *more* clever, only going down a different track. You remember that first election we had to drag through back there, that Justice of the Peace? Even if they ain't been no peace in this county since the Indians—"

Jessie nodded. "And not much justice either." That was the election Varona had come within fifteen votes of winning, eight of them given to the white grocer who ran against her by the same hands—the worn black hands—that had taken, each, a clump of folded-up bills at the back door of the courthouse on voting day. But the other seven votes? Varona had always, with the certainty of all her years in Wolfville, blamed her new neat airtight house for those lost votes. She had found, that year, that she could get a government loan for no more money than her neighbors were giving the landlords for their reprehensible shacks, and giving and giving into perpetuity. She told everyone she knew that they could live in the same kind of house, with paper seals on the brand-new windows, and shiny chrome on the flush toilets. "If I'd still a been in the shack and the shithouse with the falling-down door and all, and the Pepsi-Cola tin on my walls, those folks wouldn't have Judased me like they done. Ain't no one deserve nothing, huh. They ain't seeing no one get too far out in front. I told 'em but they none a them believed me. I don't know but what they don't really deep down inside think they don't *deserve* no chance to get out of the mud. See, even my own peoples got me down for a uppity nigger."

That was a loss Jessie was afraid would break Varona. She did in three bottles of Johnnie Walker in twenty-four hours over the seven unbought votes and then began planning her comeback. And she upped the ante: instead of justice of the goddamn peace she might as well be mayor.

"Well, sugar," she was saying now, smiling broadly, "I guess they just decided they let me sit up there in that big chair, even got a name on the door—MRS. V. JACKSON, MAYOR—then they come up like termites, you know, eat the seat right out under me until I'm sitting there, got nothing under my behind but the dust in the air!"

She documented the uselessness of the job, which was not useless: all the grant applications she'd filed, the housing she'd seen to (and now that she had a title, people listened), the services to individual constituents, the speeches she'd give to rapt schoolchildren as Mayor Jackson—it had to mean something. "Jessie, now, look at that street out front there. You see any asphalt out there yet? They *widening* Rose Street down there across town, 'beautifying,' what they call it, got 'em pots of flowers, new lamps in the street, and we still got us rats in the pipes over here. We had a baby just last week, his mama found a rat sitting in the bed with him getting ready for his dinner. She pulled that child right out of there but the rat just kept on sitting like he owned the place. Mayor! You think anybody consulted me about buying them flowerpots? And then I got to talk to my own peoples over here, explain how come I can't do half the stuff I promised 'em I'd do?"

By now the Johnnie Walker was out and Varona's eyes were heating up. It was because she couldn't look forward to it any more. Even losing had had its pungency: something worthwhile they had cheated her out of. How could it be that all of it stayed theirs, victory and defeat? What was humiliating was that their power substituted for brains—and they didn't even need a ticket of admission to watch her shame. Just lined up for it. Jessie poured herself a glass. She hated scotch but she hoped she might halve the distance between them.

"And don't be looking for no Casey neither. I do believe he got him a lady ain't interested in no politics whatsoever, no way, somewhere up around Greenwood. He like to stop over there coming home from work like he found him a gas station, you know? Get him a little service for the road." She shook her glass roughly. "Fill 'er up. Then he come on home and eat. He saying I bitch too much about things I can't fix. Well. I got me a lot of mens seem like they got better things these days than coming on home to the lady mayor."

Varona watched Jessie put the glass to her lips and shook her head. Then she said, in a voice of a different color, "Well, tell me about this little cracker child you got here. Pretty little boy, ain't he."

"Oh yes," said Jessie. "He makes me do a lot of things I'm not proud of, though. I get anxious and—you know. Heavy handed with him. And then I get sorry, when it's too late."

"Oh honey!" Varona said. "Sound like anybody who got a kid, a dozen kids. You hold their head right under. And then you say, Whoa there, what the hell am I doing, and 'xpect this boy to come up tolerating being anywhere around? Whoo, don't I *know* it!"

Jessie put her lips to the scotch and waited for it to burn through to some kind of feeling. "And I don't know if I'm making any headway. How the *hell* do you take a little savage—I mean, he *is* a savage when it comes to everything, except manners. What do you do?"

"You probably keep your mouth shut, sweetie. I know that's harder than if I say, Go fly this boy to the moon and get him back for breakfast. And Teddy's worse, I just bet. Because we know he got him a bad habit, don't we?" She winked.

"Do we?" The scotch was settling like a slight mist across her eyes and the bridge of her nose.

"Oh, you know, he forever giving a lecture. He even go round trying to convert the converted. Used to lecture me something fierce and I already believed. He don't *ever* relax, lambie, and you better not learn that off him. That is one man that got a hard-on for the truth if I ever saw one. I always thought he could make a hellfire preacher that could raise the dead and get 'em to apologize for the sins that killed 'em."

Jessie gave her a smile so sad and undefended that Varona looked away; probably it was more of her visitor than she was willing to see just now at her kitchen table, this poor old white girl. Jessie was embarrassed.

But, having given Varona nothing, she thought it would be unfair to look for sympathy for herself. She asked Varona about her plans. "Don't know," was what she said, "till I pry the tiger's mouth a little wider still and get a better look in. You know I feel like this is the end of the line for me right here. I ain't about to leave this place, I know everybody's grandma and grandchild and what they eat for supper and whether they like the taste all right, till it's too much of it for me sometimes. But I know it, and that's good as a paper from some college somewhere. If I can only figure out a better way to use it."

"Run for Congress. You're smarter than all our congressmen standing one on top of the next." That was what Teddy had always dreamed of doing, if only someone had suggested it. He had never accepted how absurd it was, considering how people elect men they're comfortable with, black or white; had never accepted that, the way he sat on the cusp between them, neither was comfortable with him.

"Oh—" she sighed, and then the bedroom door swung open with the squeak of a small animal caught by the tail. It had an ominous middle-of-the-night sound but there was something a little bit conditional about it. Someone was going to peek around it to see how its opening was being received.

"O'Neill?" Jessie sat forward in her chair.

She heard a garbled answer.

"Come on out here if you're awake."

O'Neill in his flannel winter pajamas, composed of a battalion of bears with drums strapped to their bellies, walked flatfooted into the room pretending to rub his eyes. "I got sick."

He had, no mistaking it. Jessie put one arm around him and looked into the dark little bedroom where he had managed to leave a pile of his dinner on the floor beside the bed—at least, not in it. Jessie felt his forehead.

"It's nigger food and a nigger bed," O'Neill explained sotto voce with patient exasperation, as if this were only what one could expect. "That's what you get. You didn't *say*."

Jessie held him by his narrow forearm, roughly. "Oh, yes, I did too 'say.' I most certainly did." She'd have shaken him, or worse, if Varona hadn't been there. Varona wanted to clean it up, presumably because it was her house, but Jessie wouldn't let her. It was nothing less than grotesque.

Jessie, wiping the linoleum with a paper towel, tried to force the best interpretation: not that O'Neill thought Varona was the nigger he said she was but quite the opposite, that she was obviously good and kind and that the conflict was too much for him. She remembered her mother telling her how she had vomited the first time she ate meat that was not kosher. It was the beginning of change, and it felt like a ripping.

"Oh, little man," Varona was saying from the doorway, to which she had been barred by Jessie. "My Matthew, he use to chuck up every other meal when he got excited 'bout anything. High school band? Up it come, pits and stems and tails, all of it. We readying for a trip to Memphis? Well, he'd go and lay out everything he ate the last week so we could take a look and be sure and admire it a little." O'Neill stared at her coldly but she laughed. "Think we was helping him pick out what shirt he want to wear."

While they were so engaged, the front door opened and a young voice called "Maaa?"

"Back here, Simon. Come show your face!"

A tall narrow young man appeared, so thin that he went straight from his chest to his shoes, his beltless slacks down at their last possible holding point before disaster. Jessie saw Simon every few years; she had missed this last growing spurt. His face was still a boy's, its planes soft, as if they could still yield to any influence and harden kind or harsh or canny. "Man, what you doing down there?" he asked her. "Praying?"

He nodded hello to O'Neill, who stayed in the shadows of the bedroom. "Well, I guess you're in there if they say you are."

"Now he's gonna eat," his mother said with an irritated satisfaction.

"Well, why not? You'd be on me if I didn't. All I do all afternoon. I pass that food along in front of me at the register and I don't even get to lick my fingers."

"There's a pork chop and some beans in there," she said. "You want me to heat it for you?"

"I can do it." He moved into the front room and O'Neill peeked around his door again. Perhaps Simon in the flesh did not inspire such riot in his soul.

"You want to come out and sit with us a little?" Jessie asked him gently. The child sat on the couch, the enemy couch, stuck in a corner with his flannel knees drawn up while Simon talked to Jessie from the kitchen table.

He was probably wondering, Jessie thought, and softened a little, why these people were not his parents. Did he really know where his mother was?

They talked about ambitions, which Simon called illusions. They guessed at the starting salaries of a dozen nonexistent jobs. Simon gestured with a gnawed rib bone. He was a gentle, soft-spoken young man, earnest, perhaps a bit vague, nothing of his mother's irreverent energy in him, only the isolated brightness of her eyes. He wanted to be a veterinarian and have a practice of pigs and cows, not people; wanted nothing to do with politics. Politics was a nasty business that got everyone exercised and made people spiteful. "Half the bad things you hear about, they're retaliation for some-body taking something away from someone who didn't want to give it, that's all." He shook his head. Varona cast her bloodshot eyes to heaven and then closed them. Her son was walking on her grave, digging his heels in. Jessie wondered if he was oblivious or if Simon, like his father, was punishing Varona. If so, why? Jessie needed to know why: because she had failed or because she had succeeded?

"But he don't understand nothing about discouragement," Varona was saying to Jessie, banging the end of the table with the flat of her hand. "He don't see how it's a privilege, getting discouraged. One thing for me to lose my faith, or you, we been there and back and we seen it for ourself and fought against it and fought some more—Simon, here's a woman, her hus-band didn't have no *skin* on his face whole years at a time so you can vote when you get your age—so now we can sort of relax if we got a mind to, and let down into it. Another thing for a spring lamb here to say, Oh what the hell, I won't even bother to make it through to fall, eat up, get fat, I just go'n lay me down right here under the butcher's knife, wait my turn for the blood to flow. Make me wish I kept my damn mouth shut all these years." She had made remarkable progress with the bottle. She glared at it now, just the bottom covered. She seemed unable to decide whether it was worth turning over and shaking. All she could do was scowl at it.

"You want him to leave?" Jessie asked. "Get out of town?"

Varona looked around her. "Ain't seen no college anywhere round here now, or did I miss one someplace? Sure I want him out of town, what he gonna do in a town with six hundred and forty-seven in it, half of them hoping he'll never make a dogcatcher out of himself let alone no veterinarian? And somebody else's cotton fields looking right in the window at him when he pees? You seen anything he can *do* round here?"

"You didn't have to keep your mouth shut, Mama," Simon said, sitting back from his supper. "I got eyes. You don't chew my meat up for me, do you? Only you got to let me have a little respect for the way I see it, that's all. I'm not going to live my life fighting all the time, all the time looking to sound off at somebody, twitch my fingers just itching for something I can rearrange the way I like it. You got a son who's going to learn to *settle* for a few good things and relax." He turned to Jessie, his calm features sharp, his mouth working nervously. "My mama, she sleep standing up, she one of those people they're gonna have to break her in pieces to get her to lie down in the graveyard." He breathed out, hard, a long "pphhh." "She'll be reorganizing the heavenly choir, make sure there's more black folks got a 'meaningful voice.' "

Jessie would not look at Varona. O'Neill, she saw, was drugged with the hour and the voices; he was keeping his eyes fixed blindly on a calendar hung too high up on the wall, where snow-capped mountains suggested they turn their thoughts to Switzerland. They talked on in this bleak twilight tone, slashed through from time to time with Varona's bitter saving laughter. And it looked like Casey wasn't coming home tonight.

When Jessie carried O'Neill back into the bedroom the smell of ammonia had penetrated the air. Breathing it felt like breathing in a vacuum, seemed to leave no air in her lungs. On her way to her own bed she stopped to look through her window at the dented moon. The endless stripped cotton field that lapped Varona's lot was cold as a meadow under snow. Switzerland again. In spite of everything, she'd always thought she'd rather starve under a Mississippi sunset, or under such a moon, than starve on 125th Street facing an airshaft. But what good is the clarity of the moon unless you are already at ease? O'Neill is starving, Varona is starving, Casey is wherever he is because he's hungry for something, only the man who owns the cotton field is not starving, and who knows, who even knows about him? And the moon shines hopefully on us so we can find each other in the dark as if we were food, she thought, to fill each other's mouths. But we will still be hungry in the morning.

·   ·   ·

When their trip to Birmingham was over and they were on their way home across that margin where the states seemed to overlap in colorless darkness, Jessie realized that she felt sore from her confrontation with Roger and Alexis's friends, achingly sore from a kind of overextension in their direction which was met and met again with a soft surface friendliness and a bedrock hardness beneath.

She had begun by asking Judy Carmichael to suggest the names of the Tysons' friends who might be helpful to her. Judy herself had been profoundly unhelpful, she could not say whether by virtue of lack of imagination—"What can we tell you about them? There just isn't a thing to tell, they were just clear as rainwater, those two!" (That *just* had begun to show itself as a contrivance which Judy overused: the minimizing, trivializing swipe of it across any slightly soiled surface!) Or was it a more complicated deviousness, of which she might or might not be aware herself?

Jessie had called her from home before they left for the delta and Varona's, she had given a little clap-hands of her voice and said, Yes, what a wonderful lucky time to visit, there was going to be a birthday party at the home of Donna Durgin, for Donna's twins, at which would be gathered, as if by providence, many of the special friends of Alexis and Roger and even of O'Neill, who could be reunited with his little friends while the oldsters (she laughed at the exaggeration) talked. They could sit in the kitchen and discuss every single thing.

At first Jessie had thought, agreeably, what a stroke of timing that was. Then, when sense overtook her she remembered women-in-crowds—well, anyone really, she granted, but perhaps women especially because they are more finely tuned to each other's signals than they will allow themselves to be to their *own*: they would be busy as a fire brigade handing water buckets down the line trying to anticipate each other's opinions and answers, and the children would bang in and out of the kitchen in search of solace or soda or social arbitration.

But it was worse. They sat in Donna Durgin's kitchen and, between distractions, lied to her.

There were four of them, plus a random detachment of other mothers who had not been especially close to Alexis and Roger and so either passed through or sat and were treated to a running interpretation of events that tended to make Jessie feel unreal, a part of the narrative furnishings rather than the convener of the meeting. She was half of "And fortunately there was an aunt and uncle from Jackson," who could have been anyone; who certainly seemed to be absent.

Donna Durgin, blond, dressed in gray slacks and a pink blouse with a voluminous bow that seemed to flow naturally from the soft hollow of her neck, was cute as a baseball player's wife. She had a sort of silent attendant in someone called Tooty or Tutti or Toodie, who was a rather unlikely sort of friend for her, a gray inhibited woman with nunnish close-cropped hair who seemed far too serious for such a name. (Our campaign for dignity, thought Jessie, is going nowhere until there are no more Muffies and Pookies and Tooties and Tushes.) This Tooty sat at the table listening doggedly, giving off the air of someone who was here on sufferance and would be subjected to severe questioning when they adjourned and took their smeary-faced children home. (She turned out, as Jessie pieced it together, to be a sister-in-law, a mandatory presence at family parties whose style was beside the point.) Then there was a plump, bitter giggler called Peg who was a lot younger than the others; she referred to herself in fact as The Child Bride and rolled her eyes, which were as dark and compact as olives. Jessie had not a doubt in the world that the eye-rolling connoted pregnancy-before-marriage, and a life culminating there: there was no affection in her references to her husband, who stayed resolutely nameless; there was not even neutrality.

"Do you know what he did this morning?" she demanded first thing when she entered the room, letting Donna's saloon doors swing behind her—it was a Western kitchen, they sat under a massive brightly lit wagon wheel that Jessie would not have liked to see fall from its heavy swag chain. "You-all might not appreciate it but it is, right now, this very minute, open season on the common snipe?" She turned to Jessie, to whom she had not yet been introduced. "We already went through crow and gallinule, you probably know that, and these disgusting things called rails. And sora. You ever see a sora, dead and bloody all over those feathers? Uph." Her eyes widened as if she were being pinched. "I've never been what you'd call frail but you couldn't get me to touch a healthy one and he wants me to gut *two* last time. I was thinking of maybe putting a Baggie full of those *innards* in his lunch pail."

Jessie stared at her.

"Well, he decides he's getting up before dawn this morning to go get him some snipe"—she pronounced it *snop*, which did not help Jessie's comprehension of the story, nor had she quite known what Peg wasn't when she denied being *fry-al* or considered putting the Baggies in his lunch *pile*—"with his cousin Bo. Bobo, that's the one that'd rather pinch than say hello? So at quarter to four there he is shaking me in the bed so I'll go on get the coffee ready and fill him up a Thermos of it, and then come on back and wake him like he ha'n't an *idea* morning has even started coming on."

"And you did it," Donna said bleakly, holding the kettle under its thick feather of steam.

" 'Course I did it." Peg rolled her pit-black eyes again. "He don't give a woman a whole lot of choice, you know."

Donna poured water into instant coffee, looking into each cup vengefully as if she were drowning something live in the bottom of it. She seemed to know; at least she didn't argue.

The other women were a good deal more genteel in their relations with their husbands; Jessie wondered if Peg made them uncomfortable or very comfortable indeed, in the lesser shadow of whatever might afflict their own marriages. (Judy's huge pale husband, Lovett, for example, whom she had briefly met, seemed to be distinguished chiefly by his absence. He was, in spite of his pallor, a very successful something-or-other, Jessie couldn't remember what, who was this year president of the chamber of commerce. Judy complained cheerfully that the boys were holding him ransom—if she could come up with half a million they would let him back home for visits.) All their husbands, in fact, must be reasonably successful at whatever they did: this was an expensive section of town, shaded by carefully selected pines, gated and gardened and bereft of human traffic. A bad neighborhood at Halloween, Lydia would tell her. Deserted, too much space between doorbells.

Of course they remembered Jessie from the time of the funeral. Tongues clicked at the memory, heads shook with the kind of satisfaction witnesses cultivate in the presence of uncontagious catastrophe.

"O'Neill is looking good," Donna told her in a conspiratorial whisper when he had gone off a little shyly with his old friends. He had caught Jessie's eye a few times, a dependency she found astonishing. That he looked good seemed to Jessie something one might tend to say about an adult, whose looks were more vulnerable to change. Of course O'Neill looked good—his pain or confusion was unlikely to have carved shadows of insomnia or infant neurosis on his cheeks. He had, at least, the child's invincibility of flesh, if not of circumstance, didn't he?

"Well," she began, "I think he's doing all right considering." She let the "considering" hang ominously, a petition for their help, while Judy explained to Tooty who had just moved here from Houston, a city where all was not as it was alleged to be—she had her own ominousness of phrase—how the child's parents had been—she snapped her pudgy fingers noiselessly; they seemed too padded to make a sound. Tooty gasped and put her hand to her chest as if to ward off a blow to her own heart. It was explained, again, that Alexis, a dear, never got to go anywhere while Roger tended to move around at a good clip. The first time she heard the story so told it did not occur to Jessie to put out a hand to stop it in its rolling. When the whole thing was rehearsed again in a version revised to amplify what the neighbors already knew—this to a pregnant woman named Martha who had joined them, and whose little girl clung to her knees and would not join the party until she was enticed with a green balloon that Tooty produced from her purse that said *Get Right with Christ* in child's script—Jessie intervened to ask what it meant exactly that Roger had travelled a lot.

"He had a lot of cities to go to," Judy told her. "Sometimes he got to skip around in those little company planes? You know, the baby jets? All that danger he passed through and not a nick on the man!" She shook her head, swathed in elaborate layered curls that must have been heavy when they shifted. "He was a fairly prominent man, I would call him. You have to give him credit for that, Jessie. You might have come upon a plaque he had that called him Mr. Insurance of 1976, I think it was? Did you see that in the house? That was what some of those flower arrangements at the funeral were? Some of his out-of-town contacts that were just so shocked and unhappy they had lost him."

"What were they like as a couple?" But Jessie had presumed more trust than she had bought. The question, like an astringent, made their faces tighten.

"Oh—" Donna began and then flicked her hand up the way she might have done had a fly settled on her fingertip. She did not intend to finish the sentence. What did that mean, that flip? Happy families are all alike? "Look." Jessie pulled her chair closer to the table. "Please understand me. I'm not particularly interested in gossiping about two people I barely knew." There was a disquieting little grunt of assent. "But I have their two children in my house and what I need to—"

There was a pounding and clatter and half the birthday party spilled into the kitchen, the boys pulling their guns at the saloon doors. Something seemed to have burst and they had broken out of it under pressure. Donna's twins were, to Jessie's surprise, not very attractive children—their blondness had something embryonic about it still, their skin loose and pale, as if they were made of white bread and granulated sugar. (Were they really going to look, finally, like their mother?) The boy was wearing a pair of rust-colored velvet jeans, belted with a huge brass horse's head, and his sister wore a long matching velvet dress in which she was having understandable difficulty getting around. She was intent only on jumping on her brother's back; he stayed a step or two ahead of her, looking anxiously over his shoulder, as if he were under attack. To judge by their complaints, everyone was ruining their party. Donna, her face expressionless, connoting hard-won control, put a hand on the head of each of them as they caterwauled; they looked like jacks in the box which she was about to push back down. To Jessie's delight, because mystery was so much more satisfying than cosmic equity, the gray cipher Tooty's child was beautiful, a deep dark gypsy-colored girl, the whites of whose eyes were absolutely blue with full-blooded health, a suspicious hint of hybrid vigor. She came to rest for a minute against her mother's taut thigh, saying nothing, only smiling a little. There were many kinds of victors in the world, and many kinds of spoils.

"Where is O'Neill?" Jessie asked doubtfully.

"Gone someplace with Chilton?" she was told with that eternal questioning dip that seems to beg approval for the answer. There followed, however, a bill of particulars: that he had taken two ice creams, that he thought he could do any old thing just *because* . . .

The cause of the interruption was Peg's little boy, Junior Lee, who had wet himself all the way down his leg and was hiding, it was reported with elation masquerading as chagrin, in the coat closet out front. Peg rose wearily with a look that declared such victimization, either her own or her son's, to be no great surprise. The others threw out a sort of smoke of comforting cheerful noise to cover the embarrassment.

When Peg came back walking her very small son, she was muttering, "He's all curled up playing dead, I mean, not breathing, and all these winter coats are hanging in front of him in that cleaner's plastic, Lord, he could have killed himself if he got his *nose* caught in it! Donna! What are you doing, selling overcoats on the side? What is all that?" She ruffled her son's hair, which was short as a dog's razor-back ridge. "Black as a nigger's ass in there and I'm supposed to find him!"

Jessie opened her mouth to cry out objection and closed it again. There was laughter but only her own sudden movement made her think the laughter had an edge of nervousness in it. It did not. They did not hear with her ears.

Peg shook Junior Lee lightly and he murmured up at her that it wasn't his fault he didn't know where the bathroom was. "Dumbo, you play here all the time!" his mother protested, but he said, looking down at his sneakers humbly, "Yes ma'am, but we always do it behind a tree!"

Jessie sat clutching her fingers in her fists. Peg had not said that to provoke her, it was worse: it was only what one said, it was what one laughed at. The children were dispatched in a flying wedge, even the one with the soaked and stinking pants, who had decided to rejoin the others like a man as soon as his mother threatened to take him home. "Just don't sit down on my upholstery, honey!" Donna called out, covering her eyes melodramatically, her fine fingernails straight up like the pink points of budding tulips.

And they would not give a millimeter: AlexisandRoger stayed a single word. There was bitterness afloat in the room, or sourness, rather, toward the generic husband—it was the resigned gallows humor of the servant class discussing the employers in whose lives their own are implicated so that every slight, though it is felt and recorded, is finally justified. What sisterhood the women felt—Jessie smiled to think how they would shout down such a word—was mostly negative: they had so many small rank secrets in common, some of which shamed them when it ought to have been their men they shamed, and a number (not quite equal because pleasure is not exactly commensurable with pain) of comforts and satisfactions. Why could there not be more than two sexes so that everyone could be accommodated? Her assumptions about so many things were more dissimilar from these women's than they were similar. But it hurt to think that. She was a traitor to female solidarity. Well, how many ways could one divide oneself? The women who threw stones at small black children, were they women before they were racists, were they allies first, or deadly foes? Oh, to love mine enemy, she thought. To embrace these "girls" as mine. . . .

Alexis and Roger were known by this sex, for example, to be good dancers, generous with steak and Southern Comfort at their parties. Alexis did every little public duty with a smile and when she was secretary of the Women's Circle she had been responsible for the best treasure hunt, the very best ever, which showed evidence of imagination and care. "Yes," Jessie said ungraciously, "I heard all that and then some at the funeral."

Well, then, they seemed to say.

"Well, what kind of things do you want to know?" Peg asked impatiently, leaning her chair back so that she looked like a teenager finished with dinner, whose parents are keeping her beyond the limits of her endurance.

I don't know but they are *gone*, Jessie longed to say. Why do I seem to be the only one missing them? Is this how they would like to be remembered? What a cruel thing, then, to leave your memory in such casual hands. Butterfingers! her mother would call her whenever she dropped things from inattention. They would all be the first to swear piously that Life Goes On in the Memories of Loved Ones. Were these their only viceroys to posterity, here sipping Maxim and talking about how Alexis had been lucky for someone who bought her kitchen curtains by mail order, sight unseen?

"It's just such a *country* thing to do," Judy was saying. "Considering she never did anything tacky if she could help it—"

It was an abiding mystery. Her blood had beat hard and strong, Jessie gathered—there were vague allusions to her rebelliousness, echoes off the edges of the main text, unexplained. But wherein, besides in her curtains, did it abide?

"How would you like to be remembered when you die?" She tried that on them as lightly as she could, feeling off balance. She supposed she didn't know them well enough to ask a frivolous question like that, let alone a serious one, without sounding a rebuke. But no one took it hard.

"Oh, for my snipe pot pie!" Peg answered and saluted. "I want him to put that on my tombstone. 'She never pleaded headaches,' that goes on top. Like him." She laughed joylessly. "Produced a son and heir who peed in his pants till he was twenty. Unh . . . baked a pie with his hunting rifle in it." ("But what a flaky crust," Judy prompted. All of them laughed breathlessly between suggestions.) "Let's see . . . talked to her mother-in-law on the telephone once a day at least, to give an up-to-date report on the li'l darlin to the woman who loved him best."

"Yes, lord," Donna Durgin said and bowed her head. "And died with a fresh manicure and her hair just set so she'd look good for the send-off."

Jessie joined the laughter nervously. She hadn't a clue, admit it, to what the lives of these women were like. How much did they pity themselves or each other or look forward to such afternoons as this, how much did they dream of escape? And how, after all these years, could she not know?

Women-in-groups had always, in her life, had a special purpose, they did not "hang out," nor did they coffee-klatsch. Her mother's friends conspired, however poorly. They planned meetings, they divided up flyers and stood pressing them into passing hands on cold winter street corners. Sitting at a table they grimly analyzed degrees of commitment, of political treachery, so on and on, and all their personal talk seeped around the edges in a constant lubricating flow. In college her friends had done the same except for the more massive layer of hopeful sexual innuendo that got analyzed as well. And then, Mississippi. They might not have stuck to the point, she thought, but the point hovered and cast its organizing shadow: they clustered around it, chose sides, wore themselves out on earnestness and sat down together to regain their strength and have some reviving laughter. Women who lounged and chatted and laughed without a program, whoever they might be, were as unfamiliar to Jessie as a fish might be, confronted over a coffeepot. She was unfit, she thought, for civilian life, although she was about ready to attempt it. *That* was the other sex—the one that did not hunger, every waking hour, for change, for improvement, for control. Secular women . . .

Still, she felt pain for poor Alexis: that she had not, whoever she was and whatever like, queen of the civilians even, lingered more tangibly among them. It was not necessarily her fault, there was no way to know. Is someone who is barely perceived guilty of being impenetrable or only of choosing friends who are blind? To be generous, it was probably meeting them all in a mass that made Alexis invisible: she could huddle or be huddled out of sight, caught between the shadows of her friends, and barely be missed. Alone in the room with any of them her ghost would certainly exist to be reckoned with. Judy had ordained this, that the anonymity of the small crowd, averaging out impressions, separates Jessie from her prey. Now here she was wishing she could protect that prey from her protector.

Afterwards Teddy told her it was her own fault, she had done it wrong. She had gone at it full frontwards. Had shown her face, her possible claws, her need.

"But I'm not devious. Why should I have to ask questions sideways?" she demanded. They were on the phone; she was near tears with frustration and the feeling she had accidentally lost something the children desperately needed. "Not a word about them but those insulting generalities. They talked about how O'Neill had a little asthma along with his allergies and I said we never saw it, which they found strange as if I were lying or covering something up. Alexis's peace roses and Roger's famous humidor full of five-dollar cigars."

"Well, they do it that way, you know, so they can answer you sideways. Jess? No Southern woman's going to look you in the eye and give it all away in the first half hour, that'd be treason."

"Me? Because I don't belong here? Or anybody?" They hated her as she had always hated them, then: generically and without extenuation. They would concur: why were there not at least four sexes the way most jails or bathrooms were segregated, years ago? She needn't think she was the only one who felt the chill of distance.

"Oh, Jessie." Did she weary him so, then? "No one of them would ever have asked like that. You can't ever forget there's a certain etiquette."

"You're crazy, all of you, you know that? And I don't even believe this—this Southern Mafia with its code of honor and its secret passwords and all those willful women sitting in a circle protecting the family honor. You've sold yourself a myth and you use it to justify playing cat and mouse, that's all. For the fun of it. They were just kicking me around." She thought for a minute, overwhelmed by the crooked weight of bad logic. "Anyway, whose family is it, theirs or mine?"

Teddy laughed. It was irritating how comfortable he sounded with all this hocus-pocus. There was a lot he accepted without thought, as if it were genetic. "You can think it if you want, hon, but the proof of the pudding is, did you learn anything you wanted to learn?"

Yes, but she wouldn't pursue it: that, whatever they were, he was one of them.

. . .

And she learned to drive the Corvette, that too. Dimly she realized, as they approached the garage, she swinging the keys to the house on a little silver chain with a leather luggage tag on it, that she had dreamed last night of crawling through the window to get to it, of a shelf collapsing under her weight and paint cans splattering, the side of the car splashed with blue and yellow and gouts of red that looked like blood.

But they entered decently by way of the door next to the garage. She had wondered if O'Neill would have any reaction to seeing his house thus disembodied; she sincerely hoped he would. When he struck the dusty white car on its tumescent front fender and seemed bent on making his way straight into the driver's seat, she stopped him with her hand. "O'Neill, do you want to go have a look around?" Next time they were here, she didn't want to tell him, someone else would own the house.

He stared at her angrily. "We *did* that. When Helen was here. We looked around. Why do I always have to go in there?" He put his hands on his hips like a furious woman. "We don't live here any more, in case you didn't know."

Angry that she deserved his correction, for he was right, she slammed the solid door of the car; it was magnified in the small garage. O'Neill was jamming at the switch that raised the automatic door but the electricity—how could she have forgotten?—was off. Would she have to take the damn thing off its hinges to get it open?

O'Neill, taking advantage of her innocence in the face of household machinery, gave her a contemptuous shrug—what did she know, anyway? He had been right all along!—and pointed to a chain in the corner that would raise the door manually. She could see that it hurt him to be too small to be the one to yank it.

The car bucked at street lights until she learned how to run it through first and second in one smooth decisive motion. Cornering she felt like someone hanging on to a horse by the pommel of its saddle—not that she wasn't in control but that there was such a very narrow space between her control and her submission, and a half-turn in the wrong direction she knew could give it all out of her hands. Whether the car demanded this or her expectations of the car she couldn't say—intimidation tends to come before the fact—but one way or the other, her hands had trembled on the cold indented wheel.

O'Neill, his eyes blazing approval, tried to say a few things to her but at first she was in no position to listen, she only bit her lip and shook her head until the action of the clutch began to feel recognizable to her foot. Jessie had never been particularly queasy about what she drove, it was not a subject that much compelled her one way or the other, but Teddy and Skelly and all their friends, facile and unchallenged in their machismo, had made nasty jokes at the expense of every woman who'd ever touched their cars. It was the men who had the bizarre scrapes and the real accidents— she hadn't known a single woman who had had any serious trouble in a car unless there was a man in it, beside her, with his hand on her thigh—but the derision was an attitude, a given; the more prudent they were, the harder the men laughed.

Now they were out on a highway that passed a shopping mall and then there was only clear gray road and Jessie opened it up. It did feel fine, not for the power it gave her, she wouldn't have called it that (especially since she felt an itch to ride over the edge and into the trees to abort it as if it were pain), but for a kind of anonymity. At that speed there was no ego, she had no name or sex or destination. If birds felt power in their vaulting perhaps it was power, but she thought not: it was in no way *hers*. Such movement was something to endure, to survive—to think you were causing it, or more than marginally participating in it, took an unlikely arrogance. Why did men think such cars reflected on their potency or were fueled by it? How odd, she thought remotely, taking the car from the grittiness of third to the easy momentum of fourth that barely touched the highway and then overdrive where it seemed to flash out ahead of itself, to be drawn forward like a lick of flame, matter and yet not matter.

O'Neill held his face stiffly upward as if he were in a convertible and the wind were showering rough breath down from his short hairs to his shoulders. "Aah-aaah," he sang, truly happy, for the first time happy, and hungry for more.

They drove for nearly an hour without more than seven words: "Here?" as she turned onto a likely junction road, and "No, this doesn't look too good" when they found themselves in a tiny town, poor white, dishevelled, that looked like a backless Hollywood set. "Too slow," O'Neill complained as they moved discreetly down the main street. But Jessie couldn't stand the eyes on her, the calculation of her wealth and luck like columns punched on a cash register. A small cluster of children seated on tricycles and plastic dirt bikes actually pointed.

"Wow, look at 'em staring at us!" O'Neill crowed, closing his eyes joyfully against the glare of admiration. His hands lay open, palms up, on either side of him to make it clear that he was in the grip of this wonder, passive. He was being taken, he seemed to say, Icarus at ground level, floating free.

"O'Neill. Listen. You don't have to get your jollies from making other people jealous, you know?"

He kept his eyes closed but she could tell that some whirring thing in him had stopped its motion to listen.

"I mean . . ." She was suddenly self-conscious, heading on in straight again. But she was in her own unstoppable gear. "I don't like to feel good just because I can make other people feel bad. Does that make any sense to you? There are a lot of ways to feel good that only have to do with *you*."

"All you like is boring stuff and talking." He gave her one short, sour look and then flattened his lips as if he were his sister, that act of swallowing back. She thought he would like to punch her in the arm or shout some child's obscenity at her. Shout then! she thought. Object. Protect yourself. She didn't worry that she provoked him, it was only that the provocation was never radical enough, it didn't seem to go sufficiently deep or come pitched in the right key, perhaps, to lance his single wound. But he was surely afraid of her: had he not lived in a houseful of consequences, within earshot of a father who would brook no challenge? That much Jessie had figured out, and it made her turn away in pain from the hard-heartedness of her first impressions.

So they returned to stable the car.

"Why can't we take it with us?" O'Neill pleaded. "Leave your dumb old car and drive this one back. *Please*." He bobbed up and down on the words as if he needed the bathroom.

Jessie gave him a few good reasons which he found uncompelling.

"I'm staying," he told her as she climbed out. "I don't want to drive in that dinky thing any more. This is my daddy's car." He crossed his arms in front of his chest and put his lower lip out in a parody of stubbornness.

It was beginning to get late and she was eager to be on the road, this time with a destination. "O'Neill," Jessie finally said. "I am going to go check around the outside of the house to make sure everything's all right, and when I come back I want you in the other car." Let him save face, come out without being watched. She went into the yard, which was patchy brown and gray under the shadow of winter, where the grass had gone on growing while no one was looking, like hair in the grave. It belonged to no one now.

When she came back O'Neill was gone.

She called and searched and gulped back anger with a little of the bitterness of fear: he might have run off anywhere, it could take hours to track him down in a city strange to her, not to him. She would need to call in help. How would the silent chorus of disapproving Southern ladies like to fetch their husbands and their dogs and flashlights and beat the bushes with her?

Then she heard him laughing. She thought he was laughing. He was under the car, pressed low to the oily cement, and that was no laughter, he was crying steadily and to himself. His hiding seemed no demonstration for her punishment, she could feel how he wanted to be alone, invisible, out of reach of any kind of debt of behavior or comfort. Perhaps he wanted not to be at all.

Nonetheless. She called, she bent and tried to see where he had lodged himself and could barely find a dark obstruction between one dangling part of the car and another. He had made himself small as a cat and he sucked air and heaved it, heaved and sucked, until his breath had that convulsive hiccuping lunge to it, all crashing in against the lungs, nothing hissing back out, so that she began to fear he would hyperventilate and pass out, all beyond her reach. What about that asthma? This would be the time for it to attack. Yet she still didn't think he was doing this to her. There was a difference between anger, which could be aimed and assuaged, and grief, which was private from beginning to end.

"O'Neill!" she called in the dark garage. (The lights were gone along with the automatic door.) "O'Neill, sweet boy, come out!" She had never felt more stupid, searching for something to call him, not even for an argument, just a name, as she would try her own children's favorite endearment to see which one would prick their insensibility and, making them bleed helplessness, give her a feeble chance to move them. What had his parents called him, what dear dead names had they taken with them?

Jessie was undone. She stood and found, as if she were someone else, that she was crying along with him in a contagion of shivering and exhaustion. They were both so far from comfort—she wished she could tell him that, and move him to a pity he could wield himself. She had no idea how long he was down there but it must have felt somehow good to him, better than it looked: he stayed and stayed. As the last light out in the yard and driveway was struck blue, she saw a black slow stream inching toward her feet where she stood empty-handed beside the open car door. The light on the roof of the car was like the modest eye of a children's flashlight. He had knocked a hole in the oil tank or he had wet himself under there in the blinding dark. Probably wet himself—then he was lying with his knees and his stomach in it, moaning now, beyond consolation, an animal that intended to lick its own wounds. She hoped he wouldn't put himself to sleep. If she tried to pull him out—say she could even reach him to get a hand around his ankle—she would surely hurt him, scrape him above or below. "Honey, come out and let me warm you up!" she called to him bleakly, the command in her voice retracted like a closed knife blade. Christ, what was she to do, take a deep breath and drive the damn car over him? Start it up to scare him out, the way she sometimes had to do when Mickey Mouse stayed stubbornly curled beside a wheel? If she alarmed him in this state he might never forgive her; it would be dangerous, like waking a sleepwalker. He wanted his father and mother. He wanted them and could never have them back. He had sobbed out "I hate you!" and "I don't want to go with you," which might easily have been so, or might have been propitiation, extreme evidence of his love for his parents which he'd thrown out to placate whatever invisible force was keeping them from him, flung down like steak to a dog. "Never" is not a word that says very much to small children; she was no child and it didn't say anything to her that she believed. She turned her head from it whenever it came near her life, she would not entertain absolutes. But that, after all, changed nothing: absolutes were not to be undone by her absence of faith.

It was wholly dark at last except that the car light was a pathetic little moon, a played-out yellow under a cloud. Jessie, beyond all hope of movement, sat down in the driver's seat with her feet outside the car and put her arms up on the cold leather. O'Neill's solid flesh would comfort her too, if he would only let it. It was unfair not to let her warm him, let her show him how many good things were left all around the outer edge of the gaping hole which he would keep open forever. He made her feel inconsequential, invisible: yet he was a fact in her life and she in his. Before they knew it, he would have lived as long with her, then longer than he had with his own parents. They had to acknowledge each other. She laid her head gently against her arms as if it were someone else's which she had promised to guard, eggs in a nest, easily broken, and she slept too.

.   .   .

When she woke up, she decided to promise him the car. That was the only lure that would charm him out. She would call out to him, as the lavender light rose, like smoke, to the window and the gaping door, "All right! Okay, O'Neill, we'll take it home with us!" and her skin prickled suddenly with a kind of embarrassed pride at the idea of it, as if someone were looking at her and revising his opinion upward. It was impractical, absurd, ugly, she thought, but all she had to do, really, was drive to school and store and back—such was the measure her life had shrunk to—and she could do that in a fast car, what the hell. The children saw her, too, they must, as Judy had put it: an aunt from Jackson. Where had her vividness gone? Her rebelliousness? What was the last unexpected thing she had done? Teddy's suffering, his losses, had blotted up all her attention, had made her settle, both feet flat, with no qualms, on her steadiness—her work, her children, her yoked forward movement. Balance. Ballast. She would stop being cod liver oil and a heavy pair of shoes and drive the frivolous fast car, mockingly sit there behind that lurid fiberglass erection, and not apologize.

She sat in the carved-out soft seat and stared straight ahead, out at the garage wall that shone with lights the windshield struck, thinking how she would look driving up to the house on Willowbrae Drive, the nasty sound that exploded like derision through that exhaust pipe, sputtering power. Then she knew she couldn't bring it home. Oh, it would be lovely, vengefully lovely, to gun that motor and sound like an army (of capture or liberation, depending on one's situation) but she could not so assault her neighbors with this vision of the luck of their catch. Since when does an extra child or two bring such spoils on its head? To most folks, it means tighter times, more mouths to break the bread for. Not that all of Plywood wouldn't love to own one, everyone; on the contrary. They would love one and the Carlls would have one. Son of a bitch!

And when they moved, they were going to ride down a new street among alien neighbors, giving a false accounting of themselves at best. To drive a white Corvette, Teddy behind that thrust of hood like a cop behind a nightstick, when what he most wanted was to serve notice that, by a fluke, one of the have-nots was coming into the community of haves. (The moral equivalent of a have-not, anyway.) He would be happy, she thought, if only somebody remembered his name and burned a cross on the lawn to welcome them. There was no way they were going to tool down whatever Lane or Drive in a little hot-shot dual-exhaust that set them down with noisy effrontery on the side of the rich.

It was that bootless thing, a good deal less useful, even, than charity, that made them give things up, refuse to have even what they could afford, because there was a world worse off that could have nothing. Andréa used to say, "Damn right I have a decent house, you think I could get my briefs written on a rickety old table in back of some shack somewhere just to show I'm one of the natives?" Sometimes it angered Jessie that she and Teddy derived satisfaction from what they chose to forgo: there was not meant to be compensation in renouncing, every religion said so. And they did it in half-measures, too: they gave up so very little in real fact. They were moving, now, after all; they would live in a very fine house and badmouth it, low-rate it, oh, it was so self-righteous and no one gained an ounce from their squirming guilt. That was their Simone Weil streak, she would say to Teddy: Simone Weil who starved to death because there were workers and prisoners all around her who had nothing to eat. She who ate what they ate and when it ceased to be enough, took the sentence as a doom, broke herself into passivity, denied herself choice just as the others were denied it. Well, Jessie loved and hated Simone Weil—like all saints, she was blessed and unforgivable, her death put not a morsel in a single human mouth; all it stanched was the hunger of her own voracious conscience, before it rattled and gasped out. And that, Jessie thought, solved no problem but the crisis of one woman's ego. And yet, and yet . . . she had forever been haunted by the act. She had always had to work at suppressing awe, which was a kind of envy, that someone had so followed through—she thought of a dancer's body in total extension—had so purely resolved a motion to its ultimate outcome, had obliterated the distance, white-skin privilege, class privilege, the luxury of self-conciousness. What she had refused was a hi-erarchy that valued one life over another, like a child who took every promise literally. The glare of her simplicity hurt Jessie's eyes.

She had sunk down on her backbone in the leather that was so soft it felt edible. She moved the stick shift idly through its little square, that clear pattern so ingrained it lives in the synapses, and saw herself pulling it into the concrete driveway, into the ruts where Teddy parked the slow brown tired car. Put this there, she thought with a little breath of shock, and you'd better pack your bags. That was the line below what they called the bottom line. She could hear Varona say it: when you ready to kiss the man goodbye, girl, that's when you come and take this here thing out of where it come from, ride it right on over him. This car's nothing but a going-away car, don't you know that when you see it, all hot and shiny?

She slid out of the seat with her lips pressed tight together on relin-quishment, and went to call gently to O'Neill.

. . .

Driving home her mind played loosely, almost drunkenly, over a hundred surfaces, chief of which was Alexis's face: she had had a wide brow and a sharp nose, almost prominent. Assertive. There was a mystery in her. If she were still alive she might be difficult, she might present a paradox or two, but death had halted the play of light across that surface and left her a conundrum to be solved, if only the evidence turned up.

The road dipped a bit through a long valley; yellowish winter grass rose up a gentle incline, matted like the hair of an animal. Lions are that color, she thought, that indifferent sickly yellowish brown; you'd think they'd have more vigor in their hides than Alabama in November. Something about the angle of the rise felt familiar. She dug and dug for it; when they got to Meridian and past, to Chunky, to Hickory, she was still searching. Maybe it was one unforgotten day when she was very new in Mississippi and she had found such an incline and climbed it, full of suspense at what she would see on the far and downward side. She had been in Winona only about a week or so and she was already falling, falling fast, into the crack of a steep-sided disappointment. Everything she had hoped to do she was smiled out of doing: she would not be the one to walk through the fields wearing a sack across her shoulder, taking names: white girls didn't do that. Nor would she, for a while yet, knock on doors in town. The freedom schools—one held, vigilantly, under a tree in a broad meadow owned by a black family, the other in town in a little firetrap room behind the barber shop—were at the moment overstaffed. People were standing around with nothing to do. She was assigned to the freedom library like it or not, and she distinctly did not like it. She had not come all this distance to stamp books, did not see why the giving up of individual ideals had to be hers alone (for the revolution; her father had done that) when every single other person had pulled what he or she had wanted. She was caught somewhere between paranoia and a simpler gratitude that she was here at all, where she wanted to be. Teddy and half a dozen others had been here longer: they knew what was best. (They said they did.)

Already Teddy was hulking large between her and everyone else. They were finding places to be alone, nights; she was distracted, obsessed, almost, with the feel of his body, the rise and fall of his words on the most unexpected syllables, the firmness of his gentlemanly hand at her elbow, so unlike the abruptness of New York boys. It was a subversion of her attention that she resented at the same time that she yielded to it gratefully. And it stood between her and the others, as visible as if she wore a "T" on her forehead: she was Teddy's girl and needed no friend before him, needed no man beside him. They made room for her, but not for herself; they respected her because they must: she walked in his aura. She was exhilarated and depressed in the same instant; then Teddy would come up behind her, turn her to him, no matter where they were, and suck a kiss so sweetly from her lips (right in the middle of conversation, as her lips formed an important word) that speech and opinion, hers at least, were put in their place. He was shameless. She didn't know, though, if he was calculating. She could not seem to get him to focus on her discontent, and the last thing he would concede was that his having annexed her had rendered it impossible for her to make her own way. When she was unhappy with her job assignment, he told her he'd take care of it. Sometimes he understood her anxieties, sometimes he didn't and she didn't know which was worse.

What she did know was that she was never alone. And she had not seen Mississippi, whatever she meant by that. Well, she had not gone out into the streets by herself; she had given over her car, in spite of the fact that she did not believe in unilateral sacrifice, to the rural canvassers who needed it more. (Teddy advised her to do so without a scene.) She had never gone into the mildly hilly countryside and she felt she would not be truly there until she had touched some of the ground with her own feet. Probably she was thinking of her mother's dust-colored Alabama, broad in her vision like Western table-land, stark as the top of a mesa. (On the long ride down to Mississippi she had been occupied with a young man named Joe something, whose skin was dark and pitted, and who had an early vintage Afro, who had appropriated the seat beside her so that he could try to blow in her ear all the way from Ohio to Memphis. It had been made amply clear in Ohio that to resist the advances of black suitors was to put yourself in danger of being willfully misunderstood. Still, in Memphis when they stopped to eat, she had urgently begged one of the other women to be sure to sit down next to her. Not very insistent, Joe turned his attention on another white girl who pretended to be asleep the rest of the way.)

Now, on this day that she sensed would be the last of her free time before she became what she tended to refer to as a bloody librarian, she had decided to walk out of town a little way to get her bearings on the crust of this local earth. She headed out the old highway west of town, passed a dark store at the frayed edge of the closed section where a young boy in what might have been his father's broad-brimmed hat waved to her in solemn circular motion: it looked like the very precisely meaningful signal a trainman or a yachtsman might make.

There was something like clover all along the margin of the highway, deep colored, tart, the intensity of those red-hot cinnamon candies she had loved as a child. She picked some but had no buttonholes or bobby pins to keep it in and finally had to drop it. Cars went by at an irresponsible clip; some slowed; when they slowed and swerved, remarks were made; she refused to pay attention. This side of the village was all black—anyone who walked here presumably knew that. Anyway, consider her dungarees and sandals, she thought smugly, her heart thumping, consider a certain look of unconstraint. Once a flashy yellow Mustang stopped and a white man asked her (as unintelligibly as any Negro) if she needed any help. She smiled neutrally and told him she was just fine. She could feel herself already trying to soften her accent a little—hypocrite. He must have been a salesman, she had thought, by his sanitized shirtsleeved look and by the interior of the car (dangling amulet of baby rattle, display cases piled on the back seat, a seersucker jacket neatly hung on a hook at the far window: she practiced taking in details just in case) and he didn't say anything more. But the glance he gave her as he pulled up the window on his air conditioning was the first of a certain kind of look she was going to become accustomed to: it seemed to be charitable at the surface: lady, you couldn't know what you're doing here, I want to believe you're only stumbling through. But what rode beneath the surface was a nervy disrespect: so whatever you get from the likes of worse than me is better than you deserve. He apparently had a second thought, he opened his window again so she could feel the keen edge of cold he kept inside there. "Hey, y'all ought to get turned round, do you know North goes the other way?" The word "North" was broken into at least two syllables; it tried to call forth the sexy and the murderous, the hideously depraved, implied alleyways and unspeakable acts, all in a rise of the eyebrows and a buckle in the voice. But what Jessie had was a marvelous warming flash of the Automat—when he said North that way she could feel for half an instant the cool concave little marble pit at the bottom of the old window section under all the rectangular glass doors and the shiny gold knobs where your money's returned if they're out of buns or vanilla ice cream. She gave him a jaded look and walked on, unwise, she suspected, because her speed, which was prudently hasty, acknowledged that she had understood him. Her heart somersaulted at possibilities avoided. Later it would come to seem that such an encounter—merely verbal—was the height of forbearance and hospitality.

She had passed a culvert and come at last to a rise of hillside off to the left of the road where two goats were delicately ripping up grass. This was the hill she had glimpsed in its similar oblique rising this morning, a few acres that had felt the same geological nudge from below, gentle, unprepossessing. One of the goats, the gray one, had looked up at her as she came near, and had gone on watching as if she interested him. It was a funny delicate creature with a set of retractible ears. She had never actually had occasion to be so near a goat before. He didn't even smell, at least not out there on that minty-fresh slope. She'd hauled herself up the little incline and dared to reach out to pet him along the bristling razor-back of his neatly crewcut neck. His friend or brother loped slowly over on the narrowest possible deer legs with a kind of high-heeled brittle walk. He too wanted to be petted, or so it seemed. Thus it came about that Jessie Singer, girl reformer, one early July day with much self-consciousness tried to find the perfect attack to give maximum pleasure to two flea-tormented goats (for so they turned out to be, not to mention their other intimate afflictions, from the diseased front left hoof of one to the born-in humpback of the other).

The nuances of their conditions she picked up from the old, the very old lady who came toward her then over the soft brow of the hill, dainty in her black patched dress and the kerchief which rode so low over her forehead that not a wisp of hair poked out. Half pirate scarf, half nun's surplice, she had thought, smiling, and the woman hailed her with a raised hand, unsuspiciously, incautiously. (It wasn't incautious, Jessie would learn, to greet a white face; to the contrary. But she had come expecting an armed camp and prisoners' impulses, not wary and servile prisoners. Little she knew.) Reluctantly Jessie had removed her palm from the goat's cool mane and come halfway across the hill to speak with her. She had burlap tied onto her feet too. Jessie thought, shamefaced, how she had a lifetime of tender irrelevancies to unburden herself of, for example, how she had learned as a child that if her head and feet were warm, the rest of her would be warm too: not in a dress as thin as this one.

"Blackie jus' tellin you hello," the woman called to Jessie. "He don't genally take to strangers good."

"Well, he's being awfully nice to me," Jessie assured her, scratching his hard neck vigorously. It felt like a vegetable brush.

The goat fit his damp muzzle into her dry hand and made small anxious thrusts, searching between the fingers. They were strangely like babies, their satisfied tiny motions the same. While Blackie licked her hand, Sam raised his head and called out in a voice like an old Ford; up close it was quite alarming.

They had a nice talk, a wonderful talk, she had thought, reassured, feeling: things will be all right, I'll be able to do this, look how she trusts me. A lot had run together for the old woman: her children and other people's—she had nursed everybody's, Jessie gathered, and now the goats. People asked after them when she went into town to get her commodities and they had bugs in them. (The goats or the commodities? Or the people? Jessie couldn't have said.) The goats were clearly superior to her sons (one of whom was called Sam just to confuse matters) in that they had no intention of boarding the orange and tan I.C. that went hurtling past—it did a sort of demonstration run for Jessie over the far side of the hill—on the way to Chicago.

They walked slowly up toward her little shack and Jessie felt her pace slackening with discouragement as they came close enough for her to see. There was a kind of glamor to such poverty in photographs; if it had texture, that became the grittiness of art, uncompromising vision, good matte paper. Someone proudly put his name on it while it remained changeless. Similarly, her father's Poverty was all rhetoric, peoples, not people; and even that Jessie came to from the safety of the second generation. On this hillside she found herself pushing back as much reality as she could, arguing that the old lady was really a victim of age and aloneness. She even had a certain vigor about her in contrast to her frailty, she was black as good potting soil, and she didn't sound the least bit vengeful.

"I needs one thing or two at a time is all," she confided. "Ain't no sense you moanin on the bones of things got no *thanks* in 'em, they be picked clean soon enough by they own buzzards." Jessie liked that very much, insofar as she could comprehend it; she was pleased just to be able to understand this toothless speech. So they walked up over the hill to that house, which was worse than picked bones. It looked abandoned, condemned; never built was more like it. A gardener would never have stored his tools in such a shed for fear they'd rust. It had no light, its windows were small as her own sunken eyes. Jessie tried to see in but could make out nothing but isolated glinting objects: a bulb, something like pale clothes or cloth hanging like wraiths. Out front, like an artist's quaint arrangement (if he were jaded by beauty outright), she had placed an old wooden straight-back chair that must have been part of somebody's dining room set. "One thing I does better than my house, you know," she told Jessie, laughing, and yellowish spittle collected at the corners of her mouth, "I passes water, see, my pipes be good, house don't even got none to break when the hardfrost come!"

This seemed to please the old woman inordinately, she laughed and rattled and coughed and discovered Blackie at her back when he honked along with her; they made a party of it. She bent her dark neck over his head and squeezed him and he beat the ground lightly with his narrow paws: goat delight.

They talked a bit more, platitudes about the North. Jessie assured her she was right, her sons ought not to have left Mississippi. She blamed school for Sam's leaving, especially. Whispering, she said that if he hadn't learned to read and all, he wouldn't have wanted so much he couldn't have. Jessie at the time thought this a unique view among the "underprivileged": the kind of instance that had been brought before the contingent of volunteers in their sessions in Ohio to incite their optimism and bring them to believe in the solubility of problems was a man named Steptoe who had learned to read in a program of the kind her mother had worked in so abortively, and who sat now like Abe Lincoln in a cabin without electric light, poring over any books that came his way, ten or twenty a week. He was sending his sons to college, by hook and crook and federal loan. The old lady's laissez-faire attitude shocked her.

"But maybe," she argued, "maybe if he can read and do good work he *can* have all those things."

"But now look, they's things he shouldn't ought to have." She looked at Jessie through her veiny red eyes, sufficiently victorious to bring about a smile that moved the various runnels on her cheeks and chin in complex reformations. The geography of her face was mesmerizing. A goddamn Puritan, Jessie thought, though, pulling her eyes from it: *ought to* have? Her goats and her gospel were morally satiating. It was a convenient arrangement.

Jessie said goodbye and thanked her for her company and walked home very slowly. Sympathize as you may, she thought now so many years later, sympathize humanly, but survivors—marginal survivors—turn out to be the enemies of progress. In all the world only government officials and little children are more deeply conservative. What a credulous innocent she had been.

But late that same afternoon she was sitting on the little porch of the freedom house reading the newspaper in a quiet hollow of the day: silver bowls on sale, and silver-plated bun-warmers, it's never too early to begin to buy back-to-school wash-and-wear at Penney's. And then she had heard the strangest sound, it was a huge, unbelievably loud booming; later she thought it was most like hundreds of boxcars rolling straight down a hill. It had been getting dark but she did not know enough about the local cast of light to say if it was prematurely dusky, and had she known more, there were always those torrential summer storms around this time of day, which looked terminally forbidding and passed in twenty minutes. The booming passed too—just at the horizon among the darkest clouds, it seemed to be, and it moved on up the highway and left an extraordinary silence, a hollow in the air. All around the little yard and up and down the barren sandy block everything seemed to be dancing in a huge updraft, the way cinders fly when a bellows blows on them. That was how the papers flew up off the porches and the dust whirled and came spinning wildly down. The gate next door banged and banged. As she watched, a window across the street slid right out of its frame and landed in the dirt with a trivial high-pitched tinkle. It flew into shards like a cocktail glass just knocked off a table, something done in by a careless elbow.

Jessie was stunned. It was altogether the way things might be at a safe distance from a bomb, behind its impact: sudden disarray and then a chilling silence but no bones broken. The clouds on the horizon were breaking up, moving on, and that maddening sun was, as usual, poking through the way it did after a rain. The woman who lived across the road, who had come to peer through her broken window with her eyes wide, came out onto her cinder block front step, carrying a tiny baby. "Why ain't you crouch on down behind you sofa!" she shouted at Jessie. "That were a twister just passed us by! Don't you got folks in there could tell you to get in out of the way?" At which news Jessie was aghast and not so much terrified, in retrospect, as sorry she hadn't paid closer attention. What an extraordinary event! It had been a bona fide Act of God and she hadn't even realized. "I didn't see any funnel," she objected, as if to protect her reputation for common sense.

"Don't matter, you just couldn't get it in sight, it were a twister, cyclone." She shook her head. "They specially called out the highway there on the radio, say it bearin down along just this way and on out past toward Greenwood. Ain't you got no radio in there?" She was scolding Jessie and maybe challenging, a little, the way these black and white children lived all together in that house. And of course, Jessie thought, a mama is a mama. The young woman shook the baby in her arms as though to get his agreement; his dinner must have sifted down as she bounced him.

And at that moment Teddy and Tommy drove up, slapdash, to the noncurb. "Hey, we were riding behind that the whole way!" Teddy called out cheerfully, swinging his long legs out before the rest of him. "We were hoping to God it would miss here." He was elated. He looked as if he'd won a bike race.

"Isn't that dangerous, couldn't it have turned on you or something?"

Tommy came up, laughing, on her other side, short and secure in his weightlifter's body. "Sure, I tried to tell him there's a Mississippi law against travelling too close behind a tornado, it's a moving violation."

Teddy proceeded to tell her what the thing looked like from behind: it did sound animal, like a Martian growth or a maddened bull on one wild leg. Jessie asked if anyone had been hurt by it.

"Oh man—this whole shopping center over west of town is gone—just—" He snapped his fingers. "I think a lot of casualties, probably." He was still smiling.

"My God." All she could imagine was Mont-Saint-Michel.

"Well, don't worry. It missed us out here." He whistled through his teeth. "They can have out west."

"What do you mean 'they can have out west'?"

"Oh—" He shrugged and went up on the porch and in, letting the screen door slam. Tommy was unloading groceries from the trunk.

Jessie marched into the house behind him. "Teddy, aren't you going to see if there's any help you can give, they're probably—"

His face told her a peremptory no, beyond challenge. She stood and ran her fingers through her curls. There was a radio with a chipped green case on a turned-over bushel basket that served as a table. "How do you get this damn thing on?" she called out, rattling all the buttons at once, and when Teddy came up behind her he said very sternly, "Take it easy, Jessie. Nobody needs you over there."

"What are you talking about, they must need everybody, they always—"

He passed his hand, in a parody of soothing, down her neck and over her shoulders, as if she were a wet cat. "They don't need us and we don't need them, all right? You think if this roof fell in right here or this whole side of the village collapsed everybody from over west would come running to wipe up all them hot-blooded li'l pickaninny children?" He distorted his voice to deliver those words and if Jessie had closed her eyes or turned her back she could have been convinced that she had never met this young man.

"I thought those were your people. I thought you couldn't give up on anyone in your beloved community. All those bricks or cornerstones or something. Or do you only say that to girls you want to lure into your bed because it makes you so appealingly vulnerable and large hearted? I remember every heroic reference to your own redneck cousins. 'They know not what they do.' " She had such bitterness in her mouth that she wanted to spit.

"Don't simplify it, Jessie. You-all are talking what you don't know up close."

"What is it that I don't know?" All of a sudden it was you-all. She took his hand off her shoulder where it was playing offhandedly with the material of her shirt, trying to divert her anger.

"Remember, I told you everything was political. . . ."

"Right. Not that you made that up."

"Well, that means *every*thing. Every nasty act and every act of generosity . . ."

"Right. So? Do an act of generosity and it will come back to you twofold. Or even if it doesn't."

"You think they'd embrace us if we came over there in a mixed car and picked up brooms and started sweeping up the broken glass? Not on your everloving ass they wouldn't. And even if they did, hon, even if they did, we've got us some priorities of our own. I wonder if you've noticed. Can we do everything? We can barely get anything done." But it was his vengeful smile she saw and saw, trying to look sorry, not succeeding. He was harder than she'd thought. No—flatter. He didn't have as much dimension as she'd dreamed. Just as his annexation of her independence made it hard for others to know her, so those others, and this constant gruelling urgency, kept her from knowing him. Perhaps it was his bitterness that had done the flattening, an acid that had burned the edge off certain feelings. What he meant by his folks—she saw now how she had misunderstood—was the ones who had already changed. Reformed. The ones who were like himself. The others he hated exactly as they hated him. SNCC hadn't understood; neither had she. But what did she know of bitterness, of being cast out, damned by her own mother? He might be right: absence of compassion breeds absence of compassion.

She turned from him and went back to the porch where she picked up the Jackson paper again: there was a wedding announcement for a token Negro couple that took nearly two pages in the Colored News section: every pair of gloves and silver shoes was described, and every alma mater and diploma in business science zealously, proudly noted. The subhead called it The Wedding of the Year. When she closed her eyes on stinging tears she imagined she saw the bodies of Blackie and Humpback Sam flying head over heels—her own Chagall—doing small-plane tricks, figure eights and loops. Newspapers flew all around them, the old lady's straight-back chair came apart and rung by rung it fell, and all of it was cartoon funny. The invisible funnel had roared over the highway culvert toward Carrollton and rammed, she knew it had, into the hillside where the little family lived with nothing to hide behind but half-filled sacks of rice and powdered milk crawling with vermin. Over west, the kids were out buying bathing suits on sale, not school clothes as the newspaper suggested. Barbecue starter and fishing line. It wasn't the fourth of July yet. Goddammit, Teddy, she thought, breathing the tears back down, the good Lord ought to grow a tree for you like he did for Jonah, a gourd with a booth, whatever that is, and sit you in it and teach you a lesson when the green gourd withers. I hope you inherit no more than a goat and watch it disappear in a whirlwind and then live to see the sun come smiling out. If your sympathies exist two at a time, she thought (now, today, bearing O'Neill's sleeping body home), they call you soft, and they always will. Andréa called her soft for letting that boy-thief go free. When the goats flew past the windshield in her memory, wasn't that O'Neill's tiny face flying with them as she had seen it crying out delight when the raggedy children watched their loud hot car go by? If she turned him over now he would be peaked and wet, his cheekbones bruised deathly dark. She had never dared walk up the highway again to look for the woman and her goats. She had locked them where she locked her disappointment in Teddy, out of the demanding light. Did anyone ever learn to love Nineveh, or Jackson or Birmingham, somebody else's city?

A girl in school (White), Barbara Lingum I think her name is, came up to me in the hall and asked if she could talk to me. She asked me a lot of questions—where was I from and did I like it here and on and on—until I said why should I answer all this. "What about you?" We were standing just against the wall near the water fountains, heavy traffic lane, so she said would I meet her after school, she thought she had an idea I would be very interested in.

Well, since she is kind of nice-looking and well-dressed with short medium-color hair in a little flip, bright little coffee bean eyes and a kind of rabbit face (I mean she looks "together") I thought Oh, why not. Then I went back and forth on it all day but finally I went where she said. Nothing the least bit interesting ever happens here so I was hoping she had some wild idea for me.

We went out far from the buses. Well, to get right down to it, do you like to go to school with all these—and she didn't say it but she waved her hand at the whole mess of kids getting on the old yellow buses, it looked like all of Africa was there. I told her no, of course not. I only know a few crazies who do, I said. Do you agree?

I knew she did by then. She only goes to Barber Jr. High because her father is Disabled from work in a factory and he gets very little support and her mother "flew the coop" a long time ago. Her father is a song writer and he is expecting to hear from Nashville any day about a lot of songs he sent them. But meanwhile the last thing they can afford is Jackson Prep or any other academy. So Barbara is stuck with this weirdo place that she calls Babble Jr. High. But, she goes, did I know that there is something we can do to make it harder for them to send us here forever? The Klan is doing their organizing right out in the open, they have a membership rally next Monday at the Holiday Inn, I think it was, or one of those, right downtown near the medical center. No one is hiding it or anything. They are proud and it is legal. She goes "I don't know about Birmingham but here it is not shameful or looked down upon." And they have a youth group. Wouldn't I like to join? That was why we were standing over here on the ugly old dead lawn in the cold watching our buses close up and take off without us.

Well. That was a surprise all right. She might even be a good friend to have, there is nothing strange about her like that Abneice or whatever her name is, the fat one. And I was interested that she had lived a long time without any mother and she seemed to be just fine. A couple of other kids are in the youth group, a boy named Tabb and some other one I don't remember. Mostly some kids in high school, not so many in jr. high. Her older brother was in it, he had a meeting at their house once and she said it was like a lot of things came clear to her right in her own living room. Like for me maybe in my church, she said. Then she started going to the rallies and they are the real fun. And the people are nicer than you might automatically think. She told me about dues and some of the things they do besides meetings, there may even be a little "hanky panky" we could work on with the grownups, nothing dangerous, just some small "disturbances" to keep people nervous as cats. (That's what she said.) "The Klan is mightier than ever!" She raised her hand and looked a little silly, frankly. When I told her my Daddy was in it when he was very young she said he would be proud of me if he knew I was going on with it.

But actually that was the only time I had a second thought. I don't know as I want my Daddy being proud of me since I know how I spent the last few years hating him so much. (Dear Lord please forgive me but I can't hide my thoughts from You so why even try?) I was the one who was wishing he would somehow die or disappear, so why should I want to be his good girl all of a sudden. My mother's good girl hated the Kluckers and their evil ideas. She thought they came from bad homes.

Since I missed the bus I decided to walk home and think about it. Even though it was a long long walk I have not come to any conclusion yet. Frankly I might like doing it right under Holy Teddy's nose just for the fun of it. Because he wouldn't know and couldn't even stop me even if he did know because he does not own my brain. I don't know. Mom always said Sleep on a doubt and it will turn one way or the other. So I will do that.

The next day but I still don't know. I stalled off Barbara, her name turns out to be Lingham, it is Old English, she said. I told her I didn't have time to think about it. First of all I don't want to hurt anybody (physically). (She swears we don't do that. It is all psychological warfare.) On the other hand, if Teddy and Jessie find out maybe they will want to get rid of me back where I belong. I don't care if they think of me as a Monster, that's okay. If they ever get to like me it will be dangerous to getting out of here.

Then there's Andy. More and more he is becoming my friend. He has this sort of special look he uses for me, I can tell: it is his sort of "protective gaze." When I am in it I can remember a little of what it is to be warm and comfortable. If he found out I was in the Jr. Klan, imagine! I could never look him in his eyes again.

The subject itself I don't know about. I am scared to think of the colored taking over and I do not recognize them in school or anything as being much like me. But do I want to make them unhappy and "nervous as a cat," that's something else. Why make them suffer when I would rather just not live near them. I have to think about this some more.

Later that week, Lydia happened to step on the cotton-polyester rainbow that ran the length of Helen's sleeping bag, which had fallen crumpled off the couch, and tripped, narrowly missing a chair, which could have opened up her skull. She thought she had put her foot down on a pile of rocks, but it turned out when she investigated to be *Algebra for Beginners, Your World and You, Spelling Fun (Advanced)* and a green notebook barely written in. Lydia was no hypocrite: she liked school and thought everyone should be in it, especially those who had acknowledged no other plans for the day. She told her mother about her discovery when Jessie got home, her eyes pale and large with virtue and satisfaction.

Jessie had planned to take the girls out after school to look at some new houses up north near the reservoir. She wanted everyone's enthusiasm and engagement, it was their assignment to care about the search and cheer it on. She did not ask Helen where she had been; she trusted Lydia to follow her lead.

The bare bulldozed earth around the recently finished houses had not yet begun to heal—it looked like fresh graves everywhere. There seemed to be an extravagant dedication to unfinished wood surfaces. Was this new? When had paint gone out of style? There were no sidewalks either, like the worst of neighborhoods: a sign of class. There were double garages instead.

Jessie drove bleakly around and around, hoping to be seized with enthusiasm by a house style called Riviera or Buccaneer. Lydia liked certain houses much better than others, but there was no pretending that her choices were like her mother's. "The long ones are better than the tall ones," she announced confidently, without bothering to specify why: taste was an absolute and argument beside the point. (Naive as she was, Jessie had to concede she was probably right.) "And green! No way. A green house! And I wish we could get one where you wouldn't see that ucky garage first! They all look like garages with houses attached."

The only principle of her own that Jessie uncovered was that she seemed to prefer plain consistency to the extravagant ambitiousness which brought about those wood and brick Georgian ranch houses, the New England colonials fronted with plantation mini-columns. It had been rumored that this was an integrated neighborhood which, if it were true, would constitute its only recommendation. But in all their circling they saw not a single human soul outside by which they might verify the rumor, not planting, not polishing; only a small brown terrier tied to a garage door who was practicing baying without a moon. It was enough, this neighborhood, to make Jessie lonely for the beached cars and the bare sufficiency of Willow-brae Drive.

Helen, as usual, watched in silence and, in spite of the lack of finesse with which Lydia interrogated her about her favorite kinds of architecture—she herself most loved long Spanish California houses suffocating under purple flowering bougainvillaea—Helen would not be moved. "I never thought about it all that much," she said, not unkindly, only as if she'd been asked an exotic question. Lydia was beginning to cultivate an odd expression when she looked at her cousin, somewhere about halfway between patience at the breaking point and outright amusement at all she and her friends would have called "weird." This was expressed in a vaguely superior and disrespect-ful near smile that suggested she had only asked the question to see what kind of bizarre response it might bring forth. Helen gave her little more than her benign silence or a distracted generality for her trouble.

Jessie headed over to an old established all-white subdivision whose cross-streets came off a boulevard at angles, estates on one side, more modest houses on the other. No one, she thought, could object to living in these houses, except on deepsworn principle. Aesthetically they were unimpeach-able, their corners comfortably blunted, broken in by wear. Financially the neighborhood had always been beyond them. But everything, of course, had changed, deepsworn vows and principled impoverishment—how odd, how very very odd luck could be, and so mixed she could not tell if what had befallen them was good or bad.

They turned a corner and coasted slowly down a street of stucco, brick and decently aged greenery. A green-stamp Eden, shady and secure. Jessie imagined the comfortable kitchens, a hundred matching canisters all up and down the block, spectrum of spice racks from simple maple through unglazed pottery through transparent Plexiglas, something for everyone. Tall-ceilinged living rooms and velvety pile wall-to-wall. Framed family pictures in the den, and a few diplomas from Southern schools. You could do a lot worse, she thought. It would be so comforting to relax into a roomy house with unpredictable corners, bookshelf space, a second bathroom.

And headed for the bus stop at the boulevard end went somebody's "girl." There went Johnnie or maybe Sarah or even Lurene, a heavy dark woman with a forehead that glowed with sweat, who wore no uniform but needed none to announce herself: why else would she be in this place? Her shoes were run-over, with little windows for her bunions, and her walk was the shuffle of someone who has moved too much furniture and scooped up too many dust-devils for one day. She moved ahead at good speed, on her way to her own late dinner. They coasted past slowly.

Jessie, though not much given to generalizations, knew this woman. She and Teddy used to call her out, after her ten-hour-day, to meetings. She used to sign petitions; if she put her name down on the voting rolls, she was another triumph as she lifted her pen. She had gray linoleum in her living room, or maybe some sort of plaid? Six (living) children right down to her "baby," whose picture in army uniform sat on top of her TV? She grew zinnias and tomatoes on dead downtown soil behind her house, and made green tomato preserves just before the first frost. Every spring, the creek flooded her yard and lapped at her back stoop, or came right into the kitchen. Her feet, out of those shoes, spread like fungi, Chinese black mushrooms or—what were they?—tree ears, splotch shaped, flattening in every direction to be free. Her weight was as much a fact as her existence, as her sex. She was nice or not nice, happy or not happy, it was only certain that she was, at seven o'clock, eager to be home for her own dinner and late again.

They watched her arrive at the corner just as her bus came. The driver stopped grudgingly, without pulling closer to the curb. She stood for an extra few seconds in front of the stop looking at him as if she had a question to ask, and then gathered herself together, concentrating, like an athlete about to pole vault or ascend the eight-foot beam. She took a large shoulder-raising breath, then rolled up the steps, her assorted masses moving in opposed directions like someone's arms and legs stirring under a blanket. It must have hurt her to elevate herself so, one foot to the other, balancing all of herself, hips, bust, shoulders, above. Inside, then, her round indistinct face was at the window, frowning behind dust. She looked like an old photograph, someone's unrestored ancestor.

Lydia was looking out her window.

"Would you like to live in one of these houses, do you think, Lyddie?" Jessie asked her neutrally.

"They're nice," Lydia answered cautiously. In touch with old realities, she had thought them well out of reach.

There was no reason to sully her dream of grandeur with sociological second thoughts, but it took all Jessie's forbearance to stay quiet.

Then, slowly, suspiciously, "Would we have to get a maid?" Lydia asked as the bus doors folded shut and the woman was borne slowly, almost majestically away. "*Grandma* has a maid, doesn't she?" Apparently she knew surrender when she saw it.

When Jessie thought about it later she gave herself every chance to repudiate its ever having happened but could not do so and would not check with Lydia for fear of inciting an unbecoming contempt. But what she heard then was Helen making a sound that was both a snort of challenge and a laugh outright. It was a bitter damning noise, but at least it assured Jessie that Helen was not only paying close attention, judging as she went, but was waiting for something that might make her life bearable and familiar: she was not dead to them. Of course not.

After two days I am still stalling off Barbara and getting worried. She seems to be trailing around with me to make me give in, and now this Ronny Tabb person who's an awful pimply nasty character in high waters who it wouldn't surprise me if he is some kind of pervert, he is surrounding me too. He is someone I would not want to be in a dark alley alone with: "unwholesome." They make me feel like a criminal, or like I have something of theirs I won't give back and one of these days they will take it.

I am writing in this diary while I stay home today to keep me company. I cut school because it is so boring and I did most of the work so long ago I have already forgotten it. But instead I am "buying" more time before I give Lingham and Tabb my answer, so that is why I am lying low. It's so easy to cut school! They're so unorganized Barbara said they only catch people once in a while. I left home with all my books when everybody else did today and instead of going to the bus, since they all go in a different direction I just walked around a little and then came back. Maybe they will never find out. And if they do, maybe they'll believe how much I hate it here. I slept some and watched some soaps, careful not to leave any trace, even smoothed out the couch cover I sat on, and then I went through Andy's things—I don't know what I was looking for, nothing special, but it was very exciting in an odd way. He is a slob like everyone else in this house except Lydia who for some reason is very neat. His socks are in his sheets and his clothes all rolled in a ball on his chair. No girlie magazines under his mattress or even cigarettes, he is very pure! I laid down in his bed and thought about some "indescribable" scenes if we were married. But I have to say if he did not neaten up and wanted to live like a pig we would definitely have some problems. Maybe we would have to live on a desert island and if we didn't have any clothes to worry about he couldn't roll them in a ball! Just a sweet blond body with those long arms and that special look in his eyes, blushing in places I never saw before!

Then in the afternoon I went up in the direction of where the bus would leave me and walked home real slow with my books and all. No one saw me, but just in case. The neighbors on this block don't pay much attention to me. One woman wearing an incredible red velvet pants suit that was like a whole moving theatre curtain who was getting in her car across the street said "Hi there" but I made a face, I guess I was scared that anyone saw me, so she will probably not repeat herself next time. (I felt dumb.) They may live in this nigger dump of a neighborhood but I don't notice Teddy and Jessie exactly "hanging out" much with the people on this block. She has some friends who are these sort of classy "working woman" Negro types, very tasteful dressers (no theatre curtains) with big important looking purses that go with their shoes—one woman came over yesterday who is a teacher with Jessie. And they probably are all living in white neighborhoods!

Now when I look at someone like that who's sitting at the table with Jessie and they are studying some kind of social studies plan or something, they look like me and Julie Ann when we did our homework together, I am saying to myself Can you really go out of this house to a Klan rally, jr. grade? Could I bring them information if Teddy or Jessie ever gets involved in anything they should know about? I don't owe anybody anything here! It is silly to think I do. Still I would feel wrong about it. That is only human.

I am praying on it, Lord, You know I am, but You still haven't told me what You require of me. I am going to stay out of school one more day hoping for an answer.

Once in a while Jessie remembered that she had a body, and took it swimming. She would slip into the warm water at the Y with the same relieved yielding she felt when the sheet and blanket settled around her for sleep. All of them used to come to the pool years ago—back in the time when sex was not their only exercise—and Teddy would lead the children off the diving board like a mother duck walking her babies out into the world. Hitting the water they made the sharp sound of a rifle report, and Andy's shout, or Lydia's, would leap up triumphantly to echo off the hazy tiles. Then, as the children's social calendars began to bloom with their own notations, their moments as a family became rarer and rarer until the idea of going swimming with their parents would have been a humiliation. Well, fine, that's healthy, Jessie supposed, pushing into her crawl, reaching out a cupped hand to hold the bright impossibly blue water. But this is mine now. (And in her throat she felt like a crosstide the offense of being an embarrassment to her children.)

She swam as she did almost everything else, vigorous where others might opt for discipline or even for beauty. There had always been something wrong with the coordination of her arms and legs in the breast stroke, her thrust and kick unsynchronized, but that didn't slow her down or diminish her pleasure. She did five laps, her head remarkably empty of details and obligations; this was better than any consciousness-dousing drug she could imagine, nothing impinged but the cool weight of the water and the misty disembodied sound she made when she slapped against it, and they did not seem part of nature. Contained as it was, the pool felt like some intermediate element halfway between a lake's freshness and the flat assertions of plastic. Suspended there, long and curved as an eel in her eggplant purple suit, she was free of herself and all the others, uninhabited, saturated by joy which still was—how casy to forget—as easy a medium to move through as this water.

FIVE

Teddy was on a three-day trip across the bottom of the state when Jug Dixon called. On the phone, when you couldn't see him in his half-decent sports jacket and polished shoes, he was such a shit-kicking country boy, Jessie thought; it was easier to picture him on a tractor or sitting at a kitchen table leaning his huge elbows on oilcloth, drinking half a gallon of milk and wiping his lips with the back of his hand than meeting with governors and moral spokesmen about interracial reconciliation. That seemed like a ventriloqual act. But where was the voice coming from?

"Anything I can do for you, Jug?" she asked, skeptical. There tended to be only one thing, with variations, that women could do for him.

"Well, darlin," he said, never in a hurry. "There might could be. You gonna be talkin with the man, you think, before he gets ready to come on home? Lor, there's a bunch of you over there these days, int there?" He implanted a chuckle in the middle of the sentence somehow, just so, like a raisin in a plump cookie.

"Yup," she said. "Yup to both questions. He usually calls in some time when he's away this long." She had her shoes off; she wiggled the toes of one tired foot.

"Well, listen, sweetie. You tell him for me—now he dudn't have to come home specially—but tell him we got us a little fight on our hands, okay? For when he gets back. Tell him to keep the motor-car running."

"What do you mean 'a little fight,' Jug?" You can tell me, she didn't say, since it's damn clear you want me to pass it on fast.

He pretended surprise and reluctance. "All right, Jessie. Listen." Was he hooding the receiver with his palm or had she seen too many movies? Would he pull up the collar of his trench coat and hunch into the wall? "Klan is rumbling a little down Rankin County. Hoxey, Mourning Dove, in around the river over there?" His voice had grown husky, maybe serious. "Sort of cousins of the Klan, know what I'm saying. Not real heavy duty yet. A lot of angry amateurs. But you know that can be the worst damn kind, fellas like that think they first discovered revenge."

"Is there any real danger, do you think?" One ought to pay attention, she supposed, even if he seemed to be dramatizing—Jug had had plenty of access to real facts about real events, years back, you didn't have to like him to want his information. And it was usually sound. It was what he didn't give you that made Jessie wonder: she was sometimes sure he played both sides against the middle, reconciled black and white by sharing secrets, making a mess of gray in between. There were the days when news from the black community—internal dissension, for example—would somehow seep through and influence white strategy. No matter what accomplishments he brought home, she couldn't trust anyone who could talk and drink with the governor and walk with his arm over the shoulders of the governor's men. Jug was what Teddy, untroubled, called the necessary price; the information, he insisted, flowed both ways. He was valuable.

"Can't say if it's for real. I only just heard this and I'm just now going down to have a look around for myself."

"Has there been some particular incident—"

"Oh, a little something—sheriff roughed up some black kids and the kids weren't having any this time. Things been brewing a while, lot of lil petty irritations, you know how it gets." At least he granted that much attention on her part. "But they're putting out some real threats, particular people and all, and I thought ole T.C. might want to come along is all. So you just let him know I found him a little action. Saw him last time I thought he's gettin kind of itchy. So you have him give me a call."

Jug's condescension did not amuse her. A little action. He made it sound like he'd found Teddy a woman. She was looking into the dark wood of the kitchen cabinet as if it weren't solid, seeing the two of them skulking through the brush in the scrub woods of Rankin County looking for trouble.

"You want me to call him where he is, Jug?"

"As you will, sister. I haven't got my trusty finger on the pulse out there like I said, I don't know if we got us a crisis or just a lot of noise, know what I'm sayin. Might be like the old army trick where the guy in the tank turns off his lights and drives round and round the village till it sounds like a whole fuckin brigade. Pardon my Chinese."

"Got you, Jug." She had had her fill. "You'll see him when you see him. I'll tell him you called." It was Jug's wife, she thought, who was married to the one-man regiment.

Hoxey, Mourning Dove: those two scabby little places felt like African villages twenty miles out of Jackson, so near the airport you could read numbers on the bellies of the planes from your backyard. The towns were shadeless, impermanent looking, tribally ingrown. Hoxey was white, Mourning Dove black; they shared a lot of the same family names, which meant they'd been plenty friendly, two by two, in the past. The thought of the towns depressed her, with or without the Klan or the Klan's cousins stirring things up. Not many people out there worked; they were trying to keep busy, probably keep their body temperatures up. She decided she wouldn't tell Teddy till he came home in the natural course of things. Jug had been, she knew it but Teddy in his eagerness might not, running his finger down his sucker list looking for cheap help. Bored and restless, it would say beside Teddy's name, maybe invisibly. Hot to trot, with a wife who didn't used to talk back and a houseful of kids to make him feel like Gulliver caught lying flat and useless in a crosshatch of threads in Lilliput. Yet there was something *real* happening out there. Her fury at Jug and his slimy tone was getting in the way of that. (There is always something real, she argued back. Politics, she had learned at a very early age, was the art of separating the events you could make something out of from those that simply happened and went on happening. Most of the atrocities just slipped on by. . . .)

Almost perversely, as if to make something self-fulfilling, when Teddy called she asked his advice about Helen, how she was holding out on them. She could hear the juke box in the background, it surged behind their connection as if their voices had to travel a long way under the sea.

"You could follow her when she leaves for school."

"I know. But Teddy, you can't see me doing that, can you? Skulking around corners and stooping beside parked cars?"

"You could confront her."

"You're getting warmer. I could certainly see that. But I have the feeling it wouldn't be worth much. I mean, in direct proportion to how automatic it is. I don't think we need to increase her sense of persecution." She could hear Teddy yawn, his breath sucked right out of the receiver. "Domestic crises bore you, don't they?"

"Hey," he said. "You think I'm down here in beautiful Picayune calling you from a truck stop because I can't stand the heat in our kitchen?"

She stalled a long second. That nasty song about the YMCA heaved in the background with the throb of waves. "To tell you the truth, hon, I don't actually know what you're down there for. It's been a lot of years of truck stops and Introduction to Economics. Life is short."

"Try buying a pound of hamburger meat on your alternative salary these days. What are you doing, Jessie, trying to pick a long-distance fight?"

She sighed. Her conversation with Jug had incited her; she was grim with her anticipation of Teddy's absence, literal and emotional, when his adrenaline got going. No wonder he was bewildered.

"You'll think of something to do with Helen. You're good at that kind of thing."

"I'm getting tired of having you on the road, do you know that? I wish you were here. I'm tired of your playing so damn dumb about so many things, when it suits your convenience." You are in Picayune, she thought irritated, but I don't know where you *are*.

"So you could put your problems in my lap or your own sweet self, lady?"

"Oh damn it, Teddy, don't try those old moves on me! What do they mean? You're down there while I'm struggling with these kids—"

"I'm not down here for kicks, do you think?"

"And I can't seem to—" She stopped.

"What?" he asked patiently. "Jessie? You can't seem to *what*. You wanted to move and we're moving. You don't like my job—well, I don't like it either, you're right, it's a waste, it's an early death. I know that as well as you do. But I'm not the only one who can't find the way to go, in case you hadn't noticed."

She was chastened. "I'm sorry. I'm as confused as you are. Only twice as busy." She was appalled, suddenly, at the necessity of confronting what it was she wanted: she hadn't the slightest idea what it was, she only knew what it would feel like not to be alone. She kissed him goodnight into the stone-cold receiver her anxious breath had warmed a little. She was failing him as surely as he was failing her. It was bad enough to disapprove of yourself, but what must it be like to feel disapproved of, and scolded like a child because of it. She picked up the phone again, but he was all alone in Picayune watching the truckers playing the lurid lit-up machines, cut loose from her. Then, not having told him about Jug's call was like a salty little corner of vengeance she had to suck on till it melted.

Nothing. No sign.
Then right at dinnertime Barbara Lingham calls me! Jessie goes

"Well, you have a friend." I just told her we were eating, could I call her back, but she said she would so I couldn't get away. When she does she says just try it once. Like a new candy bar or a strange food or something. Just come to an organizing meeting, why are you afraid? She says "Think of your father and you'll come."

You know what I think of when I do that? Along with a lot of other things, my father the night Mom locked him out of the house in his robe saying "Go back to your girlfriend!" (which she pretended we didn't know about which would be a laugh but she never said anything to us about it, I guess she just couldn't) and Daddy taking off all his clothes and sitting on the front porch tailor fashion. And when we came around from the back to go to school he was sitting there like an Indian or something and he said "Your mother has stripped away everything from me. Let everyone know that." I was so afraid he was going to stand up with everyone walking by I ran back in the house. I wanted to call the police. Mom said "He is trying to make you blame me for what he does" and "It is all or nothing with him, he is either all decency or he goes crazy like this!" And all I could do was hide in the bathroom. I hated both of them so much. And O'Neill said he stood there naked as a baby with his hands on his hips for an hour, cursing our mother. The Lord said that children ought not look upon the body of their father, or strangers look upon it either, or another woman not his wife. And then on Sunday don't you think he went to church like nothing had ever happened? The only thing that kept me from killing myself for shame is that particular morning not very many people went by so he couldn't really show off as much as he wanted. Hearing about it like they did is just not so scandalous. And my mother I think got more sympathy than anything else: everybody knew about dear neighbor Donna Durgin. Sometimes when I think of HIM I just get a hot blur in front of my eyes, it burns away all details and any other reasons for loving him. In other words I would not do anything for that man because he was literally insane.

We are moving! I don't know how soon exactly but Jessie took us to see some houses today (only from the outside). She seems to mean it. They will never buy anything as beautiful as our house in Birmingham (but at least we'll have some blessed Room and my own "belongings" will come. Teddy is against moving, you can tell when the subject comes up. But here is where Jessie seems pretty strong, she just laughs at him and says he wouldn't notice if he lived in a doghouse!) And also he is away a lot. So I guess what does he care that we are all over each other?

(Not that I would mind with Andy.) I wonder if my peeping Tom had anything to do with it? If so, I'm glad.

My mother could never be strong because Daddy was (sometimes only) so crazy he was dangerous. Teddy I would say is repulsive—that scar, I had to sit next to him in the car once, it is so gross but his children or at least Lydia kisses him goodnight right on it! It is far worse than Bonnie's father's false teeth in a glass that she has to put up with. But even if I can't look at that red stripe cheek, he is not actually dangerous, he is pretty gentle I have to admit and even pets the cat and gets dreamy talking to it. It is when he talks to me or even his own kids that I can't stand it, he is always lecturing someone or giving a whole long history of something nobody wants to hear. Sometimes it even looks to me like Jessie can't either, she looks like someone who is making secret fists, either bored or angry. Well, I can understand that because when he gives O'Neill and I one of those lectures about how dangerous it was to be the first white people on this block or whatever he's going on about, I am making the same kind of fists so that my nails even cut into the palms of my hands.

How long had Helen been out of school? And how was she covering for herself? Jessie knew she could check the attendance records but that would arouse suspicions they could do without. She did want to hope that what Lydia had just told her was a one-day whim but with every cell of her intuition she doubted it. For all she knew the girl had somehow managed never to go back after her very first day; she was afraid to wonder where she might be spending her time. Jackson, unlike a larger or more complex city, did not provide an unending supply of anonymous pleasures. Compared to New Orleans, where she and Teddy used to go for R and R, just to see some random, unaffiliated faces, it was a swollen small town where you were bound to be spotted on any corner by one of your neighbors.

Andréa and Tommy came over for dessert the next evening. Their daughter, Cleo, clamored in ahead of them, shouting out long nonsense syllables of greeting. She had the head of a Persian lamb, all tight and glossy, that looked as if it would keep her warm in winter. The first thing she did was belly-flop on Mickey Mouse who lay innocently sleeping on Andy's jacket, which had been left where he flung it, on the armchair. A surprised syllable slid, moist, from the cat's mouth.

"We're never going to move," Jessie announced as they settled in. She told them about the houses she had seen. "At this rate we'll build two more stories on this house and have the first high-rise in Plywood Barracks."

"You don't need one of those new suburban houses, Jess. You need what I think is called a great Victorian pile," Tommy said. "You certainly have enough kids to qualify. The kind that gets made into a school or a funeral home?"

Eventually the children assembled around them, sitting with them only because they wanted dessert. (They made this clear, without words, by the indolence of their posture.) Asked to, they had all worked together in the kitchen, miraculously, to glue together with whipped cream a box of thin chocolate wafers. Andy had played uncontrollable beast, unconvincingly, and prevented anyone from helping him slather the cream on the sides with a spatula. "Bully!" his sister called him. "We'd have let you have the bowl if you wanted it that badly." That was Helen in a soft, ingratiating voice. Jessie strained to hear from the other room, but there were only the sounds of effort, approval, mumbling, giggles, and then the tap water running in the dirtied bowl. Cleo had gone in to them and was imitating the rise and fall of their speech, thrilled to be allowed to stay.

Then, waiting for their share, they sat outnumbering the adults. Jessie watched Helen studying Tommy without expression, his trucker's body— he was chunky, strong, all his shirts strained at the shoulders—and his surprisingly delicate face. He had always worn his fair hair very short, almost crewcut, just a little slide of wave, old fashioned, as if to reassure his political enemies that he was no hippie. It was the kind of look that Jessie found provocative on conservatives, a call to arms. On Tommy it was an inside joke. Tommy taught American civilization at Millsaps, that decent white college, and had an unstrainable patience with students and faculty alike who came to him innocent of what he called history. Most of them seemed to think they'd grown up in a garden spot—no irony there—and he saw it as his duty to teach them to discriminate between their perceptions and those of others not like them. Years ago he had called the lot of them "my little South Africans," but that was changing. He was a man of hope and sinewy will and he spun his students into the dim gleaming of con-sciousness with all the mad trust of a spinner of straw into gold. Andréa, her tan arms round and smooth as a soft stuffed doll's covered in cut plush, sat inclined in his direction, a little of her studied independence yielded to his solidity, his courtesy. She had put a many-colored Mexican scarf over her shoulders.

Even with their differences, however, the children were separate from their elders. They formed, where they sat, a little cabal of shared instincts that implied, leaving out every detail, that youth was superior to middle age or, at least, was allied against it. They thought it a sign of superannuation that anyone would gather together just to eat dessert (although they wanted some) and sit facing each other with such propriety, talking. Jessie watched them huddle, their eyes on the fluffy white log they had prepared for the center of the table, and remembered the astounding capacity of her babies when they were in their strollers, or even earlier, in their carriages, to seek out any other child, baby or not, in any room, in an open conspiracy of delight. Andy, and then Lydia just like him, would gravely follow the movements of a child of any type or color up to around the age of ten, and smile encouragingly—with some kind of relief, was it, or merely a shared knowledge?—at the slightest acknowledgment. The cant of the four of them toward each other, subtle right now, Andy with his foot on one rung of Helen's chair (a surprisingly intimate gesture, actually) suddenly informed Jessie where Helen's salvation, or hers in Helen's eyes, would come from if it came at all. She and Teddy would have as little to do with it as the girl could conceivably manage: the three of them, with O'Neill bringing up the bottom end—he was terribly quiet tonight, still under the chastening effect of his time alone beneath the car as if he had sat up all night with his daddy's body—the four of them would arrange it, tacitly perhaps. How could she have been so slow to comprehend? That first encounter at dinnertime, when Andy called O'Neill on his hideous niggering—why hadn't it been evident that he spoke on a different wavelength which did not resound as painfully as hers or Teddy's in his cousin's ear? She couldn't solve it all just now but she felt a quick stab of hope that rose in her chest like fear. She bent to pour the coffee.

.   .   .

When they'd heard about the truancy caper, Andréa and Tommy had diametrically opposed responses.

"She wants your attention," Tommy said without hesitation. "She wants you to discover her and show her how much you care by dragging her back by her pony tail."

"Tom-mee!" Andréa laughed. "Nothing of the kind. That girl wants a little freedom!" She widened her eyes, innocent and certain of her instincts. "She needs time to think things through. Jess, you're too close to the whole thing to see how her whole world has turned over, I mean completely upside down, not just around the edges like yours."

"The edges!" Jessie gasped. "Some edges."

"Look, kids do a lot worse under less godawful circumstances. You're lucky she's not suicidal, or out getting high or running around with—"

"Exactly," Tommy said. "And that's why it's the perfect time for Jessie to step in and go on record before she does begin doing those things."

They regarded each other with an amused tolerance. Tommy had grown up in Ohio nearly alone, raised by an old and frail grandmother while his mother worked hard to support him. Andréa, the professor's child, had been fussed over until, as she loved to say, she grew lace between her toes where other people had athlete's foot. "We don't say a single surprising thing, do we?" She laughed and reached for her husband's hand. "You see how objective psychological interpretation is, how free of individual bias. And what did Teddy say when you told him?"

"Oh, he was predictable too. He said I'd figure out what to do."

"Bought you off with a gallant compliment. That sweetie pie."

"Right."

"You know what he's so busy with that he can't concentrate a little on something like this? You better be careful, girl, maybe he's got himself some little assistant principal who buys his books down Picayune way, likes to look into his big blue eyes."

"Your nasty mind! Andréa! Well, it's probably worse, actually. It's nothing at all, I think. I'm coming to the painful conclusion that the less there is to think about—because God knows he doesn't have to think about his new editions and his workbooks and all that—the less he thinks. It's the Theodore Principle of Diminishing Attention." She was ashamed of herself for mocking him.

Tommy and Andréa, never having heard such a tone of disgust from Jessie, frowned at her like doctors registering a dire list of symptoms. Jessie touched her finger to the plate where the whipped cream log had been. It felt to her like a sad and hopeless gesture when just a few minutes ago she had discovered a hint of direction. Chocolate crumbs stuck to her finger like a dozen ants; she brought them to her tongue thinking, if Helen is asking us a question—*me* a question—does that mean I have a choice of answer or does that answer have to be "yes"? And what form does "yes" take? The only word she was sure of was "Help!" and she didn't know whom to ask it of, Teddy or Helen.

· · ·

But this was a helplessness to be indulged only at night. In the morning she had four children at the table in various states of undress, two working sleepily at raisin bran and two at sunny-side-ups.

"Sunny-sides-up," Lydia protested earnestly.

"But it's only one side." Andy. "Two eggs, one side each."

"But who ever heard the word 'ups'?" And so on.

At moments like this, which were so frequent in the Carll house that the children assumed the world proceeded by fits and starts of verbal analysis and good-natured nonsensical argument, Helen and O'Neill stared at them aghast. Nothing is so intimate, in the life of families, as such instants, habitual and unnoticed: the way time is filled between memorable moments, the airy invisible medium in which everything solid floats. They didn't seem quite certain of the tone of the discourse, whether its speed and lightness would tolerate imitation, so that when O'Neill tried to enter he had the stricken face of a beginner at jumping-in, making a treacherous leap as the long rope circled over. "Who knows how you say two merry-go-rounds?" His eyes skittered from Lydia's face to Andy's and back, shamelessly searching for their approval. His sister was not included in the riddle.

"You just *said* it," Lydia laughed.

"No, wait. Carousels!" Andy offered.

"Close." O'Neill waited the proper instant. "Give up?" He was merry with himself. "One merry-go-round and *another* merry-go-round! Get it?"

"Oh, O'*Neill*." Helen rolled her eyes. "Andy's was better." Just as shameless, Jessie thought; Helen gave her cousin an encouraging smile.

"Did you just make that up?" Lydia asked.

"So?" O'Neill was defensive.

"That's pretty funny," Lydia told him with a look that strove for magnanimity. "That's *excellent*."

His face went slack with relief. He smiled, for himself, not for her. Handed a rope, the swimmer does not always remember to be polite. "Can I have another egg, please?" he asked Jessie, emboldened. "Our daddy didn't even let us talk at the breakfast table."

"Why not?" Andy poured himself another glass of milk and did not question the connection between jokes and second helpings. "Did it interfere with your digestion?"

O'Neill laughed a little wildly, as if there were something forbidden even in the memory. "Something about breaking up our discipline? Or something?" He appealed to Helen for help.

She stared at the dregs of her egg, which lay thick in her plate like a smashed tube of cadmium yellow. "It broke discipline. He liked to pretend we were at military school. It made us too—I don't know—giddy or something. Happy." She said the uncomfortable words very neatly, broken into separate syllables like something that would receive its rhyme in the next sentence. "He wanted us to say grace and keep our mouths shut and our eyes forward."

"But you can't eat with your mouth shut," O'Neill added earnestly. They sounded a little like a vaudeville team—who's on first—in the driven fixity of their responses, their eyes gone slightly glazed with recollection. That was the way they had filled the spaces at meals, then. "So I never got more than one egg. Sometime I want to see if I can eat a whole dozen. Could I do that, do you think? Maybe on a weekend where I can rest a little in between?"

Jessie and Lydia and Andy looked at each other in alarm. Then Jessie saw Andy reach forward, a small movement not intended to call attention to itself, and place his hand gently on Helen's sky blue sweatered arm just above the cuff where it hardly began to broaden from the frail wrist. His face reddened. Helen kept her head bent slightly as if she were saying a solitary grace. Astonished, Jessie saw tears cluster at the tips of her eyelashes and thicken in the corners of her gray eyes; for an instant they swelled like magnifying lenses in Andy's eyes as well. His fair skin was absurdly transparent; he could make no secrets of his sympathies, ever. Blood rushed up. The blotches of angry color looked like they should hurt.

"You miss him," Jessie ventured softly, hopefully.

Helen squeezed her eyes tight, which pushed her tears out where they clung resisting gravity, mesmerizing the roomful of them. She made the clenched face of someone who is being battered but will not cry out; there was something fanatical, Jessie decided, in such resolution. It was what one expected of a political prisoner, not a thirteen-year-old orphan girl at breakfast.

Andy traced one finger across the pressure point on the underside of her wrist. If he could keep his gentle instincts in the face of everything, she thought, he would grow up to be a superb lover. So that was what happened to the closeness of mother and son: you made nervy speculations about such matters and felt you had a proprietary right since you were the first one he loved, and perhaps you were responsible. . . .

No one breathed. The moment dwindled and passed. Pain seemed to be drawn back down into the hollow vessel of Helen's body visibly, the way the blood receded in the capillaries of Andy's cheeks, his inflamed nose, his lips that had gone dark as a chilled swimmer's. How hateful martyrs are, and the suppression of rightful feelings, that ungenerous pinching-off, Jessie told herself. Why had her father taught her that? Why would anyone want to perpetuate such stoicism in the world? (She was grateful for her own father's spontaneity, his noisy demands, his hands open wide in their habitual gesture of expectation, generous and ready to be seized by some comrade's.) Helen, she thought, could Helen be taught such a thing? Would howling be more unseemly, really, than this punishing silence? It was self-indulgent to hold a roomful of people, as if unconsciously, as if helplessly, in your grip; to watch through the slits of your eyes how everyone hangs on those precious tears, awed because you will not let them fall. Was it because she had betrayed her father and loved him in spite of everything? Did she think it disloyal to remember him being cruel, was that why she wouldn't cry?

"It's okay, Helen," Jessie murmured, and wished they were by themselves somewhere. "You haven't noticed anybody perfect around here, have you?"

But Helen stared straight ahead as if she hadn't heard.

Jessie took us to see this movie "Heaven Can Wait"? Warren Beatty is something else but I didn't think it was so funny spoofing heaven and making it all silly and full of these dumb puffy clouds. Bad taste. I am not talking about dying or not dying but the whole concept of such a show, bargaining not to die or go to heaven and all, like God is some used-car salesman. I heard Andy and Jessie discussing if it was the "wrong" kind of movie for us. Well, it didn't upset me except for being sort of insulting to someone who wants to see God, thank you.

I know my little brother believes maybe they will come back to us somehow, on the way out he goes "Oh it's like when Teddy died that time, remember?" And then I know what he's not saying, he decided he'd better not ever say it to me because I will only shush him but I see him thinking it. He will wake up one morning and it will be just like this story I once wrote when I was about nine—how this little girl prayed and prayed to get a horse and then on her birthday morning she opens up her eyes and it is looking right in her bedroom window, black with white star "glowing" on its forehead. Only O'Neill sees them standing there probably holding their suitcases, with their coats on. And he will say to his longlost Daddy the way he always does, "Did you bring me anything?"

When Teddy drove up to the house on the evening of his third day of absence, he found Jessie and O'Neill, one long shadow and one short, standing at the open door. He was in high spirits, having sold a dizzying quantity of his wares, and so he called out cheerfully, "Hey, you guys waiting for me?"

But they were not. Jessie had one arm wrapped protectively, tensely, around O'Neill's shoulder, not for camaraderie's sake. "He's having trouble breathing," she called to Teddy. "We're getting a little air." She was holding the storm door open with her hip.

O'Neill blinked at Teddy fiercely as if they shared a code conveyed by the eyelashes. In the bad light Teddy got down on one knee on the cold porch and looked into his face, but there were no answers in it: it was pale, worried, and tight as a small knobby fist.

"Whenever I come home in a really good mood there seems to be a crisis waiting on the doorstep," he said, standing up slowly, his hand ambiguously on O'Neill's head.

"Ssh." Jessie smacked him in the arm with the side of her hand. "Egotist. What kind of thing is that to say." She had been panicky, nearly afraid to catch her own breath when O'Neill began to wheeze. He had eaten a bowl of ice cream after school and then, coming into the living room, had risen on his toes and opened his eyes wide as if someone were clapping him on the back with every inhalation. Jessie was convinced that if she had never heard in that accusatory way about O'Neill's asthma in Birmingham, he would have none now. That was thoroughly inexplicable, but she had no doubt it was true.

"What have you done for him?"

Jessie looked over the boy's head at her husband, who seemed always to be a spectator. "I can't think of anything. He sat in a blanket a little but that didn't help at all, and he doesn't know where his medicine is. I didn't even know he *took* medicine! Helen's not here, I don't know where she is, she's worse than the cat. . . ." Jessie let the door close.

O'Neill was at that moment, in fact, poking his finger at the cat who was watching him from the coffee table with predatory concentration. When he wheezed, trying to get the breath out, Jessie thought, and was ashamed, he sounded like Mickey Mouse worrying up a hairball. "I think it's him!" O'Neill whispered in a sucking voice, between rasps. "He's doing it." He gasped and brought his breath up a long slow careful way like a full bucket tipping up to the top of a well. Jessie held O'Neill to her, hard, as if she could squeeze the damaged breath out of him by main force. She was not smothering him into it, surely; maybe she could smother him out of it. Everything was a passive cry these days, every goddamn action a reaction to something that stopped its breath or at least its words: asthma, that cliché, notorious stifler. Truancy, silent opting-out. Varona's depression. Teddy's emptiness. Why couldn't anyone *talk* about what hurt? Why couldn't *she?* She wanted to kick something so hard a chunk of frustration would finally come dislodged and the world grind noisily back into motion. Teddy gaped, pulling helplessness down around himself.

She went to the phone. "It's okay, I'm calling the doctor, O'Neill." She got a busy signal, dialed again and was relieved to hear the rasp subsiding gradually, quieting as though he were retreating into another room. Thank God.

"Calling the doctor seems to work," she said and laughed, relaxing. "I'll remember that."

But the joke was lost on him. Still breathing hard, he made his way to the den with odd circumspection, stunned by the attack the way he had been by his long night of tears in Birmingham (when there had been, Jessie realized, no asthma. Probably emotion had nothing to do with it after all). Most of his entrances and exits were occasions for the laying-on of exuberant hands—objects fell, were tweaked, rearranged, removed; the room was overwhelmed with activity, laid waste by a kind of innocent busy destructiveness, no animus in it. Sheer energy flooded it like light. But now he murmured an unintelligible word and, hands to himself, seeped away toward the den and the TV. Jessie studied the place where he had stood as if a spell had rendered him invisible. What did manipulation *mean*, then? When the children were little they cried to be held. "Don't pick him up!" cautioned some friends, some books. "Do you want to spoil him?" "Go to him, hon," Varona had said on the day she dropped off a stuffed duck the color of egg yolk for Andy's crib. "He cryin, he want something, and maybe that somethin is just you. When they that little, you the best thing there is. Babies don't cry to chase you away, that happen they wouldn't go *on* like that." Maybe O'Neill liked to be held, to be worried over. Maybe he had liked it when he crawled out of the Corvette's shadow and hid in hers. Could it be that simple?

"Jug Dixon called," she finally said, fatalistically, watching Teddy take it in. A glimmer of dead light was what she saw, the noon sun straight down on Hoxey and Mourning Dove, on their interchangeable primordial bleakness—broken toys, rusted oil cans, too many lounging men with bad teeth and unhealthy yellow eyes and all the hopefulness of lifers. She imagined Teddy driving up frantic in a swirl of dust with that eager-to-serve-you look of a McDonald's order-taker. A different form of entropy, theirs, it suffered fewer fits and starts and reversals than middle-class wind-down. It spread like mildew, under things, inside them, rotting out the center of anything that faced out of the sun. "He wants you to call him."

"Now?"
"Yesterday."

*I wasn't here (I was at the library) but this afternoon O'Neill had a
bad fit with his breathing. He couldn't find his medicine. I could kill
him for losing it. Could it be the cat? Would they get rid of it if we find
out that's the problem? I bet they won't. Or did something happen? I
am so furious, I don't know why, I don't even know who I'm mad at but
I just wanted to strangle something with my bare hands when I found
out. It was a good thing Mickey Mouse was outside or somewhere or I
would have been tempted. I even wanted to squeeze O'Neill to death,
which is very un-nice because he's the last one I should blame. He could
actually die that way. People do. Daddy's cousin Lorna's daughter was
at a party with a lot of smoke and maybe some drinking or something
and she actually did die of her asthma, no joke. I yelled at him something
terrible about his medicine, I said he must want to die or something or
else he would know where it is* AT ALL TIMES AND KEEP IT WITH HIM. *I
made him cry I was so mad. Then even though I knew I was monstrous
I felt better.*

Teddy came home after midnight ecstatic. Jessie was reading in bed,
her hands outside the blankets, cold, the rest of her warm in pliant flannel.
Teddy flung off his clothes like a man on the shore of a lake on a sweltering
day. He flattened himself against her, his whole body celebratory.

"Whatever did you find that's set you up so?" He was crushing her
book.

"Oh, the assholes!" Teddy answered. "They have themselves in a ridiculous situation and unless we blow it somehow, they're going to leave
behind an organized community where there's never been one before." He
took her by the elbows and buried his face exuberantly in the flannel of her
breasts. "You know what that place is like—Mourning Dove. Think about
it, what a melancholy thing to call a place you expect to be happy in."

"I'm sure nobody ever dreamed of being happy there. It's just that you've
got to live somewhere. And so? What happened? Hey, I can't hear you if
you do that." She was caught somewhere between pleasure at his firm
comforting weight against her, and embarrassment that an evening out with
danger could excite him, body and spirit, far more than she could, safe and
warm. His face was chilly and his day's growth of beard scratched.

"Oh, Jess. What it is is one of those classic scenes. Okay. Picture: Black kid—name is Tango—he's walking in Hoxey with his girlfriend. Girlfriend's pregnant and they're on their way to where she works to pick up some stuff that belongs to her because she thinks she's about to have this baby and she'll never get a chance to come back for it? So they're walking along and the deputy sheriff—named Rye, who's this dedicated cretin?—he says something nasty about the girl or the two of them, I don't know what it was, something about her very visible condition." Teddy was sitting up now and Jessie watched the little fuzz of light, like peach fur, traced around his profile as he spoke: lamplight, the aura of his animation. Becoming, whatever it was. "And Tango got mad, which was the intention. He says he didn't hit the cop, he only insulted him back and kept his girl's hand and kept on walking."

"But?" She has heard all this so many times before. Still it is real. Still the victims will bleed their own real blood before the telling's done.

"But. End of the story—no, middle. Where we are now. Tango's been in this little shithole jail nearly a week and he's mincemeat, we went to see him and they've done a job on him. Grisly, I mean. The girl's in the hospital here in Jackson, she went into labor and the baby was born in jail very premature—I don't know if they really thought it was due or if they can't count or just what, that part's a little hazy. But it died, anyway, with who knows what kind of assistance from whom. And at this moment—well, I sure as hell hope not right this second, I hope everybody's sleeping although you never know with those bastards—there are two ugly camps. Tango's friends have been around demanding an investigation and now there's a nice little ad hoc group of sheet-heads out there daring them to take a step. A lot of people have been laid off from the clothespin factory, you know, in Hoxey, so there's a little too much free time and it weighs heavy, especially when the pocket's empty. There's been one firebombing but it hit an outbuilding, and a couple of—"

"Well, and where are you in this." She asked the question, Teddy would tell her later when they argued over it, without a question mark. That told him exactly where she thought he should be.

"What do you mean, where do I stand? What kind of question is that?" It was his old much-practiced innocence that tottered on the edge of affront. Sometimes she could see his eyes change first, they softened and widened the way even Andy's and Lydia's never did about to be disillusioned by someone's cynicism.

"Teddy, you were made for simpler times. You're a black and white man, aren't you."

"What are you talking about?" He had drawn measurably far from her so that they seemed to be addressing each other across a broad table.

"For one thing," Jessie began, playing with her cuff, half-sorry, half-delighted to do this to his mood of exaltation, "I don't trust Jug."

"Why, all of a sudden?"

"It's not all of a sudden, you know I've never trusted him. Don't sound as if you're performing for an audience that needs a thorough introduction to the characters." She sighed. "He never gets his hands dirty, for one thing. He stands there looking like he's busy but he's only taking notes so he can give the details to his 'contact' at the capitol. First he makes things happen, then he tells tales on them. A provocateur. And you have been known to think so too. Who else has he called in on this one?"

Now Teddy was agitated. He pulled his long legs out from under the covers and sat, feet on the floor, his back to Jessie. She hated to see him cold. "There are a lot of other people. Dandridge. Keith Shulman from the Lawyers' League. A *New York Times* stringer is supposed to be coming." He looked at her over his goose-pimpled shoulder. "Dandridge is getting a bunch of Jackson State kids and faculty over there to march. What are you doing, Jessie?"

"To *march*?" She sunk her face in her hands and breathed steady deep low breaths to calm herself.

"There's a young girl who carried a baby a good long time and then lost it in a pissy jail cell. Where's your feminist consciousness on that one? I don't think they ever had a doctor for her."

She didn't appreciate the hostility that ran, deep, beneath the question.

"There's a bunch of folks out there that everybody's forgotten, and that pathetic town, and now they're in some deep trouble. That Joyce was right. Is it really any different from ten, fifteen years ago? Do they deserve our defense less than they did back when Huntleybrinkley did a story like this every goddamn night?" Teddy stood up and walked across the room, his hands moving absently at his bare sides as if he were looking for his pockets. He turned to her, more earnest, even, than she, his face absorbed and dark in his anger. Had they not advanced past that first didactic encounter in the back seat of that borrowed car? Jessie made fists to keep from laughing: a man cannot really argue politics or moral commitment naked in a wintry room. All of him bobbled, his elastic cowlick, his bony shoulders, his chilled penis retracted, about as assertive as a tuft in a couch cushion. Even his feet looked pale, nervously shifting, moving, toe joints rising, falling like the felt-covered hammers inside a piano. He didn't seem to care how silly he looked; she wasn't sufficiently serious. It came as a rebuke to realize that.

And, rebuked, she weakened. "Teddy," she said to him quietly. "Teddy. You are a man with four children and a wife. At this very moment not a single one of them is functioning very well and we'd be very happy if we could have a little piece of your undivided attention." When she had finished, she gave him a wide innocent smile.

He stood quietly, the frame of his chest moving visibly with each breath as if he had been running. However he lectured her, patronized her, she thought, he couldn't bear to hear her criticism. The ripple of movement across his face and body, like a cat twitching its fur, might have been chill and might have been impatience.

"Aside from any other reasons I might have for wanting to keep you alive, I frankly don't think you have the right to volunteer your services for this bit of local terrorism just now." She looked away embarrassed; she ought not to weaken her case by using words like terrorism, which she didn't even mean. "Heroism," she amended, sheepishly. "You won't like that but it's what I think."

"When will I? Have that right, I mean. When, then? You sound like those parents who didn't want their kids to come down here in sixty-four, you know that? Those shivery hysterical grandmas you had so much easy contempt for." Teddy's long chin jutted stubbornly. "Is that what you've become? Already? And not even over a child's decision?"

She smoothed the ribbon of the dark red blanket. It was smooth, it felt like a rim of raw flour, magically immaterial under her fingertips.

"Come on, tell me. When can anyone be spared? Was anyone who's died since the beginning of this thing dispensable?"

"That isn't what I mean. You know it isn't. Don't distort."

"Well then, enlighten me. Let's measure off our distance."

"I think Jug Dixon is using you, all right? I think he wants to stir something up and this is—"

"You think he's making this happen? Staging a confrontation? He got this kid Tango—"

"Come on. That's not the way you make confrontations, don't make me seem more naive than I am. Let's say he's fanning it instead of helping to put it out, if you like that better. It would be of more service to the people of Mourning Dove if you told the *Times* stringer to go back to New Orleans or wherever he came from, and not to give the damn thing any publicity at all. You're glorifying those goons by paying attention, and you're only forcing their hand."

"My God, Jessie, I don't believe what I'm hearing. Every damn do-good chickenheart in the state of Mississippi and everywhere else in the country said that close to twenty years ago. Tiptoe, whisper, or you'll be to blame for the violence you call down on your heads. I don't believe this." He sat down abruptly at the edge of the bed as if he'd been struck.

Jessie made herself lean over and put her arms across his shoulders but he would not soften. "But it isn't twenty years ago. You're all alone out there. I think Jug is desperate for something to happen to open things up a little—and that's admirable enough, I guess—and he knows you are too. Which is all very noble, and God knows I agree there's been a premature freeze, with a lot of people caught drowning under the ice, if you want to look at it that way. But wishing isn't having. Plus—" She put her head on his shoulder but he ignored it; she felt like a coquette. "Plus you have certain very binding commitments just now that make your absence—dangerous at worst and inconvenient at best."

"Don't tell me about my commitments, I've counted them very carefully. I've been out one fucking evening—"

"So far. So far." She dared him with her eyes when he turned to glare at her. She watched him read her face feature by feature.

"That's going to be a self-fulfilling prophecy, mama. I never asked to be responsible for four goddamn children—"

"Well, guess what, Teddy. Neither did I. Alexis didn't ask to be killed either, as far as I know. So what." They sounded like hissing children.

"Anyway," Teddy went on, trying every direction. "I'm sorry. That was a stupid thing to say. But look, aren't you the same woman who keeps at me about my pathetic job, how I'm wasting my talents, how I've given up? Isn't that you? Or have I been misinformed about your opinion?"

"Yes, that's me. But I didn't intend—"

"You didn't intend. Well, thanks. *You* didn't intend. You know what this is called? I remember from my psychology class—it's the good old classic double bind. I'm damned if I do and I'm damned if I don't. And you don't know *what* in the hell you intend." Teddy took a deep breath that seemed to meander lazily through the moist close-branching by-ways of his lungs like cigarette smoke before he let it out slowly. Jessie listened to it come. "Jessie," he said then in a defeated voice. "You do surprise me. You were a good friend when things were hard in a certain way, you know what I mean? A sort of limited way, when we were all caught up in a kind of simple danger. Life and limb. But now that I need you for something else—" He put one hand over his eye, as if it needed soothing.

She was speechless: it was her analysis of him, Teddy as the first giraffe to eat from the tops of the trees, the hero who couldn't adapt. She turned away from him. She had been thinking that she'd rushed this confrontation:

two weeks from now when he was strung out and short-fused, when his shirts stank of the special sweat of terror which made simple exertion smell sweet, when every voice made him twitch with anticipation, when his bladder twinged every five minutes and he yawned the way you do when you're nervous and can't seem to hold enough oxygen—two weeks in Mourning Dove, in the line of fire, would have been time enough for this discussion. She got into bed and pulled the ribboned blanket edge over her shoulder for its comforting touch more than its warmth (because it too had steeped in the chill of the air), and made herself close her eyes. He was right that she had no idea what she hoped for him, except that somehow miraculously he be useful and contented, and that he stay with them and hear them, all of them, when they talked. But under the covers her face burned with humiliation and bewilderment. You were a good friend once, he had told her. And now that I need something different . . . They ought to be able to laugh about it, the coincidence of terms, the congruity of their dissatisfactions. Even though her eyes were closed, the hot tears brimmed and spilled and soaked the blanket edge. If they had just been able to laugh, she would have known it would be all right.

I got all the info. from Barbara about the youth rally and said I would decide at the last minute. I wish I could just know her for a friend, not a scout leader type. For instance, how does she buy her clothes? I guess her father just gives her the money and drops her at the store (if he isn't too "out of it" to drive?) She doesn't talk about what injury he got. Because, for instance, I don't want Jessie's help buying clothes, I would end up ridiculous. And I don't have one single friend to go with, like to the mall or Highland Village.

It is a few minutes later and I can already see how that is pity for myself. I let it come out for a little while, it feels better. But I can still catch it in time before I get all soggy. I can take Lydia's bike or get a ride or a bus and just do it myself. When you are an adult maybe you know exactly what you look like in the mirror and you don't have to bring someone to tell you (?)

"What are you going to tell your mother?" Jessie asked tonelessly.
"Oh, my mother. I'm not ten years old."
"But on Thanksgiving you expect your family to show up, it's not

unreasonable of her to think we might want to be there. We said we were coming months ago."

Teddy made an ambiguous face, a half helpless, half malicious smile.

"You *look* ten years old," she told him, tracing his lips with her finger.

"Look." He closed his mouth so decisively he almost caught her vagrant finger. "We are going out to Mourning Dove and we are going to boycott Thanksgiving with those people and a whole lot of others. Our children are going to be made to understand why we're there and not sitting in an overheated dining room eating that compressed wood Aunt Tush dares to call a turkey."

"But they're also going to understand that their grandmother and their great-aunt, who have nobody else left, are eating their compressed wood entirely alone."

"I'm sorry." He did not look sorry. "We can't be in two places at once, though, can we, so we have to make our choice."

"But your choice is cruel. And if you're concerned with educating these children, you'd better remember that while you're teaching them one thing you're also teaching them another."

Teddy covered his eyes with the long stalks of his fingers, weary. He rubbed the bridge of his nose with one hand as if he had just removed a painful pair of glasses. "Okay." He took a deep impatient breath. "Okay. I'm teaching them there are larger groups than the family that you can swear loyalty to. Is that what you have in mind, approximately? I am teaching them that women tend to take a narrow view of anything that threatens their beloved family."

"Teddy, my father did that." She was proud of the evenness of her voice.

"Precisely. And your mother never forgave him, true to form for her sex, and you've never forgiven him either. Which is why you have it in for me, although I'm not planning to be away for two years. As far as I know."

She stared at him coldly. Let him say it all.

"I have always supposed he had to do what he did, Jessie. You don't walk away from your life casually. Some people call that heroism, you know."

" 'Had to' doesn't tell me a damn thing. He chose to, and he chose himself irrevocably out of his wife's and his daughter's life. Heroism." She looked swamped with tears, her face going spongy soft beneath her attempt at control.

Teddy took her hands, held them to his chest an instant and then kissed them slowly, sighing, so that, viewed from a sufficient softening distance he might have seemed to be yielding. But the gesture was meant to be sufficient consolation. "Jess. This is one day. You're all coming with me, we're going together. This is an act of solidarity with a couple of dozen endangered people who can't afford turkeys or cranberry sauce to begin with, and, to make matters a little worse, who are being stalked right now by goons with rifles and kerosene in Coke bottles who think they're waging guerilla warfare among the tarpaper shacks. We're trying to give whoever might be listening a message. And I don't want O'Neill and Helen to see us at odds over it, if you're so concerned about lessons learned."

She let him hold her hands although she felt she was surrendering freedom of movement to him; Mickey Mouse raised his tail like a flag and leapt out of arms when his feet were constrained. "No, we are not coming with you. The world is *not* listening, Teddy. The world has got its own problems these days. The world is much more interested in Jonestown or whatever. Something sexy. What about *this* world right here under your roof? And what do you tell your mother?"

He dropped her hands and turned his back on her. He had his old angers too. "That's a question of a different magnitude. Any damn thing. Flu. Car trouble. I don't care. Tell her we'll see her at Christmas. Tell her we'll bring the goddamn tree."

I had a dream that must have been that character, Jimmy Jones, he was at my window and he was calling me. He sounded like Andy so I went! (Of course I didn't know it was a dream.) But when I looked out in the backyard, it was raining and lightning, and there were all the people from Jonestown, white and colored, all laying face down in the yard, naked every single one. And Teddy and Jessie were in the pile too. They were thin with scrawny rears.

I think that was because—this makes me feel funny to write it—I heard them before, way after I fell asleep I got up to go to the bathroom and when I went past their door guess what I heard. Well, it was a lot of breathing, both of them, with a few words thrown in, and the bed moving a little and then—I would swear that couldn't really be very pleasant if it makes people sound like they are dying and then thoroughly dead! I wondered if there would be any survivors! This house is much too small. All the years we lived in Vestavia I never heard any such thing and even if my parents were "at" each other a lot, especially recently, I know from logic that they were having sex together anyway, even when people who truly hate and despise one another seem to, they conveniently forgive each other at night a certain number of times per week (they say). (I think if you could do it just once to find out, then you wouldn't have to just keep on, but people seem to so I will wait to decide. "You are too young to know every little thing," Mom would say like she always did.)

I haven't had to look at them this morning (I am writing this in bed), they will not be embarrassed but I will. I wonder if their children grew up hearing things they shouldn't. I wouldn't want my brother to know anything like that, it would scare him, he would think another set of parents was going to die before the sun comes up! Can you just hear me asking Andy to find out?!

Mostly it is just one more thing that makes me wish I was home. I don't belong here. Dear Jesus, I don't think You listen to me any more. If I am abandoned I would like to know WHY.

I am having to get up and go to school today. I will think of something to tell Lingham somehow.

We talked in gym. There is a membership meeting in so. Jackson the Friday after Thanksgiving but there is no way for me to get there. I tried thinking if I was meant to go, little problems like "transportation" would just solve themselves. "My father and I will pick you up," she says right on cue. "Seven o'clock. No sweat."

So I sit there during dinner, I'm thinking these people would die (one already did!) to keep the Klan out, how can I do this even as a half-joke? Then Teddy—right while I'm going over all this in my poor head!—invites all of us to this anti-Klan demonstration in some little town some place! I cannot believe it. Like, I really believe mysteriously he was reading my thoughts. It is something awfully strange, you have to admit. I'm thinking Do I OR don't I? and he's saying "These f——— are getting ideas again, we can't let them pick off this defenseless bunch of people," the way he talks you can see all these little, like, frail children, huddled up behind trees and doors yelling "Teddy, HELP!"

But Jessie definitely does not agree. Here is this same woman who was just moaning in his arms last night and she's calling him a (pardon the expression) "asshole." (No, that was some friend named Jughead who she says is leading him around by his nose.) But it wasn't hard to see she wanted to call Teddy one too. I'll bet.) What does this mean about her feelings about the KKK? I can't tell.

Anyway, O'Neill pipes in that he wants to go. I said, "No, you don't," but I got overruled. Teddy gives me that cold know-it-all smile.

"It won't be dangerous," he tells me. "He can learn some valuable things from a march." Well, what if I don't happen to like what they want to teach him. I don't count for anything all of a sudden, the dear older sister has just as much of an opinion as some stranger. Teddy is smooth as the serpent.

Before he went to sleep I came to O'Neill's bed and sat on the side and warned him his uncle Teddy is trying to brainwash him. But he is so confused and he is also more scared of getting in trouble than I am. I could care less. He goes "Maybe they'll shoot at us!" and his face gets all pink with excitement. "Teddy says there are these places where people actually got killed and stuff, and we can go visit them, he says they ought to make them just like the Civil War monuments with markers and everything. So people will always remember. He told me I have to learn all this stuff just like his own kids. It's History." Then he says, "One place there's this dam"—this is disgusting—"and they buried these three guys under it, first they whipped them and they burned out their car and then they dragged them—" and I said "O'Neill, you better stop right now before I throw up." I told him he enjoys all those gross stories too much, if he's going to listen I don't think he's supposed to be thinking oh goody, dead bodies and blood and chases and all. Anyway, what I am trying to do is get him to see it's like cowboys and Indians and suddenly does he realize he's riding with the Indians? Just whose History is it? But he can't, he is a soft touch, as they say, for an adventure, and maybe even for a day with Teddy as a "father." Talk about throwing up. He started crying and told me to leave him alone. He goes "You don't want me to have any fun." I almost told him about Lingham and the Klan kids, take your choice of "fun" but what's the sense of that, he doesn't know what's happening, he is a little child and this is even confusing to me.

Thanksgiving dawned, one of those tender sunny days that could have been early spring except for the weariness of its light; it lacked the energy to cast hard shadows. On days like this one Jessie was beguiled into loving Mississippi; it seemed to be making its concessions to comfort, if only she could make hers.

Teddy and O'Neill were eating a good heavy breakfast because there wouldn't be much food later in the day. Teddy was giving orders as if his command of the troops had already begun: yes, O'Neill could wear dungarees if he wanted to. Yes, he could bring his little camera, thousands of great photographs had been taken on days like this.

"Couldn't we have turkey tomorrow?" O'Neill begged, not for the first time. "I don't see why we've got to give it up today and keep on giving it up." He suddenly had an idea. "We *are* going to be home tomorrow, aren't we?"

Teddy was tying on his work-boots. His movements were different on a day like this, eager, angular, like the children's on the first day of vacation, as large as if he were already outdoors faced with some physical challenge. "Let's hope," he said to O'Neill. "Don't ever know."

He winked at Jessie; he had decided, apparently, that O'Neill, who was going as their representative, would enjoy the promise of danger and uncertainty and that Jessie, who was not going, ought to understand the plan, at least, and cooperate. But, how could he have forgotten, she hated to have anyone wink at her: it was a mark of insincerity, even if she, winked at, were not the one who was being fooled.

. . .

There was not a thing to say for their day except that they were there, in Yazoo City. No new adjectives presented themselves, no opinions were reversed, the only thing Jessie knew by day's end that she had not when they set out was that, however convenient it might be for Teddy to think he and she were interchangeable, his mother didn't consider them so: in Teddy's absence no one got credit for putting in an appearance. Jessie apologized to the children and lied to Dorothea about the car trouble that had kept Teddy in Picayune. Even a little lie buttressed by sterling intentions was compromising in their presence, an incitement of their worst instincts, and all the worse because it was not believed, was not sufficient. Dorothea had been stood up. There were always buses. There were planes. "And boats," Andy murmured to Jessie to show his loyalty.

"But he has to work tomorrow," she lied, certain that Dorothea would never grasp the intricacies of the school calendar.

Stern, lionlike, Dorothea reminded her, "I was his mother yesterday." Her expression was so shamelessly self-satisfied that Jessie could have been convinced this had some bearing on her statement.

"And you will be tomorrow," she told her mother-in-law, getting into the rhythm, wondering what in the world she meant. Talking to Dorothea was like breathing the air above the tree-line—you were light-headed and probably irrational but once you got used to the feeling that you had something as unfamiliar as helium in your lungs there was something dazzling and restful about having no responsibility. Now it was almost as if no one were listening.

The children were impeccably polite, as if in compensation for Teddy's truancy, and Jessie asked a hundred questions about family members she would never meet. But in the end it all counted against her: had she truly belonged she'd have known Uncle Jennings and Great-Aunt Tilla and all the rest, and, knowing them, been constrained from asking potentially embarrassing questions. Jessie envied the children mightily that they were allowed to hunker together, run in the yard—even Andy ran with them— and keep their mouths so becomingly shut.

Teddy and O'Neill were home when they got back. It had all, O'Neill said, been super. He showed them the sign he had carried: it said, with a helpful picture of a round wingèd lump on yellow legs:

THE KKK IS THE TURKEY!!!!!!

There were a lot of kids although most of them couldn't stand still and one kept knocking him on the head with his sign. Best of all, when they were out on the highway, walking the narrow piece that connected Hoxey and Mourning Dove, a bunch of fast cars came by and scattered the marchers who were all over the place just dozing along, talking. Nobody got hurt, he said, but boy did they jump!

"We," said Teddy. "We were among them, if you remember."

"Well, we. Yes, sir. We jumped too. I sure did like that."

Teddy frowned at him. "O'Neill's got some sense of humor. He liked it better than dodgeball. But it was a good march."

"A lot of people?"

"Small. Tight."

"Not many, you mean."

"Enough. It's a town with some problems—two hundred people, two churches, two congregations that avoid each other as if the other one's contaminated, and one of the preachers was behind the march, so—"

"The other half boycotted. Great."

"But there was a lot of good feeling, and we kept all of Hoxey in their houses, as far as we could tell. Nobody was venturing out."

"Well, Thanksgiving's not one of your big shopping days. Where would they have been going?"

"The only problem, as he said, was coming back there's a section of road where they caught us and nearly hurt some people."

"And how did the marchers feel about that?"

"Like they ought to—mad. Victimized but not cowed. Somebody nearly lost a couple of real little kids, though."

"For nothing."

"Jessie, you weren't there. You can be as jaundiced as you want if you know what you're talking about. You-all were sitting in a parlor full of antimacassars."

She went into the kitchen to put on the tea-kettle. O'Neill had gone in to watch TV. "And did the rest of the troops turn out as promised? The kids from the college and all the rest? Was *The New York Times* there?"

"You'll believe the *Times* but you won't hear me."

"I've never believed them yet. For one thing, they tend to talk to you."

"Two kids from Jackson State came and one from Tougaloo, and Dandridge put in an appearance but he had to leave before the march began. He gave a little pep-talk."

"I'll bet he was dressed to kill, with his mustache waxed." Dandridge was a young black lawyer who was so pretty he had groupies. He wore boots and a black silk carnation, and he made Jessie queasy. She had also heard that he carried a gun. "And what do you think your nephew got out of the day besides a terrific scare on the highway? Did he think you were at the demolition derby or what?"

Teddy smiled and nodded. "He said—this was on the way home—he said he was glad he hadn't gone to Yazoo because he liked getting to hold his sign up as high as he could."

"It could have been anybody's sign. Roger's. It could have said 'Nuke the whales.' "

"Could have. But it was ours. One of these days it'll make sense to him."

Another little exhibitionist in the making.

"I told him about some of the big marches—Selma. Meredith. I told him how they don't always use cars but they usually use something with an edge on it to try to turn you around. You know how you get the donkey to do what you want, Jessie."

"I do?" The thin shriek of the tea-kettle was calling her.

"Yeah. First you've got to get his attention."

"Right, so you hit him over the head with a picket sign. I'll remember that." She went in to get the kettle. "Did he say anything nasty about his fellow marchers?"

"Nothing worth repeating." Teddy was beginning to look depressed—did that mean she had succeeded at something? He sat studying a ragged cuticle on his thumb, digging at it with his long index finger. When he raised his head to watch her pour water over the tea-bag, which flopped in his cup like a cigar butt, she thought belligerently, don't give *in* so easily, man. I don't need to be right. I don't want to be. Convince me. His mobile mouth turned down in self-disgust to remind her that he could do this to himself better than she could. What they lacked, both of them, were killer instincts; they could injure, tear flesh, but they seemed incapable of finishing what they started. The Floyd Pattersons of marriage. He was in a familiar spot after a short remission of pain. But she would not apologize.

We went to see Grandy. Frankly it would be merciful if she died, she doesn't make any sense any more. It was one Boss Boring Day. Andy said he likes to go because this is where his Daddy was a boy and he walks around trying to see him there running under the magnolias and climbing through the crepe myrtle where this telephone pole is still there all around it and he used to climb up on these metal rungs and be up in the top of the bush like a great climber when he really wasn't. I guess he meant my Mom was the same (a young girl, I mean) but I'm already busy just trying to see her a couple of months ago. That is quite hard enough for me, thank you. Grandy tried to talk to me about her, she did make that connection which I thought was pretty good considering. But what could I say. She goes "Your mother."

"Yes." (me)

"She's home?"

"No, she isn't home."

"She's here."

"No."

But then when I thought she really wanted to know and I was beginning to get a little upset because I was going to be the one to break it to her for the umptee-umph time, she changed the subject to something about these gardens in Louisiana that she wants to visit in the spring that are solid miles of bulbs. I hate to say it but she is "stark raving mad." Andy just threw me this look, he is taking his father's place here. It said "Don't be angry, have pity, just have everlasting pity on her." I do. She is more of an innocent babe than her grandson O'Neill. Only since she looks like a grandmother that is awfully hard to remember.

O'Neill came home from the rally so tickled. I am losing him, there is no other way to say it. He sold himself for a fast dangerous drive in a car, next to someone who feels like a Daddy, which is what my brother wants to have more than anything in the world. Even with all the differences between his real Daddy and this one. Well, I have to admit

I know that feeling, a father is still a father no matter what. I know that's what always kept us good, not really anything like what you'd call Respect.

I went in the bathroom after O'Neill came home from picketing where I can get a bit of privacy for a while and actually cried for him. It is a fact: I have not cried once for just myself. I am proud of that anyway. Or maybe I was crying for Mom because what I would hear behind their bedroom door was such frightening shouting and Daddy slamming drawers and threatening. If I had a stick or something I should have hit him with it. And if I hit him a good one I would never have had to convince Mom to go with him that last time to make it all Final. And I would not be here now in Shantytown and they would not have dirt and worms and, oh dear God, would have none of it in their eyes, above and below and everywhere. Help me, help me, please, I am going to dissolve with such thoughts in my mouth like worms in my heart and soul. When I get like this I am a disgusting slug with salt poured down on me, shrivelling, vanishing. All of us shrink down to a little clump of skin and hair and then nothing.

The letter came with a Birmingham postmark but no return address so as, Jessie guessed, not to encourage further inquiry. Unfolding it, she had the queer breathless sensation she was handling a ransom note; she half-expected it to be composed of letters cut out of magazines. But it was in a slightly chaotic green ball-point script that seemed to be rushing off toward some relief at the right-hand margin, and signed quite legibly Tooty (Therese Uplheim) Durgin; under that, printed, Mrs. Joseph Durgin as if three distinct people had lent their names to the message.

That message said without much equivocation:

Dear Mrs. Carll:

It was good to meet you the other day. You are very confused about what was going on over here and I don't blame you. I have just moved here a short while ago and it is still shocking to me what I have moved into. I think you will want to know that I learned your brotherinlaw Roger Tyson and my sisterinlaw Donna Durgin for a long time were having improper relations and everyone over here knows it. That is why they were all so quiet that day. When it is time for gossip, mostly nasty, take my word for it that is not a quiet bunch, but they will protect each other in a pinch, which is the code of honor of criminals. It is all a filthy business but it is true so you should know it. Mrs. Tyson probably went out to Seattle to keep an eye on him because who knows what else he had up his sleeve (or to have it all out with him far from the children and neighbors, now no one will ever know). Probably they cracked up their car having an argument. Other than that I should say that my sisterinlaw seems to be a perfectly nice person but I don't know her well, only last year I came into her family by marrying her brother Joseph. But I'll say that if I don't find the moral atmosphere to improve here I myself will not hesitate to move my child (from a previous marriage, I was widowed) so that we can find a better influence. This is a sordid business.

I hope you don't resent my sending these words of truth. People's sins should not be allowed to disappear so easily as if they never were. In this case I have not a second doubt that iniquity followed them out all the way to the west coast and scourged them there, one guilty, one innocent, which is sad but as you know often happens as with drunk drivers having wrecks with the sober. (That same occurred just last week in a suburb of Birmingham, a drunk and a small child and you can guess who got killed. They never seem to, it always makes me wonder if the liquor is a kind of armor, nothing wants to get near the stink.)

I hope you can use this information somehow, although I don't know how. I am not trying to cause trouble but I was raised to believe truth must find a home. Good luck in your endeavors.

Your's in Christ's compassion,
Tooty (Therese Uplheim) Durgin
(Mrs. Joseph Durgin)

There wasn't much evidence of Christ's or anyone else's compassion in the letter but Jessie was glad to have it nonetheless. She was, in fact, nearly sick with excitement, her hands shook, her mouth was dry as midsummer. She didn't know what she would do with the information either, but every confirmation of one's instincts is a kind of compliment, isn't it, she thought, and the compliments add up to a flattering sense of self. She could use some flattery just now. The *bastard*, she murmured out loud. The *worm*. She felt closer to Alexis than ever.

After she had folded the note back into its severe envelope, she considered the chances that this Tooty was insane. There was a distinct possibility:

she had had that peculiar unfocussed intensity, balanced, bobbing, on the edge of some fanatic unwholesome grimness. Her severely shorn hair, her raccoon-shadowed eyes, some out-of-synch details of her plainness that hadn't even registered in Jessie's memory. She had known girls with that killjoy look, dedicated to a half-cracked sobriety at a woefully early age. Usually they wore uniforms—it takes an excess of high spirits to seem happy in a uniform—and went to parochial school. (As a child she had given a good deal of inconclusive thought to cause and effect: did reciting the catechism endlessly from a thumbed little pamphlet make you humorless and boring or did only humorless and boring children get sent to St. This or That's in the first place?) She was shocked, now, to realize what kinds of prejudices *she* had harbored. Never having called them that she had never counted them against herself, nor worked at their obliteration. They seemed, in any event, to have faded like childhood freckles. It was something to keep in mind.

.   .   .

The day after Thanksgiving, a skinny *New York Times* called the march from Mourning Dove to Hoxey "a sad exercise in yesterday's tactics." The reporter had counted the marchers and, in that pseudoneutral tone which beguiles by innuendo and juxtaposition, pronounced the twenty-four of them (including children) inadequate to the purposes of self-defense or of intimidation. He showed faint amusement at the spirit behind the signs. (O'Neill's was specifically cited. He was ecstatic and stared and stared, wanted and was given his own copy of the paper, laughed and danced a little in disbelief.) But the reporter also suggested that most of the slogans had been initiated by "the twin shepherds" of the demonstration, "experienced white civil rights activists Frank Dixon and Ted Carll who were kept busy in the basement of the God So Loved the World A.M.E. Church stimulating the courage of the marchers and issuing admonitions, second-nature a decade ago, to meet violence with calm and to keep the line of march solid, singing as they went." Recent University of Mississippi graduate, lawyer Fred Dandridge (off to eat turkey at the home of friends in nearby Jackson), was quoted to the effect that while such marches were good for morale, they were " 'an exercise in nostalgia. The legal system is finally beginning to be responsive to inequities and atrocities perpetrated against blacks, and that is the arena where this kind of problem will be settled.' " He was seeking an injunction to prevent residents of Hoxey from entering the neighboring town.

The reporter had access to a few of the troublemakers from Hoxey who denied they were being kept inside by the demonstrators. " 'We were eating turkey and pulling on our wishbones,' Edward Shepley, 30, an unemployed lathe worker, said. 'I was wishing we could get this country back on the track.' After the incident in which the high-speed automobiles interrupted the marchers on their return to Mourning Dove, Shepley took credit on behalf of the Rising Sons of the Ku Klux Klan, a new organization, with apparent pride. 'I was working off a big meal and those marchers were so weak from giving up Thanksgiving and singing on an empty stomach they just couldn't move fast enough. I'm sorry I didn't get one.' Law enforcement officials refused comment."

" 'Our stomachs always empty' was the response of Mrs. Owena Ferguson, 68, whose great-grandson Tilbert Malley barely escaped injury. But the approaching new year, in spite of the lively spirit of defiance in this divided town"—this was the reporter being oracular; it was a feature article and he was finally allowed to admit to judgment—"hardly promises any improvement."

Teddy flung the paper down and smashed one fist into his open hand. "Asshole. They think they've got to send a fucking *reviewer?*"

"It *is* bad for business," Jessie agreed. "But did you think he'd write a blurb just to cheer you on and recruit sympathy?"

"Not a blurb. He could have talked to a dozen other people and gotten another story entirely. Creep came with his mind made up like it was his bed at the goddamn Holiday Inn. He never talked to me. Christ, it sounds like he talked to you."

The children were waiting to go to the schoolyard with Teddy for a game of Frisbee. Lydia, glancing openly at Helen, flicking her eyes to her cousin's face as if Helen were a judge, was embarrassed by her father. She probably thought him correct—he was usually correct—but unseemly and vulgar in his rage. Lydia had recently confessed to Jessie that sometimes she found herself wondering if Helen's gorgeous royal iciness might have been inherited from her father's side of the family. It was her ideal to be enigmatic and serene.

"Your chances are pretty slim in this household," her mother had told her, stroking her slick dark curls. "Anyway, I wouldn't call what Helen's father had dignity and I don't think that's what she has either."

"What does she have then?" Lydia had looked ready to argue. Jessie recognized the idolatry that was natural to her age. Aside from the Communist Fathers, whose grave pictures she had cherished at her daughter's stage, she had had no one real—and yet wasn't it the case that whenever anyone had asked her what she was going to do when she grew up, she

would give a perfect accounting of her cousin Ruth's unglamorous achieve-
ments, with a little ill-fitting duty to the Young Communist League thrown
in: I am going to the University of Chicago and make Phi Beta Kappa and
be a social worker and get married when I'm twenty-five to a doctor or
maybe a lawyer. So much for revolution. In her head she saw them working
side by side for the Party, like her own parents, but the desire to be her
cousin overwhelmed duty. She hadn't known Ruth very well because of
the age difference—Ruth's mother was Jessie's mother's oldest sister—and
because she had stayed in Chicago with said husband (who was a chiro-
practor, not a doctor, but why quibble?). And she had never been in Chicago, didn't know what a social worker was, let alone what the "making"—
she thought that meant some kind of creation—of Phi Beta Kappa could
possibly be. All the specifics of her ambition were bogus and had to do
with something else. A kind of bonding, an assurance that one would grow
up recognizably a woman, not a kangaroo or a boulder? A simple shoring
up, with blood-company, of the lonely spirit of a child who spent too much
time alone? It made sense, she supposed, that was what made everyone so
tediously avid nowadays for "proper role models." But proper had very
little to do with it, except at a distant remove, or she'd have longed to be
Emma Goldman or some Bolshevik friend of the family. (Then again, her
parents had no young *friends*, maybe that was what was necessary for im-
printing. With geese it was mere movement!) What did Lydia like about
Helen's reserve, what foreign need did it answer in her?

Jessie tried to describe Helen. "I think what you call dignity is something
she's crouching behind, actually, sort of for protection. Do you know what
I mean?"

Lydia wrinkled her nose, betraying the very absence of dignity she
decried; perhaps it had to be inborn. Every one of them had a face like a
voice that could not be lowered. "You make it sound like a couch or something. Like where they tell you to go in a tornado."

"Well . . ." Jessie considered. "She's had a bit of a heavy wind in her
life, wouldn't you say, so that's not a bad comparison, a tornado. And she
just might be keeping her head down for now."

Lydia sighed, long-suffering. "Did you find out where she's going instead
of school?"

Jessie said no.

"If you let me stay home from school I'll follow her. She'll never see
me."

"Two hooky players. No way. We'll figure it out. Listen—"

Lydia had looked across space at her then, her dark blue eyes attentive in a wholly new adult stillness of expectation. Jessie felt as if she hadn't looked at her own daughter for a month, distracted by these other, these exiled, children. Too many people for the single eye to see, she was going to neglect or abandon somebody, surely, find an unfed corpse in its bed one of these mornings, someone who had slipped out of the frail net of her attention and for one of a good many reasons could not provide for herself. For himself.

"What, Mom? 'Listen,' what?"

Jessie was so deep in her dream of abandonment she could hardly remember. "Oh. Listen, Lyddie. Do me a favor. She's a brave girl and she's doing the best she can, believe me. But don't envy people like your cousin who go all limp and quiet, okay? That's not a terrific ideal. Well, not limp, starched stiff maybe—but who don't tell you things. It makes everything very hard for her and for the rest of us who want to help her. How can I say this? She's—if you were drowning, would you try to save yourself or would you tuck your arms down at your sides and just sink like an obedient stone?"

Lydia had looked at her with something between perplexity and skepticism. She squinted one eye as if that might help her see what her mother was talking about but she opened it again, still bewildered. Jessie watched the complicated folds around her eye come smooth. "Well, I've been thinking about it." And Lydia took a deep difficult contentious breath. "*I* think she's trying to save herself. You think Helen ought to go to school even if she hates it, but I think that sounds like it would be the worst thing. Yuck. And if she asked you you'd only get mad and yell at her." She looked righteous, from long experience, and a little bit afraid.

"Do I yell? Me?" But Jessie was ready to concede. Lydia knew something about power, a subtle thing it was not given all children to understand, or adults either. "Oh, baby, that's called passive resistance!" she had said, and gave her a congratulatory kiss on the top of her head.

Jessie thought of the conversation now, watching Lydia regard her and Teddy coolly, how they stood locked in their distances, inflamed by each other's stubbornness. She clutched a brown and white Frisbee shaped like an Oreo cookie, held it against her chest like a stamped-iron shield. Jessie was overcome by admiration—this little girl hadn't even had to boycott Thanksgiving to understand what refusal might be; how hard and hungry you had to make yourself to live in opposition.

This is the day I had to decide whether to go to the meeting. And something happened that I think was just ordained to be. God is still

*guiding me after all, every road is only more complicated than it looks
and I am not a good reader of the Signs. (Rev. Carstairs used to say you
have dislexia (sp?!) of the soul.)*

I stayed home again and slept on the living room couch because I
didn't want to think. I kept imagining Teddy's face if he ever found out
I went to the Klan rally and that scar of his filling up dark red with
blood the way it does when he gets mad. Color of nightcrawlers. Yucchhh.
And me there just in my long sweater and tights, no jeans or anything.
And about noon or so there comes this rattling of the back door and I
go into a complete panic. What would happen if anyone found me here
defenseless and only ¹/₂ dressed? Maybe it was the Peeping Tom! So I
picked up this very heavy round rock shaped like half a grapefruit they
use it for an ornament, a "geode" it's called, this very smooth milky blue
stone like glass inside and outside it is rough as a coconut, and I'm ready
to throw it or smash at him if he comes after me. It is heavy and would
really make him regret getting up in the morning. Or should I hide? I
can't decide and I'm breaking out in this sweat so I sneak up behind the
kitchen door and I'm trying to see through the crack under the hinges,
not daring to breathe.

And what do I see but Andrew Carll himself, the Prodigal Returned,
and he's making himself one of his banana and peanut butter extrava-
ganzas. So then I just lost all my cool, I shouldn't have but I was so
relieved I just shouted out his name and he jumped and knocked the
whole (JUMBO!) peanut butter jar off the counter and I came out and
we just sort of fell in each other's arms for laughing! We were laughing
and howling until we both had tears all up and down our cheeks and
then in a while—it was like a dream, I am not sure it even happened—
he is just sort of hugging me not laughing any more. And I hung on for
dear dear life. We said not one word. It was so good and comforting I
thought, my life is saved, my whole life.

Finally with me up against him I begin to feel just what I felt with
Tim Knight that time, poor boys just give away their deepest emotions
and desires, he is getting all hard up against me like a broom handle
held to my stomach, and then when I kind of half-glanced down, I didn't
really mean to only I wanted so much to see how I could do that to him
not even trying. Then he blushed the deepest purple and let me go, kind
of gave me this gentle little push and turned away to begin cleaning up
the peanut butter and glass with a whole roll of paper towel. It looked
like an explosion did it, it was everywhere, on the cabinets and halfway
across the room. "Don't walk through it in your bare feet!" He sounded

sharp with me so I thought I'd better put my shoes on, and my jeans too.

It turned out he came home from school at lunchtime because he was going on a tennis match up to Canton and completely forgot his uniform and racket. So he got a ride over to eat and pick it up and was going back but he was in no hurry because all he had in the afternoon was 2 study halls backtoback. And we talked. Some of the time he actually held my hand: it was not !!! like before, it was just, you are a friend of mine and it is natural to sit near you and maybe even protect you. And, Diary, do you know I spilled out all my confusion. I just thought, he will know what to do, he can advise me for my best interests and not despise me or cast me out. I asked that first: If I told him something really terrible, something that would make his parents want to kill me, would he have to side with them and hate me too? What would it take to make him stop liking me? He said, slowly so I stared at the words as they were coming out of those specially pink lips of his, very sober, "Helen," he said, "You couldn't ever do anything I wouldn't understand! Just try it and see."

Well, that was easy for him to say. So I told him what I was thinking of doing. Tonight, I said. At seven.

He wanted to know why. He was shocked, but he was trying to be nice and calm because he promised. Do I really hate black people so much. Did they ever hurt me personally? He was very cool and logical but I could tell he was sort of mad, no matter what he said in words. I tried to tell him no, I don't hate anybody, he knows I don't. It seems to have more to do with being true to my family background. Against what I am being exposed to all of a sudden. How would he like it if everything he grew up with disappeared over night and suddenly, say, he was in Birmingham in our house?

"Not your whole family, not your uncle. Or your grandfather," he said, "from what my Dad tells me about him. They are your family too. Your grandfather would have thought my Dad was a hero if he had lived long enough, it is only your grandmother that is the problem. Not to mention the other side of your family that I don't know." "But that is only half!" I had to remind him.

It wasn't my mother either, I had to admit. She was beginning to change. Only my father. And even he thought the Klan was "a bit much," he was tamed down to where the Citizens' Council was good enough for him, or what was left of its "good old days."

So we talked and talked about Daddy and I said some awful things I have never told a single solitary soul, how much I hated him and wanted him to give us all a divorce, not just my Mom. And told him about Donna Durgin, our dear neighbor, which I never told anyone before, even my own mother would never say it and neither would I to her, that I knew. Knowing about her was just always around, like a terrible smell or something. And I said about how I made my mom go to Seattle with him, how she didn't want to but I thought maybe it would help their Marriage like a second honeymoon, or else would be their last "stand" and they would agree to get a divorce finally. I told Andy how he beat on her and sometimes on us, why couldn't she finish it once and for all. Well, of course I never said to her You should get divorced from Daddy but I kept telling her how all the best magazines and all say "Get a new lease on life, take a vacation together." I thought with a new fluffy nightgown and breakfast in bed and champagne in one of those buckets, maybe he would look at her, she was his beautiful wife, 1,000 times prettier than Miss Donna Dyed-Blonde Durgin, and he would say, "Oh, I am better off at home!" So she finally listened to me and thanked me for such good advice, and that was the reason she called his secretary and they planned how it would be a secret, the secretary got plane tickets for both of them and Daddy didn't even know until he sat down on the airplane next to her, in her best suit and her hair done.

Then when I began to tell all that to Andy I thought I would faint, I got such a hideous pain in my guts, it wasn't the words it was the pain that made me start to cry. It crossed from under my heart down to the top of my thighs. Like lightening cutting across me. I doubled up with it like I was breaking right in half. I had to put my knees up and head down and push them against my chest to make the pain ease up a little.

Andy is rubbing my hand, my arm, and just saying my name to comfort me. And after a long time he goes, "Look, I'm not a psychiatrist so I don't know, I can't figure out why if you hate your father so much you want to march in his worst footsteps." That's as far as I ever get either, I don't understand any of it. Then he says, "I think you must hate my father too, while you're at it, don't you. Do you hate all fathers?" I agreed, yes, his father made me very upset and angry, but not all fathers. I gave him reasons but he just smiled. I think he looked I would call it tender about his own father, not about me just then. I went a little farther because to be honest I was jealous of that smile. "If you really want to know," I was sort of taunting him, "I think your father is a fool."

But this was his son so he defended him. He said he had some differences of opinion with Teddy but fathers are human, didn't I know that. "I am going to be a father some day—if I'm lucky—" He blushed at me. "And I'm probably going to be a mess of some kind that I can't even imagine now. But I hope my son will go on loving me anyway. And I don't know when sons are supposed to stop being just ordinary people and begin being gods just because they have kids. Anyway," he goes, looking very near his own tears, the centers of his eyes got rounded out like they were these lenses, "I have this awful feeling sometimes that my mother is going to sock it to him one of these days, you know—I mean, leave him. Like you wanted yours to do. I just get this horrible feeling she's more unhappy than she ever says. And he's not going to know what hit him." He puts his head down in his palm and I guess he's trying to gather himself together again. "My father," he says like it's a big pronouncement, "is a very passionate man."

I thought he meant all that sex between he and Jessie. But he said how much Teddy wants to do good in the world—he believes all this— how his best days were over when he was quite young and nothing he does any more seems to work out. Whoever's fault that is. And he won't sell out to the new times. My father used to talk about when he was young that way too but when I said that Andy wouldn't listen. "No, admit it sounds like what Teddy was involved in had to do with loving and helping and your father was only interested in keeping people back, things that were violent and full of anger. It is not the same thing." It was like My father is bigger than your father, only it was goodness we were arguing about! Anger is everywhere, it's true, whenever I turn around. It is like wars, where does it stop? And then I had this feeling too, it was like a black ugly wave. Which was, well, let your parents get divorced then, so what? Why should you be spared when the rest of us aren't? You'll be lucky if divorce is the worst thing that happens to you.

I was sitting there with my shoes off under the table and there was still glass, big hunks of it and little tiny slivers, I could see them under the counter. I got up, I was feeling nasty and hot inside, blind. I was like being pulled down under a wave and couldn't breathe right. And I smashed my foot down right in the middle of it. I don't know what I thought I was mashing there but it was my bare ball of the foot. I picked up a big piece like a diamond with thick sides, and I didn't even think why I was doing it, I just pushed up my sweater sleeve and pulled the thing down my bare arm, it went like a rock you skim across water, just skipped down the inside soft place that always looked too pale and weak *anyway. It was beautiful the way I made the stripes, they were invisible and didn't even hurt and then after a while so slowly the blood bloomed up like coming from way deep under, seeping up to run in these tracks and I knew they had always been there. Like they were just waiting to be used. I still didn't feel it much but I was watching Andy's face crack into this horrible shape and I think he was shouting at me. That seemed to take a long time getting to me and his words never came clear. He was very angry though. Anger again and everywhere. Even the gentle people are hiding it inside, their "concealed weapon." I didn't know why he was so mad at me because I didn't hurt him, except that I was making bright blood everywhere, in the squooshy peanut butter under my feet and now it was splashing on the counters. I said "Don't hit me!" because he was coming at me with that face and that was all for a while. I put my head down on the table. He patted me very gently, sort of on the ear, and it was so nice to have someone caring about me like that I didn't even mind my arm stinging.*

He fixed the cuts, there was really only one, the rest were just these little scrape marks. Didn't say a word, just kept on going "Tth, tth." They weren't very deep and I pleaded with him not to tell on me. He keeps going "I have to, how can I not tell them" and on and on, so I finally made a deal with him. It wasn't really a deal because I had already decided in my heart but I said if he didn't tell, I wouldn't go to the meeting with Lingham. In fact I want them to know I am this desperate but I am deathly afraid at the same time. I can't say what this fear is but it overtakes everything. I would rather have pain than fear, something that hurts is very simple and pure—sort of orange and yellow and fine instead of a tunnel of dark and bluepurple like being afraid that shadows everything. The lines down my arm are perfect only they aren't deep enough, they are only vague scratches. Maybe I like things to have happened already so you know the worst. I told him nothing will ever happen to me. It is nothing he can understand and nothing I can explain.

I will wear long sleeves, it is winter, and they will never know. Or I can always say I fell down in gym and got gashed on a sharp rock. It is so weird how reasons don't leave marks. True stories and lies come out into the open air and they make the same ripples in the air waves so your voice sounds the same. Only God the One Listener knows because He can put His finger on your soul and hear the truth vibrating there, just the way when I was little I would put my finger on my canary McManus's feathers and take the warble right out of his throat, from him to me.

I told Andy it was good he wasn't wearing his tennis whites yet and then I showed him how you get blood out of cloth with cold water. It is one of those things girls know, along with not being too surprised at how bright red your blood is. In his eyes he looked like he was the one who did something wrong and was sneaking to clean up the mess. It's funny (though not funny ha-ha), he is bigger, older, and a boy, but it looks like I can make him feel however I want to.

With some will and a sense of almost conspiratorial closeness, they bought a house. There was a bit of luck and coincidence running their way but they believed they had it coming. Helen, out from under what was just possibly the weight of Lydia's critical admiring gaze, came forth with a dozen emphatic opinions. And when the real estate agent asked Jessie for a ballpark figure of what she could spend, she closed her eyes and smiled and brought out a number that sounded like a joke, like ordering a double scotch on the rocks: something that others might have done routinely but that made her feel like a stranger to herself. The agent, however, only nodded; there was no reason she should know what a funny-tragical moment it was when Jessie (whose nearly nonexistent savings sat with Teddy's in an unaccruing account shrinking in value by the day) pretended to join the capitalist class.

They talked about equity, they talked about sliding interest rates and assumed mortgages while she blindly assured the agent that the bank would find the two of them good risks—gypsies, Dorothea bitterly called them. But they wouldn't be consulting Dorothea.

The second house they saw, on Rebus Road, would serve. Jessie felt as if she had the flu, or a galloping head cold that prevented her from tasting and smelling; she was giddily missing the sense that any of it mattered. She was a millionaire and this was to be her fourth, or was it her fifth, house, a convenience for her occasional trips down here. Good roof, good furnace, good mortgage. It was a house of no particular age, full of angles and up on a little rise trimmed with azaleas and oleander. She knew Teddy would approve: his father, the civil engineer, had taught him the rudiments of geography: was it up off the level in case the dam ever broke? (The *dam?*) Truly insignificant details like that, Jessie decided, amused, dispassionate, can sell you anything if you pile them high enough. They take on a life and a texture of their own. Shelves in the garage. The cellar walls were dry and would stay dry. A standing freezer. Did they deserve a standing freezer? Didn't everybody? She only wished the house weren't brown, the one they were fleeing was brown and heavy spirited, a handful of Lincoln Logs.

Andy would see the room they meant for him and turn pleading eyes on his mother. There was space for models and uniforms and posters, the walls a deep blue like the good November sky, and his own bathroom too. He could make a pit out of it and no one would have to see. Each of them could have such a room, O'Neill's a little smaller than the others but big enough for litter. Lydia, sighing, would have to yield up her dream of purple flowers and a hacienda; this was a bird in the hand. Café curtains would be just right on her windows. Helen measured off her room in paces, looked relieved, actually said she liked it. She would have a window seat. Jessie marvelled at the ancient division of preferences; she was too weary to dream of trying to change them, whatever the truly contemporary woman might envision in her kingdom of future equality: Andy with a window seat, Lydia asleep beneath posters of sharks and stingrays.

As for Helen. Jessie decided she had her mother's perfect middle-class matron's sense of propriety. The dining room, she suggested, could be formal? They could buy all this (terrible oatmeal-colored) wall-to-wall carpeting that made friction sparks, and the long dimming drapes too? Jessie's hopes—she saw them now for what they were—that Helen's hostility might be the mask of a rebel, an artist, a natural alien—disintegrated. She took in every symbol of the defeat of Jessie's asceticism with a chillingly practiced eye. The dishwasher was second best but the garage door had an automatic eye. Jessie smiled, light-headed again. "We had that kind at home," Helen assured her, having come alive so dramatically she was like a thirsty plant given a soaking, her leaves suddenly uplifted, beginning to shine. "Don't I know it," Jessie answered bleakly.

The agent asked Jessie if she wanted to show the house to her husband before she committed herself. Surely it was safe for a day, half a day.

"No, he'll be all right."

"Men don't seem to care as much," Mrs. Ashcroft mused, grateful. "When it comes to houses they like to please the woman who's going to spend her time there." Was she someone's little woman, Jessie wondered, with her football shoulders and her forty-six-inch bust?

"My husband would just as soon live in a Quonset hut," Jessie told her. "We're going to surprise him."

Jessie really meant it. There is a house for us! It isn't too bad either, not what I would pick if I was doing it but they don't make that much money and Jessie keeps muttering about modest tastes, hard enough for Teddy to accept where it is, blah, blah. He would live in a shack if she would go too. The best thing is it is a much better element over here, and people at least have some taste, nicer cars, some look like they have gardeners like we used to. I get my own room with a humungus closet and some fun corners. I have a lot of ideas what to do with it and will maybe buy some magazines for themes and stuff and try to make it all match. I saw an article, "How to Antique Your New Furniture." I am less depressed to think I can finally close the door and be alone, FREE AT LAST! I am up a few stairs with O'Neill on one side and Andy and Lydia are like down a few, it is all split up levels, a little like at home. Only the nearest bedroom, with a bath in between, is The Sex Maniacs. Just what I need for neighbors.

I wonder how long it will take to mess up this house like the last one! I don't ever see Jessie cleaning up. She does work for school or goes to meetings of those women or reads a book or something like that, and I don't know who she thinks will keep everything from getting buried but there are people who just don't care. Mom used to make us put our dishes in the dishwasher even if we didn't want to so they could be sterilized. And the towels in the hottest water with bleach. Last week Jessie told Lydia to turn the washer on cold because we were using too much money to heat the water!! Whatever it is that she thinks is important, it is not sanitation.

Someone who does care. I went home with Lingham today, just couldn't come up with a good excuse not to. We went on the bus together, you're not supposed to do that but she fixed it up some way, and then when the bus driver winked at her I thought, Oh wow, this girl is an operator, she has some secret connections, who knows how many. So we went pretty far across town, I don't know where because I almost never go anywhere in this dumb city. She lives on a scruffy street called Heber with some nice old trees but a lot of broken sidewalk and houses right up to the street. I don't want to say poor white trash but . . . I was absolutely shocked. (Because this girl wears nice skirts, never pants, the kind of Gunny Sacks that are trimmed with lace, the pretty spriggy kind of flowered fabrics—it turns out she makes them—and even has these different matching accessories, bags and bows and things.) I don't know how she does it, it looks like no one ever gives her a single thing.

There is this dark porch, screens with holes so big she says birds can fly in the openings and do. Then the living room is just—it was sad, is *all I can say. There is an old couch, one of those foam rubber things and she made a cover for it but this was a few years ago and she is 14 now so you can imagine how grubby it looks. And it was never a very nice color to begin with, sort of washed-out pink that reminded me of the inside of someone's mouth.*

There are shelves made out of boxes full of brickerback she had collected and found and made like thimble dolls and little paper bouquets and clay dogs, and a table that is an overturned peach basket. All this sounds funny which it isn't—I mean, it actually is a good job of looking like furniture, and she keeps it so scrubbed and nice I don't know when she sleeps or does her homework or anything. Also she said no one is ever in there except her and her older brother Jack who drinks and is unreliable and broke up some real furniture they had when he was Stoned. Her father was sleeping when we came in, he was in a huge chair in an old robe with his head way over on the side, puffing and snoring. He is very blonde and actually kind of nice looking for a father, especially one who drinks and is not worth much. He reminded me of a sailor, I don't know why. He is where her brother learned drinking, obviously: "It is his only indoor or outdoor sport for that matter," she tells me, and sometimes she gets furious and sometimes he makes her want to cry for him because she knows this is no kind of life for him either. Sounds like my father, a little. "His fingers are smashed up but he can hold a bottle just fine" (very sarcastic).

She has some movie actors on her wall, John Travolta from "Grease" and someone dressed up like a general. Then she has Geo. Wallace and Lurlene, an ancient photo dead so many years, and the grand dragon of the KKK all dressed up like someone on Halloween.

Everything in her room is so immaculate I do admire her a lot. She has no dresser, only drawers piled up but the socks in the top one are like little snowballs rolled all pure and white. The wallpaper in her room is worn through in one place and she took a crayon to it, she showed me, and filled in the exact pattern of lace and roses and leaves so I wouldn't have known it was different. It must have taken hours!

She is one young girl alone in this house without a mother or sister or friend and she must feel good for keeping everything so decent. All her brother is good for is tearing it up and once he came and puked on her bed (her word) calling her Miss Sissy. She says he is always furiously angry at anything and everything and so is her father. She forgives them because if she was angry too who would keep the family running? "We would fall into smithereens so what would be gained?" is what she says.

(Her brother, by the way, carries a knife and once stabbed a nigger, they don't know whether he died, it was in Sidon and he didn't wait to see.)

We fussed with each other's hair, I was honest and told her that little curl the way she has it looks old-fashioned, like somebody's mother in a picture from the 1940's or 50's. And she showed me a pattern she is cutting for a nice brown checked blouse with a stand-up collar, sort of but not quite "mandarin." As for her Klan group, which I was praying we wouldn't have to talk about, she just said "I hope you will come and see it is not roughnecks or murderers or anything like you read in the papers." She said I would be surprised at how decent everybody is, and who some of them are, I might even have heard of them. But I told her— re-iterated (new vocab. word!)—that I don't know Jackson like she does being born here, and won't bother to learn it either because I am getting out as soon as I can figure out how. When I said that I had this funny memory, it made me smile, this poem my Mom used to read me and then O'Neill,

> *Don't you ever go down*
> *To the edge of the town*
> *Without*
> *Consulting*
> *Me!*

I told her a very little bit about Teddy and Jessie who are crazy about niggers and how he took O'Neill to that rally. I was honest, that it is hard to live right there and say I would plan to go against them even if I never want to help them like my brother. So she goes, "Listen, my dear friend" (she has that snotty kind of tone she uses, it makes her sound really older) "I have had to grow up very fast, and gratitude is something you can't afford if you have to be tough. It is like gum on the bottom of your shoes"—that is exactly what she said! I think she probably read that somewhere—"It keeps you from moving where you have to go. My Father says Social Security pays him because they owe it, not because they are trying to be nice, he put his money in, he should get it out. And no one else deserves his thanks and he won't plead with anyone for anything." She is strange for sure. In some ways she seems a grown-up woman but not worn down yet.

She says she doesn't like boys and never will because they distract you and bring you down. The way she talked I saw a bunch of vampires with blood on their fangs! That is just as well actually because I have trouble thinking of her for example the way I was with Tim Knight or dream about Andy. You do have to soften yourself when you're with them, but so what? I would like to be something like Barbara for selected purposes only. She is one of those my mother would say beats the devil from her door and he comes in the window (to make her grim, I mean, and make her eyes shine with vengeance about something once every five minutes.) But I wouldn't want to get on her bad side either! Incidentally, she does not have Religion in her corner, which could make a big differ- ence. I wanted to tell her that maybe we could do a trade, I would come to her membership meeting if she came with me to look for Jesus one Sunday morning and I could introduce her. But of course the problem is I am in my bed Sunday morning these days, not going to church out in the open. So maybe that will wait.

I went home by public bus, which she put me on and said just go straight. Every single person on it was Negro right down to the bus driver who sang all the way out there and really thought he was funny. (He was, sort of, making comments on things we were passing like a bunch of little children from a school or something walking and holding onto a rope he said they looked like they were climbing up the side of Mount Everest, and once a woman running along the sidewalk on very high heels, looking ridiculous, a blond woman and once upon a time I don't think such a man would dare say anything funny about a white woman, though I may be wrong.) The colored passengers didn't bother me but I felt so obvious like I was naked or something! A woman smiled and a cute little girl in a furry coat (mother said nobody makes cuter children) sat next to me and kept trying to catch my eye. But I was thinking about two kinds of KKK, the one that drags these same people out of their houses and kills them in the moonlight out in the countryside with mother and children crying at his feet vs. what Barbara says, how they have a computer now and a big office staff and their name in phone books like a business someplace. But I realize she never said where. When I got home I looked and there isn't any listed in Jackson.

Saturday morning. We all had a race around the block (except Lydia who was staying hunched over her drawing like she was studying for a test.) And it was odd, when I let go and really was galloping along not thinking of anything I suddenly felt like my legs belonged to my mother. I could sort of feel what her body felt like from inside, what it was like to be in it. This did not make me as sad as it sounds. It was more what Rev. Carstairs used to call "exaltation." Exaltatay, Jubilatay! I know I am going to look a lot like her, I don't know if that is why or if any daughter (or son) would feel how they are basically connected. Now it makes me very sorrowful how it is getting dark before dinner, the lights are not all on yet and it is the worst time of day or night. I always feel it in my throat. Emptiness. But that is an everyday feeling, nothing new. Only that when I was running I could have been her, Alexis Jeanne Carll Tyson, and would have thought, Oh I have a little daughter, her name is Helen Marie, and would have wondered where she was. And she, I guess, would have been watching.

Lingham keeping her distance. Obviously is disappointed, I failed her expectations. Oh well.

We have to run around the track in school. I am pretty good but some of these girls are phenomenal. They move like birds. One of the dumbest girls I ever saw (in math) was so fast I couldn't actually see her, only blurry lines where she was and then wasn't, like in a comic strip. I found I was wanting to dance again when I finished running today. Something that felt good about moving. You don't have to think about anything, it is your arms and legs that think. A relief.

If I still feel this way in a while I may go to one of those dancing schools. I hate to give Jessie the satisfaction though.

Jessie was right about the reactions to the house, every detail. Brought to see it, Andy, independent Andy, took her hand like a suitor and looked into her eyes beseechingly, till she had to laugh. He was a second-generation antimaterialist, and that was a contradiction in terms: he loved things shamelessly.

Teddy did not come to see it; he was more involved in thinking rhetorically about the neighborhood, its kitchens and broom closets manned by old friends in servants' clothing. They took the house, then, and tried not to think about what Jessie called "all that." Did that mean they gave assent? "What are you implying when you say yes? I mean, implication is nine tenths of—what?" Teddy was doing a performance. "*A kiss but nothing below the neck. I like your mind but not your politics. I vote for your stand on handguns but not on capital punishment. Leave my mother out of this. I will keep my own religion but we will bring them up Catholic. I pledge allegiance to the flag. I only work here.*" Jessie thought of the street around dawn, washed in a thin gray light like an underexposed picture. She thought of it at midnight, unpeopled. Andy, who no longer let her near him very much, hugged her like a five-year-old.

Teddy had been gone a lot, between work and Mourning Dove where he went to eat grits and ears, but on the day of the official closing they both stayed home and woke feeling a little soiled by the indulgence. Then they sat obediently in the office of the bank vice president, a red-faced man with aggressive wavy red hair. He had not blinked at their names or their faces, which disappointed Teddy, however convenient it might be for today's purposes. (They would not have wanted to ask for a mortgage in 1965.) His indifference to Teddy's outworn notoriety meant that the bank officer was new in town, newer than ten years anyway. If Teddy mourned, Jessie was relieved.

They signed their names again and again, tight lipped, even before they went into the roomful of lawyers for the closing. Andréa had sent someone from her office, a favor. Teddy said when he saw the pale curly-headed blond Tony Hill, "I hope Andréa didn't send that albino over here because she was trying to make things easy for us. He looks like he stepped out of a Wheaties ad."

"You *are* out-of-date, I always knew it. Wheaties!"

"Jack Armstrong, the all-American boy?"

"Oh, honey, I don't think Jack can cut it any more." She laughed.

But Teddy wasn't in the mood for laughing. "Some people mortgage their futures," he murmured, "but we're signing away the past."

Jessie played violin over her arm and watched him fidget, a child in a tie and jacket. "You left your sense of irony back in the last decade, you really did," she told him. In spite of everything, in spite of the arrival of Helen and O'Neill and all the circumstances they brought along like unwieldy luggage, this was still something he was accustomed to thinking Jessie had forced, with her delicate constitution and her neurotic fears. A Dorothea who needed pampering.

Teddy had described, as they drove to the bank, a house in Mourning Dove through which he had watched the moon rise. "They patched the roof but a good wind ripped it all up again."

"Why are you telling me that?" she had asked irritably. "Am I supposed to give up my roof because a stiff wind blew through Mourning Dove?" Teddy had grinned without comment. "You think we ought to get an outhouse because your friends don't all have plumbing?"

There was a young black vice president to take care of black business at the bank—t.c.b., baby. Jessie and Teddy looked at him on the opposite corner of the little fenced arena where they were corralled with their earnest money, their affidavits. He was extremely earnest, brow permanently wrinkled like some of Jessie's third graders over their sums. If anyone made any mistakes in here they weren't going to be *his*. The man was better dressed than anybody in the bank, he must have gotten paper cuts everytime he put his hands on the creases in his trousers. "Hey," Teddy whispered, nonetheless. "There's a cat with clammy underwear." He was hanging on so hard you could see it in his shoulders, the way his elbows seemed pinioned to his sides for fear of making an offensive movement. This business of working for *the man*, it cost something. The outer pressure had seeped in, he looked as if he might burst from it. Andy had told them how a friend's little brother had put their kitten in the microwave oven. It didn't burn, oh no, it waited till somebody took it out and then it exploded. Jessie thought that was what he looked like he was considering doing: he was dressed for matters of state but it was only his vest that was holding him together.

Their red-faced v.p. was finishing up with them, smoothing the shorn sides of his hair as if in preparation for his next customer. The waves in front never moved, they were like a stone ledge over water. "Now, you know I want for you to be real happy with our service, Mr. Carll, Mrs. Carll." He bowed to each of them ceremoniously. "And if there's any—" He saw Teddy watching that dark pinstriped back as it bent and rose and sat again. "We try," he said very quietly into his shirt collar, eyebrows up to his flushed forehead for a defense. "We do try, hard as we can, to sort of keep things in the family." That was a code phrase; it was supposed to work like a wink to solidify their genteel conspiracy of color.

Both of them smiled and took a deep breath. Jessie sat on her hands. Would endangering their mortgage win her thanks from that desperate black v.p. who was smiling now, with studied impersonal cool, at a nervous old black couple come for some bad news about their fate? Would it gain him anything? He was giving the bank's dismissal to those two rumpled figures who bent avidly in his direction as if for comfort. If he didn't do it, somebody else would. She was sure he was apologetic. He was talking fast, using his hands a lot for reassurance, all in the family.

For herself, the best Jessie could do was to tell herself, We will always stay orphans. But she was not sure how: they had just bought (twenty years at 15½ percent) into the bosom of the family. Helen and O'Neill, and the others too—their own poor others—would be happy to lean their heads on that pale white bosom, so much broader than her own, and relax.

·   ·   ·

Andréa had hired a new lawyer for her office. He called innocently to ask about the house they were trying to sell. Teddy, who was home for the first time in a long time, told him about it with enthusiasm. After he had finished, Jessie took the phone. "Listen," she said and laughed, embarrassed. "This is not the kind of question I like to ask. I mean, I don't want to give you the wrong idea but—since I don't know you I don't—umh, to be perfectly frank—I don't know if you're black or white. Now listen—no," she said. "No, it's nothing like that, Andréa can assure you. You only need to know that you'd be crazy if you were white and bought this particular house." She explained. This was fact. She hated to have the children hear this, even though they knew what they knew; hated to organize it for them, to hear how it sounded, abrupt and ugly and acknowledged.

"Well, I sure succeeded in beating back his interest," she said as she hung the receiver back on its hook.

"Great," Teddy said. "We're going to end up carrying this house—"

"You don't take it seriously, you still don't. I want to tell you, the power of your will is something terrible to behold."

He shrugged.

O'Neill stood squarely before her. "I don't understand something at all. I thought white people hated black people."

Jessie nodded. "Some do. What don't you understand?"

"Well, do black people hate white people too?"

"Hey," Teddy said. "I think the kid's on to something!"

Jessie glared at him. "O'Neill," she said and put her arms around him so she could give him a little warmth. Her children had never had to learn this, it had always been with them, in the air they breathed. "Being disliked and hurt and kept from living a life the way you'd like it—that's bound to make people pretty angry, isn't it? Don't you think you'd be angry if you were treated that way? If you were hungry, let's say, and you couldn't just go sit down and eat a hot dog somewhere, even if you had money to pay for it? Or live in a house you like, things like that? And if you're mad, sometimes you can end up hating the person you blame."

She watched him think about it. She had never seen a child swallow, inch by inch, a large idea and have its progress register on his face the way it did on O'Neill's. He looked like a minor machine whose ON button has been pushed, his energy devoted to grinding and sorting. He twisted his mouth to one side and then the other as if it were trying out balance for a change. She felt she could almost see through the inside of his eyes, see herself standing with an encouraging patient look. "Complicated," he said to himself but he kept on grinding.

"Complicated," Jessie nodded. "Most things are, there's no use pretending they're not."

He sat on the stool and swung his legs rhythmically in their blue corduroys. He had the beginnings of the rather sad gentle perplexity of those who accept doubleness in anything: not this or that but this and that. It made him look alone, she thought, isolated with his own perspective on the world, hung at a great height, dangling. And aged. Or ageless. But, having exacted this much conformity, she could begin to recognize him as one of her own.

Today I thought I would go running myself just to try it. So after school I went down to the track before I had to get the last bus, and I put my books and jacket down and just took off like I heard a shot. It was so good! I ran until my side hurt and my ankles started turning over. But when I was really streaking along and the buildings across the field were rushing past so they looked like one endless long train it was finer than fine is fine. And what I thought was someone who hates where she is ought to know how to run because you never know. Maybe it will come to that and you will have to cross some border and be free. It is the last thing I would ever want to read but we are doing these slave stories for language arts, and there is this one little boy, he gets away from these they are like guards who look for runaways, they are called patarollers? And after he is sure he is safe he says (he's still squinched down in the bushes somewhere), If they caught me after I led them all around they would cut my legs off to keep me still. But as long as I have my legs there is no border so far away that I can't run up to it and across! And then he realizes he lost his little sister somewhere, he thought she was just behind him, and at the end you see him walking on back down to the road where he came from and you know what is going to happen. And he disappears into the shadows! It is an awful story.

But anyway, two more things. One, there is no french to learn for running like in ballet, all those words always mixed me up, I could do the step without the words or the words without the step but it would get me crazy doing both. And two, I like the feeling sort of behind the running too. My legs are my strongest place, when they go and go and chop the air I am not even Helen, I have no name, I am just God's free animal. He feeds me the yellow line on the inside of the track and I seem to swallow it down, and then there it is again.

There was some ballet on television tonight, it was Maria Tallchief's story, and I could see Jessie looking at me asking Do I dare talk about DANCING again and then deciding no. It's funny when you are 1,000%

sure what somebody is thinking, especially a grownup who is supposed to know about you but not the other way around. Like in the comics when they put a big question mark over somebody's head, do I, don't I?

About the dancing I feel that it was like the time a few weeks ago when I saw their cat Mickey (Mouse) back up a dog, a pretty good-sized one like a hunting beagle sort of with huge ears right off the front lawn! Mickey raised his one paw and hissed so you could actually see these little pearl-colored pickety teeth of his, and the dog just inched on back, it was like an accordion that scrunched up into itself and got tall and narrow. Then it took off like a "bat out of hell." So I feel I guess I accidentally did that to Jessie who doesn't want me all "discombobulated" (sp?) again. I looked at my point shoes hanging on a nail in my closet, they are like dried rose petals that used to be beautiful but are now mostly forlorn and a little wilted and I couldn't decide what I feel anyway. I wonder would it be disloyal if I ask them for some good running shoes, that was so fine that day and all my muscles and joints were the next thing to cheering. I will bring it up with Jessie some time soon. What will she say about her theory that I am such a "bigot" when even she will have to know the track team is 9/10 colored. I bet she will not say anything. One of the things you forget when you get grownup is you don't know how to apologize any more.

They heaved their ersatz belongings into a U-HAUL. Andréa helped, all for the privilege, she said, of getting to drive down the loop of Rebus Road with her head in a handkerchief singing "Swing Low, Sweet Chariot" so the neighbors could get themselves ready.

But it was not the sort of street that invited visible curiosity. Jessie said "I always thought moving was something people did just to amuse kids, it was always better than Ringling Brothers, Barnum and Bailey. You'd look at the furniture and giggle, all those awful lamps and lumpy old armchairs coming out or going in, and the boxes of one-armed teddy bears and potties and plastic lemon trees? Where are the kids gawking from their tricycles?"

The children, even without greeting committees, stepped lightly with their burdens; they were, after all, feathering their own nests. When finally O'Neill sagged, sat down in the frame of the front door to pant for sympathy, Lydia hissed at him. "O'Neill, get *up*. You've got your own room to collapse in now."

Teddy glared over their scurrying with the helpless fury of an evicted tenant watching his belongings being piled on the sidewalk. Even when he bent to the lifting and hauling he worked at a detachment that would express his disapproval. Finally he stopped work altogether.

"You're a bad sport," Jessie said, close to his ear as she passed him, swaying, with a kitchen chair in each hand. "And selfish at that."

"What does sport have to do with it?" He looked unsympathetically at the ant-file of obedient carriers.

"Oh, high drama! You think you won't have any more influence on them now that we have three bathrooms and a front hall closet? You take the house more seriously than they do!" She wanted him to stop sulking if only to carry cartons of books. "Symbols are where you see them."

"Birnam Wood is coming to Dunsinane!" Andy propelled the *ficus* before him, his face hidden in its dry quivering leaves. "Look out, Daddy!" He dive-bombed his father.

"Your father is a nonparticipant. He is registering a protest," Jessie told him. "Just leave him alone to have his little funk. When we put all his things in the wrong places he'll come out of it." She sounded like a television commercial, she knew, the contemptuous kind she most depised in which husbands and wives betrayed the audience's hostilities—or the copywriter's perception of them—by assaulting each other's dignity and laughing about it. They always forgave and embraced after the product name flashed on.

She wanted to try one last time. She put a box of dishes down on the doorstep and said, "Teddy? Honey? Please don't think I don't realize how much we're leaving behind in that house. I know it. And I know you never wanted things to change—"

"Things? Oh, shit, Jessie, don't patronize me. I don't know what 'things' you take seriously enough to put in your list of changes. Look at us. Just look at us." He swivelled his head around irritably.

She obediently looked around her—the children were climbing around on the truck, leaping off it with the kind of cries one hears around a swimming pool; Mickey Mouse was rubbing his gray hide against the lamps and suitcases on the lawn, sniffing. She could imagine worse. "Life goes on. We're all *here*, we're okay. Consider the alternatives."

"This is childish of me, okay. I admit it. I don't want to let any of it go."

"So many years, love. How did you—how did we stop changing with it? If we missed a turn—" She was embarrassed; every metaphor made her think of soap opera.

Teddy was smiling bleakly at her. "Don't include yourself just to be charitable. It's nice of you but actually you don't share this condition. And apparently it's not contagious."

"A couple of months ago—right after they came—I was telling Andréa that I wanted it to be *before* again, before that phone call from Birmingham?"

"But you've managed, Jessie. You've come around somehow, you're doing your big girl's duty. And I can't—it's like—my life isn't *big* enough for this."

"What does that mean, you can't?"

"I *can't*—"

"You won't."

He straightened and brushed off the front of his shirt vigorously, as if he had to be especially neat to take leave of the discussion. "And here's where the sympathy ends."

"Well, I have a hard time telling the difference between incapacity and unwillingness, frankly. When Lydia tells me she can't practice her flute—"

"I'm not Lydia. Whatever my failings, please have the grace not to compare me to an eleven-year-old. And not to scold me like one. You're asking me to justify something I know is irrational. And I can't."

Jessie looked abashed. "I'm sorry. I didn't mean to do that."

"Jessie, I've been thinking of leaving."

She stared at him and thought his face ought to look different, having said that. A man could not say that to his wife, close his hand tight around her heart and squeeze until she had no breath, no blood in her limbs, and not be transformed. His face was not transformed, his blue eyes were clear, color of reflected sky, and his wide thin mouth was not distorted by his pain. She let him say whatever he had to.

"But I can't. I won't. I promise you. I just—" He shrugged. "I just have to figure out how to go on with this."

She sighed and it sounded like someone else's sigh, she was that disembodied. "You won't but you had to tell me."

He grinned sadly, and bobbed his head in acknowledgment. "Right."

"Scrupulous honesty to the bitter end."

"Not because of you—not to punish you or even get away from you, in spite of—how little help we seem to be to each other these days." He paused, bemused. "I don't sound like myself, talking to you. It feels like an empty room and there's this echo—"

"What, then? The children?"

He shook his head. "I don't know. Please. Not one thing. I don't know."

"So be it," she said without feeling and reached for the box of dishes. When she picked it up it rattled suspiciously; something had broken on the truck. "Goddamn," she said to herself as she walked away from him. "The good dishes, the ones that match."

When they were finally done with the unloading—Tommy, Andréa, Jessie and the children—they couldn't find Teddy; his car was gone.

"You know," Tommy said, "the paradox about Teddy and this certainty he has that moving over here is the end of commitment and decency and all the rest is that he of all people isn't acknowledging that anything much has changed for the better around here. You'd think he might be impressed that the people on this street could care less who your friends are nowadays, when they would have frozen you out—or burned you out, even better—fifteen years ago, but he's—" He shook his head.

"He's in love with his pessimism." They were in the kitchen; Andréa was splashing cold water on her cheeks. "Who would believe this is December, I feel like an oven."

Tommy offered to go out to get some beer. "Take the kids along for sodas," Jessie shouted after him. "They deserve a little pay." She turned back to Andréa.

"But if he's so pessimistic," she said, "how can he be spending so much time out there in that godforsaken little town?"

"Oh honey, *you* know. Terminal self-defeating pessimism gets itself involved with lost causes with great relish. Then there's something to blame when it all goes wrong. You really think he believes they're going to change anything, he and Big Jug-head?"

"Oh, absolutely. I do. I think they're convinced they beat back a real threat and they can build something out of it, and then watch it spread. The Second Coming."

"Watch out!" Andréa called as if she were someone else, in church. "I think you're naive. Underneath—two, three layers—Teddy Carll does not believe. He has a tragic undersoul, that man. I think he believes that maybe one out of a hundred is elected—like he was—and the rest will never be saved, but he can die trying. He already did, after all." She filled a glass of water from the tap and handed it to Jessie.

"That's a funny attitude for someone who's involved day in, day out in the same commitment." Jessie didn't think in terms of undersouls, nor did she much like others to claim greater understanding of her husband than she. And she was not going to tell Andréa what he had just said to her. She had begun to wonder if she'd dreamed it.

"Oh Jessie, you know what I mean. Teddy's walking a mighty peculiar edge. He spends ten years selling the history of Western civilization and freshman comp. textbooks and suddenly he gets the call—I mean, he gets *a* call—and he's spending every waking hour solacing this town. It doesn't make a whole hell of a lot of sense and it's totally futile politics. I don't get the feeling it's politics at all, in fact. I get the feeling he's working something out all of a sudden, I mean urgently—maybe it's this house or this family he can't recognize any more—and he's using these people to bring him to it. Those things are always self-serving while they're doing their little bit of good. But it sure ain't no mass movement. It's charity work."

"I don't know," Jessie whispered, draining her tall glass of cold water. "I think you're right, basically, he's provoking something, and I don't know if it's in him or in me or just out there someplace. Maybe he's picking a fight to prove he can still land some punches."

"Well. Could be. As for Jug."

"Yeah. You know what I've always thought of Jug and his hidden agendas."

"I've been asking some questions around and I haven't turned up any of those ulterior motives the man's so good at. But I will, honey, I know I will."

No wonder she felt distant from him, Jessie thought: he was on his way out that narrow strand of highway, she was sure of that, till it stopped at the sloppy edge of the Pearl River. While they stood here relieved to be finished sweating, he was probably sitting in the dead dark rear of the bar where half the village rotted its days away, writing them all off as betrayers in Calvin Kleins, barefoot in thick pile the color of suet.

. . .

By evening the next night, Andy had made a friend who lived diagonally behind them and who seemed interesting, he said cautiously. Good thing: he flew one of those motor-driven miniature airplanes, an object of daunting power. But—bad thing—he wore a jacket all the time. On basketball days the boys at Andy's school wore sports jackets (to impress the other team with an unnatural propriety). But to wear one at home! It was a sick idea. The boy went to St. Thomas's a few blocks away, a parochial school which had existed forever and was not one of the academies established solely to overcome integration; it even had a few unimpeachably black students. In this neighborhood one could, without having to declare anything too vigorously, buy into civilized values. Jessie was grateful for such schools, in spite of their limits; Teddy loved to mock their squeaky clean safety.

O'Neill had unearthed two little boys and a game girl (provisionally approved; he was skeptical) and Lydia was taking long walks around the corner to flirt with a blond-haired girl who looked to be around her age; they had not yet exchanged a word.

Jessie had suggested to Helen that she might want to paint her room a more cheerful color—it was a blue gray so flat and dark she found it depressing, like the gunwales of a ship. (Lydia, bless her, declared it pigeon-feather colored, without the rainbows.) But who could guess what someone else might need? Jessie remembered sitting in the forced gaiety of the Women's Crisis Center a few years back, the big brilliant blue and orange poster of a still life on the opposite wall, painted in a fresh breeze by a woman with a calm hand on her heart. Why had they done the walls in this coercively happy yellow, she had wondered. Perhaps someone in pain would be better soothed by a sorrowful acknowledging blue, a deep bruised purple, a searing blood red. Who were they to have made simple assumptions, as if the women who came there were kindergarten children? Now she imagined Helen lying in bed at night, her lamp burning bright circles in the blue, feeling her darkest thoughts well met there.

Jessie watched her shelving her books with such compulsive care that she wondered how the girl had survived the melee of the other house with her sanity intact. To someone as orderly as Helen, the casual mess and the disreputable state of their belongings must have been a continuous assaulting noise or a rotting smell lodged in her nostrils without relief. As it was, Jessie caught her looking into the living room where their sparse furniture sat lonely and, in grander surroundings, almost aggressively shabby, with a complex look of superiority and impatience. Children are as capable of condescension as any adult, she thought, and a good deal less tolerant of extenuation.

And, although Andy and Lydia, before their final departure, had walked slowly around the yard on Willowbrae Drive working hard at permissible sentiment (here was the cement slab where Andy broke his big toe and the doctor had told him he didn't even get to miss school, and this the tree behind which Lydia used to pee, invariably on her shoes), every one of the four was visibly, physically relieved to be here. It was their first unanimity.

Jessie was the only one who had not run off to take a deep-dish bath in privacy. Teddy had drifted home, been met with irony and a set of requests to move unwieldy objects, had gone to bed without a word—Teddy, Jessie whispered to herself, our first night in a new place, our bed beneath this window facing in a whole new direction! Aren't we going to have any new experiences together? He had crawled into bed, in fact, on the wrong side and had hugged his edge, leaving a gap between them that could have been swabbed with poison. Fifteen years and you can't just change sides on me, Jessie objected silently. How could she sleep, how would they even make love when he would have to approach her as a stranger, moving against her from out of nowhere? He was the man who was going to leave her; he was the man who had changed his mind. She was the woman who was supposed

to be grateful. She lay alone on her side in a panic promising herself he
would come around. If an event like a crosstown move destroys a marriage,
she reasoned, the marriage was holding with Crazy Glue. When she woke
to unfamiliar sunlight, bold squares on the tan carpet, perfect for her plants,
he was gone.

.   .   .

Jessie called her parents to tell them about the house. The tone and
rhythm of her mother's voice on the phone made instant announcement,
always, of her state of mind, no matter what she actually said. She was a
thoroughly direct woman when you were with her but she seemed, somehow, to think of the telephone the way an ostrich might: if she could not
be seen perhaps no one would know a thing about her. Discoveries were
made face to face or not at all.

Tonight she sounded stranded, lost in space. She talked as if she were
hypnotizing herself staring at a little dot in the distance.

"Nothing at all is the matter, why do you say that?" she insisted. Finally,
when Jessie would not let her go, she reluctantly said, "Well dear. This is
all hard to explain on the phone. You know. Do you possibly—have any
plans to visit soon? With the children?"

"Should I? Would you like me to?"

"Well, I'd love it, of course. When am I going to meet my new grand-
children?" Jessie could read the tone: it was an SOS.

"How's Daddy? Is anything—"

"Daddy is all right. Within limits. He's—"

"What?"

"His health is fine. He's had a little cold."

"Mother."

"Is it a bad time, Jessie? With your new house and everything? I should
probably come to you."

"It's a good time, Mother. I could use some time away, actually, and
the kids will be on Christmas vacation."

"You can leave them with Teddy? They wouldn't mind that, would
they?"

Jessie was taken aback: she hadn't intended to leave them home. But
something urgent was happening, so urgent that her mother had abandoned
grandmotherly solicitude.

The children were separated by larger spaces then ever; there was going
to be less physical closeness in this house; also less friction. When it came
to space, Teddy was out in it, launched in his own orbit. Unpacking, she

held a wine glass by its frail stem, turning it between her fingers, thinking it looked like a mouse's tail attached to the transparent body of the glass. Did Steuben make crystal mice, rats, rattlers? The glass roach: from a series called Real Life. If she disappeared for a little while they would manage. Christmas vacation began on Wednesday and Teddy didn't have to work. No one was buying books when schools were out. He usually sat in a tent of paperwork and dozed. No one needed anything he or she couldn't provide if they pulled together, just as well not to let them lean too far out from each other anyway. (Was it centrifugal or centripetal force which would do them in?) Teddy could screw himself. She put it as bluntly as she could to hear how her anger sounded. Then she placed the glass carefully in its new cabinet. Better to be coldly angry than glass-breaking mad and have to replace the glasses. That was the sign of someone still in control. Teddy would have to settle in when she was gone. Her decision appeared to have made itself, justifications and all. He could even have both sides of the bed. When screwing oneself, one may approach from either direction and expect to be welcome.

SIX

Her parents did not live in one of the logical places. Those practical co-ops built by the Ladies Garment Workers' Union in the west Twenties or the rangy old high-ceilinged thick-walled rent-controlled apartments on the Upper West Side, with as much square footage as any house—those were the logical places, which would have welcomed them as familiars: tired radicals in need of bookshelf space, willing to tolerate old kitchens, claw-footed bathtubs, unadorned lobbies.

But they lived, out of place and at great expense, in Brooklyn Heights. They had moved soon after Jessie left home and so she came as a visitor, objective, even critical, without the built-in bias of a child who has grown up at an accommodating angle in those rooms. She had been appalled at the useless extravagance of the house. What did two people, without at-tendant children, without so much as a single space-consuming hobby, need with the two floors of a duplex, its marble fireplaces, no two alike, its parlor floor chandelier, its fine French doors and its garden with the granite girl balanced on a toe, inviting birds to bathe in the shell of her open hand? Jessie thought the house a cruel jest, forced by her mother on a perpetually unforgiven Jack Singer: a punishment that most vengefully calculated its harsh effect, like the rape of a nun or the robbery of someone's last dollar. Jack Singer among the coupon clippers.

She had called them from the airport, not earlier. That way, no one would attempt to meet her. She took a roundabout series of airport buses and two subways, overwhelmed by the thoroughly different feel of space and time underground. Compared to the weight of the city, Jackson felt new, bare, lightstruck, a town of cards, leaning one against another along the visible surface of the earth, susceptible to scattering by a single harsh breath. She had always been grateful that Jackson had no subway to doom its passengers to a relentless confrontation with their own lack of variety. There wasn't enough diversity, ethnic or intimate, in Mississippi, to make people-watching a viable sport.

She walked the long lovely blocks from the subway, deserted in mid-afternoon except for occasional cars and taxis and here and there a distant overcoat or a fast-moving child cutting across a street in a bright parka. Winter constrained every neighborhood, then, not only her new one, in its suburban reticence, made unnavigable by the absence of sidewalks. There was a fuzziness in the air, a gathering dampness that made the brick and the fancifully painted brownstones seem to run, liquid, behind her gaze. Film shot through a soft filter. Her parents' house was two in from the far corner of Willow Street. It had its own tree, in winter retreat, and against the steps a pair of dark green garbage pails sat like palace guards with their hats chained on. The house had an exterior so anonymous and unimpeach-able, lacking in idiosyncrasy which she could identify, that she felt she was approaching, with their address on a paper closed inside her fist, the home of strangers.

.   .   .

Her mother was in something she referred to twice as "fine fettle."

"What do you suppose that actually means?" Jessie asked her, receiving a cup of coffee gratefully from Elizabeth Singer's well-kept hands. "Fettle? Does it have to do with horses, do you think?"

Her mother smiled. "It could have something to do with fetlocks, I suppose. I can't really imagine." She brought the cream in a pewter container and, tilting it over Jessie's cup with her eyes widened and mouth just open to denote expectancy, waited. "Say 'when.' "

Jessie said, "When." Her mother, she thought, still a lovely woman with that broad forehead, had the good manners of the kind of hostess she had once held in contempt. She had, in fact, the genteel existence of such a woman: her closet, her calendar. It was a bad joke the way money had materialized in her parents' lives. Even in fairytales, the fisherman and his wife dream so hard about waking up rich that it's almost work; the spinners of flax into gold or the little tailor struggling to cut his magic coats grow desperate before dawn and are saved for their decency and earnestness. But her parents . . . Money, to Jack, was filthy; Elizabeth's parents, who did not share that opinion, left her a good deal of it when they died. And

Elizabeth, having learned that long painful lesson in independence when her husband was underground, invested the money without consulting Jack: it was all in her name. She turned out to be very good at money, better than she had been at a cut above poverty. "You know, Jessie," her mother had told her once. "Nobody cares what sex the signature on the check is. In sufficient quantities anyone's money is respected." Except by Jack, of course; the more sufficient the more ignoble. And what was that about respect? Had her mother's life, begun just off Madison Avenue in an apartment with servants, turned out, like many a poor woman's, to be obsessed with the overcoming of some deep deprivation of parity? With whom, then? Men? WASPs? Better Reds?

"Come see, darling," her mother said, leading her by the hand. They entered a little room off the kitchen that Jessie remembered as a serving room, but which now held an easel and all the accoutrements of an amateur playing professional. Overplaying; the professionals Jessie knew had to husband their supplies carefully.

"Hey, not bad." On the easel was her mother's idealized vision of the Brooklyn Bridge, hazy and purple, an extravagant dusk or dawn breaking behind the solidity of the twin castles. "Very nice, in fact. Mother! Are you going to turn out to be a late-blooming genius?"

"Oh, a Grandma Moses. I'm catching up in years, anyway." Elizabeth Singer looked down modestly. "Actually, I've begun to volunteer at the Brooklyn Museum—I've been giving tours, dear—and so I get to take free classes." She smiled a little sheepishly, as if the idea embarrassed her. "I take my sketchbook with me now wherever I go and I sit down on benches in every unlikely place and do you know what I see?"

"I can't imagine."

"I see dozens of other women—some men too, actually—sitting there like me with their heads at a queer angle trying to catch the essence of something we've never seen before. It's odd, a little army of us, all blooming late, just before the frost." She laughed. Jessie was touched. . . . The tough defensive woman she had become after those years of service to her husband's zeal was hard to find in the well-coiffed, carefully made-up matron she had become. Each role seemed to devour the one before it. Perhaps she was a Russian doll with all her former selves lodged, undigested, inside? Or else they were long since distributed into her blood and sinew and were everywhere palpable at once. Jessie put her arms around her mother, who was much smaller than she was. Good legs she had, slender waist, face only beginning to soften, as if it were relaxing, with permission, into wrinkles that streaked her cheeks upward, cat's whiskers. Looking backwards took less energy; when Jessie was home the future lay at her feet like a canyon. It was good beyond words to be a daughter for a while; impossible to believe she was mother to so many.

. . .

"Your mother and I have separated," Jack Singer told Jessie after he had hugged her and looked her over without divulging his judgment. "Did she get around to telling you that? Between servings of French pastry and quiche?" But Jessie was confused—he was smiling. He looked in pretty good fettle himself; both of them could have advertised the benefits of a health club for the gently aging.

"What do you mean?" Jessie laughed nervously. "Mother—"

Elizabeth Singer had gone into the pantry for something and was only now coming back within earshot, holding a green can of olives rather tenderly, as if it were alive. "Mother, what is this Daddy is telling me, that you've separated."

Her mother gave a long-suffering sigh and turned to feed the can to the electric opener on the wall. The small impatient movement of her head seemed to suggest that, incorrigibly careless, her husband had lost a shirt button again or had broken one of her favorite dishes. "You'll have to ask him. He has separated from me, dear, you don't hear me saying I've separated from him, do you?"

Now Jessie laughed out loud. Her parents had been far more difficult to themselves than to her, and they had made every gesture, the political and the emotional, and finally the apolitical, broad and sweeping. All their lives they had leapt with both feet into everything they had done. They had never, as far as Jessie knew, done anything laughable before.

"This is not a subject for comedy," her father told her, still smiling. "Your mother seems to think I've made myself a laughingstock by dissociating myself from her and her symphony tickets and her benefit dinners and her social affairs at the houses of the numbskull wealthy." He looked hard at his daughter, studying her to see if she would mock him. "There's been enough of this female liberation business, I'm liberating myself while I still have some time for self-respect." His eyes moved around the room quickly, suspiciously.

She needed time to think about it. "Well, where are you living? What are you doing with yourself?"

"Hah!" cried Elizabeth Singer. "Ask him where he's living and see what you get. The man is getting senile. He has lost every capacity except the automatic functions."

"Mother."

"Well, ask him again. He hasn't answered."

Her father looked conciliatory. He shrugged and said, "Here. I'm not leaving the house, there is no other place where I could get as good a deal now, but I'm paying rent." He looked at his wife. "She's a landlord once, those people in the upper duplex, she can be a landlord down here too. No favors. I ask nothing, only peace and a simple way of life. I want you to know I would not be sitting in here at this hour chatting with your mother if you weren't here. We have our cooking schedule that we adhere to."

"No favors," Jessie's mother echoed, disgusted. "All of a sudden I'm a widow with a boarder. He sleeps out there on the sleep sofa, opens it up with a huge thunk as soon as he knows I'm asleep, shakes the house to its foundations. His clothes are in a cardboard box in the hall closet. I offered to bring down a dresser but he would rather cram everything into bags and boxes so he can shame me every time he puts on a wrinkled shirt. It's his hair shirt, after all."

She got up and rummaged around in one of the kitchen drawers, came back carrying a handful of notes on cheerful paper from an expensive note-pad: little technicolor chickens pecked around the edges inquiring WHAT'S HAPPENING? Her mother had always loved stationery, the way others loved silk blouses or lush jewelry, a sensual indulgence, though of which sense it would be hard to say. These days she wrote to Jessie on embossed paper that felt like the inside of a seashell.

The notes were addressed emphatically to no name. PLEASE BE MORE CAREFUL TO WASH YR. DISHES & SILVER. THERE ARE NOT ENOUGH CLEAN ONES FOR ME. THANK YOU. No signature. LEAVE SOME HOT WATER FOR A SHOWER! THIS IS THE THIRD TIME! Jessie blushed for her father; thinking harder, she blushed for her mother too. Both of them were watching her for a sign of preference, of special sympathy. She would give none. "You are being children, both of you," was all she could say, her cheeks hot and her eyes teary. "Either that or this is a comedy act and you both keep a very straight face." She stood up abruptly and told them she was taking her suitcase to her room. "It *is* the same one, isn't it, or have you decided to quarter the Weathermen in there, or a troupe of bareback riders or the local Moonie sect or something?" She found herself, to her astonishment, close to tears. It is difficult, the very first time and forever after, to feel sorry for one's parents, to worry and plan to care for them, because then there is no more refuge, no retreat, for the homing child. But to be forced to laugh, not even amused but humiliated . . . "I'm not up to this," she murmured. She supposed they would accost her separately now to plead their cases and that she would counsel some solution that would placate them vaguely without being heard, and leave the raw wounds unattended. The last time they had had a go at each other—the first time—Jack Singer had received a party courier who had released him from his exile and drunk a glass of schnapps with him to celebrate the successful conclusion of his heroic performance, and sent him back to rejoin his regiment, as it were; only then had he discovered that his cell's particular war had been over for years. As for his marriage—none of them raised a voice back then, if anything they had carried on at a numb middle level. Jack Singer would ask a question (critically: you wear all these shoes, Lizzie? You have a couple of extra feet stashed somewhere?) and it would be answered by default—a silent, resistant smile—or by a crushing Yes, I wear them. I like shoes. Her father would bend his head, though not literally, in acquiescence: he was a man, prodigal, being borne by an angry woman.

"But what sense does it make, Jessie?" he asked her, outside the bathroom where, towels on her arm, he caught her almost immediately. (Elizabeth, wife, was downstairs cooking dinner.) "She was mad at me, I could understand that, I really could, I agreed, for ruining her marriage. For leaving you, leaving her. Fine." He chopped the air with his hands; it was a gesture taught to presidents to spice up their national addresses. "But do I have to apologize till I'm ninety? When she starts to throttle the corpse—here I was, I was what she didn't want to lose and when I came back what did she have left for me? A gnawed bone. So what was she saving? Where was the famous doomed marriage? Who doomed it? She made herself a career out of rubbing salt in my wounds."

"Daddy—" He was obsessive and would always be. He bit into his words deeply, shaped them with sharp corners and Bronx glottal stops, spit them out with Bronx fricatives. His bald head winked at her in the bad light of the hall, showing her, unchanged after all these years, how vivid the knotty and unadorned skull could be, coursing with blood, ideas, anger. When she was very little, his head had been the globe of the world.

"And the worst of it is, I come home disillusioned, I'm feeling used, I'm torn with disgust at the Party, disgust at the world, disgust at myself, and what does she have waiting for me? Do you happen to remember? Ah, tss, you were too young, what do I want from you?" He sighed; she had failed him. She remembered nothing but his disruptive presence, as if he'd been a boy emerging from the girls' room at school: a reason to stay clothed, to hide your sanitary napkins in your own closet. "She made a feast to welcome me home, and it was like specially selected poisons, one course after another—caviar and a very good wine, filet mignon, I remember this unbelievable dessert, it was an English trifle in all those fussy little layers, all wearing this whipped cream, you'd think it was lace. It was—" He paused to make sure that she saw how his eyes were watering. After all these years—she had been thirteen—he could squeeze feeling out of the event. The insult of that meal had nourished his anguish, been the center around which accreted a thousand other insults, and so, never confronted by a change of weather, it would never melt.

"But that sounds awfully nice to me. She must have thought you hadn't had anything really good for two years—"

"Nice? Nice!" He looked away, affronted. "Is it nice to kill a man who's been through famine by jamming his head into his plate at a feast? People die that way. Jessie! Starving people came out of the death camps creeping, crawling, and do you know when they died, after all that? Tell me, do you know?"

"Death camps. Daddy, I'm a little slow—"

"They died, young lady, when they ate. Nobody thought to restrain them and they burst their shrunken stomachs with ordinary food." He lowered his chin emphatically to say, You see.

"But you were never exactly starving."

"And anyway, here's the thing. When did we ever eat like that? Whose food was that, caviar and two-inch steaks. For that I languished two years in those hellholes afraid to come home at night for fear I'd see an FBI agent waiting for me on the stoop, or pick up the phone and hear a mysterious click? So I could come home and see she couldn't wait to show me, my wife and daughter are living like ladies-in-waiting in splendor."

"We never lived in splendor, what in the world are you talking about? Splendor!" Christ, all that junk they bought on employee discount, the changes of underwear, the earmuffs, the pop-up toaster after all those years of remembering too late the toast laid up against the electric slabs, smelling the smoke, scraping it with a knife. Christ, he's raving like Teddy, she thought dumbfounded. He's made a good meal into a symbolic attack on his ideals the way Teddy's making the new house into a guided missile, a goddamn atomic warhead.

That must be what happens—it was the only explanation—when you get to the bottom of the barrel and there's nothing left but sediment. Not the ideals but the sloughed impurities of the ideals, thick and crude, a perversion of the taste you began by loving. Paranoia and irrelevancy. She sank against the linen closet door.

"She was never serious, that's the thing you have to know. She never cared—I should have known when she told me FDR was her idol, and

Harry Hopkins!—after all she saw with her own two eyes, how nothing was ever going to change for the poor and the working man." He was shaking his head at the contagion of folly, convinced he was immune.

"Daddy, you're still on the working man? Hasn't thirty years of history carried away any of that?"

"What? What is 'that'? You think I'm sentimental. Are you telling me the working man is obsolete? Are there no more slaves to capitalism in this day and age, just because some people sit and press buttons on those computers? And even the computer people, do you know they're going blind from watching those little screens all day? Like living underwater when you aren't a fish. Feh! You should take all your 'history' and try to feed somebody with it, your black man even, see how many calories it has." He sounded like an old man who might stop her on the street to harangue, one of those characters she dreaded who had his single line of ancient melody and nothing else behind it. ("Parents are like that," Andréa always said, "because we are their children. When they're not talking to us they seem sufficiently complicated. We simplify them.")

"How did we get from Mother to 'my black man'?" She wanted to warn him of how much was at stake when he talked to her this way: she was on the edge of disillusion where the walking was getting slippery.

"Your mother was a political dilettante and, if you want to know, I was charmed at the particular angle she used to hold her head when she listened to me. Among other things. It was a case of entrapment."

She hugged the towels to her breast for protection. They were shades of taupe or mauve or something else that didn't sound the way it was spelled, a sweet piece of the spectrum that hovered near the violet end. Her mother had talent in the decorative department too. All those personal skills, art and money, suppressed by allegiance to the Central Committee.

"It's not fair to hold her responsible for not being what you thought she was. She was doing what she could, which was more than most of her class of girls in 1935 or whenever, and you came along and upped the ante, from all I've ever heard about the matter."

"All right," he said amiably, and roughed up the hairs of his mustache. "All right. Say your mother was playing in the grapefruit league and when she fell in with me she found herself playing hardball. Only there aren't many women who play that game, you know. That's what it comes down to. I don't care what they're saying about women these days—"

"Really," Jessie said. The towels felt like a fleshy bosom. "You think political seriousness comes on the XY chromosome, don't you. You and your son-in-law. Has it ever occurred to you that men make it very difficult for women to play the roles they might like to?"

"Testosterone. I'm convinced. Politics is an aggressor's game and it's determined by hormones who'll be the most masterful player. The hunter, the warrior. And the woman really wants to be at home. The bourgeois family is a web the female spins to catch us and keep us."

"Oh, Daddy, that cliché. You are so confused. I mean, if you thought that why did you run right into the trap? And why would you never take her political interests seriously?"

He waved a hand at her, swatting her questions away. "Her politics." Jessie put her arms around him gently. His body had the hypertonic resistance of a small child's when he lies kicking on the floor and knows that any comforting touch threatens surrender. And was he telling her he had never wanted a daughter?

"That's a classic Marxist view of the family and it happens, whatever you may think of Marx, to be one hundred percent correct, allowing for the occasional exception. It serves its purpose, nobody can argue with that, but it also makes tension and it will always keep us at odds. You remember that. It's what's kept the species alive since the caveman."

"Daddy, I don't think I even want to argue with you." How sweet and unfamiliar her voice could become; it was sticky with a condescension she couldn't control. Given a different set of circumstances he could have been a hard-hat, a redneck, whatever mean generality of a type, hot headed, ignorant; what they lacked of his dialectical persuasion they could make up in two-dimensional, self-justifying, hectoring zeal. He could also, she thought miserably, have been most of the men she'd dealt with in Mississippi, the ones who'd said that a woman's place in the Movement was on her back.

She turned from her father and pushed into the small guest room, whose walls faked sunrise at any hour. Dignity, she thought miserably. Is it a hormone too, that dwindles in the glands, a tide like vigor and clarity, that turns and ebbs, another defining chemical, not specific to one sex like estrogen or testosterone, but human? But no, that wasn't fair: she knew too many dignified old men and women, and too many young ones without courage or tact or taste.

What an irony, that Jack Singer had yielded to that masculine acquisitiveness that had needed her mother. Living for the Party, as he had from the age of seventeen, stripped you—tried and failed to strip you—of the randomness and urgency of sexuality, of glamor, of conspicuousness. Jessie believed the libertine in him joined up hoping to become a Puritan, disci-

plined, damped down, honed to a single point. He never had to tell her he
had failed. She didn't consider that his fault; when he went underground
and spent those years with a succession of other women, not Jessie's mother
and not her, she considered *that* his fault: the wrong discipline at the wrong
time. But the Party should never have pretended that intellectual discipline
saved whole souls—it only saved the accessible part that lay out in the open,
a sacrifice to change.

. . .

Dinner was stiff. Her parents concentrated far more on ignoring each
other than on turning their attention to Jessie. She gabbled on because she
loathed silences even when they were kinder than these; she said more about
the Tyson children than she wanted to, painted them all too simplistically
as hyperenergetic boy and moody quiet girl, and seemed to make Roger
and Alexis downright lurid. She felt fair to no one, but under the influence
of her parents' belligerence, subtlety would have been an inaudible whisper.
I am too easily led, Jessie thought gloomily. For someone who considered
herself independent, she was damnably impressionable and eager to accommodate. She suspected herself of having mistaken, her life long, noisiness
for independence. The whole damn Ingratiating syndrome was nearly as
hard to avoid as a genetic inheritance. She and her mother had been feisty
girls who, when the crisis came, couldn't bring their teeth together around
a single flesh-and-blood ankle. . . . Jack Singer gulped his coffee as if he
were late for an appointment, and left them to each other.

"Oh, Jessie," her mother said, weary. "You just can't imagine what it's
like to have a lifetime of disappointment taken out on you."

"Oh, I'm afraid I can, Mother. Even if it's only half a lifetime."

"You know, I find I get more upset about the little things than the big
ones." She touched, self-consciously, protectively, the gray turtleneck sweater
that showed under her tailored green blouse. The grace she had grown into
was no longer incidental: it had become her politics, her platform, her
principle. Jessie found her lovely but painfully remote.

She said nothing. She took in the serene forehead she had memorized
as a child, saw the wrinkles like lateral scratches, the creases between her
eyes like the kind you make in pie crust with thumb and third finger. Seeing
her mother so rarely made it impossible not to study her afresh each time;
it made it hard to advance into intimacy. She had a dancer's face, Jessie
decided, a sort of strength and simplicity of feature which suggested pro-
fundity and seriousness. Certain kinds of beauty seem frivolous; her mother's
was grave. And there were few women her age who could dare to comb

their hair straight back like that, and hold it in a clip like a schoolgirl. It was indeed a face that could entrap a man, and thereby entrap herself as well. "Oh, Jessie. Darling, I shouldn't have bothered you to come."

"Don't be silly. How could you not have? It's true, obviously, and he's not making a secret of a thing. He's just dying to be noticed."

"Well, I shouldn't have taken you away from your new house and your children, all those children, you've been so overwhelmed—"

Jessie smiled bitterly. She wasn't going to burden her mother with her own confusions. But hadn't she sat at Varona's table the same way, suppressing her own anxieties? It was beginning to seem inevitable that when she sat down alone with any woman she would hear this cry of distress and bewilderment, and hear the echo begin inside her, passively, like a twopenny motor. (And Alexis—if she had sat across the kitchen table from Alexis, holding her hands, what kind of story would she have heard in the sweet blue Alabama evening with the mimosa tree shaking its pink feathers teasingly against the window?) Brooklyn Heights was all brick and narrow streets that ran deep as gulleys between the kitchens; Wolfville was flat and irrevocably empty, and her own Willowbrae was a warm-weather quickie— bad workmanship with no foundation, home as fast food, disposable and cheap. Rebus Road was only one cut above it, more sprawl, better sewage. The litany reassured her, it made disaffection seem inevitable. (Not Andréa. Did Tommy make the difference, or did Andréa herself, her sanity and certainty, her profession harder and sharper than anything around it, law the diamond cutting edge?)

"Oh, Jessie. Your father wanted to change the world and it wouldn't just change when he shoved with his hip. That's the oldest story, isn't it? And then, to add insult, his own colleagues seemed to punish him for even trying. I wish there was something brilliant to tell you about him, dear." She sighed. "I never minded your father's union activity; that seemed to make a lot of sense and it showed some results. But the rest—" Then, her favorite mannerism, she ran one finger slowly across her lovely forehead as if she were pushing every obstruction before it, leaving a clear field. "He never understood that. He thought I was out to undo everything. Ever since—" She got up to reheat the coffee, placed the glass carafe carefully in a pan of bubbling water. "He wanted to go to Spain, you know. Going to Spain was like—what would it be like now? I can't think what—"

"Going to Mississippi when I did?"

"Even that was more special, that tended to be only young people of a certain age and class. There hasn't been anything quite like Spain. It was the graduation ceremony for all those young men, and it was a terribly, a profoundly masculine commitment too, you know. I didn't know any women who went, although there may have been some. But we had just gotten married and very quickly I—you know I lost that baby, which was very upsetting. That would have been your brother." She sighed for it. "Your grandmother had had more miscarriages then she could count and I was panicked, I was sure I was going to have the same trouble, I had grown up afraid of that. So—" She made a little face, self-deprecating or perhaps deprecating of the way chance has its way. "So he stayed home then, for my sake, and to be honest with you, I think he began to resent me right then. I've never told you this, I'm not sure he even remembers it that way. He gritted his teeth and just stood bitterly in the traces like an old work horse who had no more hope of running free in this lifetime." When she poured their second cups of coffee, her hand shook. "Well, I never knew what to do about that. It was my fault, I suppose, but it wasn't my fault at the same time. I mean, I didn't ask to lose the baby, I was devastated, and maybe I could have been stronger about it, not taken it to heart the way I did but—I was very young and very frightened, and I hadn't been very good in my brief little life of world-burning, maybe I gave up hope too easily and didn't really believe any of it was worthwhile, I don't know. But the fact is—" She sipped her coffee contemplatively. "How can I know— it's more than forty years since then, how in the world can I take apart forty years to search for the one year with the worm in it? He made one bad decision to stay and maybe that's why he was so obedient when they ordered him underground. Everything grows out of the things before it. I know you think it's amusing, this pseudoseparation, but your father is a terribly un- happy man who's looking for some comfort wherever he can get it."

"And you can't decide whether to be angry or to offer yourself as a sacrifice."

"I can decide. Don't ask me what I can decide. But I'm not your father. I can't *do* what I decide, is all. I can't get rid of him, I can only try to make myself immune. I've deafened myself so that I don't really hear him when he rants at me." She smoothed her perfectly smooth hair. "He has some human moments every day. A few. I only wish he wouldn't drag me down with him in public. I have a very hard time when he does that. And then, of course, when we go out to someone's house, and I want him to be friendly and gracious, he tells me I care more about my hostesses than I do about him. I'm afraid I take it very badly, which is exactly what he wants. So we don't go out together any more."

Jessie laughed. "Do you remember that old movie, what was it we used to laugh at? That Hungarian, or whoever, it was probably Peter Lorre, who kept saying, 'Dawn't prah-voke! Dawn't prah-voke!' "

Elizabeth laughed too, quietly, neatly. "Well, that's it. I run around pleading with him not to provoke and that seems to give him his only delight. It's much easier, you know, to pour all his anger and bitterness down a single throat. He doesn't have to look anywhere else for blame, and he doesn't have to swallow it himself."

"Mother," Jessie began. Why not step forward and claim her share? Who was she protecting? "I know this feeling, I'm—Teddy is very unhappy and restless and I think he tends to take some of that out on me. Although he does a job on himself too, believe me. But look—what do I *do?* You know? I still have twenty or so of those years you're counting—"

"And you're afraid. Well, you ought to be. Oh, Jessie. Dearest." Her mother reached out to touch her, fingers on her wrist as if to intuit her pulse. This is, Jessie thought, one way to know you're grown up: realize you've got your mother's problems, side by side, not even like menopause at your own good time. Nongenerational.

"Mother. I don't—this is hard, but—I have to admit I understand the difficulty Daddy's had living with this opulence. It offends what little he has left to believe in, that must make sense to you." She looked at the handmade Portuguese tiles around her mother's sink; to think she and Jack Singer had lived on Sullivan Street once, with a bathtub in their kitchen. "You have to admit there's been a certain perversity this whole long time— I mean, since he first left and you began to—you know what I mean. Change. There are so many unlikely kinds of weapons to use to hurt each other, I can't believe you don't see how you've— Surely you've recognized that. Whatever your reasons." She seemed incapable of finishing a single sentence. Her mother sat looking like someone being pelted by hail or scratchy sand, her eyes squinted half-shut against it, her mouth crumpled like a piece of dried fruit.

"Maybe," Elizabeth Singer said in a remnant of a voice. "I can't claim to have been very forgiving back in 1954. I suppose I'm to blame for a lot of things. But let me warn you, Jessie, especially with this women's lib around to tempt you these days. You make things unpleasant for your Teddy at your peril. Given enough time, he will make things bitter for you if you oppose his freedom early on."

"But Mother! You were right, weren't you, not to want Daddy to go when you didn't think he *had* to? Your common sense *ought* to have prevailed. You're not telling me you should have yielded—"

"I'm telling you that our circumstances are out of our control but the way we react to them isn't, not really. My circumstance was that I bled away a baby I wanted desperately and somehow I let that make a chain to tie your father up as if he owed me what I couldn't have. He thinks I was jealous of his political dedication and maybe I was. And now I suppose your husband looks around and he sees four children all of a sudden instead of two, and if he's panicking—which is what I think I hear you saying—if he's panicking you need to let him run free until he comes to his own conclusion about what he can and can't do."

Jessie knew she should tell her mother that Teddy had almost left her. Left them. But if she'd said the words out loud, she'd have to hear them. She had never had an unmentionable shame in her life, a humiliation that made her want to put her fingers in her ears rather than hear it spoken. She wondered how long she could suppress this and live with herself, let alone with him. "Just—are you saying just keep your mouth shut and stay and babysit these children and let him go out and get himself shot or something like that, for nothing, and just—" She had come this far, leaving everyone behind, to sit and be counselled in self-defeat by her self-defeated mother. Just, just, just: Judy Carmichael overused it too. She had said it three times, the word for helplessness, for bearing something she didn't want to be reduced to bearing. Unjust. "You've drawn the wrong damn moral from the story. The story's great, Mother, it's perfect, yours and mine have a lot in common. But why should I let Teddy get away with that? He's been sitting on the sidelines for thirteen years and now that he's decided to act, he's making a huge mistake, reading the possibilities all wrong, he's so desperate to do what he wants to do, like a last gasp—and you think I should just stand on the sidelines bowing? If they annihilate him—which they well might—do you recommend throwing myself on his funeral pyre too? Then we can leave four orphans to the world. You can bring them up, in fact. I'll put you down as their guardian."

Her mother watched her silently. Her face had come untwisted but now it was empty of expression, wiped clean to the point where Jessie knew hostility had to be hidden behind such blandness, such banked invisible heat.

"No anger?" Jessie still needed to taunt her. "Are you sure all that anger Daddy's bathing in is his, or are you enjoying it too without having to compromise your dignity and disturb your hair?"

Elizabeth Singer looked at her nails, "I get regret, Jessie. All right. Will that satisfy you? It's very late in the game. I get sadness for both of us, and for all the people your father has bled for because he couldn't touch their lives. He was always so far away from anything that could give him real satisfaction. I suppose he was happy when he was overwhelmed by Party responsibilities, mostly he loved being too busy to breathe, what with meetings and leafleting and organizing in the shop. But that's transient, that pleasure, if it doesn't lead to anything. He's lived caught halfway between, somehow, where nothing very much grows. But I had you." She looked hard at her daughter. "I had—for a while I had my family, both of you. If that baby had lived, I'd have had him too." She closed her eyes. "Be grateful for your children, Jessie. Don't make them into gift horses that you can look in the mouth. You have a much better chance of making your mark on the world by concentrating on them, close to home. Teaching them. Or take them along with him, if you can. Stay together."

"What, so they can spend their time hugging the hearth, teaching *their* children?"

"You're the one who's confused now, my dear daughter. Are you defending Teddy's right to leave you for his heroics, or are you arguing my part, which says 'Stay here and cultivate your beautiful garden'? I think you've forgotten which side you're on."

.   .   .

Jessie seemed to spend the rest of her visit on the phone. She couldn't get an answer on Rebus Road; perhaps the phone was out of order. But when she called to check they told her there was no problem; her party must be out.

She tried to reach an old Movement friend, but she had moved to Hawaii. That struck Jessie as an unlikely match: plain round little Diana, shaped like a muffin with raisin eyes, on a beach against a billboard blue sea. This was a caricature of Diana and of Hawaii but it was all she could conjure. Another old friend was delighted to hear from her; they would meet for lunch.

Jessie had some time to kill before noon and she found, without any trouble, her own worn footsteps: some ran toward the department stores, others into bookshops long since replaced, added to, drenched in fluorescence, bursting with stacks of huge objects made to be discounted, and paperbacks featuring magnified eyes and breasts and thighs with naughty garters that invited snapping. In the mid-sixties when she'd come to the city—it was always The City, no matter how irrelevant to her state of mind—she was never able to concentrate. Books lay outside her line of vision, her eyes flicked over them and rarely stopped. Her real life was entirely pragmatic, more engaging than any fiction, and it lay elsewhere.

The years between were calmer; she could hold her gaze still as a flashlight beam and, contented, read by it. But here she was again. She prowled the aisles of Barnes & Noble nervous as a sighted leopard, and tried to consider Christmas books for the children. But it was exhausting, this plenitude; it made every book seem like every other.

The sun hit Lord & Taylor flat on its Christmas trees and angels; strung in harsh light all of it looked calculated. The windows were opulent and silly, every model bent implausibly by a sadistic designer into a position that would have hurt a live woman. The secret of that best-remembered moment of her childhood in The City, when she and her mother had skated and walked in the gathering mist, putting Jack Singer's dereliction behind them, was darkness relieved by a galaxy of lights. That and the comfort of her mother's hand; they had held hands in her big warm pocket. Today she felt like an orphan: her parents were dissolving, changing form, flickering out. They had compromised their authority. If they thought of her at all, they pictured a grownup not in need of reassurances of their solidity. . . .

Peter Pan and Wendy, the smudgy lost boys and the looming pirates in the store window danced in holiday coexistence in a Never-neverland done up in red and green for Christmas. She studied it. Captain Hook was handing Wendy a big box tied in a flamboyant red satin bow. She curtsied. He took it from her, made a wide circle and brought it back to make another offer. And again, with tireless mechanical patience. Wendy, she thought, struggling to remember—she is the lost boys' mother—her brothers', Peter's— all the time she is far from her own poor parents. Everywhere you turned you could find your own reflection.

She met Merrie at an Indian restaurant so beautiful, full of wood and profound colors, the smell of spices laid like another color on the air, that she felt herself relax. There are many worlds, she reminded herself, and Jackson is only one of them.

Merrie was nearly unrecognizable, and all for the best. They had been comfortable, if not intimate, friends for the year that Merrie had lived in Mississippi. She had always been cheerful, hard-working, efficient, but she had a dark and pessimistic side which she tried to suppress. It would gain on her at night, an edgy depression, a terror that seemed to float in the windows of her little house as the good-smelling dark came down. Evenings smelled of the grave to Merrie, of futility and stealth, and the Mississippi countryside was decidedly the wrong place for her. She tried to blame her jumpiness on an experience she had had with a man once, when he'd caught her alone down near Batesville and she had hidden in an okra field all night. But Jessie saw something deeper than that. Merrie tried drinking but it made her sick and too sleepy to do her work; she gave herself desperately, dispassionately, like a terminal patient, to one man after another, black and white interchangeably, but they had nothing for her: she would sit up in bed at night and cry. Teddy called her a succubus; she frightened him. Perhaps she was a flag of defeat waved in everyone's hopeful face. Finally she gave up and went back to Barnard to finish college. In the city, she said, it doesn't matter what time it is, it's always light enough. Jessie had always thought of her as an ordinary girl—well, woman—strayed into an extraordinary situation, a civilian picking her way across a mined field. She had predicted for her the solace of the everyday.

She seemed to have achieved precisely that. As tall as Jessie, once gawky but today almost commanding, she was a series of lavenders and purples flowing lushly one into another like a watercolor exercise on tweed and silk and wool. The color of Elizabeth Singer's towels. The world of style seemed to have run to plum while Jessie remained random, beige and blue and leftover Sears green.

"Merrill Lynch," Merrie said, "and don't look shocked, Jessie, it's not as if I've turned to a life of crime." Her long face, under a good, complicated haircut, was animated. She had a wide happy mouth and honest dog brown eyes. She never mentioned her hideous depressions—could they, Jessie wondered, have been metabolic? "Nor to the values you think of when you think 'Oh, money.' But it's—I'm using my mind, Jessie. It is so *good*. I have to work very hard because I'm not really trained, you know. It's all been OJT—"

"OJT."

"On-the-job training. You know. But I can't doze off, believe me, when I'm trying to figure out where somebody's life savings are going. It's like playing Bach: not cut and dried, because there's room for interpretation, but it needs discipline and care and I don't think, frankly, that I've ever done anything harder." Something about the way she said, "Frankly," nasal and confiding, made Jessie think of debutantes and alligator shirts; yet she had tried something else, something more, alien. And had she stayed in the South, she'd be doing this by now anyway: looking for her mind. "As for redeeming social virtue—" and she sighed. "People work for money, money works for people. Investments make more things we believe in possible. It is not," she said emphatically, looking ready to clinch a sale, "contrary to our social ideals that people make the most of their earnings." And Jessie supposed you could do it in the light.

"Why do you assume I'm thinking that?" She was settling into the enchanted sense of satisfaction the spices cast over her like a warm net and had ceased to think anything. "You shouldn't be so defensive. What do you think I'm doing that has such great significance? A as in alligator, b as in bear? I play with Cuisinart rods and separate small squabbling children all day."

"What are Cuisinart rods?"

"No, no." But it didn't matter, she was ready to nod off. Maybe they put hashish in their curry? She and Teddy used to store their grass, such as they had ever had time and patience for, in a bottle marked FENUGREEK. Maybe someone in the kitchen here did the same and this time had forgotten.

"You know what I think, Jess." Merrie wiped her mouth energetically with a huge red napkin. "Difficulty is what's missing for most people when they get to our age. The edge. You know? Competence is the worst enemy, that and experience, isn't it paradoxical? They make us go soft. I used to tell that to my mother when she told me to wear a girdle. Remember girdles? Well, if your muscles can't do it themselves, you're kidding yourself." She was a lucky woman, Jessie thought, not confused, only challenged. Her children went to private schools: no Carll guilt seemed attendant on that fact. She had a summer place—"just a place, I wouldn't dignify it any other way!"—in Sag Harbor. Jessie didn't envy her acquisitions, only her attitude. Or were the night tremors chronic, suppressed under tension again, waiting to erupt. Did the lunch-hour swimming, the Nautilus exercise machines keep down the secret tics and phobias, the scarred and ruined parts? Her husband was an astronomer at the Goddard Space Flight Center uptown. "And he'll always be happy if he's just got his equipment. The thing about the stars—they don't change but he says they're like a modest woman, they show you a little more, give you a little more, each time you look." So he was the one who worked in the dark then, under the demanding sky. Jack Sprat and his wife. She was awed at the neatness of the arrangement.

Merrie paid for the lunch. Jessie hugged her and went home through the teeming Christmas hordes, her stomach knotted with anxiety, turmeric, jealousy, superiority. She tried her Jackson number again from a phone booth and got no answer.

"Andréa," she said then, having pulled her friend out of a meeting. "Do you know where everybody is? It's been days and I'm getting panicky."

Andréa's laugh had the effect of a freely falling knife. "Oh, honey, things have been happening here that you're not going to like."

"I just left!" She held her breath a double beat and murmured, "Okay, I'm ready. Hit me with it."

"Well."

"Well. Andréa!"

"Well, the reason you're not getting any answer is that they have—you could say they have all decamped I think is the word, out to that little shithole town Teddy loves so much."

"Mourning Dove."

"Yeah, well, you know I don't mean Venice. I don't think he's spent more than fifteen minutes in that house you went to all that trouble over. He calls it 'Jessie's neighborhood,' and the feeling I get is he goes home to change his underwear and put a little cat food out once in a while so Mickey Mouse won't revert to the wild."

"Oh Jesus. And the kids are with him out there?"

"Jesus might just be the one to call on right about now. He has—listen, lovey, he needs to tell you a lot of this himself." She sighed a heavy sigh, the kind that works best if there's a lot of bosom behind it. "I think you're going to find that this little trip has cost you."

Jessie's neck crawled with frustrated anger. "Cost *him*."

"No. Listen, Jessie. He's found out some shit about Jug—"

"What do you mean?"

"Well, basically all your suspicions about the man were correct, but Teddy was so eager to have a buddy I guess he couldn't see what was right in front of him."

"But there was a kid in jail?"

"Oh yeah, there was all that. There's always something rotten some-place, we know that. But it turns out Jug, bless his heart, is up for a job with a new group, some housing and welfare coalition, this is out of Washington, and it was urgent that he come on all fresh and hot and shiny looking like an activist right now, even if he had to make the action. That's the way the wind was blowing with these folks, they didn't want a paper pusher. So Jug set it up and then took off. Are you with me?"

Jessie closed her eyes; there were things she saw too well and others she heard too well. She was ready for sensory deprivation. "I'm with you."

"Well, all I can figure is, when Teddy found out what his good friend was up to, why he needed his services all of a damn sudden, instead of telling Jug where he could put it, all he could do was redouble his efforts himself. I mean, you've got to admire him, the man's got some pride."

Jessie grunted. She had had too many occasions for that phrase in the past few months; it usually meant that if you didn't have any common sense, at least you had a few uncompromised principles left. "And the kids?"

"Well," Andréa said. "They stayed at my house most of the time, if you want to know. Cleo couldn't get over her luck. We had sleeping bags everywhere, it looked like a disaster relief center. But I think he was going to bring them out there for a couple of days for a real treat, so they're gone now. Andy put himself in charge, he took the little kids to the movies, one of those Walt Disney matinees where the price of admission was they had to bring canned goods for the 'kids without Christmas'—generic beans for the generic poor? Like a small town—that was kind of nice, actually. Lydia must have spent five bucks on barbecue beans. And I know they went roller-skating one day while Daddy was off playing Santa. And Jessie?"

"Yeah." Bless Andy who could take care of anything that needed a calm, even hand. But she hadn't wanted Helen and O'Neill to be parentless in her absence, and Andréa and Tommy were at work all day.

"Jessie," Andréa went on. "Listen, I want you to know I did this. I took that lil ole silent girl of yours out to lunch with me. With Miss Lydia along to sort of run interference."

"Did you really?" She was aghast. "Did she come?"

"Of course she came. She's my house guest, she'd better have come. I took them in to Holmes on the mall, that pretty restaurant they have. Just like a couple of ladies. Sat in those big throne kind of rattan chairs they've got and starved, you know the soup and half a sandwich routine, like the whole world's on a diet?"

"Maybe they ought to donate the other half of each sandwich to those generic kids you mentioned. Well, how did it go? Was she civil?"

Andréa laughed. "Oh Jessie, your expectations. More like cowed than civil. Honey, if you want to know, I think the girl's more of a little scared grieving thing than some of the other forbidding kinds of horrors you and T.C. put out about her. All the racist gunk? What does she know? She was polite as you please and couldn't find her voice where she put it, and even tried to ask me some questions about my work, if you can believe it! Sometimes I think it's politeness gonna save the South, just like it was a blight all those years it kept anything nasty from showing. People are going to be decent to each other in more and more places as a by-product of—"

"Could she meet your eyes?"

"Oh shit, Jessie. 'Meet my eyes.' That's the trouble with the two of you, you look at the whole world like it's all a page or two out of Henry James. The whole civilized universe does not have an obligation to meet your eyes or mine and get off on this simultaneous moral reverence of yours. Or gratitude either. That's what I told Teddy: man, it's a luxury to step up and even *like* the person who pulls your name out of the hat says you've gotta live with them."

"André . . ."

"You see enough of what I see in my line of work. . . ."

"Come on, now, you sound like an emergency room doctor all of a sudden."

"Could be one, honey. I just could be, what with the child abuse, the abandonments, the general drag-assed emotional neglect and flat-out cruelty. Some of it's every bit as bad as a razor fight."

"But what does that have to do with us? I don't see you saying about your little Cleo that she deserves whatever she might happen to run into even in her daycare center. Aren't you over there barking at her teachers to shape up and be stimulating, be a little more this and not so much that all the time? You're not about to be satisfied making do."

"Well, all right. Of course. I only mean you've got exaggerated expectations of what a thoroughly decent kid who's been through an abominable experience might be ready to give *you* so soon. It seems like all the shaping up's on her side. And I want to tell you she's got one of those tight little faces you could trust to keep a country's war secrets. It just closes right back over whatever you feed it, not a ripple."

"Yeah," Jessie began. "It's not exactly a clown's face. . . ."

"Now, what I'd really like to see is what would happen in a very laid-back—*unjudging*—*ordinary*—situation, where she didn't get pushed to any conclusions about what's bad behavior. None of this committee agreement about how to—uh—belong—in the Carll household. Do you know what I'm saying?"

Jessie refused to rise to the bait; she could not afford to get angry at Andréa right now. "Is there such a thing? Andréa? Really? No shared assumptions?"

"Oh sure there is. Absolutely. I've got mine and they're as obsessive as yours. But I'd suggest trying to keep them unspoken as long as you can, not make them into confrontations just because this little sister looks so cool she makes you think she's brought a whole cosmology of the devil along with her."

"Oh, do I need a lecture now, André? Teddy must be a wreck, I don't know where my family is—"

"Jessie, I don't know. I'm sorry. This isn't the time anyway, I've got to go back to my meeting. We're about to tackle the redistricting they're going to use to put all our elected folks' desks out on the street."

"André, wait. How can I get to them? If they're out there now, is there someplace I can call?"

"No phone where he's staying, you ought to see it. I think he told the kids to pretend it was scout camp and they're going to eat mashed potatoes out of an envelope. Teddy's running around like he's getting the place ready for the next summer Olympics. Single-handed."

"Poor Teddy. What a double-cross."

"Well, he doesn't want to live on your block anyway. He thinks he's Jimmy Jones. Write him a letter. He's surely picking up the mail." She said her usual unsentimental goodbye and was gone. There would be a map of the eighty-two counties of Mississippi spread out on the table over which she and her cadre of lawyers would bend, focussed as surgeons at an operation deciding on the place to lay the cool edge of the knife. They were making plans that would take them in an orderly fashion to one court after another, rising in painfully slow progression to the point at the top. So Teddy's method was not so methodical as that. Neither was he. Nor she. Why did she have to have a guarantee of victory before she would join his battle?

A woman was banging sharply on the phone booth door with the edge of her dime. Her face was inflamed, under a hat that looked like a butternut squash, green and yellow and squat. Jessie picked up her bag and folded the door open.

.   .   .

Jessie came home from her lunch with Merrie mesmerized by the light; the absence of light. The New York horizon was impenetrable, its buildings made an indented mass against a bled, colorless sky. Figure and ground reversed back home and sky prevailed, scored with toothmarks, discreet bites taken out, but tentatively: the capitol, the bank and insurance company buildings, the new federal skyscraper at the end of Farish Street holding together black and white Jackson with a single snap. She walked very slowly down her parents' block wondering how the children at school would see this deep oxblood-colored place, all crowded brick and massive wooden shutters, when their eyes had been formed by longer vistas of light. And if they'd grown up in Colorado, in Washington, where the mountains looked like billboards for the infinite, would they be different children?

Her mother met her at the door in her tweedy walking suit, distraught. She was relieved to see Jessie. "Do something for me, will you, dear. I'm too tired to do this today."

"Sure. Do you want something at the store?"

Elizabeth Singer stood holding on to her suit lapels as if they could support her. "Your father," she said, "is down at the police station." Jessie opened her mouth to exclaim but her mother went right on. "No, he's all right, don't waste any worry on him, this is his idea of a second occupation, now that he's retired. He very nearly lives there and in some of the other precinct houses. He seems to have his favorites. Let him explain. I'm going to get dinner."

"Mother—"

"He's a poor old fool, Jessie, who has no pride and dignity left. He's made himself a bone in as many throats as one man possibly can and he will not be swallowed. It's pathetic." She took off her suit jacket and, slipping it onto its padded hanger, told Jessie where to go to collect him, and what the procedure was. "Most of the time they don't even bother to book him, they just bring him along to get him out of trouble."

"But what has he done?" Shoplifting? Peeping in windows?

"Sometimes if they're not too busy they bring him home in the squad car and that saves me a trip. But the neighbors!" She smoothed down her skirt and came to the door with Jessie. "I think they must assume he drinks." She lowered her voice as if they could hear her. "What else could they possibly think?"

What he had done, this morning at least, was stand, singing union songs, in the path of a crane at a construction site near the Brooklyn Bridge that was ringed with picketing workmen. A one-man passive resistance band, very dignified, totally immovable.

He was in high spirits, not restrained by cell or handcuffs when Jessie came into the bright and noisy room; he was down at the far end having a spirited conversation with a young clerk who was leaning over her typewriter to listen. He waved at Jessie as if they were in a train station, a great crowd roiling between them.

"Your father," the on-duty officer told her, "seems to think it's still 1968." He shook his head without malice and that broke Jessie's heart more surely than anger, which she could have resented. The year 1938, more likely, she thought. They had their chance to humor him quite regularly, and as a crank he had no power to threaten them, they probably thought of him as a sort of superannuated bag-lady with a mouthful of Jane Fonda's slogans. Jessie smiled and thanked them and cringed when Jack Singer, at the door, raised his fist and shouted, with a concentrated defiance that made him look the way he must have forty years ago, "We shall prevail!" The typewriters ticked and the phone bleated and everyone called out goodbye. Jessie helped him shrug on his overcoat in the wooden hall.

"Who shall prevail, exactly?"

"The Electrical Workers' Union," he told her mildly. "This is a city project and you wouldn't believe the outrageous contract they're being offered, it's an offense to decency." He catalogued the offenses but Jessie barely listened. This was absurd, a joke, except that it wasn't funny.

"Are there so many strikes you end up in your own neighborhood all the time?"

He laughed. He was exceedingly pleased to have had a typical day's work to show Jessie. "There's a lot, and there's the prison up on Atlantic Avenue, don't forget, and a lot of tenants' groups these days, you know, and I don't mind stepping on a subway once in a while if I have to." He frowned. "What kind of malice did your mother put out about me?"

"Oh," Jessie answered, "Daddy. She's just tired and embarrassed. What do you expect her to think when she's got to spend half her time picking you up like—" A lost child, she thought, but was not cruel enough to say. "I don't think she believes this is very productive."

"Being the eight-millionth dabbler to paint the Brooklyn Bridge, that's productive. For the art supply store with its rip-off prices, for them it's productive, but I can't see who else. Can you? What is this self-expression when no one else is watching? Tell me. The tree falls in the forest for whom? The chipmunks? Be honest, do you need to see another vase of chrysanthemums or a bag of apples spilled out on the table there? Cézanne already did that, Jessie. I go in the kitchen, she's sitting with her nose on the edge of the table, she's looking up at fruit. *Up*. What's she doing? She's studying the shadows. It isn't even the oranges, it's the spheres and their shadows. Who needs that when there are still a lot of important things to be done in the real world?"

"The real world? No, don't bother telling me what that is, my husband reminds me every chance he gets." She turned the corner with him, linking arms.

"The best time," Jack Singer said, patting Jessie's hand, "was when I came up before Judge Sadler, do you know him, Martin Sadler? On—I don't know what, a charge of obstruction, it must have been—and the next night we were having dinner over there at his house. Ah, priceless. Your mother's friends. She has no taste at all. In fact if she has any criterion it must be What will hurt him the most?" Jessie looked into a store window while they walked: BOOTS REDUCED / EVERYTHING MUST GO. $100 – $450. "Most of the time I would come with her—I don't any more, she can go alone like any other woman without a husband, we're all sputtering out by now anyway—and when I come I sit, that's all. Feet flat on the floor, attention straight ahead. I'm a good boy, right? You want me, I would say, you got me. They want to feed me this stuff then let them feed me, I don't even thank them. It doesn't concern me, her vapid friends impressing each other with their nouvelle this and that in the kitchen, there's never anything nouvelle about it even if they say it in French and use raspberry vinegar on it." He blew out and riffled his lips like a horse.

"So you know where I took my plate that night? The judge was probably relieved, he didn't want to eat with a criminal—in with the help is where. With the servants. They're more interesting anyway. They had this kitchen like something in a restaurant, so I gave them a little help getting the dinner out, you know, one course right on the heels of another and then the guests get heartburn and heart attacks and they wonder why. So when we were done serving, we sat down and had a good old time over the dregs." He laughed. "It's as good a line of work as any."

"And what did the servants think?" Jessie asked.

Her father shrugged. "Who knows? It was a change, anyway. Look, a man my age with nothing to lose . . . I'd rather I *had* something to lose, of course, but if I don't I don't." His eyes glittered. "At least I can still irritate the hell out of them."

They were coming down his own street. "When the men were running amok at the House of Detention down there—that's what the newspeople like to call it, running amok although believe me, tootsie, you know the last thing they have in there is any place to run any way at all, in fact that's what they were protesting, the overcrowding. But anyway, I gave the police such a hard time in the street, what with taunting and leading songs and taking away their sawhorses and their NO PARKING TODAY signs they usually put up for parades, they actually had to lock me up for a day. I was telling a lot of old stories in the street about the time we struck the biggest coat-maker in the city, and way back to my first shop, the thugs and the saboteurs. And I taught some of these kids, they think they're organizers, they were there to cheer—I taught them some old tricks. They call themselves organizers! They're full of theories they studied in school about why people land behind bars but they don't have a plan, no theory, no system, no discipline."

Jessie could feel her father's arm tense with excitement under her own. Memory was enough to do that to you.

"So you know when they threw me in this—well, it wasn't even a cell, actually, but close enough, a room with a good lock—I felt such nostalgia from when I used to be a professional pain in the ass, it was like . . ." He shook his head and Jessie saw that his eyes were bright with tears from the simplified past. If we knew how long we would have to live in it we would never make a decisive move, she thought, and Teddy's eager ill-used face flew up between her and the parked cars, the splotchy tree-trunks, the single brick house long as freight train, cut up by walls, that was the 200 block.

Her father's fiction was that he still had some effect on the way the world moved; her mother's was that she had been excused and had none at all.

How strange it was, how disembodying: they entered the old quiet house that held itself with massive dignity and walked in to the dinner Elizabeth Singer had prepared, and there she fed them like any wife and mother whose family had returned from work or a long simple stroll on the Promenade beside the gun-gray river. Elizabeth had assembled her face tonight as a mask that betrayed exhaustion but no hurt and no humiliation. Jack Singer whistled, blew on his soup, put in so much salt Jesse had to keep herself from scolding—he was not, after all, O'Neill—and grunted while he cut his meat as if to protest its toughness (it was very tender) as a personal insult. "Tell me, Jessie, is this salty enough?" He shook his head in wonder. "I don't have such good taste buds any more. That's another reason I can do just fine without the vinegar made of kumquats and all the subtle sauces. Zing. It doesn't have that zing any more unless I load it on."

"It's probably sitting there in your arteries, Daddy, little spreading salt-piles."

Her father shook his handsome shiny head. If it hadn't been for an assaulted wrench of her eyes, no one could have guessed that Elizabeth Singer suffered her husband's sorrow and his vindictiveness in the same moment. Jessie considered this, cutting her beef with the side of her fork. The two of them, grief and anger, must alternate in her like pills and liquor, one quickening her spirits to sympathy, the other depressing them. He shot a look at his wife quick as a flirting boy, found her studying him, her mouth a dash of pain, and turned his sulking eyes away again.

All of a sudden Jessie apologized and went to New York to visit her parents (the Communists)! One time I talked to her mother when she phoned and she said she wanted to meet me but I don't know, I think I would be afraid. (She sent us a present of shirts once, probably she was trying to be nice and get in our favor.) Anyway, I don't know why Jessie went now when we are only 1/2 unpacked but she gave us our Christmas presents which we had to wait to open. (A nice blue gingham dog-shaped pillow for my new room, which I really like, a subscription to Seventeen and a good Irish sweater that looks better off than on, frankly.—I feel like a football player, but one in fashion at least!—For O'Neill a great tank that goes by remote control and a Victorian village or something to build out of a cardboard book. And a whole big bunch of Battlestar Galactica stuff.) I have some small presents for them too, barettes for

Lydia, and for Andy I found a Shakespeare record of this (sappy) woman singing Sonnets. For Jessie I will get a pair of the silliest color tights I can find, I saw some called tropical fruit colors and I think she would look good in mango or kiwi (yuck). And for Teddy I don't know. Do you think I could find some cianyde (sp.)?

It will not be any kind of real Christmas but that's good, it might as well not try to be like it was at home or it would have been very hard. (Although last year I have to admit my parents nearly killed each other over DD, how she stole over to give Daddy his gift, very cute, and Mom tried to pretend she didn't even know she was there and when she left threw the whole room at him. I unplugged all the candles on the tree before she could pull it over and burn down the house. And even at that she never figured out I knew, or at least would admit it. She thought I was a little baby where such things are concerned. That or she had some pride about it and was ashamed that her child would know? It is not for me to say which.)

But without Jessie we didn't really plan to do anything much. I remember Andy said of course Christmas is not a Jewish holiday but they are (except Jessie) half Methodist and they usually at least do something and have a tree. Once in a while they went to church when he was little. But now Teddy announces he is going to that Mourning Dove for a few days where the demonstration was that time and the picketing O'Neill couldn't get enough of. And when he comes back to get us we will all go out to help them celebrate, and we will take presents! That is where his feelings lie, of course, I forgot. (I don't think he ever knew what Jessie got us, for example, even though the cards were signed both of them.) At first he sort of said, well maybe I shouldn't go, but I know Andrea would love to have you over for a few days to visit. So we did.

Andrea and Tommy (they are the Smiths) have a nice den with old dolls up on the shelves, the kind you keep from your grandmother and one of those that turns over, this way it is blonde and white and when you flip its skirts it is colored but both have the exact same face sewed on in different colors. And a nice house in general, nicer than Jessie and Teddy's. She also took Lydia and I out to lunch at this place, inside a department store, and was very nice, you could feel her being an aunt, even if the wrong color! We went through the mall and she bought me some bath soap, it looks like spaghetti and it's in a Ronzoni kind of box, and for Lydia a little sketchbook in hard black covers, I thought Lydia would die in the aisle of being grateful. Their parents don't really give them a whole lot and I think she is hungry for some small "luxuries" like that. Although I liked the feeling someone was trying to be especially nice to me it was funny, I have to admit that one good thing about being here with these people I can't stand and all, I at least haven't felt "special" all the time the way I would if I was in Birmingham as the orphan child somebody had to take in and people would be falling all over us to make us happy happy happy. Maybe I am crazy but that is how I feel about it.

About Andrea. When she said "Merry Christmas!" I suddenly realized I ought to get something for her only I didn't have any money, about a dollar in my bag which would buy you one ribbon and a Santa sticker. I felt awful about that. I think for a Negro she isn't like anyone I ever knew, even though Mom always said there were plenty who could live in our neighborhood and be as good as anyone else, and some even had that kind of money. Lurene was sure of herself the same way but only in the kitchen or wherever, with a million opinions about what to use, Ajax or Comet and she gave the same kind of look if you did something wrong or said a dumb thing. (Bon Amy was the right answer for all time with her.) But if I saw her in the street she was cold and quiet like she almost didn't know me, and no apologies either. Andrea is just like any white woman only I think she is actually much smarter than most. (Like she is much neater and more precise than Jessie.) I shouldn't be surprised but I am that I can (almost) forget what color she is. It is probably that she is leading us around and we would not dream of sassing her or telling her what to do the way I could Lurene, nicely, Mom would always say, but firmly. I would never want Lingham to know what I am thinking on this subject but I am seeing now that Daddy was really always talking about poor people not just black people. I don't even know what some of the awful habits and contagious problems are any more that he was protecting us from. Maybe Lingham being pretty poor herself she never got to meet any Negros like Andrea who are actually lawyers and doctors and things. I am not sure.

Anyway, we went home with Andrea and she made us grits and chicken livers in the morning for breakfast with some herbs or spices or something that smelt wonderful to wake up to. Sometimes I think I would like to be a lawyer too but not the kind of thing she does that is all to put white people in their place, which seems to be the place black people used to be in. I am confused but it is fairly interesting.

Days we have been doing a lot of dumb stuff with Andy being the Father (he thinks he is the Big Adult or something). I stayed home when they went to see "101 Dalmations" (barf) but I gave in when he had money for us all to go roller skating. Poor little Lydia—she's almost as tall as I am, not exactly little!—needed to be held up, she's not at all athletic. I thought about it a lot, she is like she only sort of faces in, the way some buildings have all their windows out of sight from the street. That sounds crazy, I know. Very private but a lot is actually going on where you can't see it. We went around with our hands crossed in front and she was nice, she thanked me a lot. She also said she hates having her parents away at night. I wanted to say How would you like them to never be coming back but I didn't because first it would be mean and second it might make her wish she hadn't said anything. You have to keep thinking ahead two steps, it is no way to relax. I do have to admit I was pretty panicky myself last night even with Andrea and Tommy in the next room, I felt like something trapped at the bottom of a bowl with steep sides I can't climb out of like some insect someone dropped down in there. I can't explain it. Maybe I was actually missing Jessie. Wouldn't she be surprised.

I am finished, I am leaving. I am putting this diary out where anyone can read it. Let them understand what happened to drive me to this.

My Uncle Teddy Carll is crazy. He makes my Daddy look like a normal man. I would swear in court that what he did to my brother and I was cruel and vicious and he did it on purpose to show us how much he hates us and has never wanted us here. His own children can do all this because they don't feel the same way at all, they are not bothered. That is their business entirely then. Is this what happens when I let my principals down a little, what I said about Andrea?

I cannot believe it was just this morning but with my dear uncle leading he comes and gets us from Andrea's so we can go on this, what my history teacher was calling a Forced March like in Russia across the endless snow or something, we go to K-Mart and buy all this junk, just for anybody. I mean have you ever seen anything so dumb. Baby clothes and fruitcakes and a purse and some hats, Santa Claus himself, just all thrown in a big bag. The only time I ever saw such a mess of goodies nobody asked for was when this girl in school Flo said her father took her for one of those Divorced Dad's Sundays and had this big pathetic jumble of gifts he thought she'd like and he didn't even really have much sense of how old she was and what she'd like so there was a little of dolls and a little of Jordache. Teddy did it with tools and flashlights and anonymous junk like that. And we ride out to Mourning Dove and he makes a big deal of it. There is a church service getting ready to go on *and he stands in front of this seedy building with two steeples both with paint peeling and just—with the minister helping, they are very buddy-buddy—it's like a grab bag. Some people didn't get any and a lot were swapping the wrong stuff. Big deal. Will people love him for it or be any happier if they're already miserable? (I'm learning how much it takes, Lord: misery is a hole that goes so deep it is never filled up.) My opinion is he threw away a lot of money on nothing, not even a lot of thanks. This is his stratagy, he calls it: make people "comfortable" with you and then ask them to do for themselves some of the things that need doing. Bribery is what it sounds like, I will give you candy if you wash behind your ears. Because my mother always said charity just makes people feel you are condescending to them anyway, so they don't really thank you except skin deep.*

After that I can't even write it. All I want to say to WHOEVER READS THIS *is:*

We were abused to have to stay where we did. Teddy said it was a 1 or 2 day vacation and it would be "good" for us like going camping which I hate anyway. It was this old house painted (I mean chipping) the exact color of grass stains on your pants knees, and falling over. I heard somebody died there last month or something so it was empty. Probably had germs everywhere, O'Neill kept saying. He looked very spooked, his eyes were going real fast over everything looking for I don't know what. We were supposed to sleep on the floor like survivors of something terrible, a tornado or something, in our sleeping bags. Surrounded by filth and cat stink. This little sink with rust stains, no hot water was turned on, and the toilet made me so nauseous first I would not go at all. Then when it made me feel so sick not to even pee I was going down into the woods near the river. And washing in the river that was so cold I thought I would catch pneumonia.

Meanwhile where is my uncle Teddy? At first it looked like he was going to spend today with us. But then after a while he is nowhere to be seen and so happy when we do get a quick glimpse of him, he is pretending to fit right in and be Wanted. I don't think anybody noticed, frankly. He kept trying to talk to people about beginning to demand their rights about this and that and the other. Lydia played with the babies around—(there are lots, them breeding like rabbits) and so did I a little, what else could I do? Andy was always driving around with a boy he liked, who must be the blackest person I ever saw, like from Africa, not even one littlest bit of mixture in him. The boy kept staring at me,

I don't know what Andy told him. He was teaching Andy driving and Andy was walking like he was six and a half feet tall all of a sudden. You would think nobody else ever learned how to drive before. O'Neill had fights in the woods and got buried like Indians in a mound under the leaves till he came down with a chest cold. The leaves are moldy and frozen through, when you pick up one a whole bunch comes up with it.

Tonight at supper—we were mooching off someone who didn't look like they could really afford food for 4 more strangers—Lydia asks Teddy if she can talk to her mother in New York and Teddy says maybe but that's all he says. Probably he does not want Jessie to know he has kidnapped us on this stupid so-called vacation or roughing it with the natives. Then Lydia gets daring and asks why are we here anyway, will he please explain it. (She is polite.) (This is while our "hosts" are not in the room so she won't hurt any feelings.) O'Neill is coughing meanwhile and doesn't even have his medicine with him in case the asthma jumps out at him, which I wouldn't blame it if it did. Andy is humming under his breath till I want to scream—I think that's his way of keeping from getting too mad, not even knowing it himself. Teddy has been talking to this negro woman, she is something else, she has a comb stuck in her hair—I see this at school sometimes—just as if it got caught in there, it is so thick, and she just left it there. And Teddy looks so dopy he is like another teenager in the family, I can't believe he is the Head of this Household: he is skinny in a checked shirt and has his chair sort of tipped backward with his arm across the back of it. He is letting a beard grow but on the scar side it is all blotchy and won't cover the red places. He is always "a marked man." But he is so comfortable in this slum with these people who are beneath him, and now at last he has his children with him to show it off to them. I don't know why he just doesn't move out and become one of them. Maybe he could get a good sunburn and pretend he was born of a mammy, a pickaninny just a little on the light side!

"I wanted you-all to meet my friends" is sort of what he said. "These folks missed the parade last time it went by and they want to get in on it this time." At first I thought he meant another real parade like Thanksgiving but of course he was talking about all the Agitation and Riots and so on from a long time ago. Although I didn't see any parade getting ready to go anywhere with him leading.

So then I guess he decided we could talk to Jessie in New York. So he calls her from a phone in this bar. I didn't want to go in. Lydia and Andy went and O'Neill ran in after them and he came out with a Coke very happy. She told him about the store windows in New York, the way they did them for Christmas. He was excited that he talked to her, I think he felt better. I wondered if Lydia complained to her, but probably not with her Daddy standing there.

Then! When we got "home" and turned on the little light in our borrowed house I saw this shape I thought was a cat, big and puffed-up looking, in the hall. And Andy says "Rat! Hey. Mega-rat!" It is going to burrow under the stove. No wonder there is this sort of sweet stink over everything, it is their NEST in the insulation under there. Rat turds, I guess, steamed.

Mega-rat. He thinks that's funny. So does Teddy. Andy says "Let's catch him and roast him" and they go and bend down to peek under the stove. But that is it for me. Positively the end. It does not have to do with niggers or no niggers or anything nicer I could call them, I liked it at Andrea's house, clean with rugs and soft towels and a nice smell, it has to do with Teddy forcing us against our will, that he made us come out here. What a Merry Christmas, he is really thoughtful.

O'Neill is snuggled down in his sleeping bag, he is so tired, but I ask him if he wants to come with me. He says "Where?" but when I answer he is already asleep and breathing through his mouth so loud it is like the Death Rattle. I am writing this waiting till everybody's zipped in their bags and then FAREWELL. I do not apologize, nothing fancy, it is the middle of a nightmare, midnight in my Soul if they want to know. They are all perverts in a way, even Andy because he never criticizes anything, let alone is Contemptuous. How can Teddy dare to do this to us? Andy doesn't even ask or find it weird. Even his little sister was asking those questions over supper that showed she wasn't too happy. Even for a day he shouldn't have forced this down our throats. We are children, basically, and not being consulted.

I took a flashlight, some crackers, my parka, all the money I could find in Teddy's wallet (not much, about $22) and considered leaving a note to Andy. But I have lost such faith in him, he is weak, without any bite. Wish me luck, I don't know how far I'll get. Dear God, be with me. I am not looking for trouble. Only some kind of sanity and decency. I actually wish Jessie would come home. I may not like her but at least she isn't crazy.

YOU CAN READ ALL OF THIS, I DON'T CARE!!!!!!!!!!!!!!!!

Returned by force. It was sleeting. Just my luck. I actually fell down twice, hurt my elbow, knees wet. Feet so so so cold and somehow parka didn't keep out dampness. Don't even know which direction I went in in the dark. Felt like an animal, a rat myself, skulking along highway. Once a car came by and drowned me in light, I prayed they wouldn't stop—who knows who it could be. What have you come to? I kept asking myself almost like a marching song, measuring the way with it. I only got about 2 or maybe 3 miles if that. They didn't miss me till it was light. Then they drove up really slow like they wanted to sneak up on me. Andy nearly fell out of the car when he saw me. He screamed my name at me like it was a curseword. I told Teddy I will take him to a court or something, I am calling Dick Reidy and will get him in trouble. There must be a word for keeping someone against her will. Slavery. Ha. I hit him in his scar, scratched and made him bleed, tried to dig through to the bone. Look, I showed him my arm. Me too. Only the scar is almost gone. Although I couldn't arrange to die like some special people. If I died I would not ever want to come back. Just howled. Would not get in his car. They grabbed me and stuffed me in like a sack. Hit Andy too, he is such a nurd, right where I knew it would hurt most. I had them scared. Teddy goes "Why did you do this, we are going home tomorrow anyway." "I want to go home today." "Okay, today." "Right now."

I cursed all the way home, every single stinking word I could think of, horrible sharp words Daddy would kill me before he let me say any of them out loud, I can't even write them here. O'Neill cried back to Jackson. He kept saying Don't, every time I called Teddy another nasty word. I couldn't hold them in. It was like going into the woods to do those bathroom things behind a rock. I couldn't not or I was going to smash up altogether like glass splinters. Woke up in bed. Flowers from Lydia on a tray. She must have had to buy them in this season, nothing is growing out there. Sleep and more sleep. Too tired to escape again right now. Later I am going to get free of their selfishness. Praying calms me down: even words, calm as a boat on the stillest waters. When I open up my Bible it tells me this Psalm without my even going looking. I know that this is right because it always happens that way, the perfect words seem to be waiting for me as if God wanted to whisper them in my ear as soon as I was ready to listen. "Give ear, O God, to my prayer; And hide not Thyself from my supplication. Attend unto me, and answer me; I am distraught in my complaint, and will moan; Because of the voice of the enemy, Because of the oppression of the wicked; For they cast

*mischief upon me, And in anger they persecute me. My heart doth writhe
within me—" And while I am reading this silently the door pushes open.
I would lock it if I only had a key.*

*"Will you get up before Jessie comes back?" This is Andy. These are
his first words to me since they dragged me home here. Very kind.*

*"And terrors of death are fallen upon me. Fear and trembling come
upon me, And horror hath overwhelmed me." I just say these out so he
can hear what he is interrupting. Then I catch my breath. "No, I will
not."*

"She will be very upset."

*"And I said, Oh that I had wings like a dove! Good, then let her be.
You don't care about me or her either, you're just protecting your father."*

*"Will you stop saying that thing? What can I do for you?" He takes
my hand. Chilly! I pull away. Both hands on my Bible which has travelled
with me through everything, the white velvet familiar as beloved skin. It
is getting a little grayish, I wonder if I can clean it somehow? "Then I
would fly away, and be at rest. Lo, then would I wander far off, and I
will wait for Thy name." Here: I will write what I said to him. I said
"You? You can f—— off."*

I see in his eyes that I can still strike deep.

*"You don't have to worry, my father by coincidence is finished with
Mourning Dove. They aren't really interested in doing anything long-
lasting there. He says organizing is impossible." (I don't even know what
organizing means but it doesn't matter.)*

*"Good, I hope he's miserable he wasted all that money on ugly
pocketbooks and baby crawlers."*

*"You're being a baby, Helen." He said that to me. Nothing soft or
sympathetic and no apology for what they did to me.*

*So I repeated what I said before. "F—— off right out of my room."
He closed the door behind him. "For it is good, in the presence of Thy
saints." I held the Bible to my cheek where it was cool against me. I
know where my strength is hidden.*

*I don't think they even read my journal. In addition to everything
else, that* is *insulting.*

They were home again when Jessie drove up from the airport—she
wondered if Teddy had hurried them back furtively before their coach
turned into a pumpkin. (But how odd; they had gone to his version of the
ball only to sit in the cinders.)

The children were not kind. "You should have seen it," Lydia said when she and her mother and O'Neill had gathered for a reunion over English muffins and tea with milk that was her favorite form of cozy celebration: she knew the British did something like this at about this same cool and darkening time of day and it had a kind of glamor about it. "Like—the bathroom where we were, it had a mirror, I kept pretending it was a crystal ball, it was all under this haze? And this nasty little sink that was, like, one big rust splotch?"

"Splotch. I love that word, *splotch*." O'Neill pretended to drop something from a great height, opening his hand to let it fall down fast. "Sp-l-aahh-tch! Bl-aaahh-tch!"

"And, like—" Lydia continued.

"Lyddie. Once upon a time it was only stoned musicians who said 'like' as often as you do." Jessie hugged her and then sat down and poured her tea, leaving room for half a cup of warm milk. "And what did you do with yourselves?"

"Oh, nothing. God. Andy was learning to drive from this kid and he almost knocked down a whole barbed wire fence. And—I don't know. O'Neill, what did we do?"

"Nothing. *I* don't know. All the kids were—first they were scared of me, then they ganged up, so I had to fight 'em. I almost rolled in the river, we were down there. Then we played Choctaws in the woods and made mounds to bury everybody in. But it was all leaves because you know that ground is a rock out there."

"Daddy was mad a lot because he said we were missing our *opportunities*." Lydia put her hands on her hips to indicate her impatience with this tack.

"Just what opportunities were those?"

"I don't know, he never said. Mostly he was sitting in this place they have called Barky's, it's like a bar and grill or something? And he said that was where the people were unless they were in church. So he sat with them all day when we were there." She thought some more while she buttered a muffin meticulously. "We gave everybody Christmas presents, that was nice. The little kids. Because they don't have a lot of, like, clothes without ripped-up knees or, like, they're all worn down, things you would give away, you know?"

"Except it was Christmas," O'Neill interrupted. "They got very fancy. And Teddy made us dress all up, he said it was disrespectful—" he maneuvered through that word very methodically—"not to get as fancy as everybody else for Christmas."

"Not to God, he means." Lydia looked very happy sitting back, sipping from her mug with a daisy on it. Jessie felt guilty and angry that she had, in the children's minds, brought them back to the luxury of order. What an irony. "Disrespectful to all those people who put on their suits and dresses and all. He couldn't even find his tie!"

"Anyway, we had to stand around and shake hands like we owned the place," O'Neill continued. "Who wants to own a bunch of shacks that are all falling down and a string of scraggly dogs and nothing but a billion little—Nigra—kids." The word took impressive care; that was about as far as he could go. He said it as if it were a gift to her.

"And Helen? Where is she?" Jessie finally asked when the girl had definitively failed to make an appearance.

They seemed to have to think about this. "She's sick," O'Neill finally said, as though this had been a hard question asked in school and he wasn't sure he remembered but would be glad to take a guess.

"It was cold there," Lydia added by way of explanation.

"But she's better since we came home." O'Neill looked very eager to please. "Boy, I'm glad we're home."

"Now that we've got this house," Lydia said fervently, "we've got to use it!"

Jessie, bewildered, went up the few steps toward Helen's room. Helen had hung a sign stolen from a hotel. It had a picture of an ostrich on it, viewed from behind. DON'T EVEN THINK OF DISTURBING ME! But she knocked on the door nonetheless, and when no one responded, she opened it and tiptoed in.

They must have told Jessie I was just sick. She came in to see me and put her hand on my forehead, one of those things Mothers always do. She asked was I coughing like O'Neill? I wanted to say No, not coughing, but dying inside. But I could tell how stupid that would sound so I just didn't say anything. I have some pride at least. She brought me a very tall glass of hand-squeezed orange juice. It wasn't what I needed at all but it was nice of her—I feel she is a Victim right now like me, no one is telling her everything that happened when she was away. For her own sake I am considering telling her how he first left us all alone and then made us guinea pigs for his social experiments. If you want to know, I'm surprised he didn't have us drinking in the bar with him. But if she thinks I am crazy what will happen to me?

Andy was going to a New Year's party. He couldn't hide his excitement: it was in Eastover at what was rumored to be the most extraordinary house represented at his high school. He didn't much like the boy who lived there who was fat and nasty and acted as if he knew no one liked him, but he was going to overcome his scruples, Andy told his mother, and put up with him. His pool was shaped like a valentine and once they had filled it with beer and jumped in.

Teddy had gone out without a word. Jessie had a feeling he was drinking in some café on Farish Street, trying to ingratiate himself with a bunch of black men who had nothing better to do than feed the jukebox and sit in the bleakness of a new year that felt just like the old.

The other children, though they protested that they wanted to stay up till midnight, fell into sleep grudgingly one by one. Jessie carried O'Neill to bed and, later, pulled Lydia's comforter out from under her long legs carefully—she was thoughtful enough to have given out on her own bed—and tucked it gently around her, all the blue and white animals in the ark disappearing head first into her shadow. She was embarked on a long slow process, adorning her wall with an elaborate-colored mural of the same animals, full of inspired details. She was painting the name of every animal into its body like a Nina in a Hirschfeld cartoon.

New house, new year, new life. New loss. Teddy had barely been home since her return. She would just as soon be alone with it, practice his absence like a sacrament, taste it, smell it, see how it felt: nothing in her hands. Instead of turning on the television set to watch the great bright ball drop above Times Square (which, infuriatingly, fell over Jackson an hour early, implying that only Eastern Time was real) she sat in the kitchen with a glass of scotch. She still hated scotch, it was like a punishment for having adult problems like everybody else's, for feeling like a character in a book, and stared at the kitchen clock. The clock was old and handsome, and the children took turns winding it with a big brass key; probably it had ticked on evenly through the Civil War. It had come out of Teddy's Aunt Adelaide's house, which he always referred to, rather sloppily but with relish, as "the plantation." (Well, in fairness, however small it had been, if it was a farm and had slaves it was a plantation; why did she resist?) Oak, hexagonal, it felt like the kind of clock schoolrooms had on their front walls fifty years ago, beside their framed Stuart's Washington afloat in clouds of incompletion. Jessie had hung it first as a kind of centerpiece. Now she stared at it, at the imperceptible advance of its hands with their fine curlicued tips that looked as if they'd been drawn on the clock face with India ink. It was time that did it all, they floated in it, in its solution, and everything disintegrated slowly as if it were water. There was public time—at a sufficient distance it was called history—and there was private time that beat like a small hot heart inside the body of that history. All those fluttering failing hearts, trying only to sustain one body at a time. You couldn't escape the public part, you were in it and it in you—like DDT in an apple, maybe, part of each cell as it grew, not washable, not sitting on its skin waiting to be peeled away. But you could escape the private, apparently: Teddy could by vanishing, sitting (like that ostrich on Helen's door) with his head in the dark.

The scotch singed the end of Jessie's nose, made it itch, made her sneeze. Sneezing alone in a large room was as peculiar as laughing: it seemed to be an act in need of an audience. Maybe that was what his everyday life felt like then: something you did alone only if there was no one to watch. Narcissist. She sat between adversaries, pouring the laundry starch from the bottle labelled scotch. He had said that the first time around, when they were new together: everything you do, Jessie, has an effect that multiplies. Ripples outward from your touch. When you work with unplumbable need which will never run dry, you are like a doctor confronting pain and accident. All these years he had sat parched, watching need being plumbed by others; now that he was back in his medium, fluid, he did not want to come home any more.

At four o'clock Andy came in. She'd have worried more had she not been drifting in and out of self-pitying sleep with her head on the table. He announced that the party had been cool but the pool, its shape invisible, had been sheeted like a corpse for winter. "I'll have to get invited in a better season," he said and kissed his mother on her smeared face. Jessie had awakened with her mouth sweet and full of cobwebs and she thought for a moment that she could taste candy, she had been dreaming of an altar made of chocolate; the children had jumped on the altar the way they used to bounce on the king-sized bed on Sunday morning. But it was that scotch: she had drunk it in one year and was going to regret it in the next.

"What do you think Daddy's doing tonight?" he asked at the door, wistfully, as if Teddy were in a foreign country.

"Oh, probably remembering when we were young and the world needed us for every little thang. Or so we thought. They never needed us for as much as we imagined even then."

"Oh Mom, that's silly, and it's not true either." He would not let her betray any of it. "Hey, you don't look too great this year, y'all," Andy said, coming back to put his hand on her cheek. Slowly, thoughtfully, he did their ancient secret handshake, clasping knuckles, reversing direction, seizing arms, ending with a jaunty knock on the head. Jessie let him lead her through it awkwardly like a bad follower in a two-step. She hit her forehead with her fist and then knocked on his, her teeth clicking like a wood block.

"I'm okay, love. Worry about him if you want to worry. Why would a man like your father spend his time in a dark bar pretending to have no better place to go? Those are the most—desperately unchanging—places. Time stops. I remember one we had in Tolewood, where the only thing that moved was the arm on this big poster of a man socking away the Schlitz. It was on a piston or something: up and down, up and down went the glass to his mouth. I used to get hypnotized. I'll bet it's still going."

Andy leaned against her, as unsteady as she; together they made a stable structure that held for a full minute, then broke apart into wobbly arms and legs.

"I hereby nominate you Man of the House," Jessie said bleakly. "*Happy New Year.*" She finished the scotch with a terrible face and turned out the lights slowly, in the kitchen, in the living room, thinking how the room, the house, was like a child whose father had rejected it. Would it ever get free of its air of guilty innocence?

.   .   .

"Mom," Andy said excitedly the next afternoon. "Can I show you how I drive?"

Jessie laughed. "Well, I don't know. I heard some kind of nasty rumor about your unnatural relationship with a barbed wire fence."

"It's okay, I'm great. Really. I'll know more than the teacher when I get to Driver's Ed." He moved her confidently toward the car. And there he was, blushing, trying to turn the key as casually as if he'd been doing it for years, looking out the window. They took off with a jolt and Jessie tried to balance her pride in her son—he hardly seemed hers, but some ready-made adult who came with all his competencies intact—with a certainty that he was going to take them into a telephone pole. He drove a little too quickly around a few corners, speeding up wherever there was a short straightaway. A pinkish orange dog walked with dignity in front of the car, looking at it without the slightest urgency.

Having been away from Andy for a week was like coming home to find the most familiar room transformed; nothing was quite the size she had remembered. She felt an unbearable fragility about his bravado as though, if she were to put her hands tenderly on his cheeks as she had done so often in the past, she might shatter him; and yet very soon he would be as hard to touch as wood.

"Andy," she said, having planned no such interrogation. "What did you think about last week when your father sort of left you in charge of everything?"

He glanced at her quickly out of the corner of his eye. "Can I pull over? I'm not good enough yet to talk and drive. It's crazy, I still have to turn the radio off when I'm in traffic." He laughed, embarrassed. "What did I think? I don't know. I told him to go, he wasn't sure he should leave us over there with Tommy and Andréa but—I think he was afraid you'd be mad. I didn't mind doing stuff with them, O'Neill and Lyddie were so grateful, they kind of clung a little, you know? And Helen—" He paused and his cheeks flamed with uneven rays of color. "I didn't see her until he took us out there. Except she did come skating, I guess. I don't know what she was doing but I didn't think I had the right to order her around. Anyway she wouldn't have cared what I said."

Jessie nodded; she suppressed her desperate curiosity about their falling-out. As Andy had said about himself, she didn't have the right. "And what can you tell me about Daddy?"

He widened his eyes and looked straight at her. "My daddy." He sighed and sucked his teeth. "I don't know. I think he's—he was very depressed when we came back. He said it was stupid what he was doing in Mourning Dove, he had always known that, he couldn't make everything happen that he had in mind, and nobody really seemed all that interested in getting organized anyway." He had obviously not mentioned Jug, the instigator.

"He's right. How can he of all people not realize what a huge stone he's pushing and what a high hill it is?"

"Well, I don't know but he had some idea he could—I think he feels worse than he did before when he was sort of dreaming of—I don't know, a comeback, I guess you'd say."

"Like an entertainer, huh? A personal victory. As if those people were some kind of show he could write, starring himself. Oh Andy, your poor father. I don't like to say that but . . ." She let the sentence dwindle; looked out the window at the tepid sky. Was he arrogant or suicidal?

Andy reached over and touched her arm shyly. "I respect him a whole lot, Mom, only it's hard to watch him so hopeless. Nobody said he had to go out and save the world."

"It's an old bad habit."

"You know what he told me? He said when you married him he was like a general, and now he isn't even a foot soldier. I mean, I think he's afraid he disappointed you."

"Where's the war, I wonder." What self-pity, she thought. She didn't want to be implicated. But a wisp of the question hung at eye level like smoke: had she really driven him, somehow, into this crazy self-defeating action?

"Let's head home. Now that we're all depressed together." What had Andréa called it? Simultaneous moral reverence? Something about family-pack ideals, like chicken wings, cheaper in quantity?

Andy watched her carefully.

"I'm sympathetic with him, Andy. I've been wishing all these years he'd find some way to use himself and all he knows. But what he's trying to do . . ."

"It's like he doesn't know how to do any of the things people are doing now, isn't it? He could be a lawyer or something. Or work for, I don't know, for welfare. Or *against* welfare and try to get it changed. It's so confusing."

"But he doesn't want to. That's what you have to understand. He's a revolutionary who wants to keep his allowance and have his meals cooked. He was a hell of a movie star, honey. No, that's not fair. Let's go before I say anything else I don't mean."

Andy jerked the car into gear and when he got it not quite safely into the middle of the street he breathed out hard, as if his effort turned mysteriously into carbon dioxide. He reached over and turned on the radio.

New Year's Eve. No reason to get up. Where will I be next year?

There is no such thing as Time. My parents have entered into Eternity, they are beyond the pitiful counting of days and years here in the mud of the daily world. The perfect pain is followed by the perfect numbness of heaven. If I could die I would be as old as they are, and as young, and I would never change and never be without love again. I see them putting up a marble stone to me HELEN MARIE TYSON *and my dates are 1966 – 1979.* SHE BECAME A DOVE PERFECTED. *And even Teddy would stand in front of it and be sorry, since he will never understand that earthly survival is as nought. Poor Grandy will try to figure out where I am, and Mom too, why both of us never show up at her house any more, and she will say something like "Ribbons and tongues and snapping turtles." And she will never know. But when she comes to join us her mind will be healed and it will all be clear as the sky I am looking at outside the window while I'm writing this: blue into black, and the winter moon is either wincing or smiling, I can't tell which where it heaves up out of the loblolly pines that guard our backyard from Menace.*

Lingham just called. She said she tried to get me last week. Imagine if I said, Oh Barbara, I was spending a few days with some niggers and some rats, you should have been there! I am surely in the most peculiar position anyone has ever been.

She was calling to ask me over. I chickened out. I said I was sick— it was simpler. Anyway I am. I wonder if she wants my friendship or only my membership. That is the awful thing about people like her (and Teddy). They can never be like, regular. *I do not trust any of them, whatever they Stand For.*

Although what would happen to the world if there weren't any fanatical people in it? Mathemeticians have to be crazy, and actresses, lawyers. I think about that sometimes. Priests. Mother always talked about being moderate in your love and attention but I wonder. It's like my dancing, I hold myself at the edge and can't decide whether I should jump in all the way and swim hard or just hang at the edge and float.

Life resumed its natural contours in the new house, which was in no single way remarkable except for its capacity to enrage Teddy. Jessie was convinced that he believed the advent of O'Neill and Helen had somehow brought their very house along and dropped it around him like the cardboard boxes under which they captured the occasional mouse; that it would soften, in the course of things, his moral fiber till it too resembled the Tysons'. He managed to arrange to be out almost all the time: either his work kept him on the road without the usual respites or he was mysteriously elsewhere.

When he did come home, he often smelled of beer, surprising her each time with that sweet acidy edge, like rotting apples. Drinking had never held the slightest attraction for Teddy—life was too unpredictable, he would say, to give up your edge (if you were lucky enough to have one). One beer for companionship; he'd been like a man in perpetual training. But there were all kinds of beer-drinking down here, the redneck teenager-never-grown-up and the out-of-work black man sitting in the dark eating pork rinds and quietly cursing. She knew which one Teddy was catching up with, reaching for camaraderie, matching curse for curse, hoping that in the dust motes, the unaired fried-grease rancidness, he might pass for a friend.

He did come home one evening, though, and after dinner met with an editor for a New York publisher who had come to show him a huge collection of Movement photographs, to ask for help choosing a hundred for a book.

The editor was a long-waisted wiry young woman, sunburned from what might have been Christmas in the Bahamas. She must have been ten when Teddy was having his face rearranged, Jessie thought unmagnanimously, as if—not as if, because—that left her unimplicated in a way that mattered.

The woman tried very hard for dignity when she spoke with him but Jessie was amused to see that Teddy made her girlishly nervous. Every time she asked him a question her skin mottled and flushed right through her sunburn. She listened to his answers with her lips slightly parted. Once he showed her the small pale spot his face made in a crowd of demonstrators. "We were on our way to the Fairgrounds Motel," he said and his eyes engaged with the sight of it, hard and soft at the same time. "That's what we called it, we were thrown in the animal pens down there at the fairgrounds and we were even too many to keep in one place—" and Jessie saw the way the young woman's features jellied with admiration and the peculiar combination of pity and awe that many women reserve for war heroes and athletes injured in the line of duty. Her response was like the insinuating arrangement of knees and legs that she would have worked out had they been seated side by side on a couch in a darkened room.

A groupie. Jessie threw her a scornful look and left them alone.

Teddy drove the editor back to her hotel room and came home at three o'clock. Jessie, one eye open, watched him undress in the opaque dark.

"You must have taken the long way around," she said flatly.

"I drove her around town, I had a lot to show her."

"I'll bet."

Only his shirt caught and reflected a dim light, and then his pale underwear, turning and bending. "You get sarcastic like that, Jess, you have all the sweetness and charm of a sheriff."

When he had stacked all his clothes on the bedroom chair and started, naked, toward the bed, his whole visible body was extinguished; he was nothing beside her but breath and weight.

. . .

Teddy was going to New York to see the editor of the photograph book. He was a paid advisor now.

"Good," Jessie said matter-of-factly, remembering the skinny young woman in her careful casual clothes and turning away from her dazzled gaze. Out of those dress-for-success "separates," she would look like a tough sinewy squab. I am harder than I thought, Jessie whispered to herself, standing stiffly in the hall looking into the living room. "We could use a little extra bread, we have to replace this couch."

Teddy stared. "Replace the couch. Why?"

"It's had nine lives at least, come on, in all these years. I believe there have been more babies conceived on it—you remember who used to sleep on it. I remember Steve what's-his-name hiding under it once when it looked like somebody was about to shoot in the window. I don't think you were here but I told you. And that guy from CBS spilled his spaghetti right off the plate—he was here for some demonstration or other, remember he had an incredible mustache?—and it tipped and just sli-i-id right down between the cushions? Come on, Teddy."

"Come *on?* We ought to bronze it if it's seen all that. You want to get some fashionable hunk of Danish wood in here? Or one of those white damn things like Andréa's that you'd be afraid to sit on?"

"Why don't you take a picture of it and send it to your editor up there for her book? The famous T. and J. Carll couch, Movement artifact warmed in its day by the nether end of every significant civil rights figure."

"What's the matter with it?"

Jessie looked around the living room hopelessly. "Exhaustion. Incapacity to keep up with the modern world. Teddy, let's not haggle, all right?"

"Are you going to get like your mother and replace everything comfortable with something glossy and new? We used to make love on this couch once in a while, you know."

She smiled. "I do know. But you won't soften me up by making me nostalgic, you'll only make me angry." And would he go to lunch with the editor and then come back to her office to caption the pictures he'd chosen? Or did he have other ideas for lunch hour? He struck her as vulnerable in ways he hadn't even begun to acknowledge. Or ways he had, which she would be left alone to discover. She had always trusted him but distance and the wantonness of possibility drifted between them now like a fog. They stood together in the hall and studied the blue green striped couch, which was as frayed and mottled and full of petty woundings and healings as the skin of an aged barnyard animal.

· · ·

Time, Jessie saw, was easing the Birmingham cousins into a passably ordinary life. O'Neill was calmer in school; having yielded in Mourning Dove, he seemed to make no visible distinction between the black children and the white. What problems he had—angered, he threw blocks, hurled chalk at the other children or flung it at the ground as if it could penetrate the floorboards like straw in a tornado, and called nasty imaginative names, "Pig Winkle!" and "Nurd Ball!"—she suspected had been with him always.

The extra burr at the end of his taunts, the visible delight he took in mastery, she guessed was a combination of his father's nastiness and his own relief at being out from under it: from victim to victor through a lonely corridor.

Helen, though: Helen had closed around her wounds with some hasty unhealthy scarring. Surely her remoteness was not natural. She had worked hard on her room, silently, without consultation; had made it into a warm nest, lined with a softness Jessie was unaccustomed to in her house. They had let her buy wall-to-wall carpet, a lavender blue—"periwinkle," she called it and Jessie heard how O'Neill's "Pig Winkle!" echoed his sister; she was relieved to think they must have conversations out of her sight. Helen had had some of her old furniture shipped from Birmingham and she painted it white and methodically stenciled purple forget-me-nots in the corners. Then she had hung posters of unicorns and rainbows and loving couples in a perennial mist as if they stood locked under Niagara Falls.

"Whatever happened," Teddy asked Jessie, "to girls and horses? I mean D. H. Lawrence horses? What is all this lily white and gold unicorn fever?"

"Delicacy and independence," Jessie said. "Not masculine strength to seize them and overwhelm all their Victorian scruples." It was a holdover from the flower children, that was clear, all this greenpeace. Could a generation of rebels grow up on unicorn milk?

When Teddy was present, Jessie had a hard time not concentrating on his absences. When he made love to her she was distracted by her memory of his back, retreating; of Teddy sarcastic, of Teddy at the Ramada Inn deflowering that political virgin. She was learning a separation of body and feeling that she knew was as common as contentment, more common, maybe. For now she gave good weight, in a manner of speaking, for every touch he gave or asked for. But she was wary and felt herself in a state of suspension.

.   .   .

The editor, returned to New York, wanted Teddy's own book. She called; she wrote him a letter that made Jessie blush, though he showed it to her proudly. Its praise of Teddy and his talent felt like a blurb inside a dust jacket. Brilliant, uncompromising, lucid. Apparently she dealt with fiction.

"One picture is worth a thousand words," Jessie said. "Why don't you stop while you're ahead."

"There's a lot of excitement over the photograph book. A lot. She thinks the time has come around for a reassessment of the Movement."

"How can you reassess what you're still in the middle of? I think this is the worst possible way for you to spend your time, if you want to know."

"Jessie, you have too damn many opinions, you know that?"

She had been clipping and planting on the front lawn, getting ready for spring, which was rumored to be approaching. Teddy was standing above her; it felt like an angle in a movie: intimidation. Long shadow cast across heroine. She had the clippers. She refused to be intimidated. She chopped and listened to the dry clap of the blades. She chopped again.

"Jessie," he repeated. "Do you have the slightest idea how much pleasure you take in throwing ice-cold water on me? No, wait." He put his hand up to keep her from objecting. "Do you-all know that most problems are made by two people, not one?"

"Please don't 'you-all' me. That might be thrilling to a New York girl but I wasn't either of those things any more last time I looked. And no, I'm not aware of taking much pleasure in this cold water throwing you accuse me of."

"I have been trying, I really have, to understand what it is you want of me so I can *do* it and be done with it," Teddy said. "But you are so damn cold. Do you know how fucking cold you are to me?"

She put down her clippers and stood up very slowly to keep from getting dizzy. They were knee to knee. "I think you're telling me that it's been my fault, the rotten times you've had the last ten years or so. Is that what I'm hearing?"

He frowned at her and something in the assured set of his face made it clear that he'd been through this analysis once already with someone who agreed.

"What you're hearing is every time I try to do something—Mourning Dove is an example—I've got to drag along the weight of your skepticism."

"I didn't have anything to do with Mourning Dove, Teddy. You didn't need my approval. What was wrong out there was that you, who are offering yourself up now to do a formal analysis to be printed between two hard covers—you made an incorrect reading of the possibilities of the times, based on your own desperation. I'm sorry that Jug used you, I really am. That was despicable of him although it wasn't any particular surprise. But you're angry with the messenger who brought you the bad news first."

"And you were delighted."

She bowed again to her clippers, which were so heavy they tipped her hands forward like a divining rod. "I was not delighted, that's ridiculous. Look, I know that every time anyone tries a passion and exhausts it—I mean, the whole country even, fashion, politics, anything—that's a passion they can't experience again for a long time. So you can end up worse off than before. I know that, Teddy—after Mourning Dove, there's one possibility fewer in the world. But I just can't believe that looking back to the old victories is going to help you get on with your life. You're not a historian, I swear you're a goddamn necrophiliac."

"Not everyone," he said meaningfully, "is as destructive as you are."

She snapped the clippers at a sagging forsythia branch. "Are you trying to scare me?" The branch fell in slow motion through the bush and snagged on the lowest branch. "Because I will not give up my right to my opinion just to keep you agreeable." Or faithful, she wanted to add, but could not.

"You've got the clippers, lady. I can see you just turning to me and making an end to my unruliness."

"You flatter yourself, Teddy. I wish you were a little more unruly. I swear it's your ruliness we've been suffering all this time." She hadn't wanted to be right about Mourning Dove, she thought. How good to have been wrong. But he had as many ulterior motives as his friend Jug: he had wanted to fail there. Andréa was right. He had chosen an impossible campaign so that he could hang his flag of surrender. She almost looked up to tell him that but she knew with a lurch that his desire to talk about this was like those passions she had talked about: once it failed, he would be angrier than ever. And then it would all split open.

· · ·

The worst of it: that she couldn't tell him what this felt like. She imagined that Helen and O'Neill must have wanted to talk to their parents, quietly, perhaps in their beds, about the pain of losing them. It was a cruel paradox: Teddy was the only one who understood her and knew what she needed. If this passed, she would confide in him later how lonely she had been not knowing it would pass. She could feel her jawline tightening, caught herself holding her breath in the car coming home from school.

So it continued. He was never home, beyond pretense or apology. He would finish his travels for work and drive to the airport without even coming back to unload his laundry, let alone see his children. He was off to New York or goaded by his editor, to some university somewhere to consult with an academic historian—what disdain he had had, once, for desk-chair analysts!—about the death of the New Left or the limitless powers of government in private affairs. When had he decided so unequivocally that the Movement had been a failure, and that its demise had been entirely unnatural? She tried to engage him in conversation but he was listening to distant voices, the ones that supported his paranoia, and anyway, he never stopped moving long enough to hear the end of a question.

Jessie was bewildered: could this be *all*? Could this marriage wink out like a cinder in cool air, starved for the oxygen of Teddy's attention? Implausible. Or was it, as he alleged, her approval that had atrophied? Would there be no confrontation? Or would they feel no heat if they did collide?

Her married life, she thought, felt like the last paragraph in one of those great Victorian novels. Every breath of Dorothea Brooke is duly noted, every stirring of hot feeling, tepid regard, heart-stopping cold—she could hear the grass growing, that was her problem, Jessie would imagine the infinitesimal rasping sound of the green shaft lengthening and Dorothea, rapt on the lawn, attending—and the whole rest of her life was done in a single paragraph! Cheat! Snap of the fingers, so much for her. And him. And them. So much, then, for this love affair with Teddy Carll that had absorbed her for so long she was someone barely recognizable, a young girl, on the other side of the mountain of it. She was too logy with depression and boredom to be angry; if she wept her tears would be a dripping faucet, ignoble. All she wanted was to tell him how empty and unfamiliar it felt. But he wasn't there for her to tell it to.

I actually got bored in bed and went back to school. There's nothing interesting happening. Slogging through. I do not touch shoulders with anyone. In gym I stand to one side. I get into my gym shorts with my back turned.

There was an awful fight in school, everybody assumed it was Racial. But it was two colored boys, only one with a knife. The other one pushed him through a big window in the front hall. The hole in the glass was beautiful, I looked at it on the way out: like a sun with uneven rays all around. I don't know if they got hurt, or if they will have to pay for the window.

When it is warm and I have to wear short sleeves my arm will be healed. It will only have one little scar. I can barely remember doing it, that is why I'm glad I write things down. Andy and I haven't healed up either, you could say, and I don't think we ever will. We just have to stay far away from each other like on two sides of a wall, he is on their side and I am alone over here.

Yesterday on the school bus I forgot to get off. I didn't remember where I was, what city or where I live, and so much of it looks the same anyway: low houses and azalea bushes and clusters of stores like little crowds of people. I got off at the end and walked around a little and then I remembered. It comes from not concentrating. I feel like I have had a knock on the head, hard.

*Interesting: Teddy has been home less and less. That's better for me.
I can pretend I am keeping him away with my death ray vision that
sends secret thoughts through the air! (O'Neill says he has that and he's
serious.) I think he is sort of coming apart. I can see Jessie frazzling up—
she gets all grim and uses short snappish words for everything, and she
throws Mickey Mouse off the furniture where he has positively lived for
years, and worst for us she is making lousy meals. One morning she was
in the kitchen I was sure she had been crying. Why couldn't I be given
to a peaceful household? Are there any? I don't suppose Teddy has a
Donna Durgin (although who knows?) but he sure isn't paying any
attention to this wife. Andy and I are barely talking, so I can't ask him.
I catch him watching me but then he looks away. I said something to
Lydia about it and she just stared at me like it was the most shocking
news. Maybe if these two split up, O'Neill and I will get sent back to
Alabama (if anybody wants us). I just learned this word in school, "Extra
dited" (or maybe it's all one word) that means when a criminal gets sent
back where he came from. Well, I am ready. This is beginning to worry
me a little, where we would go.*

*I wish I could go to sleep and wake up when I am an adult. 17 or
18, on my own. If I could graduate (just dreaming) with my class at
Sunnifield Academy, standing on the front step for our picture, holding
each other around the waist. The girls always wore a flower in their hair
for the picture. Then we would break and separate to mingle with everyone's parents and just like Cinderella, after one cup of Jenny Eiller's
mother's good mystery punch I would be gone!!! They would find my cap
and gown in a heap on the bottom step and never solve the mystery of
where I came from or went. I saw on t.v. this year's Miss Jr. America
went to Sunnifield three years ago but odd I didn't even know her name.
Even if she was before my time, you'd think she'd of been famous for
something while she was there. A "slow bloomer."*

Jessie, at work, was introducing the father of a new child to the school.
He was a "single father," he told her, who had custody. His son Adam
clung terrified to the pocket of his suit jacket. Jessie walked beside the man,
who could have been her age or a few years younger. He stood close to her
radiating, like a stove that could warm a room, a firm inquiring sexual
presence. He was, she supposed wearily, what the school had in store for
itself, a sign of the solidity of its success. He was tall and regular featured,
husky, square faced, in an impeccably white collar (he knew how to do his

own shirts, apparently) and a three-piece gray suit, shoes shinier than the newly waxed hall floor. He wanted Adam to be centered, and to relate well; he would appreciate input as well as feedback; that was where he was coming from. The Eastern, the Freudian and the electronic mingled in his imagery with all the wantonness of the reds and blues and yellows of the littlest children's finger-paints. He was what she too had in store, undoubtedly, if it came to that: an import—he was from Rhode Island and had been transferred to Jackson apparently without qualm or curiosity. Its history and mythology did not necessarily accompany it into its long neutral future. She sighed. Could she possibly prefer such innocence to Teddy's obsessions? Would she have to educate a potentially interesting man in the old urgencies while she learned the new ones (kilobauds, chips, whatever computers forced into the bloodstream)? Somewhere there must be other scarred old veterans—a union organizer? An antiwar campaigner? Anybody with scars; she would have to hope he was not a pile of smothered ashes. The amazing thing was to think about Teddy and his editor—she did have a name, it was Lynet Figulietti and Teddy wanted her name used—and to wonder where he got the patience. Well, he had always loved to teach and preach to anyone who needed him, and no one else seemed to these days, unless you counted children. The missionary position, Jessie thought bitterly and took the visiting father through the doors of the cafeteria where a sour tide of tomato soup broke over her and threatened to make her sick. The biliousness of withdrawal pangs. She hadn't felt that way since the last time she was pregnant.

.   .   .

Every now and then Teddy seemed to touch down among them, at his own good time. He had one hell of a nerve, she thought, like a teenager who moves out and comes home for a solid meal when he gets hungry. But she was not about to tell him to stay away.

On the afternoon of a Saturday warmer than spring, Jessie saw him pitching a ball to O'Neill across the backyard, the way he had with Andy in another life. Teddy bent his front knee, held his long back leg extended, leaning into his pitch. Ah, lovely. If she hadn't known him she'd want to know who he was. They were using a whiffle ball and as it flew toward O'Neill's bat, which he twitched nervously off his shoulder, she heard the odd whistle the wind sent through the ball's slit spaces. It sounded like a knife, a sword slicing air.

O'Neill pushed himself off balance missing the ball; Teddy shouted

correction. But his attention was cruel, Jessie thought, knowing how suddenly he might withdraw it, like a passing shower that teases a parched
garden. Let the flowers, the carrots strengthen their roots without water if
they are to live that way. Let them adapt to drought. It might be another
month before Teddy noticed O'Neill was there.

.   .   .

It was a good party: she had danced most of the night. These days she
was relieved when she didn't have to talk with anyone earnestly about her
"situation." Most of the time she came home from such discussions thinking
of herself as a candidate for "Queen for a Day": get this poor woman out
of the kitchen, help her dry her tears and have a good time!

Now, exhausted, she sat on the arm of the couch and listened. Andréa
sat straight up in her chair, her legs crossed like a secretary with a steno
notebook on her knee. It was clear halfway across the room that she was
defending something.

Teddy slumped indifferently in his corner of the Turners' couch. He
was surrounded by salmon-colored flamingoes in a dark forest; the throw
pillows on the couch were, absurdly, satin quilted into the shapes of pastel
birds. "But he was, he really was just another 'boy,' only he had whiter
teeth and a nice straight back and people followed him because he looked
like their idea of an African prince—"

"Who?" Jessie asked.

"Stokely," Andréa answered in her satiric voice. "Teddy's expounding
his newly enlarged theory of white control of the black psyche. It's the one
that begins with the FBI in our alphabet soup and all of us spooning it up
hungrily, and swallowing down every little command without knowing it
because, see, they're clever and they've shredded them all up so they look
nutritious, like carrots and celery—"

"Come on, Andréa," Teddy said, unaroused.

"Well, that's what you're saying, isn't it? The turn toward black power
did not originate with black people, it was mandated entirely from some
office in D.C. and then sort of slipped in—"

"To tap a lot of feeling that was already real and valid. Don't make me
into a moron because you don't like the implications of what I'm saying.
I'm only talking about how Stokely, or that black power march Meredith
did, the one down the highway to the capitol, remember? I'm saying that
if it hadn't suited LBJ on down, if they hadn't said 'enough is enough, let's
put an end to some of these changes and start turning the white friends

around before things go too far,' then none of that slogan-shouting and fist-raising would have turned into headlines. Come on, you agree with me, Andréa, why are you giving me a hard time?"

Andréa sighed, exasperated, and took a long drink of rosé from a glass that was thin as cellophane.

Joe Turner, an amiable man who puffed on his pipe as regularly as he breathed, bent toward Teddy and spoke in a voice that sounded confidential. "Something about that tone, Ted. Something cavalier about it, you know? Dismissive?" He waved his hand before him. "You don't think we had sufficient feeling to be able to come up with the next stage to—"

"Joe. Joe." Teddy roused himself and concentrated hard in his direction: Joe was a dark-skinned man with a tiny head on a large sloping body; he had the look of a Buddha doll arranged from pieces built to different scales. "Feeling, yes. Power, no. But look, you're in good company when it comes to powerlessness. Who did you ever respect who got on the controlling side of anything much?" Teddy opened his eyes wide in Jessie's direction as though he expected her to second the motion.

"You're saying black leaders, not to mention the grass roots, originated nothing, no useful emotions, no strategy, no weapons?" Joe asked.

"No comfort either." This was Andréa, shaking her glass in a slow angry circle. "So that's why they showed you out to the gate of Eden and gave you a push, huh, Teddy? In fact, they let you stay there just so long and then they heard their master's voice again—had nothing to do with all those reasons you understand so well. You always were a protector of the white ego, Teddy. Something really gratifies you about knowing where the power is even if you don't approve of it."

Teddy drained his glass, then raised it to her. "More in sorrow, friend. I know you think I'm some kind of a crypto-bigot, you always have. White folks have got to watch their tongue with you."

Joe leapt in to reassure him that they were only having a difference in interpretation. He tried to surround them with pipe smoke.

"Bullshit," Andréa said and drained her glass. "This is no difference in interpretation, Teddy always plays both sides of the street. It's an interesting habit, he manages to score baskets for both teams and foul players every time he turns around."

"Andréa," Jessie began, without the slightest idea of what she wanted to say.

"Now listen, child. You're living with a dangerous man here, he is so morbidly confused—I really mean this—he is so turned around, he doesn't know which end of him the words are coming out of."

"Oh Christ," Teddy said and sighed all the way from his feet.

"No, listen, friend. You know I'm as cynical as the next one about who controls what when we hear it on the tube, 'an authorized source' this and 'the people' that. But there are certain facts and certain events that you are not going to assault and one of them happens to be that folks like you, with your insidious wise-ass know-it-all 'sense of history' and all that nonsensical poop, brought down on your own heads one hell of a lot of what happened to you back then. Teddy, you were a brave man but it was not your Movement. You did plenty right and we did plenty wrong but in the final analysis you were there to do what we all thought needed doing, and when folks like Stokely started pushing back—"

"When folks like Stokely started pushing back, that was the end of the forward movement, and the beginning of—"

"Of something you can't deal with, Teddy love. Of a long quiet time of unflamboyant action and behind-the-scenes tinkering, and that isn't visible enough for you. Aren't you the one who always says he doesn't want a job with an in-out box?" She winked at Jessie.

Jessie, divided, did not smile back. Neither did she look at Teddy, who had gone to pour himself another drink.

"You're married to the only macho man," Andréa said, her eyes still vital with points of angry light. "Can't let us have a single little thing of our own." She looked to Joe for agreement but he was lost in contemplation, his head encircled by smoke like a mountain peak in cumulus.

.   .   .

He came home feisty, not quite drunk, full of sex and resolution. Jessie moved away from him when he sat down close to her at the kitchen table. She was remembering a conversation he'd had early in the evening with Tommy and Fred Dandridge, the lawyer who had hot-footed it back to Jackson for his turkey on Thanksgiving. Teddy was trying yet another bit of political paranoia on them—what was it? What? She strained backwards. Oh, it was the Guyana nonsense: how the American government had paid Jimmy Jones's way to take his Commies and black visionary fools out of the country, kill them in the jungle, try to do it quietly. "But then that congressman . . . the whole thing hit the fan." She had seen Dandridge and Tommy exchange something even less than a glance, Tommy sending up a signal like a spot of light, Dandridge meeting it, acknowledging it. Amusement flickered an instant above Teddy's head. She wasn't alone in thinking him half-crazy. "You make it sound like Snow White," Tommy had said.

"Kill these people and bring me their hearts." Fred Dandridge had laughed and slapped his thigh in its pinstriped pants.

"You've never elaborated your paranoid theories so vigorously around here, Teddy. What's going on?"

"There's been enough evidence by now to put it together that way."

"But even if what you've always said is true, if all the big events, the assassinations and riots, are manipulated—I have no trouble believing that— why do you take away from people their natural reactions? Don't you think all the strife and struggle you went through were real and justifiable?" She sat high on the kitchen stool with her hands clasped around her knee, flushed with self-consciousness. She felt as if she were talking to a man she had just met. "What I find awful is that you're so arrogantly sure of this incredible simplification. Turning into a master of self-justification, somehow, fitting all your own disappointments into this theory—"

He turned from the refrigerator. "Is this leftover pizza in here?"

"I wouldn't expect you to know since you're never here any more. Yes, it's pizza. Pepperoni."

He took the box out carefully. "What do my own 'disappointments' have to do with this so-called theory? Which is not theory, by the way, but documented fact."

She stared at the cold pizza as he turned the box top back. Jesus, it looked like coagulated blood on yellowed flesh. "Well, why do you feel you have to deprive people of their natural reactions? You were there, you know how complicated the whole love-hate, jealousy-contempt, need-resentment business is." She closed her eyes. "Things had to change."

"Dialectical thinking is what undid your father." Teddy, with a hard smile, slid all the slices of pizza onto the tray and pushed them into the toaster oven. He closed it as emphatically as a slammed door.

"My father's personality undid him. No one is without needs. Let's not get into that. You insulted a lot of your good friends, calling Stokely a 'boy'!"

"The Central Committee undid your father. Don't overpersonalize. And Stokely *was* a boy, only he didn't know it. Victims rarely do." He was arranging a napkin and a plate for himself. "You think Martin knew who set him up to be shot? Are you one of those people who thinks James Earl Ray had a pathetic childhood?"

Jessie came down off the stool with a stomach-tensing jolt. " 'Overpersonalize?' What the hell kind of word is that? You don't talk that kind of language." Some wives, she thought, could smell another woman on their husband's body, she could hear her words; it was embarrassing. "You are

really at the edge and you're the one who doesn't know it. Next thing you
know you'll be ranting on a street corner next to Skelly Washington. Skelly
shilling for Jesus, and you for J. Edgar Hoover. And my father in the
background singing the Internationale." She covered her face. "Oh Teddy."

"I can't stand people," Teddy said, crouching to peek through the murky
window at his pizza, "who love to make politics into pop psychology so all
the forces are more their size. You-all want to make every action into a
decision you take over the breakfast table or in front of the mirror, go right
ahead. It's all metabolic, right? How did you sleep, what did you eat the
night before, how are your bowels, did he tell you he loved you or did he
only fuck you till your ears rang?"

"You are trying to be a bastard—"

"And what's your diagnosis of your husband? Did I get involved in this
mess so I could get some 'Nigra' pussy? Or was I looking for my father?
Or working out childhood frustrations—"

"You were more likely sticking it to your beloved mother, if you want
to know. I don't think compassion entered in, and I don't think justice
entered in. I think it was more like anger and rebelliousness—"

He was staring at her with wide unsteady eyes.

"Oh, I don't even mean that. You're the one who wants a simple one-
word explanation, don't make me do it. It was a dozen things and they came
together like a—point of intersection on a graph. A confluence of rivers."
She flung her hands around in the air, vaguely, trying to make peace, to
muddy up the flow of the conversation, soften its rush to destruction.

"Oh, a confluence of rivers. That explains it. If that's what you've
understood of me all these years," Teddy began.

"If I'm one of your 'pop psychology' specimens, I can say the same thing
to you, you know. Your pizza's burning."

He turned to push the button on the toaster and to retrieve the charred
pieces, on which the sausage was strewn like black checkers on a reddish
ground. While his back was turned, Jessie, too overcome for speech, slipped
out of the room and then out the front door, looking for air that didn't hurt
to breathe. She sat on the step of the front porch and thought about how,
once, when her women's group met, in that time of hope, one of her friends,
Natalie, had said that her husband had been so busy making money when
they met that she hadn't noticed that his inner life cast no shadows; perhaps,
in fact, he had none at all. She had been so distracted by love that she had
never missed it. (By love, they all assumed she meant sex, but she had
meant more than that: there were a lot of charms that could obliterate
inconvenient fact.) The inner life, though: it was suddenly something solid,

an organ of the body, intimately sunk, deep red with rich circulating blood, whose necessity for survival had not been proven, and here was a man born without one like someone without an appendix, possessor of a single kidney. They had discussed the symptoms at the time, commiserated with Natalie about her poor unsuspecting husband's defect, and she had thanked them for their sympathy. (And later it was a trial to meet some of the women from the group, how sad this was, because they were embarrassed at how little in their lives they had been able to change for all their insights. Natalie was making do with a new job and a new hairdo, "a whole new image." Those who had succeeded in doing what they knew they needed to were long gone, retrenched out of sight.)

Well, and now here was Teddy, her hero with his one outdated song to sing. As if on an x-ray, she could see exactly where the empty space gaped. It wasn't kindness that he lacked or passion or, God help him, earnestness, it was the capacity for honest reflection. An unexamined love is not worth loving, she thought—had she read that or did it only sound like something you might encounter on a plaque somewhere?—but Teddy had found it sufficient that his love for the world that needed him be demanding, that he keep moving in its service, too tired for reflection. Her grandmother had been like that: too busy to sit down, too purposeful ever to give a thought to pain, let alone to dying. And when her first illness befell her, at eighty-two, she was aghast and unforgiving; never having seen so much as a shadow, a smudge of weakness or a slackening of strength, she fell into a darkness so profound she had no desire to survive it.

·　·　·

The day they called Jessie from school to pick up Helen—she was comatose in the nurse's stuffy cubicle, her shoes off, a pathetic fuzzy green blanket pulled over her where she shivered on the cot—Jessie understood that things had been more complicated than she had realized.

"This is the orphan?" the nurse whispered to her when she arrived, implying that Helen was famous. She was holding a sheaf of papers to cover her mouth. She seemed to be granting Jessie exemption or at worst forgiveness for whatever might have befallen this distant charge of hers. The nurse was a heavy sweating pink woman with gull gray hair curled so tightly Jessie winced when she saw it; it looked as if it hurt. "Yes," Jessie admitted, "Helen was an orphan, I suppose, but she's our child now." It was a strangely melodramatic category to put her in but Jessie had the distinct feeling that Helen had attracted her attention and seduced her interest in such domestic details because she was one of the few "decent" white girls at the school, where irregular arrangements were otherwise rampant. What did being an orphan have to do with it? Jessie's knees nearly buckled when she heard how Helen had been flat out, her lips tinged blue purple. She was fine now, sitting up, pale and silent. What had happened?

The nurse dismissed food poisoning (hence the school's responsibility). "Because it was too soon, I believe she barely begun to eat when she was struck down." Did she get this way with her period, she asked. Jessie was sure she would have noticed. She had no fever, no signs of any kind upon her. "Some kind of hysteria then," the nurse suggested firmly, implying that such fits were common. Perhaps they were; the only adolescent Jessie knew well was Andy, who did not seem subject to anything remotely like hysterical suggestion. The nurse had shaken her wattles for emphasis; she knew what she was talking about. "At least it didn't spread, let's be grateful for small favors. More often than not, one of them goes off all the rest will follow, nine-pins, just bing-bang-bang." She made scallops in the air that must have represented falling bodies.

Certainly Helen was not about to confide her secret. She walked out to the car staring straight ahead, picking up her feet and putting them down gingerly as if they were on a narrow promontory over water.

Hopelessly Jessie pressed her for an explanation every way she could. Helen said she wanted to go to sleep. After a while she came out and told Jessie she was going to take a shower. Jessie, encouraged, said "Fine." But after half an hour, she went to rattle the door. Of course, of course, there came no answer. Leaning against the closed door in the dark hall of her own house with a hysterical girl on the other side, Teddy nowhere she could ever guess, no one telling her anything she needed to hear to make sense of any of it though she was strong, she thought, and poised to hear it—that was the first time she felt real anger massing in her chest, light, not heavy, buoyant because it was not turned against herself. She felt as if she could fly right off the ground with it, this agitation like a two-penny motor. But where would she go with it?

Later she found Helen on the floor in the laundry room, leaning one shoulder against the wall like a propped-up drunk. The girl had washed her quilt and sheets—whyever in the world?—and then given up on them half-way to the dryer; they sagged and stretched and puddled on the floor in front of the machines. Lifting dead weight Jessie felt her back muscles twang a warning. The girl was light but not easy to get on her feet. "For God's sake, Helen, have a little *pity*. Help me, will you please." She was struggling to get her shoulder under Helen's.

Helen looked at her surprised. Her face was mild and empty as a sweet child's awakened from a nap. Jessie pleaded with her, laying her down on her striped bed, to talk a little, to make herself feel better by unbottling her pain. She studied Helen's eyes: maybe it was drugs. That hadn't occurred to her, nor—strange—had the nurse mentioned it. The nurse undoubtedly didn't want to admit that white girls of a certain class had such problems. Amazing, considering what she must see. But there was something else in Helen's eyes as her head rolled back on the pillow. They were welled up and hurt-looking, they had a startled defensive light-sensitive squint, as if she were about to duck away from a blow. Her secrets were more complicated than a handful of pills.

A minister if not a psychiatrist? A few days in the hospital under surveillance? Antidepressant drugs? Jessie lay down on her own bed and, knowing she should stay on duty outside Helen's door but terrified to be awake, slept.

This is how it all started.
Now I am reaping what they sowed.
A boy in my school asked me out!
He is almost white, with just sunburned looking skin and green eyes, and so I suppose he thought he had a chance. He just came up to me in caf. where I was sitting alone doing nothing, only blowing on my soup, and he said "Can I sit down?" Not disrespectful or anything but still. And then he goes, will you go out with me? I don't remember exactly what the words were, I was so shocked. I just stared. I couldn't do another thing. I would have moved away but I had all my books and my soup and dessert weren't even on the tray, I don't like to eat on the tray, it feels tacky. So I played just like an animal, stayed totally still and stared at him without even one single word or so much as a blink. I remember that snake I once saw that Judy Carmichael's cat scared—it just tried to convince me and the cat that it was no snake at all, we were only dreaming snake. Finally when he must have thought he had a deaf-mute on his hands the "brazen" boy shrugged and left. I couldn't eat after that and sat wishing I had screamed at him or hit him with my tray or something to go on record against such things. (Another word I just learned, we are still studying prisons and The Legal System: deterrence.) Then I looked around to see if the others were watching anyway and they weren't. In a minute or two, the more I thought about it and saw my Daddy's face turning bright red like he was having a fit everything turned black and white and spotted and spun around like when you stand up

too fast. I was afraid I was going to faint. I put my head between my knees and then that was ALL.

Jessie came and got me. She had to. I am so tired now I can't even lift my chest to breathe. My back will not support me. When I close my eyes that boy with the green eyes who is definitely brown is taking up the whole view and I don't want to remember his face. My vision blurs like it did after Daddy paraded his naked self on the front porch. It is the way I feel only when I don't want to go on any longer. If he went out with me and then would stand against me like Andy and Tim Knight and all boys and men. It is a feeling like putting your head in Clorox or something and trying to look around: hot and blind and like my face will flake right off.

I tried to call Lingham but couldn't get the numbers straight. I will join with her now, I made a mistake and will fix it, if it is not too late. I will prick my finger for a promise or anything they ask. I asked Jessie if I could take a shower, wash my hair. She was glad for me, thought it was good. It is to get the dirt off, everything on me feels dirtied by this whole thing. Why would he think I would go with him, do I give off that feeling? Mom said women who "get it" are asking for "it" every minute under the surface and men know the signs.

I washed my quilt and sheets but I couldn't get them out to dry, too heavy. I was in the corner of the laundry room sitting on the floor which was cool. Arms and legs hurt from scrubbing. How do I get inside, that is still clean till they get in there. I wish our religion had nuns, you could stay closed up and whole forever. Could keep your private places like a little child, round and hard and locked. You could be married only to Jesus Who would love you at a distance.

When the washing machine shook and hurried in SPIN *and then "Ahhhh" like a deep breathing-out and stopped, it reminded me of Teddy and Jessie that time they were so-called making "love."*

I wish something really hurt, that gives me something to think about or not think about and feels better all around. I am thinking what it can be. Not dangerous, just a sharp clear pain like lemon in a cut. Funny how instead of feeling ripped open by pain I feel sealed up in it like one of those plastic bags they close with heat. And nothing could get in to me.

Lingham came to visit. I opened my eyes and there she was. We sat and talked about nothing, we don't really have a lot to say. She told me about that Tabb beast. Yukk. She says he is either going in the army or going to be sanctified for Jesus, depending. She says he is more of a gentleman than he looks. (I think she likes him although she says boys are against her principals.)

So I thought all right, and I told her about this boy that asked me out and (I was hoping this) she said she would get him. I wasn't sure which it was and she said any nigger *with green eyes in the school she would sniff out and do something maybe to his locker, or worse. As a warning, just like I wanted to. Worse to come if he approaches any other white girl ever again. I am actually thinking how he got the light eyes and skin, either by a white man on a black woman OR vice versa, which is all sickening. I see them all in the days of slave quarters in the master's big bed. Making mongrels. (Or not the master's bed, his wife would be there: in the little shack somewhere or out in the woods after dark.)*

Jessie said I slept 15 hours after Lingham left. Woke sticky and stinking hot and took a long shower, 2nd of the day. Almost fainted in heat. My arm that I cut has only one mark under the water. Like a butterfly in haze. Look what I said: "in heat." That isn't what I meant! The shower is the only place I feel comfortable, I don't know why. The water makes me blind coming down, my every part (of my body) getting hit hard and sort of soothed both somehow at the same time. The shower is better than pain for making me feel empty of my terrible thoughts. I cannot do anything to myself but if I did it would be in there, under the flowing silvergray water. It would be peaceful, just slipping down as if I was only more of it myself, all the wet falling, tears, rain, blood. The way Mom and Daddy went to rest: tears, rain, blood, the way to heaven shiny and slickened.

Jessie wants to know can I go to school. Otherwise I will have to be shut up somewhere (she doesn't say it that way but must mean that. The loony bin). What to do with me? I am a Strategic Problem, and I have been ever since we showed up here. She looks awful. I almost pity her: no husband and now me for good measure. She is definitely be-draggled.

I said, if you want to know what to do with me, "Send me away!" "Please," I said, "send me somewhere to a school I can live with, that is all I need." She said that was a long discussion for when I get well. I said I won't get well *here, I said I would even show her my diary for proof. No, that is an invasion of strictest privacy, she said. "I don't doubt you so I don't need proof. You can keep your secret diary for yourself."*

Helen took the threat to heart: the next day she was back in school, silent, the hollows under her eyes shadowed a bruisy blue. Jessie caught her with quivering lips at the dinner table. She seemed to be a perfect candidate for anorexia but she picked at her food as she always had, dutifully, with resentment. Every one of them walked as if in pain, Jessie and Andy and she. The younger children went about their business less depressed than bewildered. The house was silent as if an invalid, or Sleeping Beauty with a good many years to go, were shut in at the top of the split-level stairs, in any one of the bedrooms. The younger children met and passed in the wide hall as if chastened. It might have been the greater physical distance between them that had slightly altered their relations; or it was a waiting similar to Jessie's, a suspension of ordinary watchfulness while things between Teddy and Jessie floated unsettled. She only knew that she felt like a visitor in someone else's house, a place familiar from long frequent visits but never comfortable enough to be confused with her own. Teddy's curse seemed to lie over them like a tangled net, rising invisible around their ankles and knees as they moved from room to room.

. . .

Teddy had left for work the morning after their encounter over the pizza and he had not come back. Jessie had no way of following him around town but assorted rumors floated back to her. So far, to her knowledge, he had stayed with Fred Dandridge, with several black ex-Movement friends, Kenny who sold real estate and lived in a far grander house than theirs, an institutional-looking building with a circular driveway out near Hanging Moss Road, and George who worked as a hospital lab technician and lived, sweltering and freezing according to season, in a tiny frame house on brick stilts. She tried not to imagine what he must be telling them, dragging no defeat but some sordid self-serving justification through every neighborhood in town. His paycheck showed up in their bank account reliably.

"Don't worry," Andréa assured her. "He shows up over here he's not getting past the welcome mat. That thing is selective about who it lets in the door." She was unequivocal. "You know I don't think shrinks are our saviors but, I say, if he doesn't get himself some help, honey, he's going to wake up a bin case one of these mornings. He and Helen, both of them, are in need of a lot of repair.

"Here it is again, friend," she said to Jessie. "He can't be ordinary. The boy is just not built to be another kid on the block. I'm surprised he wasn't a juvenile delinquent. But see, he had niggerloving, that was good enough to do his revenge number for him."

But that wasn't what Jessie needed to hear: everyone's reductions were an insult to the truth, everyone went round in a circle saying what was most consoling, whatever justified one's feelings. To have no doctrine was to have no protection.

.   .   .

On Valentine's Day Lydia finished a giant card for Teddy that she had labored over for weeks, an intricate rice-paper heart crammed with line drawings of every kind of face she could think of, every color, every race, rimmed with gold paint: a loving, teeming crowd. "Do you want us all to sign it?" Jessie asked her, too casually. In the middle under lace, in something like Gothic lettering, was written *Daddy, I love you!*

"No," Lydia said, whisking it angrily off the table, "it's not yours. Get your own if you want one."

"Do you know where you're going to send it?" Jessie asked her gently. "In case he doesn't happen to come home in time?"

Lydia looked hard at her. "I thought you knew where he's staying. O'Neill said you knew."

She sighed. "I guess O'Neill doesn't want to think he's mislaid another father."

Lydia, ripping the valentine slowly in half with excruciating control, and turning it to continue in quarters and then eighths, said, "How could you not know where he *is?* He's your husband, isn't he?"

When Jessie began to laugh, Lydia crumpled into tears and threw the scraps of paper at her, aiming for her face. They fell slowly down like many-colored flower petals. "That's the dumbest thing I ever heard. You can't just lose a father and you know it."

Jessie didn't insist. Her bitterness sounded indistinguishable from cruelty and that was the last thing the children needed from her.

.   .   .

Late that night Lydia met her father at the front door. She was returning to her room from the bathroom; it was not clear where he was returning from. Jessie was grading papers at the dining room table when she heard the key turn in the lock, and then Lydia appeared out of nowhere to stand staring as the door swung open. (Perhaps she slept badly every night, Jessie thought sadly, like the parents of teenagers waiting to hear the front door slam.) Teddy, his features softened as if someone had gone at them with a soap eraser, looked into his daughter's face and then, over her head, saw Jessie watching them. At first he looked perplexed, his brow drawn tight like a slow student who thinks he has seen a problem somewhere before but isn't sure how to attack it. Then, when Lydia threw herself at his waist, half-pummelling and half-embracing him, saying nothing but "Daddy, Daddy!" he sent Jessie a look of such fierce pain, of such helplessness, that she wanted to shout "Look out, Teddy!" fully believing he was about to be hit from behind. "You don't know what you're doing!" she wanted to say, but said nothing: the grief in his eyes protested that he was being taken from them by a force he could not control. But perhaps he did know: there was murder and there was suicide and why would he not know if he was perpetrator or victim? He said nothing to Jessie but picked up Lydia, who clung to him like a monkey, her knees out sharply to the sides, her arms around his neck, and took her up the few steps toward her room.

To her surprise, he came back down again and stood before the dining room table which was strewn with her third graders' homework, construction paper covers on their homemade books: MY RABBITT and HOW I RODE MY BYCICLE. When she said to his silence, "You're playing with me, Teddy," he smiled brightly but otherwise the prisoner, she thought bitterly, stood before the jury without expression. She couldn't say that for fear he'd laugh and the air would clear, though nothing would be resolved. "Teddy, why? What's making it all come apart right now? Why can't you talk to me about it?"

He seemed to be analyzing her face, studying it for subtleties of expression she knew it did not contain. "Listen, there's only so much inarticulateness I can deal with. I've got this girl who skulks around the house communicating with no one, least of all me. Now I've got you coming and going." He swayed slightly before her. "Well, add your little book to the pile, then. Write me a letter. Go to the typewriter and send me an explanation of this silence of yours. After all these years of talk, and all the back talk, just give me a hint about why you want to fall apart all by yourself, okay? With no love and comfort from me." She struggled against tears; her throat burned.

"I don't have anything to say." He stood and delivered it with his hands empty at his sides. "I can't forgive self-pity in anyone. In myself it smells like vomit and it's in my nostrils, I can't get free of it, all right? Does it make you feel better to hear that?"

"Why, though? I don't understand what's happened to bring about all this grandiloquent disgust all of a sudden! Teddy."

"I can't talk about Mourning Dove with you. I can't talk about the Birmingham children with you, or where we've moved ourselves to, over here in supersuburbia, I can't talk about my future with you—"

"Teddy, I'm right here—"

"All I can say is there's a part of me—the least presentable part, maybe—that stamps its foot and demands a statement of allegiance, Jessie. We were here first—you and I. Doesn't that mean anything to you?"

She had no answer for him; she wasn't even sure she knew what he meant.

"You know what I think? You're not going to like this but I think maybe you've been the adventurer, not me, or the opportunist—whatever the right word is. You got what you could use of this whole experience—'doing the South,' I guess—and that's it. And now you're bored."

Jessie was dumbfounded. "Fifteen years?"

He shrugged. "So? Maybe you're a slow learner."

"Like those women who used to come down here from New York when things were at their worst, remember, and have 'Wednesdays in Mississippi' to show their solidarity? I've had thousands of Wednesdays."

"Sort of, right. And of course there were some distractions along the way. I mean, a couple of kids. So you didn't have to think about me much, or where you were. And now we've come to the end of it."

"You're very imaginative. I like that. I just collected you, you're another notch on my gun."

"Like that Trotskyite boyfriend you had in college whose politics began to bore you. Do you have any memory of saying that? I'll never forget it, this cold wind blew through my gut when you were blithely telling me how you woke up one day and you said, 'If I hear another word about Bukharin and Stalin and all the rest of them I'll scream,' and you never went out with him again. And I thought, that's going to happen to me. And it'll be about as reversible as trying to change the features on my face."

"You believe that!"

He looked at her sadly. "Yes, I believe that."

"Everything we've seen and done, every bit of help we've been to each other." She barely had breath to make the words; she felt as if she'd been kicked in the stomach.

"Well, I don't know, Jessie. You don't seem to have anything to tell me that'll help me make a single change in the way I act, the way I think. But you seem to be mightily dissatisfied."

"But whenever I suggest something you don't like, you tell me I'm not 'supporting' you. If you're only going to count what I say when I agree with you and cheer you on, I might as well keep quiet." None of it meshed; her words, his listening. There was glass between them. She put her face in her hands so that she wouldn't have to see him standing before her like a needy child; when she lowered them he was gone.

Lingham and I did a Bomb Threat on my school. She found out the names of the three green-eyed male Negroes in the school and when I came back I studied every crowd very hard and identified the one who made the pass at me. It was McCoy Nelson, someone told me he is rich, his father is a big undertaker. (They always bury their own.) So then she walked out of school today at 1:45 and I stayed behind to see it and enjoy it thoroughly. She called and asked to speak to the Principal, Mr. Hover, and said to him in a disguised voice "There is a bomb in McCoy Nelson's locker. Let him look in his black heart for the reason why!" At least that is what she promised to say and I don't think she is the kind who lies— she is still very awesome to me for her strength of mind and how serious she is about everything she gets involved in. When she gets going she will not even stop to smile. She reminds me of a very ferocious monkey.

So they evacuated us and I had figured out where he was during that period—you can sneak around because nobody much cares and if you're smart and you get caught in the hall you can always have some alibi ready. I was watching to see if Mr. Hover or somebody would come to get McCoy Nelson to ask him just what was in his heart that was putting everybody in such danger (and scare him like we intended). But—big disappointment—they never came for him and I don't know if he ever got his warning. I watched very carefully. Maybe they had a list of locker numbers. But we all put on our own locks, so I don't understand it. Could Lingham have chickened out?

I do remember once when Teddy was talking about something—that Mourning Dove stuff probably—and he said Acts of Terror are harder to pull off than anybody ever realizes and lots of times people get hurt themselves. I remember it because he was saying when those "boys with the gunracks" came driving through the middle of the crowd and almost got he and my brother, one of them knocked into a tree in his excitement, I guess, and creased up the front of his truck. But did Teddy laugh. And he got talking about some Klan conspiracy that happened a long time ago where a perfectly ordinary well-respected woman that no one knew was involved in anything got killed in a shootout when she went with some others to bomb some rabbi's house, this was in Meridian, Miss. and had a government informer with them or something. I kept picturing

Lingham while he told the story, she met the whole description perfectly. It was scary, I saw her with her little white collar lying dead in the back seat of a car and both her feet were arranged perfectly in clean socks and those docksiders she showed me she got at a church bazaar rummage. She was really proud of them.

Well, anyway, about the Bomb Threat, trying that kind of thing I didn't regret because there was no way anybody could get hurt, only a little "inconvenienced." But I was mad that the boy never got the punishment coming to him. Let him have nightmares before he thinks his simple money can make him as good as white.

Jessie says let's get you a dress for Easter and I will take you to the nicest church, St. Thomas's. This is a borderline I am on, which way I will go, with her or against her? I can feel it, I am not CRAZY. *Sweet pain or nothing? I never bought a good dress without my mother. She comes in to lure me: a nice blue? (That is my color, everybody knows that.) Maybe even a bag and shoes. Then I think No, I am not that easy to conquer with things like baiting a trap. A blue dress could be a mess of porridge.*

*Then again it could be a laying-out dress if
I will leave that sentence unfinished. I am still looking for a beautiful pain to give myself and my flesh. All of it rhymes:*

pain	*strain*	*lain*
rain	*brain*	*stain*
sane	*insane*	*vain*

And Andrea and other Negroes would come to my funeral, I can't believe it. That's the thing, they have me in a corner like a Beast. Teddy would probably sing a spiritual over me. And worse still, he would be oh so relieved if he never had to see my face again. There's another word for the list—again. I just bet if I wasn't here any more he would come home and make peace with his own family. Well, then, there's a good reason to stay around.

It had been a punishing winter, icy, with a snow or two. The bridges this year had seemed to be one endless frozen slick. Jessie could never call this snow even though she saw the flakes come hesitantly out of the sky and whiten the ground for an hour. A "snow" was not something you stepped on once, stepped through, and brought up bare ground.

Easter was finally coming, none too soon, and they were preparing another family convulsion over where their loyalties would take them: there was Dorothea, who called herself one day to invite them. Jessie worried about why Aunt Tush hadn't done the phoning as was customary, asked if she was sick, got a reply about cologne and lip blush, gave it up. Like a child who had laboriously memorized her lines Dorothea could only repeat her invitation and repeat it again. Perhaps it was progress that she had made the call? Jessie stalled her off at the risk of confusing her. They would have to get over there one of these days, with or without Teddy.

Then there was Helen, who had come to Jessie one evening and asked, looking down and all around—the more she cared, Jessie had finally learned, the more her emotion bore down on her and smashed civility into a thin powder of vagueness—if perhaps they could go to St. Thomas's on Easter Sunday, and maybe even on Good Friday. Jessie was delighted: a desire! A benign and earnest wish! Without hesitation she said, "Of course you can. Of course. How lovely. Maybe I'll even come along." For that she received a stricken look that told her that acquiescence was more than enough; she didn't have to ruin it by being abject.

Relative peace had restored itself at Helen's borders; she was quiet but not visibly edgy or depressed. Her control felt like a maintenance dose of a levelling drug. They were going to buy her a dress for Easter and she had timidly invited Jessie, her chauffeur by necessity, to stay with her, a pretend mother.

It had begun to rain in the early afternoon and by the time Jessie pulled up to the side door of the junior high, great gusts of water were smashing across the open lawn. Jessie thought that must be the way the dust bowl had looked, rolling opaque clouds whirling and gusting, filling empty space with a wild solidity that came and vanished and, like something surfacing, rose again across the field. Helen ran toward her with her books on her head. "Help!" she laughed, shaking herself when she had sat down. "That's scary, it's—it weighs so much, the rain."

"May flowers," Jessie mumbled, heading toward the street, but she couldn't see it. The curb and the road were uniformly silver; she felt her front tires prodding the curb. "Uh-oh." She put her lights on and backed up a little, trusting there was no one close behind her. The rearview mirror was completely useless. "Maybe we should wait till it slows down a little."

"I heard there was a tornado in Texas that killed a whole bunch of people," Helen said in her dim unemotional voice. "I hope we don't get any of those."

Jessie drove haltingly into the street but she realized she couldn't see where to pull over, nor could anyone see her. You could be just as tense at five miles an hour as at fifty when you were driving blind. "Honey, open your door and tell me where I am, will you?"

Helen pushed her door ajar and a huge wing of water splashed up, noisy as a flowing stream. "Ooph, wait. I can't even see from in here. I guess I have to step in it to see where the curb is." She waded out with one hand on the window of the car as if she feared she might lose it. "We're practically out in the middle. I never saw anything like that!"

So Jessie, who could have kept her eyes closed for all the good they did her, eased them forward at almost no speed, praying she wasn't crossing an intersection. Somehow—with luck and the repeated reconnoitering of Helen who was so wet she had begun to chatter—they inched up to an empty corner that must have been a bus stop. Jessie kept the car running so that her lights would not sap the battery. Steam rose on the windows as if they were ascending in a plane through heavy clouds, and the old car rumbled and skipped. If Helen had been Lydia it would have been a good moment for confidences and for cuddling, but sitting without a necessary word, in a fog of neutrality without content or curiosity, felt nearly sufficient. It felt, in fact, like the perfect expression of Jessie's general mood these days of emotional deprivation which, like a dearth of oxygen, made her muddled and dangerously, unnaturally peaceful.

She gave Helen her gray and white Mexican sweater to stop her shaking, and the two of them sat looking blankly forward, drowsy, nowhere in the world, nothing before their eyes but the spots and streaks and segmented snakes of their vision itself.

No dress. Rain instead. It is a sign, I should have told her No, I wouldn't go. God thinks I was getting ready to sell myself for a blue cotton dress and accessories. Tomorrow I will say I can't try again or I will be punished.

I had this horrible dream like I had before. People in cars on a highway with Mom and Daddy all washed away in the rain—must be this terrible downpour I could hear tearing up the yard. I thought I recognized faces in other cars: Mrs. Toulon who died when I was in her 3rd grade—lost all her hair and we couldn't look at her, then they got that man substitute, and my tap teacher who always smiled, her mouth was an O in the dream. Jessie has this picture in their room, a woman on a bridge with her mouth like some sucking tunnel, her face is folded in half. You can almost hear OOOOOOO That feels very good to write. SOOOOOthing.

In the dream there is always the same big drain at the center divider of the highway (also an O with a grate on it) and they all slip around, a whirlpool, and go down into it. A big ripping sound woke me up, it was something tearing right off slowly, then it was speeding up. Waited to hear a howling pain, whatever ripped, but only got ssshhhhh, endless washing sound of leaves and rain against each other. Is it raining in Birmingham on the cemetery? I always wonder: Jesus, are all their arguments over in the rain of heaven? Do they lie peaceful beside each other? I would go into their bed when they were still getting along and lie right between them so comfortable. The head board was carved I always thought like a peacock and I would look at it, it was wood but I could make up colors like it was a tail all spread out. My father had a little cleft in his chin and I would put my finger on it. He would say "Who's there?" He had these big veins in his neck. His chest was covered with hair like baby ringlets, only starched. I can't believe he was the same Tyrant who hit me later and Mom was afraid of. Now I think they are back in that early time and they are in eternity together not in the clothes they were in but in his striped pajamas and her prettiest (maybe her wedding) negligee, ecru with lace around the top. It seems right, so they are lying there naturally. And her hair just done and he is holding her hand. I know Rev. Carstairs said heaven wasn't really like that, only in kindergarten Bible class they let the little kids think of it that way, but that is how I like to see it and who does it hurt to make it beautiful and comfortable too?

In the morning they saw that a limb of the live oak on the front lawn had come down close to the house. It lay across the grass like a tremendous animal—"a big dead horse," O'Neill said and poked it with his foot as though it might respond. There were loose twigs everywhere, a feeling that the neighborhood had been shaken hard so that everything loosely attached had snapped off. The wind had been so wild that Jessie had felt the house tremble and throb like a small boat about to tear loose from its moorings. So light and plastic and new, it made old house noises she couldn't imagine it could bring forth. The children were soundly asleep or she'd have had a congregation of them in her bed for reassurance. She'd have liked that; she had been going to bed these nights as if into exile. Teddy's flight had made her flee toward them in perfect counterbalance.

Hustling the children into the car for school, she noticed how much debris had been let loose by that wind. Puddles still stood in every declivity, shaking under the steady rain like pudding. One house down the street had cardboard and a pale green blanket where the front window should have been. Could the wind have done that?

There was no rain when she drove home, but twice they heard on the car radio an advisory from the National Weather Service: there was a possibility that the river would flood, there had been record-breaking rain up north. The announcer spoke of flash floods but he sounded matter of fact enough and played his Kool and the Gang records on cue.

But before dinner Andy came into the kitchen after a phone call to say that his friend Rick's street in Presidential Hills was under two feet of water. He had had to walk his bike home through it.

"Some of these newer neighborhoods have really lousy sewer systems," Jessie said. She was making a large pot of spaghetti and peas; sometime between October and today she had gotten the knack of cooking for all these mouths. "You'd think they'd do something about it."

But as the evening continued, so did the bulletins. The rain had stopped, finally; there had been so much of it that there was going to be trouble. "Friday the thirteenth is coming, folks," Andy said and whistled the old "Dragnet" tune. "Dum-de-dum-dum."

"You're a real pistol today, aren't you?" The newscaster said that the usual creeks were flooding in what he didn't call the poorest parts of town, the hollows. Little Cany Creek, swollen, did in its neighbors as a matter of course. A little girl, deaf or retarded, it wasn't clear which, and probably black, though that was conjecture on Jessie's part, had disappeared into a culvert. Something about her handicap implied that she was a casualty of her own shortcomings, not of the river. (That was the kind of thing Teddy would say.)

Jessie mixed the peas into the spaghetti trying not to think of the child in the swirling water. She wondered instead where Teddy was this minute, with whom he was eating, whether he was welcome there or suffered for decency or old time's sake. It had been close to a week since he had been home in "Jessie's neighborhood."

Andy and Lydia were poking each other and snarling. Jessie told Andy to stop being provocative.

"If I'm going to be the man of the house," he said pulling his chair back roughly, "since there isn't any other one—" (he looked at her without sympathy)—"I'm going to be as provocative as I want to be. My father provoked himself right out of here."

"Andy." Helen had never rebuked anyone but her brother before. "Don't be nasty."

He served himself first, flinging the spaghetti sloppily onto his plate. "Well, maybe the rest of you aren't, but I'm sick of goodness and virtue and church out of church. Everybody for himself. I hope Daddy's having a good time wherever he is."

"You keep up that tone and you're going to be by yourself alone in your room," Jessie told him quietly.

But Andy was forking peas viciously. "I'm too old for that, Mother. I could drive that car away if I wanted. I'd just as soon eat by myself anyway."

"Then do. Have your adolescent rebellion somewhere I don't have to watch you get peas all over the floor."

He took his plate and fork and left the table, making sure to give his chair a kick on the way out. It spun into Helen's and half toppled but she caught it and steadied it and then, looking frightened, using her fork like a comb, continued her careful separation of strand from strand of spaghetti as if it might be hair that harbored something she had to search for but didn't want to find.

. . .

Very early, before sunrise, Jessie opened her eyes to what sounded like a radio in the distance. She strained to hear the voice as it lifted—how peculiar—out of a silence so dense and deep she felt as if she were on the shore of a lake that swallowed sound. This was no Plywood Barracks where people liked to jive at three in the morning; even the cats on Rebus Road were dutifully altered into discretion and never sang along the backyard fence. She went to the window and looked out but there was nothing to see, only the first cracks in the night sky, a good clear day beginning to seep through the color of egg, yolk and white together.

At six Andréa called. "Are y'all okay over there? I couldn't tell how far the warnings were going."

"What warnings?"

"They've been out with bullhorns, where've you been, child? You better get yourself in gear."

"Bullhorns. Ah—" The radio.

"They're telling folks up northeast to get out of their houses because the river's really coming. You'd better get yourself a truck or something, Jessie, and—"

"Andréa, a truck? Over here? Are you kidding?"

Andréa cleared her throat patiently. "I know you wake up slowly, hon, but collect your wits now and listen to mama. First thing, turn your radio on and listen up. When you hear what's in store for you—man, you picked the place to move to, I want to tell you, all you white folks gone get your feet wet—then get those children out of bed and you either haul your furniture up on some cinder blocks or something, or if you're a pessimist you get a U-HAUL on over there and take it someplace before all that stuff floats up to the ceiling. We'll come help you. Is Teddy there?"

"No more than usual. If he's not around here on a good day, I don't expect him to come around in a pinch." Jessie looked up to see Andy and Helen at the kitchen door, shoulder touching shoulder, wide-eyed as Hansel and Gretel looking in the witch's window.

"As the 'man of the house,' " Jessie said to her son when she'd thanked Andréa and put the phone down, "you'd better get ready to do a hell of a day's work."

He ignored her tone. "Where's Daddy?"

"Where do you think he is. You children don't really seem to have grasped the simple fact that your father's irresponsibility has—" She paused to watch Helen's face dissolve into a vague wash of pain; tears must be massing up behind and making her skin soggy. "Never mind that. You heard the bulletin?"

Helen said, "You don't really think it's coming, do you? We aren't anywhere close to water."

"No. But nobody ever thinks anything's coming, Helen, winter or night-time or anything, right? When it's light out it feels like it'll be light forever." She opened the back door, regretting that she'd said that. Oh Helen. One bitterness ought not to feed another.

There were traffic noises down on Ridgewood Road, the rush of air in truck brakes like the sound of large animals sighing, and she could see movement in a few houses, open doors, lights, shadowy shapes passing behind windows. A helicopter was beating, threshing in the indeterminate distance. That was the sound of true emergency to her, propeller wings monotonously, threateningly stirring up wind. Helicopters could only mean surveillance or salvation, and it was never a good day when you needed either.

·   ·   ·

It was not a good day. Jessie rode the brakes of her skepticism hard, it was so unimaginable that real water would travel hundreds of miles down-stream to come licking under their solid front door with the metal lip below it. They weren't in the floodplain. And they were on a hill; at least on a slight swell, a raised shoulder of earth. Andréa wasn't thinking of the specifics of their situation, didn't understand geography.

"Let's go see," O'Neill suggested. He was eating his second Pop-Tart, looking forward to some genuine excitement. It was an amazing day when no one even discussed the possibility that there might be school. "Let's drive up to where the houses are already in the river!"

"We shouldn't," Jessie said. "The last thing they need is spectators." Then again, there was no other way she could concede the threat of this so that she could do anything to secure them. "We'll see if we can drive around a little. If we're in anybody's way, though, we're coming right home."

Out on the block it looked like an ordinary fine sharp clear spring day that had brought the neighbors out to tend their holdings. Only the tending was bizarre: some people called Sandler, up two houses, were hoisting their television set onto the roof. Jack Sandler in his floppy madras bermuda shorts was trying to hand it to his teenage son, Steve, who was grappling with it at an angle meant to keep him aloft; but he couldn't hold on to the huge set and to the roof under his feet; he did a little dance, up and down, trying for purchase. "Only the electrical items!" the father shouted to Jessie when she called to him. "If your other things get a little wet they'll dry. But anything with wiring, y'all better get it out of there!" Farther down people she didn't know—most of her neighbors were barely familiar faces to her—were weighing down a car with Confederate license plates so that its springs nearly touched the driveway. They looked like Okies. The sun was barely over the rooftops and the backyard pines.

"Everybody's so hysterical!" Lydia said in a stage whisper. "The river's so far away I think they just like being all involved. Don't you, Mom?"

Helen stared hard at her to assess the authority of her disgust. Then she studied Jessie for her answer.

Jessie shrugged and turned at the corner. They headed north. There was a snarl of traffic—U-HAUL, RYDER, HERTZ, all the bright trucks were passing each other, almost a convoy, gears scraping under the hands of amateur truckers. They shouted to each other, good humored, through rolled-down windows. The concentration of loaded vehicles made her think of a lifetime of news pictures of refugees on all the long marches, Cambodia, Hanoi and long before, all across Europe, war planes strafing as they passed over. Ants, self-absorbed segments of a larger flow. Mostly they were heading down from farther north and toward her from the east, where the river looped and coiled, some of it cleanly, sharply defined at its edges, some of it boggy, buggy, soft and full of water lilies in the inland reaches. There were estuaries and minilakes among the finest houses. The estate where Andy had celebrated New Year's Eve had a miniature lake across the street, and a little inlet with a curved Japanese bridge over it; so he had said. Jessie never had occasion to see such a neighborhood.

They were stopped finally and turned back by the police. Helen cried out when she saw the traffic barricades as if she had been slapped. They parked the car in someone's empty driveway and walked up to see beyond the barricades and "There it is!" Andy said in an awed voice: it was blue brown and muddy, and crinkled silver lay across the top of it like aluminum foil that had been used and flattened out, folded in a thousand hairline cracks. They couldn't see it moving toward them or toward anything but it was halfway up to the windows of the brick houses, up the mailbox poles. There were cars whose underparts were invisible and one small rental van, which had started to make its getaway pointed at them, abandoned in the middle of the street. "I wonder how much they missed by," Jessie said respectfully as if she were viewing the body of an escapee cut down in mid-flight. If only someone would tell her what to do: Andréa had tried, Teddy had not tried. She turned to lead them back to the car. "Come on, Helen!" Andy called. Helen was standing stricken with her hands across her stomach as if it hurt, staring down the long block which had become a river, listening to the bark of a motor and then the slow sighing exhalation of the water as the first boat—in time there would be hundreds—came hesitantly toward them.

.   .   .

She drove the children back to the house and sat in the driveway, dumb, while they clamored for directions, every thought come to a standstill. Her mind had seized up like a motor. I am a passive person, she thought, the word PASSIVE a sign in lights, the letters spaced out loosely, slowly. ("Of course we never gave you a lot to do," Teddy used to say about the Tolewood days when they'd stuck her in the library. "You've got a million opinions but no idea of what to do next. You're always waiting for someone to tell you if you can dare." But whatever she'd dared he'd laughed at.) Now she thought of fields, pastures, broad and open, dotted with grazing cows. She saw herself sleeping under a tree in a rain of apples. What to do, where to go? Should they pack and leave, escape what most likely would never come or hold tight and wait, turn it away with their concentration? *Seat cushions may be used for flotation*, the stewardess's voice was always saying. *In case of inclement weather*. No, *bumpy air. Unexpected turbulence*, that was it. Forever unexpected. Who says chance favors the prepared?

"Mother, for God's *sake*." Andy was at her sleeve, pulling at her. She would feel so stupid packing these things they'd just unpacked a few months ago. It could never get up the hill, water seeks its own level, it doesn't flow up inclines full of greenery and infant alyssum and whatever that ground ivy was: cedum?

"What do you think? Andy?"

"About what? You mean, should we hoist the TV onto the roof? *I* don't know." He looked around still snarling, still the new irritable Andy who'd lost respect for his mother. "Where the hell is our daddy when we need him is what I'd like to know. He could give us a phone call at least. I hope he drowns out there."

That felt like a hard slap between Jessie's shoulders; it cleared every passage. She opened the car door and felt her height as she unfolded out of it. "Listen. You guys sit tight, listen for the phone. If you want to, get some of your things together, are you listening, O'Neill?" They were all over the lawn, running and tagging each other, drunk on the pleasure of their safety alongside such danger. Only Helen stood like someone too fragile to move; she seemed to be listening to something the rest of them couldn't hear. "Take the things you care most about—"

"What kind of things?" Lydia began.

"And pack it up in plastic bags and put some clothes in, at least one whole change of clothes. You never know."

"Can I take my comics and stuff like that?" O'Neill asked. His mouth stayed open; he was ready to make a list.

"Where are you going to be?" Helen still looked queasy.

"I want to take you all over to Andréa's and then I'm coming back, up to Sedgewick and River Road and see if I can help out."

"Mama!"

"Lyddie, don't worry, I'll be all right. It's not even the least little bit dangerous, none of this is anything but inconvenient. And there's no way it can get up here. But whatever happens, it comes very slowly, and I'll be back. Do you understand that? Nothing's going to happen to me or to you while I'm gone. And maybe your father will even show up."

"Can't we come?"

"Oh, honey, I'd feel better if you were nice and warm. You can play with Cleo when she comes home from daycare. Andy, do you want to come?"

He began to answer when Helen caught his glance and held it without saying a word. She looked like a starlet in one of those horror movies whose wide-eyed white face the camera loves to play over to excite the audience: schoolgirl horror.

"Helen, relax, please," Jessie said sternly. "This is not a crisis. Believe me. If everyone is alert . . ."

She looked so doggy and dependent that Jessie tried to restrain her harshness. Did the child need to remind them that she'd already suffered sufficiently? Nobody's counting, Jessie wanted to say. You can't bring over the balance from one set of books to another, even if you're on good terms with the book-keeper.

She was ready to take them to the car when Lydia grabbed her arm. "We want to come with you," she said so firmly there was no sense appealing her decision. This was a hard family in which to propose even the temporary disappearance of a parent: let it be.

"Okay. Boots for everybody, though."

"Boots!" That was O'Neill, insulted. "Why don't we go barefooty, our feet'll get wet anyway. If it's really a *flood*."

So challenged, she let them prevail. They trooped out in a line, with Helen at the far end already so wan with fear that Jessie knew she would be weighed down by concern for her.

Nonetheless, for a few hours she felt good: brainless and resolute and indiscriminately useful. She waded through ankle-deep water until it touched her knees to offer her services lifting, hauling, throwing small items into large bags, shoving indispensable articles into wooden rowboats, flat-bottomed aluminum fishing boats, speedboats, one tipping canoe. Where had all the boats *come* from? A huge gleaming yacht, all wood and brass, sat uselessly moored in a yard like a woman so overdressed at a picnic that she couldn't get down on the ground to eat.

While Jessie moved boxes into a rowboat, Lydia rescued a rubber tree and O'Neill stumbled beneath a cage of crying kittens. They laughed a lot as they hauled; it was oddly invigorating to repeat the movements they had staggered through making the move from Willowbrae to Rebus Road, only this time in the widening eye of danger. The children were caught up in the odd celebratory mood—*they* were not the ones in trouble, their energy flowed out with the simplest magnanimity. Only Helen hung back; she trailed after Jessie, holding her arms around herself in a parody of protectiveness.

The water was rocking at their knees by noon. Andy walked past Helen wordlessly, carrying a delicate carved rocker to a rubber dinghy, where it sat with its dignity unimpaired. They moved files marked XX SECRET XX a small gray computer as contained as a cat, an empty birdcage whose gold toothpick door swung squeaking on miniature hinges. "Do you think the bird escaped?" O'Neill asked, poking Jessie. "Who would worry about an empty cage on a day like today?" said Lydia. "Weird." Jessie helped someone carry a set of formal portraits wrapped in blue blankets, one of them—the blanket kept slipping—of a young woman whose expanse of bare soft pink neck and shoulder looked like romantic legend, not anatomical possibility.

Here and there someone did not mind showing visible pain: one gray-haired woman, perhaps the one whose portrait Jessie had just hefted, sat sobbing at her kitchen table where still water gapped like roomy wide-mouthed boots around her calves. Helen came right up to her and stared. When the woman looked into her face she gave her a guilty smile and walked away, head down, the smile still on her lips. But for the most part there was grim silence or the businesslike call of orders and responses. Someone had a tape deck that played the same three twanging country songs again and again like Muzak, your woman and my man, my woman and your man.

In one living room a baby in a slicker sat in its infant seat on top of a shiny Italian Renaissance sideboard that had been hoisted onto blocks. It chewed contentedly on its fingers a few inches from the ceiling. The baby's father told Jessie, "They're letting water out of the reservoir a hundred thousand feet a second, get the pressure down so it won't burst. Keep the damn thing so high for the fishing and boats these days there's no room for new water." He was a blond crewcut collegiate type with full lips the color of bubblegum—a very clean machine, Jessie would have called him, not the sort who tended toward disillusioned indictments of authority.

"You must not be a fishing man," she said amiably. She was holding a toaster oven to herself, getting crumbs all over her chest.

The young man stood on the top of a table to reach his baby down. He was not inclined to sound amiable. "Whole damn city could go under, somebody said they're sandbagging the sewage plant. I want to tell you, there ought to be an investigation of the Fish and Game Commission when we dry out. If we ever do." That would have been Teddy's approach, she thought; there are no natural disasters, only manmade botches. (And he was probably right in this case.) The baby crowed with delight as it swept through the chill air making the arc of a bird, landing against his father's chest that looked warm with exertion and anger.

"Where's Helen?" Jessie asked the children. "You can all go get some ice cream if you'll go together."

"She's crying out back," O'Neill told her soberly. "She went around the house, I saw her. She's under the wisteria."

Wisteria, hysteria, maybe she should have stayed home with them, a gesture of protection. She had dared to hope Helen might reach out of herself at least a little bit in crisis. Somewhere there must be a critical point beyond which a terrified soul cannot reverse its direction, but she refused to think Helen had come to that. "Do you think she's—is she always like this, honey, when things are a little—when it's kind of scary?" Secondhand children are like secondhand cars, Teddy had said once, cold, cold: you don't know what you're getting.

"Well . . ." O'Neill made small tentative damp noises, considering. "We never had a *flood* in Birmingham—"

"Oh, I know, O'Neill, I didn't think you had one of these exactly. But is she pretty brave usually?" Would he know? She was his older sister and all he had of his own to put his faith in.

"She never did cry when Mommy and Daddy—didn't come home. I did. Judy—Mrs. Carmichael?—Judy told her to be brave like Daddy would want and she just put her hands over her face and didn't ever. She said it was okay for me because I'm still—"his voice faded on this, ashamed—"you know. Like—little."

Jessie pulled him to her. He put his arms around her neck. "Okay, big little boy. I'm going to go talk her into some ice cream. Why don't you come and help?"

They found Helen standing alone behind a house that seemed to begin at window level; she was in the water waist-high gazing out over the level lake of the yard as if she could see a horizon miles distant. Jessie tried breeziness with her but got no response. Finally she touched her arm gently and said, "Helen, let's go home." Helen turned to her slowly, her eyes fixed at the wrong level as though she were blind. "We've had enough," Jessie said, and wondered if she should be alarmed at how boneless Helen's arm felt in her grip. They moved slowly around to the front of the house, Jessie propelling, Helen sagging like an invalid. The other children, huddled, staring, must have looked to her like accusers.

On the way to the corner they met a capsized makeshift raft that had bumped into a larger boat and lost half its goods into the freezing water, so that Jessie and its owners and the children had to reach in to their necks to retrieve them; they bent over the thousand fractured lights and put their noses in. Up close the water stank, though she couldn't name the smell. O'Neill did, eagerly.

A few blocks later a frightened three- or four-year-old girl stood howling on one side of a street where a few inches of transparent water trickled down the center like a moat. Lydia ran to pick her up and carried her across to her parents who were too distraught, lashing a tarpaulin over furniture, to have missed her. She kicked Lydia violently in the gut and tried to break free, a cat carried against its will. She put the child down beside her mother, who was pregnant and sunburned, freshly rose pink, as if she'd spent the day at the beach on a blanket. "Oh thanks," the young woman said absently. "Aren't you nice. I told her to stay right here."

"They do wander," Lydia said smiling. Jessie could see how adult she felt, putting a whole generation's distance into "they."

All of them kicked up spray, walking back to the car exhilarated, kids tossing up a spring puddle. Helen walked with her head down, as far from them as she could. Andy didn't really hope Teddy would drown, Jessie thought, but she wasn't surprised at his anger at both of them. Finished, she said to herself, grasping only the tip of it. Without appeal. If he showed up again when the floodwaters had been sucked back up—down?—and put his hands on her, expecting her to turn and smile and part for him as if she were water, he'd see. Her back was what he'd see. The Birmingham cousins were down to a single parent.

They came into their house shivering in soaked dungarees and shirts and in the silence realized how busy with people the morning of rescue had been, how almost gay, in spite of all the pain they had seen. They had not been playing, that was the best thing about it. They had earnestly met real need. Then how lovely, how satisfying, to dry out, drink hot chocolate, feel safe and generous and exhausted. They put the stereo on and festooned the bathroom with their wet clothes; then, without Jessie's urging, all of them crawled onto their beds and napped for the rest of the afternoon. Jessie considered going in to reasure Helen, but Helen was on her own: sleep rescued her instead.

.   .   .

They watched television all evening, saw the water breaking wild over the reservoir spillway, rushing savagely beneath the aerial camera, an un-recognizably wide swathe. Lydia began to cry. Andy put her on his lap; her feet touched the floor. "It wasn't anything *like* that," she objected. "What if that came where we were moving all that stuff?" She managed to be alarmed in retrospect.

"Even if the water comes all the way up here it won't look like that, right, Mom?" he said. "It just sits there like a lake. You *saw* it with your own eyes. It's just muddy and still and kind of cruddy but it isn't coming to getcha!" He tried to make her laugh, lunging at her.

Mom said right. Helen wasn't Catholic but for the short time she sat with them, before she retreated in a kind of upright crawl, she worked her fingers in her lap as if they held a rosary. The phone rang twice, an unfamiliar double ring like a twitch and recoil. The first time her heart raced but it wasn't Teddy, it wasn't anyone: random firings. The next-door neighbor, Bubba MacIntyre, a thin man who carried his middle-aged paunch as if it were a sack of mail between his thin arms, knocked timidly at the door. Did they have any sleeping pills, he wondered; his wife was "touchy." Jessie apologized: they were always too exhausted—these days, too depressed—to need help sleeping.

O'Neill said he hoped the men with the bullhorns would chase them out at dawn, he was a helicopter half the time and the rest a soldier with a megaphone made of the rolled-up *Clarion-Ledger* informing them that the dam was not going to hold more than another three minutes. Then he started counting down. "O'Neill," Helen shrilled at him when he got to eighty seconds, "you're doing that just to upset me."

"Why you?" her brother asked. "That doesn't have anything to *do* with you." That was when Helen hunched away to her room.

Jessie called Andréa but the babysitter told her that Mr. and Mrs. Smith were at an emergency meeting of something that sounded more like Alcoholics Anonymous than it could possibly have been. Because such things continued come hell or literal high water, the children watched an English comedy and entered into an hour of unintelligible speech. "Nay-oh, nay-oh," Andy said like a bleating Cary Grant. "That's the way they toke in *Green*land." O'Neill and Lydia would try again, holding their sides; they were manic. "Nay-oh, New*found*land. Dear me."

Jessie's excitement had become weariness in the joints and an unnatural watchfulness; adrenaline like coffee had chewed up her nerves. She sat and worried about Helen who just a few weeks ago had lain in the dark testing out the borders of her sanity. Danger was not what she needed right now. Christ was apparently only one of her secrets, her fetish, and He was not sufficient balm. She remembered O'Neill walking across the room touching wood, paper, plastic that looked like wood. (Would he have felt unprotected had he known he was knocking plastic veneer?!)

The younger children went to bed silently, very late, and Jessie whispered reassuringly to both of them that nothing could possibly happen while they slept. "I want Daddy," Lydia said, wobbling toward tears. "I didn't think it would be like this." Jessie laid her head on Lydia's pillow for a long minute, wondering which "this" she meant, letting her daughter's warm tears wet her cheek. When we come through this we'll be different, Jessie thought, we'll have managed something large without him. This was called abandonment. Desertion, inadvertent, willed or otherwise. Taking care of business somewhere else. It would hold in a court of law; closer to home, it would leave more room in her bed when the children trooped in one by one before dawn.

It is flooding outside!!! Everybody is stone-face calm, I can't under-stand how. (Except for Lydia—she is scared like me, which is only normal.) O'Neill dragged us off to see it coming and he had such a good time you'd think it was a country fair. Then later Jessie made us go help people escape, we had to carry all their stuff out to boats and rafts, I didn't want to touch any of it, I just could feel the cold on my legs like they were disappearing from my feet up. Crowds and cops and everything in slow motion. I can feel it advancing, if I put my ear to the ground like an Indian I would hear the waters shaking. It is the scowl of God, I can't explain that better, only it is flat and endless and cold and it is no coincidence. It is brown as a sewer and the sun is shining on it. Is there no safe place in this world? I think if I lived on a tall mountain the wind would come to blow me off and if I burrowed in a tunnel, the ground would collapse all around. Now I understand all of it: Teddy in his bar or his lovenest will be saved. Everyone at home here will go under. This is happening only in the best parts of town! I see that. Canton Club Circle they say is where so much money is. Gone. All on the Eastover side. Gone. Such beautiful furniture going under. Carpets were drowning and pretty kitchens, I even saw a blanket chest like the one we bought last year just standing there like a coffin, it was sinking under the water, I saw the lake in this dining room come up right to the lip of it and then go in. Jessie says Don't worry, it will stop long before it gets to our house, but I do not see any reason why water running on a flat place will stop. I am at my desk shivering cold. Learning how my Mom and Daddy's death was actually easier and merciful because they only saw it coming for a few seconds if at all. (I keep seeing Daddy's hands around Mom's throat, not on the wheel, did it happen that way?) I would say we can escape this but I personally know the flood is meant for me, so they will not take my hand and drag me anywhere. If it comes Andy says we are probably going to Andrea and Tommy's. "Oh good," Lydia goes, "we can play with little Cleo." Not me.

All of them were asleep, catnapping like soldiers in the trenches, trying to spell each other but giving in, when someone knocked sharply at the front door and rattled it as if to break it open. Jessie didn't know if she said "Teddy!" out loud or only thought it, but by the time she was at the door, barefooted, no one was there. She opened it and gasped, having forgotten, in an hour's exhausted sleep, how real the water was: there was no street, only a long shallow stream flickering like mercury, shaken gently by the chill breath of the breeze. It was so beautiful she could not be afraid of it, and that, she thought, was sinister. Far off, where the tiny cupping of the breeze could not be seen, it lay as thick and still as a field of snow, a surface imperturbable as something geologic, ancient, unchanging. They were still dry on their incline, but that safety was about to give out: the house across the way, in a broad decline, was beginning to look like a houseboat, its windows just above the water line.

Lights were on, inside and out, but Jessie thought she'd better turn off the electricity. The children might panic in the dark—oh God, flashlights? candles? Who were the people who thought of everything in time?—but wouldn't they be electrocuted if they touched something with their feet in water? She heard the rapping down the block, a voice raised in warning, then a minute later its repetition like an echo, a reflection. When she went to wake the children she tried to sound cheerful. "O'Neill, you've got your wish. We have to evacuate."

"Neat-o!" He sat up straight. "Do we go to a shelter and they feed us and all?"

The children put Mickey Mouse in the car where he would stay dry; he had a look of cat-concern in his eyes, Lydia was sure she saw it. They left the windows open enough for him to breathe. "But if the water gets up to there and then it comes in the car!" Lydia cried. "Please can I take him in the picnic basket, Mama, please?" Jessie took another look at the cat; he did look anxious, shut up in there, water or no water. I've been very bad at predicting how far this thing is coming, she thought, although she had been no worse than those in authority. Even downtown Jackson was washing out this morning, Capitol Street becoming a swamp. The fairgrounds was, according to the radio, reaching for cliché, "a primordial sea." Who's to say? "Take him along."

"But keep him away from me," O'Neill shouted. "I'm not carrying any cat, what if I get sick?"

The furniture on the neighbors' roofs looked like a village. Boat traffic obeyed the rules of the highway, kept to its lanes. There was honking, motors clacking, threatening. Around the corner, on a terraced block much higher than theirs, O'Neill reported people sitting in lawn chairs as if nothing were bearing their neighbors away. It was bad enough, Jessie reflected, to be so busy that she'd given less than a thought to Town Creek, Cany Creek, all those clogged capillaries that were flooding out the often-flooded; this was the year for the exempt to be chosen. Helen, who hadn't so much as muttered good morning, said matter-of-factly, "Don't worry, Neill, those people are going straight to hell when the time comes."

She will never be mine, Jessie thought.

What began to smell (it was vague but they didn't imagine it) was coming from the waste processing plant: there was a tinge of sourness in the water, just a hint lying above and separate from the fifteen other smells, of earth and chemical sharpness, of fish and miscellaneous filth. When the water rocked and came away from a wall, it left its stain, a nameless brown gray slime. "Soon," O'Neill said to Lydia with relish, "we can find some leeches and then some snakes, they're gonna be washing up everywhere!" He studied her face as it, predictably, crumpled. Why did I have to have such a stereotypical girl-child, Jessie wondered; it went deeper than window seats and unicorns. "See," O'Neill went on, having ascertained his effect, "they've got to lie down sometime and rest just like anybody else."

Jessie went through the house as quickly as she could, stuffing clothing into plastic garbage bags, twisting the colored ties around the necks of the bundles viciously. She heaved the bags onto the cluttered top shelves of the closets, packed the bulletin board of outdated photographs in cleaner's plastic and slung it over her shoulder with her clean shirt and shoes and change of underwear. Then she stopped and stared at the living room which she didn't love yet, the wide light room that had undone Teddy, had made him want to sleep on a dirty floor for penance or purity. When they came back her asparagus fern that she never watered enough would be limp, the old SNCC posters—she had capitulated and hung them—would be stained brown as if by proximity to fire. O'Neill's two new angelfish might make it but then might not, depending on just what it was that came floating under the door. They would rise right up and out of their bowl, their redundant patch of water, the goldfish too, and the mollies, at large on an unending surprise sea. Imagine the angelfish swimming happily down Rebus Road, under the bottoms of boats, left at Ridgewood and out toward the interstate that led toward the Gulf of Mexico! When she told that to O'Neill he laughed with her and she began to elaborate on all the fish would see: the finger pointing to God on the church in Port Gibson, and catfish farms where their cousins lived, plantations near Natchez, and the Atchafalaya Swamp where there were panthers. They were the only two perverse enough to be having an adventure, not a catastrophe. Jessie felt herself surviving this with goodwill, with energy, with relish. The others went out of the house first, grave and hurried by their imaginations, Andy standing behind Helen who would not acknowledge him. Lydia stopped at the door, then dashed back for her good set of magic markers; she had obviously fought with herself about their status as luxury or necessity and had reversed the decision at the threshold.

But Jessie had turned back too: the phone began to ring just as she got to the end of the flagstone path. "I don't believe it," she would say to him. "Another minute and you'd have missed us. Where *are* you?"

But it was only the flood again: nothing at her ear but a raucous buzzing, a high tension wire sound that was like those cicadas that scream along the pea green bayous north of Bogalusa. The phone was dying; she was hearing its terminal shriek.

This is Goodbye. What do they say, D-Day? I understand now the flood is for me, it is not the sharp honest pain I wanted but "ceasing on the midnight without pain" (my favorite poem). I am going to slip under and be out from all this, and leave all these people to each other again. Jesus sent this to me, it is a punishment and a salvation both, which is the way He can make all things happen at once.

In case:

I am sorry, Jessie, because you were actually pretty decent, especially considering your background. Only you should have taken this diary when I offered it the first time, you would have understood me better. Don't grieve for me because this problem (me) should never have been yours. I know sometimes you were on my side because I am a girl so it was sort of a principle with you, you thought a "mother" should be with a "daughter," but I appreciate that you tried to make me feel at home. Good luck in your struggle to keep your home together but I say Let Teddy Go. Maybe he will find a colored woman to make him happy.

There is only O'Neill left, my beloved little brother. I don't have to say goodbye to you, in the Hereafter we will be brother and sister again. Be strong and try to understand me. I am in a state of exaltation. Not everyone gets to know exactly when they are supposed to die.

(One last thing: I do not wish ill to anybody except to Teddy because he and my father deserve the death of Sodom and Gomorrah or the drowning of the sinners when Noah was saved! I hope he sees this.)

I am falling asleep on the page, there is a splotch of ink. I should be very wide awake for this, I am probably entering OBLIVION in a few minutes and then eternal life which makes me ecstatically happy. But I keep yawning exactly like when I am nervous. (Before I played Gretel last year I yawned and went to the bathroom, again and again. Very unromantic.)

What I am doing is, I am putting this my diary in a tan plastic garbage bag with a note in crayon so it won't wash off. READ THIS. *I had to cut most of the bag off above the tie. It looks like strips of skin. Even though this kitchen is going to be an ocean floor soon I put the scraps in the trash basket because I got good training in neatness and am proud of that. And I am putting it inside Jessie's pocketbook so she will have to find it soon. It is sweet-smelling in there, I think she must sneak chocolate bars or something. I am noticing a thousand details per second!! Then I am taking the bag to a place that is dry this minute, although who knows how long?*

Water take me now. I am going to wade in, for my last baptism. I will lie down under a silver wave, just sink down easy and when I wake I will be near my mother, and can rest there. And near my God Who sent this flood for me and nobody knows that. He can make all things happen at once. When I say to Him "Yes I am happy to come" I can feel Him saying—a conversation almost except the voice is not out loud— We will see. You will put yourself in position to come to me and if you are not saved then you deserved to die, but if you live through my Flood then it was fated that you are innocent and you shall have to live in this vale of tears a while longer. That was what they did with witches! The idea makes me feel strange, is He saying I am a witch like in Salem? Or (worst): Is He saying He doesn't know if I am guilty or I am innocent? No, this is for me, this is how the person discovers for theirself and comes to believe the verdict. I hear His voice ready to give me a Sign. Christ will lay my question at the foot of the cross and I will watch what happens and I will be convinced. Guilty or innocent I will soon know. Actually it is a lot like Abraham and Isaac only I am no boy! That is the scariest part of the whole Bible but of course it's okay in the end because God is good. Will He send a ram in the thicket and then unbind my ankles and I will stand and live? I would just as soon lie down and be taken for a sinner.

When they read this they will understand that I was more important than they dreamed of. This would be called Helen's Flood if only people knew! It all works out and the body is only a shell and it can sink, it will not detain me. Look, I can say to Andy, I died pure. Corruption is Yours, Salvation is Mine. I slipped away from you all. I deserve to die and I deserve heavenly forgiveness, that is the joy of Jesus Christ, both at the same time. "Whom wilt thou find to love ignoble thee save Me, save only Me?"

I am feeling how the water is beautiful and cold like metal. I actually saw a snake that might have been dead, I couldn't tell, it was just floating. A black one, about as wide as a bicycle tire. I hope no water moccasin gets O'Neill because if he sees one I know he will reach for it. He has played with the whole world but I never learned to do that and now it is far too late. If I sink like a rock will there be snakes at the bottom? Dear God, I hope not, even if I will not feel them, please, God, protect me from any insect or snake coming near me, the whole thought of it makes me shake all over. Now it is funny, that I thought if I was in danger I could run fast and get away from it. I close my eyes and see the water just touching the lip of the blanket chest, teasing, then seeping a little staining the inside of the lid and finally pouring in until the whole thing is only a casket of dirty brown water that has been everywhere first.

But I put my Faith and Trust in a world with nothing ugly in it. You shall decide. I am on my way.

When Jessie rejoined the children they were running in circles like ants whose hill has been destroyed. O'Neill shrieked at her, "Helen's gone! My sister's gone!" and Andy, stock still on the curb, water over his ankles, stared at her as if she were an apparition.

They had stopped when she ran back to the house, looking at her for their signal, and right out of the middle of their circle—what had felt like a circle—Helen had slipped without apology. They hadn't seen her go, her back had not been visible making its way down the block, she had not run, kicking up cold muddy water as she went. Perhaps she had ducked behind the house? Lydia ran to see and reported nothing but the neighbors' yards turned to the endlessness of the Gulf of Mexico, that dark unagitated slime that licked at the ankles for a quarter of a mile. Their daffodils were gone, their tulips showing a bit of pink and yellow like the ears of cats. Andy said, "Maybe the house!" and tried to run but the water prevented speed and made him look like an exerciser lifting weighted ankles. O'Neill had given himself to noisy tears and ragged breathing in Jessie's arms. A dead cat, white with root-beer brown stripes that circled it, regular as barrel staves, floated past with that mesmerizing evenness of will-less objects borne on a slow tide. Jessie bent O'Neill's head down to keep his eyes off it. Its fur was tamped down. If hiding was a joke of Helen's at a time like this, she would pay for it. But Jessie knew her niece didn't play practical jokes, not a chance. If she had a sense of humor it had never shown itself.

Even the shallow water could exert a pull, magnetic, if you stared at it long enough; there was a prehistoric look to it, spread so placidly where it ought not to have been.

But it was implausible—impossible!—that she had met with an accident. This water was as threatening as a bathtub with the drain half open.

Slowly they walked, each in a different direction (O'Neill, sagging, attached to Jessie's side like a leech surfaced from the scum) calling her name. Jessie was distracted by the mocking beauty of the water, the dreamy reflections like arty photographs, concentric circles at the foot of poles, wavery outlines of architectural shape, all of it deeply, distressingly quiet. Though the block was still not deep enough for boats, it was no longer safe going for cars. Her neighbors therefore went on foot, carrying their plants, their cardboard boxes. Mrs. Sandler bore her roasting pan, big enough for a Thanksgiving turkey, aloft over her head. Jessie inquired of everyone. No one had seen Helen but everyone reassured her. Certainly this was not drowning water. She must have remembered something somewhere. Perhaps they should wait right where they were so that she could find them when she came looking.

Jessie's knees were weak. Andy, coming toward her from the house, was in a state of agitation she had never seen him in, not since he was little and subject to nightmares. His face was red, his eyes locked; she saw him laboring even to raise his feet. When he arrived at her side, sweating hard, he raised his hand and dangling from it, its bottom dripping—the house was succumbing, every inch of the downstairs under an even inch or two of water—was Helen's plastic bag of clothes and miscellany, the rescued pittance Jessie had forced them to pack. "And you looked everywhere?"

"Everywhere," he insisted. "In every room. I didn't look under the beds."

O'Neill set up a howl like a dog. Lydia clutched his arm as if it were a pump and wrung it. "We'll get help," Jessie whispered as if she were keeping a secret close to home. "We'll get the police, maybe she got ahead of us and turned up somewhere. She was very eager to get out of here."

"Maybe a church?" O'Neill breathed desperately between gulps. "She would feel comfortable in some church, maybe."

That was a thought. They walked as quickly as they could, straining against the drag of the water, which was calf-height now and painfully cold, slapping vindictively against their skin. This is not happening, Jessie felt herself thinking, this is a dream, ridiculous. (Only bad things felt like dreams; why not good ones?) She was intensely ashamed, humiliated, as the pack of them bore themselves forward like banished sinners from a refuge. They would find help for themselves, dry off, warm up, lie down, rest their leg muscles, but that was hardly the point. She had eluded them or stumbled and gone under, hit her head, and Jessie was to blame, guilty for her innocence of Helen's true condition. For she had had a searing vision as the wet cat lazily, comfortably swept down Rebus Road turning a shoulder this way and sinuously that, of Helen doing away with herself for spite, for pity, for anger, for hate, her soft shoulder-length hair slack beneath the surface, her pale skin paler still. You can drown in three inches of water, she used to warn her children. Helen had no one to warn her of anything she needed to know—no wonder she drew this danger to herself and yielded to it.

They had walked as far as the shopping center without a word. Anyone seeing the mother and her three children would have assumed they were furious with each other, so set were their faces around silence. When they arrived in front of a phone booth, Jessie took her place at the end of a line of four who were chatting with that elated sense of importance that crisis brings. One old woman, thin as a river bird, was saying over and over, "I always thought it was worse than living in a holler, where my son put up that house. I always thought so, and I told him so."

Even before she found a policeman Jessie was calling Andréa and Tommy to invite herself and the children to their house. No use taking up a place in a shelter, depressing everyone further with thin soup and three inches of resting space. When she reached into her canvas bag for her wallet, her hand encountered a small thick shape inside a plastic bag, cinched at the top with a blue Baggie tie.

· · ·

It took more than an hour to drive over but Andréa arrived in her car to take the children to her house. They didn't want to go, it was a form of abandonment. But O'Neill was so agitated that Andréa intended to stop at the hospital to see if the doctor thought he was in danger of an attack. He and Lydia had lost size, they sat with their shoulders huddled down like rebuked children much younger than themselves. Andy wanted to stay with Jessie—he had absorbed the years the younger ones had sloughed. "We should call churches," he told his mother authoritatively. "She really might have lain herself down on the altar—you know, like a sacrifice?" But when he tried to call the nearest church, he discovered the phone lines were overcrowded. There was a hot-line, Andréa told them, for emergencies. If they put themselves in the hands of the hot-line people, who had radios and other gear, they wouldn't have to do this themselves. Jessie fought a short battle with herself about the shame of making this disappearance public. But what a luxury shame was! And hadn't her judgment betrayed her? She surrendered.

She had only read the last few pages of the diary. They were such a theatrical number, she thought, but that didn't make them any less threatening. "Water take me now." At Helen's age, exhibitionism was partly for others and partly for the self, and the self would listen hungrily. She needed time, she knew, to begin at the beginning because the question was, who was Helen's deepest anger for, herself or others? And the religious part, which she was in no position to understand: did one literally try to hasten death—to see God, to be rejoined with the prematurely dead? The diary had the impenetrability of a code. She only knew that she ought to have read it sooner, on that day when Helen held it out to her, all her desperation right in her hands. Jessie's refusal was a stone that had migrated to her chest and hunkered there now—it was another of those irrevocable instants that have their momentary logic, only to lose it to time. What had she been thinking of?

Andy was standing in front of a drugstore window staring in at nothing. His reflection, in a red and blue Rugby shirt and chinos, was wavy as moiré, as something glimpsed, in fact, underwater. At the bottom lay, as if sunk, a display of plastic lawn chairs and white Styrofoam coolers with sky blue lids—if Easter was here, could summer be far behind? "I'm going to go to every church from here to the reservoir," he said in a tone so bottom-heavy Jessie took it as a kind of penance. "I'll walk and I'll hitch rides on other people's boats. I'm going to get the cops to give me a list of churches." He had seen over his mother's shoulder that his name was one of the last things Helen had written in her diary.

"There must be forty of them," Jessie objected glumly. "City of churches." At least he had somewhere to go. "Can't we let these hot-line people keep warm calling them all up for us, instead of traipsing all around yourself?"

But Andy shrugged and walked off, his shoulders tight. He knew the value of keeping busy. Overhead a giant spider of a helicopter seemed to dangle in an invisible web. They had to shout to be heard.

"Wait a minute! Where will I find you?" She meant, Don't leave me. He assured her he would get himself to Andréa's by sundown; he was not in a mood to be fussed over. She had wanted to ask him one more time if he had checked the house very carefully but he broke into a run as if he were escaping and disappeared into the crowd, moving against its flow before she could say a word.

Which left Jessie to throw herself, mortified and frightened, on the mercy of those appointed to be helpful.

They sent out an all-points bulletin. A man in a khaki slicker plied the streets in a khaki boat and shouted Helen's name through a bullhorn. Had she wanted to answer, Jessie insisted, she would have answered long ago: she knew her name. But the man persisted; he had no more alternatives than she did.

Jessie, who could not sit still and wait to hear what they had not found, slowly made her way back to the house. It was shocking, the transformation, the absurdly neutral assertion of water into every opening. Yet, if it hadn't been for this—whatever it was—of Helen's she would still feel as she had yesterday when she'd made herself custodian and handler of other people's beloved possessions: that the flood was a phenomenon that interested but did not touch her, that it was not so much a nightmare as a fascinating event like the landing of astronauts returned from orbit or the dynamiting of a mountain, say, to build a tunnel. It engaged her interest but not her sense of the tragic. There were certainly thousands of challenging manifestations of behavior all around, the howlers and the stoics, the volunteers and the unmoved, but the only unanswered questions concerned property. (Would it survive or float away, would the veneer buckle or the rug be stained?) She could, she realized, walk away from Rebus Road without looking back. That was where this callousness came from: if it weren't for the children who lived in it with her, the children dry and safe now at Andréa's, across town, she would be gone by evening.

On Sparrow Drive, two blocks behind Rebus, a silver gray Mercedes, color of camouflage, floated purposefully past, driverless, on the wrong side of the street. British instincts. She could not imagine why it hadn't waterlogged and sunk.

When she found the house, which had been rendered indistinguishable from the others on the block, only the top few feet of its downstairs windows showing, she couldn't move the front door. Either it had swollen shut or the weight of the water, inside and out, prevented its movement. Exhausted, in a fit of rebelliousness, she hesitated a few seconds, then scaled the dogwood that stood in the yard, so that she was like a child poised over a swimming hole. She put one tentative foot on a branch, found it solid, and sank down on it, legs akimbo. There were still these relieving moments when one's body moved like a child's and none of the epithets fit: stepmother, bereaved aunt, wife on the edge of divorce. She sat still and, none of those, felt the hard hide of the tree under her thighs as if she were playing horse-and-rider in somebody's backyard. Her burgundy red legs dangled down, tights sopping. Would Teddy ever come back to find out what had happened to them? Two of those four children were *his*.

Closing her eyes would be dangerous, sleep too attractive; she could fall into the water if she relaxed her grip. Instead she pulled Helen's diary out of her soggy bag, stripped it carefully of its plastic swaddling and inspected it from the outside: it was a dark red fake leather, worried or stressed or whatever they called it when something had those lines on it—crazed?!— and if it had ever needed a key, it needed none now. The clasp, a fake brass tarnished purple, fell back loosely. This time she began at the beginning.

.   .   .

When she had turned the last page Jessie made herself go back and reread the pages she had fled across the first time as if she were being pursued. She wept until her chest hurt: Helen's poem about dancing school. The sounds of their love-making, hers and Teddy's. The morning Helen thought she ran on her mother's legs. When she stared down out of the tree it seemed fitting that she was alone on a kind of island, unapproachable. This was not the moment to separate her feelings into strands, she could do that when the mystery had ended and the water was drawn back: it would be like the sorting of the worldly goods of the dead again, guilt, blame, forgiveness as tangible as possessions. Now all she felt was grief for Helen, so simple, so searing that she knew she had never before felt pure sorrow for her; always the pain had been adulterated. Always it had been admixed with pain for herself. And here they were.

She had known two early suicides. Now she thought about them, sick with fear. One had been a boy she had liked in high school—oh, Richie Peltz, with his slender arms and his keen critical eyes. She pictured him in her honors English class, straight-backed, hair short, ears stuck out the way boys looked in the fifties, but never to change, to grow the sideburns and neck curls and mustaches of the sixties, never to harvest that barely budded manhood. He had been smart like the rest of them but ballasted, too, by a sort of relieving ordinariness; had been captain of the swim team, had played a sweet saxophone. And when he was in his early twenties, going into the foreign service, living in Washington, something like that, he had done away with himself. She never heard a single detail, which made it worse, and so she never quite believed he had done it. And Julie Jowett, Skelly's girl for a season, who had worked with such dedication in the dangerous days— she was the one who could stay up all night without flagging—a few years later went home to Texas and the only word any of them ever received was that she had killed herself. Who could guess the drama they had escaped, the insoluble hideous soul-disintegrating dilemma? She had tried and tried to imagine but all she had felt for the two of them was fury, an animal's sense of betrayal at desertion from the pack. And now, having lived what she'd only guessed at the time—that one's life does change, does clarify, become a tincture of another weight and color and smell and taste, so that nothing one did, for better or worse, survived its moment with its imperatives intact—she pitied them, and was more angry still. They were children and should not have been let loose with the weapons to do themselves irreparable harm.

Helen, she said to herself softly, in wonderment. Was it possible she had foreclosed on every chance of escape, of relief? Could she really have made herself a sacrifice on her own makeshift altar? Where in the world would she have erected it? Where, Jessie pleaded with herself, was she waiting to discover whether God loved her if nobody else did? Or had He, somewhere out of sight, tossed her back to grow into a full-sized sinner?

.   .   .

Teddy was sitting in Tommy and Andréa's living room when Jessie came in. "Andy's taking a shower," he told her as if he had never left home. He looked awful, his hair long enough to curl around the bottoms of his ears, his gaunt cheeks unshaven. She was too weary for combat. "I tried to call you but the phones were crazy."

So he had been there, at the other end of that shrieking.

"Couldn't you have come over? The children really needed you."

He hesitated. "I was in Mourning Dove and the road was wiped out between there and the highway."

"Are they all right out there?"

"No, they're pretty devastated. It's—" He looked down miserably. "It's a mess. I ended up getting over here in a helicopter the Corps of Engineers sent out to survey the damage."

"You're kidding!"

Jessie waited to see if he had any apologies to make. Apparently he had none; he was here. And I, she thought, ashamed, think about that town as if it were the Other Woman.

"She wasn't in any of the churches," Teddy offered quietly.

"Jesus, I can't call the cops another time. They have nothing to offer but a man and a megaphone."

Andréa and Tommy had, without an uncertain gesture, overridden the motel anonymity of their house with African fabrics and the complex reflecting surfaces of sculpture from Dahomey and Uganda. The living room

seemed to be filled with slick black bodies in wild positions of agon and
celebration, each growing out of the one below as if from a single root.
Teddy sat on a white couch in his dungarees, leaning against flamboyant
purple and black pillows. Jessie was exhausted; she had nothing to say to
him.

"I looked for you at the house," he said.

"Amazing what changes can take place while you're someplace else."

"Even while you're there. The garage looks like a goddamn marina."

"Here," she said and gave him Helen's diary. "You might as well take
a good look at this."

He turned it over slowly. "You make it sound like a real thrill."

"You won't like it."

"Is that why you're giving it to me? Is this her weapon or yours?"

"It's truth-telling time."

"You expect a thirteen-year-old hysteric to tell me any truth that's going
to matter to me?"

"You'd better find out how things look to her. And you'd better try to
figure out what she's telling us about where she's gone. You never told me,
by the way, about the last time she took off."

"After Mourning Dove?" He was rubbing his stubbly chin with his
hand, considering. "You'd have crucified me."

"Maybe you deserved it. Although the Jesus image doesn't sit quite right
on you."

"Ah, Jessie," he said wearily, and stretched his long legs out in front of
him. He opened the diary. "Here goes nothing."

.   .   .

When he was finished he was a sickly white. Andy had come in wearing
Tommy's blue terrycloth robe. "God, Daddy, you look mulched," he said
and laughed a little too vigorously. They had been speaking very quietly,
containing their feelings the way one might in church or at a funeral. Andy
was agitated instead.

Teddy sat with his head dropped back between his shoulders as if he
had been shot. Jessie wondered if his eyes were open.

"You know, it doesn't matter what she's telling us about where she is.
Can you really see any way to make this whole thing tolerable?"

"To her or to us?" Jessie asked bitterly.

"How could we have her back in the house after we know some of these
things? And she would *know* we know."

"Well, she wanted us to hear them. Maybe she had to get them said and listened to once and for all, and she'll be ready to begin again. If you'd rather see her drowned, well, I suspect she sort of picked that up somehow."

"That's a hell of a thing to say. But the Klan? Did you read that? Just consider what you're harboring here."

"Oh Teddy, what am I harboring? Good question. What does all that mean? You haven't given her a single thought the whole time she's been with us. She's only got so much to fight with. It's so pathetic."

"Pathetic!"

"Pathetic. Aren't you big enough, strong enough to allow her a choice of weapons? You had one."

"I had one."

His rhetorical style had always sounded mocking to her, that repetition was never meant to be acknowledgment, always judgment.

Andy had taken the diary from his father and as he read he rubbed his fingers across it, pressing for secret meanings.

"Do you want to stop talking to Helen the way your mother stopped talking to you? Would punishing her that way make you feel noble in defense of your honor?"

By his breathing she could see how angry he was. Andy looked from one of them to the other, frightened, holding a page halfway turned. O'Neill, in the bedroom with Lydia and Cleo, had begun to cry at the top of his voice. She went in to hold him against her. She felt hollowed out with fear, light as an empty pod. When she looked at her hands and feet, they seemed to be moving without her will.

"Mom," Andy said in a whisper, when she had set O'Neill down and returned.

"I'm thinking, why leave your diary."

"Well, suicides do that sort of thing all the time, they leave notes so everyone will blame themselves. I mean, I suppose that's where the real satisfaction lies. It surely can't lie in dying."

He winced. "I just have this funny sort of depressed feeling that she wanted to, like—stay close to whatever home. I still can't—I don't want to prove anything, I don't know if it's a mystery you solve, I just think, sort of psychologically speaking—" He looked at his father embarrassed, his giveaway color reddening the tips of his ears. "A note is one thing, it's final and full of—it makes you feel guilty. But this feels like—one side of a conversation, sort of, doesn't it?"

"Oh, you're wishing, Andy. You don't want her to have said the last word. And to God."

Teddy snorted. "People have a right to say goodbye to whoever they want to."

"Thanks for permission," Jessie said. "That's your democratic impulse, it still twitches once in a while like a beheaded chicken." She put her arms around Andy and rested her head on his shoulder. Darkness had seeped into the room as if it too were water. It stained the ceilings and the furniture, obliterating them all in the same gradual flow. No one touched the lamps.

She stared at Teddy. She had no part in his life now. She wondered if he understood how momentous that knowledge was, and yet how impossible it would be to find the precise moment of disengagement—it was like the twilight coming down to steal the details of the room, which were visible and then not visible, with no line of demarcation between. People could surrender to their weakness, she thought, and make it their most hideous strength. Abandonment followed abandonment, like a chain reaction collision on a foggy road. "You won't have Helen in the house. Has it occurred to you that you don't seem to live there any more?" Why did he look at her that way, as if she were only trying to exasperate him? "Are you going to tell me you don't mean it, you'll be back when you get good and ready?"

"I don't know what I mean. But look, what could we do with her, she'll never let herself be happy here. She's set herself up as a kind of deepsworn enemy. She hasn't heard a thing we've said since she came—"

"So you talk a little more, and patiently. Although kids don't learn from that anyway, this is not a freedom school! And if you want her to learn tolerance, you could begin by showing a little more of it yourself." She drew her fingers through her hair fiercely. "Anyway, little children talk about enemies, Teddy. O'Neill is around the right age for good guys and bad guys in teams. Red Rover Red Rover, send Teddy over. Even your poor sister got beyond that kind of game. She was generous enough to be forgiving."

Andy got up and lost himself in the plant jungle under the front window. It was Tommy who tended the superfecund greenery with magical effectiveness. Once he had explained that the house he grew up in had nothing live in it but himself and his grandmother, and his mother who slept all the time she wasn't working. "When it comes time to do your own life," he had said in his straightforward Midwestern, "you either perpetuate your childhood or you stand on it and finally kick it out from under you." Andy looked out at them like one of those faces in children's drawings that waits to be found in the foliage.

"Do you want to know what Helen's always made me want to do?" Teddy asked. "I want to pinch her arm when she's sitting there picking at her food the way she does. That's a diabolical thing to say but I want to pinch her till she screams. She's one of those empty Southern girls I grew up with, only instead of raucous the way Alexis was, she's voiceless like a little cut-out doll or something, and all I can think to do is hit her or pull her hair or make her *react* somehow." Jessie opened her mouth to respond but Teddy went on, plunging his fist into his open hand. "Jessie, why do you think loving a family is unconditional? I don't have to love all comers just because they're here and make a claim on me."

"I can't talk about you, Teddy. She's a child and you're not a child, you're responsible for your thoughts and actions in a way she just isn't prepared to be. But look—why did you expect your mother to forgive something she didn't share and couldn't understand? Just tell me that. What does ideology have to do with any of this?"

Teddy's face was dark with anger. "It doesn't. Ideology doesn't have a damn thing to do with it. I'm talking about acceptable human behavior. And why do you have to keep dragging Dorothea into this? Do I have to be psychoanalyzed before I'm allowed to be disgusted by a strange girl at my table picking through the food like we're trying to poison her, and then getting herself involved with some murderous ruffians who would dynamite us out of our skins if they thought they could get away with it? I'm only trying to be honest about the way I feel. I'm sorry I'm not all lovingkindness like you are, but what should I value more, telling it the way I feel it or forcing fake compassion out of my mouth? I can't *do* it. I'd like to be agreeable but I just cannot do it."

He turned his face just slightly toward her. She was astonished to see the pitted moon landscape of his cheek glittering, the gnarled relief of hills and furrows slick with tears. They took the meager light and fractured it and she thought, and then suppressed it, too awful to be acknowledged, his poor cheek looks like one lobe of his brain uncovered, moist with blood and fluid. How terrible, she thought, to be so bare, so inside out. Shouldn't a man who has been as far away as death be forgiven everything? She wished she could go and put a kiss on his cheek without his taking that for hope.

. . .

Jessie and Andy dragged themselves, against a great counterweight of depression and futility, to emergency headquarters to put out another plea for information.

"It's black on black *in* black out there," a man in fatigues told them. "What would y'all like for us to do? We got boats, we got a helicopter, we got lights so bright you could make a movie in em. What do y'all want for us to *do* with em?"

"If we could play the voice of Jesus through a megaphone," Andy muttered to his mother. The man heard him and looked at him slowly, all over, reassessing his impression. He shrugged and they shrugged back.

O'Neill spent the night hunched beside Andy on the couch in the guest room. He seemed beyond tortured breath, quiet in the stillness of shock. Jessie did not talk to him much, she only held him tight to her chest. She had said soberly, "Don't worry, O'Neill. I'm pretty sure she's somewhere hiding out from us and we'll find her." But without specifics she wasn't hopeful and she didn't want to have to repeat that. Andy held forth in the optimistic way he had perfected through years of luck and competence and so, as the highest bidder, he got to keep O'Neill beside him. Lydia kept trying to catch her brother's eye so that she could register despair but he only frowned at her to stop before O'Neill saw her.

Lydia came and sat in her lap for a long time without saying a word; if she wanted to be a baby, that was fine with Jessie, who could use some wordless warmth against her chest. "Sometimes she was like an old lady, you know what I mean? Like so many—"

"Whatever you're going to say, Lyddie, don't say 'was.' Say 'is.' If we're lucky."

Lydia bobbed her head obediently. "Is. Okay. And now—even if I saw her again I don't even know if she'd be the same any more."

"How do you mean?"

"I don't know. She'd just be different."

"We'd have to make her feel like she's not, though. We'd have to—" Jessie made a circle of her arms and Lydia stepped into it.

"Like that?"

Oh God, Jessie thought. How easy it was for Lyddie to stand there. Her child development books said children were not supposed to understand abstractions till they were something like thirteen. Lydia had been good at the big questions from the age of two. "Like that," she said, and squeezed so hard that Lydia grunted and broke the spell with her laughter.

Teddy sat up alone in the living room. Jessie lay on a mattress on the guest-room floor imagining the quiet lapping of the water like an animal's tongue against the closed door. Danger, danger everywhere and not a drop to drink: Helen had understood. The wild silver Mercedes bobbed and lurched behind her eyes. Even the Haves have it, the plummy parts of town brought low. It was a pretty unimpressive apocalypse, she thought, but if you wanted one badly enough . . . Because there was no absolute safety, Helen had rejected relative. That was so self-defeating Teddy should have sympathized.

She lay thinking about escape routes from her balked life as if she were steering one of those flat-bottomed boats through the unexpected waters. What if, she thought, imagining the insane luminosity of her front yard, what if they finally left, all of them left? Before the new house promised to resolve their confusion that was all she had wished for. What if they went to New York, say, where they would all be new together, and shared the handicaps all around, the unfamiliarity, the strain, the foreignness? That was something better than escape. A sharp light struck off the rocking surface behind her eyes; she could not stop seeing water. If Helen were with them— Jessie made herself believe she would somehow turn up at the door, sheep- ish—they could find a school for her that was so different from anything around here that the girl could never have dreamed it. All the dynamics of their lives were so much more mutable than a child could know! She would tell her about Richie and Julie, the suicides, who were so arrogant in the face of all they could not imagine, all that could still have happened to deliver them. She would congratulate Helen for holding out, for wait- ing. . . . Who could have dreamed the roof would be casting its shadow on a lake this morning, looking like a dock? Teddy could rip the house down to its studs or sell it as is, live in it, make it into a home for black reactionaries, anything he pleased. Giddy, she thought, I'll call Lynet, Teddy's editor, ask for help finding a place in Manhattan to live in with all those children. She would confuse the woman (who would call Teddy and say, What is going on!); she would jiggle all their roles a little, make strange things happen. She was too old to ask anyone's permission. The only absolutes were that she had four undefended people in her care. However inept they were, she and Teddy were not undefended.

Three people. When Andy tiptoed in and knelt by her bed, she had to re- vise the plan: as of this instant, three people. He shook her shoulder tentatively.

"Mom, are you awake?"

"Mmm. All night. What?"

"I want to go back to the house. I have this funny feeling."

"What."

"You'll think I'm crazy. I—you know where she talks in the diary about cutting school and just lying around the house, staying home all the time? I mean, she never did anything really—like—dangerous."

"So?" Like the time you found her home, Jessie was thinking, breathless, and you didn't tell me about it. The time she scratched up her arm with glass. No one let me help!

"You know I didn't check the house *that* carefully. When I went back in. I mean, I just sort of ran through opening doors and shouting. I wasn't expecting her to be hiding, we just figured, remember? that she might have gone back for something."

Jessie was out of bed before he had finished. "Let everybody else sleep," she said. "The less they have to be awake right now the better." Nor did she want Teddy with them; she could not predict what he'd do if they found the girl: yell at her, embrace her, weep for the two of them.

It was Easter Sunday and up and down Tommy and Andréa's block, neighbors in brilliant flowered dresses and innovative hats emerged smiling from their front doors. They seemed to have decorated themselves with the same attention to variety that the builder had strained for in the decoration of the facades, no two alike come what may. Jessie tried not to be irritated by all that good cheer; Andy bowed his head, not as humble as he looked, so that he wouldn't have to meet anyone's smile. Even the little boys who liked to do wheelies on the street were tamped down into suits, sheepish and respectful. Andréa would keep O'Neill and Lydia. O'Neill, awake, lay in front of the TV cartoons in a half-stupor—Valium in a children's dose—which terrified Lydia more than his hysteria, which she could at least share. The doctor had given them very specific instructions of symptoms of brewing trouble to watch for, and Jessie enlisted Lydia's aid as a kind of nurse to distract him.

They borrowed Andréa's car and parked as close to their neighborhood as they could and hitched a ride in a beautiful wooden canoe. Jessie knew that the emergency squad would take them over but she demurred. In another mood, Andy would have laughed at the block—"Lake Gitchee-goomee," he muttered as they took the noncorner, gliding out into the middle, but he wasn't smiling.

"Forget something?" asked the young man, who told them that he'd built his boat and had never had a chance to use it before. "Gettin baptized in pure-d sewage, int that something?" They thanked him and jumped out into water shoulder high, so cold their legs throbbed, hurt and then went numb in the first two minutes. Jessie found that she could move fastest when she lifted her feet off the ground and danced forward—it was an unexalting form of flight. Somehow they got the back door partially open and, gasping, floated into the dark hall. What a time for buoyancy. . . . The house felt like a cave, abandoned underground, sour-smelling and unlit, sunk in a silence that, merely empty, it could never achieve. It was not hollow but dense, actively black in all its corners, amplifying; each movement of a limb, the sound of water slapping on water, was like lips parting, except that magnified it had an evil sound, as if they were disturbing something that liked to live alone, depth rocking on depth, bottomless. "Holy shit!" Andy breathed, then looked at his mother to see if she might take offense under stress. But she wasn't listening to him.

There were only a few inches of water at the topmost level of steps. Andy pushed open Helen's door. "I only took a quick look in here yesterday," he said softly and then recoiled: at his feet a brown snake, dislodged from beneath the door, quivered spastically, feeling its freedom. "Helen!" he called timidly, stepping out of its way. Even quiet, his voice had a hollow echo. "Are you in here?"

The moist grotto silence hung around them. "Watch out," Andy cautioned his mother, "there's a snake over there—look. I don't know what it is, just keep your distance."

There was a vague sound, a rasp of cloth, from somewhere. "Helen?" He stepped through the water, his full shoes making a gulping suction sound, and pulled open her closet door with the noise of a samurai warrior landing a blow. It was so dark in the closet that neither of them could see but Jessie, emboldened, parted the hangers and ran her hands urgently through the soft hanging cottons. When she grasped flesh, cold and unresponsive but live flesh just the same, she let out a triumphant shout to match Andy's and pulled the hunched-over figure toward her, hard against her chest. Helen came without resistance. She flopped like an oversized doll. Jessie, staring into her averted face, discovered she was shaking her as if she needed waking. The violence of her movement felt like anger. "Helen!" And "Helen!" she cried again across no distance. Helen's head lolled back and rolled to one side; she seemed to be trying to focus. Only her dungarees had been wet; they could see by the way the water now spread its darkness like blood across her shirt that she had so far been well out of the worst of it.

"Helen," Jessie said very deliberately, as if she were speaking to someone in a coma who might hear or might not. "You're safe." She could not say "You are saved," it was too presumptuous, and too accepting of Helen's premise. She held the living girl in her arms and felt it all slide off her, regret and anger and relief like separate streams of icy water splashing and mixing in the brine that covered her ankles. "Do you understand me?" When she put her palm gently on Helen's sagging cheek and pushed it up to face her, she felt like a ventriloquist righting her dummy. "Do you understand that we love you? Is that enough of a sign?" Subtlety was for the securely blessed, she thought.

Helen's light-shocked eyes circled and circled her face like someone in a plane looking down at the distant ground. "Did you read it?" Her voice sounded rusty.

"I'm only sorry I didn't read it sooner. I can't—I don't know how to ask you to forgive me." She knew how stiff the words sounded, but they were all she could summon: she was in the presence of a stranger. We all need exoneration, she thought, overcome. Someone to pronounce us innocent. We are never free of it. That was the word Teddy wanted from his mother and would never get; it was the one he had gone to sleep to dream while they were rushing down the highway between the kudzu valleys, the difference between approval and acceptance. Her mistake had been not to know helplessness when she saw it, not to see how loss leaves each victim soiled, even defaced, by a different fingerprint. She rocked the girl who, body against her body, breathing evenly as if in sleep, allowed herself to be rocked.

"Where's my brother?" Helen asked, lurching around to see if he was behind her.

"At Andréa's, he's okay. But you had him stupefied with fear." She might as well bind the girl into it, guilt and all; the web was there, they were all bound in it.

Putting her shoulder under Helen's, walking her against the weight of the water, Jessie was thinking how—so strange—two accidents had torn her family's life across, this way and that: Teddy landing in the bright bed of leaves, Alexis and Roger slipping across the median in the rain. And she, now, felt they had been in yet another wreck from which she was dragging Helen, half against her will. She could feel how the overturned bulk of their lives had crashed down hard and the wheels were still spinning.

Outside the sky was mockingly brilliant, the sun's clarity an outrage. The history books would make symbolism out of it, the flood and Easter and heavenly light. Jessie and Andy supported her between them like Helen's Christ himself, she thought. They were going to have to find a passing boat or a CB they could call out on. Helen, limp, could never walk out to dry land. She was barely standing with their help.

"Something's coming," Andy murmured, leaning his hip against Helen and swinging his arms which, like Jessie's, kept tensing in the aching cold. Their legs were beyond consulting for feeling: sun or no, the water was an assault.

Oh, it was coming, all right. It was a big paint-peeling rowboat listing to one side, much the worse for wear, and flying from the mast, which was something like a broomstick, were a Jolly Roger, white bones on black ground stretched one way, and a massive rebel flag in vaguely electric colors that would glow like a spirit in the dark. On the high side of the boat was a sticker that said DRINK COORS! A young man, shirtless and freshly, achingly sunburned, gave a whoop that cut across Rebus Road and seemed to bounce and spread in concentric waves on the silver stippled water. Behind him and his triumphantly raised beer can sat Teddy squinting helplessly into the blaze of light.

"Oh *shit*," Jessie said, and Andy breathed out hard as if she had punched him in the solar plexus. "Daddy!" he shouted, and dropped his side of Helen to move in slow stifled motion toward him. Half of Helen crumpled in slow sections into the water. But she was not without hope, Jessie thought. She was safe or saved, and knew it: raised her head out of the stinking water and wiped her face, unsmiling, with her own two quivering hands. So much for the chastening of the flesh. And she will smile yet, Jessie found herself thinking. If surviving was the crime that had driven her to the back of the closet—surviving when her parents had gone under—then she was still guilty. But this minute she was pulling herself up straight, she was arranging her stringy hair behind her ears, she was studying her fingertips which had wrinkled as she stood there. She looked curious.

So Jessie was free to face Teddy, who was hugging Andy and then, very slowly threshing the water, approaching them, wincing in the slap of chill while the young man and his commandeered pirate boat held on to his broom-handle mast with his head at a sentimental tilt to watch the family reunion. Teddy must have told him he was coming home.

"You're a little late to see the resurrection," Jessie said bitterly. Helen made an animal sound deep in her throat and stared at her. Like a colt, she was up on her own two feet, standing firm.

"Helen," Teddy said in a hopeful voice. He smiled encouragingly at her, squinting into the glare. "Jessie."

Jessie shivered. It was too late for more than Helen's resurrection. "Ah, Teddy. I'm sorry." She shook her head wistfully. "I haven't got the strength. It's not your fault, not all of it."

"You said we'd all begin again. . . ."

That was what sentimental alcoholics promised themselves and everyone else, hundreds of times. But the two of them were too deformed by their pasts, she thought, to be so endlessly malleable; they had to live bent out of shape to fit each other. When she told him about New York, about her resolve to put Helen at her ease by displacing the lot of them, there was another thing she was going to tell him: that she had one answer, at least, to the question of who he was, who he had become. He was the hunger artist of the seventies. He wanted to perfect his fasting; he would never let himself be satisfied again.

She turned, emboldened, to Andy, churning the water into bubbles like a hundred winking fish-eyes. Because he didn't really understand difficulty nor, she imagined, the difference between hope and resignation, because he loved whom he loved so ardently, he clasped her hand, her fingers, her forearm, her elbow; snapped his fingers; bounced his knuckles off her head: the old salute. He thought she was going to turn to Teddy and welcome him back.

Electric as a lure across the water, the stripes and stars of the rebel flag bobbed just at the corner of her eye. If only she could lie back and be fatally, amiably, uncomplicatedly irresponsible, float down Rebus Road toward the ruined estuaries of her swank neighbors, leave this yardful of adversaries to themselves to grapple and stare into each other's confusions as if they were mouths that would speak panacea. Damn. She was going to bring them all pain.

"I'm cold," Helen said in a voice familiarly, childishly demanding. It was not the voice of a sacrifice.

"Okay, let's go." Sucking up the flood with a straw would be easier, she thought, than what they had ahead of them. Smiling, near tears, hot above, cold below, and exceptionally tired, Jessie clasped her son's hand—his nearly grown-up hand—in one of hers and Helen's in the other.

Teddy, as she turned from him, stood exaggeratedly still in the harsh light waiting to be recognized. His long unbent shadow struck out dark across the water, lying behind him like the one felled pine in an open field. How odd, Jessie thought, that the field is the color of the sky. She stiffened herself, afraid he would call to her, but he didn't. All she could hear was the intimate lick and suckle of the instant, which was deepening around her. She would walk in it a good deal longer before it became the past.

A NOTE ABOUT THE AUTHOR

Rosellen Brown is the author of two previous novels, *Tender Mercies* and *The Autobiography of My Mother*; a book of short stories, *Street Games*; and two books of poetry, *Cora Fry* and *Some Deaths in the Delta*. She currently lives in Texas with her husband and two children, and teaches writing and literature at the University of Texas.

A NOTE ON THE TYPE

The text of this book was set in a digitized version of Janson, a redrawing of type cast from matrices long thought to have been made by the Dutchman Anton Janson, who was a practicing type founder in Leipzig during the years 1668–87. The diary entries were set in Electra Cursive, a typeface designed by W(illiam) A(ddison) Dwiggins for the Mergenthaler Linotype company and first made available in 1935.

Composition by Crane Typesetting Service, Inc., Barnstable, Massachusetts.

Printing and binding by The Haddon Craftsmen, Scranton, Pennsylvania.

Typography and binding design by Dorothy Schmiderer